The
MX Book
of
New

Sherlock

Holmes

Stories

Part XXXIV
"However Improbable . . . ."
(1878-1888)

THE MX BOOK OF NEW SHERLOCK HOLMES STORIES

PART XXXIV
"HOWEVER IMPROBABLE...."
(1878-1888)

SOUTHAMPTON STREET

359

EDITED By
David Marcum

OFFICES

TRADITIONAL HOLMES
ADVENTURES
COMPILED FOR THE
BENEFIT OF THE
RESTORATION OF
UNDERSHAW

First edition published in 2022
© Copyright 2022

ISBN Hardback 978-1-80424-105-9
ISBN Paperback 978-1-80424-106-6
AUK ePub ISBN 978-1-80424-107-3
AUK PDF ISBN 978-1-80424-108-0

Published in the UK by
MX Publishing
335 Princess Park Manor, Royal Drive,
London, N11 3GX
www.mxpublishing.co.uk

David Marcum can be reached at:
thepapersofsherlockholmes@gmail.com

Cover design by Brian Belanger
www.belangerbooks.com and *www.redbubble.com/people/zhahadun*

Internal Illustrations by Sidney Paget

CONTENTS

Forewords

Adventures

(Continued on the next page . . . .)

(Continued on the next page . . . .)

These additional adventures are contained in
Part XXXV "However Improbable . . . ."
(1889-1896)

Part XXXVI "However Improbable . . . ."
(1897-1919)

(Continued on the next page . . . .)

(Continued on the next page . . . .)

PART III: 1896-1929

PART IV – 2016 Annual

(Continued on the next page . . . .)

PART V – Christmas Adventures

(Continued on the next page . . . .)

PART VI – 2017 Annual

(Continued on the next page . . . .)

The Unwelcome Client – Keith Hann
The Tempest of Lyme – David Ruffle
The Problem of the Holy Oil – David Marcum
A Scandal in Serbia – Thomas A. Turley
The Curious Case of Mr. Marconi – Jan Edwards
Mr. Holmes and Dr. Watson Learn to Fly – C. Edward Davis
Die Weisse Frau – Tim Symonds
A Case of Mistaken Identity – Daniel D. Victor

PART VII – Eliminate the Impossible: 1880-1891
Foreword – Lee Child
Foreword – Rand B. Lee
Foreword – Michael Cox
Foreword – Roger Johnson
Foreword – Melissa Farnham
Foreword – David Marcum
No Ghosts Need Apply (A Poem) – Jacquelynn Morris
The Melancholy Methodist – Mark Mower
The Curious Case of the Sweated Horse – Jan Edwards
The Adventure of the Second William Wilson – Daniel D. Victor
The Adventure of the Marchindale Stiletto – James Lovegrove
The Case of the Cursed Clock – Gayle Lange Puhl
The Tranquility of the Morning – Mike Hogan
A Ghost from Christmas Past – Thomas A. Turley
The Blank Photograph – James Moffett
The Adventure of A Rat. – Adrian Middleton
The Adventure of Vanaprastha – Hugh Ashton
The Ghost of Lincoln – Geri Schear
The Manor House Ghost – S. Subramanian
The Case of the Unquiet Grave – John Hall
The Adventure of the Mortal Combat – Jayantika Ganguly
The Last Encore of Quentin Carol – S.F. Bennett
The Case of the Petty Curses – Steven Philip Jones
The Tuttman Gallery – Jim French
The Second Life of Jabez Salt – John Linwood Grant
The Mystery of the Scarab Earrings – Thomas Fortenberry
The Adventure of the Haunted Room – Mike Chinn
The Pharaoh's Curse – Robert V. Stapleton
The Vampire of the Lyceum – Charles Veley and Anna Elliott
The Adventure of the Mind's Eye – Shane Simmons

PART VIII – Eliminate the Impossible: 1892-1905
Foreword – Lee Child
Foreword – Rand B. Lee
Foreword – Michael Cox
Foreword – Roger Johnson
Foreword – Melissa Farnham

(Continued on the next page . . . .)

(Continued on the next page . . . .)

(Continued on the next page . . . .)

(Continued on the next page . . . .)

PART XIV: 2019 Annual (1891-1897)

(Continued on the next page . . . .)

(Continued on the next page . . . .)

The Adventure of the Headless Lady – Tracy J. Revels
Angelus Domini Nuntiavit – Kevin P. Thornton
The Blue Lady of Dunraven – Andrew Bryant
The Adventure of the Ghoulish Grenadier – Josh Anderson and David Friend
The Curse of Barcombe Keep – Brenda Seabrooke
The Affair of the Regressive Man – David Marcum
The Adventure of the Giant's Wife – I.A. Watson
The Adventure of Miss Anna Truegrace – Arthur Hall
The Haunting of Bottomly's Grandmother – Tim Gambrell
The Adventure of the Intrusive Spirit – Shane Simmons
The Paddington Poltergeist – Bob Bishop
The Spectral Pterosaur – Mark Mower
The Weird of Caxton – Kelvin Jones
The Adventure of the Obsessive Ghost – Jayantika Ganguly

Part XVII – Whatever Remains . . . Must Be the Truth (1891-1898)
Foreword – Kareem Abdul-Jabbar
Foreword – Roger Johnson
Foreword – Steve Emecz
Foreword – David Marcum
The Violin Thief (*A Poem*) – Christopher James
The Spectre of Scarborough Castle – Charles Veley and Anna Elliott
The Case for Which the World is Not Yet Prepared – Steven Philip Jones
The Adventure of the Returning Spirit – Arthur Hall
The Adventure of the Bewitched Tenant – Michael Mallory
The Misadventures of the Bonnie Boy – Will Murray
The Adventure of the *Danse Macabre* – Paul D. Gilbert
The Strange Persecution of John Vincent Harden – S. Subramanian
The Dead Quiet Library – Roger Riccard
The Adventure of the Sugar Merchant – Stephen Herczeg
The Adventure of the Undertaker's Fetch – Tracy J. Revels
The Holloway Ghosts – Hugh Ashton
The Diogenes Club Poltergeist – Chris Chan
The Madness of Colonel Warburton – Bert Coules
The Return of the Noble Bachelor – Jane Rubino
The Reappearance of Mr. James Phillimore – David Marcum
The Miracle Worker – Geri Schear
The Hand of Mesmer – Dick Gillman

Part XVIII – Whatever Remains . . . Must Be the Truth (1899-1925)
Foreword – Kareem Abdul-Jabbar
Foreword – Roger Johnson
Foreword – Steve Emecz
Foreword – David Marcum
The Adventure of the Lighthouse on the Moor (*A Poem*) – Christopher James
The Witch of Ellenby – Thomas A. Burns, Jr.

(Continued on the next page . . . .)

Part XIX: 2020 Annual (1882-1890)

(Continued on the next page . . . .)

The Adventure of the Matched Set – Peter Coe Verbica
When the Prince First Dined at the Diogenes Club – Sean M. Wright
The Sweetenbury Safe Affair – Tim Gambrell

Part XX: 2020 Annual (1891-1897)

Foreword – John Lescroart
Foreword – Roger Johnson
Foreword – Lizzy Butler
Foreword – Steve Emecz
Foreword – David Marcum
The Sibling (*A Poem*) – Jacquelynn Morris
Blood and Gunpowder – Thomas A. Burns, Jr.
The Atelier of Death – Harry DeMaio
The Adventure of the Beauty Trap – Tracy Revels
A Case of Unfinished Business – Steven Philip Jones
The Case of the S.S. Bokhara – Mark Mower
The Adventure of the American Opera Singer – Deanna Baran
The Keadby Cross – David Marcum
The Adventure at Dead Man's Hole – Stephen Herczeg
The Elusive Mr. Chester – Arthur Hall
The Adventure of Old Black Duffel – Will Murray
The Blood-Spattered Bridge – Gayle Lange Puhl
The Tomorrow Man – S.F. Bennett
The Sweet Science of Bruising – Kevin P. Thornton
The Mystery of Sherlock Holmes – Christopher Todd
The Elusive Mr. Phillimore – Matthew J. Elliott
The Murders in the Maharajah's Railway Carriage – Charles Veley and Anna Elliott
The Ransomed Miracle – I.A. Watson
The Adventure of the Unkind Turn – Robert Perret
The Perplexing X'ing – Sonia Fetherston
The Case of the Short-Sighted Clown – Susan Knight

Part XXI: 2020 Annual (1898-1923)

Foreword – John Lescroart
Foreword – Roger Johnson
Foreword – Lizzy Butler
Foreword – Steve Emecz
Foreword – David Marcum
The Case of the Missing Rhyme (*A Poem*) – Joseph W. Svec III
The Problem of the St. Francis Parish Robbery – R.K. Radek
The Adventure of the Grand Vizier – Arthur Hall
The Mummy's Curse – DJ Tyrer
The Fractured Freemason of Fitzrovia – David L. Leal
The Bleeding Heart – Paula Hammond
The Secret Admirer – Jayantika Ganguly

(Continued on the next page . . . .)

Part XXII: Some More Untold Cases (1877-1887)

(Continued on the next page . . . .)

(Continued on the next page . . . .)

Part XXV: 2021 Annual (1881-1888)

(Continued on the next page . . . .)

(Continued on the next page . . . .)

Part XXVIII: More Christmas Adventures (1869-1888)

(Continued on the next page . . . .)

Part XXIX: More Christmas Adventures (1889-1896)

(Continued on the next page . . . .)

Part XXX: More Christmas Adventures (1897-1928)

(Continued on the next page . . . .)

The Adventure of the Chained Phantom – J.S. Rowlinson
Santa's Little Elves – Kevin Thornton
The Case of the Holly-Sprig Pudding – Naching T. Kassa
The Canterbury Manifesto – David Marcum
The Case of the Disappearing Beaune – J. Lawrence Matthews
A Price Above Rubies – Jane Rubino
The Intrigue of the Red Christmas – Shane Simmons
The Bitter Gravestones – Chris Chan
The Midnight Mass Murder – Paul Hiscock

Part XXXI 2022 Annual (1875-1887)
Foreword – Jeffrey Hatcher
Foreword – Roger Johnson
Foreword – Steve Emecz
Foreword – Emma West
Foreword – David Marcum
The Nemesis of Sherlock Holmes (A Poem) – Kelvin I. Jones
The Unsettling Incident of the History Professor's Wife – Sean M. Wright
The Princess Alice Tragedy – John Lawrence
The Adventure of the Amorous Balloonist – I.A. Watson
The Pilkington Case – Kevin Patrick McCann
The Adventure of the Disappointed Lover – Arthur Hall
The Case of the Impressionist Painting – Tim Symonds
The Adventure of the Old Explorer – Tracy J. Revels
Dr. Watson's Dilemma – Susan Knight
The Colonial Exhibition – Hal Glatzer
The Adventure of the Drunken Teetotaler – Thomas A. Burns, Jr.
The Curse of Hollyhock House – Geri Schear
The Sethian Messiah – David Marcum
Dead Man's Hand – Robert Stapleton
The Case of the Wary Maid – Gordon Linzner
The Adventure of the Alexandrian Scroll – David MacGregor
The Case of the Woman at Margate – Terry Golledge
A Question of Innocence – DJ Tyrer
The Grosvenor Square Furniture Van – Terry Golledge
The Adventure of the Veiled Man – Tracy J. Revels
The Disappearance of Dr. Markey – Stephen Herczeg
The Case of the Irish Demonstration – Dan Rowley

Part XXXII 2022 Annual (1888-1895)
Foreword – Jeffrey Hatcher
Foreword – Roger Johnson
Foreword – Steve Emecz

(Continued on the next page . . . .)

Part XXXIII 2022 Annual (1896-1919)

(Continued on the next page . . . .)

The following contributors appear
in the companion volumes:
Part XXXV – "However Improbable . . . ." (1889-1896)
Part XXXVI – "However Improbable . . . ." (1897-1919)

Editor's Foreword:
The Dramatic Moment of Fate
by David Marcum

*"Now is the dramatic moment of fate, Watson, when you hear a
step upon the stair which is walking into your life, and you know
not whether for good or ill."*

— Sherlock Holmes
The Hound of the Baskervilles

In early 2022, we celebrated the 168th birthday of Mr. Sherlock Holmes, (born on January 6th, 1954). We're racing toward his *bicentennial*. That's a true *Good grief!* realization. (And if you think those next thirty-two years to 2054 won't fly by, you're either kidding yourself or still very young. By the time these current volumes see print, we'll almost be celebrating Holmes's *169th*!)

When I was a ten-year-old kid, discovering Mr. Holmes in the mid-1970's, the days of gaslight and hansom cabs were already long gone – but I knew some people who still remembered those days. Just imagine the changes that they lived through. My grandparents were born into the era of horse-drawn vehicles. (My dad's father and mother bought the first automobile ever driven in their small town.) They lived to see the world go from that type of existence to a man landing on the moon. Now, with our own exponential technological advances, we're also seeing changes moving at an even swifter pace. But for many, there's something deep inside that looks backward to different, supposedly simpler, times – and those are farther away with each passing year.

The Holmes Era – essentially the final third of Queen Victoria's reign and the Edwardian era, give or take a few years – conjures up definite images of dark and mysterious London streets and passages, often occluded by rolling fogs. Cabs and carriages carry finely dressed people past pedestrians who could have never afforded a cab ride in their entire lives. There was the rigid formality and ritual for those who *had*, and the scrambling, dangerous, and often short existence of those who *had not* – with all of them living jammed together in the space of just a few square miles.

London's wealthiest sector – the wealthiest sector, in fact, in the whole world – was located within just a few blocks of the City's poorest. These societal extremes must have been mightily confusing. There were

1

expected rules and behaviors that could not be violated. And while the cities pulled all of these conflicting layers tightly together, many rural areas remained just as remote as they had been for centuries. The countryside was dotted here and there with pockets of industry, extending their influence a bit more each year by way of railway tendrils – but only along profitable paths, leaving other vast tracts in isolation.

It was a time when science was revered and pursued by some – academics and gentleman amateurs – while at the same time many embraced superstition and ignorance with enthusiasm and anger by way of mediums and spiritualists. Often it was far too easy for the ignorant to proudly believe that the impossible was possible, consciously choosing to ignore science and knowledge and fact.

And in the midst of this chaos – rich and poor, knowledgeable and willfully ignorant – one clear note began to be noticed, quiet at first, almost beyond hearing, but gradually becoming stronger and more steady, resolving the various discordant tones around it. This note – possibly one could liken it to a steady air on a single Stradivarius string – brought in some small way balance to societal disparity, and light to shadowed and intentional disregard of knowledge.

This resolving influence was Sherlock Holmes.

The human mind is, by nature, drawn to the mysterious, from big questions like what happens after death, to the small, such as what's around that next curve or over that far hill. In the years when Sherlock Holmes was in practice, England was a peculiar stew of modern science and method, along with centuries of acceptance that humans were at the inevitable mercy of an overarching Fate on a grand scale, or mysterious, deadly, and immediate creatures in the shadows right outside the door. Holmes believed that answers could be found – *must be found* – or else mankind, at the bottom of things, had no course but to be blown without choice in whatever direction the fateful wind sent him.

"*No ghosts need apply,*" he famously told Watson in "The Sussex Vampire", refusing to believe in a supernatural explanation for a series of mysterious wounds. This four-word quote is often pulled out and referenced to indicate that Holmes had no use specifically for belief in *ghosts*, but to understand its wider implication, the entire quote must be recalled:

> "*But are we to give serious attention to such things? This agency stands flat-footed upon the ground, and there it must remain. The world is big enough for us. No ghosts need apply.*"

2

He refers to the "*agency*" – the team of Holmes and Watson – being "*flat-footed*". Defined by Merriam-Webster, this means "*proceeding in a plodding or unimaginative way*" – or perhaps in a better light, "*in an open and determined manner*".

Holmes often decries the lack of imagination shown by the Scotland Yarders – they accept the easiest explanation without attempting to see to a deeper layer, or to imagine what might actually have happened. But when Holmes himself shows imagination, it is in a "*flat-footed upon the ground*" way. No ghosts – or any impossibilities for that matter – will be considered, for to do so opens a door that cannot be shut, and the involvement of too many possibilities. If murder suspects include both the likely human candidates and the countless dead who might have involved themselves, then there is no possibility for resolution.

Holmes had no use for the impossible. Why waste time considering something that is *impossible*? Eliminate it, and one will inevitably narrow in upon the true solution, however improbable. In The Canon, he references this method a number of times:

> "*How often have I said to you that when you have eliminated the impossible whatever remains, however improbable, must be the truth?*" and also "*Eliminate all other factors, and the one which remains must be the truth.*" – The Sign of Four

> "*It is an old maxim of mine that when you have excluded the impossible, whatever remains, however improbable, must be the truth.*" – "The Beryl Coronet"

> "*We must fall back upon the old axiom that when all other contingencies fail, whatever remains, however improbable, must be the truth.*" – "The Bruce-Partington Plans"

> "*That process . . . starts upon the supposition that when you have eliminated all which is impossible, then whatever remains, however improbable, must be the truth.*" – "The Blanched Soldier"

Too often, because Sherlock Holmes is such a heroic figure, there is the temptation to place him in impossible stories, with situations ranging from absolutely incorrect, where he's living and working in the modern world instead of the correct time period, to having him face actual monsters, serving as a pop-in substitute for Van Helsing or Kolchak the Night Stalker. If a story has these impossible aspects, *then it isn't a*

3

Sherlock Holmes story, but rather a *simulacrum*, with a *faux* Holmes acting out all the Holmes-like parts and making the familiar motions in a situation that would never have actually been a part of Holmes's experience.

Besides the incorrect stories where Holmes is frozen and then thawed in modern times like an amusing duck-out-of-water, or the impossible situations of a modern-day character having absolutely nothing in common with Holmes but a stolen name, there are the efforts to have him battle aliens, vampires, werewolves, and ancient Lovecraftian horrors, and at some point in the story, one is dismayed to find that these turn out to be actual aliens, vampires, werewolves, and ancient Lovecraftian horrors. They might be well written by an author that one respects – but when encountering these, listen for that one clear note, quiet at first, almost beyond hearing, but gradually becoming stronger and more steady. This note has lyrics to resolve the discord:

> *"But are we to give serious attention to such things? This agency stands flat-footed upon the ground, and there it must remain. The world is big enough for us. No ghosts need apply."*

This resolving influence is Sherlock Holmes, and *No ghosts need apply*.

This series of anthologies started because the True Sherlock Holmes was being slowly worn away and diminished. There was a rise of simulacrums – modern Holmes, damaged Holmes, broken Holmes, monster-fighting Holmes. That version was creeping into the public perception of who Holmes truly was like a penumbral shadow sliding across the sun. Too often aspects of these incorrect versions were being included in what were supposed to be representations of the True Holmes, and it was feared that soon the True Holmes would be lost in the umbra.

These volumes have always had the overall basic requirement that the stories *must* present Holmes and Watson as *heroes*, and that the stories can stand alongside the original Canonical efforts that appeared in *The Strand*. It turns out that there was a need for stories like that, as many authors wanted to be part of such an effort, and many readers wanted to experience it. When I first started soliciting stories for these books in early 2015, I truly believed I'd be lucky to get a dozen for a small paperback book. As that year progressed, more and more authors heard about the project and wanted to contribute, and that small beginning led to three simultaneously published hardcover volumes with over sixty stories – Parts I, II and III –

4

the largest Holmes anthology of its type at that time. We've since surpassed it in a number of ways.

From the beginning, all author royalties have been donated to the Undershaw school for special needs children – called "Stepping Stones" back in 2015 – which is located at one of Sir Arthur Conan Doyle's former homes. As of June 2022, the books – now at 36 massive volumes (with more in preparation) and with over 750 traditional Holmes adventures from over 200 worldwide contributors – have raised over $100,000 for the school. I'm incredibly proud of this achievement, and more thankful than I can ever express for the contributing authors, and also the fans who have bought the books.

But even more important to me is the presentation of adventures reaffirming the True Sherlock Holmes.

After the first three volumes, I actually believed that there would be no more, but within weeks, contributors – both previous and new – wanted to know about being in the *next* set. It didn't take much convincing to keep going, because by then I was quite addicted to people sending me new Holmes adventures nearly every day. The various decisions had already been made regarding the books – sizes, cover style, format, *etcetera* – so it was just a matter of soliciting more stories. That was very successful – so much so that we ended up publishing two sets per year, an *Annual* in the spring, and a themed collection in the fall. These themes have included several sets of Christmas Stories and Untold Cases . . . and seemingly impossible cases that have rational solutions.

When the first set of these was announced, *Eliminate the Impossible* (Parts VII and VIII, 2017), a Sherlockian who only wants to have Holmes facing real monsters, despite Holmes's own words to the contrary, commented on social media at the time that these were "Scooby Doo" books. He was correct – these do have Scooby Doo aspects, where, at the end of the story, Holmes unmasks the supposed monster or ghost to reveal a very-human villain. (One might turn it around to say that *Scooby Doo* was Holmes-like, because in their world – at least for many years until the stories shifted and were ruined when they faced actual supernatural villains – no ghost needed to apply there either.)

There might be ambiguous aspects to the stories in these *Impossible* MX anthologies – maybe there is some unexplained side aspect that might be an actual ghostly encounter – but the solutions absolutely cannot involve real supernatural elements as the solutions – because that's a cheat.

At times, I've had to turn some stories away, as the contributors haven't understood the brief. (Having Holmes, for instance, deduce that he's a character in a fictional story might seem to be a clever idea, but it doesn't fit the scope of these books. Likewise, neither does having him do battle to the death with a real vampire, only to turn and find that Watson is now a vampire too.)

Although a few contributors indicated that they couldn't come up with ideas that fit these requirements, in many other cases it has actually stimulated more clever story ideas. In 2019, the concept was repeated with *Whatever Remains . . . Must Be the Truth* (Parts XVI, XVII, and XVIII). Again, the theme inspired some really brilliant stories from our contributors.

By fall 2021, it was time for me to come up with the idea for the next themed set – because the theme had to be announced in late 2021 to give time for the stories to be submitted by the June 30th, 2022 deadline. Having used all the other pieces of Holmes's famous quote, *However Improbable* was the natural title for this collection:

> *. . . when you have eliminated the impossible whatever remains, however improbable, must be the truth.*

I'm not sure what to do about a similar-themed set a few years down the road. Quite likely I can start using pieces of Holmes's other famed quote from "The Sussex Vampire":

> *"This agency stands flat-footed upon the ground, and there it must remain. The world is big enough for us. No ghosts need apply."*

"Flat-footed Upon the Ground"? Possibly. *"The World is Big Enough for Us"*? No, that sounds too much like a James Bond title. Probably *"No Ghosts Need Apply."* Stay tuned . . . .

When announced, contributions were solicited to receive stories much like the previous sets – primarily cases that seemed supernatural but weren't. But then a fun thing happened: The contributors began to nudge and expand the requirements, opening them up a bit. I received a number of seemingly supernatural-that-aren't cases, but also new stories about seemingly impossible crimes – wherein the impossible was eliminated, leaving the improbable truth. I was thrilled, and it was – as always – great fun to see all the clever impossible situations that the contributors contrived, and how Holmes cut through the tangles to a solution. As expected (and required), he's a hero, and that's what he does.

The beauty of reading Holmes stories – and I read a *lot* of them – is that from their basic underpinnings, they can jump in any direction. The stories in these books have to fit certain givens: Holmes and Watson must act like Canonical Holmes and Watson. The dates in their lives and the history through which they move have to be acknowledged and respected. The contributors can't make any changes like killing major characters. Rather, these characters can be used, but then they have to be put back on the shelf, as good as new, for the next person. After satisfying those basic requirements, every new story is a surprise. It can be a comedy or tragedy, a romance or a technical procedural. It can be narrated by Watson or Holmes or some other person. It can be epic or small, a private affair or something that might lead to global war. It can be set in the city or the country, and in England or on the Continent, or in the United States or Tibet – as long as the time-frame fits with the other events of Our Heroes' lives.

In *The Hound of the Baskervilles*, Holmes states, *"Now is the dramatic moment of fate, Watson, when you hear a step upon the stair which is walking into your life, and you know not whether for good or ill."* I know of what he speaks. Nearly every day, I receive a new Holmes story in my email inbox, a submission for the MX Anthologies, or one of the other Holmes books that I edit. Each arrives with infinite possibility, and I can't wait to read it and see what previously unimagined adventure is about to entangle The Detective and The Doctor.

When I was a kid, first meeting Mr. Holmes, I soon realized there weren't enough stories about him. Sixty is really a drop in the bucket for The World's Greatest Detective. New stories appeared on a very irregular basis, and I wished so much for so often that I might have more of them. Now, by way of these books and the modern publishing paradigm and the incredibly gifted and generous authors who contribute to this series, my wish has come true.

I'm amazingly lucky to have the opportunity to see these stories first, fresh from the Tin Dispatch Box, and it's always a thrill when the various collections come together and can be released to the wider world. Now, with this new set – Parts XXXIV, XXXV, and XXXVI – there are more Holmes stories than there were before, and that's a very good thing. I hope you enjoy them, and with any luck, we'll be back soon with another round – because there can *never* be enough stories about the traditional Canonical Holmes, whom Watson called, *"the best and the wisest man whom I have ever known."*

"Of course, I could only stammer out my thanks."
– *The unhappy John Hector McFarlane,* "The Norwood Builder"

As always when one of these collections is finished, I want to thank with all my heart my incredible, patient, brilliant, kind, and beautiful wife of thirty-four years, Rebecca – every day I'm more stunned at how lucky I am than the day before! – and our amazing, funny, creative, and wonderful son, and my friend, Dan. I love you both, and you are everything to me!

With each new set of the MX anthologies, some things get easier, and there are also new challenges. For almost three years, the stresses of real life have been much greater than when this series started. Through all of this, the amazing contributors have once again pulled some amazing works from the Tin Dispatch Box. I'm more grateful than I can express to every contributor who has donated both time and royalties to this ongoing project. I also want to give special recognition to multiple contributors Josh Cerefice Arthur Hall, Tracy Revels, Dan Rowley, Tim Symonds, and Margaret Walsh. Additionally, Ian Dickerson provided not one but two "lost" scripts from the Rathbone and Bruce radio show by Leslie Charteris and Denis Green.

Back in 2015, when the MX anthologies began, I limited each contribution to one item per author, in order to spread the space around more fairly. But some authors are more prolific than that, and rather than be forced to choose between two excellent stories and let one slip away, I began to allow multiple contributions. (This also helped the authors, as their stories, if separated enough from each other chronologically, could appear in different simultaneously published volumes, thereby increasing their own bibliographies.)

I'm so glad to have gotten to know so many of you through this process. It's an undeniable fact that Sherlock Holmes authors are the *best* people!

I wish especially thank the following:

- *Nicholas Rowe* – In 1985, my deerstalker and I were on the front row for the opening-day showing of *Young Sherlock Holmes.* I was a college sophomore and skipped a class that afternoon to be there. (I'm pretty sure that this was the first Holmes film that I ever saw in a theatre.) I'd also bought the novelization, which I started reading that night – waiting until then to be surprised by the film. Although I did have some

8

reservations about a non-Canonical early meeting between Holmes and Watson in their younger days, pre-January 1ˢᵗ, 1881 at Barts, I found the story to be wonderful and exciting, and in particular, Young Holmes was portrayed to perfection by Nicholas Rowe.

Fast forward to 2015, when my deerstalker and I were back in a theater, this time on the opening day of *Mr. Holmes*. Over the previous couple of days I'd re-read the novel upon which it was based, Mitch Cullin's *A Slight Trick of the Mind*. That's a pretty bleak story, and while I give credence over written original versions over film adaptations, in this case I heartily recommend the latter over the former. While I was enjoying how the tone in the film had shifted from the despair of the book to hope, I was also thrilled to find that Nicholas Rowe was back as Holmes – playing a cinematic version that elderly Holmes (played by Ian McKellen) goes to see in a theatre.

I was incredibly surprised when Sherlockian author Paula Hammond put me in touch with Mr. Rowe, and truly amazed when he agreed to write a foreword. Nick, thanks so much for being part of this and your support.

- *Steve Emecz* – From my first association with MX in 2013, I saw that MX (under Steve Emecz's leadership) was *the* fast-rising superstar of the Sherlockian publishing world. Connecting with MX and Steve Emecz was personally an amazing life-changing event for me, as it has been for countless other Sherlockian authors. It has led me to write many more stories, and then to edit books, along with unexpected additional Holmes Pilgrimages to England – none of which might have happened otherwise. By way of my first email with Steve, I've had the chance to make some incredible Sherlockian friends and play in the Holmesian Sandbox in ways that I would have never dreamed possible.

Through it all, Steve has been one of the most positive and supportive people that I've ever known.

From the beginning, Steve has let me explore various Sherlockian projects and open up my own personal possibilities in ways that otherwise would have never happened. Thank you, Steve, for every opportunity!

- *Brian Belanger* – I initially became acquainted with him when he took over the duties of creating the covers for MX Books, and I found him to be a great collaborator, and wonderfully creative too. I've worked with him on many projects, with MX and Belanger Books, which he co-founded with his brother Derrick Belanger, also a good friend. Along with MX Publishing, Derrick and Brian have absolutely locked up the Sherlockian publishing field with a vast amount of amazing material. The old dinosaurs must be trembling to see every new and worthy Sherlockian project, one after another after another, that these two companies create. Luckily MX and Belanger Books work closely with one another, and I'm thrilled to be associated with both of them. Many thanks to Brian for all he does for both publishers, and for all he's done for me personally.

- *Roger Johnson* – From his immediate support at the time of the first volumes in this series to the present, I can't imagine Roger not being part of these books. His Sherlockian knowledge is exceptional, as is the work that he does to further the cause of The Master. But even more than that, both Roger and Jean Upton are simply the finest and best of people, and I'm very lucky to know both of them – even though I don't get to see them nearly as often as I'd like – in fact, it's been six years since out last meeting, at the grand opening of the Undershaw school (then called "Stepping Stones"). I look forward to getting back over to the Holmesland sooner rather than later and seeing them, but in the meantime, many thanks for being part of this.

- *Paula Hammond* – Paula has been a regular contributor to these MX anthologies in recent years, and while she wasn't able to send a new adventure for this set, she amazingly "introduced" me to Nicholas Rowe. Paula: Very much appreciated, and thanks for the support and being part of these books!

And finally, last but certainly *not* least, thanks to **Sir Arthur Conan Doyle**: Author, doctor, adventurer, and the Founder of the Sherlockian Feast. Honored, and present in spirit.

As I always note when putting together an anthology of Holmes stories, the effort has been a labor of love. These adventures are just more tiny threads woven into the ongoing Great Holmes Tapestry, continuing to grow and grow, for there can *never* be enough stories about the man whom Watson described as *"the best and wisest . . . whom I have ever known."*

David Marcum
October 2nd,, 2022
143rd Anniversary of
"The Musgrave Ritual"

Questions, comments, or story submissions
may be addressed to David Marcum at

thepapersofsherlockholmes@gmail.com

11

Foreword
by Nicholas Rowe

I have a confession to make. In life as in fiction, one half of a couple may admit to a past affair simply in order to appease his or her conscience, when best advice might just be for the guilty party to say nothing and carry on without off-loading – Why cause unnecessary hurt? Mine will be a different breed of confession, but I am driven to make it because the secret has been with me for too long now, and I have a sense that I may be among friends here, an unofficial member of a global appreciation Society that worships with varying healthy degrees of dedication at the altar of Arthur Conan Doyle and his creation, Sherlock Holmes.

The fact is that I am a dilettante in this field, or rather an interloper. My "membership" of the club, so full of *bona fide* Sherlock Holmes devotees who have read all there is to read about the Great Detective and who may have gone so far as buying the meerschaum and donning the deerstalker, was thrust on me out of the blue when I was only just out of school. Christopher Columbus (Wait . . . I'm not THAT old . . . I'm talking about the film writer/director) had written a screenplay for Paramount Pictures that imagined Sherlock as a schoolboy, meeting John Watson for the first time, and falling in love with an eccentric inventor's niece. It had the three of them getting involved in an adventure with an Egyptian sect brought to the streets of Victorian London. It was, to all intents and purposes, my first real experience of acting in a film, throwing me in at the deep end playing a character so loved and "'owned" by millions of people . . . and I had only ever read *The Sign of Four*. My knowledge of Holmes and Watson was confined to the brilliant world created by the unbeatable Basil Rathbone (happy to argue about this) and the brilliant Nigel Bruce. At some point I got hold of a clever biography of Holmes and remember a small incident at the Reichenbach Falls . . . but that was it.

Since then I have dallied from time to time with Holmes – a little cameo in Jeffrey Hatcher's *Mr. Holmes*, enjoying Clive Merrison on the radio, watching old re-runs with Jeremy Brett as your man, and of course Benedict Cumberbatch. The eventual success of my first foray (it wasn't an instant hit in the cinema – far from it) made me understand just how robust this character was, and how much appetite there was to see ever more of him. I could have done more research – probably should have done – but (Your Honour), we were all guessing just a little, playing

12

around with characters from a sacred future, but who were for now still in their embryonic form. We perhaps felt we could allow ourselves a little more artistic licence.

So, I have made some excuses, but have I resolved anything?

Maybe . . . As I consider the achievement of David Marcum in compiling a whole new world of Sherlock Holmes stories, hundreds of them, and the bravery and enthusiasm of the many writers who have created them, I tell myself that I just need to relax a little. I am at least in the good company of people who fly the flag for the future of Sherlock Holmes.

Nicholas Rowe
June 2022

"Why, You Are Like a Magician"
by Roger Johnson

You'll remember the incident in "The Adventure of the Beryl Coronet". Sherlock Holmes is gleaning evidence at Fairbank, the house from which the precious diadem has been stolen. When he asks the young mistress of the house, Mary Holder, whether a surreptitious nocturnal visitor is "a man with a wooden leg", her reaction is rather dramatic:

> *Something like fear sprang up in the young lady's expressive black eyes. "Why, you are like a magician," said she. "How do you know that?" She smiled, but there was no answering smile in Holmes's thin, eager face.*

Magicians have proved to be good detectives, of course – in fiction, at any rate. The Great Merlini solves apparently impossible crimes in long and short stories by Clayton Rawson, who was himself a notable magician. On television, there's the equally brilliant Jonathan Creek, who creates the tricks and illusions for an unappreciative egotist named Adam Klaus. Because he knows how these things work, Creek can spot the tell-tale clues that most of us miss. All thirty-two episodes were written by David Renwick, who is otherwise known for his comedies – which shows that you don't have to *be* a magician in order to *think* like a magician.

Members of the Magic Circle are forbidden to reveal their secrets except to *bona fide* students of the art. That, of course, is a restriction that can't apply to the conscientious detective story writer. Derren Brown, David Blaine, or Dynamo don't tell us how they achieve the miraculous, but Clayton Rawson and David Renwick do just that, because a real detective story must have an explanation. The all-time master of the impossible mystery was John Dickson Carr, author, under his own name or as Carter Dickson, of seventy novels and numerous short stories, all devilishly clever and nearly all compulsively readable. It's only fitting that his biography by Douglas G. Greene is called *John Dickson Carr: The Man Who Explained Miracles*.

The "impossible crime" is usually epitomised in the locked-room mystery and its variants, in which a murder or other felony is committed in a space to which no one has access. This was Carr's specialism, but he wasn't the first: Consider Poe's "The Murders in the Rue Morgue", for instance, or that grand Father Brown story "The Dagger With Wings" by

G.K. Chesterton. Or – and it's time we introduced Sherlock Holmes – "The Speckled Band".

The apparently impossible becomes even more disturbing in a sinister atmosphere, which is something that all these writers excelled at. There are effective weird touches, for instance, in "The Copper Beeches", "Wisteria Lodge", and "The Blanched Soldier". And this is from Conan Doyle's description of Stoke Moran manor house, the setting for "The Speckled Band":

> *The building was of grey, lichen-blotched stone, with a high central portion and two curving wings, like the claws of a crab, thrown out on each side. In one of these wings the windows were broken and blocked with wooden boards, while the roof was partly caved in, a picture of ruin.*

The supernatural is no more than hinted at in that particular story, but in Sherlock Holmes's most famous case, *The Hound of the Baskervilles*, its presence is almost expected. The same is true of "The Sussex Vampire" – with that title, it would have to be – and "The Devil's Foot". The latter case, which Holmes calls "The Cornish horror", plays out in a landscape that almost outdoes the Dartmoor of *The Hound*:

> *It was a country of rolling moors, lonely and dun-colored, with an occasional church tower to mark the site of some old-world village. In every direction upon these moors there were traces of some vanished race which had passed utterly away, and left as it sole record strange monuments of stone, irregular mounds which contained the burned ashes of the dead, and curious earthworks which hinted at prehistoric strife. The glamour and mystery of the place, with its sinister atmosphere of forgotten nations, appealed to the imagination of my friend, and he spent much of his time in long walks and solitary meditations upon the moor.*

But it's mystery that Holmes loves. Our great detective has no truck with the supernatural. That's as it should be. And that why those stories – and the stories in this book – are so satisfying!

Roger Johnson, BSI, ASH
Commissioning Editor: *The Sherlock Holmes Journal*
June 2022

An Ongoing Legacy
for Sherlock Holmes
by Steve Emecz

Undershaw
Circa 1900

The MX Book of New Sherlock Holmes Stories has grown beyond any expectations we could have imagined. We've now raised over $100,000 for Undershaw, a school for children with learning disabilities. The collection has become not only the largest Sherlock Holmes collection in the world, but one of the most respected.

We have received over twenty very positive reviews from *Publishers Weekly*, and in a recent review for someone else's book, *Publishers Weekly* referred to the MX Book in that review which demonstrates how far the collection's influence has grown.

In 2022, we launched The MX Audio Collection, an app which includes some of these stories, alongside exclusive interviews with leading writers and Sherlockians including Lee Child, Jeffrey Hatcher, Nicholas

Meyer, Nancy Springer, Bonnie MacBird, and Otto Penzler. A share of the proceeds also goes to Undershaw. You can find out all about the app here:

https://mxpublishing.com/pages/mx-app

In addition to Undershaw, we also support Happy Life Mission (a baby rescue project in Kenya), The World Food Programme (which won the Nobel Peace Prize in 2020), and *iHeart* (who support mental health in young people).

Our support for our projects is possible through the publishing of Sherlock Holmes books, which we have now been doing for over a decade.

You can find links to all our projects on our website:

https://mxpublishing.com/pages/about-us

I'm sure you will enjoy the fantastic stories in the latest volumes and look forward to many more in the future.

Steve Emecz
September 2022
Twitter: *@mxpublishing*

The Doyle Room at Undershaw
Partially funded through royalties from
The MX Book of New Sherlock Holmes Stories

17

A Word from Undershaw
by Emma West

Undershaw
September 9, 2016
Grand Opening of the Stepping Stones School
(Now *Undershaw*)
(Photograph courtesy of Roger Johnson)

It seems not so long ago I was writing with news from Undershaw, and here we are again with even more achievements to report. The school is now well into our new academic year with an unprecedented number of students on our roll, and we are busy firming up our place as a Centre of Excellence for SEND education, not only in our locality but further afield.

As an example of the positive culture we have at Undershaw, we received the most wonderful feedback from a work experience placement student we hosted recently. Here's what she had to say about our school from the time she spent with us:

> *Coming to Undershaw was a fantastic experience. I really appreciated the opportunity to spend time with your students, and even to take part in some drama improvisation! Your students were articulate, confident, and thoughtful. Sports Day was a real highlight for me – I felt it was inclusion at its best. The range of activities on offer, and the careful thought*

18

that had gone into the design of the day to ensure that every child could enjoy and achieve was inspirational.

Earlier in the summer we took our accolades to new heights when Undershaw was awarded a Gold Award by the Skills Builder Programme. This is a framework which identifies eight vital life skills, such as problem solving, leadership, and listening. When mastered, these skills ensure our students are fully equipped to take their places as economically and socially independent young adults. At Undershaw, we work tirelessly to ensure our students are immersed in every feasible aspect of their academic and character education, both of which furnish them for their rich and dynamic futures, wherever they may lie.

Undershaw is making a mark as a great seat of learning, proven this year with a fantastic set of GCSE, BTEC and Functional Skills results. We are so very proud of the results which are testament to the students' hard work, resilience, and perseverance. The way that they approached the examinations, having had their previous learning and opportunities to practise with mocks disrupted by the pandemic, is remarkable. Our students move on with a great set of qualifications and achieved the school's first ever Distinction grades, but just as important, they have developed their social and communication skills, built their confidence, and have become the most delightful group of young people. We look forward to hearing all about their next steps and their future successes.

I often say we have the best "job" in the world, as we are privileged enough to witness these remarkable students, who may not have had the best experiences in education before they came to us, find and fuel their passion under our tenure and ready themselves to spread their wings. My inbox is awash with emails from alumni telling me of their latest triumphs as they carve out their niche in the world. I will leave you with the sign-off from one alumnus who wrote to me recently and signed off with the words, *"Thanks for the confidence in me"*. That just says it all.

On behalf of all the wonderful students, committed and talented staff, and the families we support, I extend my heartfelt thanks to you all for being by our side. Undershaw would not be the school it is today without the selfless dedication of all at MX Publishing. We are honoured to have such friends in our midst.

Until next time…

Emma West
Headteacher
October 2022

"Undershaw," Hindhead, Conan Doyle's House.

Editor's *Caveats*

When these anthologies first began back in 2015, I noted that the authors were from all over the world – and thus, there would be British spelling and American spelling. As I explained then, I didn't want to take the responsibility of changing American spelling to British and vice-versa. I would undoubtedly miss something, leading to inconsistencies, or I'd change something incorrectly.

Some readers are bothered by this, made nervous and irate when encountering American spelling as written by Watson, and in stories set in England. However, here in America, the versions of The Canon that we read have long-ago has their spelling Americanized, so it isn't quite as shocking for us.

Additionally, I offer my apologies up front for any typographical errors that have slipped through. As a print-on-demand publisher, MX does not have squadrons of editors as some readers believe. The business consists of three part-time people who also have busy lives elsewhere – Steve Emecz, Sharon Emecz, and Timi Emecz – so the editing effort largely falls on the contributors. Some readers and consumers out there in the world are unhappy with this – apparently forgetting about all of those self-produced Holmes stories and volumes from decades ago (typed and Xeroxed) with awkward self-published formatting and loads of errors that are now prized as very expensive collector's items.

I'm personally mortified when errors slip through – ironically, there will probably be errors in these *caveats* – and I apologize now, but without a regiment of professional full-time editors looking over my shoulder, this is as good as it gets. Real life is more important than writing and editing – even in such a good cause as promoting the True and Traditional Canonical Holmes – and only so much time can be spent preparing these books before they're released into the wild. I hope that you can look past any errors, small or huge, and simply enjoy these stories, and appreciate the efforts of everyone involved, and the sincere desire to add to The Great Holmes Tapestry.

And in spite of any errors here, there are more Sherlock Holmes stories in the world than there were before, and that's a good thing.

David Marcum
Editor

Sherlock Holmes (1854-1957) was born in Yorkshire, England, on 6 January, 1854. In the mid-1870's, he moved to 24 Montague Street, London, where he established himself as the world's first Consulting Detective. After meeting Dr. John H. Watson in early 1881, he and Watson moved to rooms at 221b Baker Street, where his reputation as the world's greatest detective grew for several decades. He was presumed to have died battling noted criminal Professor James Moriarty on 4 May, 1891, but he returned to London on 5 April, 1894, resuming his consulting practice in Baker Street. Retiring to the Sussex coast near Beachy Head in October 1903, he continued to be associated in various private and government investigations while giving the impression of being a reclusive apiarist. He was very involved in the events encompassing World War I, and to a lesser degree those of World War II. He passed away peacefully upon the cliffs above his Sussex home on his 103rd birthday, 6 January, 1957.

Dr. John Hamish Watson (1852-1929) was born in Stranraer, Scotland on 7 August, 1852. In 1878, he took his Doctor of Medicine Degree from the University of London, and later joined the army as a surgeon. Wounded at the Battle of Maiwand in Afghanistan (27 July, 1880), he returned to London late that same year. On New Year's Day, 1881, he was introduced to Sherlock Holmes in the chemical laboratory at Barts. Agreeing to share rooms with Holmes in Baker Street, Watson became invaluable to Holmes's consulting detective practice. Watson was married and widowed three times, and from the late 1880's onward, in addition to his participation in Holmes's investigations and his medical practice, he chronicled Holmes's adventures, with the assistance of his literary agent, Sir Arthur Conan Doyle, in a series of popular narratives, most of which were first published in *The Strand* magazine. Watson's later years were spent preparing a vast number of his notes of Holmes's cases for future publication. Following a final important investigation with Holmes, Watson contracted pneumonia and passed away on 24 July, 1929.

Photos of Sherlock Holmes and Dr. John H. Watson courtesy of Roger Johnson

The
MX Book
of
New
Sherlock
Holmes
Stories

Part XXXIV
"However Improbable . . . ."
(1878-1888)

However Improbable
by Joseph W. Svec III

Watson sat in contemplation,
wondering what to do.
Sherlock sighed in affirmation,
saying that it's true.

"When you have eliminated,
through precise deduction,
the impossible, you'll be elated.
There will be no obstruction.

For then whatever does remain,
however improbable,
or strange, or odd, or even arcane,
it's not just probable.

It must be 'truth', I say.
I know that it is so.
Mark my words this very day,
as onward you do go.

Use these words as your guide
in all you come across.
The answer then will never hide.
You'll ne'er be at a loss."

Watson nodded, "Yes, I see.
Your words they are quite true.
A bit verbose, if you ask me.
To recall, hard to do.

When you have eliminated
excess words and rhyme,
then it will be abbreviated
to a shorter line.

Keep it simple and precise,
easy to remember.
Short and sweet and quite concise

like a burning ember."

"Watson, you are brilliant!"
Sherlock then replied.
"Your words they are resilient,
and can not be denied."

A one line phrase for all time,
a true deduction tool!
It will solve most any crime.
A simple basic rule.

Here it is my trusted friend.
Tell me what you think.
This will be the perfect end.
We'll put it down in ink."

"When you have eliminated all which is impossible, then whatever
remains, however improbable, must be the truth."

The Monster's Mop and Pail
by Marcia Wilson

"Now that," said my friend Sherlock Holmes, "was an odd little case."

Such comments were common to Holmes when he was cleaning, for he was completely vulnerable to how his scraps of paper and newspaper clippings could plunge him into a past memory. This was why the work of a single day had taken us most of the week, and I admit I was easily distracted when I saw him the way I did now, with a faraway gaze and a strange smile on his thin lips.

From what I could see, he was holding an envelope stamped with the Yard's stationery sigils. When he saw I was watching he chuckled and pulled out a pound-note folded inside.

"It wasn't my first case with the police – by no means! But it was a watermark moment, Watson. This was the case that broke the wall between my work and their regard."

"That was some years ago," I mused. "And you haven't spent the money?"

"I honestly didn't think of it. The letter that came with it is neatly pasted in my album, but it tells you something of my focus that I felt my true payment was in finally being taken seriously."

"Have you discussed this case before?" I tried not to look too eager, but I was growing dull and stupid under the monotony of clearing our rooms for spring.

"I don't believe so. Hmm! Mrs. Hudson will have our lunch in a few minutes. I shall do my best to entertain you with my recollections.

"Before I met you, Watson, I was eking out a rather precarious career in Montague Street. It had the advantages of being proximal to sites of learning, as you know. That advantage was negated by the fact that no one could possibly not know everyone else's business in that quarter. Since discretion was part of my stock in trade, I had to take precautions to gain the trust of my clients. It was nothing to don a disguise three days out of the week, and I remain a little vain about my self-created skills in leaving and returning to my own address with the least amount of attention.

"Adding to this problematic lifestyle was the very nature of my consultatory. Things have changed a great deal in a few years, but at the time I was no different than any of the other experts employed by the police."

"I find that hard to believe," I protested.

Holmes shrugged.

"The nature of the job was very different then. The police were accustomed to visiting an expert in whatever field had been affected by a crime – be it a laundry-mark, or a queer scratch on the lock-plate of a door. The expert rarely left his office and gave a quick answer on the spot. It was a simple, straightforward method of getting information that led to arrests and for the most part it worked for all parties considered.

"The exception, of course, is when there were muddled-up, jumbled cases where a single expert's testimony could crack a case by sheer luck! Imagine if you will, a hapless inspector forced to consult first a locksmith, a tailor, a greengrocer, and a shoemaker because of the sheer plethora of a clue-rich scene of crime. How was the man to know which clue was useful, and which was dross? In the dogged pursuit of evidence, the policemen found themselves fast out of money and time.

"Every dedicated policeman keeps on hand a collection of experts and informers. Most of them are paid out of his own pocket for a few minutes' talk and, believe it or not, the policeman does well in protecting even the worst, most criminal of the citizens on his personal beat. This is a delicate net of intelligence, spun of the frailest floss. In keeping with the confidential nature of one's informants, the men go to extreme lengths. For example, Lestrade would go to Gregson's usual beat to collect information for his hated rival, because Gregson would be too well-known. The same courtesy is always returned. I've often thought the Hapsburgs would tip their collective hats on how the police have systemized their connections.

"Montague Street, again, was less convenient for my clients, so when they did come to my door they were often aggravated, with pockets already drained from fruitless queries, and feeling the pinch of deadlines.

"I was attuned to this problem and resolved to keep myself alert to a solution, for this would be my best way of keeping my bread and cheese – as well as encouraging my reputation.

"My opportunity came one chill spring day with a knock on my door. For the first time in my profession, I had the pleasure of an inspector come to call."

"Was it Lestrade or Gregson?" I guessed with a smile of my own.

"It was Lestrade indeed. He had independently noticed I refused to take their pay when my services came to nought. He was also reaching the height of his jealousies with Gregson, and his bafflement was a sight to behold. Even today when I am feeling a little dark about the inevitable loss of my abilities, I conjure up that memory.

"I bade him come in and poured coffee against the chill in my Spartan little rooms.

36

"'I'll be frank with you, Mr. Holmes,' began Lestrade. 'We have a proper mess. Have you heard about the incident at Hathorn Mewes? Ross George was found yesterday morning, collapsed dead on the floor of his room with odd wounds on his forearm, as if an animal had got to him. But there's no signs of any animal at all in his rooms and the door was locked from the inside.'

"'The Mewes are crowded enough. I am surprised his neighbors cannot contribute something.'

"'They're an offish lot right now. I can't give you details. I'm on my own here, and while I'm sure things will improve in a few weeks, I need to solve this case now.'

"The concession galled our little friend to his core, but I understood what he was saying. 'I have time for you today, Inspector. Finish your coffee while I get my things and take me to the crime.'

"That got his attention, for the 'indoors consultant' was deeply ingrained in the policeman's mind. Still, he had asked for my help and those were my terms.

"The problem was apparent. Ross George was how the police (and I) knew him, but the public knew him as 'The Impervious Ivar, Master of Mysticism'. He was a nefarious mesmerist with an admirable ability to gull the most incredulous victims into parting with their money. He had an amazing talent for reading the assorted strengths and weaknesses of the public and preying on them, and from this livelihood he barely set foot inside his Mewes address. Dining out and supping as a seasonal guest among the bored elites was more his fancy. A party of significance meant seeing him in his white silk turban and black suit, plying his tricks for trade. There were rumours that his true abilities lay within his memory, which was alleged to be without fail and thus a crumb of gossip or scandal from ten years past could be brought to his mind when he needed a favour or loan. If that is true, we can be grateful that his laziness kept him from more than a self-indulgent life. He would have been a fearsome spy for hire!

"His stock in trade was a selection of stern suits and turbans, elaborate white shirts with continental ruffles and pleats, and a large, scaly thing wrapped well in a roll of cloth tucked under his arm or kept in a very dark suitcase with a wire-cased window. The public reported seeing the occasional black-and-forked tongue flicking out of it. He pretended to consult with this thing as part of his act and never let anyone see it. Naturally the public was hasty with ignorance and some colourful fairy tales had emerged regarding this beast. It was commonly accepted as a demon that whispered counsel to his ears, a thing that would vanish in a puff of infernal smoke when he died.

37

"The police had an unsavoury problem before them. George was the darling of foolish but wealthy and well-connected socialites, and probing too deeply into the case could harm the reputations of several old families. I doubt many people really believed he had arcane powers, but in light of things one can't be too careful as to who one puts on the guest-list!

"A dead man, strange wounds, a locked room, and a missing demonic familiar was truly a problem."

"I have to agree," I assured Holmes, but the entire scenario could make anyone's head spin, and I told him so. "It wouldn't take long for the worst of the papers to claim a supernatural element and turn this death into a farce."

"Exactly. His last social engagement was a weekend party for Sir Lionel DuMonte, and the ink covering the event was barely dry. By default, the police would be investigating the guests for potential connections. Time was running out, and I was far from the respected amateur that I am today. I might have had the freedom to beat the corpses in the morgue, but it was quite another privilege to examine a body that is under police authority.

"Now fortified with strong coffee, we bundled up in Lestrade's cab and sped for the Mewes. Lestrade was able to supply a few details regarding what was known of George's last day, but there was little I would call useful. Once the make-up, beard, and turban were off, Ivar became George, and a more forgettable person you will rarely see. In a building as crowded as his tenancy, he was barely known and aloof. Fears of his demon had snared the superstitious people and he didn't encourage their friendship.

"The police had excellent sketches of the room where George had been found. It was a small, single lodging with a wash-stand, wardrobe, folding-bed, and a shelf stocked with what appeared to be cleaning supplies. There was a sketch of the body, on its front and sprawled loosely with a small pool of blood coming from the man's left arm. Once seeing the room with my own eyes, I was impressed at how accurate and flawed it all was."

"I don't understand what you just said."

Holmes shook his head, still smiling ruefully. "No charcoal masterpiece could have recorded the real state of that room, Watson. It was clean. Even with that dry puddle of blood, it was positively sterile, and to see something like that in a place like the Mewes? Astounding.

"I should have mistaken Mr. George's room for temporary lodgings were everything not so carefully kept. Everything gleamed with care and polish. A hand-built shelf boasted as neat a collection of soaps, unguents, and cleaning-rags as you could imagine. A stout tin pail filled with water rested under the shelf. A single wardrobe and a folding-down bed set against the wall were the only furnishings outside of the single wash-stand with pitcher and bowl. The shaving-kit hung on a hook on the wall by the mirror. The window glowed with what could have only been daily washings and the only illumination was a mirror-backed wall lamp. The bed was pulled up and tucked away. The police artist had been exemplary, but again, nothing could have adequately translated this absolute war against grime.

"In ten minutes I had scoured everything of note in that small room. It took me longer than I like to confess, but once I realised why I felt something was wrong, it was painfully obvious.

"'Lestrade,' I asked, 'where is the mop for this bucket?'

"He stared at me and said to his knowledge there was no mop, and all had been under police guard since the discovery of the body. PC Roach confirmed this, for he had been guarding the doorway for the past four hours, and PC Dale before that, and no one had seen anything removed. They may have thought me quite mad, but were polite enough to keep silent as I examined the mop-pail. It was scrupulously clean, without a speck of corrosion or stain inside it. A light layer of dust from the air of the room floated on top and that assured me the water had been standing in the pail for a considerable length of time.

"I don't recommend this, but after wafting taught me nothing, I dipped my finger into the pail and tasted it. It was to all appearances clean, clear (if stale) water from the well.

"'Lestrade,' I said, 'we are missing something important. Why is there not a mop?'

"'I tell you, there is none.'

"'That is important.' And for the moment my curiosity was satisfied. I went to the door to examine the lock. It was an old-fashioned iron latch where the bar is slid straight up, and then to close it, it is lowered into the horizontal sheath. A tongue-and-groove fell through the centre, locking it all in place. It was similar to the latch in my own room, and I wondered if George suffered the same problems as myself. A little rocking back and forth, opening and closing, showed that one could lock this door on their way out if they tipped the bar up in a waiting position, then carefully shut the door mostly shut. A sudden, quick slam jolted the metal and it fell down of its own accord. It didn't happen every time, but once out of every two or three attempts.

"'Well! That's one mystery solved!' Lestrade clapped with a grin. 'Anyone could have locked the door after themselves by slamming it.'

"'It doesn't happen every time, but yes. If we presume another person was in this room when George died, this would be how he or she could lock the door on their way out.'

"Maybe this person had the mop." Lestrade said with some sarcasm.

"If there was a mop."

"Lestrade stared and whistled. 'I thought you determined there was a mop!'

"'Not just yet. Do we have time to view the body?'

"Lestrade hesitated, and finally nodded. 'There ought to be no problems if you're with me,' he said, and from there we diverted to the little morgue the Yard was renting for the service. In the brief length of time the coroner, a man named Honeycutt, had discovered a small purple contusion in the scalp of the corpse, and a strange puncture wound inside a puncture wound."

"Holmes, this is a very odd case!"

"I doubt anyone would disagree with you, Watson. To illuminate your confusion, the dead man had a nasty-looking collection of scars on his forearms, and one on his left shin. They were bite marks of some powerful creature with a short, squat jaw and hooked dentalia along each side. If you saw the teeth of a mako shark during your Australian days, you would find the shape very similar, if smaller.

"The freshest bite was on the man's left forearm, and it was inside one of the deepest tooth-scores that Honeycutt found the tip of one hypodermic needle. I'll give the man credit, for he was an old Navy surgeon with a sour pessimism that presumed all the bodies under his care were victims of foul play – thus it was his duty to expose it. He died not long after our meeting, Watson, and I sorely regret not having the chance to know him.

"Honeycutt had precious little evidence, but the hypodermic needle appeared to be clean under the microscope. It was his suspicion that someone had murdered George by injecting a simple air bubble, hoping to disguise the work by doing it inside the tooth-puncture that had opened the small vein in the arm. By this time Lestrade was getting a bit excitable, and I begged him to allow me some time to check with some of my informants, as I had some suspicions, but it would do no good to betray the Yard with false leads. In the meantime, would he mind investigating the possibility of recent debts incurred by Mr. George? Specifically, someone related to his stage-work or a particularly enthusiastic follower of his folderol?

"Lestrade agreed and I left under my own power, where I spent the rest of the day at the London Library. It was a fruitful three hours for us both. I was returning home when Lestrade's cab pulled up. He had been on his way to meet me with his own news.

"'I don't know how you thought of this, I swear I don't!' he blurted as he pulled me inside with his constables. 'I found his banker and it wasn't five minutes of chatter before I found a note for fifty pounds from Albert Webb, due yesterday. He was George's own agent!'

"'What a demonstration of faith in his client's abilities!' I clapped. 'The payments seem not to have gone well.'

"'That's one way of stating it,' Lestrade agreed. 'My men and I went a-knocking at his office and there he was, prepared to give himself up – he thought we had more evidence than we really did, but I could scarce discourage him from confessing before witnesses.' Lestrade's grin was positively gleeful as he added, 'You'll never guess what he had in his office, too!'

"'Ah, did you find the Gila Monster?'

"Poor Lestrade's face dropped in the most satisfying combination of horror and dismay I have yet to see equaled. He sputtered for breath as the constables simply stared at me, wide-eyed with awe."

I had been on that side of Holmes's genius enough times that all I could do was laugh in sympathy for the poor policemen.

"A Gila Monster! Here in London, Holmes? What a bizarre case! I saw one once in a private zoo and I had nothing but admiration for the keepers brave enough to put up with its sluggish humours. What wicked teeth! They don't need their venom to cause a great deal of harm! But how did you know what it was from the clues?"

"I did not!" Holmes laughed loudly, in high spirits. "That was why I went to the library! There are few scientific questions that cannot be answered by a good reference shelf! I operated under the logic of a small animal, possibly reptilian from the paddle-shaped punctures, and by process of elimination I found a few large lizards, but nothing granted me my 'Eureka!' until I found a warning about their strong jaws.

"Gila monsters, once latched on their quarry, are extremely reluctant to change their mind, and their jaws are stronger than the average man's fingers. Anyone who keeps them has to be aware that they may be bitten without warning. The bites are excessively painful and the venom in the bottom of the jaws causes faintness, weakness, and a host of other unpleasant side-effects.

"The best and swiftest method of getting a Gila Monster to let go, said the books, was to submerge the lizard into a quantity of water. It will let go to breathe and you can free yourself."

"The pail of clean water!" I marveled.

"Indeed." Holmes pulled up his after-dinner pipe and was admiring the envelope with its pound-note.

"But how did you determine the killer was related to George's stage-work?"

"We know that there was a familiar, real or constructed, as part of his performance, and yet in that clean room there was no proof such a thing even existed. I had seen that strange leather suitcase for myself when I saw him perform, so the absence of it was deeply suspicious. Who would go through the trouble of stealing such a thing? Someone who had some belief that he was entitled to it!

"The conclusion was a *denouement*. George needed money and put up his Gila Monster as collateral to Webb, who had been planning to break free of George and make his own fortune in mesmerism. George's expenditures were greater than his savings and he had nothing to pay. According to Webb, they had argued enough that he was infuriated over the reneged debt. He needed his money back, and the sooner the better. He had seen George suffer the bites of the lizard often enough that he could easily arrange things that it bit him during their meeting. As usual, George laid down on the floor to equalize his fainting spells and lowered the Gila Monster into the pail. Once it let go, Webb took his chance and injected the fatal air bubble into George's blood, though it was difficult to do with the blood flowing freely out of the bite-wounds on this arm. Very quickly he popped the lizard into its case and departed, cool as you please, being sure to slam the door until he heard the latch fall into place.

"Word of my little coup was swift to reach the ears of the Yard *en masse*. It was very shortly after that I had new bargaining powers, and I used this to my advantage. A consulting detective willing to leave his comfortable office and padded chair to do his own investigative work *and* who bills only once for his time and expenses, is a far cheaper and more discreet solution to visiting multiple experts who may or may not have the answers a policeman needs. And so, Watson, my reputation began to build, but nothing tops good real estate! When I had the chance to move here, closer to the pulse of London, I was able to hold up my half of the costs thanks to my elevated income. A far better and less draughty place than old Montague Street, and of course, I have far better company."

The Wordless Widow
by Gordon Linzner

"Watson! You're up! Excellent!"

Sherlock Holmes's high-pitched voice echoed through our quarters at 221b Baker Street as he entered the sitting room. I had, of course, already heard of his heavy tread coming up the stairs, although he could move with a deathly silence when the need arose.

It was our first summer living together, one of the warmest in London's history. Holmes had freshly returned from a rare early excursion to Scotland Yard. With no present cases to occupy him, my friend was inclined, when the mood struck, to spend the day in research. He took a particular pleasure in studying police methods in person, at the same time becoming familiar with the local constabulary.

"As awake as I can be," I admitted, grateful for the distraction. I tossed aside my copy of that day's *Daily Telegraph*, having already scanned its pages several times while barely absorbing a headline here, a paragraph there. "I trust your morning has been more productive than mine."

Those who regularly follow my little recountings of our adventures have undoubtedly noticed how often I felt compelled to draw my friend Holmes out of a gloomy mood, whether mental or drug-induced. These actions met with varying degrees of success. The reader may not be aware, however, that, over the years in which we shared rooms, my friend often provided the same service for me, for in those days I often struggled with wartime memories and experiences.

I had slept in late that day, copying Holmes's usual habit, and so had been unaware of his early departure. The previous night had been a late one for me, during which I foolishly indulged in a long and ill-advised series of distractions. Consequently, my pension for the month was sorely depleted. I now sat with ankles crossed, my mouse-gray dressing gown bunched up over my knees, one slipper dangling haphazardly from my left foot, trying not to think about how I would survive over the next fortnight.

"It was enlightening, at least," Holmes replied, raising a thick dark brow. He pointed a long finger toward the tray on the table beside me. "Are you finished with that?"

Most of my breakfast remained untouched, even though I'd waved off the maid's attempt to remove the tray not long before my friend's return. Holmes of course read my expression, as he does all too often.

Before I could answer, or even nod my agreement, he scooped up the last hard-boiled egg, juggling it in one hand.

"You seem particularly energetic this morning," I commented.

"Do I? I just had a fascinating discussion with Inspector Tobias Gregson regarding one of the most obvious open-and-shut cases he'd ever seen."

"A little too obvious, I gather from your tone?"

"You're getting used to my ways, Watson. Shall I share the details?"

"I couldn't stop you if I wanted to." I straightened up in my chair, then bent to retrieve the wayward slipper that dropped to the floor. "I'm all ears."

"The body of a dock worker named Wallace Clayton *(Holmes began)* was discovered in an alley near Paddington Basin, three days ago, in the early morning hours. He'd been shot through the back and apparently dragged out of sight behind a rubbish bin. The constable on duty that morning, a man named William Hammershaw, nonetheless managed to stumble across the corpse. Robbery was clearly not the motive, for a quick examination found his identification and several pound notes untouched on his person.

"His wife, Mary Clayton, an expectant mother, claims she had spent that entire night at their flat in Kensington, mostly asleep. She'd retired early, exhausted from burden of childbearing. Her husband wanted to visit some friends of his at a local pub, but promised he would not be gone long. Not until the following morning did Mrs. Clayton realize he hadn't returned, when Gregson and his team came to their flat, waking her with the sad news.

"The wife or husband is almost always the obvious suspect, and fingers were quickly pointed in her direction. During the previous week, the couple had been heard arguing loudly. None of her neighbors could confirm she actually had been home that entire night. According to Constable Hammershaw, at least one witness claimed he saw her, or someone who looked very much like her, wandering near the Basin at approximately the time a gunshot was heard. Unfortunately, he failed to note that witness's name. A hansom cab was also seen speeding through the streets about then, but again Scotland Yard has so far been unable to track the driver down.

"The new widow told Gregson that her husband had gone out to meet some friends, though she didn't know exactly who. She readily agreed to let them search her flat for possible clues to their identities. That was when Constable Hammershaw, who'd volunteered to accompany Gregson's men, suggested they search the bedroom, and there they discovered the pistol hidden beneath her mattress.

"Mrs. Clayton insisted she'd never seen the weapon before, had no idea how it got there. She was brought to the station for questioning. An examination later determined the bullet that killed her husband could have been fired from that type of gun. Furthermore, it seemed impossible that anyone could have slipped into the flat to tuck the weapon under the mattress if she was, as she insisted, sleeping there the entire night.

"Under Gregson's interrogation the woman abruptly threw a fit, tossing her chair aside and threatening to overturn a table. There was some concern she might be endangering her unborn child. Once the police restrained her, however, she fell into an unnaturally quiet, almost catatonic state, and wouldn't speak further.

"Gregson decided that, rather than keep her in a regular prison cell, they would place her in solitary in an asylum, where a medical staff could look after her

"That is where she has been for the past forty-eight hours, eating little, saying less, staring blankly at the stone walls of her cell whenever the officer in charge or one of the staff looks in on her."

"This sounds quite sketchy to me," I replied, once Holmes finished his narrative. "The woman didn't even try to create a reasonable alibi. I'd guess she's counting on a plea of insanity to save her from the gallows."

Holmes nodded. "Possibly. Of course, should that fail, she'd still be kept alive long enough to give birth, in about three months. I'll know more later, as I have an appointment to visit the prisoner at Edgecombe Asylum this afternoon."

I leaned forward in surprise. "This hardly sounds like your type of case. Where's the mystery?"

"Gregson knows my interrogation techniques. He believes, in my unofficial capacity, I may be able to draw out Mrs. Clayton with better success than he had. It is, if you'll pardon the expression, worth a shot."

I winced at the pun. "Really, Holmes . . . ."

"At the very least, the visit should help me further explore the criminal mind. I believe an outside medical opinion would be of great assistance. Would you be willing to accompany me?"

"I don't know if I'd be much use. I'm a medical practitioner, not an alienist."

Yet Holmes knew I would relish not only the distraction, but another opportunity to see him at work. I suspected he also wished to demonstrate that, inconvenient as my trauma was, others suffered far worse. In our few months together, I'd learned to read his real agenda. He clearly wanted to free me from my torpor, if only for a few hours.

"Afterwards," he added, "we can enjoy a late lunch at Simpsons. My treat."

That sold me. I changed to my street clothes, grabbed a tasteless slice of cold toast to chew on, and followed Holmes down the stairs and out onto Baker Street.

"Consider this, too, Watson," Holmes continued as he waved down an approaching hansom cab. "If Mrs. Clayton is telling the truth, and is truly innocent, then we have one of those 'impossible' crimes you're so fond of hearing me talk about. How could anyone place the murder weapon under her mattress if she slept there the entire night?"

The carriage ride to Edgecombe Asylum seemed to take less time than checking in at reception.

"My name," my friend repeated, his voice growing sharper as his six-foot frame leaned over the admission desk, "is Sherlock Holmes. The gentleman at my side is a medical professional, Doctor John Watson. Inspector Gregson notified your office this morning that we were coming!"

The haughty woman behind the desk looked up, meeting his gaze coldly. "So you already said," she snapped, shuffling her paperwork beyond his reach, though Holmes had shown no interest in it. "I still require written verification. And I have nothing to indicate there would be two of you."

Holmes turned to me, rolling his piercing gray eyes. "See, Watson, why I find women untrustworthy." In years to come, he would keep such reactions under better control.

The woman paused. "What did you say?"

I started to respond before my friend made matters worse, when we were interrupted by a deep calming voice behind us. "Mr. Holmes!"

My friend spun around, his sour expression transformed into a welcoming smile. "Lionel Becker!" he greeted warmly. Turning to me, he added, "I helped Doctor Becker sort out a trifling matter last year."

"Trifling!" Becker gave a sharp laugh. "Those missing papers could have cost me my career! Instead, thanks to your efforts, I am now in charge of Edgecombe Asylum." He addressed the woman behind the desk, as she warily focused on the three of us in turn. "Nurse Evans, is there a problem?"

The nurse's demeanor grew suddenly condescending.

"No problem, Doctor Becker. I was just, ah, sorting out the paperwork."

"I can tend to that later. I'll vouch for Mr. Holmes, and if he in turn vouches for his friend, that's good enough for me."

The nurse did not look up again.

"She just started this week," Doctor Becker whispered, once we were out of earshot. "She's just over-cautious."

"I may have over-reacted," Holmes admitted. "I'll apologize on the way out."

The doctor led us down a corridor lined with heavy narrow wooden doors. Tearful groans and muffled curses echoed from behind some of those barriers. At that moment, I questioned my wisdom in accompanying my friend. A brief, confident glance from Holmes, however, helped steel my nerves. Though I'd only known the man a few months, I knew he would never deliberately risk the well-being of either my mind or my body.

"How is the lady doing?" Holmes asked the doctor as we continued down the shadowy passageway.

"She's hardly spoken a dozen words in the two days since the police brought her here," Becker replied. "She spends most of her time sitting quietly on the edge of her bed, staring at the walls. Barely touches her meals, though she seems to enjoy her tea. In my opinion, she isn't only depressed, but severely traumatized by her actions. I shouldn't be surprised if the jury accepts an insanity plea, assuming the case even reaches a courthouse. Perhaps your colleague can shed some light."

I raised a hand in self-deprecation. "As I told Holmes earlier, I'm a doctor of the body, not the mind."

"Every bit helps," Becker assured me.

Near the end of the hall, a thick-set constable, roughly my own age, leaned against the stone wall next to a particular door. He was idly twirling his truncheon, but hastily pocketed the weapon beneath his long, dark-blue uniform coat as he noticed our approach.

"Good day, Doctor Becker," the constable greeted.

"And to you, Constable Hammershaw," Becker acknowledged. "How is Mrs. Clayton doing today?"

"I've heard not a peep from her since arriving for duty this morning. The room might well have been empty, save that I did look in on her first thing. I gather that this gentleman is the Mr. Holmes we've been expecting?" The officer tipped his tall hat in my friend's direction.

"You have the advantage of me, Officer Hammershaw." Holmes offered a slight bow, then indicated my presence. "This is my friend and colleague, Doctor Watson. You discovered Mr. Clayton's body, did you not? And accompanied Inspector Gregson to interview the new widow."

47

"That is so. I'm hoping to eventually move on to detective status myself. I asked to join the inspector in order to acquire more first-hand experience."

"In fact," Holmes continued, "I'm told it was you who suggested searching the Clayton residence."

"For information about the dead man's friends. I hardly expected we'd find the murder weapon."

"You seem a bit . . . nervous."

"Anyone would be, in these surroundings."

"Officer Hammershaw was also part of the team that brought Mrs. Clayton in," Becker added.

"I volunteered for this guard duty," the officer confirmed. "Want to see the case through personally."

Becker nodded. "At first my staff wasn't sure his presence was a good idea, given what we heard of Mrs. Clayton's initial hysteria. When she lapsed into her current withdrawn state, however, the woman seemed indifferent, almost oblivious, to her surroundings. I saw no harm in keeping the constable as an observer. He might even add some insight."

"A not-unreasonable assumption," Holmes agreed.

Becker gently tapped the narrow pass-through hatch in the center of the door. "The last thing we wish to do is startle Mrs. Clayton," he told us. "She's jittery enough. Although now it's past one, almost lunchtime, she should be expecting a visit." He leaned toward the door. "Mary? It's Doctor Becker. I'm sliding open the hatch in a moment. Some gentlemen with me wish to speak to you. They are neither police nor journalists, I promise."

There was no reply.

I raised a querulous eyebrow.

"She never responds," Becker whispered, "but now she's been warned of our arrival. I pray you have more success than our own staff in getting her to open up, Mr. Holmes." He slid open the hatch door to peer within. "Mrs. Clay . . . ? Good god!"

Doctor Becker hastily pulled a set of keys from his side pocket. While he unlocked the door, my friend peered past his shoulder to see what had shocked the doctor.

"We'll not get any information from her now," Holmes observed grimly.

The four of us rushed inside, Becker in the lead, Constable Hammershaw taking up the rear.

Mary Clayton lay face down on the narrow bed, her rumpled hospital gown exposing the back of her knees. Her right arm was outstretched, its fingers lightly clenched. Her left dangled off the edge of the thin mattress. The inner sides of both wrists were stained dark red.

Becker hurriedly knelt beside the woman, grasping her left hand. I joined him with equal concern. After a minute, he turned to me.

"Doctor Watson, could you confirm the lack of a pulse?"

I raised the woman's right hand. As I did, a small metal screw slid from between her fingers onto the thin mattress. Holmes retrieved the pin, holding it up against the dim light for a better view.

"I had already guessed as much from her pallor," I said when I finished my evaluation, "the coolness of her skin, the blank open eyes. Yes, Doctor Becker, I cannot detect any pulse. Mrs. Clayton has passed away. Possibly an hour ago, no more than three. The official autopsy will be in a better position to narrow it down."

"Thank you. Our policy at Edgecombe is to pay special attention to every death. There are too many stories throughout England of patients buried alive in error. We aim to be more humane than, say, Bethlem Asylum in Surrey."

Hammershaw gave a sharp laugh. "At least the people of London have been spared the cost of a jury trial."

"That's a bit cold-hearted, Constable," I replied harshly as I rose to my feet. "The woman and her unborn child have just passed on."

The constable looked back at the body. "My apologies, Doctor Watson, if I offended you. The stress of police work sometimes affects my empathy, or so I've been told. Still, the woman did cold-bloodedly shoot her husband in the back, and what we have here is an obvious suicide."

I chose not to reply, instead watching Holmes go over the scene.

"I originally intended to become a doctor," Hammershaw continued, unbidden. "I had to abandon my medical training early on. Finances, among other things. Another reason I requested this duty."

"To spend time in a hospital setting?" I grew impatient with his inappropriate rambling.

He sensed my reaction. "Yes, well," he muttered, growing taciturn. "I'm just saying, I see no need to waste more time and money on this case."

Holmes, who'd been ignoring this exchange, suddenly knelt to examine one leg of the bed. "Someone on staff may have been careless, Watson. See? This is one of the screws designed to hold the bed in place, and here is the site from which it's been detached – no easy task with one's bare hands. The tip has been roughly honed as well, sharp enough to leave those ragged wounds on her wrists." He looked up, frowning. "Those fresh scratches on the wall seem the most likely place for sharpening."

"I notice relatively little blood on those wounds," I said. "Certainly not enough loss to cause her death."

49

"You observed that, too? Excellent! And not much staining the sheets, either." Holmes raised the dead woman's right hand, examining the fingers one by one. "There should have been indentations in her flesh, scratches or light scars, where she would have gripped the screw. Yet, I see nothing. Check her left hand, to be certain."

"Holmes!" Doctor Becker exclaimed. "You of all people should know not to disturb the body further – particularly if you suspect foul play! I'll arrange for Scotland Yard to send us an official medical examiner."

"I promise, Doctor Becker, not to disturb the body any more than necessary. Doctor Watson here is more than qualified to oversee."

I agreed. "This is hardly my friend's first examination of a potential crime."

"Watson, look here!" Holmes called. "This tiny bloodstain at the back of her gown, halfway down the spine. The garment was so rumpled, I almost missed it."

"I see it as well." Without waiting for Becker's permission, I rolled the gown further upward to fully expose the flesh. "Here! An entry point so small, it could easily be missed in a casual examination. Made by a stiletto, perhaps, or more likely a sickle knife. Entering at the right angle, the blade could easily penetrate the heart. Death would have occurred in seconds."

"Yet my scan of this sparsely furnished cell revealed no such weapon," Holmes replied thoughtfully. "Nor does it seem possible that anyone could inflict such an injury on oneself, no matter how agile. Note, too, the skin around the wound is cleaner than that of the rest her back, as though recently scrubbed – "

"Clean of blood?" I finished.

Holmes nodded. "Add to that the unlikeliness that any woman this far along in pregnancy, even one determined to end her own life, would lie face down, rather than on her side or back . . . ."

"Then you're certain this is murder, Mr. Holmes," Becker stated. "In a locked room, with a constable barring the only access?"

"I do not invent these details out of whole cloth merely to show off, Doctor Becker. There is no question in my mind. We are looking at a murder, not a suicide."

"Then, much as I appreciate your detecting skills, I now insist the scene remain further undisturbed."

Holmes nodded. "Absolutely agreed, Doctor Becker. Seal off the room while we wait for Inspector Gregson and his team. I've seen all I need to, for now."

"I'll prepare the staff for their arrival." Doctor Becker re-locked the cell door and hurried back down the hall.

50

Holmes stared after him for a long moment, lost in thought.

"Should we join him?" I asked.

"Waiting in Doctor Becker's office would be far more comfortable than standing in this corridor, sweating," Constable Hammershaw advised. "I speak as one who's been here for several hours already, as well as yesterday."

"Your advice is appreciated, Constable," Holmes acknowledged. "Nonetheless, I prefer to wait here."

Hammershaw grunted. "I swear to you, Mr. Holmes, I will not abandon my post. Nothing will affect this scene without my knowledge."

"I expect no less." Holmes signalled me to join him further down the corridor, beyond the constable's hearing.

"Have you come to a conclusion?" I whispered as Holmes leaned his tall frame against the stone wall. His eyes remained fixed on the now-disgruntled constable.

"I believe so. I still need to fit together one or two pieces."

"I sympathize with your reluctant attitude. After all, you have a history with Doctor Becker, and from what I observed something of a rapport."

"Only as a former client, Watson."

"Nonetheless, as the head of Edgecombe Asylum, he can come and go as he wishes, has access to all patients as well as any medical supplies, and equipment he desires."

Holmes raised a thick eyebrow. "Pray, continue."

"I thought his reaction to your examination of Mary Clayton suspicious. He seemed somewhat distraught when you discovered that wound on the woman's back. He might not have wanted that found."

"An interesting theory. What do you think would be his motive for murder?"

I shrugged. "That is yet to be unveiled."

"Well. Let us see how things develop."

I knew then Holmes had a very different theory, but he declined to offer further speculation.

Inspector Tobias Gregson and his team arrived at Edgecombe Asylum within the hour, to be greeted curtly by Holmes. William Hammershaw remained on watch outside the cell, frequently peering in while Gregson and his officers searched the cramped space from top to bottom, and then again once the body was removed.

Neither probe took them much time to sort through the few furnishings, including the little-used chamber pot.

51

"If what you say is true," the inspector told Holmes outside the cell, once his crew were finished, "we are talking about not one, but two impossible, or at least highly improbable, crimes. Mary Clayton's suicide only makes sense as an effort to atone for murdering her husband, or at least regretting the fact that she was caught."

"Except," Holmes countered, "even the most mentally disturbed woman would be unlikely to also take the life of her unborn child."

"Of more significance," Gregson replied with a nod, "as you kindly pointed out, is the fresh and freshly cleaned wounds barely visible on her back. Not only could she not have inflicted that injury on herself with such precision, but my men were unable to find whatever weapon caused it."

"I should have been surprised if they did," Holmes replied. "There is, however, one thing that ties these two 'impossible' crimes together." Holmes turned his attention to Hammershaw, who remained in position by the open cell door, pretending not to eavesdrop. "Constable: You discovered Wallace Clayton's body hidden behind the bin in that alleyway, did you not, and immediately notified the Yard?"

"I did. I had only just started my morning round."

"You also accompanied Inspector Gregson when he went to inform his wife."

"You did act a bit overbearing, Constable," Gregson put in, "but I must admit your instincts were sound. A quick search of the flat led to our discovery of the pistol. The vehemence of her denials only strengthened our suspicions. We had no other choice but to arrest her."

"Much as I value your presence and input, Inspector," Holmes interrupted, "I should prefer to hear the story from the constable's own lips."

"Is this an interrogation?" Hammershaw snapped. "I have nothing to hide!"

"Did I say you did? I am merely trying to gain some insight from your viewpoint."

Hammershaw looked at Gregson. "Is this necessary, Inspector?"

"I don't yet see it, but Mr. Holmes's input has proven of great value to us in the past. I see no harm in your cooperation, and shall allow his inquiry. For now."

"Thank you, Inspector," Holmes replied. "Now, Constable Hammershaw, may I see your truncheon?"

"What has that to do with this matter? The woman wasn't bludgeoned!"

"The sooner you indulge me, Constable, the sooner I will be gone."

With a growl, the thick-set man pushed aside the flap of his long coat and slowly removed the short, thick stick from his side pocket. He waved it in a non-quite threatening fashion before my friend.

Holmes barely glanced at the truncheon. "Now, if you would be so good as to show us what else is in that pocket . . . ?"

The constable hissed. "What are you talking about?"

"Then you won't mind turning that pocket inside out."

"This is insane! Inspector?"

Gregson clearly saw where this exchange was going. "Just humor the man, Constable."

Hammershaw's free hand inched again toward his pocket. Then, abruptly, he raised the truncheon, swinging it at Holmes's skull. My friend instantly spun around, blocking the attack with his left shoulder.

The force of the blow almost threw him to his knees.

Before Hammershaw could strike again, he was pinioned by Gregson and the other constables.

I rushed to my friend's side. "Are you all right, Holmes?"

"I'm fine, although I suspect I may feel the bruising come morning. I anticipated just such an outburst."

"Is this what you were looking for, Mr. Holmes?" asked Gregson. He held up a thin object, half as long as the truncheon, wrapped in a stained brown cloth.

"Undoubtedly." Holmes accepted the package, carefully unwrapped it, and held it out, nestled in the cloth, for the benefit of Inspector Gregson and myself.

"A sickle knife, as you surmised, Watson. If I'm not mistaken, there are also a few specks of dried blood on the blade. This instrument is thin enough, and long enough, to easily penetrate between the ribs and through to the heart, leaving little trace. Death would be almost instantaneous."

"Not even time for an outcry?" I asked.

"Mrs. Clayton may have been too resigned to resist, though I think it more likely a sedative was administered prior to the attack. Access to such medication wouldn't be difficult in a facility such as Edgecombe. A full *post* mortem should confirm if that was the case."

"As if the people of London hadn't enough excuses to distrust the police," Gregson grumbled. He turned to Hammershaw, who was now securely restrained by two of his own men. "Why the devil did you murder that woman? Revenge? Were you friends with her husband? Do you not trust the law to see justice done?"

"I've nothing to say," Hammershaw replied. "You and this Holmes fellow can make up all the fantasies you like. You'll get nothing more from me."

"That remains to be seen," the inspector replied, eyes blazing.

"I very much doubt they were friends, Inspector," Holmes interceded, "but the two men certainly had some interaction. A few inquiries at local pubs in Paddington should place the two men in proximity that night. No, I see only one clear motivation behind the death of Mary Clayton, and that was to prevent this case going to trial. Should the evidence prove it was indeed impossible for her to have killed her husband, the hunt for Wallace Clayton's real murderer could only go in one other direction."

"You're certain, then, she didn't do it?" Gregson's eyes widened. "How do you explain the pistol under her bed?"

"That was what convinced me she'd told the truth. Why hold onto the weapon? Why not dispose of it? Why agree to your searching the flat? No, Inspector, the pistol was planted in Mrs. Clayton's bed during your search, and only one person had motive and access. Whatever reason Constable Hammershaw had for killing Wallace Clayton, he obviously felt his best option to divert suspicion was to frame the wife.

"He requested this duty, watching over her cell, to doubly ensure his part in the affair wasn't exposed. Once he learned that an outside investigator was going to look further into the matter, he decided her suicide would not only underscore her guilt, but also preclude both a trial and further investigation. He practically gloated over the consequences of her 'suicide'. Instead, of course, his actions had the opposite result, giving me more, not less, to work with."

Gregson sighed, then addressed his officers. "Get this monster out of here. I'll meet you at the station. I look forward to a long chat." He turned back to my friend. "Will you be joining us, Mr. Holmes?"

"Oh, I don't see that's necessary. You now have enough information without my further intervention. This is your case, Inspector. I'm simply a casual onlooker, making some minor observations. I intend to look into one more small detail, but I promise to advise you should I uncover anything significant. After which, I owe my friend here a much-delayed lunch. Actually, given the lateness of the hour, more of an early dinner. You know how to reach me if you need to, Inspector."

"You still seem upset, Watson," Holmes said as we settled in at a small window table overlooking the Strand.

Our brief detour to the facility where William Hammershaw had studied for a medical career had indeed left me distraught. "That a hospital supposedly dedicated to the well-being of its patients would keep secret the name of a student expelled for such dangerous outbursts? I shudder at the abuse those souls endured, even for such a short time! The University of London, where I received my own doctorate, would never have condoned such behavior."

"The scandal wasn't much of a secret, since I knew where to look. Perhaps we should blame the Metropolitan Police for not properly vetting their new recruits. In any case, the matter is now out of our hands."

I leaned back in my chair, arms folded. "There's one thing about this case I don't understand."

He offered a thin, uncharacteristic grin. "Only one?"

I shrugged. "One of the things I don't understand, then. Edgecombe's staff move about those halls frequently. How did Hammershaw not only accomplish his murder, but set it up to look like a suicide, in so brief a time?"

"He did so in stages, my Good Doctor. Hammershaw required but a minute here and there. First, he had to sedate Mrs. Clayton, by injection, or chloroform, or more likely tampering with her morning tea. Then he returned for the stabbing. Later he'd remove the bed screw with which to slash her wrists. Somewhere in that timeframe, he cleaned up what little blood the knife left, as best he could, so as not to attract attention. I'm uncertain if he realized the other consequences of those time gaps, given his limited study of medicine."

I nodded. "Hence so little blood around the wrist. Between the moment of her death and his slashing the skin with the screw, her blood would have stopped flowing."

"Precisely."

"Although there was little he could have done about that, even if he realized the problem," I conceded.

"I've no doubt he would also have better rearranged the position of the body, had we not shown up when we did."

"That explains your ready dismissal of my theory that Doctor Becker was the guilty party, though he had the best opportunity. He would have known to compensate for the discrepancy."

"That, along with his lack of motive and – well, if you wish, I can go through the entire list, though it would be somewhat tedious. Ah! Here comes the trolley. A bit of Simpson's excellent beef would not go amiss at present, eh?"

As I had often done before, and would many times do again, I had to admit Holmes was right.

The Mystery of the
Spectral Shelter
by Will Murray

We were returning from dining at The Empire in Mayfair, Sherlock Holmes and I, when we happened to hail a certain hansom cab for the journey back to 221b Baker Street.

I am often struck by the realization how much of a role coincidence plays in our lives – particularly in regard to Holmes, who oft times gives one the distinct impression of being a natural lodestone for coincidence. Of course, such things cannot be. There should be some sensible explanation. Perhaps no explanation can be had. It is just one of those peculiar freaks of life.

We climbed aboard the cabriolet and closed the folding doors. The driver threw the locking lever and shook his reins, which drummed along the roof over our heads. At once, the horse lurched ahead, and soon fell into an easy trot.

The night was cool, for it was October – one of the foggiest Octobers in recent memory, as I now recall. The year was 1881, not very long after the American President, Garfield, died so unexpectedly.

As we made our brisk way home, we discussed this and that over the creaking and squeaking of the cab. I no longer recall the details, but something in our conversation captured the attention of the driver. Perhaps it was the number of times I referred to my good friend as "Holmes".

From his sprung seat-perch behind us, the driver called down during a pause in our exchange.

"Would you be Mr. Sherlock Holmes of Baker Street, himself?"

"I am," replied Holmes.

"May I have a word with you, my good sir?"

Reaching up, Holmes opened the trap through which payment is normally surrendered.

"You may indeed. What is on your mind, Driver?"

"I have told no one of this before, Mr. Holmes. It is, well, frankly too uncanny for ordinary conversation."

"How so?" I could tell by Holmes's tone that his interest was piqued.

"I've been a cabman all of my life, sir. Many are my experiences, but I've known nothing the like what I encountered the evening of Thursday last. Do you recall it?"

"The evening? I recollect that it was positively soupy."

"Exactly. The soupiest fog I've ever seen. I mention this feature because it lends itself to a better understanding of my account."

"Pray go on," said Holmes, with no trace of impatience in his tone.

"It was like this, sir: I was passing through Holborn when the fog rolled in. It was so miserable that there was nothing to do for it but to pull off the street. I couldn't see my own horse's head, and she couldn't make out what was in front of her. Nothing could be accomplished on such a night.

"I stood for nearly an hour at the cab rank by the Old Red Lion. It was a clammy night, you may also recall. And I felt a chill coming on. As you may know, by law we cab drivers aren't allowed to leave our cabs when on duty. And there is the risk of theft if we do. I decided to chance it and seek the cab yard, for I knew that it was folly to expect any fare under the circumstances.

"Carefully, I urged my horse to carry on. And it was on Eagle Street, south of Red Lion Square, that I happened upon a sight that was both wonderful and a little bit astonishing."

The man paused, as storytellers so often do when they are coming to an important juncture in their tale.

"There, in the middle of the way, stood one of the green cabmen's shelters set aside for men of my profession. I'm sure you know what I'm speaking about, Mr. Holmes."

"I do," replied Holmes. "They were Lord Shaftesbury's idea, if memory serves. A growing number of them are scattered throughout greater London. Modest oak huts where simple food and drink are served. Entry is barred to all except drivers such as yourself."

"Exactly. I came upon one such establishment. I've never known that one stood on that particular street, but they are building them where they can, wherever the road is wide enough to permit it, the middle of the road being the preferred spot for construction. The lights of its windows showed through the fog, promising the prospect of a cup of tea and a grumble, so I drew up, tied my horse to the tender, and noticed with disappointment that the trough was devoid of drinking water."

"That by itself is peculiar," remarked Holmes. "Such establishments are usually run with exceeding conscientiousness."

"Precisely, sir," returned the driver. "I've never encountered an empty water trough at any other hospitable shelter. As a rule, they are cut from marble, but this one was carved from common oak. I imagined it must have sprung a leak. Yet I pushed through the door, and there I paused. You may not be familiar with the interior of these structures, Mr. Holmes, for they are built along the lines of a garden shed. A small kitchen is set at one end and the greater portion is given over to a table shaped like the letter '*U*'."

"I can envision it. Go on."

"I was half-in and half-out when I froze in my tracks. The fog followed me in a bit, but I could see plainly a driver seated at the table. I recognized him at once, and called out a greeting. Yet the fellow didn't respond. He didn't deign to turn his head. I thought this odd, and it caused me to hesitate in the doorway. I looked him over closely and saw that he neither moved nor blinked his eyes. It was as if the poor fellow had frozen in place. But of course that couldn't be.

"I repeated my greeting, this time addressing him by name. Again, sir, he neither moved nor spoke. It was as if he were stone dead.

"Befuddled, I looked in the direction of the kitchen. A stocky man stood there. I didn't recognize him, for his face was a profusion of mutton chops and whiskers. He was staring at me. I didn't like the way his black eyes were fixed upon me and that, as well as the uncanny way in which the other man sat in his chair as stiff as a board, caused me to immediately retreat.

"I untied my horse and betook myself away."

The driver fell silent. The rataplan of shod hoofs on cobblestones continued unabated as we moved through Mayfair. "What do you think of that, I ask you?"

"Remarkable story," said Holmes quietly. "Is there more to it?"

"In a manner of speaking, yes, there is. I made inquiries among my fellow drivers as to Red Mackinaw, as we called him. He always wears a Mackinaw coat. We have special names for one another, you see. I'm called Old Houndstooth, of example."

"I'm aware of the tradition," said Holmes.

"I'm sure that you are," replied the driver. "No one with whom I spoke had seen Red Mackinaw in more than a month. I couldn't discover where he lived, and so couldn't inquire there. The man had departed utterly from his old haunts. Yet I saw him on that pea soup of a night, alive – and yet seemingly not."

The driver fell silent.

Holmes had been smoking his pipe, and puffed away at it for some moments in deep thought.

"You appear to have left out one portion of your story, Driver."

"If I have, you may remind me at your leisure."

"Whether you returned to the shelter subsequent to your strange encounter."

"Oh yes! Thank you for reminding me. My experience has me so shaken that it may have obliterated some of my wits. I did go back several nights later. I feared to, but at the same time I felt a strange attraction.

"Now, sir, I cannot swear to it, on account of the beastly fog, but I believe I came upon the exact spot on which the shelter stood. And as God is my witness, *it was no longer there!*"

"But you admit that the fog might have confounded your sensibilities," pressed Holmes.

"I don't deny it. But I rattled up and down that road and discovered no shelter. There was no mistaking the street. I know it well. The shelter was no longer there."

Holmes took his pipe out of his mouth and asked, "Driver, would you be so kind as to take us to the precise spot?"

"I'm not afraid to, if that is what you are asking."

"I don't doubt it," stated Holmes. "But I would like to see that spot with my own eyes."

"Very well, sir," said the driver, redirecting the horse, and wheeling toward Holborn.

I was astonished by this request. The story told by the driver had all the marks of a common ghost story. I didn't take it seriously in the least, but Holmes evidently did.

"What do you expect to find there?" I asked.

"I expect to find a void where the shelter once was."

"You credit the possibility that such a shelter existed at that spot?"

"I don't discount it. Beyond that, I have no firm or fixed opinion. I trust you don't object to coming along with us?"

"Not on any grounds," I responded. "But I'll be very much surprised if anything comes of it."

Eventually, the cab turned onto Eagle Street and drew up to the spot where the driver believed the green shelter once occupied. It was a macadamized island amid the road's cobblestones. We all three dismounted as Old Houndstooth pointed out the local sights.

"The reason I'm certain that this is the spot, Mr. Holmes, despite the fog of that evening, is because that chimney pot with the cracked corner was visible to me."

"It is a common enough chimney," Holmes observed. "That crack is distinct, I will admit."

Holmes stepped out into the street and examined the patch of macadam where the green shelter might have stood. He studied the ground intently, paced off a certain length, and then paced the width of that length. Satisfied, he came back to join us.

"The portion that is macadamized measures approximately the length of a horse-drawn carriage. That is the length of green shelters, which are uniformly built. If your shelter existed in reality, Mr. Houndstooth, that is the only spot in view on which it could have stood."

"That's my belief as well, Mr. Holmes. But what do you make of it?"

"Very little at the moment. Tell me: During the brief interval when you stood paused upon the threshold, did you smell anything?"

"Such as?"

"Such as food, for example."

"No, I didn't smell food cooking."

"Nor coffee?"

The driver shook his head. "No."

"Yet the driver who didn't move was presumably drinking something, was he not?"

"Yes, there was a tea mug set before him, and a cottage pie, but I smelled nothing of the sort."

"Did you notice steam arising from either?"

"I did not."

"How far along had the other man gotten into the cottage pie?"

"I didn't see that he had, Mr. Holmes. To my eyes, he had yet to dig in."

"Did the cook also appear immobile?"

"No, not so much immobile as standing fixedly, with the steady yet avid gaze of a crow. I didn't care for the look in his dark eyes, for there was no human warmth or greeting in them."

"I see. Now tell me, was another cab in evidence?"

"No, sir."

"Peculiar, wouldn't you say?" prompted Holmes.

"Now that you mention it, devilish peculiar. Red Mackinaw's rig should have been standing before the water trough – but it wasn't."

"Was there anything else about the immobile driver that struck you as odd?"

"There was, sir. It might have been a trick of the light, but the color of his eyes seemed off."

"Off in what sense?"

"Red Mackinaw's eyes were blue, you see, but on that night they appeared to be the wrong shade of blue."

Holmes's grey eyes grew bright. "The difference was that distinct?"

"As different as chalk and cheese, Mr. Holmes."

"Thank you."

Turning away, Holmes commenced a promenade of the area. He moved between the passing cabs and carriages, crossing from one side of

60

the street to the other, walking up, then down and all around with that long-legged stride of his, eyes bright, head cocking this way and that.

Coming to a streetlamp, he paused to pick up something from the ground. He seemed to have some difficulty doing so, and I couldn't see from this distance what he had discovered.

Upon his return, Holmes showed us the tip of his finger. Attached to it was a tiny chip of green.

"What is this?" I asked.

"I would prefer to direct that question to our friend, Mr. Houndstooth," said Holmes. He held the finger under the man's nose and the fellow studied it intently.

"That is a paint chip, I imagine."

"Indeed. Do you recognize the color?"

"It is green. That is obvious to the eye."

"Unquestionably. But many shades of green exist. Do you recognize this one in particular?"

"Well, it is dark green, but that's all I can make of it."

"This paint chip," stated Holmes, "is the shade called Buckingham Green. If you will look about, you will not see a building or door that's painted this precise color."

I looked up and down the thoroughfare and saw that this was true. Before I could ask Holmes the significance of this, our friend Houndstooth suddenly became excited.

"My word! This is the exact color that they paint the shelters!"

"It is," said Holmes quietly. "It's a distinctive green, customarily reserved for commercial buildings, and specifically for the cabmen's shelters. But for this, I would doubt your story. But having discovered a paint chip of this color, I must give it some measure of credence, even though it is otherwise inexplicable."

The driver broke out into a strong grin that made his aged eyes crinkle. Relief seemed to wash over his face. "Thank you, sir. Thank you, Mr. Holmes. I thought I had gone daft. But you have restored my faith in myself. I saw what I saw on the terrible night. Sadly, I don't know what to do about it."

"I would like to look into this matter," stated Holmes. "Take us to the offices of the Cabmen's Shelter Fund, if you would."

"At once, sir."

Once again, we three all climbed aboard the sturdy hansom cab and went rattling off.

Not long after, we were in the Cabmen's Shelter Fund offices, and Holmes was speaking to the gentleman in charge.

"I know nothing of any cabmen's shelter on that street," he said in a bewildered tone of voice. "There must be a mistake. Such a shelter cannot exist – otherwise I would know about it."

"You're certain of this, I take it?" asked Holmes.

"There is no higher authority who could contradict me on that score," the fellow assured us.

"Thank you, sir," said Holmes. And off we went.

Rattling through London once more, I asked, "What do you make of that?"

"It doesn't dissuade me from a growing conviction that the shelter existed on that night. I cannot otherwise account for it. But the possibility intrigues me more with each passing minute. I'm determined to get to the bottom of it."

"Why is that important?"

"Because of the missing driver. I fear for his fate, for a man's eyes don't change color, not even in death."

At those words, I felt a cold chill creep up and down my spine. I fell silent. I'd never known Holmes to pursue phantoms, or take cases that had nothing at the base of them. The seriousness of his words and the grave expression upon his face told me that this was no minor matter.

Old Houndstooth dropped us off at Baker Street. In parting, Holmes said, "Return to this address in one week. I may have answers, or I may not."

"Thank you, sir," said the driver and gave his reins a toss. I watched him disappear into the gas-lit evening.

We sat around the hearth after that, smoking and discussing our peculiar encounter.

"I cannot imagine what lies at the bottom of this present mystery," I ventured.

"Nor can I," admitted Holmes, charging his pipe with fresh shag. "I would have dismissed the main story except for the fact that he saw a confederate, and the fellow was strangely unresponsive. A man can mistake a building in the fog, but he will not err in regard to a comrade. The men who drive cabs and carriages are a close fraternity. When they congregate in their little shelters, they do so without the intrusion of the general public. Men such as you and I, despite our station in life, aren't permitted through the small doors to take meals with the common cab drivers. We aren't of their profession, and so are excluded. No, Watson. I believe our Mr. Houndstooth did encounter his friend, who hasn't been seen in some time."

"A building, no matter how modest, cannot easily disappear."

"Ordinarily, no," agreed Holmes. "But this one seems to have appeared out of thin air. And if it was able to do that, I would venture to say that disappearing back into thin air cannot be any more extraordinary."

"If it's gone as you say," I wondered, "how can you puzzle out the mystery of its existence?"

"By waiting for another fog of equal consistency to the one in which it first appeared."

"What! Do you think it might return?"

"Friend Watson, I'm certain of it."

"And what makes you conclude that?"

"By the simple fact that the door was open for Mr. Houndstooth."

I didn't understand the thrust of that statement, but I could tell from the veil coming over Holmes's sharp grey eyes that he was falling into one of his deductive trances, and I would probably get no more out of him.

I picked up the evening newspaper and began to peruse it. When Holmes was ready to reveal more, I was confident that he would do so.

For the evening at least, I put the strange matter out of my mind.

Over the course of the following week, Holmes came and went from our shared rooms. He spoke little, and what speech he offered had to do with personal matters or the news of the day.

If progress was being made in the mystery of the spectral shelter, I couldn't read it in his austere features. In as much as he didn't bring up the subject, I took that as a silent suggestion that I refrain from doing so myself.

I will note, however, that various members of the Baker Street Irregulars, principally their nominal leader, young Wiggins, came and went almost daily. No doubt Holmes had pressed them into service, for the net he cast was a wide one.

On the eighth day, Old Houndstooth pulled up before 221b. Mrs. Hudson brought him up.

"Hello, Mr. Holmes," he greeted, removing his rather weather-worn top hat.

"Come in and sit down, my good fellow," invited Holmes, waving an aromatic pipe in the direction of a wicker chair.

"I don't mind if I do," said the man.

Once seated, he asked, "Have you learned anything?"

"I regret to inform you that I've discovered little of substance."

Old Houndstooth looked perfectly abashed. He appeared to have put great store in my friend's deductive abilities. No doubt he had heard the increasing rumors of Holmes's accomplishments from the gossip of his fellow tradesmen.

"That doesn't mean, however, that I haven't made some progress in my investigation," added Holmes. "For in criminal investigations, absence can be as significant as substance."

"I'm most interested, of course."

"Do you know a driver who goes by the name of Bob Flash?"

"I've heard the name, but I don't know him. Not personally. We cab drivers, you might say that we are a veritable legion."

"No doubt," murmured Holmes, pausing to puff on his pipe. "By making inquiries, I've learned that Bob Flash, who was a regular patron of a cabmen's shelter familiarly known as the Green Garden, hadn't been seen in four days."

"Peculiar, that," mused Old Houndstooth. "Do you think it has meaning in regard to the matter at hand?"

"You may recall that there was a fog on Wednesday last."

"I do. It wasn't so terrible as the previous fog, but it was bad enough."

"On that night," Holmes recounted, "I prowled the length and breadth of London, changing cabs often, and collecting such gossip from the drivers as I could. I failed to sight the phantom shelter. However, I heard about the absent Mr. Flash from a driver I questioned. By making inquiries at the cab yards, I further learned that his horse and cab were never returned, and he hadn't been heard from since that last day he was seen."

"Blokes in my trade go missing every so often," muttered Old Houndstooth. "I don't conjure any special significance to it. The driver sits high on his box day after day, and in all types of weather. Then catch their death of cold quite often. Not all of them expire, but some do. Perhaps Bob Flash has departed this mortal coil."

"I suspect that you're correct. In fact, I'm quite certain of it. My interest is where might the *corpus* be found?"

"I cannot imagine."

"If my theory is correct, it will be found in the cabmen's shelter that you so briefly visited."

Holmes said this in a calm manner, but it caused me to all but rise from my chair. As for Old Houndstooth, he gasped wordlessly and his mouth fell open rather awkwardly.

After he had gathered his wits, the fellow closed it with a snap, and then asked, "Do you mean to tell me that he has joined Red Mackinaw?"

"I do. He's taken the seat that was reserved for you, except that you didn't deign to sit in it."

"What is this you are saying? I don't understand."

"I cannot name either the suspect or guess his motivation, but I've come to suspect that someone is collecting cabmen such as yourself."

Now Old Houndstooth's eyes were wide. I could tell that he wished to speak, but his tongue refused to function properly.

"I'll answer the question struggling to emerge from your lips," said Holmes. "You specifically weren't chosen. The green shelter was merely a snare for the unwary. Any cabman who entered on the night that you stood upon its threshold would have met a similar fate. As it happened, you eluded the trap, even if you weren't aware of that fact."

"I confess that I fail to comprehend the full import of your words."

"That, my friend, is because I've only begun to form a theory. I'm still constructing it, shaping the clay into a vessel capable of holding the entirety of the solution. As I say, I don't know the name of the suspect, nor his motivations. And I can only guess at certain particulars. But they begin to form in my brain, rather like a nascent fog gathering."

"If what you say is true, what is to be done about this problem?"

"Only this: The green shelter has appeared twice that we know about and disappeared each time. Upon each occasion, a thick fog enveloped London. I'm a persistent person. I will investigate each fog as it rolls around, until this ghostly structure is located."

"Then what will you do?" asked Old Houndstooth.

"I feel that I must enter it."

"Would that not mean your undoing?"

Holmes paused. "It conceivably might, I suppose. But unlike your unfortunate fellow cabmen, I won't be caught unawares."

Old Houndstooth sat silently as he absorbed the full import of Holmes's words. Finally, he spoke up. "You are a brave man, Mr. Sherlock Holmes. A very brave man."

"It isn't bravery that will unravel this riddle, but cleverness. We're dealing with a clever criminal with a strange twist of mind. I must be more clever than he if I'm to win out."

"Is there anything I can do for my part?"

"There is. I know it's highly irregular. When the next fog appears, I should like to borrow your cab for the evening."

The fellow hesitated. "I could lose my license, you know."

"And I could lose my life. But it's only a request, not a demand. You must make up your own mind. You have your risks, and I have mine."

Old Houndstooth thought about it several minutes. Finally, he said, "If it weren't for the fact the Red Mackinaw was a chum, I would fear to lose my livelihood. I will bring my cab around during the next fog. You may depend upon it."

"Very good," said Holmes.

That was the end of our discussion, Old Houndstooth politely took his departure, after which Holmes fell into a deep reverie.

I offered only one comment. "I don't understand what lies in back of this grisly matter, but for the moment I don't care to know more than I've just learned."

"You're very wise, Watson. It's a disturbing and troubling problem. I don't think it can be fully solved unless I brave the lion's den myself."

Several days passed without any noteworthy occurrences.

Inevitably, as it must, another London fog swept in, all but enveloping the City in a thick greenish shroud that chilled one most disagreeably.

As it was gathering, Old Houndstooth drew up to Baker Street, dismounted, and knocked upon the front door. Mrs. Hudson brought him up.

"Old Houndstooth, it is you!" cried Holmes. "What admirable timing."

"My cab awaits your pleasure, sir," he said gravely. "Kindly remember that I must return it to the cab yard by no later than midnight."

"I will endeavor not to disappoint you, my good fellow. You may enjoy the warmth of our hearth until I return. Mrs. Hudson will bring up a cold supper and all the tea or coffee you care to drink. You'll find cigarettes and cigars set on the table."

"Good hunting to you, Mr. Holmes."

Having previously made our arrangements, we took our departure. I was to pose as a passenger whilst Holmes drove the hansom cab. He had bundled himself up in a heavy coat, counting that his uncustomary attire wouldn't be noticed in the fog. The only concession he made to his assumed profession was to borrow Old Houndstooth's aging top hat.

And off we went. Clattering over the cobblestones, sweeping through the mist-choked roads in search of something that might or mightn't have any substance. At least, that was the way I imagined the way of things.

London fog is a strange spectacle indeed. As dusk descended, one by one, the gas lamps had been set alight. They made strange spectral beacons guiding us through increasingly deserted streets.

Before terribly long, most city dwellers had sought the warmth of their hearths. The cabs and carriages that normally bustled about retreated to equally agreeable shelters.

I opened the trap over my head and asked, "Where away?"

"I don't know for certain. I've eliminated certain areas, owing to the fact that known cabmen's shelters occupy prominent places there. I'm seeking a locality that is on a highway, for the road must be wide enough to accommodate a shelter, but also one that has the advantage of being discreet."

66

"Discreet to whom?" I asked.

"Discreet to the one who is collecting unfortunate cab drivers."

I thought the term "collecting" a disquieting choice, but said nothing.

All 'round London we wound our way, occasionally encountering a passing driver conveying a passenger hastily homeward. This was a particularly thick fog and we nearly collided rounding a turn, but Holmes was adept in nearly all things and guided his unfamiliar horse safely by the moving obstruction.

I will not test the reader's patience by describing in great detail the way we progressed in our peregrinations, other than to relate that we passed through Charing Cross, St. John's Wood, and parishes in between.

Seated as I was below and slightly ahead of Holmes, I served as guide as much as I could in my efforts to perceive obstacles in our path, for seated high on the box, as cabmen called their high perch, Holmes could see only the back of the head of his horse and what lay beyond.

Despite my obvious advantage, Holmes's vision was much keener than my own. He had a quite brilliant instinct in that way. Of course, he knew the streets and byways of London better than most cabmen who plied it.

And so it was that Holmes spied the illuminated windows before I quite made out what they were.

"We must now proceed with caution," he called down. "For directly ahead lies a cabmen's shelter sitting in the middle of a road where no shelter is supposed to exist."

Squinting my eyes, I stared ahead through the rolling fog. It was quite cold and made my lungs ache slightly. I could discern nothing more than faint row of rectangular lights in the road ahead. From my coign of vantage, they could represent anything at all.

"Are you quite certain?" I asked. "I cannot make anything out of them."

"By their position in the road and the arrangement of the illuminated window panes, I'm possessed by a ready certainty. And if you will taste the air, you may detect the faint odor of a wood-burning cook stove."

Once this was brought to my attention, I did indeed recognize the familiar smell. I reached into pocket for my army revolver. Holmes had instructed me to arm myself before we set out.

Slowing the horse, Holmes pulled up to the blurred building swirling in the fog. It was yellowish, but with a greenish tinge. No doubt the fog made the softly glowing window panes appear more green than they truly were.

I all but held my breath as the horse fell into a slower gait. I became aware of the wheels rolling over the slick cobbles and the clip-clop of shod hoofs striking brief-lived sparks against the pavement stones.

When the looming structure ahead resolved itself in the swirl, I could discern that its shape was wide and its color was green. I was looking at one end of a cabman's shelter. There was no question about it: This wasn't the end with the window for those who ordered food to take away, but the blind end.

Holmes guided the horse to one side, where the tender and water trough were set. Pulling up carefully, he drew back on the reins and the horse dutifully took up a stance with her head above the drinking trough.

Dismounting, Holmes tethered the beast, and paused to look down into the trough. I peered down as well. Although its surface was moist with fog-condensation, the wooden trough was otherwise dry. Kneeling, he struck a Lucifer alight, then peered beneath the structure, coming to his feet after a momentary inspection aided by its fitful flame.

Holmes glanced towards me and nodded silently. I knew that look. He found what he had been seeking. I felt a chill ripple up and down my spine.

Pressing close to me, he whispered, "Remain seated. I will enter. But be prepared for any eventuality, no matter how startling. I've thrown the lever that unlocks the hansom doors."

I lifted my revolver to show that I was ready.

With my curt nod of understanding, Holmes went to the entrance and stepped in. The door closed behind him. My attention went to the glazed side windows and I could see the outlines of two seated men. I studied their silhouettes closely and noted that they didn't move or react in any manner to Holmes's entrance.

This realization made my blood run cold. I gripped my revolver more tightly and waited, for there was nothing more that I could do under the circumstances.

I watched to see if Holmes's lean body would pass in front of the windows, but it did not.

I heard the soft pawing of horses nearby, and could smell their coats, which had become saturated by the cloying fog.

Unexpectedly, there came a shout, followed by the noise of objects being upset – metallic objects, I believed.

To my astonishment, I heard a snorting of horses, followed by the wholly unexpected lurching of the shelter. It commenced moving, causing the horse tethered before me to pull away, whinnying in abject fright, her hindquarters jolting the cab.

I believe I possess wits equal that of almost any man – any man other than Holmes, perhaps. Although the green shelter marched ahead directly before my eyes, my brain was slow to comprehend the seeming impossibility. Also, the rearing of the mare added to my confusion.

Nevertheless, the green shelter moved as if on wheels, yanking on the horse's traces tether, pulling her along with it.

Holmes's voice suddenly cried out, "Watson, free the horse!"

My hand was already in my other pocket as I leapt from my seat. I hastily unfolded my pocket knife, while reaching down for the traces with my free hand. There was no time to untie them, so I cut from behind the knot.

That was enough to free the poor animal. Grasping the tossing mare by her neck, I steadied her as best I could. It was all that I could do to hold on. The beast was spooked – not that I could blame her.

The door banged open and Holmes sprang out of the departing shelter, no longer wearing his top hat.

"Quickly, Watson! Into your seat!"

Holmes moved like a veritable bolt of lightning, sweeping up the dangling reins, and carrying them back to the driver's perch. He mounted with the agility of an acrobat while I scrambled back into my own seat.

Cracking the whip, Holmes impelled the skittish horse into motion.

"What on earth is happening?" I shouted out.

"Nothing that I didn't expect," returned Holmes tersely. "The shelter is mounted upon concealed wheels. I imagine they are cased in India rubber."

"What is making it move?"

"A team of two horses at the other end. The attendant is standing in the hutch window behind them, managing the traces. I almost had him, but he fought back from the fortified advantage of the kitchen, which was separated from the dining room by a half-wall and counter, which he yet commands."

We were following the shelter at a brisk pace. Due to its size and bulk, the ungainly structure didn't move with great speed, yet it passed along the misty highway at a reasonable-enough clip. Holmes was able to keep up with it, but he showed no appetite for attempting to overhaul the odd contrivance.

I comprehended the wisdom of that course of action. A hansom cab is a reasonably stable style of carriage, but it is exceedingly light. Two horses hauling a structure as large as a growler could easily trample us into kindling and broken bones.

Calling down from his seat, Holmes said, "None of this spectacle exceeds my expectations. I knew that the shelter had to be mobile in some way. A team of horses and wheels was the only practical possibility. It explains why the horse trough was of wood and not marble, and was dry. A marble trough would have been too heavy and unwieldy for convenient transportation. Nor could a wooden trough have held water for long as the shelter was moved into place under cover of the fog."

"I imagine not," I said. "But I still don't comprehend the motives behind this startling trickery."

"That is something I've only formed the most indistinct theories. We will have to get the truth from the attendant now driving the shelter to what I imagine to be a stable."

"He cannot hope to elude you, can he?"

"He cannot, but in his blind panic, the bounder is doing the only thing that his crazed brain suggests – so he seeks the imagined safety of his own domain."

"It's a mad thing that we are witnessing."

"Quite mad," agreed Holmes. "But it will not be long before we have our answers, as well as our men. Do you have your revolver in hand?"

"It's at the ready," I replied.

"Let's hope you don't have to discharge it, except to wound."

My eyes were on the rearmost window. Through the glazed glass I could glimpse the silhouette of two diners. Their bodies shook whenever the shelter was dragged around a turn, but otherwise they showed no signs of animation. It gave me an uneasy feeling to watch them seated thus, erect yet somehow lifeless.

"Are those men dead?" I called up through the trap.

"Not merely dead. They are stuffed like trophies."

"Good Heavens!" I exclaimed. Beyond that, I had no words.

Onward we raced through the fog, through streets I couldn't recognize in the swirling greenish mist, forcing myself not to cough as I inhaled the wet condensation.

I don't know where we ended up. Not at the time. Later, I learned it was in Kentish Town, not far from Hampstead Heath.

Finally, the shelter which had been rocking and rattling as it moved swiftly between the ranked gas lamps jerked to a rough and clattering halt before a long mews, for the lane proved to be a cul-de-sac that balked the horses' progress.

The mare likewise pulled to a halt.

"Steady, Watson!" hissed Holmes, throwing the unlocking lever whist dismounting from his perch.

70

As I leapt from my seat, he raced ahead, carrying the horsewhip. Together we sprinted, half mist-blind, until we reached the front of the peculiar conveyance.

Upon seeing that the hutch window behind the nervous horses was vacant, I cried out, "I don't see him!"

Looking about and raising the whip, Holmes gave it a crack.

The two horses bolted, half-turning due to the way being blocked by a mews.

As the green hut passed before our eyes, it revealed a crouching man whose face was a profusion of mutton chops. Angry-eyed, he came to his feet, a horsewhip of his own in one hand.

This lashed up and out, and Holmes took the stinging blow on one shoulder. With the grunt of pain, he sank on one knee, then forced himself to his feet and sent his own whip snaking out. The tip took the cap off the man's head, for it swept down and then sideways with such deftness that the whip might have been an extension of Holmes's own nervous system.

For nearly a minute, they fought with their whips, landing blow after blow, dodging, neither man giving an inch, nor pressing his advantage more strongly than the other – this despite the unfortunate fact that Holmes was armed with a shorter whip than his opponent.

Holmes's heavy coat took the brunt of each blow. He suffered no wounding of the flesh. Then came a snap and crack, and the ruffian's whip drew blood from Holmes's right ear. Fortunately, Holmes recoiled in advance of the blow, sparing himself the loss of that appendage.

I could take it no more. Lifting my revolver, I shot the cruel fellow in one shoulder. The bullet struck true, caused him to snap around, the whip falling from his spreading fingers.

After the fellow had fallen, Holmes turned to me and said with great sincerity, "I'm not sure that was necessary, but I cannot say that it wasn't. I commend you for your aim, if not your timing."

We went over to the prostrate man, who was grunting and cursing inarticulately.

Reaching down, Holmes took hold of one of the man's mutton-chops and stripped it off. It had been attached by gum, for it was false.

The face revealed was unknown to either one of us. It was so convulsed with fury and baffled rage that we might not have recognized it even if we had known the fellow intimately.

From a pocket, Holmes removed a police whistle and blew it once, sharply.

A policeman showed up in short order. After Holmes identified himself, he commenced a summary of our experience which satisfied the man, even if it also confused him.

71

"I'm required to summon an inspector," the officer said when Holmes had completed his account. "For this is far beyond me."

"Please notify Inspector Lestrade," said Holmes. "We will guard this man while you do your duty."

The policeman rushed off to notify Scotland Yard.

Holmes addressed the prostate blackguard. "What is your name, fellow?"

"It isn't for you to know, nor I suspect to ever find out."

"It shouldn't be hard to discover it," said Holmes tersely. "But I perceive that you are a taxidermist by trade."

The man's expression became absolutely blank. His mouth made uncouth shapes, but he couldn't get his words to emerge. Finally, he blurted out, "How in the devil did you know that?"

"By your foul handiwork, you murderous scoundrel."

My mind flashed to the two seated figures in the now-stationary green shelter, and I recalled that Holmes had said that they had been stuffed. I began to comprehend that much of the ugly matter, but most of it was still beyond me.

In short order, the inspector put in an appearance and we were forced to repeat a portion of our accounts.

The criminal was taken into custody without delay.

A wagon was summoned from the morgue, and the bodies of Red Mackinaw and the other cab driver were removed from the shelter. This was done with difficulty, given that they were stiff, their joints and limbs not flexible in any way.

I observed this awkward operation and offered my medical opinion.

"I must agree with you. I believe those men have fallen victim to a taxidermist with peculiar notions."

"What's this you say?" demanded Lestrade.

"These men have been murdered and subjected to the taxidermist's art," I confirmed. "If you examine their faces closely, you will see there is a residue of wax or tallow used to preserve the skin from putrefaction. No doubt their eyes are of painted glass."

Lestrade went to one of the victims, lifted his eyelid slightly, touching it with the tip of his finger.

"You are correct, Doctor. Glass."

Holmes addressed Lestrade, saying, "If you don't greatly mind, Inspector, I must return this borrowed hansom cab, for the hour is growing late and the driver is waiting in Baker Street, no doubt fretting over its whereabouts."

"I should like to accompany you, Mr. Holmes," said Lestrade, "so that I may have your full statement."

"I'm happy to oblige, if only you will wait until we reach 221b before I must divulge all of my discoveries, for I must tell everything to the owner of the cab, and I don't wish to repeat myself unnecessarily."

"Of course. We must wait until matters are set to rights here."

The bodies were hauled off and the green shelter was moved to the side of the road to await its ultimate disposition, whatever that might be.

Then Lestrade and I climbed aboard the cab as Holmes took his perch. With a crack of the whip, we were off.

"It is the most grisly thing I could ever imagine," muttered Lestrade. "Men stuffed like trophy animals."

"It is bizarre beyond even the outrages of that notorious pair, Burke and Hare," agreed Holmes.

"I'm eager to hear your story, Mr. Holmes. But I will exercise patience."

Eventually we reached Baker Street, alighted, and soon forgathered around our comfortable and familiar hearth. After introductions were made between the inspector and the cabbie, Holmes took up his pipe, lit it, and began recounting the entire affair for the benefit of all.

I will pass over the portion which the reader already knows.

"First, there was the question of the physical reality of the ghostly structure," Holmes was saying. "Although we were of short acquaintance, I judged Old Houndstooth to be a fellow of sober disposition. While under other circumstances I might have suspected him of concocting a wild story to cover for the murder of Red Mackinaw, that fact that he brought the matter of the man's disappearance to my attention bellied that possibility. And there was the green paint chip I discovered. A minuscule thing, true, but telling. Had Old Houndstooth here planted it for me to discover, it would not have been so tiny and difficult find.

"Once I had satisfied myself that the cabmen's shelter was a thing of substance," Holmes continued, "I realized that it could only have been moved by human agency, which would require a team of horses and suitable wheels. In as much as Old Houndstooth didn't notice any wheels, they must have been concealed under the sill of the structure, which you recall isn't much larger than a common Clarence. Therefore, only a brace of horses would have been necessary to haul it about. No doubt they were present on the night our cabbie friend here discovered the shelter near Red Lion Square. They may have been tied to the opposite side, or more probably hitched to the front for a rapid escape."

Old Houndstooth spoke up, saying, "I do recall hearing horsey noises, but they weren't visible in the fog, and I imagined them to be associated with a cab not in evidence."

"I spent a great deal of time scouring London," continued Holmes, "looking for a stable commodious enough to not merely conceal the remarkable shelter from prying eyes, but to hold both horses as well. Such a place needed to be out of the way so that the comings-and-goings of the contrivance wouldn't be noticed. Of course, a thick fog would account for its stealthy perambulations.

"I confess that I utterly failed to locate the stable. No doubt it's one belonging to the mews where we ran down our man. I'm sure Scotland Yard will ferret it out in due course. That particular detail is no longer important.

"Reasoning from the fact that the perpetrator must perforce operate on sufficiently foggy nights to conceal his activities, as well as to catch unwary cab drivers in his snare, I understood that my best course of action was to await future fogs.

"On the second occasion, despite vigorous searching, I was unable to spy the green structure, and so another cabman fell victim. It's unfortunate, but I'm but one man, and even with my youthful Irregulars out and about, adding to the search, our numbers were insufficient to accomplish anything useful."

Lestrade interrupted to ask a question that had instantly leapt to my own mind, "Why didn't you enlist the aid of Scotland Yard in this undertaking?"

"While I've known you for some time, Inspector, and you know me in turn, you do not know me well. Had I gone to your office to alert you that a madman had counterfeited a cabmen's shelter for the purposes of capturing unwary drivers in order to stuff them like trophies, would you have believed me? I have a well-deserved reputation for eccentricity. You might have ascribed my claims as an imaginative product."

Lestrade considered that question at some length. Reluctantly, he gave his answer.

"I wouldn't have given it the credit I give it now, no. Not even your growing reputation would have persuaded me that such a preposterous thing could be true."

"Thank you, Inspector. You have your answer. Now, to continue.

"On this third occasion, I decided that I must risk entry into the shelter in disguise, if I could find it. I reasoned that the shelter wouldn't again turn up again in Holborn. Therefore, I could discount it as a possibility, believing that the perpetrator wouldn't return any place he'd previously set up shop, as it were. In case Scotland Yard was on the scent, he might also avoid nearly places. But I also reasoned that such a cumbersome contraption as a shelter on wheels couldn't travel very far without risk of misadventure or chance discovery. That latter I believe could be passed off to the credulous as the transportation of a ready-made structure from the place of construction to its eventful destination. Altogether, I concluded that I must confine my search to greater London, which greatly reduced the compass of my efforts."

"That is sound thinking," remarked Lestrade.

"Thank you," returned Holmes. "This simple process of elimination proved to be the correct method, for in searching other environs, I happened upon the shelter long before dawn could break. Upon entering, I saw that two men sat frozen at the U-shaped table. The attendant, he of the false whiskers, greeted me by asking, 'What will you be having, sir?'

"'You, sir,' I returned. 'I will be having you.'"

"The fellow looked startled at my words. At that point, I reached out with both hands and endeavored to seize him by the coat lapels. And there ensued an awkward struggle. But for the wooden counter separating the kitchen from the dining area, I would have had him then, for it would have been a simple matter to knock him to the floor.

"Unfortunately, he took advantage of the barrier by kicking the partition with such force that he propelled himself backwards, thereby breaking my hand grip.

"Turning, he seized the traces of his standing team of horses that trailed into the kitchen area through the take-away window and gave them a sharp snap. So impelled, the team broke into a run, and I was knocked off my feet, losing my top hat in the process.

"This setback would have been momentary, for I could have regained my feet easily and climbed into the kitchen, conceivably overpowering the man, but I heard the startled whinny of Old Houndstooth's mare and knew that she and Watson, as well as the hansom cab, were in peril of being dragged to their destruction.

"Crying, 'Watson, free the horse!' I pushed aside the folding doors and tumbled out.

"Watson had succeeded in cutting the ties, and we endeavored to follow the hurtling shelter to its destination. I knew that it couldn't escape us, so we didn't press it too hard. This proved to be a wise course of action. The bounder had no place to go except back to his stable, unless he was willing to abandon his property and horses. He was foolish enough not to.

"And the rest, Inspector, you know."

Old Houndstooth had been listening in a respectful silence. Now he asked a question.

"Why did this man engineer such a mad scheme?"

"I don't quite know," admitted Holmes, "but I think when you use the term 'mad', you have put your finger on the only possible motivation. No doubt he robbed the drivers he poisoned. Beforehand, I imagined the tea he served contained a tincture of strychnine, or something similar that would swiftly kill without damaging the body he wished to preserve. Robbery couldn't be the motive. Considerable effort had been made to falsify a green shelter and mount it on custom-built India-rubber tyres, the latter detail I confirmed by peering under the structure by the light of a Lucifer. These tyres allowed for the safe and nearly silent progress of the entire arrangement over cobblestones. One could rob a cab driver just as successfully without going to all that laborious bother. Add to the fact that he essentially embalmed bodies and set them at his table suggested a person who is both determined and demented."

Holmes turned to Lestrade.

"I imagine the motives in their entirety must come from the lips of the perpetrator. That will be your responsibility to extract, Lestrade."

"Yes," said the inspector, rising to his feet. "And now that I've heard your account in full, I must go and see to inveigling a confession from this strange murderer."

Old Houndstooth also stood up, saying, "I thank you for your efforts, Mr. Holmes. And for the safe return of my cab."

"Think nothing of it," returned Holmes. "It was an intriguing puzzle, even if it did lead to an unpleasant resolution."

"Not as unpleasant as it might have been," returned the driver. "Weren't for you, a third driver would surely have fallen victim to this rotter."

Holmes nodded in acquiescence, adding, "If it weren't for you bringing this to my attention, no doubt that would have been true."

Old Houndstooth turned to the inspector and asked, "I would be pleased to give you a ride to Scotland Yard, if that's your wish."

"That would be delightful," returned Lestrade. "I didn't look forward to finding a cab at this late hour in this pea-souper."

"And I would appreciate your assistance in recovering my top hat, Inspector."

Lestrade laughed rather grimly. "Of course! It will make a rather memorable souvenir, I should think."

After they took their leave, I addressed Holmes. "I have no doubt that this is a case of criminal insanity. But it is more extreme than anything I could imagine."

"Bizarre is the only word for it," agreed Holmes.

"One point intrigues me: However did you leap to the conclusion that the missing man had been stuffed like a hunting trophy? As I recall, you arrived at that notion rather rapidly."

"That was the most elementary deduction of all. You will recall Old Houndstooth's observation that Red Mackinaw's unblinking eyes were an

76

entirely different shade of blue. This could only be explained by the insertion of glass eyes into the dead man's eye sockets. No other explanation was possible."

He returned to his pipe and there appeared to be nothing more to say. Not an hour after the criminal had been apprehended, all of it seemed to recede from memory like some evil dream conjured up by the nasty fog.

There isn't much more to the story than I've told. Inspector Lestrade wrung a confession from the man, whose name was Leo Ott. He was a carpenter by trade, which explained how he was able to fashion so cunningly the false shelter. He was also skilled in taxidermy, and knew something of embalming human corpses, a trade he learned from his late father. Perhaps being sired by a tradesman engaged in so unsavory a business contributed to his queer way of thinking. But that is mere conjecture on my part.

The cabs of the missing drivers were located in the same stable that had concealed Ott's queer invention and its team. The horses belonging to the deceased cabmen weren't immediately found. Scotland Yard ultimately determined to its satisfaction that they had been sold for meat, as re-selling them as beasts of burden would entail too many risks and questions.

According to Lestrade and the newspapers, Ott had never been married and enjoyed few friends. When asked why he had an engineered such an elaborate scheme for such a peculiar and unprofitable result, the man spoke simple words that were repeated in newspapers and magazines the world round.

"I was getting nothing much out of life," he was reported to remark, "and this seemed to be an interesting way to pass the odd evening."

The sheer banality of this remark was widely reported at the time. No further explanation was ever given.

"Mad as the proverbial hatter," I murmured as I read the account in the newspaper.

"Madder, Watson," replied Holmes gravely. "Much madder."

When, just before his hanging, the man was asked to repent, Ott steadfastly declined.

"It was the most interesting undertaking of my life," he stated with a simplicity I thought utterly bereft of conscience. "I regret nothing."

These last three words proved to be his unsavory epitaph.

No one claimed the body, and there were no services to speak about. Ott was buried in a pauper's grave and quickly forgotten – even if his evil deeds lingered in the minds of Londoners for some few years thereafter.

77

The Adventure of the Dead Heir
by Dan Rowley

It was late fall, and Sherlock Holmes and I had been sharing rooms for less than a year. He had taken me along on several of his cases, the first being the Lauriston Garden affair, which I may write up some day. His habits, while a bit peculiar, were becoming more familiar and easier to live with. There still was the constant stream of assorted, slightly odd visitors, his "clients" as he referred to them, in his capacity as a consulting detective, which he distinguished from governmental and private detectives. He believed he was the only one such extant in the world. And he still spent time away almost every day, visiting laboratories or hospitals or some of the less-savory precincts of London.

We were comfortably ensconced in our sitting room after a generous breakfast, both reading the morning newspapers. Suddenly, Holmes lifted his penetrating eyes from the paper, straightened his lean body in the chair, and flared the nostrils on his hawk-like nose. "Ah, Watson – Mrs. Hudson is on her way up the stairs. She has just let someone in the front door, Gregson from the Yard, if I judge correctly."

"Holmes, I am becoming somewhat accustomed to your methods, but pray tell how do you know it is Gregson?"

He smiled. "This time there wasn't much to deduce. You were immersed in your reading and likely didn't notice, but I normally keep all senses alert, even when pursuing the newspaper. I heard Mrs. Hudson open the door and greet the visitor, whom she clearly knew. I could tell by the gait and sound of his footsteps as he came into the entry hall that it was Gregson."

Before I could reply, there was a knock at the door to the sitting room. At Holmes's beckoning, Mrs. Hudson appeared and informed us that it was indeed Inspector Gregson who wished to see Holmes, who bade her to see him in.

Gregson shortly came in and greeted us both. He removed his overcoat and, at Holmes's indication, settled himself next to us before the fire. He of course hadn't changed a bit since we had seen him last, rubbing his hands and pushing back his flaxen hair from his brow. Holmes believed he was the most intelligent of the Scotland Yard detectives, although that was faint praise. Holmes found him to be quick with energy, but not very imaginative or innovative.

"Mr. Holmes, thank you for seeing me with no notice. I've been called to an unusual case that I believe could benefit from your talents."

"Why a personal visit this time instead of a letter?"

His white face blushing, Gregson replied. "You may recall that, in the Lauriston Garden matter, Inspector Lestrade was there with me, and I felt it better to stay there with him. I am the sole inspector in this matter, and felt it was more expedient to come directly to you to explain the situation and allow you to ask questions." He presumably was referring to the rivalry Holmes had discerned between the two inspectors. In the earlier case, he must have felt he needed to keep an eye on Lestrade, which wasn't a factor here.

Holmes nodded. "Is the site secure?"

"Yes, sir. Your admonition about a 'herd of buffaloes' trampling through the scene stayed with me. I only need to be told once. I have two constables posted at the location, one downstairs and one on the floor above with strict instructions to allow no entrance or exit from the house, or no egress into the room where the crime was committed."

"Very well. Tell me what you know so far. Leave nothing out." With that, Holmes leaned back and closed his eyes, but undoubtedly intensely concentrating on every word.

"I was at the Yard very early this morning when I received word of a suspicious death in Belgravia near Eaton Square. I made my way there rather quickly and was astonished with what I discovered.

"Apparently the master of the house, Norman Chapman, had left word with his valet last night that he needed to be awakened no later than eight o'clock this morning, as he had a meeting with the family solicitor. When the valet approached the door to Chapman's bedroom at eight, he knocked but received no answer. Upon attempting to open the door, he discovered it was locked, apparently from the inside, as Chapman had the only key and there was none in the keyhole on the outside. After several more tries at arousing Chapman, the valet began to become alarmed. By this time, his repeated pounding on the door and calling to Chapman had awakened several members of the household. One of them went outside and hailed a constable.

"Luckily, the constable was a quick thinker. He decided to lever open the door and instructed the valet to fetch the proper implement. The valet returned with a fire iron from a nearby fireplace, one that had a thin wedge-like edge. Using this, the constable pried open the door. Upon looking in, the constable realized something was amiss and ordered no one else to enter. He went over to feel for a pulse and determined Chapman was dead.

He came back into the hallway and instructed the valet to summon another constable. When the second one arrived, the first one told him to send word to the Yard and then return and guard the downstairs to ensure no one entered or left the house."

"It is indeed fortunate that the constable acted so promptly," I observed. "But what about the death was suspicious?"

"When I arrived at the house, it was quite evident to me that foul play had been at work. Chapman was about twenty-eight years old, thin, but with signs that he'd been gaining some weight, which because of his rather short stature was more noticeable – his clothes seemed tight, and so on. He had sandy hair that was beginning to recede, clean-shaven, and rather average features. When I came into the bedroom, he was fully clothed, lying diagonally across his bed. His clothing and the bed clothes were in a considerable state of disarray. And his body, especially his face, was severely contorted, as if he had suffered convulsions prior to his death. I asked the family if he had any medical history of seizures or other similar disorders, but they said he did not. I also asked if he was in the habit of experimenting with chemicals. They again confirmed he did no such thing.

"I began to suspect some kind of poison. I questioned the valet, who said Chapman had retired at approximately ten the previous evening, seemingly in good health and fine spirits. The valet had knocked on the door after finding it locked at about midnight to see if Chapman required anything before he retired. Chapman called through the door that he needed nothing more, but was going to stay up a while longer.

"I asked the family if they had heard anything during the night, but they hadn't. I learned that Mrs. Amelia Chapman, Chapman's step-mother, had been ill and accordingly had a nurse on duty during the night. Upon questioning the nurse, I learned she had been awake all night in the dressing room between Chapman's room and his step-mother's. Although there is no connecting door between the bedrooms, the nurse had left the dressing room door into the hallway open all night to have better air circulation. She assured me she would have heard anything in the hall, but did not."

"The condition of the body does indeed suggest poisoning of some sort," I said, "but why do you seek Holmes's assistance?"

"An excellent question, Doctor. You see, I cannot for the life of me figure out how the poison was administered. I checked, and the windows in Chapman's room were locked as securely as the door. He was healthy at midnight and dead by eight. But it seems no one but a spirit could have entered the room. There is no evidence of any poison in the room."

This aroused Holmes from his deceptive torpor. "There must be a logical explanation, Gregson. There may well be some evidence in the room to show how it was done."

"Yes, Mr. Holmes, there may be, but I decided there was enough curiosity here that it would be better to bring you in at the very beginning, knowing as how you might prefer that."

Holmes sank back in his chair and again closed his eyes. After several minutes, he opened them and gazed searchingly at Gregson. "There could be some points of interest here, especially if the scene is relatively undisturbed, a luxury I haven't often had. Allow me to ask a few questions before I decide. Other than the constable checking for a pulse, has anyone touched the body?"

"No, sir. I didn't, and I gave strict instructions to the constable to allow no one into the room, not even the coroner, until I returned."

"You said there were no evidence of poison, and that Chapman didn't have a history of experimenting with chemicals. Was there any sign of food or drink in the room?"

"No food, but a decanter and glass stood on a table by the front window. I smelled both but detected no odor."

Holmes sat silently for a few minutes, deep in thought. "Have you begun considering possible motivation? Who else is in the house? You mentioned a nurse, valet, and step-mother."

"Chapman's sister and step-brother also reside there. And the sister's fiancé is visiting. I decided not to question anyone but the valet and the nurse on the assumption you would prefer that I not plant ideas in anyone's mind."

"Quite right. Watson, what are your thoughts?"

"I not yet see how a poison could be administered in these circumstances, especially given that it appears Chapman was alone in the locked room for two hours with no apparent ill effects. The pending visit to the solicitor may be suggestive at least of motive, although perhaps it was routine business."

"That raises an excellent point. Your perceptions are improving with each matter we pursue. Gregson, you haven't mentioned Chapman's father. What of him?"

"He was a colonel in the Army serving in South Africa. He was a part of the group serving under Colley that was defeated at Majuba Hill."

Holmes must have noticed that I unconsciously touched the spot of my old wound. Gregson was being polite in referring to Majuba Hill as a "defeat". The Army had been making a night march earlier that year to relieve a garrison besieged by Boers, who caught them with a surprise attack that led to a rout. It was a humiliation for the Army that I and every other soldier felt keenly.

Holmes clearly was intrigued by this matter, but he also kindly tried to deflect my thoughts. "Well, Gregson, we might as well use our morning assisting you as sitting here reading the newspapers. Watson, are you up for joining me?"

"I would be delighted."

"Excellent. Gregson, let us don our overcoats and be on our way in the cab you have waiting for us."

"How did you know I had a cab downstairs?"

"I heard it pull up when you arrived, but it didn't depart, so it is obvious you asked it to wait."

With Gregson shaking his head, we went downstairs. The cab made its way a bit to the west, and the driver decided to proceed south along the perimeter of Hyde Park. Holmes was again deep in thought, so I took the opportunity to enjoy the park's marvelous landscape. Although not as green or crowded as in warmer times of the year, I always enjoyed seeing the beautiful expanse of grass and plants in the middle of bustling London. It made me proud to reflect that, with all the change going on around us, we Londoners still wanted to maintain nature in the heart of our Imperial city.

We soon were passing Belgrave Square and turned right onto Eaton Place, which was lined with stately townhouses, gleaming whitely in the morning sun. Each consisted of five stories with a slight cornice and a flat roof. The corners of each were faced with stone of a slightly darker color, and chimneys discreetly extended above the roof line.

We pulled up to our destination, which wasn't hard to miss, given the constable standing on guard at the front door. He saluted Gregson as we climbed the stoop to enter, apparently showing no curiosity at the presence of Holmes and myself. We entered into a hallway that ran the length of the building, with doors on either side. Gregson explained, "The ground floor has the usual assortment of arrangements, such as the drawing room, dining room, library, study, game room, kitchen, and so forth. I assume you would prefer to start with Chapman's bedroom. It's on the first floor."

Holmes nodded his assent, so we proceeded to the rear of the hall and went up the stairway. As we entered the first floor hallway, Holmes laid his hand on Gregson's arm. "Before we proceed, please describe the layout so that I can orient myself."

"Certainly, Mr. Holmes. There at the front of the house on the left, where the constable is standing, is Chapman's bedroom. Moving toward the back on that side, the next door is to the dressing room, where Silvia, the nurse, was stationed. As I mentioned, there is no connecting door to

Chapman's bedroom, but there is to the bathroom that opens into the master bedroom. That is where Mrs. Amelia Chapman, Chapman's step-mother, sleeps.

"On the other side of the hall, at the front, is Edith's bedroom. As I mentioned, she is Chapman's sister. Next to that is a bathroom. And here in the back is the guest room, where Mudge, Edith's fiancé, is staying. Oliver, Chapman's step-brother, sleeps on the floor above."

Without another word, Holmes strode across to the door to Chapman's bedroom. He paused to murmur something to the constable, who was beaming at the end of it. I assume Holmes was complementing him on his diligence.

Gregson and I watched as Holmes intently studied the door and the lock for what seemed an eternity. He also looked at the inside of the door, ascertaining there was no key in the lock from the inside. We then entered the room, which was tastefully decorated with flocked wallpaper and adorned with various hunting and martial prints. Against the wall to the left was Chapman's bed, on which the deceased sprawled. To the left of the bed was a dresser and to the right a wardrobe. To our right was the wall fronting the street. It had two windows, between which was a table and comfortable chairs. On the table was a decanter and a glass, both containing a brownish liquid, which I assumed contained whisky. Also on the table was an open book and a note book. Directly across from the door was a fireplace with an ornately carved mantelpiece. The remains of the previous night's fire were in the grate. To the right of the fireplace was a large bookcase filled with leather-bound volumes. Its twin was directly opposite on the wall with the door.

Holmes went over to the body, gesturing for me to follow. We both gazed at the grotesque figure. Gregson had been correct: The bedclothes showed the after effects of quite-violent seizures, and the face was distorted in a horrible rictus of pain, which even death could not erase. The body was partially on the bed, with the legs hanging over the side.

"Watson, observe the rug at the side of the bed. What do you see?"

"It clearly is out of place and is bunched up in several places. Also the nap is in some disarray, as if something had scraped against it."

Holmes bent over to look at the heels of the shoes on the body. "Yes, I can see remnants of fibers here that appear to match the rug. That suggests that Chapman not only had seizures, but also that initially he fell to the floor and his body arched so violently that his heels dug into the carpet. He must have then had a slight moment of recovery and attempted to climb into the bed in the position we now see him."

Holmes then walked the perimeter of the room, stopping to minutely examine the contents of the dresser, wardrobe, and the two bookcases. He also tested both windows to ensure they were securely fastened. He lingered for a long time at the fireplace, lying down on the floor to look at the remains of the fire, and turning onto his back to look up the chimney. He then spent a few moments pushing around the ashes.

Gregson and I were quiet during this rather extraordinary performance. I had witnessed it before and still wasn't quite accustomed to it, but I was learning that Holmes's methods, however peculiar they might appear to others, produced results. At last he arose and went over to the table between the windows. Holmes looked at the book's title and then flipped through the notebook. He next sniffed at the glass and decanter, smiling grimly to himself. "Gregson, please ask the constable to procure a clean glass for me and have him bring in the valet." Gregson went over to the doorway and made the request. Holmes stood in contemplation until the valet appeared with the glass. He was in his mid-forties, with an erect bearing and a very deferential manner. He tried, unsuccessfully, not to look at the body on the bed.

"We appreciate your cooperation in this disturbing matter. You already have met Inspector Gregson, I believe. He has asked me, Sherlock Holmes, and my colleague, Doctor Watson, to assist in the inquiries related to the unfortunate demise of your master. I don't believe anyone has mentioned your name."

"William, sir. William Barrett."

"Barrett, I would like to ask you some questions. At approximately what time did Mr. Chapman return home last night?"

"He didn't call for me immediately, but the butler alerted me to his presence at approximately ten. I ascertained that he already had come up here to his bedroom, so I arrived to determine if he needed me for anything."

"The door was unlocked when you came here?"

"Yes, sir. I knocked and he told me to enter. He said he didn't require anything at that time. I did set the fire going and ensured there were sufficient coals in the scuttle for the night."

"Did you notice anything out of the ordinary in the room?"

"No, sir."

"How did he seem?"

"Quite normal. If anything, a bit excited."

"Why was that?"

"I believe he was about to be admitted to a club that he had been seeking to enter for some time. He had mentioned it to me that morning while he was dressing, and said that he had a meeting for luncheon to learn the membership requirements."

"Do you know the name of the club?"

"I am afraid I do not, sir. But the prospect clearly seemed to please him."

"And when you left the room at that point, can you describe what happened."

"I closed the door, and as I walked down the hallway I heard the key turning in the lock."

"And when you returned at about midnight, how did Chapman sound?"

"Oh, the same."

"Come, now, Barrett. Did his voice through the door show any signs of drink?"

Barrett looked at the floor for a moment. "I must concede that it sounded as if he had been imbibing. But based on my experience, he wasn't inebriated, if that is the purpose of your question. He often sat by his table reading and having a drink. That wasn't unusual."

"Watson, I perceive you wish to ask a question."

"Thank you. Barrett, I don't wish to put words in your mouth, but a valet often has better insight into his master than many others. I'm sorry to ask this question, but I feel I must. Would you say that Chapman's state of mind recently – especially yesterday – would rule out suicide as a reason for his death?"

Barrett recoiled. "I am sorry, sir, but I most emphatically would disagree with any such notion. The pending club admission was the least of it. While the death of the Colonel was distressing to all the family, it did promote Mister Norman into a more exalted position. He seemed to be thoroughly enjoying his new responsibilities as head of the family."

"Do you know any of the details of those responsibilities?" I asked.

"I do not, Doctor. It isn't my place."

Holmes paused. ""Quite so. One last question: You see the decanter over there on the table. Is that normally kept in this room?"

"No, sir. It's one from downstairs, most likely the game room by the looks of it. It was Mister Norman's habit, if he wanted to have a drink while he read, to go downstairs and bring a decanter and glass up here."

"Thank you. That will be all for now." As Barrett left the room, Holmes headed back to the table by the windows. He again examined the glass and decanter closely. He put his finger into the liquid in the glass and licked his finger. He then poured some of the liquid from the decanter into the new glass Barrett had brought with him. As he began to lift the glass to his lips, I couldn't constrain myself. "What in Heaven's name are you doing? That could be poisoned!"

"Trust me. I have an idea, and this is the quickest way to confirm it. If I'm correct, it will facilitate the rest of our inquiry." And without another word, he downed the contents of the glass. Smiling, he said, "It is as I thought. Gregson, please ask the nurse to join us."

After Gregson left us alone, I asked, "Do you have a theory?"

"I don't deal in theories – only facts and the logical deductions from them. There are some suggestive points in this room alone, and Barrett's observations were helpful. But we still need to question the other occupants and, as you so correctly suggested, see the solicitor."

"Yes, I was thinking that might lead somewhere, and Barrett's remark about Chapman's attitude toward his inheritance has further piqued my interest."

"Mine as well. Your presence in these investigations is beginning to be quite helpful."

Before I could express my earnest thanks, Gregson entered with a doughty, stout woman of about fifty. She glanced at the body as if seeing such was an everyday occurrence for her. Although rather matronly, her blue eyes and alert features revealed an underlying intelligence. Her reddish hair and ruddy complexion suggested to me she was of Scottish extraction, an assumption that was verified as soon as she spoke. "This officer – excuse me, *Inspector* – says you want to talk to me. He says you are helping him in his inquiries into the unfortunate death of Mister Norman. Which of you is the so called 'consulting detective' – a thing I've never hear tell of, quite frankly."

Undaunted by the brusqueness, my companion replied, "I am Sherlock Holmes, and this is my associate, Doctor Watson. Thank you for taking the time. I have just a few questions. May I ask your name?"

Unfazed by his emollient manner, she replied, "Sylvia McAlister. I don't know as I have any choice, but go ahead so that we can get this over with and I can return home. I am far beyond my scheduled duty hours."

"We'll try to get you home as soon as possible. What time do you come on duty?"

"At half-past-nine. And always punctual, I might add."

"I am sure. Could you describe last night?"

"Mrs. Chapman was a bit tired when I arrived, so I got her settled, made sure the fire was going well because she gets chilled, and went down to the kitchen to get her some warm milk."

"What seems to be her ailment?" I asked.

"A particularly bad bout of influenza. With my care she is almost over it, but still weakens at the end of the day. This morning she seems better, and she even dressed and had breakfast downstairs."

Holmes nodded. "I understand you sit in the dressing room with the hallway door open after Mrs. Chapman retires."

"Yes. I'm from up north and her room becomes a bit stifling for me, what with the fire blazing away and all, so I keep the door into the hall open to get a little more air. Of course, I leave the door into her room open too so as to hear if she needs anything."

"Did you hear Norman Chapman return to his room?"

"Quite a racket he made. If you ask me, he had been drinking again. It was shortly after I had the missus tucked in, but I couldn't tell you the exact time, as I didn't expect all these foolish questions and thus didn't look at my watch."

"Very understandable. Did you also hear Barrett the valet come to the door several hours later?"

"Yes. He asked if Mister Norman needed anything. I couldn't quite make out the reply, but I know the door didn't open and Barrett went away."

"And after you took up your station, other than Barrett, did you hear or see anything outside Mister Norman's room."

"Nothing until Barrett came to wake him up this morning. And don't you dare ask or imply I wasn't awake or not at my station at any time."

"I wouldn't dream of it, Mrs. McAlister. Just one more question: What do you think of Mister Chapman's demise?"

"It isn't really my place, but if I were you, I would look at some of the family members. I don't listen in, of course, but mark my words – there were tensions in this house. Not everyone was pleased at who was ruling the roost."

"Fine, we will do that. Unless Inspector Gregson needs anything, I believe you may go." When Gregson shook his head, she gave a toss of her head and left the room.

"Quite a specimen," I said.

"Indeed. What say we talk to Mrs. Chapman." Gregson informed us she, her step-daughter, and the fiancé were all in the drawing room. As we were leaving the bedroom, the local coroner arrived. He and Holmes had a whispered conversation, after which Holmes, Gregson, and I went back downstairs and proceeded to the drawing room at the front of the house.

It was a spacious, well-appointed room, handsomely decorated with fashionable wallpaper, comfortable chairs and sofas, mahogany end tables, and various bucolic paintings on the walls. As we entered, the three occupants rose to greet us.

A striking woman of about thirty came forward first. She was quite beautiful, with bright blue eyes, auburn hair, and a well-proportioned nose and mouth. She was a bit pale but spoke with a clear voice, her American accent very pronounced. "Hello. I am Amelia Chapman. I assume you are

Mr. Holmes and Doctor Watson. The inspector has explained to us that you have kindly agreed to help with this dreadful situation with Norman."

"Yes, Madam. We will do what we can." He turned to a younger woman, about twenty-five, slim and rather plain, who suffered by comparison with Amelia. "I take it you are Norman's sister."

"That is correct. I am Edith Chapman. And this is my fiancé, Elias Mudge, who has been staying here while on a break from his training in legal chambers." Mudge seemed a few years older than Edith, already losing his hair and a bit on the portly side. He seemed fairly taciturn, and simply inclined his head to us in greeting.

At that moment a young man in his mid-teens appeared at the door. His auburn hair and eyes told me this was the second son. Mrs. Chapman confirmed this. "And this is my son, Oliver. Please join us dear." He came into the room and shyly stood by his mother.

"Thank you for your time. If you all will indulge me, I would like to impose by asking a few questions. Mrs. Chapman, I understand you retired rather early."

"I was feeling tired after our evening meal, so decided to go to bed. It was a bit past nine. I began to prepare for the night when Mrs. McAlister arrived and helped me finish. She then went into the dressing room, where I believe she was for the remainder of the evening."

"If one leaves the dressing room door into the hall open, is it easy to hear anything at the door to Mister Chapman's room?"

"Oh, quite. David, my late husband, always insisted we close it at night so that we wouldn't be disturbed by Norman, who often stayed out rather late."

"How did your stepson seem yesterday?"

"Very cheerful. He was about to join some club. I had the impression David might not have permitted it, but in any event, Norman was quite enthused."

"Do you know why Chapman was going to visit the family solicitor this morning?"

"I'm afraid that I don't. Norman relished being a man of affairs, even though he missed David deeply. He didn't confide in me concerning business matters – unlike his father."

Holmes turned to Edith. "What did you do after your step-mother retired?"

"Oliver, Elias, and I went to the game room. Oliver and I played cribbage, while Elias sat watching and having a night cap."

"I understand there are refreshments in the game room?"

"Yes, there is a drink trolly with several decanters and glasses."

"Did you see Norman at any point?"

"He came in shortly before ten. He wanted to take one of the decanters and a glass up to his room."

"Was there any conversation?"

"Not really. He just said hello, took the decanter and glass, said something about a meeting this morning, and left."

"I realize this may be rather delicate, but did he seem under the influence of alcohol?"

To her credit, Edith blushed and looked away. "I would say he might have been a little."

Mudge finally spoke up with a sarcastic tone. "No more than usual."

Holmes turned to him. "Did you happen to notice how much was in the decanter?"

He shrugged. "Perhaps it was three-quarters full. I was having brandy rather than whisky, so paid it no particular attention."

"Did anyone else drink from the decanter before it was removed?"

"No. Edith had sherry, and Oliver was drinking mineral water."

Holmes sat there for several minutes, clearly deep in thought. He then thanked them and he, Gregson, and I went into the hall. "Gregson, Watson and I will go and visit the solicitor. I suggest you stay here and oversee things. Watson, please go and procure us a cab. I have a few suggestions for the inspector and will be out shortly."

I was able to find a hansom in short order. When Holmes emerged, he told me he had obtained the address of the solicitor from Mrs. Chapman, and we were soon on our way east toward Chancery Lane. Holmes turned to me. "Well, what are your thoughts?"

"If Chapman was poisoned, I don't see how it was accomplished. I thought at first the decanter had been poisoned, but your startling demonstration showed that wasn't the case. Chapman locked the door from the inside at ten, removing the key. I find it highly unlikely anyone would prop a ladder against the front of the house and risk being seen by a patrolling constable. Based on what the nurse said, no one came to the door after ten except for Barrett, and he didn't enter. Even if someone could have gained entry, how could they relock either the door or the windows?"

"An excellent summary. And as yet, we haven't uncovered a motive, except to learn Chapman was in high spirits and thus an improbable candidate for suicide. Perhaps we'll learn of someone else's motive from Ogilby, the solicitor we're about to see."

We pulled up in front of a weathered granite building, grimy with at least a century's accumulation of soot. Holmes paid the driver and we entered and ascended the creaking stairs to the second floor. In the hallway there were several doors, all with tarnished brass name plates. We located

Ogilby's chambers and entered. The room was dusty and cluttered with papers and books. Ogilby rose from his rolltop desk, removing a pair of spectacles. He was in his sixties, very thin with hair turning white. His nose was almost as pronounced as Holmes's, and his eyes looked at us curiously.

"I believe you must have wandered into the wrong door. I don't have any appointments at this time."

"No, it is you we wish to see. I am Sherlock Holmes and this is Doctor Watson. We are working with the police in a certain matter in which you may be able to assist."

"May I see some evidence that you are connected with the police?"

Holmes reached into his inner coat pocket. "I thought you might require that. Here is a handwritten note from Inspector Gregson of Scotland Yard asking you to talk to us."

The solicitor took the letter, which I assumed Holmes had procured when I stepped outside back at the Chapman residence. He put his spectacles back on and scrutinized the paper for a long time, as members of the legal profession are wont to do."

"Fine. I of course will cooperate to the best of my ability."

"Thank you. We understand that you represent the Chapman family."

"Yes. In fact, young Chapman had an appointment earlier today that he didn't keep."

"I am sorry to inform you that he is deceased. He was found this morning in his bedroom under some suspicious circumstances."

Ogilby sunk back into his chair. "Good Lord! That is terrible! First the Colonel, and now Norman." He paused to wipe his brow with slightly trembling hands. "Please have a seat. What would you like to know?"

We removed our overcoats and pulled over two chairs, after removing the jumble of papers from each of them. Holmes resumed. "What was the nature of the appointment this morning?"

"Simply to go over some routine matters related to the Colonel's estate."

"Could you explain the estate to us?"

"Let me think a moment." He went over to an old cabinet and removed some papers. He looked them over, again quite painstakingly, nodded to himself, and then returned to his chair. "I wanted to ascertain that all the relevant materials have been filed in Chancery and thus are public. One cannot be too careful when it comes to a client's matters."

"Quite understandable. Please tell us all about it."

"It is a bit complex, so bear with me. I will attempt to simplify for you laymen." I thought to myself that nothing was too complex for Holmes to follow, but kept quiet.

"There are three pieces to the Colonel's estate. First, there is property he inherited from his father, and that is the most valuable portion. It consists of a manor and very profitable farm in Wiltshire. The Colonel rented out the farm for a handsome sum, and the family uses the manor as a summer residence. That land is all subject to an entail, which means that it can only pass through the male line, so young Norman automatically inherited all that upon his father's death. Now that Norman has passed away, it will descend to Oliver as the Colonel's next son.

"Second, the family of Norman's mother, Mildred, was quite wealthy. Her father was some sort of merchant, I believe. In any event, at the time of her marriage, her father established a quite substantial trust. The beneficiaries are any children of Mildred, meaning Norman and Edith."

"Who is the trustee?

"An excellent question. The Colonel was the trustee, and, when he died, Norman became the trustee as Mildred's surviving eldest son."

"Are there any conditions to distribution of funds?"

"One would think you are a lawyer." Apparently it was his highest form of praise. "The trust is quite liberal in the freedom the trustee has during the lifetime of the beneficiaries. The only rather odd thing is that, if any female beneficiary desires to marry and the trustee doesn't approve of the match, the female and her descendants are cut out of the trust." I glanced at Holmes, who was sitting passively listening to this recital.

"There is a third portion of the Colonel's estate. When he remarried, his new father-in-law was persuaded to set up a trust for the benefit of Amelia and her descendants. Her father was also quite wealthy, based if I recall on shipping and railroad interests in the Midwest in the United States. Again, the Colonel and then Norman were successively trustees, with broad discretion as to disbursement of funds."

"And who will the new trustee for both trusts be?"

"I will be for the first, and for the second, I also will be until Oliver becomes of age."

"Were the family members aware of these arrangements?"

"The Colonel and I talked before he left for the war. I recommended he gather them together and explain everything. It is my experience that it is better for the testator to explain everything to the family to minimize disputes down the road. He seemed to agree with me, so I assume he did so."

"This has been very helpful. We thank you for your time and will be on our way."

"I am happy to help. I think I'll go over to the house and express my condolences."

91

We donned our overcoats and went back the way we had come. Once ensconced in a cab, Holmes smiled at me. "Well, your notion of seeing the solicitor was rather fruitful."

"I agree. We have gone from having no motive to a plethora. Mrs. Chapman could have wanted the entailed estate for Oliver or to remove Norman as the trustee of her father's trust to be replaced by a more pliable Oliver. Oliver himself could have wanted the same thing."

"And what of Miss Edith?"

"I sensed there was some tension between her fiancée and Norman. Undoubtedly you notice how Mudge made a sneering remark about Chapman's drinking, so I suppose both Edith and Mudge could have wanted to remove Chapman as trustee. That not only would double Edith's inheritance, but also would eliminate the risk that Chapman would object to the marriage and cut her off."

Holmes chuckled. "Indeed, a wealth of motives. Any further thoughts on the method?"

"I am still at a loss."

"Well, I have some ideas. Here we are, back in Baker Street." We went upstairs and he went over to a bookcase and spent some time purusing a volume. He then turned to me. "I'm going to go out and look into something. I may not be back until late, so don't wait for me."

After an excellent meal of roasted lamb and boiled potatoes, accompanied by an excellent burgundy, I had a cigar by the fire and thought over the case. I must have nodded off, because when I awoke with a start, Holmes was sitting in his chair with his favorite pipe. I was unsure how long he'd been there, but the room already was filling with smoke. "Ah, Watson, you go on up to bed. I'm going to have a smoke and think about this case." I went up to my room and turned in, no closer to an answer.

In the morning when I came down for breakfast, I was unsure whether Sherlock Holmes had slept at all, but he nevertheless looked as bright and alert as ever.

"Good morning. Mrs. Hudson is bringing some fresh toasted bread and coffee for you. You'll have just enough time to enjoy them before Gregson arrives."

"How did you deduce he is coming?"

"No deduction this time. I have sent for him."

"More instructions for him."

"No I believe I have the answer."

I knew better than to try and coax him to tell me, so I had my breakfast and was finishing when Gregson arrived, hung up his overcoat, and took a chair.

"Mr. Holmes, I've nothing to report yet on the task you set for me."

"That's fine, Gregson. I believe I already know what you'll find."

"So you have an answer for me this quickly?"

"It was rather simple once you examine the facts and eliminate certain factors as being highly unlikely. Let us start with motive, so that I can bring you up to date on our trip to the solicitor after we left you. Watson and I were in agreement before then that Chapman seemed not to be a risk of suicide, based on the unanimous opinion of those in the house as to his cheerful state of mind. And you kindly eliminated accident through experimentation with chemicals. His family is a different matter altogether. I can give you more detail, but the short version is that the estate arrangements of the Colonel provide them all with a motive."

"Extraordinary. Are you positive?"

"Chapman's death doubles his sister's inheritance and removes any veto by Chapman over her proposed marriage to Mudge. Mrs. Chapman and Oliver both benefit by having freer access to funds set aside by her father, and Oliver will inherit an entailed manor of some value. They all apparently knew of this, at least based on what the solicitor told us concerning his conversations with the Colonel.

"Let us turn to method for a moment. The door and windows in the bedroom were securely locked from inside at ten, and no one entered the room after that point, as established by the nurse. I inspected the chimney, and it is too narrow for a person. It also hasn't been cleaned for some time, and anyone attempting to lower something into the room would have disturbed the soot, which isn't the case.

"It seemed to me that the whisky was the likely source of the poison. The condition of the body, with evidence of arching of the back and distortion of the face, suggested strychnine as the likeliest poison."

"As you requested, I am having inquiries made at various establishments that purvey that substance. But how did Chapman ingest it?"

"He retrieved the decanter and glass himself. Had there been powder in the glass, he would have noticed it. I've been making a study of various poisons, and may write a monograph on it someday. Strychnine is odorless and colorless. As you correctly noted, there is no odor to any of the liquids in the glass or decanter, other than the normal smell of good whisky. The contents of the glass, which I tasted, was bitter to the tongue, as I ascertained by dipping my finger in it. The decanter, by contrast, contained unadulterated whisky."

"Holmes," I interjected, "that was a particularly foolhardy way of proving that. Why on earth would you take a risk like that?"

He smiled. "Thank you for your concern, but there was no risk. It was unlikely that a murderer would leave out a poisoned decanter in a place where anyone could accidentally drink from it. But just to be sure, before swallowing, I allowed a minute amount to touch my tongue. When there was no bitterness, I decided to swallow the contents." I had noticed before that Holmes relished a touch of the dramatic from time to time. He was willing to do that even if the audience only consisted of Gregson and me.

"So the question became how did strychnine get into the glass? Gregson, I believe your inquiries will uncover that Chapman himself was the purchaser of the poison."

"Why would he do that? You yourself said he wasn't suicidal. And he had no history of meddling with such materials."

"Several people mentioned that Chapman was excited about joining a club, and that his father might not have approved. When I examined the notebook lying on the table by the window, I discovered an address with the initials *P.C.* next to it. After checking my indices that I keep of various nefarious matters, I left Watson here and went to the address. It was indeed a club, and I gained entrance by feigning acquaintance with Chapman. Luckily, they hadn't heard of his demise. If they had, I would have pretended not to have known about it.

"Once inside, I was introduced to the club secretary. He offered to show me around, but asked if I minded waiting in his office as he had some business to attend to. When left alone, I hurriedly scanned the volumes in a bookcase and located the club rule book. I learned that the establishment's name was the *Phoenix Club*. I found the section on the initiation ritual. Just as I was finishing it, the Secretary returned. He demanded to know what I was doing. Before he could raise an alarm, I used my knowledge of the body's pressure points to immobilize him temporarily. I made haste to leave the building, returned here, and thought about the entire matter for some time.

"What I learned was the initiation ritual included ingestion of poison of the inductee's choice. Here is what I believe happened: Chapman procured strychnine. I noticed the remains of a chemist's paper twist among the ashes in the fireplace, which is how he must have transported it. He must have decided to practice taking the strychnine, either to test his tolerance or to build up some resistance to it. Watson, you probably know that, in small doses, it is often used as a stimulant. That may be why Chapman chose it.

"He went to his room and locked the door so as not to be disturbed. Given the level of whisky in the decanter, he must have been drinking to screw up his courage, and had probably been drinking earlier as well. Sometime after midnight, by then in a drunken stupor, he added the poison

94

to the glass and discarded the paper in the fire. I don't know how inebriated he was, but he must have misjudged the dosage, with the terrible results we saw. He drank and swallowed all of it at once, which would have led quickly to respiratory failure, spasms, and death, likely within five to fifteen minutes.

"Possibly he thought what was happening was part of building up his resistance. Or maybe he was so immediately overcome that he was gasping for air and couldn't call out for help, or get the key and unlock the door. In any case, it must have been an agonizing death – but it was not murder, as will be proven when you find where he bought the poison."

Gregson and I sat in shocked silence. Quite shaken, he arose. "Thank you Mr. Holmes. I will step up the efforts to locate where the strychnine was obtained. When we add Chapman's description, that should accelerate the process. I don't look forward to informing the family. Good day, gentleman."

After he left, I looked at Holmes. "This is monstrous. I have never heard of such reckless behavior. You actually have something in your indices?"

He got up and went to the case containing his books. He retrieved the *H* volume and rejoined me. "I had a recollection, and this confirmed it. Over one-hundred years ago there was a scandalous organization called The Hellfire Club, which practiced various types of debauchery too indecent to mention. One of their rituals was taking poison along with strong drink. That Club was allegedly disbanded after public outcry. Rumours have persisted that it has continued underground, as it were, including at our Universities. Apparently this current group named themselves 'Phoenix' as an attempt at irony."

"Holmes, I'm appalled that this could exist in the heart of the Empire, and involve the heir of a distinguished military man."

"Unfortunately, some people never learn that the thrill of risk taking may be far outweighed by the risk in question. They don't understand that, once you take a risk, you cannot give it back."

The Body in Question
by Tim Newton Anderson

In the first years I shared a flat with Sherlock Holmes in Baker Street, I participated in a number of interesting cases with him. However, I never imagined that I, myself, would be one of his clients.

Holmes was sitting at the writing desk when I rushed into our rooms. In the two years we had lived there, he had gradually turned it from the neat and Spartan bachelor accommodation we had first found in 1881 to something resembling a cross between a chemistry laboratory and a junk shop. One corner held a table with apparatus and bottles of chemicals, while many of the other surfaces were covered in newspapers and documents, with souvenirs of our cases placed on the mantelpiece and in other nooks around the room. At first our landlady, Mrs. Hudson, had attempted to tidy these away, but Holmes loud protests if he failed to find something in its accustomed place resigned her to lifting and dusting where she could. I was grateful she didn't put us out on the street, which I partly ascribed to her enjoyment of the comings and goings and a degree of maternal interest in her eccentric tenant.

"You will find a glass of whisky by the armchair, Watson," Holmes said as I entered, "as I saw from your progress down the street that you are in need of one."

"I'm sure you didn't need to exercise your powers of deduction too hard to come to that conclusion," I replied, sinking into the comfort of the chair and grasping the glass, "but I am nevertheless extremely grateful."

"What I can further deduce is that something has occurred in the anatomy room at Barts which has disturbed you greatly," he said. "It's barely two hours into your shift assisting Sir James Paget, and your hand scrubbing and re-dressing has been perfunctory, which suggests a hasty exit rather than simply an early finish. Your continued flushed countenance, now that you've had time to rest, indicates something on your mind rather than the exertion of a brisk walk."

"I am afraid I may lose my licence to practise medicine," I said. "That is, if I avoid actual criminal charges."

"While I may sometimes tease you about your qualifications," he replied, "I've never doubted your ability and conscientious pursuit of your profession. You are also the most honest person I know, so I must question what has prompted you to imagine this catastrophe."

The familiar surroundings of our sitting room and the beneficial effects of the whisky had started to relax me, but I still felt the dread of my mistake gripping my mind. The work as assistant to Sir James Paget had been the first medical appointment I had taken since returning from Afghanistan, recovering from the physical and mental wounds I had received there, and I was counting on my salary not only supplementing my Army pension, but providing enough savings to be able to purchase my own general practice. Whilst I had enjoyed supporting Holmes in his role as a consulting detective, I was still a relatively young man and had ambitions to have a wife and family, which would be impossible without a reasonable income.

"As you are aware," I said, "one of my duties at Barts is to book in the corpses that come in for dissection," I said. "Since the Anatomy Act, it's important that all are correctly registered to ensure they have been properly procured. The porters pick them up each morning by the Henry VIII Gate in the wicker baskets they've left out for the body dealers the night before. "

"I have followed the trade with some interest since my own work in the anatomy laboratory some years ago," said Holmes. "While the days of the London Burkists are half-a-century in the past, I know that the dealers in corpses aren't always scrupulous in obtaining the necessary permissions from relatives to sell the bodies for dissection. The Dorset Street traders have been known to persuade friends in the workhouse mortuaries to release bodies which should have been afforded a proper burial. While the trade is legal, there is the anomaly that people aren't allowed to personally profit from the sale, which is something to which the police and authorities generally turn a blind eye."

"Exactly why it is so important to keep an accurate register of the name and details of the death of the deceased and the person who sold them," I said. "We could be checked by the Inspector of Anatomy at any time, and the good reputation of the hospital would be destroyed if there were any irregularities. There have been enough protests at the practice to make every reputable teaching hospital cautious. That's why what happened this morning is so terrible."

"Gather yourself and give me all the details," said Holmes. "Rest assured I will do all in my power to help you."

I sat back in my chair and gazed at his aquiline countenance. While he hadn't been completely successful in all of the cases I had observed, he had always placed his reputation – and indeed his life – on the line for his clients, and I had no doubt he would do the same for me. The humidor was near my seat, and I reached out to take a cigar and light it with a Lucifer while Holmes took some shag tobacco from the Persian slipper where it was stored and filled his pipe, lighting it from the fire with a long spill.

"I arrived for my shift early, as usual," I said. "A new group of students has recently started, and I was aware they were keen to commence their lectures. Each must dissect at least two bodies a year to qualify in surgery, so the earlier they can claim their body, the sooner they can achieve that goal. They had already gathered in the anatomy laboratory awaiting Sir James and the delivery of the bodies by the porters. The sooner I was finished checking the details and entering them into the register, the sooner they could commence.

"As you are aware, the gender, age, and condition of the bodies, as well as factors including the cause of death and any unusual medical conditions, affects the price which is paid. Women, especially those who have died in pregnancy, are particularly prized. The vast majority, however, are male paupers who have succumbed to one of the many diseases such as tuberculosis which are endemic in the East End workhouses. Their relatives, if any, are normally all too content to have them buried at the public expense. It is important for me to do a thorough inspection of the bodies and check the results of any *post mortem* examination to determine the price, as well as ensure they haven't been obtained in any criminal way.

"Once I had removed the soiled sheets used to disguise the nature of the baskets, I checked all of the bodies and paperwork and instructed the porters to remove them to the laboratory. I can assure you that I was more than happy with my work and anticipated no issues."

"I'm sure you were your normal thorough self," Holmes said. "I assume the issue transpired after you had finished your work,"

"Indeed," I said. "As soon as I had completed the register, I went to the laboratory to watch Sir James and the students. I was particularly interested in one of the bodies which had suffered from a rare tropical disease contracted in his profession as a sailor, and whose diagnosis would prove fascinating. However, as I entered the room, I immediately noticed a problem. There had been four bodies for dissection – three male and one female. On the slabs there were now four *male* corpses – one of which I had never seen before."

"Perhaps one had been taken to another location in the hospital," Holmes said.

"My own first thought," I said. "But when I questioned Sir James, he assured me that the bodies in question were those which had been delivered. I know you sometimes question my observational skills, Holmes, but I assure you I can tell the difference between a male and a female. The names were similar – the body I saw was *Frances* Wolsley –

with an *e* – and the man in the dissection room was *Francis* Wolsley – with an *i*. It was, however, a different corpse. And worse was to come. On examining the dead body, it evident that while the woman I had signed in had died of pneumonia, the man had clearly been murdered."

Holmes raised an eyebrow in surprise, but encouraged me to continue with a hand gesture.

"It wasn't immediately noticeable in the grime on the man's body," I said, "but there were slight marks of strangulation around the neck and the eyes were bloodshot. Sir James noticed these as well and immediately carried out a further examination which identified deeper bruising beneath the skin and some ligature injuries. The attacker had been careful not leave obvious marks, which suggested the man had been grabbed from behind and pressure applied to the carotid artery and trachea. There was little doubt, however, that the man had been deliberately murdered."

"This case has more and more points of interest," said Holmes. "What did you find when you examined the register? I presume it had been altered?"

"That was indeed my next move," I said. "Most of the entry was unchanged, but the letter '*F*' had been changed to '*M*' and one letter altered in the name. The culprit hadn't changed the date of birth – the man was older than the woman I had registered by a dozen years – but if I hadn't observed the swap, the substitution would probably have gone unnoticed until the body was disposed of. With such a small change, it would be hard for me to prove the register was altered by another."

"Especially given your notoriously bad handwriting," Holmes said. "If a student rather than Paget had carried out the dissection, it is entirely possible the murder would go undetected. As it is, you now find yourself involved in a killing rather than just an administrative error."

"That would be bad enough," I said. "Certainly enough to mean the end of my employment and a stain on my professional record."

Holmes stood up and stretched his spine, which had been bent over his writing desk.

"I'm sure Sir James will be thorough in his *post mortem*," Holmes said, "but he will undoubtedly have notified the police by now, and I must examine the scene before they contaminate any evidence. Let us go there now, and quickly."

Fortunately, there was a vacant hansom cab moving down Baker Street as we exited the building and Holmes hailed it to take us to West Smithfield. It had been a year since we had both been in the hospital at the same time, and nearly two years since the fateful day my ex-dresser Stamford had introduced us there. We had both attended anatomy lectures there a few years before, but neither of us had remarked on the other in the crowded theatre, and Holmes was merely auditing the demonstrations rather than attending as a full-time student.

My friend had been correct in assuming the police would already be on the scene. A constable stood at the Henry VIII entrance opposite the wrought-iron canopy of Smithfield Meat Market, but he allowed us to pass inside. When we arrived at the anatomy laboratory Inspector Gregson was talking to Sir James. He called us to his side.

"Sir James informs me that the mystery man was killed sometime late last night," Gregson said to me. "I'm guessing, Doctor, that you have Mr. Holmes and Mrs. Hudson as alibis for that time, so that lets you off the actual killing. However, you will need to explain how a murder victim was signed into your system. We had all hoped the register would stop people killing to sell bodies to the medical profession."

"Watson has explained to me that the body he dealt with was that of a woman, and this corpse has obviously been substituted after it left his office," said Holmes. "You know him well enough, Gregson, to believe he had nothing to do with this."

I was grateful it was Gregson rather than Lestrade who was carrying out the investigation. Holmes always said the former man was the best Scotland Yard had to offer, and there was a degree of resentment on Lestrade's part at Holmes success, even though my friend had allowed the police to get the credit in some of his cases.

"I concur," said the inspector. "However, I must insist that he isn't directly involved in any investigation until we can formally clear him of any wrongdoing."

Holmes smiled and nodded. "As long as that doesn't preclude my discussing certain aspects of the case with him," he said. "He is my client, and also has valuable medical knowledge that may prove useful."

"I doubt you would avoid doing so even if I forbade it," said Gregson.

Holmes smiled again. "What have you found so far?" he asked.

"The substitution, if indeed that is proved to have happened, must have occurred outside Dr. Watson's office," the inspector said. "There was a change of shift of porters, so the bodies were left there on trolleys for a second group to bring here. There was a gap of five minutes at most, so if it happened, it must have been planned in advance and carried out by someone with intimate knowledge of the hospital and its routines."

"And do we know the name of the victim?"

"Not yet," Gregson said. "There were no identifying marks or items with the body to aid identification. My men are checking the missing person logs to see if anyone fitting his description has been reported."

"May we look for ourselves?" Holmes asked. He moved to the body on the operating table and indicated for me to follow. "As your

100

observational skills have been called into question, Watson, perhaps you would care to tell me what you see?"

I looked carefully at the corpse.

"It is the body of a man in his early forties," I said. "At first glance, the grime on his skin would indicate someone of a poor background – the sort of person who is all too common in the anatomy lab. However, if you look closely you can see that the dirt has been rubbed on – it hasn't penetrated into the fine lines on the face and neck, and there is no evidence of dirt under the fingernails, which are clean and well kept. There is an indentation on the ring finger of his left hand which suggests he was married and his ring has been taken – either to hinder investigation or as part of a robbery. There are no scrapes on the skin where the ring was, so it wasn't forcibly removed while he was alive."

I lifted up his hands and looked closely at them.

"There are calluses between the first and second fingers of his right hand which suggests he used a pen frequently – possibly a clerk. However, I would have expected ink stains on the fingers in those circumstances, so he was either meticulous in his toilet or he didn't write every day."

"Well done, Watson!" said Holmes. "And did you observe the feet?"

My inspection moved to the lower extremities.

"I believe I see what you mean," I said. "There are none of the calluses one would expect if he habitually wore ill-fitting shoes. He had been used to made-to-measure footwear."

"I'm impressed with your skills, Dr. Watson," said Sir James. "Perhaps you should be assisting me in the theatre rather than processing our supplies."

I was flattered, but until this mystery was solved I wouldn't be able to pursue the opportunity.

"Once we've examined the register," said Holmes, "I believe we'll have done all we can here."

"I'll call on you this evening," said Gregson, "to ask any further questions I may have."

Holmes said that he would be most welcome.

After a close look at the register with his magnifying glass, Holmes said what I already knew – the same ink and pen had been used for the alterations, so it must have been done after I left for the theatre – again displaying knowledge of customary movements within the hospital.

"There are several mysteries here," he said as we took a cab back to our lodgings. "Who is the man whose body lies in Barts, and how did he come there, and what happened to the young woman who was originally left on your doorstep?"

"It may be she has been disposed of in the Thames, along with so many other unfortunates," I said. "Perhaps we should ask the mudlarks if she has already been discovered."

"That is a possibility," said Holmes, "but if the body snatcher is familiar with the medical profession, would it not be more sensible to sell her to another hospital? Just like our victim, the chances of detection are small."

"I have colleagues I know at most of the teaching hospitals," I said. "I can visit them this afternoon and see if they have had any unexpected offers. I will easily recognise the woman I saw this morning."

"Excellent!" Holmes exclaimed. "In the meantime, I can investigate at the beginning of this chain of supply – with the body dealers of Dorset Street who provided the female corpse in the first place."

"Surely the dead man is the first priority?" I said.

"This is a tangled case," said Holmes. "We must leave no thread unexamined, and until Gregson provides us with a name, the woman is all we have to go on."

As I told Holmes, I knew fellow practitioners in most of the London hospitals, but in fact I tracked the missing woman to somewhere I only knew by repute: The London School of Medicine for Women.

The Dean was Mrs. Elizabeth Garrett Anderson, who had founded the school ten years earlier following her work at the New Hospital for Women and Children, which she had also founded. Mrs. Anderson was the first woman to qualify as a doctor in England, although another Elizabeth – Mrs. Blackwell – had qualified earlier in the United States. I had met Mrs. Blackwell when Sir James had invited her to meet the staff at Barts, but I only knew Mrs. Anderson by reputation. That was a formidable one. She was a handsome redhead in her late forties who held herself well. I could see how she commanded the respect of her staff and some of my colleagues, but knew that some of the less-enlightened of my fellow doctors were opposed to her work and had annulled her membership of the British Medical Association. It hadn't stopped her continuing her valuable practice, and her hospital, like Barts, operated successfully on donations that allowed her to provide health care to women in central London. She was happy to show me to her office after a short tour of the facilities.

"I have a standing order amongst the suppliers of bodies for women," she said. "Female health care is a neglected branch of medicine – too many of your colleagues dismiss some of their health issues as 'women's problems' and fail to give them the same attention they do to male patients. Are you a believer in female suffrage, Dr. Watson?"

102

"I am a great admirer of women," I said diplomatically. "I am certainly grateful for the female nurses who helped me back to health after receiving a Jezail bullet in Afghanistan."

If she had noticed my avoidance of a direct answer, she didn't pursue the subject.

"The young lady who arrived at my hospital this morning was brought in by a body dealer I didn't recognise," she said. "It's generally female dealers who supply me. They're more likely to be chosen by the female workhouses as undertakers. This dealer was a man and had I dealt with the transaction myself, I may have declined. However, a member of my staff knew that we were in urgent need of a corpse."

"Could your staff member describe the man?" I asked.

"He was tall, and comparatively well-dressed for a dealer in bodies," she said. "That in itself should have a aroused suspicions. 'Dark-haired and bearded' was the only other description she was able to give – hardly definitive, I'm afraid."

"My friend, Sherlock Holmes, is investigating, and I am sure he will be able to find the man," I said. "For the sake of all doctors, and the public, we need to be able to ensure the supply of bodies for students is untainted by scandal."

"It may profit him to start by visiting the local female workhouses," she said. "This woman was pregnant, and there are only one or two that are prepared to admit someone in that condition. I can provide an introduction – my staff and I are generally called on to attend to the mothers and children."

I thanked Mrs. Anderson and noted down the names and locations she suggested. I knew that Holmes was investigating the body dealers, but felt it would help the case if I could find the origin of the dead woman. Although Holmes was skilled in interrogating people of all classes, the body dealers would be wary of any scandal that could hurt their livelihood.

The first workhouse had no knowledge of any deceased inmate, but the second proved a more fruitful visit.

"That sounds like Frances," the Beadle told me. "That was the name she used, anyway. We get all sorts of women here, but she stood out because she was a cut above the local paupers in the way she carried herself."

"Did she have any relatives?" I asked.

"If she had, she didn't tell us, or we would have notified them when she died so they could claim the body. She had probably been thrown out of her home by her parents when she was with child – an all-too-common circumstance, I'm afraid – but even the hardest of hearts will often soften when their child dies – especially with a grandchild. Most of them relent

103

when the child is born – say it's been given to them to take care of by a dead relative. That way their daughter has a chance to make a match without the encumbrance of an illegitimate son or daughter."

"And did you make any inquiries before selling the body to a dealer?" I asked.

"You know how it is, Doctor," the man said. "We have to keep costs down, and we can't afford to employ someone like your Mr. Holmes every time someone dies. Even advertising in the papers costs money that we cannot afford."

"And of course, selling the body brings in money and saves you the cost of burial."

I looked closely at the Beadle, who was stout and well-fed, unlike his charges, who I had observed eating a thin grey gruel as I entered. I knew the workhouses performed a useful function, but that shouldn't mean providing a profit to their sponsors, or a very comfortable living to their guardians, at the expense of the unfortunates forced to live there.

"I'm guessing she had no visitors, either?" I continued.

"Not really," the Beadle said, "although there was a man who came asking after her a couple of weeks ago. Tall gent, thick black beard. He didn't know her name, but gave me a good-enough description so that I could tell him she was living here. He didn't ask to see her, though, just nodded and left. Didn't leave a card or nothing, or even say if Frances was her real name."

I didn't believe the Beadle would be forthcoming with any more information, so made my way back to Baker Street. Holmes hadn't returned, so I decided to treat myself to supper at a nearby public house. When I came back, full of good ale and an even better steak pie and mash, he was still out. Indeed, he hadn't appeared when I arose the next morning and headed to Barts to take in that morning's batch of bodies.

I'd deliberately chosen to arrive early in the hope of seeing some of the body dealers as they deposited their offerings by the door, and was rewarded by the sight of a tall man placing a basket there. I was overjoyed to see he had a thick black beard and clothes that were of better quality than one would have expected in his trade. Body-dealing was hard on clothes, and none would choose to soil a good outfit.

"Hold hard, fellow," I said. "I have some questions for you."

"What do you want, Guv'nor?" he said as he turned to face me. "The chits are all in order."

He made to leave, but I grabbed him by the arm to detain him.

"You are going nowhere until the police have a chance to talk to you."

"Don't be like that!" he protested. "I ain't done nothing wrong. I'm just trying to earn an honest living, same as you."

"We'll see about that," I said, holding firm. "What do you know about a young woman left here yesterday?"

"No more than you, Watson," the man said. He pulled the beard from his face, revealing Sherlock Holmes.

"Good Lord, Holmes – you had me fooled again!" I said, releasing his arm from my grip. "I was convinced you were our man."

"Exactly the impression I was trying to give," my friend said. "If I could fool you, I hoped to work a similar trick on the body-dealers who supply this hospital."

"And did they tell you anything significant?"

"It was what they didn't say that was telling. None of them recognised me, which convinces me our mysterious suspect isn't one of their number. It is a tight-knit community in Dorset Street. I had a hard time infiltrating their numbers, as they are extremely protective of their trade. They only agreed to talk to me after I revealed my real identity."

"So you learned less than me," I said, eager to tell him the results of my own investigations.

"Possibly," he said. "But I did confirm my hypothesis that the man we are seeking may also have altered his appearance. As you have just demonstrated, a false beard can divert the gaze from what lies beneath."

I drew out my notebook and told Holmes all I had discovered at the Women's Hospital and Workhouse.

"You have done well," he said. "I'm sure I may have been able to unearth more significant details if I had conducted the interviews myself, but what you did discover is useful. It also suggests our next step."

We went up to the anatomy laboratory, where Inspector Gregson had also returned.

"I believe I've discovered the identity of our murder victim," he said. "A William Wilson was reported as missing who fits the description. His landlady told one of my officers that he had left his lodgings in Praed Street two nights ago and not returned. I'm not sure whether she was more concerned about his well-being or the potential lost rent, but either way I believe that he is our man."

"And what do we know of this Wilson?" asked Holmes.

"He is a salesman, or rather he was," said Gregson. "A widower and something of a man-about-town. He has lodged with Mrs. Johnson since his wife died a year ago. The landlady says she has a strict policy of not allowing female visitors to her tenants, but Mr. Wilson often returned smelling of perfume, and she believed him to have had several assignations with young ladies. Apparently the perfume often differed."

"How observant of her," said Holmes.

"I believe 'nosy' is a more accurate term," said Gregson, "but a useful skill all the same."

"Did the landlady know the identity of any of the young women in question?" I asked.

"She did not," he replied. "However, she said she believed Wilson had a pattern of seeing the same person for a week or so, and then moving on to a new conquest."

"It sounds as if there will be no one to mourn his passing," said Holmes, "as well as at least one person who will be pleased. What you have told us confirms my hypothesis about what has occurred here, and I hope tonight's endeavours by Watson and me will bring the case to a satisfactory conclusion."

"Do you require any assistance from my men or myself?" Gregson asked.

"Thank you, but I believe we'll be adequate to the task. I don't believe our culprit is normally a man of violence. If you have a man stationed near the London School of Medicine for Women to take him into custody, you should have your culprit in a cell tonight."

Holmes and I wrapped up in our warmest greatcoats to stand in an alley near the back entrance to the hospital. There was a thick autumn fog which soaked through the outer layers and pained my injured leg with its chill, but was useful to disguise our presence to any nocturnal visitors. The lights inside the building had been extinguished everywhere apart from the wards, and there were no streetlamps to illuminate the scene. We stood quietly for more than hour with only the occasional stray cat for company. Just as I was despairing of a wasted vigil and longing for the warmth of the Baker Street hearth, I heard footsteps approaching and looked to Holmes, who indicated with a finger to the lips that the game was afoot.

A man entered the alley. It was impossible to see his face in detail because of the darkness, but I could tell that he was well above average height. His face was muffled in a scarf, and he wore a slouch hat which combined to obscure his features. He carried no lantern, which suggested he was familiar with the building as he walked straight to the door. He took a key from his pocket and was attempting to open the door when Holmes and I stepped out of the gloom.

"If you are here to retrieve the body of your daughter, I have to inform you she has already been removed to the morgue," said Holmes.

The man turned in shock and I braced myself to grasp him, but instead of running, I was surprised to see him burst into tears.

"I wanted to do one last thing for her," he said, "and give her a decent burial."

106

I realised that I recognised the voice. It was Arbuthnot, one of the porters at Barts. My identification was confirmed when he unfurled the scarf from his face. He was clean-shaven, as he usually was, which proved Holmes hypothesis of a false beard to be correct.

"I sympathise with your wish," said Holmes. "However, if you hadn't turned her out of your home when she became pregnant, she might not have contracted the disease that killed her and your grandchild."

The man continued to sob.

"I would have let her stay, but the wife was determined she should go," he said. "She cares too much for the opinion of our friends and neighbours."

"Which is why you visited the workhouse to see how she was doing," said Holmes. "And then you found out she had died, and you decided the man responsible for her sorry state should be punished."

"He was a worthless rake," said Arbuthnot. "Who knows how many young girls he had ruined? I'm not sorry I killed him – the world will be a better place without the likes of him in it."

"Possibly," said Holmes," but that is no excuse for taking the law into your own hands."

"The law wouldn't have been able to touch him, but I could," he said. "I was just planning to claim my daughter when she was brought to the hospital the next morning, but then I realised I could avenge her death just as well. I followed Wilson and strangled him. You pick up things when you work around doctors, and I hoped no one would notice he had been murdered. I hid his body in a cupboard overnight and then swapped him when Dr. Watson left the office."

"Why not claim your daughter's body straight away?" I asked.

"I was scared people would investigate and link me to Wilson's murder," Arbuthnot said. "By taking her to the Women's Hospital, I knew her body would be safe until I could come and get it back. I could take her to another borough and say she had died at home. I was sure I would be able to find a doctor who had passed through Barts and recognised me so there would be no trouble with the death certificate."

"I'm sure Dr. Watson will be able to persuade Sir James Paget or Mrs. Anderson to provide a proper burial," Holmes said, "but I doubt you'll be allowed to witness it."

Holmes pulled a police whistle from his pocket and summoned the nearby constable, who took Arbuthnot into custody.

Gregson joined us at Baker Street the following morning to tell us Arbuthnot had made a full confession, as I was sure he would.

"A most satisfactory conclusion," he said.

"I'm not sure much about this case is satisfactory, Gregson," said Holmes. "I feel sympathy for Arbuthnot, and little for his victim."

"How did you know Arbuthnot would be at the hospital?" Gregson asked.

"We hadn't one mystery but two," Holmes said. "The body which had mysteriously appeared, and the one which had vanished. At first it seemed that the choice of body to remove may have been a simple matter of economics – if one was to sell a corpse, then a young woman who was with child is worth more to a hospital than an older man because of its comparative rarity. However, once I had eliminated the professional element from its abduction through my conversations with the professional body suppliers, I deduced the woman's identity was as important as that of the murdered man. While the substitution could be useful in delaying, or even completely concealing the murder, there are far simpler ways to dispose of a body, including simply placing it in the Thames where the tides will prevent discovery for several days.

"Once I had decided the identity of the woman was vital to the case, it was obvious that the culprit had some emotional attachment to her and might wish to provide a decent burial. When I checked with Dr. Anderson and confirmed that a key was missing after the body was delivered there, it confirmed this hypothesis that he planned to return. Thanks to your identification of the murder victim and his character, Gregson, it was obvious to me what the connection between the two bodies and the murderer must be."

"If only Arbuthnot hadn't turned his daughter out of her home," I said.

"Alas, Watson," said Holmes. "the strictures of conventional morality determine the course of so many lives and create as much suffering as those whose evil hearts lead them to live outside of them."

The Adventure of the
False Confessions
by Arthur Hall

In more than a few of my recollections of the singular cases of my friend, the consulting detective Mr. Sherlock Holmes, I have mentioned the initial rivalry and disapproval that he experienced at the hands of the agents of Scotland Yard. Fortunately, this attitude softened in time, as the official force came to appreciate the accuracy and perception of Holmes's judgements. This was as well for them, as my friend's methods were instrumental, on occasion, in preventing the public from learning much that would have been of extreme embarrassment, had the erroneous course of official investigations been made clear. One instance from the early days of our association is, I believe, a revealing example of this.

Holmes, never an early riser, sat in his mouse-coloured dressing-gown at the breakfast table. Dishevelled and unshaven, he helped himself to coffee from the fresh pot that our landlady had produced in anticipation of his arrival.

"I must apologise for my appearance, Watson. I was careful not to present myself until I was certain that Mrs. Hudson had withdrawn."

I nodded. "I informed her that you would not require breakfast, as you instructed. I confess to not expecting you so soon, since you had mentioned that you would be in Stepney until the early hours. I trust that you managed some little sleep, at least?"

"Sufficient, for now." He drained his cup and refilled it. "It was a worthwhile enterprise, however. I was able to deliver Jonah Pickering into Inspector Bradstreet's hands. He will spoil no more young lives, I think."

I smiled with some relief. Pickering had a history of particularly despicable crimes, and Holmes had long pursued him. I turned from the window where I had been observing the constant throng of humanity below.

"I would recommend that you make yourself presentable immediately. A young woman has just entered Baker Street, appearing to be in a state of agitation. She hesitates, but I'm certain that here is her destination. Perhaps I should answer the door if she rings, saving Mrs. Hudson the trouble and allowing you time to dress."

He jumped to his feet after again replacing his cup. "I will be no more than five minutes."

He disappeared into his room as our landlady knocked and entered to clear away the remains of my breakfast. I informed her that it was likely that we would require tea very soon, and she acknowledged before withdrawing.

I descended unhurriedly, reaching our front door but a moment before the bell rang. The woman I had seen from the window appeared startled that the door opened so quickly, but she collected herself and asked at once.

"Sir, am I addressing Mr. Sherlock Holmes?"

I bowed slightly, noticing her wedding ring. "No, Madam. I am Doctor John Watson, the friend and colleague of Mr. Holmes. I presume you wish to consult him."

"Indeed, on a matter of extreme urgency."

"May I ask the nature of your difficulty?"

She cast her eyes down, and then fixed me with a desperate stare. "It is my husband. He has been arrested for murder. It is impossible that he could be guilty – yet he has confessed."

I invited her to enter and conferred with her for a few minutes to allow Holmes the necessary time to prepare himself. We then ascended to our sitting room. It didn't surprise me to find my friend fully presentable, his hair neatly smoothed and his face clean-shaven, for I had witnessed his speed before. His morning-coat was pressed and his cuffs and shirt-front shone bright in the pale autumn glow from our window.

He rose from his chair as I closed the door behind us, and I introduced our client.

"This lady is Mrs. Eleanor Crawford, of Holborn. She has explained to me that her husband is currently being held at Scotland Yard. It seems he has confessed to a murder that he cannot have committed."

Holmes raised his eyebrows. "Such a situation usually occurs when the accused seeks to protect whomever he believes is actually responsible. If that is the case, an interview may reveal the truth."

"That cannot be, sir!" She strove to keep panic from her voice. "My Andrew is an orphan. He has no one other than myself."

"Understandably, you are upset," Holmes said in his gentlest tone. "Pray come and sit with us – I think you will find the basket chair comfortable – and calm yourself while tea is ordered. We can then discuss the situation and see what can be done. The Good Doctor and I are at your disposal."

As I settled myself in my usual chair, Holmes seemed to have succeeded in bringing a measure of calm to our visitor, for she was now conversing with him quite normally.

I sat silently studying her until I heard the rattle of tea-cups approaching. She wasn't unattractive, and slim with dark brown hair and full red lips. I saw that she was lightly sunburned, and tall but not excessively so. Her dark blue costume appeared new. Her eyes reflected the anxiety she felt and, not surprisingly, her voice held a quality of concern.

At the door I relieved our landlady of the tray. I poured for us, noting that Holmes made no further reference to Mrs. Crawford's difficulty as we drank. It wasn't before our cups were empty that he judged her to be sufficiently quiet of spirit to relate to us the curious circumstances that had led to her husband's imprisonment.

"It would be best, I think, if you explained how this came about," Holmes said as I placed the tray to one side. "Pray be precise as to details."

"Andrew is the manager of an import concern, Drucker and Maidstone, in the Great North Road," she began. "Until recently, most of his consignments were of sugar, but now other items are involved."

"Coffee," Holmes interrupted quietly. "Possibly tea also."

"Yes, but how did you know that, Mr. Holmes?"

"I deduced it."

"But *how,*" she insisted curiously.

"Forgive me. The aroma persists." His eyes twinkled and his expression robbed the remark of any offence, and the lady took none.

"One gets so used to it that it's no longer obvious."

"Does your husband's employment have a connection to his present predicament?"

"It does, sir, since the man he is accused of murdering is a customer. Mr. Ishmael Avenall bought large quantities of sugar from Andrew, and was a friend."

"I imagine, then, that Mr. Avenall was the proprietor of a restaurant or similar establishment?"

"He manufactured sweetmeats for children."

"Apart from your concern for your husband, why are you so certain of his innocence?"

"Because at the time of the murder, he never left my side."

Holmes nodded. "While we awaited tea, you stated that constables came to your house in Holborn yesterday to arrest your husband. Have you spoken to him since then?"

She shook her head, visibly disturbed by the recollection. "The inspector indicated that I wouldn't be allowed to see him until interviews had taken place."

"Do you recall the name of this official?"

"I do. One of the constables called him 'Inspector Lestrade'."

111

"He and I are well known to each other," my friend smiled. "When our interview is concluded, I will visit him at Scotland Yard. But tell me: What time of day was the arrest?"

"In the early evening. Andrew had arrived home from his work not half-an-hour before."

"Can you recall your conversation, before the official force descended upon you?"

I leaned forward in my chair. Throughout the interview I had taken notes as Holmes invariably requests, and I sensed that Mrs. Crawford's reply could be important.

"There was very little," she said after a moment, "which is extremely unusual. Because of our closeness, we rarely cease exchanging words, a fact that has been remarked upon many times by acquaintances, but last night was different. It was as if Andrew somehow knew of his impending misfortune."

"How, exactly, did he strike you?" I asked.

She spent a moment searching for words. "Dazed, almost as if he were recently roused from sleep. I was alarmed because his speech was hesitant and indistinct."

"To your knowledge, is your husband a user of opium – perhaps as a remedy for a medical condition?"

"Oh no, sir. I have never known him to take such a thing."

"Had he sustained a recent injury?" Holmes enquired.

"I am aware of none."

There followed a brief silence during which Holmes appeared to be contemplating. For several minutes the only sound was of an altercation between two roughs in Baker Street. Their cries and threats reached us through the half-open window, but he was unperturbed.

"Very well, Mrs. Crawford," he said at last. "Kindly be so good as to furnish Doctor Watson with your address and any other information that you feel might be helpful, and I believe you will hear from us before too long."

She was excessively thankful. Holmes rose and shook her hand before crossing the room to the window, perhaps to see if violence had broken out. I took the lady's details and escorted her from the building, hailing a passing cab.

"Is it peaceful out there?" my friend asked as I re-entered our sitting room.

"It is, apart from a few strollers. The two young men who were about to fight are nowhere to be seen."

"They have decided to quarrel elsewhere, or not at all. Excellent." He draped his thin form across his chair. "What did you think of our client?"

"I saw nothing unusual, except that she is considerably distressed, but trying hard to disguise her anguish. I hope our investigation will quickly prove her husband innocent."

"You failed to observe that she has been married previously, and that her current marital situation is quite recent?"

I considered, but failed to follow his reasoning.

"How did you deduce that?"

Holmes laughed shortly. "Do not look so confused, for it is simplicity itself. The lady's wedding ring is narrower than its predecessor, and protects her finger from sunburn to a lesser extent. That the mark from the previous ring is still visible indicates that it hasn't been there for more than a few months."

"Might that affect our investigation?"

He shrugged. "I cannot tell, as yet. However, if we leave now, we may catch Lestrade at the Yard and still be back in time for luncheon."

"I would be delighted." I said as he handed me my hat and coat.

It was obvious as we entered his office that Inspector Lestrade wasn't in the best of moods. The desk sergeant, whom we knew well, had warned us before allowing us to proceed.

"Come in!" The inspector growled in response to Holmes's knock, but his brow cleared somewhat as he identified his visitors. We exchanged greetings and were directed to sit before his overburdened desk. Tea was offered, but we declined simultaneously.

"I perceive that you're worried," Holmes said. "Or disturbed."

Lestrade shook his head hopelessly. "You may have read of the Carrington case, Mr. Holmes. That man murdered his wife, I would bet upon it, but three times he has escaped us. On each occasion I have collected damning evidence which he has somehow managed to explain away. This doesn't sit well with me, I can tell you."

"Your feelings are easily understandable, Inspector. If it will assist you, I'll give the situation some thought immediately after clearing up another problem that I'm currently confronting. It may be that I can throw new light upon it."

The detective's relief was evident, which surprised me as he had many times expressed resentment to Holmes's "interference". I suspected, as I'm certain my friend did, that Lestrade was under pressure from his superiors to solve this case quickly. It was known that Abel Carrington had influential friends.

Lestrade smiled, his expression lightening considerably. "I would be most grateful, Mr. Holmes. This affair has been a thorn in the side of the Yard for far too long." He moved the file before him to one side and placed his elbows on the desk. "But first be so good as to explain how I can be of service to you gentlemen today. I will endeavour to oblige."

"I would be appreciative of a few minutes with Mr. Andrew Crawford, who I believe you have in the cells."

"Indeed. A strange cove if I ever saw one. A clerk came in here in a state of high excitement, telling us that he'd discovered his employer, a Mr. Ishmael Avenall, strangled in his office. Apparently, Mr. Avenall owned a confectionary factory in Highgate. I went there with a couple of constables, and it didn't take us long to discover that Crawford, who had some dealings with the victim as I understand it, was his killer."

I sensed that Holmes restrained a smile.

"And how did you reach that conclusion, Inspector?" he enquired.

"The deceased had a piece of paper in his hand. It was a page torn from a purchase ledger." Lestrade glowed with triumph. "Probably clutched in his death throes. It showed that he owed Crawford a considerable sum. The inference is obvious, wouldn't you say? Crawford came to collect his money and Mr. Avenell refused, for some reason. They quarrelled, probably came to blows, and Crawford killed him. His address was on the page, so we went straight round and arrested him."

"How did he seem to you?" I asked. "Did he admit his guilt?"

"He did, Doctor. That was the peculiar thing about it. He was like a man half-asleep. He mumbled a confession, but seemed not to know *why* he had murdered Mr. Avenall. We could get nothing more out of him, except some gibberish that he kept repeating."

"Curious," Holmes said thoughtfully. "Did you record what he said?"

"No, it didn't seem important."

"Perhaps we could learn more from an interview."

"Of course." Lestrade got to his feet and we did likewise. "This way, gentlemen."

We walked in a sombre manner down gloomy corridors. The cheerless, olive-painted walls seemed to me, as they always did, to exude misery. The inspector took us to a room containing several cells and instructed the constable on guard to unlock the first of these. In the half-light sat a man of average height, thin-faced with eyes that stared at us blankly.

"On your feet, you."

Mr. Andrew Crawford responded to the inspector's command slowly, laboriously pushing himself upright. I saw at once that his expression suggested deep shock, for he appeared to have difficulty in identifying his surroundings. He looked at all three of us in turn, his gaze blank and unchanging.

114

Lestrade made to speak, but Holmes held up a hand and addressed the prisoner. "Mr. Crawford, my name is Sherlock Holmes. I am a consulting detective, retained by your wife to help you if I can."

He paused, watching Mr. Crawford's face. There was no response.

"This is how he's been since we arrested him," Lestrade whispered, to Holmes's annoyance.

My friend paused, allowing a few moments to pass in silence. Then he concluded his scrutiny of the prisoner's countenance and asked him, "Mr. Crawford, did you kill Mr. Ishmael Avenall?"

At once the reply was forthcoming, but it was recited in the monotone of a poem.

"Yes, I murdered him. I murdered him."

I saw that his eyes had kept their unnatural stillness, and his expression didn't alter.

"What reason did you have?"

This was met with silence.

I sensed Lestrade's growing impatience, but both he and I said nothing.

"What was the purpose of taking Mr. Avenall's life?" Holmes asked again.

No answer came, and then the prisoner began to repeatedly mumble an odd phrase. The inspector nodded that this was what he'd previously described, and I could see that Holmes found it to be curious.

"Very well," he said when silence was restored. "I cannot tell if you understand me, Mr. Crawford, but I'm satisfied that there is more to this. You have my assurance that I will endeavour to discover the truth before you are brought to trial."

With that he turned and left the cell, followed by Lestrade and me. The constable slammed the door behind us, and we retraced our steps to the inspector's office.

Holmes had walked with his head upon his chest, saying little.

"Was there anything else of note in Mr. Avenall's office?" he asked Lestrade when we stood outside his door.

"Nothing. At first we thought Crawford had been disturbed while trying to rob the place, but the page from the ledger disproved that."

"Yes, of course it did. Well thank you, Inspector," he said. "Things may be exactly as you have described, but I feel it will do no harm to see if there is more to be discovered."

We found a hansom easily.

"What did you make of that?" he enquired as the horse began a fast trot.

115

"One thing struck me immediately, apart from Mr. Crawford's condition, which closely resembles the effects of severe shock. It was those repeated words, near the end of the interview."

"You recognised them?"

"That I cannot claim, but they resembled a dialect that I heard often while in Afghanistan."

He nodded. "It struck me that they were words, rather than the gibberish that Lestrade assumed."

"Perhaps we'll learn more as our enquiries progress." I looked from the window at the passing scene. "But where are we going now? This isn't the way to Baker Street."

He consulted his pocket watch. "I thought there might be time for a quick visit to Mr. Crawford's place of employment, Drucker and Maidstone on the Great North Road, before lunch. I wish to confirm something."

We arrived to be greeted by a pale-faced youth who was apparently meant to be filling Mr. Crawford's post during his absence. Clearly, he was doing so with difficulty. The strong aroma of coffee mingled with that of the company's other imports as Holmes questioned him briefly.

"And to your knowledge, Mr. Crawford displayed no animosity towards Mr. Avenall?"

"None," said the youth as we conversed in the tiny office with a single chair. "I always believed the opposite to be true. They were on friendly terms, always."

"Did Mr. Crawford appear unwell at any time recently?"

"No, not at all."

"Finally, kindly tell us: Do any of the goods imported here originate in India?"

The youth shook his head. "We once brought in a consignment of strong curry powder, but that was at least a year ago. It was never repeated because the demand was lower than expected. I can state with confidence that we have received nothing from India since then."

Holmes thanked him and concluded the interview.

"I think we'll return to Baker Street and Mrs. Hudson's pork pie," he said as we searched for a cab. "After that, I'll leave you to your own devices for an hour or two, while I make an enquiry in a different direction. Be so good as to raise your stick, for I see that a hansom approaches."

Holmes devoured his meal with surprising speed. I was still consuming my pie as he finished his coffee and left the table.

"I beg you to excuse me, but it's impossible to make an appointment for the business I must conclude this afternoon. The earlier I leave here, the more likely it is that I will find the gentleman I seek at his residence."

116

"Then you must go, of course." I watched as he put on his ear-flapped travelling cap. "But take care, Holmes. It didn't escape my notice that you placed your revolver in your pocket."

"Always astute. You are truly the single fixed point in this changing world."

With that he left, bounding down the stairs and into the street. Almost immediately I heard a cab halt to his summons, and I finished my meal wondering as to what he intended.

Shortly after, Mrs. Hudson cleared away our plates and I resolved to finally finish reading a long sea story dealing with whaling. Yet I'd I hardly settled myself when the book grew heavy in my hands, and I felt the irresistible call of sleep. It was probably the noisy closing of the front door that woke me, or the thudding of Holmes's rapid ascent of the stairs. I retrieved my fallen volume and brushed back my hair, attempting to appear as if I had maintained my wakefulness throughout his absence, before he burst into the room. His expression told me at once that his expedition had been successful.

"Ah, Watson. I do apologise for waking you."

"Holmes, how did you – "

"Your eyes, of course. They are bleary, in the way they often are at breakfast. Also, the position of the creased cushion suggests that you have adopted a reclining posture, whereas your usual position while reading is upright in your chair."

Inwardly, I reprimanded myself for believing that I could deceive him. "Your manner suggests that all went well this afternoon."

"Indeed." He divested himself of his hat and coat and poured a glass of port for both of us, before taking his usual chair at the far side of the fireplace. "I can see that you are almost beside yourself with curiosity, so I'll enlighten you as best as I can."

"Pray do so. I am all attention."

Unusually, he drained his glass in one swallow and replaced it on a side-table before leaning back in his chair.

"I have been to visit a callous murderer – a hired assassin."

I felt my eyebrows rise, involuntarily. "Good Heavens! Why didn't you allow me to accompany you?"

"It really was unnecessary. Thomas Drury knows that he has nothing to fear from me at present, although I'm now quite certain that it was he who murdered Mr. Ishmael Avenall."

"How did you discover this?"

"It was really no more than an elementary exercise. As we spoke to Mr. Avenall's replacement, I noticed traces of red mud smeared on the office floor. At this time, as far as I am aware, there are four known killers-

117

for-hire resident in London, and only one of them lives in a district where this kind of soil is common. As soon as I arrived in Hackney, I saw that Drury's rented rooms cannot be entered except by means of a patch of land with that same soil where the owner grows vegetables. It became likely that I had found my man."

"We must inform Lestrade."

"Not so fast. By now the mud has most likely been cleared away. I noticed a cleaning woman busily at work in the room beyond where we conducted our interview. Thomas Drury has escaped the hangman twice because of lack of evidence, and I have no intention of adding to that."

"Did the scoundrel admit his guilt to you?"

Holmes shook his head. "He merely stated that, if the official force has a man in custody, it proves his own innocence. Hardly a logical conclusion. He did suggest, however, a possible reason for Mr. Avenall's death, which was probably why he was hired to kill him. According to Drury, Mr. Avenall was conducting liaisons with a married woman."

"Even if that is so, how is Mr. Andrew Crawford implicated?"

"That we have yet to discover. When we have proven Mr. Crawford's innocence, I'll turn my attention to compiling evidence against Drury before delivering it to Scotland Yard. For the moment, we'll concentrate on the problem posed by our client."

After an hour or so, Mrs. Hudson served us a fine dinner of roast chicken. I realised that Holmes was in an expansive mood, and I was able to induce him to relate to me some cases from his days in Montague Street. My pocket watch showed that it was after midnight when I finally laid my notebook aside and we retired. I fell asleep wondering how he would proceed, and what strange affliction possessed Mr. Crawford.

The next morning saw Holmes in a more thoughtful mood. His breakfast was hardly touched when Mrs. Hudson cleared away our plates, earning him a concerned but disapproving stare.

We were seated in our usual armchairs, debating whether to light the fire, when the doorbell rang and our discussion ceased. Mrs. Hudson answered quickly and Holmes strained his ears to catch the subsequent murmurs that ended with her leading our visitor up the stairs.

"It's Lestrade." He turned in his chair so that he faced the door.

"A new case, no doubt, with which he requires your assistance."

"Unless he has further news of Mr. Crawford."

We both rose and Holmes acknowledged our landlady's knock by calling for entry, and she announced the inspector.

"Good morning, Lestrade," he said. "I'm sorry to see that the day began with some urgency for you."

"I'm on my way to arrest a man caught attempting to burn down several of his neighbour's houses," the inspector replied after acknowledging our greeting. "I called in as I passed because I have information which may assist you in the matter we discussed yesterday."

"That was most kind. Would you like tea?" I noticed that Mrs. Hudson had remained at the door in anticipation of such a request.

"No, thank you. I'm due in Walworth to relieve Bradstreet."

Holmes shook his head and our landlady withdrew.

"I wish you well with your investigation, Inspector."

"Thank you. I will be glad if I can conclude it today, as I have much else on hand. I wouldn't have thought it necessary to rouse an inspector early, just to look into – " He broke off, realising that Holmes had observed the indications of his haste. "But how did you know that my morning had begun in an urgent and confused manner?"

"Your shave hasn't been conducted with your usual precision," Holmes smiled. "I would suggest that it was carried out in poor light, perhaps while darkness persisted, which means that you were obliged to leave your bed in the early hours. Also your tie is slightly askew, which paints a picture of a man who must hurry. But you've stated that you have news of Mr. Crawford. Tell us, pray – has he recovered his senses?"

"I fear that he hasn't, but after you left yesterday, I chanced to meet Gregson at the Yard. He had arrested Ezra Fernworth, a saddler, who has confessed to the murder of Sir Benjamin Grappell during the burglary at Burlescombe Place."

"The dailies described the incident at great length," said I.

"Right you are, Doctor. The case was given to Gregson, and he's now strutting around Scotland Yard like a cockerel after solving it." Lestrade's eyes narrowed. "But when he boasted of it to me, I saw immediately that there was a flaw in his reasoning."

Holmes's expression didn't change. "Pray elaborate."

"Gregson took great pleasure in relating the chain of evidence that led to Fernworth's arrest, but I formed the impression that it was vague and that he is himself unsure of it. He's holding Fernworth on little more than the strength of his confession alone, and the man's response to questions proved to be so similar to those of Andrew Crawford that I thought it best to let you know."

Holmes and I glanced at each other briefly.

"Inspector, I find it difficult to adequately express my gratitude to you for bringing this to our notice," he said sincerely. "I now have every expectation that this affair will be brought to its conclusion in a day or two. You can be certain that the details of my investigation and the credit will be yours the moment I shed some light on the matter. I will not fail to

119

ensure that your superiors are aware of the considerable insight that you have displayed."

The official detective was taken aback. "Why, thank you Mr. Holmes. I did no more than repeat what Gregson described, but I'm glad to have assisted you." He produced his pocket watch, frowning. "But I see that time is getting on, and Bradstreet will be waiting. I wish you good morning, gentlemen."

He was gone in an instant. From the window, I saw him board the police coach that waited further along Baker Street.

"You were rather lavish with your praise," I smiled.

"Not at all. Lestrade has removed the one doubt I had regarding Mr. Andrew Crawford."

"You believed he was feigning his condition?"

"By no means. It occurred to me that Mr. Crawford may have sustained some injury that had caused his uncommunicative state but, unless it is a contagious condition, this is now unlikely. Another visit to the Yard is indicated, I think. Mrs. Hudson will surely keep our midday meal hot until we return."

Inspector Lestrade was correct. Ezra Fernworth appeared to be in the same pitiful state as his fellow prisoner, Andrew Crawford. Inspector Gregson seemed only too glad to allow us an interview for, by his own admission, he had made no progress.

"I can get nothing out of him, Mr. Holmes, other than the few repeated words of his confession. Apart from that, he says little. His face doesn't alter, save when he speaks in a foreign tongue."

"Ah," said Holmes as we entered a cell a short distance from that we had visited previously, "you have identified his utterings as words rather than indiscriminate ramblings. There is hope for you yet, Gregson."

The inspector returned this with a stony look. "Lestrade saw nothing, but I saw clearly that there is a pattern here, though what it means I cannot yet tell."

"Quite so. Doubtless we will learn more as our investigation progresses."

Gregson dismissed the constable on duty and we peered into the semi-darkness at a figure who seemed oblivious to our presence, for he hadn't moved so much as to turn his head at our entrance.

"Stand up, Fernworth!" the official detective ordered harshly.

The prisoner appeared to do so with difficulty, and when he moved toward us, the stronger light revealed him to be quite elderly. His eyes showed nothing, not even awareness that he was no longer alone. Holmes passed a hand in front of the gaunt and empty face without response before

120

glancing critically at the inspector. "This is the man you suspect of murdering Sir Benjamin Grappell? On account of his age, I would be interested in discovering how he gained entry to Burlescombe Place, for I know it to be steep and well fortified."

"That I have yet to learn from him, but he has confessed."

"And to what do you attribute his condition?"

"Perhaps he has been set upon by a sudden illness, or by the weight of his guilt. I have seen that happen before now, Mr. Holmes, but it will not save him from the hangman."

Holmes regarded the prisoner silently, apparently attempting to learn something of his curious state. Then, inviting incredulous stares from Gregson, he intoned a strange series of phrases. I recognised them as a passable imitation of those made by Mr. Crawford, during our previous visit.

At once Mr. Ezra Fernworth shrank back. His sudden animation was accompanied by a soft scream and an expression of sheer terror that surprised both Gregson and myself.

"Calm yourself, Mr. Fernworth," Holmes advised in his most gentle tone. "I know what ails you now. All will be well soon. You have my promise."

He turned abruptly and Gregson called for the guard to open the cell door.

"What is it, Mr. Holmes?" he asked as we made our way along the dismal corridor. "What did you discover?"

"Only that your prisoner is terrified of whomever inflicted this state upon him. There are similarities between Mr. Fernworth and Mr. Crawford, who was arrested by Lestrade, and doubtless the same person is responsible. As for *how* this was done, I know of only one possibility which I will confirm presently." He looked at the inspector sympathetically. "But I can tell you now with reasonable certainty that neither prisoner is a murderer."

Gregson ran a hand through his flaxen hair. "Very well, Mr. Holmes. You've been right on many previous occasions, so I'll endeavour to delay as I can. I would be grateful if you would inform the Yard of any further discoveries that may come to light."

Holmes nodded. "You may depend upon it."

Mrs. Hudson's Irish Stew tasted especially good that day, or perhaps it seemed that way because my appetite was keen. Typically, Holmes barely touched his food as his mind was clearly full of his intentions for the rest of the day.

"Try not to linger too long," he said impatiently. "There is work for us this afternoon."

I put down my knife and fork and pushed away my plate. "We're going to confirm your suspicions as to the nature of whatever has brought about the condition of the prisoners?"

"Bravo!" The ghost of a smile flickered across his face. "But first I must ensure that I'm on the right track. When we visited the Yard this morning, I spoke to the desk sergeant while we were awaiting Gregson. I enquired as to Lestrade's whereabouts and was informed that he would be absent until mid-day. We'll return there now, I think, to request another interview with Mr. Crawford."

"With the object, no doubt, of observing his response to the same test that caused such animation to Mr. Fernworth?"

"Precisely."

I'll not go into detail regarding our second visit to the Yard that day. Suffice it to say that Lestrade was surprised to see us again so soon, and astounded when he observed Mr. Andrew Crawford's excited state on hearing Holmes's peculiar exclamations. My friend seemed satisfied at the outcome, but would say nothing further, save that he expected to be able to bring about a conclusion to this affair very soon.

We quickly procured a cab and I heard Holmes instruct the driver that Holborn was to be our destination.

"We are to visit Mrs. Crawford?" I enquired as the hansom joined the stream of traffic.

He nodded. "Hopefully, she will not be out."

"What are we to ask her?"

"We will attempt to establish the connection between Lestrade's prisoner and that of Gregson. Clearly the condition of the two men has a common source."

Our client's residence was a villa constructed from what appeared to be Cotswold stone. As we strode up the short path leading to the front door, I saw movement behind a curtained window, so it didn't surprise me that Holmes made no attempt to raise his stick, but instead waited until Mrs. Crawford opened the door to admit us.

She greeted us in a trembling voice, and I saw at once the terrible toll that anxiety had taken upon her nerves.

"Is there any news?" she asked with a look of dreadful anticipation. "Has anything changed?"

"I believe we can offer you some hope," Holmes replied in his gentlest tone.

She led us into a small but well-kept sitting room, her eagerness to hear Holmes's explanation evident. We refused refreshments and settled ourselves on a long leather sofa at her bidding.

"Please, Mr. Holmes, tell me all!"

"First, let me assure you that I'm quite certain of your husband's innocence. We've seen him at Scotland Yard and have come to believe that both his confession and his trance-like state were induced, rather than the effects of guilt, as has been surmised."

The lady showed some relief, exhaling as her tension ebbed.

"Thank God! Will he be released when you explain your discoveries?"

"He'll be released when I can *prove* that my discoveries are valid. I expect to be able to demonstrate the truth of this affair to Inspector Lestrade soon, but to exonerate Mr. Crawford, I must identify the true murderer. In this, I believe that you may be able to assist me."

Desperation returned to her face at once. "Anything!"

Holmes nodded, and then hesitated, I thought to choose his words carefully. "Can you recall your husband mentioning, or having any association with, anyone of Indian origin? A visitor from that country perhaps, or someone he has met in the course of his business?"

"I can think of no one." Disappointment and concentration clouded her face for a moment. She shook her head despairingly. "But wait! Andrew has played cards in the evening a few times with some casual acquaintances and their friends. Some weeks ago, he mentioned that a London agent of one of the coffee exporting concerns had joined them once or twice. His description sounded foreign, but that is all I know – it was merely a passing remark that was never referred to again."

"Does the name of this man come to mind?" Holmes enquired.

She paused, then shook her head again. "I'm sorry, gentlemen. There, my memory fails me."

"Your husband didn't know this man previously? I asked.

"No, he did not, as far as I am aware." Her expression brightened. "But there may be a way to discover more. Andrew regularly maintains a diary. In it he records events both in his working life and his home. I suppose it's possible that he may have included some reference to the men who attend the card games, even if he has seldom spoken of them to me."

At this I saw Holmes's eyes glitter, as he addressed Mrs. Crawford in a restrained, but urgent, tone.

"Pray retrieve this diary if you're able. I'm sure your husband will pardon an intrusion into his privacy, in these circumstances."

Mrs. Crawford immediately repaired to the upper floor. The sounds and vibrations of her increasingly frantic search reached us, and I fancied that my friend's expression was a little less hopeful with the passing of five minutes.

Then the scuffles ceased abruptly, and she descended the stairs. Re-entering the room, she clutched a thick leather-bound volume that was clearly well-used.

"I must apologise, gentlemen," she said breathlessly. "The book wasn't where I imagined it to be. Andrew had locked it away for some reason."

"No matter." Holmes smiled kindly as he took it from her, and I altered my position to read some of the pages as he turned them. The reason for the diary's concealment soon became apparent, for Mr. Andrew Crawford had begun to gamble for increasingly high stakes. Holmes ignored this however, venturing ever further back into the recorded activities before he turned to me, briefly. "Two weeks ago. Here we have our connection. Both Mr. Crawford and Mr. Ezra Fernworth were present at an evening whist game lasting three hours. It was held, on this occasion, at the home of Mr. Lakshmi Isra, in Chelsea."

"The two prisoners were acquainted!"

"So it would seem, although I doubt they have set eyes on each other at the Yard."

As our hostess gave us a puzzled glance, I peered again at the diary while I recorded the name and address in my notebook, after which Holmes closed the volume and laid it upon a side-table before we rose together.

"Our thanks to you, Mrs. Crawford. You may rest assured that you have brought your husband's release significantly closer this morning."

We left the lady with, I felt, a hope that she hadn't held previously.

Mrs. Hudson had clearly visited Billingsgate, for our dinner was a delicious rendering of dressed crab. Holmes made a single complimentary comment which suggested to me that, in his mind at least, he had arrived at a satisfactory solution to our client's predicament. When absorbed with the intricacies of a case, he rarely remarked upon his food.

Presently, with our meal finished and the plates cleared away, we settled into our armchairs. Before I could begin a conversation with some of the questions I had concerning this affair, he rose to select a volume from his index.

"You are searching for any mention of Mr. Lakshmi Isra," I ventured.

He nodded as his eyes scoured the page. "I can recall no reference to him before now, but it is the influence that he undoubtedly wields that interests me."

"You have identified its nature?"

124

"Oh yes." He turned a page. "From the beginning I suspected the involvement of 'mesmerism' or 'magnetism' in this. As you will be aware, we have heard only hints of such a practice before now, although I understand that a false version where the effect is prearranged with the receiver of the treatment is sometimes practiced in circuses and carnival side-shows."

"This is a subject which medical science has yet to penetrate, although I have heard of individuals whose interests have strayed into it."

"Indeed." He placed the volume on his knee, thoughtfully. "I do believe that I may obtain some assistance from one such person in the morning. I'll leave you shortly after breakfast, but I don't expect to be away for long. I'm quite certain that you will be able to amuse yourself until my return."

He then got to his feet to pour us brandy from the decanter and would say nothing more on the subject for the remainder of the evening

I breakfasted alone. Holmes was already nowhere to be seen and Mrs. Hudson explained that he had left early, a fact that I had already deduced from the cold tea-pot that she replaced with a fresh one as I busied myself with my bacon and eggs. Upon finishing, I went out to complete some errands of my own. On my return, I found Holmes draped across his chair and smoking his cherry-wood pipe.

"Were your enquiries of this morning a success?" I asked.

"In abundance. I went to see a Sikh gentleman, Doctor Mahesh Singh, who I recalled from a case that was before your time, once related to me an incident that involved mesmerism. It turns out that his knowledge of the practice is quite extraordinary, and he was able to assure me that it's well within its capabilities to compel men and women to act as they would never consider otherwise."

"Such as confess to murder, though they are innocent?"

"Precisely. That is my supposition. After leaving Doctor Singh, I sought out Wiggins, who assures me that one or other of the Irregulars will be able to inform us shortly as to the whereabouts of Mr. Lakshmi Isra in Chelsea."

I nodded. "The common factor linking both prisoners."

Holmes blew out a final cloud of smoke and replaced his pipe in the rack. "Indeed. But now I hear Mrs. Hudson on the stairs. I do believe that the aroma of a well-cooked partridge was in the air as I took the stairs earlier."

Surprisingly, Holmes was in no hurry to finish his meal. As we finally pushed away our plates, I reflected that my knowledge of Tibetan religious customs and the seaworthy properties of the Egyptian *felucca* had been greatly increased.

"Holmes," I began as we drank the last of our coffee, "you have said nothing more about either Mr. Crawford or Mr. Fernworth. Are we to take further steps to free them this afternoon? Will what you have learned about mesmerism convince Gregson or Lestrade?"

"That I very much doubt," he replied as he picked up his violin after our landlady had cleared our table. "We'll indeed take further steps on their behalf, but not before we hear from Wiggins and his friends. He didn't appear to perceive the task I gave him as any great difficulty, so it wouldn't surprise me to receive a message well before dinner."

In fact, less than two hours passed before Mrs. Hudson, with great reluctance, showed a tall and grim-faced lad into our sitting room. She withdrew, closing the door softly as the young fellow stood, a tattered and uncertain figure, looking from Holmes to myself and back again. I realised that he must be a recent addition to the Irregulars. Certainly he had never before made our acquaintance.

Our visitor decided correctly and marched up to Holmes, who had long since laid down his violin.

"Mr. Sherlock Holmes, sir," he said confidently.

"I am, and who are you, young man?"

"Griffiths, sir. Wiggins sent me with a message that he said was important."

"Pray continue, then."

"He said to tell you No. 76 Albion Villas, sir."

"My thanks to you and to Wiggins," Holmes replied, whereupon the lad turned and would have left, had not my friend pressed a half-sovereign into his hand. At this he smiled for the first time as he mumbled his appreciation, saluted, and was gone.

Holmes resumed his seat, and I regarded him in silence for a few moments.

"I presume you're about to tell me that we are to visit Chelsea?" I enquired then.

A fleeting smile crossed his face. "No. I fear you must spend this evening alone. I have devised a subterfuge to gain entrance to Mr. Isra's premises, with the purpose of extracting a confession if he is indeed entangled in this affair. I'm not at all sure that it would be effective if I were to be accompanied."

I confess to feeling put out at this. My disappointment on hearing his intentions was considerable.

"But Holmes, if your suspicions about this man are correct – if he is in truth responsible for two innocent men facing charges of murder – he

126

may be dangerous. Let us make this visit together, and I will bring my service revolver to ensure our safety."

The expression that appeared on his hawk-like face then, warmed my heart but didn't dispel my disappointment. "Friend Watson – always my faithful companion. I truly regret that we cannot conclude this affair, if that is what tonight will bring, together. Whatever the outcome, you have my word that I will relate it to you in detail at the earliest possible moment."

"But Holmes . . ." I protested again, falling silent as I noticed a strange dullness to his eyes. "Are you ill?"

"Thank you, I am well. You need not concern yourself."

"There is an unfamiliar look about you."

"Oh that," he said lightly. "I am a little tired, nothing more."

I was about to object further to his intentions, but our landlady's knock forestalled me. She entered bearing plates of thick beef stew, and Holmes seized on the diversion. Several times during our meal I attempted to resume our conversation, but always he resisted. My dessert hadn't yet arrived when he pushed away his empty plate and got to his feet.

"I must apologise for leaving you so soon again. I wish to call upon Mr. Isra early, in case he intends to go out." He reached for his hat and coat. "I intend to see the end of this affair tonight, if it is at all possible."

With that, and before I could rise, he was gone.

In those earlier days, I was less likely to ignore Holmes's instructions, or I might have followed him. Instead, I wandered around our sitting room for a while like a beast in a cage. My mind was full of dreadful premonitions, awful imaginings of what could, at this very moment, be befalling my friend at the hands of this man who apparently possessed a strange and compelling force. After some time I brought reason into play, reminding myself of the skills that I already knew Holmes had in abundance and bringing to mind the evil men that he had brought to justice, their plans thwarted, in the short time of our acquaintance. I attempted to quieten my anxieties.

I forced myself to settle in my chair and immerse my mind in the accumulated medical journals that I rarely had time to peruse. More than an hour passed before I abandoned these in favour of the late edition of *The Standard*. Finally, I resorted again to an examination of my thoughts and recollections, smoking pipe after pipe until I heard the key turn and our front door open.

Someone that could only be Holmes bounded up the stairs. I put away my pipe and waited eagerly. A moment passed and he entered our sitting room, his expression telling me at once that it was likely he had succeeded.

"Holmes! Have you seen Mr. Isra?"

127

He divested himself of his coat and hat and I poured us both a glass of port.

"I have indeed." He accepted the glass and we sat down facing each other. "It is over. Mr. Isra is confined to his sitting room by the police handcuffs attaching him to a very large and heavy sideboard. On my way back, I requested the cabby to find a late office, and Lestrade should have received my telegram by now. Doubtless," he consulted his pocket watch, "he'll have his prisoner in the cells before midnight."

We placed our empty glasses on a side-table. "But how did this come about? To what extent was Mr. Isra involved with Mr. Crawford and Mr. Fernworth?"

"Both of those men will be released, as soon as I give my account to the Good Inspector at the Yard in the morning. As for Mr. Isra, I hope his affairs are in order, since he will certainly spend a good few years in prison."

"He will not face the hangman, then? He isn't a murderer?"

Holmes shook his head. "No, his crime was to make for himself a rather unusual way of earning a living."

"I am confounded. Pray begin at the beginning."

"Very well." He laughed shortly. "I am aware of my promise. Retrieve your notebook and I'll tell you all. Then, I think, it will be as well if we both retire."

At that I realised how weary I had become, and that he also must be in need of rest. I took up my notebook and pencil. "When you are ready."

All was quiet for a minute or two, save for a coach or hansom speeding along Baker Street at a fair pace.

"After leaving Baker Street, I arrived at Chelsea without incident." He tilted his head back to begin his recollections, and I noticed that his eyes were now clear. "The cabby found Mr. Isra's address without difficulty, although Albion Villas is somewhat remote from the usual routes. The house is a tall, dark structure that will not, I suspect, stand for many more years without repair. Mr. Isra proved, at first, to be a most sociable and reasonable fellow, admitting me to his home immediately I stated that I was working with Scotland Yard in accumulating further evidence of the guilt of Mr. Crawford and Mr. Fernworth. He appeared most anxious to assist me."

I nodded. "Is Mr. Isra a permanent resident here? A young man, perhaps?"

"He is scarcely past the thirtieth year of his life, I would say, and has forsaken his natural mode of dress for ours. Mrs. Crawford was quite correct when she described him as the London agent for a concern dealing in coffee. He has, however, previously attended Cambridge, and did so following his arrival from the East Punjab at least ten years ago."

"Did he disclose how he came to be associated with the two men?"

"That, and much else. Maintaining the pretence, I asked the expected questions about his connection with Mr. Crawford, making a point of mentioning that my investigation was to be long and thorough. He acted in a most amiable manner, offering refreshments which I refused, until I became aware from the hard glitter of his eyes and the gradually lowering tone of his voice that he had set his will to attempt to dominate mine. I allowed him to believe that he had succeeded, knowing that his vanity would compel him to explain what he saw as his achievements to one who would not afterwards be capable of repeating his account to others."

"He intended to kill you!" I exclaimed, although I had expected such an intention.

"Suicide was what he had in mind for me. As you see, he was not successful."

"The fellow should be imprisoned!"

"Doubtless he will be. I listened with interest to his explanation of the events that caused both Mr. Crawford and Mr. Fernworth to be incarcerated. He met Mr. Crawford through his employment of course, and Mr. Fernworth a short time beforehand at his club. Mr. Isra invited each man to his home, with the stated purpose that they should play cards, while his real intention was to obtain a measure of control over their wills. He appeared to take great delight in explaining that the practice we know as 'Mesmerism' has been in use for centuries in certain regions of the Indian sub-continent, and that he himself had been adept in its use long before setting foot in our land. He used the practice extensively to enhance his progress during his university years, and to secure a position with the establishment where he is employed to this day. Mr. Isra didn't mention exactly when the notion of using his power more profitably occurred to him, but I don't believe that his victims extend beyond the two of which we are aware."

"But if I'm correct in my understanding that he caused Mr. Crawford and Mr. Fernworth to confess to crimes of which they were innocent by means of this power, then how did he gain by it?"

"Patience. There isn't much more to tell. Mr. Isra made enquiries in disreputable places, haunts of ruthless figures of the underworld of our capital. Eventually it was realised that he was offering a scheme whereby murderers could escape punishment. He said to me that, just as in our Christian religion Jesus suffered the punishment of Barabbas the murderer, so it could be arranged, by means of his power, for others to confess to crimes of which they were innocent and suffer their penalties. The true murderers would then be no longer sought by the official force, and Mr. Isra would collect a substantial fee. I was correct in deducing that Thomas Drury took the life of Ishmael Avenall, who coincidentally knew his supposed murderer. The page from the ledger that Lestrade was so proud to discover was a deliberate ploy to mislead him. The *mantra* recited by both prisoners was put into their minds to suggest that deviation from their instructed course would result in painful death. Mr. Isra also confessed to shielding Augustus Burnham, a seasoned criminal who is no stranger to me, by falsely implicating Mr. Fernworth in the death of Sir Benjamin Grappell. The purpose of these crimes is still unknown to me, but I will inform Lestrade of the true perpetrators, before assisting him on the Carrington case, as agreed."

"Good Lord!" I interrupted. "The miscarriages of justice that this man could have caused had he been allowed to continue! The prospect is unthinkable."

"Quite so." A quick smile, vanishing instantly. "And it is fair to say, I think, that the official force experiences sufficient difficulty already."

I scribbled again in my notebook before enquiring, "How were you able to resist Mr. Isra's power? You took an enormous risk. You have stated that his intention was to induce you to take your own life."

He got to his feet and stretched. His weariness now evident. "That is true. In fact, he mentioned my fate several times, gloating over his own cleverness. I wish you could have seen the change in his expression, when I used my knowledge of self-defence to restrain and handcuff him after shedding my apparent submissive state. His technique was ineffective, thanks to the anticipation of Doctor Singh, of whom I told you earlier. He administered a temporary light hypnotic condition, which proved to be a more-than-adequate means of resistance."

He glanced again at his pocket watch. "But now sleep beckons. If I have omitted anything, I'm certain that you'll make note of it during our interview with Lestrade in the morning. Good night. I think we will both sleep well tonight."

His Own Hangman
by Thomas A. Burns, Jr.

Most of the cases of my friend and companion, Mr. Sherlock Holmes, that I have selected to record in my journals have had a clear, if not always happy, resolution. Our recent adventure involving the Speckled Band is a case in point – Holmes was able to unmask the villain and discover the means of murder, and the miscreant met a tragic, though well-deserved, end. However, we have had other cases that had some aspects which couldn't be fully explained to the public at large at the time, yet still had features of interest. The affair of the burglary and murder in Three Colt Lane was one such.

On the day that the case first came to Holmes's attention, the weather was overcast and rainy. It was a good day to stay indoors with *The Times*, *The Daily News*, *The Morning Post*, *The Telegraph* and all of the other newspapers that Sherlock Holmes took. He himself was lounging on the sofa in his dressing gown and pyjamas, his morning pipe, composed of the plugs and dottles from all of the previous day's smokes, dangling limply from the corner of his mouth. He was bored, and a bored Holmes was always a dangerous Holmes.

In an attempt to divert him from any destructive ideas, I asked him a question concerning a story I had just read in *The Post*, entitled "His Own Hangman". "Why would a man hang himself in his cell the night before he was scheduled to die by hanging?"

Holmes looked at me sharply. He knew exactly what I was trying to do, yet he couldn't keep himself from answering. "The first thing that comes to mind is that he wished to deprive The Crown of the satisfaction of hanging him. Who was he?"

"A Chinaman who murdered his master in a house in Three Colts Lane."

Holmes immediately perked up. "Ah! That would be the Quan Yin burglary."

Somehow, I had missed that story in the papers. "What is a Quan Yin?" I asked.

"It's not a Quan Yin. It's a name – *Quan Yin*. Statues of Quan Yin are an important element of Buddhist iconography. She is the female aspect of the male *bodhisattva Avalokiteshvara*, and she symbolizes compassion, acting as a patron of those in need. A *bodhisattva* is a human that has taken a vow to dedicate their future reincarnations to the

131

enlightenment of all men. The Buddhists believe that Quan Yin has been reincarnated many times. She is often portrayed as a woman seated or standing, holding a lotus flower or a vase of water." He paused to suck noisily on his pipe, then produced a vesta from a pocket of his dressing gown, lit it, and applied it to the bowl. When he was able to expel clouds of dark grey smoke, he continued. "Sir Erasmus Hadley was a noted Sinophile who had a house in Three Colt Street in Limehouse. He spent many years accumulating Chinese art and was known to have one of the most important collections in England. The showpiece of his collection was the Wengcheng Quan Yin, a statue of the finest unblemished jade, which dated from the Zhou dynasty – a unique piece nearly a thousand years old."

"You refer to him in the past tense. I take it that Sir Erasmus is no longer with us."

"You are correct. He was killed last month during the burglary in which the Wengcheng Quan Yin was stolen. I assume the unfortunate gentlemen in the newspaper story you brought to my attention was one Sam Lee?"

"That's right."

"Sam Lee was Hadley's houseboy. He was convicted of murdering his master during the theft. Apparently, Hadley caught Sam Lee in the act. The houseboy allegedly hit his master over the head with a heavy candlestick, then fled into the depths of Limehouse's Chinatown. It is unclear whether he knew that he had killed Hadley or not, but it made no difference. He was captured by police the day after the robbery, but no longer had the statue in his possession. It was suspected that he hid the piece during the time he was free, as no trace of it has been found. He was condemned to die in the Assizes and sent to Newgate Prison where the sentence was to be carried out. And now you tell me has taken his own life? Let me see that newspaper."

I handed it over.

"Hmmph. Enterprising fellow, our Mr. Lee. He tore his prison uniform into strips, twisted them, and knotted them together to form a short rope, one end of which he threaded through the grille in his cell window. The other end went 'round his neck. Then he simply sat down with his back against the wall. It wasn't an easy death – a partial suspension hanging never is. He was found by the guards who came to escort him to his early morning appointment at the gallows." Holmes folded the paper and dropped it on the floor next to the sofa, steepled his fingers in front of his face, and closed his eyes. In a minute, he opened them again and swung his legs to the floor. "Watson, get dressed. I think a visit to Barts is in order."

I had long ago ceased to take umbrage against Holmes's peremptory orders. In short order I was dressed for the street. I wore my Norfolk jacket and a woollen flat cap against the rain. Outside, the drizzle was slacking off and the sky clearing, but a fresh north wind put a chill in the air that made my cheeks sting. We walked to Marylebone Road for a cab.

The trip to Barts consumed nearly half-an-hour, as the slick cobblestones made travel slow and treacherous. Finally, our cab drew up in front of the mammoth gray-stone hulk in Giltspur Street. So much of my current life has revolved around this place. It was here that I first met Holmes, and I was currently on staff half-time. We passed through an arched entryway and went straight to the mortuary in the bowels of the building, where the stench of death and carbolic greeted us. Dr. Price, the coroner, looked up as we entered.

"What brings you here, Holmes?" he asked. "We have no suspicious deaths for you today."

"On the contrary, my dear Price, I think that you do. I've come for a look at the body of Sam Lee."

"That Chinaman? He's a suicide. Did himself in before the hangman could get to him."

"So you've examined the body then?"

"Well, no, but I got the story from the lads who brought him in."

"I should still like to examine the remains, if you don't mind."

"Why should I mind?" He waved to a line of wheeled carts holding cloth-covered corpses. "He's over there – third on the left, I think."

We approached the indicated cart, and Holmes removed the canvas and cavalierly deposited it atop an adjacent body. Sam Lee was a young man in his twenties, I surmised. His face and neck were mottled with dark red blotches, his mouth was wide open, no doubt due to his struggles for air, and there was bruising around his throat.

Holmes took the young man's head in both hands and attempted to move it. It did so easily. "*Rigor mortis* is gone," he said, "consistent with the time of death reported in the newspaper. However, I can unequivocally state that this was no suicide."

"What leads you to that conclusion?" I asked.

"Hanging always leaves a bruise on the neck and chest that resembles an inverted '*V*'. You can see the beginnings of one here." He pointed to an area just under the chin. "However, you should also notice that it is superimposed upon this vivid, circular bruise that goes round the neck entirely. A lesion such as this one is a certain indicator of ligature strangulation. Also, note the scratches and abrasions around the circular mark, where the young man clawed at the ligature in a futile attempt to loosen it. He struggled to get away from his killer, who took him from

133

behind." Holmes reached down and picked up the fellow's arm. "Look here. Another ligature round the wrist." He pointed downward toward the foot of the cart. "And he was bound at the ankles as well. It would have been difficult for him to hang himself in that condition." Then Holmes put two fingers into the corpse's open mouth, withdrew them, and held them to the light. "Hello! What does this look like?"

I couldn't help myself. "Dried bloody saliva."

He favoured me with an evil glare. "Not that," he said, rubbing his thumb against his first two fingers and holding them out again, said, "What is this, inside the bloody saliva?"

"They appear to be brownish fibres."

"Cloth of some sort, I think. Burlap? Impossible to say precisely without a microscopic examination. However, these fibres certainly shouldn't be there if our man was a suicide." A pause. "He was gagged."

"But why on earth would he be gagged?" I asked.

"So that no one could hear his screams." Holmes indicated the Chinaman's hands, frozen upwards as if he was warding off evil. "His fingers are bloody."

"Doubtless from trying to grab the noose to loosen it."

"Difficult to do with one's hands tied," Holmes said. He removed his clasp knife from a pocket and snapped it open. He inserted the point of the blade under one of the corpse's fingernails, then laid it on top of the body, in the light. He produced a magnifying glass from another pocket and employed it to examine the tip of the blade. He held the glass out to me. "What do you see?"

I took it and examined the knife. "Congealed blood," I said. "And is that . . . *wood*?"

"Yes," Holmes replied.

Holmes cleaned his hand on the canvas cover, then took the corners in his hands and snapped it out to conceal the body once again. "I've seen all that I need to. Let us be off to Scotland Yard, and thence to Newgate Prison."

The purpose of our visit to Scotland Yard was to collect Lestrade. The Good Inspector was just as used to Holmes's peremptory summonses as I was, albeit somewhat less tolerant of them. However, he had learned through bitter experience the consequences of ignoring them.

We had to change from a hansom to a growler to accommodate the extra person for the ride to Old Bailey. On arrival, we entered Newgate Prison by the main entrance and proceeded to the governor's office, to gain his permission to view the cell where Sam Lee died and to interview the guard who attended him before his death. The governor was out, but Lestrade's presence ensured that his functionary signed off on our request.

The buildings that comprised the different wards of the prison were built in a square, enclosing a space containing several paved yards in which the various classes of prisoners could take air and exercise. A miasma of dread and foreboding clung to the place like a suffocating blanket. After leaving the governor's office, we entered a yard containing perhaps two-dozen men, all roughly dressed and dirty. They paid little attention to us as we invaded their space, seemingly consumed with thoughts of their own dire circumstances. We proceeded to a massive iron gate and were passed through by a turnkey. Then we walked past a second gate that enclosed the condemned ward, where doomed prisoners are held in a group until the day prior to execution. At that time, the unfortunate one is conducted to an individual cell to await his fate. Those cells were accessed by a set of narrow steps at the end of the yard. A door at the top opened into a passage that glowed with a reddish tint and reeked of charcoal smoke from a small stove on the floor. Cell doors opened to the left of the passage. Our escort led us halfway down the passage to the cell where Sam Lee had been confined. It was a stone chamber about eight-feet-long by six-wide. A bench sat against the far wall. An iron sconce was mounted on the wall halfway down, but the candle it held was unlit. A small window high above the bench festooned with vertical and lateral broad iron bars admitted only a pitiful amount of daylight.

"This will never do!" spat Holmes, producing a small dark lantern from beneath his cloak, which he lit with a lucifer match struck on the cell's stone wall. Producing a magnifying glass, he instructed me to play the light as he directed and proceeded to scrutinize the cell from top to bottom, paying particular attention to the window and the wall that housed it. When he was finished, he addressed the turnkey who accompanied us. "I should like to question the guards who presided over Sam Lee's final hours."

The guard left, returning in a few minutes with a middle-aged man in a high-collared, navy-blue uniform with brass buttons. "I'm Rafe," he said. "You want to talk to me about the Chinaman what done hisself in?"

"Where is your partner?" asked Holmes.

"Wot?"

"You had a partner," Holmes repeated. "You didn't hang Sam Lee by yourself. You couldn't have done."

The guard's eyes grew wide at Holmes's assertion. "I never!" he said.

"Let me tell you what you did," said Holmes. "You and your partner stripped Sam Lee and bound him hand and foot, probably with strips of cloth cut from his prison livery. You drove splinters of wood beneath his fingernails until he revealed the location of the Wengcheng Quan Yin. You untied him, leaving him to think his torture was over. When your partner

135

came up behind him and slipped a garrotte around his neck and choked the life out of him. Finally, you strung him up from the bars on the window with a rope made from his own clothes, hoping to disguise his murder as a suicide."

"No . . . no . . . no . . . ." Rafe mouthed as Holmes continued his diatribe, but his protests became progressively weaker, the more details the detective revealed. As Holmes finished, the guard's chin fell to his chest, and he began to sob bitterly, doubtless from the knowledge that he too would soon occupy a cell similar to the one that had held his helpless victim.

Lestrade asked, "Why would they have untied Sam Lee before killing him?"

Holmes's words sent a chill up my spine. "Because the murderer wanted to enjoy the young man's struggle for life, I'll be bound." He glared at Rafe. "Which tells me that this weakling wasn't the killer – it was his partner that did the deed. Now you will tell me," Holmes ordered in a stentorian tone, "who your partner was and where Sam Lee hid the Wengcheng Quan Yin."

After Rafe had given us the information we sought, Lestrade clapped on the darbies and delivered the turnkey to a constable before we continued on the hunt.

We soon found ourselves in Jamaica Terrace – one of the worst rookeries in Limehouse. Walking down a narrow flagstone alley, two- and three-storey brick buildings rearing up on either side, the fine mist that fell coated the pavement with a diaphanous sheen, which coalesced in the centre of the walkway to form a rivulet that ran toward the Thames. The air was redolent with mould, fish, and soy. We could have as easily been in Hong Kong or Shanghai as in the capital of the British Empire. Only a few residents braved the weather – women in drab ankle-length dresses and men in short jackets, pantaloons, and skull-caps. None of them seemed to pay the slightest bit of attention to the daft Englishmen in their midst.

Holmes stopped in front of a plain wooden door that bore neither plaque nor number. "This is the address that Rafe gave us," he said, though I couldn't tell how he knew. "We must go carefully – his partner in crime may still be on the premises."

The door swung open at Holmes's touch – locks were a rare commodity in this part of Limehouse. The building's interior was as black as sin, so Holmes paused to light a small dark lantern he produced from his Inverness. We proceeded up a rickety staircase, stepping on the side of the treads to avoid a ruckus. There was a door on either side at the top, and another directly in front of us. After directing the lantern's beam on each in turn, Holmes chose the door in front.

We peered into a short hallway that reeked of humanity and old fish. The light picked out a bundle of clothing on the floor at the end. With a sharp hiss, Holmes ran to it and knelt. Coming up behind him, I could see it was the body of a young Chinese woman. Holmes pressed two fingers at the base of her neck, then looked at Lestrade and me, shaking his head.

The hallway ended in a small, windowless room. Holmes arose from the corpse and we followed him in there. He swept the light around until it fixed on a second body, this one a man, dressed in workman's clothing. He took up the man's hand and held it in the light, turning it over to reveal two, small puncture marks just above the wrist. "Get out!" he hissed. "It may still be here!"

I turned to do his bidding, but hesitated when I saw he wasn't following. Instead, he was using his stick to poke about in the detritus scattered about the room. Our recent encounter with the Speckled Band, coupled with the marks on the man's arm, made it easy to realize that Holmes was seeking a snake, so I kept my place in case he found it, and subsequently required medical attention.

Fortunately, no serpent was encountered. Holmes turned to Lestrade. "You'd best call your men, Inspector, for there was murder done here this day."

"Who are these people?" Lestrade asked in an exasperated tone, not seeking information as much as expressing frustration.

"The man is obviously another Newgate turnkey, likely the partner of the wretched Rafe. I suspect that the woman is the consort of Sam Lee, whom he entrusted with the Wengcheng Quan Yin just after the robbery. The Chinaman was unable to keep her identity and location a secret under torture, which has sealed her fate. However, the statue isn't here, which means that there are players in this affair whom we haven't yet identified."

"And where does the snake fit in?" asked Lestrade.

"As an exotic and insidious method of murder," said Holmes. "There is nothing more I can do here. Watson and I will return to Baker Street and ponder our next move."

Once back in our chambers, Holmes quickly vanished into his bedroom. In half-an-hour he emerged, greatly transformed. He wore a grey waist-length jacket over a black, high-necked robe that reached to the floor, and a tight black skull cap on his head. His features had been altered to appear Oriental with an epicanthic fold to the eyes and a black braid extending from under his cap down his back.

"Don't wait up for me," he said. "I may remain in Limehouse all night."

After he had gone, I attempted to interest myself in a sea story, but wild storms and the roar of cannons couldn't drive away thoughts of the case in which we were engaged. There was obviously more to it than two dishonest prison guards trying to find a stolen statue. I couldn't say why, but I felt as if there were an ominous presence lurking in the background, pulling strings like a master puppeteer. I knew that I would get nothing from Holmes until he had a solution worked out to his own satisfaction, so he could show it off like a playwright on opening night.

A soft knock came upon the door, and our landlady, Mrs. Hudson, entered at my response, bearing a tray with my dinner. After she had gone, I removed the cover to find a large bowl of smoked haddock chowder with plenty of good oat bread and butter. The steam rising into my face brought a rumble from my stomach and tears to my eyes. Sitting down at the table, I tied a napkin round my neck and tucked in.

As I was finishing the last piece of bread, which I had used to wipe the bowl clean, a sharp pain in my abdomen told me that I had foolishly partaken of one too many slices. I thought that a postprandial brandy might be just the thing to provide some relief, when another a ring at the front door, followed by another in just a moment. Thinking that Mrs. Hudson was too busy to answer the door, I went downstairs and met the postman, who handed me a cardboard box. It was approximately a cubic foot in size, and it smelt of oranges.

I carried it upstairs and placed it on the table. It was addressed to Holmes. I could see that the shipping label was embossed with a coat of arms with which I was unfamiliar. It wasn't a rare occurrence that a grateful client would send Holmes a gift in addition to his fee, to thank the detective for a job well-done. It occurred to me that a nice, fresh orange might be even better than a brandy to drive away the fullness I was experiencing. Surely Holmes wouldn't mind if I took just one . . . .

I went to the desk for a letter opener and used it to slit the tape holding the box closed. Then I opened the flaps to find a layer of brilliant oranges. I removed a particularly large one in the middle, and stared in disbelief at the broad, triangular head of a serpent that had wicked yellow eyes with jet black pupils in the centre. My surprise was absolute. I could do nothing but stand dumbstruck as the creature levitated from the box and puffed out its hood. As it lunged forward, I somehow managed to throw my arm in front of my face, doubtless saving my life, for the cobra's fangs tore into the dangling sleeve of my dressing gown instead of my flesh.

I thrust my arm to the side and pulled the entire thing from the box, with oranges bouncing across the table and spilling onto the floor. All three feet of the snake hung from my forearm. I shrugged the dressing gown from my shoulders and let it drop to the floor in a heap with the serpent

138

inside. The garment seethed on the floor like a boiling pool of lava as the infernal creature struggled to free itself from the enveloping folds of silk.

I dashed to the desk and tore open the drawer to retrieve my Webley Bulldog, and began firing into the pile of cloth like a man possessed. Five .450 calibre bullets sent splinters flying from the floor. Then the hammer clicked once, twice, three times on empty chambers before I had the presence of mind to cease working the trigger. The dressing gown lay still as death, so I took the time to extract five more cartridges from the box in the drawer and reload before I retrieved a stick from the rack to probe the folds of cloth. I levelled the gun with my right hand as I moved the silk aside with my left until I uncovered the head of the snake. The yellow eyes spitted me with hatred as it attempted to raise itself to striking position once more, but one of my bullets must have broken its back. It could rise no more than inches from the floor before falling back. I took dead aim at the ugly head and squeezed the trigger once more, watching it disintegrate into flying shards of flesh and blood. Then I turned my face away and was sick on the carpet.

It was then that I noticed Mrs. Hudson standing in the open doorway, shrieking my name. I staggered over to her, and relief flooded the dear lady's face when she saw that I was uninjured. I was extremely grateful that she wasn't in the room below when my bullets likely tore through its ceiling. The thought occurred that I should have found a safer way to deal with my serpentine adversary, but one doesn't always choose the best alternative in such a situation.

Needless to say, Holmes was livid when he returned the next morning and discovered what had transpired in his absence.

"I should have foreseen this!" he exclaimed. "I would have never forgiven myself, should you have been injured or killed, my friend. I must insist, however, that you find another place to reside for a while, until I can bring these villains to heel. I would be happy to pay your lodging at a hotel for a few days."

"Nonsense! I am a soldier. I have been trained to face the enemy head on, not to scurry into hiding at the first hint of danger. If I'm to share the excitement of your cases, it's only fair that I share the hazards as well. Besides, you need someone to watch to the rear as well."

"Good old Watson! Very well, you have won your point. But I'm afraid that I must insist that you don't leave our rooms without me at your side until this affair is finished."

"Very well, if you will agree to do the same."

"We'll see," said Holmes.

I rang for coffee while Holmes retired to his room to remove his makeup. Mrs. Hudson brought the coffee service, then retreated back downstairs to put breakfast together. No sooner had she left than I heard the downstairs bell ring. In a flash, Holmes's bedroom door sprang open and he hurried into the room, still *en deshabille*, snatching his mouse grey dressing gown from the sofa and struggling into it. A soft knock came on our door, and I removed my Bull Dog from my pocket before inviting our visitor in. I saw that Holmes also had a revolver in his hand.

The door opened to reveal a remarkable personage. He was dressed in a black topcoat with a high collar pulled up round his ears and a slouch hat low upon his forehead, concealing his features from view. Stepping into our sitting room, he said "You will pardon me for the intrusion, gentlemen," in a sibilant tone that reminded me of a buzzing insect. If he noticed our guns trained upon him, he gave no outward sign.

I slid my revolver back into my pocket and stepped forward, reaching out for his hat and coat. He moved forward to meet me, bringing the odour of sandalwood with him. I noticed he had a peculiar way of walking – feline and graceful, yet wary somehow. He readily divested himself of his outer garments, and I'm afraid I stood gaping at him like an idiot when I beheld what lay beneath them.

He was an Oriental, to be sure, but whether Chinese, Japanese, or of some other extraction I couldn't tell. He was very tall for a member of that race, and almost impossibly slender. His face was drawn and oval, and he affected a little pointed beard and a long moustache that stayed erect as if waxed. His eyes were hooded, but when he opened them and met my gaze, I was sure it was my imagination that the irises were yellow and his pupils black diamonds, much like those of my erstwhile serpentine companion. His brow was high like a scholar's and peculiar aura seemed to emanate from him, making the hackles on the back of my neck rise. I knew that I would see those eyes in my sleep for many days after this one. His oily black hair was slicked back on his head, and covered with a little pillbox hat like the one Holmes had worn with his disguise. As he passed by me, I saw a thin, tightly braided queue that ran down to his waist.

Unbidden, he made his way to my armchair and took his seat in it, laying his arms atop the armrests like a king sitting upon his throne. His fingernails were several inches long and encased in golden sheathes, which complemented his robe of deep purple, decorated with golden icons of fantastic creatures: Dragons, lions, and elephants.

"You have the advantage of me, sir," said Holmes. "May I know the name of the man who visits me in my home?"

"My Chinese name would be unpronounceable for you. You can call me 'Doctor'."

His English was letter-perfect, with a trace of an Oxford accent. "And are you a physician?" I asked him.

"Yes, I am, as much as you are, Doctor Watson, although I think you would find my methods alien to yours. Suffice it to say, we are both concerned with the health of the body and the mind."

"Why have you come?" asked Holmes.

"Because I owe you an apology – or at least, one to Doctor Watson. I deeply regret that one of my associates took it upon himself to send you a package yesterday, which may have caused you some distress. He will not be making that mistake again." He reached into his robe and withdrew a long, thin bamboo pipe sheathed in gold with the bowl mounted on top near the smoker's mouth. He looked at Holmes with those reptilian eyes. "Do you mind?"

"Not at all," said Holmes, reaching for the Persian slipper on the mantel. "May I offer you some fine English shag?"

"No, thank you," said the Doctor. "I have my own. I shall trouble you for a vesta, however."

Holmes approached him and struck the match, applying it to the open bowl. When the Doctor was exhaling a stream of white smoke, he nodded to the detective and snapped the lid on the pipe bowl closed.

"I'm afraid it's from Doctor Watson that you must seek forgiveness," Holmes said.

"And I am afraid that I cannot excuse an attempt to murder me," I said.

"That's understandable," the Doctor replied. "Nevertheless, remember that the apology was offered." He took a deep draw on his pipe and his eyes glazed over a bit, causing me to wonder if there was something other than tobacco in that bowl. "I have another matter I wish to discuss with you, Mr. Holmes. It concerns the Wengcheng Quan Yin."

"Ah. You know of the whereabouts of the purloined statue? I would much like to recover it."

The Doctor smiled a sardonic smile. "I can see that you don't understand. It is I who have recovered it from he who had purloined it, to return it to its rightful place in the land where it was created."

Holmes returned the Doctor's smile. "Knowing the reputation of Sir Erasmus Hadley, I am sure that he acquired the artifact in an ethical manner. It was taken from him by murder. Hardly an equitable exchange."

"You assume that the one who sold it to Sir Erasmus had the right to do so in the first place," the Doctor said. "Like so many other exchanges carried out between your people and mine, this one was highly iniquitous."

Holmes's tone was sharp. "What do you mean?"

"I mean that the British have a sordid history of exploitation where China is concerned. Your country flooded mine with poison because they couldn't afford the Chinese goods that they coveted, leaving a legacy of

141

death and shattered lives. Your people also sought to appropriate our culture by absconding with many valuable artifacts to which they had no right at any price."

"I assume you are referring to the so-called Opium Wars," Holmes said, "which arose in part because the Chinese government refused to allow free and fair trade between individuals."

"Insisting on silver as payment for our goods isn't unreasonable or unethical, Mr. Holmes," the Doctor countered. "But providing someone a drug that turns him into your slave is surely unscrupulous."

"The last time I looked," said Holmes, "most of the opium purveyors in Limehouse were of Chinese extraction."

The doctor smiled his oily smile again. "We aren't going to resolve the current geopolitical situation here this evening, sir. I have come only to ask that you accept the *status quo*, and understand that the Wengcheng Quan Yin is on the way back to the land of its origin. Seek it no more, and I promise that no harm will come to you, to Doctor Watson, or to any other British citizen on my account."

"That is quite noble of you, Doctor," said Holmes, drawing his pistol from the pocket of his dressing gown once more and pointing it in the Doctor's direction. "However, since you have admitted to complicity in the theft of the statue, the murder of Sir Erasmus, and in sending that little package to Doctor Watson yesterday, I think that I shall hold you here while Watson goes to summon a constable to cart you off to jail, where you obviously belong."

"Oh please, Mr. Holmes, don't insult my intelligence. You have absolutely no evidence of any wrongdoing on my part except for our conversation just now, which makes it simply your word against mine. And while I'm sure your Scotland Yard would tend to favour your version of events, I'm equally certain that the British Government would do otherwise when faced with an international incident." The Doctor knocked the ashes from his pipe into the smoking stand beside his chair and replaced it inside his robes. Then he rose to his feet in one smooth movement. "I shall bid you good day, gentlemen. You would do well to heed that which I have told you."

With that, the Doctor took up his coat and hat from the sofa where I had laid them, totally indifferent to Holmes's pistol. The detective sighed and returned the weapon to his pocket. Once clad for the street, the Doctor turned to us once more, saying, "As delightful as this *tête-à-tête* has been, I sincerely hope that we never see each other again. I fear that it would bode ill for someone." He turned with a flourish and was out the door.

"We're just going to let him go?" I asked Holmes.

142

"He was eminently correct," Holmes replied. "Other than what was said this morning, we have no evidence linking him to any crime. And since he was considerate enough to divulge the location of the Wengcheng Quan Yin . . . ." Holmes reached for a folded newspaper lying on a side table.

"What! You know where it is?"

"It really is elementary, my dear Watson," Holmes smiled.

As I waited my turn to board the launch, I was grateful for the broad-brimmed hat pushed down tightly upon my head, which kept the cold rain from running down the back of my neck beneath my heavy woollen overcoat. In front of me in line were Holmes, Lestrade, and eight of the inspector's burliest constables, clad in *mufti*, each with a stout truncheon hanging from his belt. Last to board, I took my place in the stern by the tiller. Holmes and Lestrade occupied the bow, and each constable sat next to an oar. When all were settled, we pushed off, and once clear of the dock, a stiff east wind blew over the water, bringing the earthy aroma of the city with it. At a signal from Lestrade, the oars lifted skyward like the wings of an exotic bird, then dipped into the river as the policemen began to row. The approaching sunset illuminated our destination parked a few hundred yards away, a ship called the *Hángzhōu zhīxīng*, a black silhouette against the orange surface of the Thames. She was the only ship at the East India Docks bound for China during the next several days. The oarlocks were padded thickly with burlap, so the only sound they made was a muted splash indistinguishable from the normal maritime noises. Hopefully our quarry aboard wouldn't notice our silent approach.

The deck of the junk loomed above us as we neared, and as the men shipped the oars, I turned the tiller to bring us alongside. A constable rose with a loop of rope in his hand, twirling a grappling hook at its end, and then launched it upward to snag on the ship's railing, simultaneously slowing our forward motion and bringing us closer to the *Hángzhōu zhīxīng's* side. Other grapples followed. Then half of the men held the boat steady while the others swarmed up the ropes as if they were able seamen. Once on board, they steadied the boat so the others could follow. Holmes climbed the ratlines as easily as the best of them, but Lestrade and I had to be hauled aboard by bowlines fixed round our waists. Once aboard, I produced a revolver, as did Lestrade. Holmes was wielding his favourite weapon: A hunting crop.

Our party had boarded near the bow where the capstan squatted in the centre of the deck like a giant spider – a web of anchor chain hanging over the side. The boarders had been using it as poor cover, but additional concealment was provided by a large ship's boat tied in the middle of the deck. At a signal from the inspector, the men streamed aft on both sides, where a couple of Chinese sailors dozed near ladders ascending to the quarter-deck. Those worthies were seized and bludgeoned into silence before they knew what had befallen them. As our boys mounted the ladders, more crewmen above sounded the alarm, and the battle for the ship began in earnest.

The sailors above tried to stop the attack by the simple expedient of employing long poles to push our men off the ladders before they could gain purchase on the deck. One of the Chinamen succeeded and I saw a screaming constable plummet downward to hit the deck with a sickening thud. I hurried to him. Unless I could use my revolver, my battle wounds made me a poor fighter at best, but I was a doctor and could see to the man's injuries.

Our side gained the quarter-deck without further injuries, but more Chinese sailors erupted from below, and the battle became truncheon versus knife. This wasn't as one-sided as it might sound, because the police officers were masters with their chosen weapon and the Chinamen were used to facing untrained foes. The constables cleared the deck with dispatch and stormed down the stairways to the bowels of the ship. That's when the unthinkable occurred.

As I tended to the wounded man, I heard a keening wail rise from above, to be followed by another, and yet another. Then Holmes's strong baritone echoed above the water. "Watson, for God's sake, come now!"

I mounted the ladder as quickly as I could and arrived on the quarterdeck to a scene of carnage: Four of our men lay writhing on the deck, screaming in agony with their hands clapped to their faces. I knelt next to one and attempted to pry his digits away. I felt a burning pain running from my palm down to my wrist, then I succeeded in exposing the constable's face and wished I hadn't. I swear that his flesh was bubbling, melting away so that I could see the whiteness of bone beneath! Both of my hands were now on fire as well. I spied a bucket hanging on a wall near a doorway and I ran to it. Yes! It was apparently a fire bucket and was filled two-thirds full of water. I plunged my hands into it and the relief was instantaneous. I snatched the bucket from the wall and dashed the contents into the face of the man I was treating. I saw a second bucket on the opposite side, and so was able to minister to another wretch. I could do nothing for the other two unless I could find more water. I noticed each bucket had a long rope tied to its handle, so I grabbed one and flung it over the side, using the rope to haul it back and so deluged the face of a third man. A minute later I had treated the fourth.

"No one is to venture below from here!" Holmes shouted. "We must find another way!" Followed by Lestrade and the remaining constables, he descended the ladder to the main deck. I debated accompanying him, but even though their screams had abated somewhat, the injured men were clearly still in distress, so I elected to remain and continue saturating them with water until such time that a better remedy became available.

As I was hauling the bucket up the side of the ship, I heard a slight noise behind me and I looked over my shoulder to spy the Doctor emerging from a doorway that led belowdecks. He saw me simultaneously, and he reached into his coat to withdraw a contraption that comprised a long hose mounted on a flask with a rubber bulb on the top. He directed the hose at me, and, at a loss for anything else to do, I hauled up the bucket of water and flung it at him, bucket and all.

"*Aieee!*" His scream rent the air as a vile greenish cloud materialised between us. I suspected it was death if I allowed it to touch me, so I fell backward and began crabbing toward the ladder to the main deck. But the blessed wind from the Thames was blowing the noxious cloud away from me and onto my adversary. He stumbled back toward the rail and tumbled over the side. Before he vanished, I heard a thump upon the deck. After the breeze had cleared the poison from the ship, I noticed a canvas-wrapped package lying on the boards. Could it be? I grabbed it up and used a clasp knife from my pocket to sever the cord that secured the cloth. I unwrapped it until I saw the greenish glint of jade in the light of the gloaming. Yes! It was the Wengcheng Quan Yin!

Two days later, I was ensconced in my favourite armchair in Baker Street with a hot buttered rum at my elbow. It had been prepared by Sherlock Holmes, who had been fussing over me like a hen with one chick since our return. I had some difficulty picking up my drink in my heavily bandaged hands, so Holmes sprang up and handed it to me.

"Once again, I must say that I would never have allowed you to accompany the expedition had I known what awaited us. I foolishly expected naught but a gang of unsophisticated Chinese sailors who would be no match for a group of elite English constables."

"You couldn't have known what lurked aboard that ship. No one could have done." I sipped the rum and felt it wind its way down into my belly, leaving a trail of warmth wherever it passed. "Have you anymore news about PC Pritchard?" Unfortunately, he was the only one of the stricken policemen who had survived the attack.

Holmes's tone was bitter. "He'll live, blinded and disfigured for life. The men at the Yard took up a collection for him and came up with a hundred pounds, and I have matched that amount from my savings. And by God, I swear that as long as I live, that noble fellow will never want for anything!"

"You may count on me for assistance with that endeavour," I said, and meant it. I suspected that the good constable had many more friends at the Yard who would help his cause.

"Is there any progress in finding out what that hellish stuff was?"

"The samples I have analysed indicate that it is a phospholipase toxin, possibly from an as yet unknown species of spitting cobra. It quite possibly had been weaponized by an expert chemist to make it even more agonizing and lethal."

"Who would ever use such a thing against a fellow man?" I asked rhetorically.

"Someone who places no value on human life," said Holmes. "I vow I will make it my business to track down the Doctor someday, and bring him to justice."

I knew that would be no time soon, for the elusive Doctor had vanished like the mist in the morning sun. "And what of the Wengcheng Quan Yin?"

"Safely ensconced in the deepest vault of the British Museum," Holmes said, "where it will remain until such time as it is deemed safe to display it again."

I put voice to a thing that had been troubling me since our visit from the Doctor. "I wonder if we British are committing a crime by collecting the treasures of the world and putting them on exhibition in our own land. Shouldn't we leave them in the hands of the races who created them?"

"If humanity is to survive," answered Holmes, "it must get beyond these petty notions of class and race. Treasures like the Wengcheng Quan Yin belong to all of us as human beings, not to any one class, race, or country. They serve to exemplify man's greatest potential and make it manifest, inspiring each of us to become all that we can. The crime is to lock such things away, holding them for one's own instead of making them available to all."

I must confess that a thrill went through me at his words. "Well said, old man. Well said."

146

The Mediobogdum Sword
by David Marcum

"This is intolerable," muttered Sherlock Holmes, standing and walking toward the high window. As he stood there, I knew that he would see nothing that would lessen his impatience.

I remained seated, watching him pace. Typically, he would seek calming solace from one of his pipes, but not today.

"Holmes," I said, attempting to gain his attention, but he was still lost in his own racing thoughts. "Holmes," I repeated, my tone more sharp. "You must be patient. This waiting will not last forever."

"But an entire day!" he snarled. "Wasted – and for what? All because of one man's stubbornness and stupidity."

I gestured around us. "At least it was a chance to think."

He looked at me as if I were mad, and then away, and back toward the window, as if a better answer was there. But it was no different than when he'd stood beneath it before, high on the wall, and it revealed nothing except whether it was day or night by the changes in the light.

Prison windows aren't meant to provide a pleasing prospect.

As we waited for time to pass, I recalled how, nearly a week before, Holmes and I had been summoned to Drigg, a remote village on the western coast. It had not been an easy place to reach – an understatement when considering the nightmarish travel we had faced. I could only imagine how isolated this spot would have been in the days before the railroads could even get us anywhere close.

Holmes had once saved the kidnapped child of the local Member of Parliament, in those years before I knew him, and it was this man who asked that Holmes journey so far north to such a remote location. This politician was an honorable man – a rare breed, as I was learning during my association with Holmes's investigations – and his brother was in a difficulty that, if allowed to proceed, would result in his death and a vast embarrassment for Her Majesty's Government. I doubt that Holmes was influenced by the latter, but he could not let a man die needlessly, and I agreed.

Thus, I was with him when we set out on an early train to Birmingham, and then Manchester – the two easiest legs of our journey. After that, things became more complex, and I have but vague and unpleasant memories of local trains of ever-devolving levels of comfort, and then rocking coaches and open carriages, before finally reaching our destination. With every mile that we traveled from London, I could only ponder that at some point we would need to make the same journey back again.

The investigation, the specific details of which must remain secret until the passing of at least two men, led from Drigg to nearby Holmrook Hall, where we were assisted by the owner, who turned out to be a relative of one of Holmes's college friends – which was quite useful in giving us a base from which to plan our attack. From there, our quest culminated when we worked our way east one dark night, traveling nearly ten miles into the empty countryside. There, at the site of an ancient Roman fort, we confronted the man who had set these events in motion. He had hostages, but the bravery of a local lad, known only to us as Howe, gave Holmes the distraction he needed. The captives – including a number of children – were freed, and the responsible malefactor lost his footing, falling to a brutal death amongst the indifferent stones that had settled long ago along the barren fort walls.

We had returned to Holmrook and the Hall, where the children were reunited with frantic parents, and I knew that the inconvenience and discomfort of the journey had been worth every minute. Holmes – and dare I add myself as well – had made some fast friends in this region for the rest of our lives.

After the excitement of the night had passed and morning was upon us, I felt the call of sleep, but Holmes was still alert. I asked him: Was there something else about the case that remained unfinished?

"No," he shook his head. "Rather, it's something that one of the locals – Wilson – told me about the old fort while we were walking. A legend."

I smiled. "Holmes, I've known you now for over two years. If there is one man that I would say for certain is uninterested in legends, it is you."

His expression was weary but amused. "I would hope that you'd know better than that – no one is completely predictable. I maintain a healthy skepticism, but I don't disregard that I'm intelligent enough to realize what I don't know. It's true that most legends are exaggerated twistings of past events, too often with the played-up emphasis of some false supernatural aspect, but there is often a historical basis – some actual event – that was once true, leading to a story that perpetuates for centuries afterwards. Something solid for all the subsequent twaddle to catch and hangs onto in later years."

"And this fort – what legend do they tell about it?"

"That is was once visited by King Arthur and Merlin."

I raised an eyebrow, unaware that the legendary king had supposedly journeyed to this part of the island. I associated those tales to areas much further south. "I had no idea you had any interest in such stories," I remarked.

Holmes nodded, a new glint in his eyes. "But I do. As a boy, I read Sir Thomas Malory's records, and they fired my imagination. In those days, my family traveled quite a bit, in England and Scotland, and on the Continent as well. I was thrilled to find that my father had the same interest – which pleased me to no end, as we didn't have much else in common – and it was never too difficult to convince him to arrange our journeys by way of theorized Arthurian sites." He took a deep breath. "I propose that, after we get some rest, I do a bit of research, and then we return to the fort later today – if you're interested."

Considering how weary I currently felt, the idea held little interest. Still, I too had always had something of an interest in the legendary king, though apparently not to the surprising degree held by Holmes. Even in 1883, over two years after meeting him, I could still learn new things about him – and I had sensed that there truly had been something mysterious about the old fort that seemed to call for further investigation. I nodded my agreement, and we planned on meeting again that afternoon to make the return journey across the countryside. As I ascended to my room for some much-needed sleep, I realized that Holmes probably wouldn't rest at all, instead spending his time marshalling facts for this new investigation.

I awoke in early afternoon, much refreshed, and more intrigued by the idea of our plan than I had been earlier in the day. After finding something to eat in the Holmrook kitchen, I went to the front of the house where Holmes was waiting in a dog-cart.

I was glad that he'd arranged more convenient transportation on this return trip, as we'd had to walk part of the way to the fort the previous night in order to avoid discovery. As we wound our way through the small village and onto the narrow track leading east, Holmes informed me of what he'd discovered.

"I located Wilson, who talked more about the legends he'd referred to last night."

"I've never heard of this part of England being associated with the Arthurian legends," I said. "Cornwall seems to be where most of that business seem centered. Tintagel, for instance, where Arthur was born."

"And don't forget Dozmary Pool in Cornwall, where he supposedly received Excalibur from The Lady of the Lake. But other areas have claims as well. A replica of the Round Table hangs in the Great Hall in Winchester. And Glastonbury Tor and Abbey, in Somerset, is where Arthur died and was buried."

"That's right," I added. "And after Guinevere spent the rest of her life in prayer at the convent in Amesbury Abbey, in Wiltshire, her body was taken to Glastonbury by Lancelot and laid to rest with Arthur."

I looked at the wild landscape surrounding us as we made the slow passage toward the Hardknott Pass, where the old fort was located. Our horse pulled us at a steady pace past small land-holdings, sometimes close to the road behind high hedges, and in other cases set far back, barely visible against the high distant hills. One would only know to look for these dwellings by when a dirt track joined the road, sometimes only marked by a break in the stone walls built hundreds of years before – or longer. Holmes and I fell silent for a while, awed by the rugged countryside, and the sense of long-ago history that saturated the lands all around us. And as we traveled, things only became more lonely and remote. The wind seemed to be whispering something – a story too long in the telling for our quick passing to perceive.

Finally I broke the companionable silence.

"Arthur was supposed to have visited here?"

"So Wilson said. And I confirmed it with the local vicar as well. Curiously, it isn't something that the locals seem anxious to promote. As Wilson put it, 'We need have no truck will all those visitors and tourists such as one finds crawling the rocks of Tintagel. We will keep to our own ways.'"

"Can't say as I blame him. Still, it's a wonder that the academics haven't found it out."

"Probably just a matter of time."

"What is the connection?"

"One that I hadn't heard," replied Holmes. "Sadly, my own studies into the Arthurian legends has diminished as I've grown older, although I do have a notion to make further studies of it someday. I have a notion that proofs might be determined by a full examination of certain old English Charters. I'm sure that a deeper dive into this pool can uncover many more connections – the information just needs to be assembled and compared. For instance, there is the belief that Colchester is actually Camelot – or *Camulod* as some would call it. I've been able to visit there and ascertain – "

He was starting to wander far afield as his enthusiasm grew, and I reigned him back in to our forthcoming visit to the abandoned fort at Hardknott Pass.

He smiled. "It's a ten-mile drive, Watson, but I see your point. I could talk and talk and still not get to what I want to say. I must guard against this surprising enthusiasm I'm displaying. It could very well distract me from more important things.

"Now: About the fort at the river's bend, as Wilson called it. The local legend is that some years after Arthur's birth, attempts were made on his life. Rather like Mary and Joseph fleeing to Egypt with young baby Jesus, Merlin took Arthur away in secret here – or rather near here, to Ravenglass, near the coast on the River Esk, just south of Drigg. There are still Roman ruins there to this day – a bathhouse, for instance. Then, it was an important Roman naval center, beginning in the Second Century A.D., and lasting for several hundred years."

"Ravenglass," I said. "That doesn't sound very Roman."

"Exactly what I commented to the vicar. He said that it was sometimes called *Clannoventa* in ancient times. Apparently Ravenglass is more of a corruption of a Welsh name for the Esk, *yr afon glas*, meaning *'blue or green river'*. It was here that Merlin and young Arthur were welcomed by the local King Derek. However, due to attacks that soon followed, Merlin was no longer accepted, and it was arranged that he could instead take his young ward east – to the fort where we're headed, located near a bend in the River Esk. Mediobogdum, it was called then. It was there that Merlin and Arthur stayed for several years, and where Merlin trained the young man for his future – to be the heir to three kingdoms. His reign would unite them, unifying much of Britain in a way never seen before – if one believes the legends."

"This training – that would have been based on Merlin's magic. And what he had learned living backward through time, as some legends aver."

Holmes shook his head. "That's the popular version. Other more-knowledgeable scholars theorize that Merlin was no wizard. Rather, he was an engineer of sorts – a former Roman soldier, or perhaps the son or grandson of a soldier, who was still here in Britain after the Romans had begun their retreat to the Continent. As you'll recall, their departure left a vacuum here that was soon filled by warring tribes and kingdoms of varying degrees – some civilized, and some barely above savagery. It is believed that Merlin, with his knowledge of engineering and science that he'd obtained by way of his Roman heritage and education, *seemed* to be a magician. From what I read long ago, before my Arthurian researches waned, this version of Merlin – the historical version – was a master of battle tactics, and also scientific methods that were advanced for that time as well. This was the man who had taken Arthur, the heir to three kingdoms, under his wing to raise."

"So there is no promise of magic here," I said as we drew closer to our destination. "Unlike Glastonbury, which is on a Ley Line and supposedly has connections to the unknown forces of the earth, this is just an old fort."

"Don't say it like that, Watson!" Holmes cried, a merry light in his eyes. "Aren't you usually the one telling me that there's more to life than cold scientific fact?" He gigged the horse a bit faster. "Here we have the chance to walk in the steps of one of my heroes."

"The former king?"

"The man of science who was thought to be a wizard!"

As we drew closer, we discussed that we were likely on the path of an old Roman road stretching between Ravenglass, running up the Eskdale Valley, and then on through the Hardknott and Wrynose Passes to other Roman forts at Ambleside and Kendal.

"Wilson pointed out that the remains of Mediobogdum are located on the flanks of the Hardknott Pass, with commanding views down Eskdale."

"We aren't far from Scafell Pike," I commented, and Holmes nodded.

"It's not more than two or three miles north. This would have been one of the links for troops to police the interior against the potentially hostile native population. They were never friendly or welcoming at the best of times, and as Rome's influence waned, it only became worse."

I looked around us. Now the hills on either side of the old road had risen quite a bit higher. "It's beautiful in a rough and rugged way – I expect the locals would never be happy anywhere else – but it must have been a bleak existence for the Roman soldiers, recruited from all over the world, who were posted here, far beyond the edge of civilization."

"Oh, I don't know. They were just ten miles from a bustling seaport. I expect that they found ways to entertain themselves, as soldiers do."

He glanced my way but, as a former soldier, I refused to rise to the bait. Instead, I said, "Wilson told all of this to you? An outsider? You made it sound as if they wish to keep their secrets here about their long-ago illustrious visitors."

"I believe that he could tell from my knowledgeable questions that I could be trusted."

"'Knowledgeable questions'? Does that mean that you questioned him first, in order for the topic to be broached? I had the impression that it was the other way around – that he simply started telling you about the locality during our walk up here last night."

"Let's just say that in my researches at the British Museum a few years ago when I lived in Montague Street and had more time on my hands, I came across certain documents that made references to this place. When we came here, I was pleased that I could renew my acquaintance with the topic." He looked at me. "Ah, Watson, I can see you have more questions. I'm afraid that I can't be more specific. My researches were communicated to the proper quarters at the time, and all I can say is that there is more of interest here than I can share – aspects that might have international implications should truths be revealed. Let us just enjoy a visit to a place of interest and leave it at that."

I nodded, puzzled, but knowing Holmes well enough by this point that I knew nothing else would be forthcoming. "At least that explains why you didn't ask Wilson or the vicar to come with us," I responded. "Locals such as they might have provided some useful insight."

Holmes nodded. "That's why."

Our conversation had been punctuated by long silences while we absorbed the stark beauty around us as we traveled further from the coast. Finally, before I realized it (as the location looked much like other areas around us) we reached a wider spot in the old road where Holmes pulled the horse to a stop. We had reached our destination.

"It looks different in daylight," I said, "and when approached on a cart instead of by foot."

Holmes nodded. The wind was steady and made a never-ceasing noise through the long grasses which grew all around us, stretching in varying colors to the distant hillsides. "I am not a fanciful man, as you can attest," he said, "but there is an unusual feeling about this place."

"I know what you mean," I said. "And yet, you related to me a version of Merlin that was not magical."

"True, but a visit by one man – even someone like Merlin with the reputation of being a wizard, and even if he stayed for several years – would not have had much influence over a place such as this with the feel of more ancient powers."

I laughed with surprise. "Holmes, we must get you out of London more often. You're beginning to sound more like Alton Peake with every minute."

He joined my amusement. Peake was a friend of ours who had known Holmes since he lived in Montague Street. Whereas Holmes set himself up as a consulting detective who refused any hint of a supernatural explanations during his investigations, Peake was the opposite – a consulting spiritualist of sorts who investigated events with possibly other-worldly connections. To be fair, he was open-minded and perfectly willing to accept rational solutions, but he also kept his mind open to additional interpretations.

"No fears there, my friend," replied Holmes. "I suspect that Peake would examine this site from a far different viewpoint. I simply mentioned it because certain areas, like Glastonbury or Stonehenge, seem to generate more legends and superstitions than others – and rightly so, as a visit to them seems to make their *outrè* nature quite obvious."

153

He tied the horse to a nearby post, obviously put there for the purpose long ago, and we began to climb the narrow rocky trail toward the hill where the fort was located.

"The parson was telling me that this site is much more ancient than when the Romans were here in the Second Century. He asserts that within the fort is a fairy *rath*, where the ghost of a former king, Eveling, holds court. There is some local division as to whether he was a ruler of men or elves. He showed me a volume, *Britannia*, by William Camden and published in 1607, which mentions this mysterious king." The wind seemed to pick up, and we continued our climb. "For those living here two-thousand or more years ago, belief in such a thing seems almost understandable."

Mediobogdum
Hardknott Roman Fort
The Fort at the River Bend

For those who have never visited such a site, it might be difficult to realize what one was seeing. When picturing a fort, one would expect to see walls of stone, or perhaps logs in the American frontier. This, being far older, was much diminished, and consisted simply of various low rock walls, delineating where outer and inner walls of the structure had been located. Long grass grew here and there, but in other places it was missing where footpaths had been permanently etched by curious visitors, moving between the obvious sites of interest: A taller pile of rocks providing a view, or a low spot with futile hints of possible openings into lower levels. All around us, sheep grazed, up and down the hillsides, and within the boundaries of the stones.

"It sometimes seems that legends are thicker across the British landscape than these blades of grass," Holmes said. "I have a college friend from Sussex – his name is Musgrave – who had a family riddle that was repeated for so many hundreds of years that it lost all meaning to them. And he once told me of another set of Musgraves from Edenhall, not all that far from here, just a few miles northeast of Penrith, who have owned an ornate Venetian goblet since the middle ages – they call it *The Luck of Edenhall*. Family legend says that sometime in the fourteenth century, the butler from the Edenhall branch – and trust me, the Musgraves have employed some unique butlers – came across a group of dancing fairies. They left this object lying in the grass, and the butler seized it and refused to return it. The fairies fled, but one called back that '*Whene'er this cup shall break or fall, then farewell the luck of Edenhall.*' Since then, the family has done whatever they could to make sure that the glass does not break."

I laughed and looked back and forth, unsuccessfully attempting to identify the fairy *rath*. Another question about King Arthur came to mind, something I'd recalled about the Castle Rock of Triermain located several miles to the northeast and its connection to Sir Walter Scott's Arthurian poem *The Bridal of Triermain*. But it died on my lips as a harsh voice suddenly came from the northwest, beyond the boundaries of the stone walls, where the ground dropped away toward the distant river.

"Stop!" the unseen man cried, apparently out of breath and getting closer. "You're under arrest!"

Two men climbed into our view, one a fellow in his mid-fifties, tall and dressed in outdoor work clothes, but of a quality favored by gentlemen, and the other a burly constable of approximately thirty years. It had been the older man who had called out, and he paused for a moment to catch his breath while the constable moved around behind us, as if to prevent our escape back to the road and our waiting dog-cart.

"And you are?" asked Holmes, his expression more amused than peeved.

"August Pitt-Rivers," was the man's reply. "I am the Inspector of Ancient Monuments."

Augustus Pitt-Rivers
Inspector of Ancient Monuments

I had never heard of such a title, and was inclined to laugh – an idea that was terminated when I considered the unsmiling constable standing nearby. Holmes, however, looked at the man with a sharpened gaze.

"I've heard of you," he said. "That's a new position – it was only created at the beginning of this year."

The man frowned and nodded. "That's correct – and many people wouldn't know that. I'm not surprised, however, that artifact thieves would know of me."

That rankled me. "Now hold on, sir! We are not thieves. What gives you cause for such an accusation?"

Pitt-Rivers' eyes narrowed. "We received a tip. It warned us you'd protest your innocence. Now come along – you're under arrest."

"On what authority?" replied Holmes, having lost any of the good humor that the encounter had initially created.

"On mine," rumbled the constable. He laid a hand gently upon his belted truncheon. "We can make it easy or difficult. Either way, it's back to Drigg with you. We don't take kindly to grave-robbers here."

Holmes glanced around this way and that, and I followed his gaze to where it settled – a patch of ground near one of the fort walls that appeared to have recently been disturbed.

"I assure you – " he said, but Pitt-Rivers interrupted him.

"Not now. You may make a statement in the fullness of time, where it can be properly recorded. Until then, I'd advise against resistance. You clearly aren't from around here, and you won't be difficult to locate should you choose to run."

The idea of fleeing was ridiculous, but so was the notion that we were in custody. I looked toward Holmes and could see that he was quite angry, but keeping his temper in check. He liked to see himself as an emotionless calculating machine, but he could become as outraged or angry as any man, and in those earlier days – he was still just twenty-nine then – the inner calm that he would have in later years following his return to London after his supposed death in '91 was still a number of years in the future.

It seemed that cooperation was the better path, and so we followed Pitt-Rivers down the steep slope toward the river, where a carriage was parked out of sight underneath a grove. When we were seated under the gaze of the constable, who tersely identified his name as Wood, Pitt-Rivers steered his horse back to the old Roman road, and then east a short distance to where we'd tied our dog-cart. He climbed down and attached our horse's rope to the rear of the larger carriage before resuming his seat and setting us in motion back toward the small village by the sea.

Attempts at conversation or questions went unanswered over the ten-mile route. Upon arrival at an inconspicuous building maintained for the local law enforcement authorities – apparently just the one officer we'd just met – we were led inside under the gaze of a few curious and morose locals, through a small outer office, and then into a dimly lit hallway beside a single barred cell. We were locked inside without another word of explanation or an offer to take our statements, as had been mentioned earlier. And there we stayed for the rest of the night and into the following day, receiving several acceptable meals slid through to us by Constable Wood, but not a scrap of information, or even conversation. Our demands to speak to counsel or send a message were ignored.

Holmes was becoming more impatient. "But an entire day! Wasted – and for what? All because of one man's stubbornness and stupidity."

"At least," I countered, "it was a chance to think." And it had been that. I had slept and pondered. Being in the military, as I had been not so many years before, taught a man patience, as the occasional minutes of

157

deadly excitement were separated by days and weeks of tedium and monotony. Holmes could be patient as well – when it served a purpose. If he needed to wait all night without making a sound or motion in order to solve a mystery or capture a killer – as we had done not so long ago in a sinister bedroom connected to its neighbor by a small ventilator just large enough for a devilish beast to pass – then he was in his element. But to place him in this situation, deprived of purpose or information, was, as he had stated, intolerable.

Fortunately we would soon have answers.

We heard footsteps approaching from the front of the building. The door between the rear and front opened, flooding our cell with light. It was too soon after our breakfast for more food, so possibly this visit had another purpose.

The shadow in the doorway resolved into our captor, Augustus Pitt-Rivers, the official Inspector. Holmes had explained to me that the position was a new one, created for the protection of historic sites. "But as I recall," he added, "it was created for London – and not a two-thousand-year-old rock mound in the middle of nowhere. What is he doing here? And why have we fallen into his net?"

Now the man was in front of us. Even as we both moved to the bars to confront him, he was joined by Constable Wood, who wordlessly opened the cell door. Then he turned and departed, leaving us alone with Pitt-Rivers. His mouth was tight.

"It seems," he murmured, "that you have friends in high places, gentlemen. I'm instructed to trust you. In fact . . . ." He paused to swallow. ". . . You have been appointed special investigators. I have no authority over you. I am . . . my orders are to explain the situation, and allow you to do as you will." Clearly the admission galled him.

Holmes, however, was intrigued, his curiosity replacing the outrage at our having been held since the previous afternoon. "May we find someplace more comfortable before you discharge your duty? I'd prefer to smoke a pipe while I hear your story."

Pitt-Rivers nodded and led us out and into the front room. Constable Woods was gone, but our pipes and tobacco were there – along with our bags from the inn. Soon we had found chairs and the room was starting to fill with hazy smoke, and the tension thawed a bit as the Inspector of Ancient Monuments began to speak.

"I was appointed to my position early this year. I believe that it came about because of my interest in archeology, as well as my long experience in the military. I was in the service for a total of thirty-two years, although there were periods when I was on extended leave. I mustered out in '82, and I only saw action once – the Battle of Alma in '54. My strengths lie in

158

teaching and organization. I have a strong background in archeological research, but I must admit that I mostly received this position as 'Inspector' because it was created by my son-in-law, John Lubbock, an anthropologist and parliamentarian. Yet, despite achieving my position because of this connection, I take my duties very seriously.

"And yet, there is much more to it than I initially imagined.

"I expected that I would be spending a great deal of time involved in the protection of British historic sites and ancient artifacts, but I have occasionally been – I suppose the word is *co-opted* – by other governmental agencies when necessary, and much more often than I would have believed. Such is the case now."

He drew on his pipe and then stated, "I understand that you have learned of the Arthurian connections to the fort."

We nodded, and like Holmes, I was wondering who had told Pitt-Rivers of this fact – Wilson or the parson. As if reading our mind, the man nodded. "I heard from both the minister and Wilson. The former admitted he'd spoken to you when I questioned him. The latter is working for me – he has been since my arrival a week ago – coincidentally about the same time you showed up. It was Wilson who became curious – well, concerned is the better description – when you were asking questions about Arthur's connection to Mediobogdum, Mr. Holmes, and he observed when you sought out Vicar Weems afterwards to ask more questions. When you traveled to the fort, we followed."

He shifted in his seat. "Apparently you both have some clout in London, gentlemen. Unknown to us, someone from Holmrook saw when we detained you yesterday and brought you back to the village. Word of your arrest was carried back there, and then messages were sent to London. Your friends there then notified me of your identities and new status."

As I tried to imagine who might have intervened on our behalf, Pitt-Rivers gave a small shrug. "I was unaware of your reputation, Mr. Holmes. I had no idea who either of you are, or what you came here to do – and quite successfully I'm told, in spite of the fact that it must remain a secret. When you were asking about Arthur and Mediobogdum, I only knew that two strangers were involving themselves in my business, and it's too critical to simply allow you to roam free when taking you into custody might have forced the issue and given us answers sooner rather than later."

"We need to know both the answers," interrupted Holmes, "and the questions. You have vaguely explained your interest in us, and why we were taken into custody. We still have no explanation as to what's going on."

Pitt-Rivers looked from one of us to the other. "What have you heard of King Anguish?" he said, seemingly veering into a completely new topic.

I widened my eyes, thinking that such a name sounded like something from *The Pilgrim's Progress* – Christian, Evangelist, Obstinate, and so on. Or perhaps more along the lines of *The Canterbury Tales*, with the Knight, the Wife of Bath, and the Pardoner. Such a name – *The King of Anguish* – didn't seem so unusual in that company.

But Holmes, who kept much more in his brain attic than he would ever admit, replied, "King Anguish is Ireland's equivalent to King Arthur. He was one of Arthur's early enemies, but Arthur defeated him, and Anguish acknowledged Arthur's supremacy." He leaned forward, setting his pipe aside. "How does this relate to Mediobogdum?"

Pitt-Rivers pursed his lips, as if considering how to respond. "You will have noticed – Wilson told you – that the people here are proud of their Arthurian connections, but they also have no wish to advertise them. These beliefs run deep, but are kept secret. Nothing but generalities are ever mentioned. But there are deeper legends and stories.

"You will have heard of Excalibur?" We both nodded. "There are varying origins of this aspect of the legend. Some say that the sword that Arthur pulled from the stone to show his true kingship was Excalibur, while the more common tale is that the famed sword was actually the one later given to Arthur by the Lady of the Lake."

"At Dozmary Pool," I murmured.

Pitt-Rivers nodded. "Exactly. And when Arthur died, some chronicles state that the famed sword was thrown back into the lake, but just before it hit the water, a woman's hand suddenly shot up, catching it, and then pulling it down and away from human sight for all time."

"But other accounts claim that it was buried with the dead king," countered Holmes.

"Correct. At Glastonbury. One historical account says that it was later dug up in the 1100's and given by Richard the Lion-Hearted to the King of Sicily as a gesture of good-will – although why he would do that . . . ? Others claim that it still resides with Arthur in his tomb."

"And I perceive that there must be some lesser-known story," added Holmes, "where it was buried *here* – or rather at the old Roman fort, Mediobogdum."

Pitt-Rivers looked impressed at the statement. Holmes waved a hand. "You wouldn't have mentioned it if the story wasn't leading to that point. But I am curious about King Anguish's connection to your narrative."

"The connection is that there is a revolutionary Irish group, the Sons of Condran, who have allied under the ancient reign of mythical King Anguish and are building strength to some sort of attempt to drive the British from their island. Somehow they learned of the obscure legend that Excalibur is buried at Mediobogdum – and they've decided to get it for

160

themselves as a symbol – a talisman of power. To give their cause a mystical legitimacy."

"And so you're here – "

"I'm here because of my position, and my military background, and because of certain skills that I've acquired in my past that make me useful right now – here, at this place."

"Do you think they have the sword already?" I asked.

Pitt-Rivers nodded.

"I saw a spot at the fort," added Holmes, "alongside one of the walls, that looked as if it had been recently dug up. We were . . . *interrupted* before I had a chance to examine it. Is that where you think the sword was recovered?"

"Possibly. We know that they found some kind of sword – although it certainly wasn't Excalibur, for such a thing assuredly does not truly exist. But any sword, with the weight of importance and legend and the supernatural attached to it, becomes a powerful tool for such a group as the revolutionaries forming under King Anguish's long-lost banner. And then, when you arrived with very pointed and intelligent questions – well, there was no question, at least in my mind at that time, that we must find a way to get some answers, before things progress further and we lose track of these men."

"Wilson told you why we initially went to the fort and Hardknott Pass. Didn't that satisfy your curiosity?"

"He knew some details, but couldn't establish the whole story – and that made me suspicious. And in any case, after your business there was apparently complete and successful, you continued to involve yourself – asking questions and paying a visit. The rising threat of these Sons of Condran is quite serious – I couldn't take any chances that you weren't both involved, and that your initial reason for being here wasn't just a ruse to get you into the area for whatever their next step will be."

He set down his pipe, which had long since gone out, and then turned up his hands, almost a gesture of surrender. "Since I've been here, I've learned – by way of what Wilson could overhear – that a sword was located and dug up, just two days ago, but that's all. Nothing else has come to light." His gaze focused on Holmes. "I have assurances from London that you can be useful, Mr. Holmes, and that you've been involved in affairs of this sort before – dealing with revolutionaries. I have no choice. Time is wasting, and the sword could already be on its way to Ireland. I leave the next move in your hands."

Holmes didn't nod or give any acknowledgement of the man's statement. Instead, he settled back in his chair, one hand curled around his pipe while the other drummed silently on a nearby table, and let his gaze

161

focus on some distant scene. Pitt-Rivers looked at me, as if for some assurance that this was expected behavior. I nodded, and the inspector busied himself with repacking and lighting his pipe.

Finally Holmes spoke. "How well do you trust Wilson and the constable?"

"Just barely," was the reply. "I've found that I can rarely trust anyone. I only trust you because I've been ordered to do so." There was no malice tinging this statement. It was simply a fact.

Holmes nodded. "How much have you told either of them – about the sword and the Sons of Condran, and about Watson and me?"

"Nearly nothing. Wilson told me you were asking questions during your first trip to the fort, and that you had visited the vicar. I haven't seen him since – he comes and goes. And I simply used my authority to have the constable take you into custody, and then to have you released. He didn't need to know why."

"That may be helpful," Holmes replied. "There isn't much time, and Drigg is a small place. I'll need to work alone." He stood and nodded to our bags. "You checked us out of the inn?"

Pitt-Rivers nodded. "Last night. I searched your bags to see if you had any connection to the revolutionaries." He said it as a simple statement, with no implied apology.

Holmes looked at me. "Take our things and go to Holmrook Hall. They'll be happy to let you stay. No, wait –" He stopped himself. "As I recall, there's an inn very near there. Stay there – that will prevent any of those at the Hall from being too curious. I'll be in touch – probably this evening." Then he turned to Pitt-Rivers. "I'll be leaving town now, but I'll return later. Don't look for me. I'll get a message to you when I need your help. Watson – a word outside, please."

He picked up his bag and I did the same. Then, with a nod of dismissal toward the suddenly nonplussed Inspector of Ancient Monuments, he departed. I did the same, pulling the door shut behind me.

We walked a few hundred feet, ignored – as nearly as I could tell – by the few visitors up that early.

"I plan to leave and travel somewhere close where I can effect a disguise." He checked his watch. "There's a train heading north that leaves in a few minutes. I hope that I don't have to go as far as Egremont or even Whitehaven. In any case, I'll return as soon as possible and attempt to insinuate myself into the locals and see what I might learn."

"Holmes," I interrupted, "do you believe this fellow? He checked on us, and received marching orders from someone in London – or so he says – but we took him at his word as to his position and story."

162

"That is my first priority," replied my friend. "To check on this Pitt-Rivers fellow and see if he is who he says. I'll send a wire from the Drigg station before the train departs. If he isn't legitimate, he'll find that he's suddenly in a deeper game than he's prepared to play." Then he handed me his bag. "To the inn for you, then, and I'll be in touch as soon as I can – hopefully later today."

With that he turned and walked until the next intersection, where he turned west and then vanished from my sight.

I considered finding someone to drive me the mile or so to the inn located near Holmrook Hall, but in the end, following the night of incarceration, I decided to walk. While the day was darkening a bit with building clouds, I knew that any rain was unlikely for the next hour or so. Holmes and I always traveled light, so our bags were no great burden, and I had the two of them held symmetrically. And after being in the small cell since the previous day, a walk suited me quite well. Adjusting my grip on our bags, I set off to the east.

Drigg and Holmrook

It was a narrow track that wound between houses on either side while still in the village, but in five or ten minutes I had left most of those behind, and the landscape widened out around me, with the occasional small house set back from the road, and the grassy spaces in between dotted with preoccupied sheep, intent on feeding and indifferent to me. In the distance I could see the rising mountains, although I was sure that none were the famed Scafell Pike. As the road took gentle turns, I was uncertain as to which exact direction the ancient fort was located, although it was generally in the same direction in which I was heading. I tried to imagine

163

this area during the years when the Romans were here, those centuries before and after Christ when their influence was so profound. They established cities and towns throughout the island which were still in existence today, along with the roads connecting them. They had brought incredibly influential civilizing influences and knowledge that had remained to varying degrees even after they left Britain.

From the time that Julius Caesar set foot on our shores in 55 B.C. until Constantine III thoroughly withdrew the Roman Army in approximately 410 A.D. to defend the Continental Empire from encroaching Barbarians, the influence of the Romans on Britain was almost incalculable – and yet it was simply part of the land in which we lived. I once had an American friend visit London, and we discussed his country where, except for a few native structures of unknown age in the southwestern deserts, there were virtually no buildings more than a few hundred years old. This conversation had occurred after we had passed the massive Roman wall fragments near The Tower, simply standing there by the modern thoroughfare for current citizens to touch or ignore as they chose every day. The wall had been part of the original square-mile Londinium, and various pieces were easily found. It was quite routine to read that excavations for new roads, buildings, or extensions of the Underground frequently uncovered new Roman sites on a regular basis. Having such reminders of our ancient past so easily accessible had certainly helped shape our national character.

As I reached Holmrook, the road I walked tee'd into a thoroughfare alongside the River Irt, with a sign pointing to the right, south to Ravenglass. I turned left upon the track which I knew led to the Hall. However, after only a few hundred feet, I reached a snug little inn on my left, a couple of hundred feet before the drive that led to Holmrook Hall. I presented myself and requested two rooms and a sitting room, if available, explaining that my friend would be joining me later that day. I registered under my own name, but didn't provide Holmes's. Then, after I was shown upstairs and left the bags, I went back down and asked for some breakfast.

I was pleased to learn that the Holmrook Reading Room was located at the inn and, after my meal, I made an investigation of the small library's contents. I discovered several pamphlets and books related to local Roman history, including some further information specifically about the ancient fort.

I read that Mediobogdum, sometimes locally called "Hardknott Castle", was constructed from nearby stone, along with red sandstone and other materials such as non-native timber, that the soldiers would have transported up from the coast. It was laid out according to typical Roman-fort design, and one could still see evidence of granaries, administrative

164

offices, the temple, and residences. It was roughly square with a gate in each wall. Although long since vanished, a tower would have stood at each corner, and many of the soldiers had probably lived in tents pitched outside the walls. There was no evidence that a civilian settlement had grown up nearby, as Mediobogdum was probably close enough to Drigg and Ravenglass that none was required.

The fort, as well as many like it, had been necessary because many native Britons hadn't submitted easily to the invaders during that violent time. Mediobogdum had held five-hundred or so men, and its commanding location above the valley of the River Esk had guarded an important trade route stretching over one-hundred-and-fifty miles. It had been abandoned by the early 140's A.D., although no one knew exactly why. I went through all the relevant documents and books in the library's collection, but I could find no mention of any Arthurian connections.

Afterwards, with who-knew-how-many hours left until Holmes returned, I pulled down Dickens' *The Pickwick Papers* and found a comfortable chair. Although I had read it countless times, another visit with that peculiar club was just as pleasant as always. By late morning, I ordered a whisky, and then it was time for lunch. Afterwards, seeing that the rains had arrived, I climbed upstairs to my room for a nap. I slept for several hours, finding restoration after the mostly sleepless night in the Drigg cell. I was deciding whether to continue reading in the upstairs sitting room or move back downstairs to the chair I had occupied all morning when there was a knock, and the door to the hall opened.

I found myself facing a roughly dressed man, somewhat over six feet, although he slouched terribly. He was carrying a ragged carpet bag in his left hand. His hair was ragged and gray, and the gaunt thinness of his face was emphasized by prominent cheekbones. He had a ragged tuft of a goatee on his chin, and his shifty expression glanced up and away frequently from the tattered cap still on his head.

"Come sit by the fire," I said to Sherlock Holmes. "I see you were caught out in the rain without a proper coat."

"You sound like Mrs. Hudson," he said, straightening to his full height and removing the cap. "It's been a productive day," he added.

By the light of the small fire which I built up as he found his chair, I could see how he had darkened his cheeks to shadow them. He spit out a couple of wads of cloth, probably torn from a linen handkerchief, which he'd held in his mouth to emphasize the prominent cheek bones. Although his rough clothing had helped to establish his character, what mostly made him so convincing was simply that he seemed to *become* a different person. It was a gift and a skill that he regularly put to successful use.

"I went to Egremont," he explained, "where I found a wire waiting for me from London. Pitt-Rivers' *bona fides* are confirmed – as well as our brief to assist in the recovery of the sword, and to strike a blow against these Sons of Condran. I arranged with the Egremont police inspector to obtain his assistance. He has reserved several of his men, and they're waiting just north of Drigg for our rendezvous at dusk. He also helped me to assemble this quick disguise.

"Returning to Drigg, it wasn't difficult to learn who was new to town, and who had been associating with them. I managed to confer again with Pitt-Rivers, and he didn't have that information, although his man Wilson could have obtained it easily enough. That led us to suspect that Wilson is playing both sides. I had to be careful, since even in disguise, I was someone who hadn't been seen before, and if I ran into Wilson, he might suspect my true identity.

"By asking around as if I were expecting to meet up with a friend, I found where an Irishman, Billy O'Toomey, has been staying at The Queen Hotel, and meeting with a number of shady locals each night in the pub. Apparently Billy has been recruiting for something, although I couldn't find out exactly what. However, the owner, sensing a chance to gossip, told me that Billy meets with these men in the back of a room located off his main bar, and that at some point during these conversations, he shows them something wrapped in a cloth or blanket, approximately three feet in length."

"So the sword is still here," I noted.

Holmes nodded. "That's the most likely explanation. He generally holds court around eight o'clock – which is when Inspector Hodgson will carry out his raid – with our help."

The rest of the evening passed quickly. Holmes, back in his own clothing which he'd pulled from the carpet bag, joined me as we went downstairs for an early meal. Then, in spite of the rain, we set off on foot back to Drigg, deciding that slipping into town during the twilight drizzle and reaching our destination unseen was better than arriving openly in a cart.

As we walked, I related what I'd read about the old fort, while Holmes told me some of the other Arthurian legends in this part of the country, including the legendary king's last Battle of Mons Badonicus in Bathampton. "I was involved in an archeological investigation there," he added. "Before your time – and definitely a tale for which the world is not yet prepared." As we walked through the darkening drizzle, he shared it with me, and I had to agree. Hearing the details while passing along that same road which had carried Roman soldiers back-and-forth from Drigg

166

to Mediobogdum centuries earlier was enough to raise the hair on my neck. I almost expected to see us surrounded by Roman ghosts.

We paused at a church on our right before we entered the village proper. There, in the darkness, I was introduced to the inspector and his men. "They're gathering in the inn," explained Hodgson. "This is our lucky night – it seems that O'Toomey's recruiting by ones and twos has culminated with a big meeting. We should be able to snare him and find out who all the locals are as well."

"I doubt of the locals are worth anything," said Holmes. "They are little fish, fresh into the nets. But O'Toomey will be an important link back to the larger organization. He can give us names and information. But most important, we can get the sword before it has a chance to become a relic for them to rally around."

Hodgson informed us that he already had several other men in place around the inn. We only had to join them and then the raid could commence.

I've accompanied Holmes on many such skirmishes. Some went well, but some ended dreadfully horrible. The capture of Tré Bonfardin and his Soldiers of Cromwell was successful beyond measure. Conversely, the raid upon Conner Strickland's abominable breeding dens beside the Thames went terribly, tragically wrong, and the loss from that fire always tainted the value of preventing Strickland's vile scheme. In each case, for good or bad, the event was dramatic. In contrast, the taking of Billy O'Toomey and the recovery of the sword was almost anticlimactic.

The police entered the pub while covering all the entrances to prevent escapes. They flooded into the back room, taking Billy into custody while getting the names of all the men in attendance. It was no surprise to find Pitt-Rivers' local man, Wilson, there as part of the group, and it turned out that he was a semi-important figure within the revolutionary group's counsels. Later, when the Inspector of Ancient Monuments found out the truth, he rightly understood that hiring one of the enemy as his contact person was a professional *faux pas* that would stain his reputation.

O'Toomey was taken into custody and spirited away, back to the police station in Egremont. He would be in our custody, along with our companion for the journey, Pitt-Rivers, during the return to London the following day, where we three delivered him to Scotland Yard. Although I never knew the details, I understand that the information he provided to reduce his own punishment was instrumental in disbanding and incarcerating the Sons of Condran.

We left Pitt-Rivers with the prisoner at the Yard, and then we made the short journey by cab to another building near the British Museum, a non-descript house on the south side of Keppel Street, just off Russell

Square. The door was opened by a wizened little woman who seemed to recognize Holmes, her toothless mouth smiling happily and her head bobbing as she reached and pulled him inside. "She's deaf," said Holmes, turning his head toward me so she couldn't see his face.

She pulled me in as well, and then shut the door. After taking and hanging our coats and hats, she led us down a hall to the back of the house, and into a wide room that appeared to stretch the width of the building. There, behind a cluttered desk, was an ancient man who seemed more corpse than living flesh. But his face lit up as had the woman's, and he forced himself to his feet.

"Do you have it?" was his only greeting.

Holmes, who had carried the blanket-wrapped sword from Cumbria to London, laid the object on the desk before the man. He seemed to stop breathing, and I wondered if he had died while standing upright, somehow locked in place instead of falling. Then, defying expectation, he lurched himself into motion and pulled back the wrapped cloth, revealing the sword.

I hadn't seen it since we took it from O'Toomey the night before, and while it had been impressive in the dim light of the pub's back room, it was immaculate here in the sunshine from the wide south-facing windows. The rains of the previous day had vanished.

It was something over three feet in length, heavy, and extremely shiny. It had no nicks or scratches. It was all of a solid piece – point and blade and fullard on one side of the guard, and grip and pommel on the other. No doubt, two-thousand years earlier, the grip had been wrapped in leather windings to enable the wielder to better hold it, but that had long-since rotted away. Now, without any extraneous trappings, it was simply pure metal, nearly glowing with its own peculiar light.

Holmes looked me. "This is Aldbury Aston Lonsdale – the greatest Arthurian expert in the Kingdom. Probably the world."

The old man waved a hand at this statement and then lowered it to the blade. He hovered his hand back and forth along the length of it, then gently pressed a thumb against the edge. "Razor sharp," he murmured. "Still, after all this time."

He removed his hand and then looked up, speaking to one of us, and then the other. "Very few know of the legends that tell of Arthur and Merlin's stay at Mediobogdum. The Romans had already left by then. Merlin arrived in Drigg with the young and future king after attempts had been made on the boy's life. He was given permission to move to the fort, ten miles east. Merlin was no magician – he was an engineer, with Roman knowledge and skills. He set about fortifying the abandoned site, and also training Arthur for his future duties. All sorts of knowledge – mathematics, engineering, geography, and – of course – warfare. And it was there that he gave him the sword. *This sword – Excalibur.*"

My breath caught. This was surely foolishness. Such a weapon was only legend. And yet, this man, according to Holmes, was the world's greatest Arthurian expert. But perhaps a lifetime of such expertise had clouded his old mind – he wanted to believe, so when an unusual sword was brought to him, he *did* believe. He saw what he wanted to see.

He seemed to read my mind. "You don't believe me," he said, holding my gaze. "Look at it. Any confirmation will prove it – this is a metal alloy that is unknown, as the oldest and least-known stories tell us. It came from a place beyond human knowledge."

"The Lady of the Lake," I whispered, and the old man frowned.

"Nonsense! Foolishness!" He worked his mouth, and then continued. "There was no lake, and no magical woman living in the bottom of it. The sword was fashioned from metal that fell from the sky – a meteorite! Several meteorites, actually. A Roman named Publius Varrus found them and learned how to smelt them. Initially, not knowing what else to do with them, he cast them in the shape of a small statue – which he called *The Lady of the Lake.*"

"How do you know this?" I asked. "You say it as if it's fact – but nothing definite is known of any of this – only varying and contradictive legends. Many parts of England all claim to have some Arthurian association."

"There are documents – all preserved and handed down. In my youth I traced them – read and copied them, and when I could, delivered them into the safekeeping of the Museum. They're still there . . . for those allowed to look."

"But why are they not revealed? If they are fact, they could change history."

"That's exactly why!" countered the old man. "There are secrets within these papers that, even today, could change *history*! Disunity and jealousy and resentment could grow and lead to civil war!"

"But surely after all this time – " I began, but Londsale raised a frail blue-veined hand. "Enough, Doctor. Greater minds than ours have made these decisions, and very long ago. I made the same arguments for public release of the papers when I was your age, but to no avail. I've since realized the wisdom of these strictures. You have just seen how the power of these ancient events and objects can be used. Objects with stories have power. The Sons of Condran are not the only group of that sort."

"You say it was made from meteorites by a Roman," interrupted Holmes. "How came it to Merlin's possession?"

169

"He was Varrus' descendant. Caius Merlyn Britannicus, to be more specific – with *Merlyn* spelled with a *Y*. His cousin was the ill-fated Uther Pendragon, father of Arthur. Merlyn took over the care and training of the young boy – and also provided him with the sword, which had since been refashioned from *The Lady of the Lake.*"

"And now that it's been found," said Holmes, "it must be hidden."

"For now, young Mr. Holmes. For now. But – " And he looked with great intensity at each of us. " – they say that Arthur will come again. When he's most needed. And he'll need that sword. I trust that when the time comes, he'll receive it."

I expected Holmes to answer that with a trace of a sneer in his voice, but he was only serious. "We must trust those who will now be the sword's new guardians. One can only hope . . . ."

The old man nodded and laid both hands on the blade. "If only I could hold it, but I am too weak. Show it to me, Mr. Holmes. Before you wrap it up and take it away forever, show it to me."

Holmes nodded and reached for the plain-metal grip. Getting his fingers underneath, he wrapped both hands around the grip and slowly lifted it upright before his face. It glinted and shined in the light – and yet, it seemed to have a light of its own, from somewhere deep within. It was then that old man spoke – so softly that I doubt that Holmes, just across the desk, could hear. I could not look away.

"You see it, Doctor?" he whispered. "Of course you do! It *is* Excalibur – there is no doubt! Ah, that I have finally touched it! And you see, don't you? See it? It's held by a worthy man!"

I could only nod. I don't know if Lonsdale noticed me do so, for surely he was looking at the sword as well. I don't know how long we watched – no more than seconds. Then the spell was broken when Holmes lowered it back to the desk and re-wrapped it in the cloth.

There was nothing left to say. We thanked the old man for his time and left the way we'd come. Outside, I considered asking to see the sword one more time, but I realized that it would be foolish to reveal it on a city street. In any case, Holmes spoke first.

"Do you go back to Baker Street with our bags," he said. "I have a delivery to make, and then I'll join you shortly. Perhaps in a few hours, we might visit Simpsons? I feel like celebrating."

I nodded without speaking, my throat dry. I was strangely affected by what I'd seen. The sword hadn't looked so special the previous night, in the light of the pub, or subsequently in the upstairs sitting room of our inn, but today . . . .

In any case, Holmes didn't seem to be as impressed. But then, he wouldn't be. It took a great deal to impress him, and he would never admit

170

to something that smacked of anything beyond human comprehension – certainly not an ancient sword that seemed to luminesce with its own inner light and power.

I watched as he set off along Keppel Street, and then turned at Russell Square toward Montague Street. I stood there for quite a while longer, imagining him as he carried the artifact past his old rooms before turning into the Museum, or perhaps continuing on to some anonymous building in Whitehall. Possibly someday I'd know more of the sword's story.

I finally shook myself into motion and headed the other way, toward the solid familiarity of Baker Street.

NOTES

The Inspector of Ancient Monuments

Lieutenant General Augustus Henry Lane Fox Pitt-Rivers (1827–1900) was an English officer in the British Army, ethnologist, and archaeologist. For most of his life, he was known as "Lane Fox", but he took the name "Pitt-Rivers" in 1880 upon inheriting a cousin's large estate. In 1882, he became the first British Inspector of Ancient Monuments, (a position created by his son-in-law, parliamentarian John Lubbock.) He was a strong advocate for archaeological methodology, although his position didn't give him a great deal of authority to protect historical sits on private land. His lifelong collection of historical objects led to the founding of The Pitt-Rivers Museum at the University of Oxford, and his collection from the area around Stonehenge forms the basis of The Salisbury Museum in Wiltshire.

Mediobogdum

For more information about Mediobogdum and the time that Merlin (or *Merlyn*) and Arthur stayed there, see the late Jack Whyte's *The Sorcerer Part I: The Fort at the River Bend*. Additional information about Merlin, Arthur, and the otherworldly origins of Excalibur can be found in his highly recommended *Camulod Chronicles* (also known as *A Dream of Eagles*):

- *The Burning Stone* (2018 – *Prequel*)
- *The Skystone* (1992 – Published in Great Britain as *War of the Celts*)
- *The Singing Sword* (1994 – Published in Great Britain as *The Round Table*)
- *The Eagles' Brood* (1994 – Published in Great Britain as *Merlyn*)
- *Uther* (2000 – Published in Great Britain as *Pendragon*)
- *The Saxon Shore* (1995 – Published in Great Britain as *Excalibur*)
- *The Sorcerer Part 1: The Fort at River's Bend* (1997 – Published in Great Britain as *The Boy King*)
- *The Sorcerer Part 2: Metamorphosis* (1997 – Published in Great Britain as *The Sorcerer*)
- *The Lance Thrower* (or *Clothar the Frank.* 2003 – Published in Great Britain as *Lancelot*)
- *The Eagle* (2004 – Published in Great Britain as *The Last Stand*)

The Adventure of
The Sisters McClelland
by James Gelter

In the years since I first came to share rooms with Sherlock Holmes, I have seen the consulting detective overcome many bizarre and momentous obstacles, brought about by both nature and man. There have been times, however, rare though they may be, when Holmes has faced a particular series of events in which he found himself to be the most troublesome obstacle.

Though he approached his regrettable habit of injecting cocaine judiciously and with discipline, it cannot be said that he entirely avoided any negative effects on his professional work. It is true he cast his syringe aside whenever he had a case in hand, but it is hard to think of this as a sacrifice on his part, for as stimulating as he found the drug to be, he found the work to be more stimulating still. Yet on those days in which there was no work to be had, which were once numerous, Holmes made free use of the drug. The fault, as I saw it, in Holmes's approach was that he could not know with certainty when a new client might appear and find him in such a compromised state. He had avoided such an eventuality for some time through sheer chance. But fate caught up with my friend at the outset of the case of The Sisters McClelland.

The summer of '83 was a monotonous one both for me and Holmes. Following Holmes's investigation into the strange occurrences surrounding the Roylotts of Stoke Moran, a case I have already laid before the public in "The Adventure of the Speckled Band", no more significant clients came to Baker Street for some time. Holmes loathed this professional stagnation and lamented it daily and, at times, hourly. He began to take cocaine with increasing regularity, despite my protestations, and spent his days either lying upon the sofa in the thrall of the drug, playing wild improvisations on his violin, or else pacing about the sitting room smoking his pipe for hours on end.

Between the suppressing July heat and Holmes's insufferable behavior, I often found it desirous to escape the confines of Baker Street, and so began the habit of taking long afternoon walks. My health had much improved over the course of the previous two years, and I found pleasure in taking regular exercise once more.

After one pleasant afternoon in Hyde Park, I was on my way home and had just turned off Oxford Street onto Orchard Street when a young lady knocked into me from behind. The woman cried, "Pardon me, sir!" with a rolling tongue and continued up the road at such a pace that she was soon out of my sight. I wasn't distressed by her actions, which had merely caused me to stumble for a moment but in no way had harmed me, and the incident soon left my mind. A few minutes later, however, as I approached my rooms in Baker Street, I saw the woman again. She was walking anxiously up and down the road, stopping to look at each door. I approached the lady.

"Pardon me, Madam – " I began.

"Oh!" she cried before I could continue, "It's you! My apologies, sir, if I caused you any harm before. I'm right scundered!"

She was a humble beauty in her thirties with warm brown hair, dark freckles across her pale face, and large green eyes. She wore a simple dress of brown plaid, the lace edging beginning to fray and yellow with age. She spoke in a high, musical brogue.

"You caused no harm at all, my good lady," I replied, "I noted, however, both then and now that you seem to be in some sort of distress, and was curious if there was anything I could do to assist you."

"That is most kind of you, but I fear you cannot unless you know the address of Mr. Sherlock Holmes."

I couldn't help letting out a laugh.

"Indeed, Madam, I do! My name is Dr. John Watson, and I am Mr. Holmes's close associate. I know his rooms well, for they are also my own."

A minute later, we were climbing the stairs up to Holmes's and my rooms. Before we reached the top, the sitting room door flew open, and Holmes's voice rang out. "Really, Watson, this is a most inconvenient time for you to bring a visitor unannounced, pretty though she may be. I'm in no mood to witness your attempts at wooing."

"Holmes!" I cried, offended and embarrassed. "This good woman happens to be here for you. She is a client."

Holmes appeared at the top of the stairway, and I glanced a look of embarrassment on his own face for a brief moment.

"Ah, that is a different matter entirely!" he said, with a reluctant cheer, "Why have you stopped on the stair? Bring her up!"

He vanished from the doorway. By the time the lady and I entered the sitting room, Holmes had positioned himself before the window. His morocco case, where he kept his hypodermic syringe, had been on the mantelpiece when I left, but now was nowhere to be seen.

"Welcome, dear lady," he said. "Please, have a seat in the basket chair."

"Thank you, Mr. Holmes," the lady replied as she sat, "I hope I'm not intruding, sir."

"Oh, no, not at all, I assure you."

"I didn't know who else to turn to. I'm a member of a quilting club, and one of our members, Mrs. Gale Sanderson, has spoken of you and praised your abilities on a number of occasions."

"Sanderson, Sanderson," Holmes muttered to himself. "Ah yes! I recall the case. Her son had been wrongly arrested for theft. I'm not sure what praises she could possibly sing based on that affair – it was an absurdly obvious case. Any impression that I did anything noteworthy has more to do with the obliviousness of the observer than the cleverness of my actions."

The lady was unsure of how to respond for a moment.

"I hope," she said, hesitantly, "that my own troubles aren't due entirely to my own obliviousness."

"I am sure they are not," said Holmes, who seemed to have realized his manner up until now had been less than cordial. "Watson, would you be so kind as to pass me a cigarette," he said, sitting down on the sofa. He lit it and took a long, steady pull.

"Now, my dear lady," he said, exhaling, "I know you are from Belfast but have been in London for a number of years, but I don't yet know your name."

The lady was taken aback.

"It's Mary Thomas," she said. "But how did you know I was from Belfast?"

"The accent is unmistakable."

"And that I have been in London for many years?"

"Your shoes are English made, as are your dress and hat, but they aren't new. The shoes are at least five years old, the dress at least three. What else would explain why an Irish lady would be wearing old English clothes except that she has been in England for some years?"

"They could be someone else's clothes."

Holmes smiled.

"Very good, Mrs. Thomas, but that isn't possible. All the garments fit you to perfection, and the uneven wearing of the inner soles of the shoes correspond exactly with your tendency to turn your heels out slightly when you walk, which I noticed as you entered."

"My, Mr. Holmes, you are a sharp one, just as Mrs. Sanderson testified. Surely you are just the man to advise me."

"And what, exactly, do you need advice about?"

"It is a long story, Mr. Holmes, that goes back many years, one full of vague suspicions and strange occurrences."

Holmes smiled, not his usual brief smirk, but a great, toothy grin.

"My good Mrs. Thomas, there is nothing I desire more than to hear it," he said, then laid back on the sofa and looked to the ceiling. He took another long pull off his cigarette. "Start from the beginning, and leave no detail unspoken."

"I'm from Belfast, as you well guessed. McClelland was my name, Mary McClelland. I was orphaned at fifteen, my parents having contracted cholera, and was taken in by Mother Brocca's, a boarding house for young ladies of working age. Through the boarding house, I was given a cleaning job at a clothing factory near the docks. Only weeks into this new, lonely life that had come so suddenly upon me, another orphaned girl, Cara McClelland was her name, came to live at the boarding house and began work alongside me at the factory. We doubted that we were related to any meaningful degree – there are McClellands a-plenty in the city – but we thought it would be a good laugh to call ourselves The Sisters McClelland and, over time, true sisters we became, working and living alongside one another. Eventually, we were trained and promoted to seamstresses.

"To celebrate three years of us being sisters, Cara and I went out one evening after work to White's Tavern. This was strictly against the rules of our boarding house, mind you, but we weren't the first to break them and I'm sure were not the last. That night we met John Thomas, a young English engineer who had just arrived in Belfast to take up a position designing steam engines for Hartland and Bear, the great shipbuilders. He knew no one in the city and so we invited him to share our table. The evening was great fun and I found myself so taken with John that I came back to the Tavern for the next three evenings, hoping he would return. He did on the third evening and I talked with him so late into the night I got into quite a spot of trouble at Mother Brocca's. John began calling on me and taking me on long walks. We married a few months later. An orphaned Catholic girl such as me had no reason to believe that she would ever be so lucky as to marry a charming, college-educated Londoner who could afford to buy her a house on Antrim Road, yet it had happened and I couldn't have been happier.

"John's work took the lion's share of his time, and I knew very few people outside of the factory, so we didn't have a large social circle. But on many an evening, we were joined at home by Cara, who was still living at the boarding house, and Neil Bailey, who worked in the engineer's office with John and who had become his good friend. John taught us all how to play whist, and we would play together late into the night. Neil was a marvelously entertaining fellow. John used to say that Neil loved

176

conversation so much that he would have one with himself to prevent a moment's silence. On and on that boy would talk, on everything from Byron and Shelley to theoretical advancements in steam engine design. Drove Cara near to madness, he did. One moment he would have her howling with laughter, just like the rest of us, but the next, they would be red in the face cursing one another. He could be a bit too much to take from time to time, it is true, but then so could she. He was a good man, though, there is no denying that.

"Before the first year of our marriage was over, a great change came over John. He had always worked long hours, but soon he would work at the office late into the night. He never wanted to talk about what work he was doing, saying that I wouldn't understand it. He began acting strange and distant. I blamed myself. Try as we might, I had yet to become with child, and I supposed he resented me for that.

"One evening, Neil came to the house looking for John. I told him that John was still at the office. He suddenly became very nervous and tried to depart, but I stopped and begged him to tell me what it was that John was doing at work that was keeping him so late and causing him to be so secretive. He said that we shouldn't talk about it and that for my own sake, I should not dwell on it. Neil began to come to the house less frequently after that and was much quieter when he did.

"A few weeks later, John didn't come home until well after two in the morning. I had gone to bed, but his entering the house aroused me. I came downstairs to find him sitting at the dining table, drinking whisky from the bottle. He looked almost mad, with disheveled hair and clothes. I could swear he had been weeping. When I asked him what was the matter, he simply stared at me with bloodshot eyes and then went upstairs to bed without a word.

"I couldn't comprehend what had caused this change in my husband, but the next morning, the newspaper offered a horrifying clue. The offices of Hartland and Bear had been robbed the night before."

Holmes had by now finished his cigarette and had closed his eyes. He drew a long, satisfied breath.

"The accounting offices," Mrs. Thomas continued, "which were in the building beside the one where John and Neil worked, had a large safe in which the company kept a sizable cash reserve. The safe had been cracked open and the money taken. Worst of all," she shuddered, "a guard had been killed.

"When John came down for breakfast and read the paper, he became extremely agitated and began to pace all about the house. After an hour, he grabbed me roughly and made me swear that if anyone asked me about the night before, I was to swear that he had been home all evening. I swore

177

I would do as he asked. I didn't have the heart to ask him why he wanted me to lie, or what he truly had been doing the night before. Every day I expected a police inspector to arrive at our door with questions, but no one ever came. John began to come home early every evening, but he would barely speak and never made eye contact with me.

"The Friday after the robbery, I received two pieces of shocking news that would forever change my life. First, in the morning, Cara came to visit and informed me that she and Neil Bailey had married the day before. I could hardly believe it. She told me that they had been secretly engaged for some time. When I asked her why she would keep such a thing secret from me, her sister, she replied, 'It was the secrecy that made the relationship so enjoyable.' But she and Neil came to recognize that they couldn't keep it a secret forever, and so they wed.

"That evening, John came home and told me he had accepted a new position at Martin Ash and Company in London. He was to leave the very next day and I was to pack up the house and follow him in five days' time. I was devastated. I asked him why - *why* would he rip me away from my home and the people I care about so suddenly, but he gave no reason other than the job would provide better compensation and chances for advancement.

"He left the next morning without a word, leaving a written list of instructions, such as what boat I was to take, which possessions I was to bring, and which to leave behind. He wrote that Neil would assume the mortgage on the house and live there with Cara. Never had I felt so lost than I did that morning, Mr. Holmes, and I never have again. I was to leave my sister behind, and she would live in my beautiful home. I was to travel alone to a great city I had never been to and live there with a husband I knew had been part of a terrible robbery, and perhaps . . . ."

The lady's eye went wide as she struggled to continue.

"I – I am sorry," she stammered. "I have had this thought for so long but have never said it aloud. Not only had he been part of a robbery, but perhaps had killed a man in cold blood."

Mary Thomas placed her head in her hands and wept. I offered her my handkerchief which she quietly accepted. Holmes remained unmoving, as though he were completely unaware that a woman was openly weeping directly beside him. Once the lady had composed herself, she continued.

"Neil and Cara visited that afternoon. I was in a pitiable state. They stayed with me for the next five days, and it was well they did. My heart wouldn't recover from that first morning and I began to grow weak and feverish. Neil helped me pack up the house while Cara cooked and cleaned. I could hear her sobs coming from the kitchen. Cara began to become ill, too, for I saw her retch once, and suspected she had at other times. But she had always tried never to burden me, and so did her best to hide her illness and be strong for my sake.

"My health got steadily worse over those five days, and Cara argued that I should stay a few days more to rest and recover. I feared that if I did so, John would be unhappy. He left no means of contacting him and so I wouldn't have been able to inform him of any change in our plans. Should I remain, he would come to meet my ship and be furious when I didn't appear. And so, though it was a foolish choice, I boarded the ship and left for London. When John did come to meet the ship, it was the Captain, not me, who greeted him on the dock. I had become so ill on the voyage that it was feared I would lose my life. I was burning with fever and my stomach was in agony. John, faced with the possibility of losing me, softened once more and was as kind and gentle a nurse to me as any patient could wish. After a week's time, I recovered.

"It didn't take long before our marriage soured once more. Secrets are like unseen gates that stand between us and the ones we love. We can reach through them and touch, yet are still separated. He had promised he would be making a higher salary in London, but the opposite turned out to be true. Martin Ash and Company was a much smaller operation that wasn't as innovative as Hartland and Bear. John's talents are wasted there. London is a damp, colourless city. Our house was nowhere near as lovely as our home was in Belfast. Within days, I already longed to be back in Ireland with Cara. I wrote her many letters, but she wrote very few in return. She and Neil had a baby about a year later, little Eoin. After that, I didn't hear from her at all. After a time, I stopped writing as well.

"It would be five years before I would see Cara again. She and little Eoin arrived unannounced on our doorstep, just two weeks ago. Neil was dead, she told us, taken by Scarlet Fever. He had become a gambler and a drunk and had left her in debt. She had to sell the house and, with nowhere else to go, had come to us. John tried to refuse them. I couldn't believe that the man I married had become so coldhearted he wouldn't extend hospitality to one of our dearest friends and her child in their hour of need. I wouldn't have it. I had done as he wanted without complaint for too long. She was my sister, and I wouldn't turn her away. In the end, he relented.

"The days that followed were joyous to me. It was as though the last five years had never happened with Cara smiling by my side just as she had of old. Little Eoin is a perfect darling, Cara laughs with delight every time I praise him.

"John, however, hasn't shared in our joy. He has spent as little time at home as possible ever since Cara arrived. But then, last night, I woke to hear voices downstairs. I left my room and walked down the hallway, stopping just before I reached the head of the stairs. I could hear now that

179

the voices were John and Cara's. They were trying to keep their voices low, but their anger seemed to make it impossible.

"'Surely enough time has passed by now,' said Cara. 'With Neil gone, there is no one who has direct knowledge of what we did, other than us. And no one in this town would have reason to care.'

"'There is nothing to be done!' John answered, 'The sins I have committed, I chose to commit. But those sins being done, I vowed to never allow myself to enjoy what those sins yielded.'

"'And what is my life to be?' asked Cara through her teeth. 'How am I to take care of myself? Of Eoin?'

"'Enough!' spat John and I heard him approaching the stairs. I hurried quietly back to my room and heard him climb up the stairs and close himself in his chambers.

"I didn't sleep for the rest of the night. I kept turning everything from the last six years in my mind, John's distant stares, the robbery, the dead guard, Cara and Neil's sudden marriage, our sudden move, Neil's death, Cara and John's secret conversation. I couldn't make sense of it all. That feeling of hopelessness that nearly killed me five years ago returned. Already, I'm beginning to feel weak and sickly. But this time I will not place my fate in my husband's hands. No, I will decide what my life is to be. I must know the truth. So I made up a reason to leave the house this afternoon and came here."

Holmes opened his eyes. I had come to expect that Holmes, after hearing a case presented by a client, would ask a few clarifying questions, but he simply turned to the lady and said, "Thank you, Mrs. Thomas. The case certainly had a mild point of interest or two. I believe I can inform you what it is your husband and friends have kept from you, but I must take a day to confirm one important fact. Come this time tomorrow and I will make all clear to you. Until then, goodbye!"

The lady stood up without another word, her face in an expression of confusion and disappointment. I rose with her and led her to the door.

After she had left, Holmes stood by the window and watched her walk down Baker Street.

"Damn!" he swore with a gesture of frustration. "The lady's story started out promising enough, but turned out to be a very dull business, save one interesting, but in the end inconsequential, aspect."

"Come now," I said. "You cannot mean to tell me you found nothing in this poor woman's story to be touching or intriguing."

"I found it to be nothing more than commonplace," he sighed.

"Well, I must admit, I didn't find it to be as complex as the problems you faced in Rouen last month, or during that business of the 'study in scarlet'. In fact, I believe I may have a handle on the key points of the solution."

Holmes cocked his brow.

"Is that so?" he asked. "Then pray, what are they?"

I took a moment to gather my thoughts.

"It seems to me," I began, "that these fellows, John Thomas and Neil Bailey, had a plan to rob their company's safe. It took some time in planning, as the safe was guarded and in a different building than that in which they worked. Thomas was away from home many nights, probably using his access to the one building to observe the other and learn the guard's routine."

"Sound enough," said Holmes, lighting his pipe. "Proceed."

"Cara McClelland became aware of this plot in some way. I believe they brought it to her and asked her to take part. A pretty young lady can be just the thing to distract a guard, just like how the Green Tie Gang you caught in Birmingham always employed that little blonde woman."

"Excellent!"

"Something went wrong, however, and one of them, most likely Thomas, was compelled to kill the guard. It wasn't part of the plan, and was, in fact, something they had tried their best to avoid. It weighed heavily on Thomas's heart. He hid the money, insisting that since it was gained by murderous means, they should never spend it at all. He felt the need to leave Belfast, probably because returning to the location of his crime every day was too much for his guilty heart to bear. Bailey proposed to Miss McClelland to make sure she is well taken care of even without her share of the loot. Years later, Bailey squanders all his earnings and dies. Cara Bailey, now penniless and aware that Thomas knows where to find the stolen money, comes to England to demand that he give over her share of the ill-gotten money that she is owed."

"Remarkable," said Holmes. "Really? That is your best bit of reasoning yet."

"I'm pleased to hear you say so," I admitted with a slight blush. "But, as I said, it really was quite simple."

"And yet you still managed to make your solution astonishingly more complex than the truth. Forgive me, my dear Watson, but your reasoning, while quite interesting, was in no way accurate, as it was founded upon a supposition that is absolutely untrue."

"Which is?"

"The one thing I need to confirm. I will have my proof shortly."

He walked to a bookcase beside the window where, on the top shelf, four volumes had been pulled out a few inches farther than the surrounding books. He reached behind them, lifted out his morocco case, and placed it

181

in the pocket of his robe. He made his way out of the room, but stopped in the doorway.

"I'm sorry," he said, casually, "if my comments on the stairs earlier offended."

"Thank you," I replied. "You were agitated and made a mistake. It cannot be helped at times."

Holmes took a step back into the room.

"By 'mistake'," he asked, "do you mean a mistake in decorum or of reasoning?"

"By both, I would say. It was a boorish thing to say and, had you been in a calmer state, I'm sure you would have deduced that she was a married woman."

"But I did, the moment I saw her," said Holmes. "My comment was made *before* I saw her and was based on a deduction I made solely by your voice."

I frowned.

"My voice?"

"Yes, you were speaking to the lady when you entered the house. Your usual baritone had turned tenor, as it always does when you speak with the fairer members of the fairer sex."

"Really, Holmes!" I cried. "Mrs. Thomas is a married woman."

"Come now. I may have known it by the sight of her, but you did not. You positively came to attention when I first addressed her as 'Mrs. Thomas'.

"Attraction," he continued, moving further into the room, "is one of the easiest emotions for the trained observer to recognize. The change in voice, in breath, the dilation of the pupils, the reddening of the cheek, all are obvious. A lady, I have found, can tell you much by the posture of her lips. And once you come to see attraction so readily, you will find it to be exceedingly predictable and dull."

At last, he left the sitting room and disappeared upstairs into one of the lumber rooms where he kept stacks of old newspapers. He didn't reappear until late into the evening, holding out a yellowing edition of *The Belfast Evening Telegraph*. The paper was dated four-and-a-half years earlier. Holmes pointed to an article that ran in this way:

H&B Co. Robbers Found

Investigators from the Royal Irish Constabulary have discovered the identities of and arrested the men responsible for the robbery of a safe at the office of the Hartland and Bear Shipbuilding Company, which occurred three months ago.

182

Readers will remember that a guard, Peter Brannigan, was killed and £75,000 were stolen from a safe on the second floor of the H&B's accounting office. Investigators were inclined to believe that at least one culprit worked for the company, given the apparent knowledge the thieves had of the building's security and the placement of the safe.

It appears that the job was the work of the notorious Hanratty Gang: The father, Martin Hanratty, and his two sons, Martin Jr. and Dennis. The brothers spent some months befriending the guard, Brannigan, then convinced him to take part in the crime. In exchange for an equal share of the plunder, he would tell them where to find the safe, and on a night he was on duty, allow them to injure him so as to provide an excuse for his employers as to why he could not prevent the robbery from taking place. But on the night in question, Hanratty Sr. purposefully murdered the young guard instead, so he and his sons would not have to give up a share.

District Inspector 1ˢᵗ Class William Quinn spent a number of weeks tracking down the murderous family and last night raided their hideout near Ballymoney. All three criminals were captured and most of the stolen money recovered. The case will be taken up by the next Azzies.

"I have always read the weekend edition of *The Evening Telegraph*," said Holmes after I had finished examining the article. "I recalled the case instantly, but wanted to check my memory before I shared my thoughts with our client."

"But Holmes," I asked, "if the job was perpetrated by this Hanratty Gang, what had John Thomas and Neil Bailey to do with it?"

"Absolutely nothing at all, which seemed to me to be the most likely case from the start. What had we to connect them to the crime, other than Mrs. Thomas' perception that they might be involved?"

"John Thomas made her swear to lie so as to provide him an alibi for the night of the crime."

"True, but he didn't do so until the morning after he read about the robbery occurring in the newspaper. If he knew he needed an alibi from the start, he would have made his demands of her when he came home the night before. Furthermore, if he and this Bailey fellow had spent so much time planning the crime, would they not already have gone out of their way to establish alibis beforehand? No, John Thomas had been out engaging in another sin that night, one he wouldn't wish to share with the authorities or anyone else, but he knew that if he was questioned in the case, it wouldn't look good for him if he refused to provide an alibi – thus his demand that his wife provide one."

"But what could this other sin be?" I asked.

"Once you eliminate the robbery as a reason for his strange behavior, only one explanation covers all the facts: John Thomas had a romantic affair with Cara McClelland."

"The scoundrel!" I cried. "That explains his late nights away from home."

"It is the most likely explanation for most husband's late nights away from home. It would seem that Neil Bailey was aware of the affair. Men do tend to confide these things to other men out of bravado when they would do best to keep them entirely to themselves.

"As to Thomas's late evening the night of the robbery, his emotional state, and his sudden departure to London the next week, that is easily explained when you consider the baby that Cara Bailey, *née* McClelland, had soon after. She wrote a letter to Mrs. Thomas saying that the child was born a little less than a year later, but she could have had the child months before and delayed the news to throw off suspicion. Her stomach illness as noticed by Mrs. Thomas would certainly support her being pregnant at the time.

"Now you can see the whole sad story: John Thomas and Cara McClelland have an affair. He learns that she is with child and returns home in the early hours of the morning in great distress. In order to keep his wife in the dark and guarantee that the affair is ended, he convinces Bailey to propose marriage to Miss McClelland and her to accept. Perhaps Bailey was in love with the lady all along, which had made holding the secret of the affair all the more painful to him. Thomas then accepts a job in London, one that promises less money and esteem, in order to leave his mistakes behind him. He and his wife live their unhappy lives for five years until Neil Bailey dies and Cara Bailey arrives at their door, with Thomas's secret son. Notice the boy's name, 'Eoin', which is the Celtic alternative to 'John'. She pressures Thomas, not for money but, at the very least, to acknowledge that Eoin is his son and will be cared for, at most to abandon his wife and marry her.

"As I said, the whole business was nothing more than a commonplace affair that seemed to be of interest due to a coincidence and misperception."

"And what," I asked, "will you tell Mrs. Thomas tomorrow?"

"The truth. She is a woman wronged, and I, knowing the truth, am obligated to share it with her. What she does with the truth is entirely up to her."

At five o'clock the following day, Holmes and I sat in our sitting room, awaiting the return of our client. When she didn't appear, Holmes began to pace about the room. Six o'clock came and went. Then, at quarter-past, there was a ring at the bell. We heard steps coming up the stair but were surprised when a man, not Mrs. Thomas, appeared at the door.

"Mr. Sherlock Holmes?" he asked, looking from one to the other of us.

"That is my name," said Holmes. "Who might you be?"

"My name is John Thomas."

"Indeed. Come in, sir."

He was a lugubrious fellow with pale, flaking skin. Though his frame and limbs were wiry, his belly was round and gutted awkwardly out in front of him. With his prominent jaw and large brown eyes, he must have been an attractive youth, but age and an unhappy life had worn him down. At Holmes's invitation, he took a seat in the basket chair.

"I understand, Mr. Holmes," Thomas said in a low voice, "that my wife came to see you yesterday."

"She did."

"And what did she discuss with you?"

"I am afraid, Mr. Thomas, that I insist on keeping conversations with my clients private, even from their spouses."

"It is because she knows, isn't it? She knows about Cara – about Eoin?"

Holmes considered a moment.

"She knows something is amiss," he replied. "She doesn't yet know what."

"She will soon enough, and without having to come to you. I plan on telling her all. I cannot bear the weight of it any longer."

"I'm glad to hear it. I was expecting her to come earlier this evening. Did you prevent her from doing so?"

"No, sir, I did not. Fact is, she has been quite weak the last few days, and yesterday evening after she returned from visiting you, she became quite ill. Cara nursed her all night, but today she has only gotten worse. She was ill like this once before and I almost lost her. Seeing her in this state again breaks my heart. It is because of me, because of my lies, that she is in such despair. I must free us both."

A change had come over Holmes. His eyes were shining and his muscles tense. He knelt before Mr. John Thomas and grabbed him by the shoulders.

"You say your wife is ill?"

"Yes, sir," replied Thomas, confused by Holmes's urgent manner.

185

"What are her symptoms?"

"Fever, chills, stomach pains. The doctor fears it might be – "

"Scarlet Fever?"

"Yes, Mr. Holmes, but how – ?"

Holmes leapt to his feet.

"We must go at once!" he cried. "Watson, grab your bag!"

He dashed down the stairs and out onto the street, Thomas and I at his heels. He hailed a cab. The moment one arrived, Holmes jumped on the seat beside the cabman.

"Driver," he said, "take us to – "

He looked to Thomas.

"38 Grundy Street," said Thomas.

"38 Grundy Street, Driver! And a sovereign if you can make it in less than thirty minutes."

I have never travelled in a coach through the city so fast. Thomas and I held ourselves in place with white knuckles. Holmes called out the route he wanted the driver to take. As we flew down East India Road, Holmes shouted to the cab to come to a halt.

"You there, Officer!" He cried to a constable who was walking down the street.

"Yes, sir?"

"My name is Sherlock Holmes."

"I have heard of you, sir."

"A woman's life is in danger. Hop aboard and we may be able to stop it."

Without another word, the constable climbed into the cab, which was now beyond capacity. Off we went like a shot once more, Holmes and the officer shouting for others on the street to make way. The horse let out neighs of protest, unaccustomed to pulling such weight at such a speed.

As we arrived at 38 Grundy Street, one in a row of modest brick houses, Holmes tossed the cabbie his money and leapt from the carriage. He ran to the house and threw open the door without knocking.

"Your wife," he said to Thomas. "Where is she?"

"In her room upstairs, to the left."

Holmes bounded up the stairs, the rest of us following. We charged into the lady's room.

"Grab that woman! Do not let her near the lady again!" Holmes told the officer.

Mrs. Thomas was lying in bed, unconscious. Another woman, who could only be Mrs. Cara Bailey, was standing over her. The constable grabbed Mrs. Bailey without question.

"What is this?" she cried. "Unhand me! My sister is ill and needs my attention."

"She isn't ill, and you have been far from a sister to her. Watson, how fares the lady?"

I examined the sick woman.

"Her pulse is weak and her breathing shallow. She does indeed have a fever and I noticed a rash on her neck. All these symptoms would suggest Scarlet Fever."

"Or arsenic poisoning," said Holmes.

"Yes," I said, "that would explain the sudden onset of symptoms."

"Search her," Holmes told the constable. Cara Bailey resisted, but soon the constable drew a small vial of white powder from her apron. Holmes took it.

"Rat poison," he declared.

"How could you?" asked Thomas, facing the mother of his child.

"It becomes easier with practice," said Holmes, "and she has done it before."

John Thomas' eyes grew wide as the truth dawned on him.

"Neil!" he cried. "Neil died of Scarlet Fever!'

"Doubtful," said Holmes. "Just as it is doubtful your wife's illness five years ago was due to her broken heart."

"And my vile father before that," said the lady, her eyes glaring at Holmes. "And perhaps you too, one day."

"Well, it is good to have aspirations," said Holmes. "Officer, see that she makes it to Scotland Yard. Refer the case to Inspector Lestrade and let him know I will meet him at the station to inform him of all I know about the business. Mr. Thomas, send for an ambulance. I fear your wife needs more attention than Dr. Watson can here provide."

A few days later, Holmes and I were having lunch at Baker Street. Holmes was in a much more agreeable mood than he had been in months and had spent the last hour talking of the history of the Holy Roman Emperors. As our meal ended, we received a note from John Thomas, letting us know that though the doctors had feared for Mrs. Thomas' life, she was now recovering and had returned home.

"I must thank you, Watson, for bringing The Sisters McClelland case to my attention," he said, lighting his pipe. "It proved to be far more exciting an affair than I had anticipated."

"I'm glad you came to realize the truth behind Mrs. Thomas' illness in time."

"Ah, but I should have seen it sooner," he said with a scowl. "I shouldn't let myself fall into these foul moods when I don't have work at

187

hand. I wasn't prepared to treat this case with the diligence it deserved. There is no reason my mind should stagnate between clients. There are always other sciences and histories to study that may help me in my profession, and it is with these I should occupy my time, not with cocaine and melancholy. William Ramsey is giving a speech on innovations in chemical lab equipment this afternoon. Would you like to attend? One must never stop learning."

The Mystery of the
Vengeful Bride
by DJ Tyrer

"Philips!" I exclaimed in surprise as the door opened and the boy-in-buttons ushered in a guest.

"Watson," Philips responded with a nod. There was a hint of weariness to his voice.

"A friend of yours," observed Sherlock Holmes from where he sat, poring over the day's copy of *The Times*. He hadn't long since risen from his bed, despite the day being well advanced.

I laughed and said, "Indeed. This is an old colleague of mine, Dr. Harold Philips. We studied medicine together. But Philips," I turned back to my friend, "whatever is it that brings you to Baker Street?"

"A mystery," he said, simply.

Holmes leaned forwards in his chair. "Ah, more than the mere renewal of acquaintanceship. Be seated and tell us about it."

Looking to the page, I said, "Tell Mrs. Hudson we shall require some tea and toast."

He nodded, then vanished out the door.

I settled myself and said, "So, a mystery? What sort of mystery?"

Philips shifted awkwardly in his seat. "I'm not sure you shall not think me a fool . . . ."

"Really?" asked Holmes, steepling his fingers and looking him over with an intent gaze. "Potentially foolish, but enough to have worried you for some days – or weeks. Yet, also, something you consider important enough to have come in some measure of haste."

"How?" started my colleague.

Holmes chuckled. "The latter is easy enough to discern. There is a stain of jam on your tie, doubtless from a breakfast eaten in a hurry, and one of your cuffs isn't buttoned."

Philips hand immediately fell to his wrist.

"Therefore," continued Holmes, "I am confident in assuming that you left home with some haste – which, unless you have other urgent business in London, means you were in a hurry to arrive here."

189

Philips shook his head, incredulously. "Amazing, sir. You are everything Watson has implied in his letters. But how did you know that I'm not an inhabitant of this metropolis?"

"It was easy enough to infer," said Holmes. "Your accent, for one, hasn't been polished by that common to your class and profession in London. Then there are your clothes – that tweed is much more suited to country lanes than urban streets. And, lastly, Watson's surprise at seeing you indicated he hasn't rejoiced in your company for some time – something more likely if you aren't an inhabitant of London."

"Well, sir," said Philips, "I am certain that any craniologist would delight in being able to take a cast of your skull, for it contains a formidable intellect. But you said, also, that I had been worried for some time, which is true . . . ."

"Your physical appearance: The dark rims around your eyes and a suit that fits a little too loosely. Signs of a man under pressure of worry, but only for a relatively short period."

Philips nodded and Holmes continued, as if having failed to notice the gesture.

"Something had been gnawing at you for a little while and today, you move with sudden haste to deal with it. The mystery must be a fascinating one."

"It is," said Philips. "It involves a ghost."

"A ghost?" Holmes snorted. "I am no exorcist."

I had to interject. "Philips is no fool. He's a man of science, whose interests, in my experience, run far more to rocks and fossils than the ethereal and numinous."

Holmes looked at me for a moment. Then he refocused his gaze upon Philips and spoke once more, though his tone had softened a little. "Still, unless you are touting some white-sheeted fancy out of a penny dreadful, I shall not refuse to hear more, no matter how improbable your assertions might seem. Say on and allow me to assess your claims."

"Thank you." Philips was silent for a long moment, and I could see he was choosing his words with exactness, the best to plead his case to my friend.

"It is a friend of mine – he is afflicted by what he believes is the ghost of his late wife. Haunting him. Tormenting him in some vengeful fashion."

Holmes considered him. "You aren't a man given to fancies, yet you are here, and quite worried by the story you recount. Why?"

Philips sucked his lip for a moment. "I am here because I'm worried for the health of my friend. This belief has had him quite agitated, and I fear he shall either drop from lack of food and sleep, or else from an apoplectic fit brought on by shock – or that, quite despondent, he might give in to some temptation of self-destruction.

"I am also, as Watson noted, not one to believe in such notions as phantasms. My touchstone has always been the physical and biological worlds. Yet, I have seen – "

Holmes leaned forwards again. "Yes?"

"I am loath to call it a *ghost*," Philips said, then sighed. "Yet, I cannot deny the evidence of my own eyes."

Holmes held up a hand. "I think you should start at the beginning, before you tell us what you experienced to convince you of your friend's truthfulness in these claims. Who is your friend, and what happened to his wife, and what do you know of the alleged haunting?"

Taking another breath, Philips began. "As Watson knows, my father was a country doctor, and a London practice was of little interest to me. When my father died, a bit over a year ago, I inherited his practice in the village of Hendon-under-Lumley, a most-pleasant locale. Amongst my patients was one Alfred Lombard of Lumley Hall, who rapidly became a firm friend as well."

"Lombard, you say?"

"Yes, Alfred Lombard of Lumley Hall – a banker."

"Yes, yes, I thought I recognised the name." Holmes rose and crossed to his commonplace books in which he kept a multitude of notes and cuttings and began to search through them. "A-ha! Here it is," he said, and he produced a sheet. "Alfred Lombard . . . questioned for his involvement in the Bernardi banking scandal . . . no evidence of wrongdoing . . . a report of his wife's death . . . one year ago . . . ."

Philips nodded in acknowledgement that his words were correct.

"Please continue," said Holmes returning the book to its place before seating himself once more.

Philips nodded again. "Lombard was a widower, his first wife having died before I took over my father's practice, but maybe eighteen months ago, he was involved in the handling of the inheritance of a young woman named Emily Blunden, whose late father was involved in the sugar trade. He was soon smitten by love and the two became engaged. A lovely young woman, I count myself fortunate to have known her.

"A year ago, she arrived at Lumley Hall for her wedding. The estate has a particularly fine ornamental lake of which she rapidly became enamoured and insisted should be the backdrop to a photograph of herself and her husband to commemorate their wedding. What had been a blissful day turned to tragedy when the bridge between the shore and a small island collapsed, throwing her and her companions into the water.

191

"Though my friend managed to pull the young women out of the water, I was unable to revive his beloved, who had struck her head as she fell. Emily had drowned.

"Distraught, as you will imagine, Lombard chose to let most of his staff go, save his manservant, who had been with him for many years, and the young lady who had been maid to his wife, being unwilling to leave her suddenly bereft of home and employment.

"Thus he stewed in his grief, a melancholy sight, but not one to cause me any significant concern. Indeed, in recent months, his mood had begun to lift a little, and I was certain that his heart, though sorely pained, was beginning to heal.

"Then, three weeks ago, he summoned me to the Hall and I arrived to find him in quite an agitated state, and he told me he had seen his wife, down by the lake, pointing up at him in what he took to be an accusatory manner."

Philips paused, then said, "I must digress for a moment. After Emily's death, there had been some unfounded rumours in certain quarters that my friend was somehow involved. Nonsense, of course, but it seemed that the sniping had affected him, and he was imagining himself to blame for her death in some way.

"Naturally, I didn't believe there was anything to his actual claim beyond some mental or emotional disturbance brought on by the approach of the anniversary of her death, but I soon grew worried as he began to behave more and more erratically, taking less care of himself, refusing to eat, and wandering the estate by night. Indeed, I believed it likely he might throw himself into the waters of the lake and, thus, watched him closely.

"Once, out of the window, I thought I saw a white figure down by the lakeside, one that might have been a bride clad in her gown, but it was gone in the blink of an eye and I convinced myself that it was but a trick of the light, shaped by the fancy my friend's fears had planted in my mind. But then . . . .

"It was whilst I was standing vigil over him one night that he cried out that he had seen her outside his bedroom door. I was in a neighbouring guest bedroom and ran to him, only to halt in utter disbelief as the light of my candle glittered off a patch of wetness in his doorway – a patch that, to my eyes, appeared to resemble a pair of woman's bare footprints . . . ."

"Goodness," I uttered, having become quite caught up in his telling and struck by the force of the shock that yet remained in his words.

"Yes. It was at that point that I felt I could no longer deny what my friend was telling me. But having accepted that he may well be correct in his claim that his wife has returned to haunt him, I am at a loss as to how to proceed. Lombard believes that she will come in a few days to claim his

192

soul on the anniversary of her death and that he shall then die. I fear that the state of his health might well make it a self-fulfilling prophecy, regardless of the truth."

"Knowing that you and Watson specialise in solving those mysteries most would consider impossible, you were the only people I could think to turn to, even if I'm not entirely certain what you might do. Oh, I know it may all sound ridiculous to your ears, but I pray you, please help in any way you can – A man's life depends upon it!"

Holmes rose. "Our help you shall have. Watson, send the page to fetch a cab. We have a train to catch."

Lumley Hall was a large and airy Georgian building, quite unlike the grim gothic pile I had been imagining after my colleague's talk of death and ghosts. It was late afternoon when we arrived, and a young woman in a housekeeper's uniform answered the door, showing us through to the receiving room where the gaunt figure of Alfred Lombard waited for us. With his darkly-rimmed eyes and fragile appearance, he truly looked haunted.

"Thank you both for coming," he said in a whisper of a voice as we all sat. "I know, of course, of your exploits, as recounted in the papers, and Philips, here, has furnished me with more personal details of your past." He glanced at his friend. "I must be honest and say that I was against summoning you, for it is no mortal crime that troubles me and, no matter what your prodigious skills may be, Mr. Holmes, I cannot see how they might assist me. But Philips was insistent . . . ." He made a vague gesture with his hands and fell silent.

"Mr. Lombard," said Holmes in a voice of soft sincerity, "Watson and I shall endeavour to do all we can to resolve the situation surrounding you."

He laughed without humour. "Only one thing shall resolve it, I am certain."

"What is that?" I asked him.

"My death," he said with certainty. "My wife's spirit shall see to it."

"Perhaps," said Holmes, "but I shall maintain my scepticism for the time being. I am a man of facts, Mr. Lombard, not belief. If you have no objections, Watson and I shall look into this matter and draw our own conclusions."

Lombard made another vague gesture. "As you wish."

"Very good. Now, before we do anything else, we shall need to hear your story from your own lips. Tell us what you have experienced, beginning with your marriage and the death of your wife."

"Very well," said the banker, licking his dry lips. "Very well . . . ."

193

The story was as Philips had apprised us, albeit with more detail and diversions.

"Emily wished to have our wedding day commemorated with a photograph of the two of us by the lake," he continued. "Naturally, I was happy to comply with her request. I went to fetch the photographer, while Emily went on ahead . . . ." He stifled a sob. "She was just walking out to the island in the lake's centre when the bridge collapsed beneath her and her friends. The water isn't deep and she surely would have been able to save herself, but she struck her head as she fell and, by the time I was returned and able to pull her and her bridesmaids out of the water, Emily had drowned.

"That was very nearly a year ago," finished Lombard.

He took a deep breath. "Then, three weeks ago, I saw my wife's ghost . . . ."

"When?" I asked. "Where?"

Lombard paused for a moment. "I was in my dressing room preparing for bed when I looked out the window towards the lake, as I often do, and there she was – dressed in her wedding gown, the same one she'd been wearing when she drowned."

"You are sure of this?" I asked and he nodded.

"I know what I saw."

"And you have seen her since?" Holmes asked in an almost-uninterested tone.

He nodded. "Yes. Not every night, but most. Usually down by the lake, but I have also seen her in the Hall – fleeting glimpses. She's always gone when I try to reach her."

"She has never appeared in daylight?" Holmes asked softly

"No," said Lombard. "Always late, in the darkness."

"Then we still have over an hour until we must be wary. Dr. Philips, will you be staying?"

"No. I have been neglecting my practice, and with you here . . . ." He glanced at the time on his pocket watch. "In fact, I should have been away by now." He rose.

"Very well." Holmes looked at Lombard. "Let us have something to eat and then we shall take up our vigil."

After we'd been fed, we briefly interviewed the banker's two servants, but neither the former maid-turned-housekeeper, a young woman by the name of Amanda Kay, nor his manservant, a rather-taciturn fellow called Rogers, admitted to having seen the ghost, although the former did appear to me somewhat emotional at the forthcoming anniversary of her mistress's death.

Then Holmes and I took up position in a guest bedroom close by that of our host, from which, through a narrow gap in the curtains, we could observe the lake as he did.

Having settled ourselves ready for the fall of darkness, Holmes turned to me and spoke.

"What is your opinion of Mr. Lombard? Is he an honest man?"

"Indeed, I think so. Certainly there can be no question as to his grief."

"And how about his guilt?"

"That he feels some guilt for not saving his bride is, I believe, undeniable, but I don't believe it extends further than that."

"What about the rumours?" Holmes pressed.

"Mere village gossip, I should think."

"Ah, but what if I told you that the notes I have on him revealed that his first wife, who died in a carriage accident several months before his second marriage, was the daughter of a wealthy banker and left him with a small fortune with which to console himself."

"You're suggesting that he murdered both his wives in order to obtain their fortunes?"

"Not suggesting, only repeating rumours. Yet, it must be admitted that disposing of a wife for her fortune isn't unknown."

"Yes, but surely he had access to their money equally when they were alive? Had he killed his first wife to make way for the second, I might credit it. But why kill both? And, as I said, I am certain his grief is genuine. No, Lombard is no murderer."

"You are sure?"

"I am certain," I told Holmes.

"Night is upon us," he said, peering out of the window at the darkening garden. Then he resumed his questioning, asking, "What is your opinion of this ghostly business?"

I was silent for a moment. "Well, I am disinclined to believe in ghosts, although I may not rule them out entirely. There is much, I am sure, that mankind has yet to learn about the world in which we live."

"But do you believe *him*?"

"I certainly believe that *he* believes. Now if it were just his word, I would likely assume, as Philips did, that the ghost was nothing more than a figment of his imagination and emotion. But what Philips said about seeing something himself, and the damp footprints . . . ." I shuddered. "I can see why he wonders at it."

"But," said Holmes, watching the garden, "are ghosts not immaterial? How does a ghost leave watery footprints?"

With a shrug, I said, "One hears many contradictory tales of hauntings. In some, ghosts are nothing but apparitions, insubstantial and elusive. In others, they would seem to have some physical presence and be capable of moving objects and even harming the living. Then, of course, there are the old tales of revenants and the vampire that stalks the Carpathian mountains, both of which have physical form. So I shall refrain from saying whether a ghost can or cannot leave damp marks – merely that the presence of such has me questioning how they came to be there.

"Equally," I went on, "they offer no certainty. It may indeed be that this haunting is all in the poor man's head and, perhaps, all we shall be called upon is to show him that it has no merit in reality."

"Allay his fears rather than lay a ghost?" quipped Holmes with a smile.

"Indeed," said I, returning his smile.

We waited in silence, the only sound the tick of a clock upon the mantel.

After a while, another sound impinged upon my hearing.

"Do you hear that?" I said, softly.

"What is it?"

"A distant sound – like that of a woman sobbing."

Holmes cocked his head, then shook it. The sound had stopped.

"I must have imagined it," I told him, returning my gaze to the garden below. The darkness was thick now. I yawned and stretched my neck, certain it would be a long and fruitless wait.

Then I gasped and leant close to the window pane. "Movement!"

Holmes looked. "I see nothing."

"For a moment," I told him, "I was certain that I – "

I was cut off by an agitated sound from Lombard's bedroom. We ran to him.

"It was her!" he gasped, gesturing towards the window. "It was her – I swear it – down by the lake!"

"Come, Watson!" We left the room and headed downstairs and out into the cool of the night air.

"You were saying?" Holmes said as we ran towards the lake.

"For a moment, I was certain I saw a figure, all in white, luminescent and strange. But then . . . it was gone."

"Where?"

A little surprised that Holmes took my fleeting fancy so seriously, I said, "By the lake-shore – over here."

There had been no rain, so the ground was firm and unmarked. It was possible the blades of grass were bent as if by the passage of a person, but Holmes had to admit he couldn't be certain.

But as we traced a spiral about the lawn, in search of any evidence of a nocturnal visitor to the estate, he did detect the hint of a footprint in some slightly softer ground close by a stand of trees. Crouching low to examine the spot, he pronounced himself certain of the fact.

"Somebody was here," he said, standing.

"Yes, but who? The living or the dead?"

"That, of course, is the question. Is the ghost of his wife really here to torment Mr. Lombard, or is the cause of his terror made of flesh and blood?"

"You think someone is deliberately attempting to scare him?"

"I would more readily admit it than a ghost, but again, it is inconclusive. We need more than maybes. *Who* and *Why*? Those are the questions in need of answering."

"Well," said I as we began to walk back towards the house, "we don't have long. The anniversary of Emily's death is only a couple of days away and, whether she comes for him or not, I concur with my colleague that there is a real danger that the date will trigger some deleterious physical or emotional response. As you said, we need to allay his fears."

We returned to the house, where Lombard was prowling the corridors in a state of agitation.

"She was here! She was *here*! Sobbing!"

"There was no one," said Holmes, but he glanced at me.

"She was here! She rose bodily from her coffin and stalked here to seek her revenge!"

Having so proclaimed his belief, he became even more agitated, sufficient that I worried he might hurt himself. All our attempts to calm or reason with him fell upon deaf ears and he continued to rage.

His manservant and housekeeper both came running at the loud sounds of distress as he wailed and ranted and smacked his hands against doors like a man demented.

"He needs to be sedated," said Holmes in a detached, almost-sardonic manner.

"Then help Rogers to restrain him and I'll do the deed," I said, sending Miss Kay to retrieve my bag.

"Shush, sir," said Rogers, not unkindly, as he and Holmes took hold of Lombard. "Your wife's in her coffin as sure as God intended, no doubt."

"No! She isn't! She isn't . . . ."

I injected the banker and he fell silent, slumping in the arms of his manservant, who helped us carry him up to bed.

"I'll stand guard outside his door," said Holmes, "while you go and get some sleep."

I cannot say I slept well, for my dreams were filled with ghastly pallid figures, wet and dripping, reaching out for me and seeking to drag me down into dark waters. It was as if the madness of Mr. Lombard were contagious.

I was grateful when the gentle caress of sunlight and a soft tap upon the guest-bedroom door woke me. It opened and Holmes stalked in.

"Breakfast awaits," he said.

As I followed him down, he said, "Last night, you said you heard sobbing."

"I thought I did."

"Lombard said his wife's ghost was sobbing."

"Indeed."

"If," Holmes said, "it weren't a ghost, but someone attempting to affect his emotions, it would seem the logical suspect is his housekeeper – his wife's maid."

"You suspect she seeks revenge?" I said as we reached the dining room, but fell silent for she was waiting within to provide our breakfast. Holmes gave the slightest shrug. Then we were seated.

I found my appetite somewhat restricted after the night's dreams, but ate a little buttered toast and availed myself readily of the very-fine tea brewed by the housekeeper, Miss Amanda Kay. Lombard was still asleep, under the effects of the sedative.

Philips arrived a short while later and joined us, keen to hear of our night's occupation. Upon hearing about his friend, he grew concerned.

"I should have been here," he said with a sorrowful shake of the head.

"He's quite well," I assured him. "And I'm every bit as versed in medicine as you."

"Indeed you are. I worry unnecessarily, but cannot help it. Still, I should like to examine him when he wakes."

"Of course," I reassured him.

"And did you see anything last night?" he asked.

"Nothing conclusive," said Holmes, pausing in his eating of a splendid breakfast of bacon and eggs.

The doctor appeared a little despondent and I said, "Come now, such mysteries are seldom solved in one night. Most take much effort to untangle their web of deceit."

"Of course," said he. "Of course. However, I cannot help but worry, as there is only one more night after tonight before we reach the anniversary of Emily's death."

"We shall have answers before then," I told him, "I'm sure of it".

Dabbing his plate clean with the remnant of a slice of toast, Holmes asked, "Would you say Mr. Lombard has any enemies?"

"Enemies? Why, none that I could name. He is a fine and well-respected fellow."

"Ah," I said, "but Holmes is aware of the rumours of foul play in the death of his first wife. However unfounded such claims might there be, isn't it possible someone believes them and holds him accountable? And what about the Bernardi Scandal? I know that Lombard was found to be innocent of involvement, but again, might there not be those who believe otherwise?"

"Then," said Holmes, "there are those perennial blights upon otherwise quiet country life – the unhappy neighbour feuding over a boundary, for example. Are there no locals with a grudge?"

Philips shook his head. "Not sufficient to orchestrate such a monstrous prank. Nor can I say much about the others you suggest. Reverend Makepeace, who officiated at his wedding, was caught up in the Bernardi Scandal and lost quite a bit of money, but he is a gentle soul whom I just cannot picture doing anything nefarious. Beyond that, none that I can think of . . . unless you were to count Lombard's sister."

"Sister?" I asked.

"Yes. A spinster. She lives in a small cottage on the estate, but she and her brother hardly ever seem to interact and, when forced to, there is a definite hostility between them."

Holmes glanced towards me but said nothing. Clearly the housekeeper wasn't the only potential source of sobbing.

"But," continued Philips, "don't take me wrong. Though I don't know her well, she seems a fine woman and most religious. She regularly visits the reverend and his wife."

Holmes shook his head. "A point that reminds me that the possibility of the reverend being opposed to Lombard is inconvenient news, as I daresay we shall require his assistance tonight."

"Why?" Philips asked. "Whatever do you have in mind?"

"Last night, in his agitation, your friend spoke of his wife rising bodily from her coffin as some kind of revenant. It is my intention to prove to him that he is wrong and that the source of his woes is surely someone of flesh and blood."

"How?" asked Philips.

"If you would be willing to take watch of Lombard this night, Watson and I shall prove his belief a fallacy. He seems sufficiently convinced of it that puncturing the one part of his delusion ought to free him of all its aspects."

"Whatever do you mean?"

"We shall open his second wife's coffin and stand guard over her corpse until morning in order to prove to Lombard that her body does *not* rise to walk abroad by night. It isn't that I disbelieve that you and he saw something – just the readiness to declare it supernatural and be done with it."

Philips gave a cry. "A splendid notion, sir! And no, I take no offence at your suggesting he may be shaken from his malaise in such a way." He shook his head. "I should have had the idea myself! Yes, surely that would do it."

"Then we have our course plotted," said Holmes. "Tonight, we make our move."

After Philips had left the Hall to attend to his duties as a doctor, Holmes approached Lombard to enquire whether it were possible to view any photographs taken to commemorate the man's wedding day.

His face twisted with a grotesque expression at the request, but he nodded and said, "There were some taken outside the church. The others we planned – well, I assume they were delivered, though I have never looked at them. You will need to ask Amanda."

The housekeeper's expression of distaste at being asked to locate them wasn't as intense as her master's, but it reminded me that we were intruding upon a tragedy they might have preferred to forget. I wondered if the sobbing I had heard hadn't been some ploy to disturb the banker, but rather the young woman reliving her grief. I felt an intense surge of compassion towards her.

An album was produced, within which were half-a-dozen images depicting the happy day before disaster had marred it: The bride and groom and their party. It seemed that Philips had served his friend as best man, and there were two bridesmaids, one of whom I recognised as Amanda Kay and the other I assumed to be Miss Lombard, the spinster sister.

"Watson, what do you see?" asked Holmes as he leant closer, as if attempting to discern some fine detail in the photograph.

"A happy couple and their court. Miss Kay appears delighted at her mistress's happiness, while Miss Lombard looks as sour as if she had sucked upon a lemon."

Holmes chuckled. "I cannot argue against you, but that isn't what I meant. Rather, look at the bride and Miss Kay."

"What am I looking –" Then I sucked in a breath. "They could be sisters!"

"Yes," said Holmes in a quiet voice. "It may be that the housekeeper has good reason for revenge upon Lombard, if she believes him culpable of Emily's death . . . ."

The observation left me a little shaken, and I wondered if Lombard suspected the same as we did. Holmes left after lunch, citing the need to send telegrams, leaving me to watch over our still-somewhat agitated host. He returned as the sun neared the horizon.

"I've spoken to a number of locals," Holmes told me as Rogers *geed* the horses of the wagonette that would carry us to the Church of St. Mary's, "and not a one of them would admit to any bad blood with the banker. One or two mentioned the reverend's financial losses involving the banking scandal, but none placed much significance upon it. One might truly think he hasn't an enemy in the world. Still, perhaps we can shake him from his worry."

We were travelling along darkening country lanes as the ragged streaks of red across the sky gave way to the blackness of night.

Holmes had earlier visited Reverend Makepeace to give him notice of our intent and gain his permission to enter the crypt of the church in pursuit of our providing solace for his parishioner. According to my friend, the man had been most eager to help assuage Lombard's fears, if a little uncertain at the particular means, and he was willing to ignore the various legalities involved to carry out such the proposed action.

I had to confess I had been somewhat bemused that he intended to actually carry out his plan.

"Surely," said I, "we could tell Lombard that her body was where it should be without the need to actually disturb it?"

Holmes nodded. "Yes, we could play the charade, but such is his delusion that I believe it shall require more than our word to unravel it. We require witnesses – and while we could ask them to lie, that risks a loose tongue or misspoken word undoing our work. No, best to do the deed for real, no matter how distasteful.

"Besides," said Holmes in a somewhat darker and softer tone, "I wish to see the lady for myself."

I didn't have a chance to query what he meant, for the coach slowed to a halt and Holmes exclaimed, "Ah, here we are."

I assumed he wished to pursue some thought concerning the nature of her death.

"And," continued Holmes, "it seems the reverend and the gravedigger are waiting for us." As the wagonette halted, he added, "Rogers, you may return to the Hall. Watson and I shall make our own way there in the morning."

"Very good, sir," said Rogers and he turned the vehicle and was soon out of sight.

We exchanged greetings with the reverend and the elderly man who was in charge of graves.

"Good evening, gents," said the latter.

"Good evening," replied Holmes as if responding to a greeting of exquisite manners. Then he checked his pocket watch. "It is nearly time. Do you have the keys?"

The reverend nodded and produced a heavy set of iron ones, with which he proceeded to unlock the door to the crypt that lay beneath the church.

"With any luck," said I, "we can end this madness tonight."

The gravedigger led the way down into the crypt, a heavy lantern in his hand. The sputtering light sent shadows dancing about the scene, and one could almost imagine that the ghosts of the dead truly were in the process of rising to inflict themselves upon the living.

He carefully counted his way past the niches occupied with sombre black-lacquered coffins, until he paused and said, "Yes, this is the one."

He pointed to one that bore the name of "*Emily Lombard*" inscribed in a silver plate upon its lid. With ease, he pulled it out and laid it upon the floor.

The reverend gave a shudder as he watched us. "I must say, that I find this night's work must unwholesome."

"Yet," said Holmes, "it is a necessity, and you are our witnesses."

The man crossed himself but nodded, and the gravedigger produced a screwdriver and set to work unsealing the lid.

Together we lifted it aside and each of us produced a sound of incredulity.

The coffin was empty!

Holmes was silent as we walked back to the Hall. Clearly, the absence of the corpse wasn't what my friend had been expecting, and now all his conjectures were thrown into disarray.

"Thank Heavens you are returned," Amanda Kay cried from the doorway as we approached.

"Why, whatever is the matter?" I called back.

"It's Mr. Lombard. Something's wrong!"

"What?" demanded Holmes as he jumped forward with the agility of a leopard and followed her inside.

It seemed that, despite Holmes's admonition, Philips had been called away to tend to a seriously ill patient and had left him in the care of the housekeeper. She, in turn, had left him in the library seeking solace in the written word and gone to the kitchen to fulfil his request for a cup of warm milk, only to hear him cry out in terror and return in haste to find the doors barred from the inside.

"Quickly, Watson, we must break it down."

This was no easy command to complete – the library doors were heavy and thick. But putting our shoulders to the task, we burst them open and stumbled inside, Rogers hurrying in just behind us, while Miss Kay watched from the door.

Lombard was lying on the floor, dead – or so I thought for a moment. Dropping to his side, I noticed the faintest hint of respiration. I also saw the beginning of bruises about his neck that appeared in the pattern of a woman's fingers . . . .

I looked up at Holmes and Rogers. "He's alive."

From the doorway, I heard a strangled sound and the hurrying of footsteps as the housekeeper hurried away from the scene.

"We ought to get him to bed immediately," said Rogers.

"He needs brandy," I said as the banker stirred a little, and Holmes fetched a glass.

Between the two of us, Holmes and I got him into a sitting position and dribbled the brandy past his lips. Rogers leant in close, face etched with worry.

Slowly, Lombard returned to consciousness.

"She came . . ." he moaned. "She came . . . ."

Holmes and I exchanged a look. We knew whom he meant, and our discovery of that empty coffin only seemed to confirm his words.

It was just then that Philips returned.

"Whatever is happening?" he asked, as he entered the room. He uttered an oath at the sight of his friend sprawled limp in our arms. "Does he live?"

I assured him that he did.

"The summons I received was nonsense." He looked down at Lombard. "Whether a misunderstanding or a ruse because somebody wanted me out of the way, I cannot say."

Then he said, "Your faces . . . What is it? Your mission . . . ?"

"We shan't speak of it now," said Holmes.

"We need to get him upstairs," said Rogers.

"Help us get him to bed," I said. "He will need to be sedated again."

When we were done, Holmes insisted on examining the library, but had to admit there was no way out for the windows were bolted shut and the doors had not only been bolted, but had had a heavy leather chair pushed up against them. With no evidence of any hidden doorways, there was only one conclusion that could be drawn.

"Lombard was alone in here," he said at last.

"Unless his attacker passed through the wall," said I, not facetiously.

Holmes looked at me, but remained silent.

203

"Can we deny what we both have been thinking? The coffin was empty, Holmes. This room was locked. Have you, yourself, not said that when you have eliminated the impossible that whatever remains, no matter how improbable, must be the truth?"

I shuddered at my train of thought, ridiculous, yet horribly logical.

"Well, I certainly find the existence of a ghost improbable, yet I struggle to grasp an explanation that fits the facts," I concluded.

"The coffin I might have explained," said Holmes, "but the latter point casts all in doubt." He shook his head. "I was so certain it was Miss Kay," said Holmes. "In a white gown, the similarity in likeness would easily convince him it was his dead wife returned."

I nodded. "Yes, and it would have made perfect sense for her to be guilty. After all, it was she who passed the false request for assistance to Philips, leaving her alone with Lombard. But you saw her as plainly as I did, out there with us, while he was in here, unconscious, the victim of manual strangulation by hands I can only affirm were those of a woman."

"You are right, of course, yet my mind continues to revolt at the notion." It was impossible to disagree with him, yet I was struggling to discern a purely mundane explanation for the events.

Holmes sat down in one of the leather armchairs and sighed. "A world in which the dead can rise and cadavers pass through solid walls isn't one amenable to logic and reason. In short, a world not amenable to me."

I had to shrug. "Surely reason remains. Only more variables than before need to be taken into account."

"You are right. A revenant might yet be understood by the rational mind, if only sufficient evidence about it can be assembled."

It was impossible to disagree with him, yet I was struggling to discern a purely mundane explanation for the events.

He yawned. "I do believe I shall retire and consider all that lies before us in the morning."

The house was in a sombre mood when I rose with the sun. Lombard remained abed, sedated against the horrors of the waking world that still continued to haunt him. There was but one more night before the anniversary of the death of his wife and, if he were correct, that was when she would come to claim both his life and his soul.

Even as the golden sunlight flooded in past the curtains, I found I couldn't doubt that he was right to be fearful of such a fate.

Indeed, I was left to wonder what we might hope to achieve.

"Surely, we would be better placing Lombard's fate in the hands of Reverend Makepeace, for it is more surely his province than ours?"

Holmes gave a grunt of disagreement. "I am not done yet, Watson."

Though it seemed there could be no other cause for what had occurred in that locked room, Holmes wasn't quite ready to declare the case solved and abandon the banker to whatever would befall him. I must admit I took reassurance in his bulldog tenacity to keep tearing at the apparently-insoluble facts. In all my experience of medicine, dead bodies did not make a habit of strolling about and causing mischief, and to have my certainty shaken, even for a moment, had left me feeling quite perturbed. If there was some other answer, I knew Holmes was the man to find it.

"We have yet to speak to the man's sister – his closest living relative. There may be some light she can shed upon events."

But in spite of my hopes, it seemed to me as if Holmes were clutching at straws.

Miss Lombard dwelt alone in a small cottage on the grounds of the estate and maintained a distance of separation between herself and her brother's household.

"There isn't much I can tell you," she said as she sought to answer my friend's questions. "I kept to my life and my brother kept to his. I have seen no ghostly figures, and am at a loss to understand what it is that you are seeking."

She gave a sigh. "If you must ask questions, you should direct them to the woman my brother has made his housekeeper. It seems that out of tragedy, she is the one who profits."

Having obtained nothing useful, we excused ourselves and walked back towards the Hall

"I have telegrams to send," Holmes told me. "You would do well to get some sleep, for we shall be awake again this night and I shall require you rested and alert."

Holmes, to the contrary, seemed to operate without detriment upon the most miniscule amounts of sleep, his mind ever active and working its way towards a solution. I wished I had the confidence he would find one in this case.

As he strode off down the yew-lined driveway, I turned into the house, but I didn't seek the comfort of the guest bedroom. Instead, I sought out the housekeeper.

"Miss Kay, may I speak to you?" I said, finding her in the kitchen.

"Dr. Watson, how might I help you?" There was a wariness to her, yet I discerned, too, a genuine curiosity.

"I have a question pertinent to recent events," said I, and she nodded. "Ask it."

"The first night Holmes and I were here, I heard sobbing shortly before your employer cried out that he had seen the apparition of his wife. Was that you?"

I had expected her to deny it and was surprised when she admitted it most readily.

"His obsession and the approaching date have both stirred in me memories of my mistress and the day she died, and I have been unable to help but shed tears. But I assure you, they weren't, as you seem to imply, in any way connected to what has afflicted Mr. Lombard."

Looking at her pale face and trembling lips, I was certain she was a woman afflicted with a deep sadness and that she was wholly truthful upon this point.

Then, unbidden, she spoke further. "I cannot help but wonder if this is all my fault."

"Why, whatever do you mean?"

"Mr. Lombard was kind enough to take pity on me after my mistress drowned and kept me on here, in his employ, rather than see me left destitute. He did it in memory of her, of course, but as time passed and the shadow of her death faded from him – indeed, from us both – we began to grow closer, and I dared hope that the seed of affection I sensed between us might blossom as it had for them, and that we might find comfort in one another."

She looked at me most earnestly. "He is a good and caring man, Dr. Watson."

But then she sighed. "Only then . . . well, you know what happened next, and I can only wonder if our burgeoning feelings for one another drew the ire of my . . . ."

She trailed off and began to sob and I laid a comforting hand upon her shoulder.

"You swear that your feelings for one another were of recent birth?" I asked her.

Miss Kay nodded. "Yes."

"Then dry your tears, for I cannot believe she would begrudge you the chance of happiness in her stead."

"Thank you, Dr. Watson. You are a kind man."

Lombard's sister might have despised this woman, and I could understand why she might be wary if she sensed the affection growing between them, but I was certain that Amanda Kay was telling the truth and cared deeply for the afflicted man.

Of course, that only served to reinforce the impossible nature of the mystery, for she was the obvious suspect if we were dealing with a flesh-and-blood tormentor and not a ghost.

But my doubts aside, I was ready that evening when Holmes called upon me to maintain a vigil over the banker while he slipped away and concealed himself somewhere in the grounds, ready for the night's visitation.

I provided Lombard with a lower dose of sedative to calm his nerves and sat with him as the night drew on.

Half-asleep in a chair in the corner of his bedroom opposite me, having refused to retire, he twitched and moaned fitfully. Then, with a sudden jerk, he sat upright.

"Did you hear that?" he demanded.

"Yes." There was the faintest hint of footsteps treading their way along the corridor outside the room. "It might be Amanda Kay."

We listened, I ready to act, he trembling. The footsteps halted outside the bedroom door.

"Miss Kay," I called, "is that you?"

Only silence.

I began to rise from my seat. A sudden low and hideous groan made me fall back in surprise. Lombard let out a distraught sob.

It took me a second to recover my senses, but then I was up, dashing to the door, grabbing a candlestick from the mantel as I ran past.

Flinging the door open, I looked out into an empty corridor. But looking down, I felt a tremor of fear as I saw a pair of damp marks in the shape of the prints of a woman's bare feet . . . .

A gunshot from outside caused me to break out of my reverie and, calling for Lombard to remain where he was, I ran downstairs and out the back door of the building.

"Holmes? Holmes!" There was no sign of him on the lawn between the Hall and the lake.

Then I spotted him, striding back towards the Hall from the tree line that bounded the estate.

"What happened?" I cried.

"I saw it. The white figure. Shot at it. Nothing." His words were pronounced with the staccato of frustration.

"She was here," I said in a tremulous voice. "Outside the bedroom door – she left a pair of wet footprints."

Holmes muttered something I didn't catch and strode inside to examine the floor.

I checked on Lombard as he did so. The man was in an agitated state and kept muttering, "Tomorrow. Tomorrow . . . ."

With a snort, Holmes rose and looked at me. "Tell me, Watson: If a damp-footed revenant is walking these halls, why are the only prints straight outside the door?"

Before I could answer, he added, "The evidence for a supernatural solution isn't quite as overwhelming as you seem to think, and I cannot

207

help but feel there are facts we are missing. If only we could grasp them, then we should know the truth."

I shrugged, not knowing what to say in response to him.

The next day was the anniversary of the death of the banker's wife and Lombard was in a highly agitated state, certain that she was coming for him that night. Philips and I agreed to place him under full sedation for the day and take shifts in which to watch over him. Holmes, meanwhile, was about the place making preparations.

Evening was drawing in when Lombard awakened. The agitation that had afflicted him earlier was gone – Indeed, he was in a surprisingly calm mood.

"Perhaps," said Philips, "the hour of her passing having gone by, he is recovered."

Holmes shook his head. "No, it is fatalistic acceptance of his coming doom." He turned to me. "Watch him closely, Watson. Philips, you yourself said it: A man who is certain he is fated to die at a specific time might die by his own hand, or even by an act of sheer will due to his conviction. Coddle him through this night."

"We shall watch over him like hawks," I assured Holmes.

He nodded, satisfied. Then I asked him, "But where will you be?"

"I've resolved to visit the crypt again. Perhaps the vengeful bride will not have risen from her coffin yet and I may arrest her venture."

It was impossible to tell if Holmes was serious or not, so I merely wished him luck as he turned and left, and locked the bedroom door behind him

Lombard retired to bed without a murmur of dissent, while Philips and I sat down to play a nervous hand of cards across the room from him.

The mantel clock chimed the midnight hour and I laid down my cards and opened my mouth to speak, but was cut off by the door swinging open with sudden force and slamming against the wall.

We all turned, startled, Philips knocking our card table over in his shock and Lombard sitting up in his bed with a terrified cry.

Framed in the doorway was the figure of a woman in her wedding gown and veil of white.

With a ghastly shriek, Lombard collapsed back, insensate upon his bed.

For a moment, I stared in horror. Then the bride was gone, vanished as if she never had been.

I was almost as startled as I had been by her sudden appearance, but I rose and ran to the door. If she possessed corporeal form, perhaps she was still in the house, and hadn't disappeared into some other realm of existence. I thought I caught the sounds of movement from the stairs.

"Check him!" I shouted back at Philips. "And don't leave his side!"

Then I began running.

"What's happening?" I heard Miss Kay call from her bedroom doorway.

I didn't pause to answer, but ran on, down the stairs, and out into the night.

Close to the trees, I spotted a flash of white and chased after it.

"Halt!" I shouted, drawing my revolver.

The bride was amongst the trees.

"Halt!" I cried again. She seemed to float upwards.

I fired.

The white figure gave no hint of reaction as it continued to hover between the trees and I prepared to fire again, not knowing if a bullet could have any meaningful effect upon a resurrected corpse.

There was a sudden cry and the sound of a scuffle and I turned in surprise.

Two figures appeared out of the darkness. One was the bride in her wedding gown and veil. The other, I was surprised to see, was Inspector Lestrade!

"Inspector! What –?" I lapsed into silence.

"Good evening, Dr. Watson," he said. Then, in answer to my unasked question, he yanked back the veil. I was surprised to see that it wasn't the corpse of Lombard's wife – nor indeed a woman at all. It was Rogers.

I looked around at my earlier target and realised it was nothing more than a white sheet flapping in the breeze, hoisted aloft by a pair of ropes. No longer agitated, I could plainly see it for what it was and felt a fool.

But there was no time for me to berate myself.

"This way," said Lestrade as I attempted to marshal my thoughts. "Mr. Holmes has doubtless caught the other." He began to manhandle Rogers away.

"The other?" I asked, following him.

"The other," he said with finality as we walked back to Lumley Hall.

Holmes was waiting for us in the corridor outside Lombard's bedroom with a perplexed Philips looking on as he kept a tight hold on a *second* bride, also dressed in a white gown and veil.

"Ah," said Holmes to the inspector and me, "there you are. And what is this you've caught? Rogers, of course." Holmes pulled back the other bride's veil to reveal the face of Lombard's sister. "See, Watson – not ghosts at all."

"I don't understand," said Philips, shaking his head in bemusement.

209

"Nor, I admit, do I," said I, though I felt immense relief at my friend's words.

"Really, Watson?" said Holmes. "Well, as soon as Lestrade and I have these two handcuffed and locked away somewhere for the remainder of the night, I shall explain."

While we waited for Holmes, I joined Philips in examining Lombard. Miss Kay was also attending to the banker, but it was clear that the shock of thinking his dead wife had returned for him had caused him to suffer an apoplectic shock. It was debatable whether he would recover.

Finally we retired to the library where Holmes poured each of us a large brandy.

"So," I asked, "it was Rogers and Mrs. Lombard all along?"

For a moment, Holmes didn't answer, and there was an unreadable expression upon his face, but then he nodded. "Yes."

"But," said Philips, "I don't understand. He was attacked in a locked room, and you said the bride's body was missing."

Miss Kay gave a small sob at his words.

"True," said Holmes, "but even though it seemed impossible for the actor to be anything other than a revenant risen from death, it proved to be nothing more than misdirection. I shall explain all."

He glanced towards Amanda Kay. "You see, it was all about sisters."

"Whatever do you mean?" asked Philips.

"I have no doubt, Doctor Philips, that you have an expert eye for rocks and fossils and the like, but when it comes to women, you aren't so observant. Perhaps it wasn't so obvious when each was dressed according to their station, but seeing this lady side-by-side with her late mistress in the wedding photographs, Watson and I were both struck by a surprising similarity in their features.

"Miss Kay, as I have managed to confirm, was Emily's illegitimate half-sister, and her constant companion since childhood."

Philips gasped.

"It's true!" said the housekeeper with a sob.

"But Holmes, how does that relate to Rogers and Miss Lombard, unless you're saying she's involved, too?"

"Goodness, no!" exclaimed Holmes. "Miss Kay here is innocent of any wrongdoing. But your conversation with her revealed the part she played."

I cast my mind back, trying to think whatever he meant.

"Don't you remember what she told you? That she thought she might be to blame for Lombard's haunting . . . Oh, she was mistaken in sharing his belief that her sister's ghost had returned, but she wasn't wrong on her being the cause."

"I don't follow," I told him.

"As I said, Watson, it was all about sisters – or rather, *one* sister, for there were never *two*."

"Now you're talking in riddles!" Philips exclaimed.

Holmes barked a laughed. "No, the riddle would be: When is a *sister* not a *sister*? And the answer would be: When she is a *wife*!"

"You aren't making any sense, man!"

I gasped. "Actually, I believe he is. You're saying that *Miss* Lombard the *sister* was actually *Mrs.* Lombard, his first *wife*, aren't you?"

"Precisely, Watson, precisely. You see, Mr. Lombard had a passion for money that outstripped his ability to earn it, so he sought to obtain it through marriage. Which meant, as he was already married when he met Wife Number Two, Wife Number One had to masquerade as his sister."

Holmes turned to Amanda Kay and said in a gentle voice, "I am very sorry to say that the man played a cruel deceit upon both you and your sister."

Then he continued. "I would assume murder was always part of the plan and that his first wife was willing to go along with it in return for her share of their gains, but I believe things went awry when Lombard actually fell in love with Emily, something his true wife would never countenance. With the connivance of Rogers, she ensured the bridge would break, most likely having given the bride the idea of being photographed on the island in the first place. I have little doubt she actively ensured that Emily drowned in the chaos that ensued when the three of you – " He looked at Miss Kay again. " – plunged into the water.

"Of course, there is an irony in there of her using the man she had taken as a lover to assist in the murder of her rival for her husband's affections, but I doubt she ever saw Rogers as anything other than a pawn. After all, she didn't immediately begin plotting her husband's demise, but waited, surely hoping that he would recover from his mourning and return to her.

"Except he didn't. He began to express an interest in his dead wife's sister."

"Yes," said I, "which is why you say she was right to imagine she was to blame for Lombard's haunting."

"Exactly, Watson. Realising her husband would never return to her, Mrs. Lombard began to plot his murder through a cunning ruse. Perhaps she hoped to blame it upon a spectre or madness, or it might have been that she hoped Miss Kay would be accused once it was realised she was Emily's sister. Either way, she would escape blame and, as the banker's nearest living relative, would obtain his fortune. Rogers, doubtless, assumed they would then marry."

I nodded. "Very well, Holmes, you have made your case for the conspiracy, but how did they actually enact it? I remain mystified."

"The vanishing body was no great trick," said Holmes. "Indeed, I had a slight suspicion that it might be gone. It was only when combined with the seemingly impossible nature of the attack that my certainty was initially shaken and I wondered more closely at what it seemed to imply. I suspect that Lombard's 'sister's' closeness to the reverend might explain how that poor old gent was tricked. It was be no great difficulty to learn where they hid the corpse.

"I suppose," he added, "I should congratulate their theatrics. Most distracting.

"As to what happened, Rogers knew we planned to go to the crypt in an attempt to dissuade Lombard from his belief in his wife's bodily return. Clearly, he told his lover and she headed to the crypt first and moved it to another coffin. This I was able to confirm when I returned and searched the crypt thoroughly. The reverend and she were close, so I doubt she had much trouble getting the key from him without him being aware."

"And the attack in the locked library?" asked Philips.

"As soon as Miss Kay had left, Mrs. Lombard entered and attacked her husband," said Holmes. "She then locked the door from the inside and hid. If you remember, Rogers was rather insistent we get his master upstairs and into bed. Once we were gone, Mrs. Lombard was able to slip away from where she was hiding, leaving an empty room. Thus, it merely appeared as if he had been attacked in a locked room."

Holmes shook his head. "I was a fool. Had we immediately searched the crypt and the library . . . but what is past is past.

"To finish my tale: Lestrade had ascertained for me that Lombard had no sister, and I began to grasp the plot, summoning him to join me in my search of the crypt. Meanwhile, Rogers sought to distract you away from Lombard so that his wife might murder him, either by shock or by force. I intervened, but was too late to prevent him from collapsing.

"Of course, it might be better if he doesn't recover, for besides the charges of bigamy, there must be further questions about his involvement in the Bernardi Scandal."

Holmes rose and stretched like a waking panther. "It is nearly dawn. Watson. If you could prepare the wagonette, we shall assist Inspector Lestrade in transporting the two villains to the local police station. Philips, could you check on Lombard again?"

Rogers and Mrs. Lombard came quietly, scowling as we led them out to the carriage. Philips was waiting for us with the news that Lombard had passed. I suspected that was a better fate than he deserved.

There was one question I had to ask: "Why did you decide to pretend to be the ghost of Emily in the first place?"

Rogers snorted. "The fool kept thinking that he saw her down by the lake. We took advantage of his imagination."

I shook my head at the casual way he spoke of driving a man half-mad with fear.

Suddenly, Mrs. Lombard halted.

"Come along," said Lestrade, tugging at her. She didn't move.

Her mouth opened in an 'O' and she let out a moan of terror and raised her cuffed hands to point towards where white mist rose from the lake.

"What is it?" asked Holmes, but she didn't reply, instead collapsing with a horrible sound into his arms.

"Give her some air!" I cried, dropping to her side, but it was too late. She was dead.

I looked up at Holmes, exchanging a silent look.

"What on earth just happened?" demanded Lestrade. "What did she see?"

"Well," said Holmes, looking out towards the lake, "that is the question, isn't it? One we likely shall never be able to answer." Then he nodded at Rogers. "Still, justice still needs to be served upon this one. Let's be going."

A Fatal Illusion
by Paul Hiscock

It was late in the evening, and Holmes and I were enjoying a pipe and a glass of brandy by the fire when we heard someone at the front door. Since I knew that Mrs. Hudson would have already turned in for the night, I went down myself to see who it was.

When I opened the door, I saw a boy standing there. At first I thought it was one of the young lads that Holmes sometimes employed to provide him with information, but it quickly became apparent that this was not the case.

"Can I help you?" I asked.

"Are you Mr. Holmes?"

"No, he's upstairs. Do you want to speak to him?"

"I were told to give him this."

The boy thrust an envelope into my hand and was already halfway down the street before I could open my mouth to ask who had sent him.

I looked at the message to see if it offered any clues, but the envelope was sealed, and the only writing on it was Holmes's name and our address. Since there seemed to be nothing more to be learned standing in the doorway, I made my way back upstairs.

"Are you partial to magic shows?" Holmes asked me when I walked back into our rooms.

"I have seen a few acts in the music halls, but most of them were pretty poor."

"In that case, you should definitely accompany me to the theatre to see one done properly."

"What has brought on this sudden interest in magic? I know that you don't believe in supernatural phenomena, and I wouldn't have thought that tricks intended to fool the gullible would hold any interest for you."

"You're quite correct that I have no interest in crude tricks. However, the art of the grand illusionist is worthy of study and even admiration, and it is always a pleasure to accept an invitation to see a master at work."

"An invitation?"

"Yes, the one you just collected, and have been turning over in your hands since you entered."

With all the talk of magic and illusionists, I had almost forgotten about the message.

214

"How the devil do you know what's in this envelope? There is nothing written on it apart from our address, and even if there were some secret markings that I haven't noticed, they would surely be too subtle for even you to detect from across the room."

"On the contrary, Watson, the signs are quite obvious. I could determine a considerable amount about the sender just from his choice of stationery. He used an envelope, and one of reasonable quality, as far as I can judge from here. This would suggest that he is a gentleman of reasonable means. It's certainly not the type of note we're accustomed to receiving from our associates in the police. However, the sender isn't that wealthy or important, as the paper is neither of the heaviest weight, nor monogrammed or personalised in any way."

"I will admit that I hadn't considered any of that," I said, "but still it doesn't explain why you believe this is an invitation to a magic show."

"The address tells me everything – or rather the hand in which it is written. One can tell a lot from a man's handwriting. Your own, in keeping with many of your profession, marks you out as a man in a hurry, happy to sacrifice legibility for speed. However, the author of the missive you hold is far more careful. Every letter is carefully formed. Now a young woman might take such care in a letter to her love, but her pen strokes would be small and dainty. However, the writing on this envelope is flamboyant and extravagant, undoubtedly the writing of an extrovert, such as an actor or showman."

"And which pen-stroke reveals the writer is a magician?" I asked.

"Why, that it is written in the hand of my old friend, M. Lemieux. The unique features of his writing are as familiar to me as your own, and he always invites me to be among the first to attend his show when he has perfected a new trick."

I sighed and handed him the letter. His final revelation seemed disappointingly mundane. It seemed so straightforward, once he had explained how the trick was done. Yet his powers of observation were still far greater than mine. I wondered how many people's handwriting I could recognise from across a room? Mine, probably, and maybe Holmes's. I was wondering if there were any others when Holmes interrupted my thoughts with a most rare admission.

"Watson, it would appear that I made a mistake. This isn't an invitation to M. Lemieux's latest presentation, but a request for my professional assistance. There has been a death at the theatre."

The tall, thin windows of the Alhambra Theatre were dark when our hansom pulled into Leicester Square, and when I peered through the glass doors into the foyer I couldn't see anyone inside. However, Holmes wasn't deterred. He rapped loudly on the door, and after a couple of minutes we saw a lantern moving inside as someone approached.

As the figure drew closer, we saw that it was a young man in a poorly fitting suit. He opened the door a crack and called out to us, "I'm sorry, gents. There's no more shows tonight."

"We are here at the invitation of M. Lemieux," said Holmes, brandishing the letter he had received.

"As I said, there are no more performances tonight, and I am afraid M. Lemieux is unlikely to be performing again for the foreseeable future."

"Your discretion is admirable, but unnecessary. I am Sherlock Holmes, the detective, and I'm here to investigate the death that occurred here this evening."

The young man thrust the lantern towards us to see our faces better. The bright light in my eyes made me take a step back, but Holmes held his ground.

"You don't look like policemen," he said having inspected us, "but the constable did say a detective would be coming. You'd better come in and speak to him."

I opened my mouth to say that we weren't with the police, but Holmes silenced me with a slight shake of his head and let the young man lead us into the darkened building.

I had assumed that we would be taken to the manager's office, or some other room backstage, and so I was surprised when we were led into the main auditorium. Inside, the house lights were down and the seats were empty, but ahead of us the stage lights blazed brightly. There were a few small groups of people up there, but they were gathered around the edges, all seeming to want to keep as far as possible from the object that dominated the middle of the stage. As far as I could make out it was a thin box, slightly taller than a man. However, it was impossible to see any details, as it had been covered with a large sheet that had probably once been white, but was now a dirty grey. I had seen magic tricks performed using covered boxes before, but this seemed shabby by comparison.

"I thought I told you not to let anyone in, boy!" shouted a voice from the stage.

"My name is Mr. Parker, and I'm not some stage hand," replied the young man who had let us in. "I'm the assistant manager, and until Mr. Morton returns, I'm in charge here."

I heard a few titters of laughter from the stage at this statement, suggesting that young Mr. Parker's authority was far from accepted.

"Besides," he continued, "these are the detectives you have been waiting for, Constable."

216

A man in a uniform stepped out of the shadows towards the front of the stage, and stared down at us.

"These two aren't police officers. I told you, there won't be a detective here for hours yet. They have all been called out to some to-do over in Barking."

Mr. Parker rounded on us. "You lied to me! Who are you really? Are you with the newspapers? There's no story for you here."

"I didn't lie," replied Holmes. "I would never claim to be anything as simple as a police detective. Rather, I am the man they turn to when cases transpire to be too complex for them to handle. As I said at the door, it was your illusionist M. Lemieux who asked me to come here, not the police."

"Lemieux, you had no right!" Mr. Parker said angrily. "You should have consulted me before summoning this man."

"It is my reputation that hangs in the balance," replied Lemieux. "I have no intention of trusting it to you or the police when I can call upon the finest detective in England to assist me."

"You may send me away if you wish, Mr. Parker, but I don't believe your employer will thank you when he returns," said Holmes. Then, spotting the constable about to raise his own objections, he added, "Likewise, when Scotland Yard finally sends a detective to handle this case, they will not be pleased if they discover you have rejected my assistance."

I wasn't sure if this was true. Lestrade or Gregson might accept our presence, albeit with some grumbling, but some of their colleagues were far less appreciative of Holmes's work. However, the threat seemed to work as the constable nodded and retreated back into the shadows.

"If you and your friend will come up here, I will show you everything," said Lemieux. He gestured to a small wooden staircase on our left and we ascended it onto the stage.

It took me a moment to adjust to our new surroundings. It was dazzling compared to the gloom all around and I found that I could barely make out any details in the auditorium below. There was also a disconcerting smell of burning, and I wondered if the hot lights had set fire to something.

"Lemieux," said Holmes, "I would like you to introduce you to my friend and colleague, Dr. Watson."

The illusionist stepped forwards and shook my hand. He was wearing a black tailcoat over a crisp white shirt and waistcoat. He had slicked-back dark hair and a long moustache waxed into narrow points.

"Lemieux and I were pupils together at school," continued Holmes.

"Really? How did you come to be studying in this country, M. Lemieux?"

217

"My parents thought that the English boarding school would broaden my horizons."

Holmes laughed, "Don't be fooled, Watson. His real name is Harry Lester, and he is no more French than we are."

Lemieux looked at him with a pained expression. "Are you planning to give away all my secrets, Holmes?" He spoke more quietly, and all trace of his French accent disappeared.

"You need not worry. You can trust Watson completely. However, I need him to understand that nothing in your world is what it seems."

"Why do you pretend to be French?" I asked.

"It adds an air of mystery. Who would you prefer to see perform – plain old Harry Lester, or the Marvellous M. Lemieux? Also, the accent means the audience has to concentrate more to understand what I am *saying*, and pay less attention to what I am *doing*."

"He is a master at the art of misdirection," said Holmes. "When I move among the criminal community gathering intelligence, it is vital that they don't realise what I am doing. Lemieux has taught me a number of the techniques that I use to distract my opponents."

"You were a quick study, and arguably just as skilled as I am," replied Lemieux. "Still I like to test him, and try out all my new tricks on him. I haven't fooled him yet, but his observations help me refine my acts."

"What happened tonight?" asked Holmes, suddenly grave. "You said in your letter that someone had died during your act. Were you trying a new trick that went wrong?"

"No, that's what is so distressing. I've performed this illusion dozens of times, and there has never been a problem. However, this evening . . . Well, I think you should see for yourselves."

Lemieux led us over to the covered box in the middle of the stage. As we approached, some of the other performers gathered there turned away in anticipation. I also noticed, with a sense of dread, that the smell of burning that I had detected before was growing stronger.

The illusionist grabbed the sheet with both hands and then pulled it off in one swift and well-practiced movement. It fell away to reveal a tall glass box. Smoke had stained its sides, but they were still clear enough to see the stomach-churning sight of a burnt body inside.

"The Burning Woman," said Holmes, who clearly recognised the set-up. "I remember suggesting when you first showed it to me that it was too macabre."

"Macabre is what the people want," replied Lemieux. "Illusions of death draw in larger crowds than any other tricks."

I noticed that now we were in the centre of the stage and on display, he had slipped back into his French accent.

218

"Only this time it was not an illusion," said Holmes. "I presume that was your assistant?"

"Yes. A young woman named Helena. She had been working with me for two years."

"How does a woman accidentally burn to death in a glass box?" I asked. "Why did you not smash the glass and pull her out the moment you saw that she was in trouble?"

"It isn't that simple," replied Lemieux. "It was meant to look like she was in trouble."

"You mean it was actually meant to look like she was burning to death?" I asked, appalled.

"Not precisely. During the illusion the box is wrapped in paper. When the fire is lit, the flames appear through the opening in the top of the box, and my assistant's struggles are cast as shadows on to the paper. At the climax the paper burns away, at which point the empty box is revealed – only tonight, we saw this instead."

"Haven't enough people stared at her body?" came a shout from across the stage. "Cover her up, you murderer!"

Lemieux picked up the sheet and draped it over the ghastly sight once more.

"Who was that," I asked, "and why are all these people here?"

"The police constable insisted that all the performers and staff must wait here until a detective comes. He made everyone stay on the stage so that he could keep watch over us all. As for the man who shouted at me just now – that is Philips, one of the stage hands."

"He seems particularly upset by your assistant's death," said Holmes.

"He was attracted to Helena. One might say he was a little bit obsessed with her."

I had thought that we were speaking privately, but the acoustics of the stage carried Lemieux's words to Philips, who angrily came over to us."

"That's a lie! We were in love!" he said. "You were just jealous and wanted to stop us from being together."

Lemieux shook his head. "She might have indulged your attentions once or twice in the past, but in the end she just wanted you to leave her alone."

"That is what you say, but I guess we'll never know the truth now that you've killed her!"

"I keep telling you, I didn't kill Helena. It was just a dreadful accident."

219

I saw Philips clench his hands into fists, and for a moment I thought he was going to assault the illusionist, but instead he raised his hand and pointed a finger at Lemieux's face.

"It was *your* trick, so *you* are responsible, and when a proper detective arrives, I will see that you are punished for it."

Having said his piece, he stalked off to rejoin his fellow stage hands in the shadows at the back of the stage.

"I am sorry about that" said Lemieux. "Helena complained to me more than once about his obsession with her. He would get angry if he saw her even speak to another man. She told me that she feared he might turn violent if she continued to reject him. Still, he has a point. It was my trick that killed her, not him."

"You're worried that the police are going to arrest you?" I asked.

"It's possible, but even if they let me go, an unexplained death during one of my tricks will destroy my career."

"You think the theatre will let you go?"

"Certainly. The Alhambra reopened last year, following a fire that destroyed the old building. It had a somewhat insalubrious reputation before then, and the directors have been keen to raise the caliber of the entertainment. They will not allow a scandal to bring it into disrepute again. For my part, I hoped that I might be able to create a show to rival Maskelyne's House of Mysteries, but there is no chance of that happening now."

"You are certain this was just an accident," said Holmes, "but yet you sent for me."

His voice came from near our feet, and I looked down to see that while we had been talking he had crouched down on the floor and pulled up the sheet to examine the base of the glass box.

"I need to know what happened," said Lemieux. "I've been over what occurred this evening dozens of times in my mind, and I cannot see that I made any mistakes. I hoped that maybe, with your incredible observational skills, you might spot something that I missed."

"Your assistant was meant to slip out through a trap door before the fire started," said Holmes.

Lemieux looked at me for a moment, clearly loathe to reveal any of the secrets of his tricks in front of a stranger. Then he sighed and nodded, before explaining for my benefit.

"She was meant to have escaped safely before the fire started. I would create the illusion that she was still in the box, struggling, using shadow puppets lit by the flames. She would provide the cries of distress from the safety of her hiding place."

220

"Then I need to see the trapdoor," said Holmes. "I assume it is this way."

Then, without waiting for a reply, he set off, leaving Lemieux and me to trail in his wake.

For a moment I thought the police constable might join us, but he clearly had no interest in finding out what had really happened as he just shrugged and left us to explore the theatre without him.

Holmes led us to an area below the stage. He quickly located the point directly beneath the glass box and started to examine the trapdoor mechanism. As he worked, I questioned Lemieux about the trick.

"I am surprised the solution to your trick is as simple as a trapdoor," I said. "People must have guessed."

"Did you examine the base of the box when we were on the stage?" asked Lemieux, and I shook my head. "During my act, I draw the audience's attention to it. The box is held half a foot above the ground. You can see all the way underneath it during the trick, or at least the audience think they can, therefore ruling out the possibility that my assistant might escape that way."

"You actually draw attention to the escape route," I said, incredulously.

"Of course, and after I have done so, nobody thinks to look at it again. As Holmes said, the key to an illusion is misdirection. You need to make the audience see what you want them to see."

"You make it sound so simple," I said, "just like Holmes when he is explaining his deductions."

"The two have much in common," said Holmes. "The difference is that Lemieux's stage illusions rely not only upon his skills, but upon precisely engineered machinery, like this trapdoor."

Using a broom that he had found in the area below the stage, Holmes struck the boards above his head and a trapdoor dropped open.

"As you can see," said Lemieux, "the mechanism is working perfectly. It is the first thing I checked after the accident."

"You need to look more closely," replied Holmes. "Can you see how the side of the box is hanging over the edge of the trapdoor? I don't believe it is meant to be like that."

"No," replied Lemieux, "the measurements are precise. The trapdoor should fit perfectly within the base of the box. However, you are right, someone has moved it."

"Just one inch, yet it is enough to cover the catch from above. When your assistant went to effect her escape, she would have been unable to reach it, leaving her trapped above as you set fire to the box."

221

"So because somebody knocked the box slightly out of position, she couldn't use the trapdoor?" I asked. "What a tragic accident."

"It is a tragedy," replied Holmes," but I don't believe it can have been an accident. The placement is too precise. No, someone did this deliberately."

As we tried to understand his shocking revelation, Holmes led us back up towards the stage.

"Who could have engineered such a cruel death for that poor girl?" I asked as we walked.

"I cannot believe any of my colleagues here in the theatre would have done such a thing," replied Lemieux. "Everyone loved Helena."

"Yet it must have been one of them," said Holmes. "The perpetrator needed to be intimately acquainted with the mechanics of your trick. A stranger couldn't possibly have conceived such a plan."

Lemieux thought for a moment. "The people who knew the trick best were myself and Helena, but we can be certain that she wouldn't have engineered her own death, and of all the people here, I'm the one with the most to lose from her death. Nobody will ever allow a magician who let his assistant die back onto the stage."

"Surely other people must have known the secret to the trick?" I asked.

"I suppose so. The mechanism was there on stage for anyone to see, but all the acts tend to keep to themselves. We don't discuss the tricks of our trades with each other."

"You set up the box yourself before every performance?" Holmes asked.

"Well, I checked, but I have help moving it. For something so insubstantial in appearance, it is surprisingly heavy."

Lemieux fell silent as he realised the implications of his statement, just as we reached the stairs back up to the stage. Holmes bounded up the steps two at a time and then hurried out into the centre of the stage, beside the covered box, as though he was a performer about to present his own act.

"Can you all gather around?" he said. I didn't think he shouted, but his voice carried around the whole space, and everyone immediately looked towards him. The performers and stage crew gradually stepped out of the shadows and formed a semicircle facing towards Holmes and out into the auditorium, as though they were about to give a curtain call.

"Thank you all for your patience," said Holmes. "I am sorry that you have been kept here so long, but hopefully you will be able to leave very soon."

"Now see here," said the police constable, stepping forwards to confront Holmes. "I have tolerated your presence here, since M. Lemieux vouched for you, but it isn't your place to decide when these people are free to depart. That is a matter for a real detective."

"I don't think we'll need to wait for a 'real' detective from Scotland Yard to join us. On the contrary, you are quite free to take the credit yourself for solving this murder."

"Murder?" blustered the constable. "That is a very serious accusation to make. M. Lemieux has been reckless, maybe even negligent, but I don't think we can accuse him of murder."

"I'm not accusing M. Lemieux of anything, but there is no doubt that his trick was deliberately sabotaged."

At this revelation, there were gasps of shock from around the stage. Everyone waited to hear who Holmes would accuse of this heinous act – except for Philips, who started to walk towards Lemieux. Once more his fists were clenched, but this time he didn't hold back. He raised his hand and punched Lemieux in the face, knocking the illusionist to the floor.

"You did this!" he shouted. "You couldn't stand the thought that she was in love with me, and not interested in you at all, so you killed her so that I couldn't have her."

Lemieux wiped a trickle of blood from the side of his mouth. I expected him to deny Philips's accusations, but it was one of the other performers who spoke up.

"She told me this might happen." The woman who spoke was one of a group of dancers, wearing matching dresses that I thought seemed a little too short to be worn out in public. "She said she was afraid of him." The other dancers nodded in agreement with her.

"Of Lemieux?" asked the constable.

"No, of course not. She thought of him like a father. I mean Philips. You can see how he is, and it isn't the first time either. Tell him, Stacey, how he pursued you before Helena arrived."

One of the girls, presumably Stacey, looked at the ground nervously, but didn't speak. However, this seemed to be enough of an acknowledgement for those gathered. Other people around the room started to speak up, saying how they had witnessed Philip's obsessive and violent behaviour, their accounts overlapping so that none of them could be clearly heard.

It was more than enough for the police constable. "I think you had better come with me," he said, as he approached the accused man. You can explain how you did it down at the police station."

He reached out to grab Philips, only to realise in that moment that the violent stage hand was much larger and stronger than he was.

"It would be better if you don't try to resist arrest," said the constable, but Philips had no intention of going with him quietly. He pushed the policeman aside, then took one last look at M. Lemieux, still lying on the floor. For a moment, Philips seemed to think about attacking the illusionist one more time, but then he clearly thought better of it as he ran to the edge of the stage. Then he jumped down into the auditorium and ran past the seats, through the doors, and out into the night.

Matters progressed quickly after Philips had left. The constable quite happily accepted the stage hand's flight as an admission of guilt and told everyone that they were free to leave. I was surprised that he made no move to pursue the murderer, but he seemed to think that it wasn't important and that Philips would soon be picked up by his colleagues. He departed to file a report with his superiors at Scotland Yard, and the assembled performers and stage crew wandered out after him, still muttering to each other in shocked tones about what had just taken place.

The Assistant Manager, Mr. Parker, was one of the last to leave. He came over and shook Holmes's hand.

"Thank you for your assistance Mr. Holmes. The theatre is in your debt." Then he turned to M. Lemieux, and pointed to the covered glass box. "You will need to clear this away."

"Have you forgotten," I asked, "that there is a young woman's body in there? It is evidence."

"It's stopping us from opening the theatre. Mr. Morton will be most displeased if it isn't removed before he returns, and you will lose any slim chance that he might allow you to perform here again at some point in the future."

"I will see what I can do," replied Lemieux.

For a moment Mr. Parker seemed to consider pressing the point further, but instead he just said, "Very good," and scuttled out of the auditorium, leaving just Holmes, Lemieux, and myself standing on the stage.

For a moment the auditorium was silent, then Holmes started to clap his hands.

"Bravo. I must congratulate you, Lemieux. Your latest show was meticulously staged. I'm certain that it would have been good enough to fool almost any audience."

Lemieux sighed. "But not you, Holmes. I feared as much, but for a moment I thought I might finally have tricked you."

"The simple tricks are the best. You taught me that, but it seems you failed to learn your own lesson. You tried to make me look in too many

224

directions at once. It would have been better if you had just left it as a tragic accident."

"You're probably right, and I did consider it, but you never saw how bad Philips was. I couldn't bear to think he wouldn't be punished for his treatment of Helena, or that he might start to abuse another woman in the same way."

"Please can you both explain what you're talking about," I said, interrupting them.

"It's quite simple," replied Holmes. "This whole evening was an elaborate trick staged for my benefit."

"That isn't true," said Lemieux. "You might have been the intended audience, but I did this for Helena, not you."

"You presented a compelling case against Mr. Philips. An obsessive and violent man with an intimate knowledge of the stage machinery in this theatre was always going to be the most probable suspect."

"I truly believe it was only a matter of time before he serious hurt her, especially once he found out about her fiancé."

"Sorry," I said, "but if are you saying that Mr. Philips didn't murder your assistant, who did?"

"Nobody. Helena is alive and well," said Holmes. "I would guess that she is currently boarding a train with her fiancé, heading towards their new life together."

"If she is alive, who is the unfortunate soul in that glass cabinet? That is a real body, not an illusion."

"I don't know who she was," said Lemieux. "She was dead and already burned when I acquired her body – the victim of a fire. Her identity was unknown, and she was destined for a pauper's grave. There is an attendant at the morgue who can be persuaded to provide corpses for the right price. This woman has, in death, unknowingly helped a young woman in distress, and will receive a proper and respectful burial, I assure you."

I was relieved that nobody had been killed just to accomplish this illusion. Nevertheless, I was disgusted.

"Why was it necessary to defile this poor woman's body at all? If you wanted to help Helena run away, surely you could have just performed one of your disappearing tricks."

"I considered that," said Lemieux, "but it wouldn't have been enough. Philips was completely obsessed with her. As long as he thought she might still be alive, he would have pursued her."

"And what about Philips? He isn't the most pleasant fellow, but he doesn't deserve to be hunted by the police for the rest of his life for a murder that never happened."

"Remember what I told you when we arrived at the theatre, Watson," said Holmes. "Nothing here is as it seems. That wasn't a real police officer. He was Helena's fiancé." He turned to Lemieux, who nodded in confirmation.

"I know you had to involve him in order to release the trapdoor and put the corpse in Helena's place," said Holmes, "but he wasn't a good enough actor to fool me, and his uniform was obviously fake."

"I worried about that, but he was the only person we could trust, and it was necessary. Philips would never have fled if he hadn't believed the police were after him. However, Dr. Watson is correct. It would have been too cruel to have him actually arrested. He will have a chance to make a new life for himself – just far away from here."

I turned to Lemieux. "It seems as though you knew Holmes would see through your scheme, so why did you involve him at all? Your fake constable could have solved the mystery, and nobody would have suspected anything."

"But there might have been doubts, whereas nobody will ever question a case solved by the great Sherlock Holmes. Besides, you forget, I am a performer. How could I have carried out my greatest illusion without ensuring that I had a worthy audience?"

The Adventure of the Newmarket Killings
by Leslie Charteris and Denis Green

Sherlock Holmes and The Saint
An Introduction by Ian Dickerson

Everyone has a story to tell about how they first met Sherlock Holmes. For me it was a Penguin paperback reprint my brother introduced me to in my pre-teen years. I read it, and went on to read all the original stories, but it didn't appeal to me in the way it appealed to others. This is probably because I discovered the adventures of The Saint long before I discovered Sherlock Holmes.

The Saint, for those readers who may need a little more education, was also known as Simon Templar and was a modern day Robin Hood who first appeared in 1928. Not unlike Holmes, he has appeared in books, films, TV shows, and comics. He was created by Leslie Charteris, a young man born in Singapore to a Chinese father and an English mother, who was just twenty years old when he wrote that first Saint adventure. He'd always wanted to be a writer – his first piece was published when he was just nine years of age – and he followed that Saint story, his third novel, with two further books, neither of which featured Simon Templar.

However, there's a notable similarity between the heroes of his early novels, and Charteris, recognising this, and being somewhat fed up of creating variations on the same theme, returned to writing adventures for The Saint. Short stories for a weekly magazine, *The Thriller*, and a change of publisher to the mainstream Hodder & Stoughton, helped him on his way to becoming a best-seller and something of a pop culture sensation in Great Britain.

But he was ambitious. Always fond of the USA, he started to spend more time over there, and it was the 1935 novel – and fifteenth Saint book – *The Saint in New York*, that made him a transatlantic success. He spent some time in Hollywood, writing for the movies and keeping an eye on The Saint films that were then in production at RKO studios. Whilst there, he struck up what would become a lifelong friendship with Denis Green, a British actor and writer, and his new wife, Mary.

Fast forward a couple of years . . . . Leslie was on the west coast of the States, still writing Saint stories to pay the bills, writing the occasional non-Saint piece for magazines, and getting increasingly frustrated with RKO who, he felt, weren't doing him, or his creation, justice. Denis Green, meanwhile, had established himself as a stage actor, and had embarked on a promising radio career both in front of and behind the microphone.

227

Charteris was also interested in radio. He had a belief that his creation could be adapted for every medium and was determined to try and prove it. In 1940, he commissioned a pilot programme to show how The Saint would work on radio, casting his friend Denis Green as Simon Templar. Unfortunately, it didn't sell, but just three years later, he tried again, commissioning a number of writers – including Green – to create or adapt Saint adventures for radio.

They also didn't sell, and after struggling to find a network or sponsor for The Saint on the radio, he handed the problem over to established radio show packager and producer, James L. Saphier. Charteris was able to solve one problem, however: At the behest of advertising agency Young & Rubicam, who represented the show's sponsors, Petri Wine, Denis Green had been sounded out about writing for *The New Adventures of Sherlock Holmes*, a weekly radio series that was then broadcasting on the Mutual Network.

Green confessed to his friend that, while he could write good radio dialogue, he simply hadn't a clue about plotting. He was, as his wife would later recall, a reluctant writer: "He didn't really like to write. He would wait until the last minute. He would put it off as long as possible by scrubbing the kitchen stove or wash the bathroom – anything before he sat down at the typewriter. I had a very clean house." Charteris offered a solution: They would go into partnership, with him creating the stories and Green writing the dialogue.

But there was another problem: *The New Adventures of Sherlock Holmes* aired on one of the radio networks that Leslie hoped might be interested in the adventures of The Saint, and it would not look good, he thought, for him to be involved with a rival production. Leslie adopted the pseudonym of *Bruce Taylor*, (as you will see at the end of the following script,) taking inspiration taking inspiration from the surname of the show's producer Glenhall Taylor and that of Rathbone's co-star, Nigel Bruce.

The Taylor/Green partnership was initiated with "The Strange Case of the Aluminum Crutch", which aired on July 24th, 1944, and would ultimately run until the following March, with *Bruce Taylor*'s final contribution to the Holmes Canon being "The Secret of Stonehenge", which aired on March 19th, 1945 – thirty-five episodes in all.

Bruce Taylor's short radio career came to an end in short because Charteris shifted his focus elsewhere. Thanks to Saphier, The Saint found a home on the NBC airwaves, and aside from the constant demand for literary Saint adventures, he was exploring the possibilities of launching a Saint magazine. He was replaced by noted writer and critic Anthony Boucher, who would establish a very successful writing partnership with Denis Green.

Fast forward quite a few more years – to 1988 to be precise: A young chap called Dickerson, a long standing member of *The Saint Club*, discovers a new TV series of The Saint is going into production. Suitably inspired, he writes to the then-secretary of the Club, suggesting that it was time the world was reminded of The Saint, and The Saint Club in particular. Unbeknownst to him, the secretary passes his letter on to Leslie Charteris himself. The teenaged Dickerson and the aging author struck up a friendship which involved, amongst other things, many fine lunches, followed by lazy chats over various libations. Some of those conversations featured the words "Sherlock" and "Holmes".

It was when Leslie died, in 1993, that I really got to know his widow, Audrey. We often spoke at length about many things, and from time to time discussed Leslie and the Holmes scripts, as well as her own career as an actress.

When she died in 2014, Leslie's family asked me to go through their flat in Dublin. Pretty much the first thing I found was a stack of radio scripts, many of which had been written by *Bruce Taylor* and Denis Green.

I was, needless to say, rather delighted. More so when his family gave me permission to get them into print. Back in the 1940's, no one foresaw an afterlife for shows such as this, and no recordings exist of this particular Sherlock Holmes adventure. So here you have the only documentation around of Charteris and Green's "The Adventure of the Newmarket Killings" . . . .

Ian Dickerson

The Adventure of the Newmarket Killings

Originally Broadcast on February 12th, 1945

CHARACTERS
- Sherlock Holmes
- Dr. John H. Watson
- Jack Ryan
- Joan Everett
- Pop Casey
- Ike McDougall
- Marc Blaine
- Guy Everett
- Driver
- Announcer (Bruce Campbell)

SOUND EFFECTS
- Rattle of horse carriage
- Carriage drawing to a stop
- Carriage door opening
- Footsteps on earth
- Whinnying of horse
- Scuffle
- Scrape of chairs
- Galloping hoofbeats
- Crack of whip
- Splintering of wood

CAMPBELL: Petri Wine brings you –

MUSIC: THEME (FADE ON CUE)

CAMPBELL: Basil Rathbone and Nigel Bruce in *The New Adventures of Sherlock Holmes.*

MUSIC: THEME (FULL FINISH)

CAMPBELL: The Petri family – the family that took time to bring you good wine – invites you to listen to Doctor Watson tell us about another exciting adventure he shared with his old friend, that master detective, Sherlock Holmes. You know, the lives of Holmes and Watson weren't always filled with action. They spent many a quiet evening at home in Baker Street discussing the problems of the world over a glass of port. It seems that no wine is more expressive of friendship and hospitality than port. And I'm sure there is no port wine more enjoyable than Petri California Port. Try a good glass of Petri Port after dinner some evening, or anytime you get together with your friends. You'll love the rich ruby-red color of that Petri Port. You'll love its smoothness and full body, and it's remarkable and wonderful flavor a flavor – that comes straight from the heart of luscious, handpicked grapes. Serve that Petri Port alone, or serve it together with cake or cookies or with fruit. Yes, and serve it proudly. You can, because the name Petri is the proudest name in the history of American wines.

MUSIC: *SCOTCH POEM*

CAMPBELL: And now for our weekly visit with the genial Doctor Watson. Let's see if he's –

WATSON: (INTERRUPTING – FADING IN) Now don't say "Let's see if he's expecting us." You know I'm always expecting you on Monday evenings, Mr. Campbell. Come in and make yourself comfortable.

CAMPBELL: Thank you, Doctor. And how are you this evening?

WATSON: I'm in splendid health. Thank you, my boy. Took a long walk this afternoon, and this evening I was down feeding my chickens. Had to mix up some special mash for the little'uns,

CAMPBELL: I didn't know you kept chickens, Doctor.

WATSON: Certainly, Mr. Campbell. When Sherlock Holmes retired, he took to bee farming, but I thought chickens would be a little bit more in my line. (CHUCKLING) Anyway, I never did like honey. But you haven't come here to listen to my views on farming. You want a story, I suppose.

CAMPBELL: That's all right, Doctor. Last week you told us it centered around a famous racehorse.

231

WATSON: It did, Mr. Campbell, it did. His name was Panama, and he was one of the finest pieces of horseflesh I ever saw in my life.

CAMPBELL: And you've seen quite a lot of horse flesh in your life, eh, Doctor?

WATSON: Yes, I have. In fact, you might say that horses have played a very important role in my life. If it hadn't been for a horse, I might not be sitting here in California tonight.

CAMPBELL: How did you figure that one out, Doctor?

WATSON: The murderous Ghazis. If it hadn't been for the devotion and courage shown by my orderly, a fellow named Murray –

CAMPBELL: That's right, Doctor. He threw you across a pack-horse and brought you back safely to the British lines, didn't he?

WATSON: (A LITTLE GRUMPILY) I see I've told you that story before.

CAMPBELL: I'm always glad to hear it again.

WATSON: No, Mr. Campbell. Tonight, I think I'll concentrate on telling the story of the horse, Panama.

CAMPBELL: Just how did you and Sherlock Holmes become involved in the affair?

WATSON: An urgent telegram arrived one morning as Holmes and I were browsing over a rather late breakfast. The message was from a young fellow by the name of Jack Ryan at Newmarket, and it requested my friend's immediate help and promised a big fee. We weren't very busy at that time, and the prospect of a few days on the Sussex Downs promised a pleasant change. And so, early the next morning found Holmes and myself in an open carriage, approaching (FADING) the Ryan stables . . . .

SOUND EFFECT: RATTLE OF CARRIGE IN BACKGROUND

WATSON: (ENTHUSIASTICALLY) The country here is beautiful, y'know, Holmes. The little red-and-grey roofs of the cottages, and

232

the farms peeping out through the trees over there. So peaceful and soothing.

HOLMES: (MOROSELY) Do you know, Watson, that it's one of the curses of having a mind like mine. I observe everything in relation to my own particular job. You look at those scattered houses and are impressed by their beauty. I look at them and think how easily crime may be committed there.

WATSON: Good Lord – crime with a spot like this?

HOLMES: It's my belief, Watson, based on my experience, that the lowest and vilest alleys in London do not present a more dreadful record of sin than does the smiling countryside.

WATSON: What a depressing thought.

HOLMES: The reason is very obvious. The pressure of public opinion can do in the city what the law cannot accomplish. There is no alley so dark that the scream of a tortured child, or the thud of a drunkard's blow, does not obtain sympathy and indignation from some neighbour. But look at these lonely houses – think of the deeds of hellish cruelty, the hidden wickedness, which may go on, year-in, year-out, in such places, and no one the wiser.

WATSON: 'Pon my soul, Holmes! You're in a particularly gloomy mood.

DRIVER: (OFF A LITTLE) 'Ere you are, gentlemen. These are the stables. (CALLING) Whoa, Nellie! Whoa, gel!

SOUND EFFECT: CARRIAGE DRAWING TO STOP

HOLMES: (AFTER CARRIAGE HAS STOPPED) Can you tell me where I might find Mr. Jack Ryan, driver?

DRIVER: Right over there, sir, by the fence. Talking to the young lady in the blue dress.

SOUND EFFECT: CARRIAGE DOOR OPENS

HOLMES: Thank you. Come on, Watson.

SOUND EFFECT: FOOTSTEPS ON EARTH

WATSON: By Jove, that's a very pretty girl with young Ryan.

HOLMES: Yes, and judging by his expression of doglike devotion, I think
we may assume that it's . . . well, that it's not his sister.

WATSON: (*SOTTO VOCE*) He's seen us –

JACK: (ABOUT THIRTY – OFF, CALLING) It's Mr. Holmes and
Doctor Watson, I'm sure.

HOLMES: How are you, Mr. Ryan?

JACK: (FADING IN) A great deal better for seeing you on my premises,
Mr. Holmes. (RAISING HIS VOICE) Joan, dear . . . .

JOAN: (FADING IN. YOUNG, WELL-BRED) Yes, Jack?

JACK: I want to introduce these gentlemen to you – Mr. Holmes and
Doctor Watson. This is Miss Joan Everett.

AD LIB: *HOW D'YOU DO'S*

JOAN: I've heard so much about you both. I do hope you'll be able to help
Jack.

WATSON: We shall do our best, Miss Everett,

JOAN: I'm sure you will. And now, I don't want to seem rude by running
away as you arrive, but I really must get home. I just took a canter
over here before lunch.

WATSON: I hope we shall see you again during our stay here?

JACK: Don't worry, Doctor Watson, you will. (OFF A LITTLE) Bye,
darling. I'll be over later.

JOAN: (FADING) All right, Jack. (RAISING HER VOICE) Goodbye!

HOLMES AND WATSON AD LIB: *GOODBYES*

234

WATSON: (AFTER A MOMENT) Miss Everett's a very charming young lady, if you don't mind my saying so.

JACK: I like your saying so, Doctor. And now, supposing we take a little stroll and I'll tell you what's been on my mind.

HOLMES: Just what I was going to suggest myself, Mr. Ryan.

JACK: (AFTER A MOMENT) Mr. Holmes, I came down here five weeks ago – when my father was killed.

HOLMES: I remember reading about it,· He was kicked to death by his own horse – Panama, wasn't he?

JACK: That was the coroner's verdict.

WATSON: You say that as though you don't agree with it, Mr. Ryan.

JACK: I don't. But let me tell you the story from the beginning.

HOLMES: Please do, Mr. Ryan.

JACK: Well, I haven't much knowledge of how a racing stable is run – even though my father was one of the most prominent trainers on the turf. In fact, until his death, I had been studying in London to be a doctor. But I felt it my duty to come down here and try and take care of things – for a while, at least.

HOLMES: I quite understand. Please continue.

JACK: I arrived here to find that Panama – the horse, that is – supposed to have killed Father – is the favorite for the Wessex Cup race to be run in two weeks' time. I didn't suspect anything wrong at first, although several of the stable-hands told me that they didn't believe Panama was a killer – that he was the sweetest-tempered horse they'd ever handled. But three days ago, Mr. Holmes, one of the grooms was kicked to death in Panama's stall – just as my Father was.

WATSON: Sounds to me as though the animal is a confirmed killer. Some horses are, y'know.

235

JACK: I know that, Doctor. But you see this time, although the local coroner dismissed it as another accident, I insisted on attending the autopsy. The mark of the horse's shoe was clearly distinguishable. The toe of the shoe had smashed the groom's temple above the left eye – and the heel had split his nose.

HOLMES: So naturally you suspected foul play.

JACK: Of course.

WATSON: I don't see how you deduce that.

HOLMES: (IMPATIENTLY) It's obvious old chap. Mr. Ryan, how many people are employed here at your stables at the moment?

JACK: Three.

HOLMES: And who are they?

JACK: Mark Blaine – Father's assistant trainer. Fred Bates, Panama's jockey for the Wessex Cup, and old Pop Casey, a groom who's been with my father ever since he started training horses.

HOLMES: I see. Would it be possible to go to the stables and meet these people?

JACK: Of course, though I imagine you'd like to come over to the house first and settle yourselves in.

WATSON: (MUMBLING) Must say I could do with a wash and a bit of something to eat.

HOLMES: And I – if you don't mind, Watson – would like to go to the stables first. Now, don't look grumpy. Your appetite will be all the keener for a slight delay.

MUSIC: BRIDGE

JACK: These are the stables, gentlemen. I might as well begin by letting you take a look at Panama – since nearly everyone except me seems to think he's a killer.

HOLMES: Hello – One of your grooms appears to be having trouble with
somebody.

WATSON: Yes – looks like he's throwing him out.

JACK: It's Pop Casey, my head groom . . . and the little fellow's Ike
McDougal – a bookie! Come on . . . .

CASEY: (FADING IN. ABOUT FIFTY. IRISH . . . HEATEDLY) You
keep away from here, Ike, d'you understand?

IKE: (WHINING COCKNEY, ABOUT FORTY) I ain't doing nothing.
Just takin' a look-see.

CASEY: You keep your dirty long nose outa here . . . or else I'll punch it
for you! Go on! Be off with you!

IKE: (FADING) What are you afraid of? Might steal one of your 'orses?

CASEY: Good morning, Mr. Jack.

JACK: Morning, Pop.

CASEY: It's sorry I am about that, Mr. Jack. That's the third time I've
caught Ike McDougall snooping around here. Next time I'll really
give him what-for.

JACK: Pop, these two gentlemen are Mr. Sherlock Holmes and Doctor
Watson. They've come here to try and solve the mystery of Panama's
two killings.

AD LIB: *HOW DO YOU DO'S*

CASEY: I'm glad to meet you, gentlemen, but if you don't mind my
saying so, there's no mystery about it.

HOLMES: I'm glad you think so, Mr. Casey.

JACK: Pop's been with the Ryan Stables since I was a child. He knows a great deal more about horses than I do. Just the same, Pop, I'm not at all satisfied that those deaths were accidental.

CASEY: Come over here, gentlemen, and look in his stall.

SOUND EFFECT: FOOTSTEPS. WHINNYING OF HORSE (FADING IN)

CASEY: There y'are, gentlemen. Meet Panama.

WATSON: (ADMIRINGLY) What a beautiful animal! Doesn't look like a killer, I must say.

CASEY: Don't let looks deceive you, sir. He seems friendly enough, but just let him get you alone in his stall like he did your poor Father, Mr. Jack, and Joe the groom, and you'll find out he's just a plain killer.

BLAINE: (ABOUT FIFTY. GRUFF) (FADING IN) Rubbish! Panama's the sweetest-tempered horse in the stable.

SOUND EFFECT: HORSE WHINNYING

JACK: Hello, Marc. I'd like to introduce Mr. Sherlock Holmes and Doctor Watson. Mr. Marc Blaine, my head trainer.

BLAINE: How d'you do, gentlemen. Jack told me you were coming here.

HOLMES AND WATSON: AD-LIB *HOW D'YOU DO'S*

JACK: Pop, you better get about your work instead of trying to spread the story that Panama's a killer.

CASEY: (FADING) You mark my words - that horse is bad Just let him get you alone and you'll find out.

BLAINE: Silly old fool! I think it's high time you got rid of him, Jack.

JACK: I wouldn't want to do that, Marc. He was with Father over twenty years, you know.

BLAINE: Yes, and that is about twenty years too long, if you ask me.

238

HOLMES: Mr. Blaine, is Panama given to rearing?

BLAINE: I've never seen him do it, and I've known him since he was foaled.

HOLMES: Then undoubtedly you are right, Mr. Ryan, in supposing that your groom was not accidentally killed the other day,

WATSON: I don't see how you deduced that, Holmes.

HOLMES: It's obvious, my dear chap. You will remember that Mr. Ryan attended the autopsy. The toe of the horse's shoe had smashed his temple above the left eye and the heel had split his nose.

WATSON: But I still don't see . . . .

HOLMES: Oh, come now, Watson. A horse kicks up with its hind legs. Therefore, if it had been an accident, the hoof marks couldn't have been in that position on the groom's face.

WATSON: He might have been bending down.

HOLMES: Bending down? No, old chap. He would have had to be standing on his head, and I think we may rule that possibility out. Mr. Ryan, I understand that Panama is the favourite in the Wessex Cup Race?

JACK: Yes, he is, Mr. Holmes.

HOLMES: Is there anyone who might have a special interest in ruining his chances?

JACK: (HESITANTLY) Well, I don't –

BLAINE: Oh, come now, Jack, you know as well as I do that the only horse that'll give him any real competition is King Cole – Guy Everett's horse.

WATSON: Guy Everett? Any relation to the Miss Joan Everett that you introduced us to just now?

239

JACK: Yes, her father. But it's ridiculous to suggest that he'd have anything to do with this business.

BLAINE: Is it? If you ask my opinion –

JACK: (INTERRUPTING) I didn't –

BLAINE: I'll give it to you just the same. I think that Guy Everett'd give his right arm to win the Cup, and I don't think he'd be too scrupulous about how he did it!

JACK: (HOTLY) That's a lie!

BLAINE: Just because you're in love with his daughter, there's no need to close your eyes to things, Jack. If you knew as much about horse racing as I do, you'd realize that sentiment and business don't mix. (FADING). See you later.

JACK: Mr. Holmes, I hope you don't believe what's he's suggesting.

HOLMES: At this stage, I don't believe or disbelieve anything.

JACK: Personally, I don't trust Marc himself. He only joined Father a few years ago, and I've heard some strange stories about him.

HOLMES: I see. By the way, Mr. Ryan: I should like to meet Guy Everett – the rival owner. Would that be easy to arrange?

JACK: Extremely. I was going over to have tea with Joan this afternoon. Why don't both of you come along?

HOLMES: Splendid, eh Watson?

WATSON: Oh, yes, splendid. But tea sounds a long way off. I was wondering if perhaps we might have a little luncheon first.

MUSIC: BRIDGE

SOUND EFFECT: CARRIAGE DRAWING TO A STOP

JACK: Well, here we are, gentlemen. These are Mr. Everett's stables.

240

WATSON: Beautiful place, Mr. Ryan – even larger than your own, aren't they?

JACK: Yes, but then Mr. Everett's record on the turf has been a lot more successful than my father's, I'm afraid.

SOUND: CARRIAGE DOOR BEING OPENED

JACK: We might as well leave the carriage here and walk up to the house. It's only a few hundred yards.

HOLMES: A little walk will give you another appetite for your tea, Watson.

SOUND EFFECT: FOOTSTEPS ON EARTH

WATSON: (AFTER A MOMENT) I didn't need a walk to give me – Hello! What's going on over there?

SOUND EFFECT: VOICES RAISED IN ARGUMENT (OFF)

WATSON: Good gracious me! It's that bookie fellow again – the one that was thrown off your place this morning, Mr. Ryan.

JACK: Yes – Ike McDougall! And he seems to be receiving the same treatment here.

WATSON: Something of a coincidence, wouldn't you say?

HOLMES: He's coming this way. (RAISING HIS VOICE) Afternoon, Mr. McDougall.

IKE: (FADING IN) 'Oo are you . . . ? *Aow!* Hello, Mr. Ryan. (STARTING TO FADE) Sorry I can't stop now, gents. I got a train to catch.

HOLMES: (FADING A LITTLE) No you don't, Ike –

SOUND EFFECT: SLIGHT SCUFFLE

IKE: Take your 'ands off me! I ain't done anything!

HOLMES: (COMING BACK ON) Then there's no reason why you should mind having a chat with us.

IKE: What d'you want to know?

HOLMES: This is the second time today I've seen you being thrown out of stables. What's the game, Ike?

IKE: The game? Same game that everyone plays around 'ere, Guv'nor – 'orseracing. Only I'm on the other end of it – the bettin' end. I'm a bookie.

HOLMES: I know that. But why do you spend your time skulking around the stables?

IKE: Tryin' to get tips, of course, Guv'nor. I have to try and work the odds so that I come out on the right side of the book . . . whoever wins the race. (SUDDENLY) Blimey! 'Ere comes Mr. Everett . . . I gotta get movin'. (FADING) Good day to you, gentlemen.

EVERETT: (FADING IN) (ABOUT FORTY-FIVE, POMPOUS) Be off with you, McDougall! And if you show your face here again, I'll have you arrested!

JACK: Hello, Mr. Everett.

EVERETT: (HIS TONE CHANGING COMPLETELY) Jack, my boy! Forgive me. I was so busy throwing that scoundrel off the place I didn't notice you and your friends.

JACK: May I introduce Mr. Sherlock Holmes and Doctor Watson.

AD LIB: *HOW D'YOU DO'S*

EVERETT: You must forgive my display of temper, gentlemen, but I cannot tolerate bookies. They've done their best to ruin what should be a fine, clean sport . . . Are you going to have tea with Joan?

JACK: Yes, Sir.

EVERETT: Then I'll walk up to the house with you.

242

WATSON: I understand, Mr. Everett, that your horse, King Cole, is one of the favourites for the Wessex Cup.

EVERETT: He's a favorite, Doctor, but if young Jack's Panama runs true to form, I know who'll win the Cup.

HOLMES: May I ask if you're a betting man, Mr. Everett?

EVERETT: (STIFFLY) I never bet, sir. I race for the fun of the game, and I'm always glad to see the best horse win – even if it's not wearing my colours.

JACK: You've had a pretty good record of wins, sir – compared to Father.

EVERETT: Your father was very unlucky, my boy. He had fine horseflesh . . . but he seemed to be dogged by bad luck. In fact, I sometimes wonder – (STOPPING HIMSELF) Hmm . . . but that's another matter. There's Joan out on the terrace. Go and join her, gentlemen. (FADING) I'll be with you in a few minutes.

JOAN: (OFF – CALLING) Hello, Jack!

JACK: Hello, Joan. I brought visitors.

JOAN: (FADING IN) Mr. Holmes – Dr. Watson – I'm so glad to see you again. Sit down, won't you? I thought it was warm enough to have tea out here on the terrace.

SOUND EFFECT: SCRAPE OF CHAIRS

WATSON: Thank you, Miss Everett. Charming place you have here.

JOAN: It is nice, isn't it? Mr. Holmes, have you been able to find out anything since you arrived?

HOLMES: Very little, Miss Everett, except to confirm Jack's suspicion that the groom's death was not accidental.

JACK: Yes, and the chances are that Dad's death wasn't accidental either.

WATSON: (SUDDENLY) Hello? Who's that galloping up the hill towards us?

JACK: (AFTER A MOMENT) It's Marc Blaine – there must have been trouble!

HOLMES: I'm afraid so, Mr. Ryan.

JOAN: Oh, Mr. Holmes, do you think so?

JACK: (CALLING) What's wrong, Marc?

BLAINE: (OFF, CALLING BREATHLESSLY) You'd better come back at once – It's Fred Bates . . . the jockey.

JACK: What happened?

BLAINE: He was out exercising Panama, and he got thrown. His head was kicked in – *He's dead!*

CAMPBELL: Doctor Watson's unusual story will continue in just a few seconds – time I'd like to take to remind you that one wine that seems to be the outstanding favorite among the ladies . . . is Petri California Muscatel. That's probably because, like a beautiful woman, Petri Muscatel is subtle and intriguing. Petri Muscatel is the color of burnished gold . . . and its flavor . . . Well, it's the flavor or big plumb Muscat grapes – picked by hand – carefully and tenderly when they're just full of wonderful, delicious juice. If you want to show that you really know the wine that *women* prefer . . . serve Petri Muscatel. Serve it after dinner, or later in the evening. It's wonderful – and why shouldn't it be? It's a Petri wine!

CAMPBELL: And now, back to tonight's new Sherlock Holmes adventure. The great detective and his old friend, Doctor Watson, have been called in to investigate the mystery concerning Panama, a famous racehorse that is reputed to be a man killer. Shortly after their arrival at the stables, another death has occurred. Fred Bates, Panama's jockey, while out for a practice canter, has been thrown and then kicked to death by the horse. As we rejoin our story, Sherlock Holmes and Doctor Watson, accompanied by Jack Ryan, the horse's owner, are in a carriage racing towards the scene of the tragedy.

SOUND EFFECT: CARRIAGE RATTLING AT GALLOP, ON EARTH

WATSON: (NERVOUSLY) You're going awfully fast, aren't you, Mr. Ryan?

JACK: I can't make the horse go fast enough for my liking, Doctor. Bates killed . . . it's a terrible business! He's my best jockey, and I counted on him to win the Wessex Cup for me.

SOUND EFFECT: CRACK OF WHIP. RATTLING OF CARRIAGE (UP)

HOLMES: You may not win the Cup, Mr. Ryan, but I think we can hope to solve the mystery of Panama for you. This time we can examine the supposed accident exactly as it happened. Let's hope some blundering fool hasn't moved the body.

SOUND EFFECT: CARRIAGE BEING REINED TO A STOP

JACK: There's Blaine – and there's poor Bates' body. (CALLING) Whoa! Bess! Whoa!

SOUND: WHINNY OF HORSE. CARRIAGE DRAWS TO A STOP. DOORS OPEN

WATSON: (AFTER A MOMENT) There's someone else there . . . It's Ike McDougall, the bookie fella!

HOLMES: He got over here in a remarkably short time.

245

HOLMES: The body hasn't been moved, has it, Mr. Blaine?

BLAINE: (FADING IN) No, Mr. Holmes. It's just the way we found it.

HOLMES: Thank Heavens for that. Mr. McDougall, how did you get over her so speedily? It was only a few minutes ago that we saw you leaving Mr. Everett's stables.

IKE: I got a bicycle, ain't I? I was cycling back this way when I saw Fred Bates out exercising Panama. I stopped and watched him through my field glasses. He wasn't far away from me when he came the cropper . . . so I cycled on over.

BLAINE: That's true. He came up after I was on the scene. I sent Pop Casey off for the local doctor, and told Ike to guard the body, and then came over for you gentlemen.

WATSON: But you didn't see the accident yourself, Mr. Blaine.

BLAINE: No, but I was on the scene a few seconds after it happened.

JACK: And did you see it, McDougall, eh?

IKE: That's right, Guv'nor. Through me glasses.

HOLMES: Please describe the accident.

IKE: Pop Casey was riding Tommy Boy – to pace Panama, who was three or four lengths behind 'im. They were clipping along at a full gallop. Suddenly Panama seems to shy, and Fred Bates comes off. Casey pulls up and goes back to 'im. I jump on me bike – and when I got 'ere, this is what I found.

HOLMES: Hmm . . . let's have a look at the body. (AFTER A MOMENT) I think I'll take the liberty of moving it . . . so . . . .

WATSON: Poor devil! His face smashed in . . . .

HOLMES: (AFTER A MOMENT) You'll notice that the body was lying across a trail of fresh hoofprints. Unless Panama had a fifth leg, he couldn't possibly have kicked this poor fellow.

WATSON: I don't see why not.

HOLMES: Because, old chap, the trail of hoofprints is unbroken, and yet the rider has been kicked three times.

JACK: Isn't it possible, Mr. Holmes, that he could have been kicked as he fell off?

HOLMES: That would have been even more remarkable. How could the jockey have been hit by three hoofs at once – all of them striking him in the head?

BLAINE: Of course, you're right, Mr. Holmes.

HOLMES: By the way, Mr. McDougall, you said that the horses were galloping at the time of the accident.

IKE: That's right, Guv'nor.

HOLMES: And yet these hoofprints are obviously those of a horse cantering. How d'you account for that?

IKE: (CONFUSED) I was only lookin' through me glasses. Remember?

HOLMES: (DRYLY) I see. And even through the field glasses, you couldn't tell the difference between a canter and a gallop. (SUDDENLY) Hello! What's this mark across the jockey's face?

WATSON: (AFTER A MOMENT) It's a long shallow cut . . . It wasn't done with a knife, or even with the sharp edge of a horseshoe – the edges of the cut are *bruised*. (GETTING A SUDDEN INSPIRATION) By Jove! It could have been done with a whip, though.

HOLMES: Possibly, but I doubt it. By the way, d'you notice that the racecourse is very narrow at this point? It can't be more than thirty feet wide.

247

BLAINE: What's that got to do with anything, Mr. Holmes?

HOLMES: I'm not sure, except that the trees on each side of the course make me somewhat curious. (FADING) I think I'll take a little stroll.

IKE: Wot 'ave trees got to with poor Bates gettin' killed? Seems to me your friend's a bit balmy.

JACK: I must say I can't see what Mr. Holmes is getting at.

WATSON: (KNOWINGLY) I don't suppose you do . . . but I think you'll find out before very long. By the way, McDougall – you said that you saw the jockey fall off.

IKE: That's right – through me glasses.

WATSON: What kind of fall did he take?

IKE: He seemed to turn right over in the air as he fell.

WATSON: I see. And Pop Casey was two or three lengths in the lead at the time, you say?

IKE: Yes, Guv'nor.

WATSON: Then Holmes was right. Casey couldn't possibly have reached Bates with a whip.

HOLMES: (FADING IN) No, he couldn't have done, Watson.

WATSON: Did you find anything out?

HOLMES: I found out everything, my dear fellow. And a simple tree gave me the evidence that I required.

WATSON: A tree? But how . . . ?

HOLMES: Have a little more patience with me and I'll give you the answer. I suggest we all go over to the stables, where I think I can prove to you, Mr. Ryan, that your horse is *not* a man killer.

MUSICE: BRIDGE

248

IKE: I dunnow what you dragged me to the stables for, Mr. Holmes. Wot 'ave I got to do with this case?

HOLMES: A great deal, I think.

SOUND EFFECT: DOOR OPEN, APPROACHING FOOTSTEPS

HOLMES: Ah, there you are, Mr. Casey. Is the doctor coming?

CASEY: (FADING IN) Yes, sir. He's on his way.

HOLMES: You're just in time to help us solve the mystery of Panama.

CASEY: There's no mystery. She's just a plain bad horse – a killer. I told you that from the beginning, sir.

HOLMES: I know you did – but I don't think you believe it.

CASEY: Why should I lie to you, sir?

HOLMES: Let me ask you a few questions. Was Ike McDougall here around the stables about the same time that Mr. Ryan's father was killed?

CASEY: Yes. That was the first time that he was thrown out. Mr. Ryan did it himself.

HOLMES: And was killed shortly afterwards. Was Mr. McDougall in evidence three days ago when the groom was killed?

CASEY: Yes, he was. I threw him out myself – just as I did today.

HOLMES: Exactly.

WATSON: You mean McDougall murdered them?

HOLMES: He was vitally concerned in all three murders.

IKE: You're off your chum, Guv'nor – that's wot you are.

HOLMES: Am I?

RYAN: I must say, Mr. Holmes, I wish you'd explain.

BLAINE: So do I. I can't make head or tail of this.

HOLMES: I think you'll find it's really very simple. For years, Ike McDougall has been fixing races – and stable-hands. Your father discovered it first, Mr. Ryan, and got killed in consequence. I imagine the groom was silenced the other day for the same reason. And today poor Fred Bates was killed because he was the best man to ride Panama . . . and because he couldn't be fixed to throw the race.

IKE: But 'ow could I have had anything to do with it? I was a quarter-of-a-mile away when Fred was killed today. And Pop Casey can prove that.

CASEY: That's true, Mr. Holmes.

HOLMES: I can explain that very easily – if you don't mind my searching you, Mr. McDougall.

IKE: (VIOLENTLY) 'Ere! Leave me alone!

HOLMES: Hold him, Watson.

SOUND EFFECT: STRUGGLE

WATSON: I've got him!

HOLMES: Thanks, old chap . . . now let's see . . . Ah! . . . What an unusual belt you wear, Mr. McDougall – several yards of steel wire coiled around your waist. How d'you account for that?

IKE: I . . . I was taking it home with me to mend a fence.

HOLEMS: I see. And naturally you had to keep that startling event a secret, under your coat.

RYAN: Mr. Holmes, I wish I could see what you're driving at. What's that wire got to do with Fred Bates' death today?

250

HOLMES: A great deal, Mr. Ryan. You will remember I examined the trees adjoining the spot where Bates fell today. I found scars on the bark of a tree which, which I coupled them with the long shallow cut on the jockey's face, gave me the answer to how he was unhorsed. It was the wire stretched between the two trees.

CASEY: But that's impossible, sir. I was riding ahead of him. If there had been a wire – Why wouldn't it have unhorsed me?

HOLMES: Because you knew it was there – and ducked when you came to it. In fact, you led Bates into the trap.

CASEY: I don't know what you're talking about, sir.

WATSON: But Holmes, even if he was dismounted that way, how do you account for the hoofmarks on Bates' face?

HOLMES: Oh, those? They were caused in the same way as they were in your father's case, Mr. Ryan, and in the groom's.

RYAN: And what way was that, Mr. Holmes?

HOLMES: If you'll direct me to Pop Casey's tackle box, I think I can show you.

BLAINE: His locker's right there.

HOLMES: The key, please, Mr. Casey.

CASEY: You keep your hand off my things!

HOLMES: Very well, then. It shouldn't be difficult to open. Hand me that shovel, Mr. Ryan.

RYAN: There you are.

HOLMES: This ought to do it.

SOUND EFFECT: SPLINTERING OF WOOD

CASEY: You got no right to do that!

251

HOLMES: There we are! (SUDDENLY) Don't leave us, Mr. Casey! Grab him, Blaine!

BLAINE: (OFF A LITTLE) No you don't, Casey! You stay here!

HOLMES: There's the answer to your mystery, gentlemen.

WATSON: Good Lord! A horseshoe – nailed to the end of a sawed-off pick handle!

HOLMES: Exactly. This is the weapon that killed all three men. It is the only way that the wounds could have been inflicted.

RYAN: But . . . but who did it? Casey or Ike McDougall?

HOLMES: In the case of today's murder – both of them. After the stretched wire had thrown Bates off his horse, Pop Casey went back and finished him off with this instrument. Then he quickly took down the wire and left it for his partner Ike McDougall to dispose of, while he went for the doctor.

WATSON: But we saw McDougall a few minutes before this, over at Mr. Everett's stables.

HOLMES: He had helped Casey lay the trap beforehand, and was over at the rival stables to try and establish an alibi, no doubt.

RYAN: You mean that Pop Casey was in league with McDougall?

HOLMES: Undoubtedly, Mr. Ryan.

Ryan: I can't believe it. He'd been with Father for twenty years or more.

HOLMES: Yes . . . and for twenty years or more your father was supposed to have had bad luck. I think you may find, however, with these two scoundrels where they belong – at the end of a rope – that your luck may change.

MUSIC: UP TO STRONG CURTAIN

CAMPBELL: Say, Doctor, tell me – Did Mr. Ryan's horse, Panama, win the race?

WATSON: Yes – and it might please you to know that I'd put several pounds on his nose and won myself quite a bit of money.

CAMPBELL: Why Doctor, I didn't know you bet on the horses.

WATSON: I don't ordinarily. But this time I couldn't lose.

CAMPBELL: But suppose Mr. Everett's horse had won?

WATSON: (LAUGHS) Don't worry, Mister Campbell. I only bet on a sure thing. Er – you don't happen to *know* about a sure thing, do you?

CAMPBELL: It so happens I do. (CONFIDENTIALLY) Now don't tell this to a soul . . . .

WATSON: I won't.

CAMPBELL: But if you want a sure thing . . . .

WATSON: Yes . . . ?

CAMPBELL: Just bet on the fact that Petri Wine is always good wine!

WATSON: (INDIGNANT) Oh, there you go again!

CAMPBELL: Well, it is, isn't it? You *can* be sure that Petri Wine is good wine . . . because the Petri family has been making wine for generations. They know how. That's because the Petri business has been family owned and operated ever since way back in the eighteen-hundreds. Therefore, everything the Petri family has ever learned about the art of making fine wine – all their skill and knowledge and experience – has been handed on down in the family – from father to son, from father to son. The Petri family knows all there is to know about turning luscious, handpicked grapes into fragrant delicious wine . . . That's fact. So whenever you want wine – a wine to serve before dinner . . . before your meals . . . or for any occasion . . . you can't go wrong with a Petri wine, because Petri took time to bring you good wine! And now, Doctor Watson, d'you feel like giving us an idea of next week's story?

253

WATSON: Next week, Mr. Campbell, I'm going to tell you a strange story that takes place in a sleepy village on the outskirts of London. It concerns a very elusive murderer that had escaped the police for five years – although my friend Sherlock Holmes caught him . . . *in twelve hours.*

MUSIC: *SCOTCH POEM*

CAMPBELL: Tonight's Sherlock Holmes adventure is written by Denis Green and Bruce Taylor and is based on an incident in the Sir Arthur Conan Doyle story, "The Adventure of the Copper Beeches" *[sic].* Mr. Rathbone appears through the courtesy of Metro-Goldwyn-Mayer, and Mr. Bruce through the courtesy of Universal Pictures, where they are now starring in the Sherlock Holmes series.

MUSIC: (THEME UP AND DOWN UNDER)

CAMPBELL: The Petri Wine Company of San Francisco, California invites you to tune in again next, week, same time, same station.

MUSIC: HIT JINGLE

SINGERS: *Oh, the Petri family took the time, to bring you such good wine, so when you eat and when you cook, Remember Petri Wine!*

CAMPBELL: Yes, Petri Wine, made by the Petri Wine Company, San Francisco, California.

SINGERS: *Pet – Pet – Petri . . . Wine.*

CAMPBELL: This is Bob Campbell saying goodnight for the Petri family. *Sherlock Holmes* comes to you from the Don Lee studios in Hollywood. This is the Mutual Broadcasting Network!

CUE: This is Mutual!

The Possession of
Miranda Beasmore
by Stephen Herczeg

"They are saying she's possessed – by a *demon* no less!"

"Preposterous!" I sputtered.

My good friend, Dr. Marcus Nefferson, sat back in his chair. "Any right-minded person would think so, yes." He sipped his coffee before adding, "But the Beasmores are so convinced they are bringing in an exorcist."

"Well, that should be intriguing," said Sherlock Holmes. A wry grin remained on his face as he took a long draw from his own cup of coffee.

"I simply don't know what to think anymore. My medical opinion has been thrown out in favour of the involvement of some sort of witch doctor."

"What brought all this about?" I asked.

Nefferson glanced my way, taking a deep breath followed by a sigh. "Yes, sorry, I jumped straight in without setting out the context." He drained his coffee, placing the cup back on its saucer with a slight clink. Leaning back in the chair once more, he began. "I have been the Beasmores' doctor since well before young Miranda was born. I have always found Julius and Claretha to be the most amicable of people, but extremely prim and proper to the point of priggishness. I generally have assigned the reason to their strong religious outlook. Both are avowed Roman Catholics."

"Intriguing," said Holmes. "That would be something that puts them at odds with the mainstream of Christian theology in this country, but one that I know is on the rise again after so many centuries."

"Quite, but I've never really paid attention to the fact until recently."

"Why?" I asked.

Holding his hands up to quell the questions and bring us back to his story, Nefferson waited until we both had the hint and then continued. "Miranda is central to this. Her parents' obsessions comes later." He took a deep breath and let it out slowly again. From that simple act, I could tell that the story had left his mind in a perpetual state of perturbation and remained silent while he continued. "Miranda was always a jovial and social child, but like so many of her generation, once the teenage years came upon her, that joviality left and was replaced by a dour outward attitude. Of late, she has been more introspective and has sought solitude and a life away from people. When she shunned even the weekly journey to Westminster on Sundays, the Beasmores approached me about Miranda's condition. They attend mass at the Our Lady of Victories Church, and they seem very close to the priest there, Father Rammier – Morris, I think his first name is. I've met him on occasion at the Beasmore house in Kensington."

"So very religious, which is no bad thing in these trying times," said Holmes. "What does this Beasmore do?"

"Lawyer. For his clients' defence, I think. Works out of an office in Belgravia. Anyway, I was dragged into this matter when Miranda's emotional state became much worse. Claretha, the mother, contacted me when she couldn't entice Miranda from her bed. I found the poor girl in a deep melancholy, bedridden and in a virtual delirium. She wouldn't answer any of my questions, and any utterance made little sense. The mother said she had been like it for at least two days, and once had become very violent. All I could do was administer a powder to help her sleep. I could only diagnose a clouding of her consciousness, but I didn't think it was the work of alcohol, as the girl is only fifteen, and her parents do not drink. There was something deeper that seemed to be troubling her."

"When was this?" I asked.

"Almost a week ago. I left the poor thing, with every intention of returning the next day, but things as they may be, that didn't happen for a few more days. By then the parents had decided to take matters into their own hands."

"In what way?"

"When I returned, I was greeted by this priest, Father Rammier. He had the audacity to question my motives. When I said I was simply there to check upon my patient, he remonstrated me, saying that she was in his care now." Nefferson stopped for a moment, collecting his thoughts, and calming a wave of slight anger that had crept into his voice at this remembrance. "I know I shouldn't have, but I pushed past the pesky little man and headed for Miranda's room. What I found shocked me to the bone."

He stopped again. I was well engaged now, so prodded him to continue. "Go on. What is it you saw? How was the girl?"

"Nightmarish," he said, in a whisper, before raising his volume. "The young girl had been bound to the bed by her wrists and ankles. 'What have you done to her?' I shouted and, without turning to the priest, rushed to her side, freeing her right arm from its bond. Rammier grabbed my shoulder and said, 'No, she's too agitated!' I shrugged his hand away and bent towards the girl. Her eyes were closed as if she were asleep, but her breath came in short, ragged gasps. I leant in to examine her but failed to see the right-hand ball itself into a fist and fly at my face. The punch had more strength than I could imagine Miranda possessing and knocked me to the floor. Dazed, I sat up in time to see the priest replace the binding, with quite some difficulty as the young girl thrashed around, uttering curses and mutterings that I could nary understand. Finally, the priest turned to me and said, 'You fool! I warned you!' Feeling the pain in my jaw, I was almost in agreeance. Finding my feet once more, I looked down as Miranda strained at her bonds, eyeing us with looks of pure malevolence, and asked him how long she had been this way. He said that Julius had requested his attendance four nights previous, which was the evening of my last visit."

"Could you tell what was wrong?"

"No. This was a severe change in demeanour that was beyond my experience."

"Why was the priest there?" asked Holmes. "Surely a physician was the correct person to call upon."

Nefferson sighed. "That's where it gets very strange. As I mentioned earlier, the Beasmores are very religious. They have a predilection for calling upon God, and his servants upon this world, in times of need such as this. When the father, Julius, arrived in the room, he bade us both leave and join him outside. There he told me that my services would not be required just then. I was shocked. I protested, stating that the girl was obviously unwell and in a state of mind both harmful to herself and others. I suggested that she be taken to a sanatorium for the proper treatment. I was taken aback – Julius seemed to chuckle in mirth at my suggestion, before composing himself and saying that all was in hand. They had sent for someone that would be able to assist and cure Miranda of her ills."

"Really? Who?" I asked, surprised that a layman would be called upon, or even another doctor. Nefferson was one of the finest physicians that I knew of.

"An exorcist."

I laughed out loud, before stopping and calming myself. Even Holmes had a wry grin on his face. "An exorcist? This is the nineteenth century, not the Middle Ages."

"That was almost precisely my reply to Julius, but he was convinced. He stated without any hint of humour that they believed Miranda to be possessed by a demon from Hell."

"Preposterous."

"Yes. Any right-minded person would think the same, but the Beasmores are not of that mind. And this Rammier fellow simply re-enforced their view, and added his own take on the subject, hammering home all that the church said about demons and Satan and such." Nefferson dropped his head and shook it slowly. "I was raised to believe in God. I attended church throughout my formative years. I'll admit that once I became a man of science, my beliefs wavered, but I've never lost them altogether. But this, this *devotion* that the Beasmores have to their beliefs is beyond anything I've ever seen. Add to that their acceptance, without question, that whatever troubles young Miranda can be – and *is* – a demon . . . ."

"Hmm," murmured Holmes. "I can see that their position would put you in a very difficult situation. A physician, forbidden to help his patient because of some primitive adhesion to outdated religious doctrine."

"That is part of it, though the next part of my story will emphasise my concern greatly."

"Oh, there's more?" I asked. "Go on then."

"Yes. Two days ago, the exorcist arrived."

I shuffled forward in my seat. My interest had been piqued, but was now bordering on fascination.

"I can only tell you that I don't think I've ever seen another priest like this man. He flounced into the Beasmore residence like an actor entering the stage in the final scene of an Elizabethan farce."

"My word."

"Yesterday I attended the Beasmore residence, hoping to simply undertake one of my regular visits to appraise Miranda's condition. While still in the entranceway, there was a ring of the bell, and as soon as the door opened, this vision erupted into the place. He announced himself, with a thick Italian accent, as Father Ernesto Tinnerello. He was all flowing capes and scarves, not like the quiet and demure priest beside him. I found out later that he had been sent to England by the Vatican as part of a study tour, inspecting the ancient Catholic churches that had survived Henry VIII's purges. This gave me less impression of the man than his entrance. He did not seem the type to lead an archaeological or anthropologic sort of life.

"As I mentioned, he was the exorcist. Once the introductions had finished, I asked what his interest in the case was. He simply said that he had been asked to exorcise the demon and send it back to Hell. I must admit that I scoffed at the suggestion. It had been up until that point that I had merely seen the Beasmores' insistence on demon possession as some sort of sick fantasy, but with the appearance of Tinnerello, it was clear they intended on performing some form of rite to cleanse Miranda."

"And did this not worry you from a physician's standing?" I asked, appalled at the primitive nature of the goings-on.

258

"Of course it did!" Nefferson replied in a terse tone of voice. "I knew that I had to tread lightly. There was some form of mass hysteria in the house, but I strongly suggested that I should remain in case of any untoward medical problem arising. Julius almost showed me the door, but Claretha insisted that I be present, if not to provide medical assistance, but also to be assured that nothing untoward would occur."

"And what did occur?" asked Holmes.

"It was horrible." Nefferson leant forward for a moment and dropped his head into his hands. Holmes and I looked at each other before I stood and moved to the sideboard. Bringing back three glasses and the decanter, I poured us all a stiff brandy.

"I know it's a little early, but I feel you could be well in need of this," I said, offering the brandy snifter to my friend. Looking up, he took the proffered glass gratefully and downed the fiery liquid in one swig.

"Thank you, John. I think I needed that." I refilled his glass, before placing the decanter on the table and sitting down.

After taking a long breath, Nefferson continued. "Without a word or a whisper with anyone, Tinnerello requested access to Miranda's room. He was immediately led upstairs to the young girl. I followed in his wake, ensuring I wasn't restricted from entering the room, and huddled into a corner to give me as good a view of proceedings as I could. My worry was for the child, not the theatrical display that I was about to witness." Nefferson took a sip from his brandy. "Rammier assisted the exorcist, holding the other's satchel while several items were removed and placed on a table near the bed. I spied a leather-bound copy of the Bible, a glass bottle filled with clear liquid, and a large brass crucifix. My eyes fell on the girl. She slumbered, ignorant of the goings-on around her. My heart went to her, and I hoped that she would remain asleep through whatever would transpire. I was wrong."

I shifted in my seat and had to know. "Did they wake her on purpose?"

"I'm unsure, but the Italian moved to the bed and studied the poor girl for a moment or two, before leaning over and whispering. The effect was immediate. Her eyes snapped open, and a raging snarl rang out across the room. Miranda's eyes locked on Tinnerello, and a stream of abuse left her mouth that would make a fishwife blush. I spied her parents and noticed their faces aghast in horror, unsure whether at Miranda's words or the fact that she had said them in the first place."

"Interesting. I'm intrigued how a young girl of such a delicate nature would come by such language," Holmes said, his face showing more amusement than horror.

"Indeed."

"What happened next?" I asked.

"The exorcist snatched up his crucifix and Bible and, holding them before him, extorted Miranda's sneering form with a stream of Latin. I haven't even heard the language since my school days, so all I could pick up were the odd word or two. Many references to God, to Satan, and such like."

"Did it have any effect?"

"Yes, but quite the opposite to what was expected, I assume. Miranda almost flew into a fit of rage. Her face became a snarling visage of pure hatred. Obscenities leapt from her mouth. As she strained at her bonds, I grew concerned that she might injure herself. I moved forward, but Rammier moved in front of me, blocking my way and holding a hand up to my chest. 'Do not disturb Father Tinnerello until he has finished.' I tried to push past, but the girl's father joined the little priest and grasped my arm, further restraining me. I felt that if I tried any harder things might turn ugly, so I relaxed and maintained my distance, gritting my teeth at the display before me."

"Good Lord."

"If only he had some say in it, but this was either the work of man – or worse," Nefferson added. "As Miranda thrashed and spewed her vile insults at the priest, he continued, expelling further monologues and prayers in archaic Latin, which only elicited more snarls and expletives. All at once, Tinnerello stopped and turned back to his satchel. Withdrawing some long-tapered candles, he lit them, filling the room with a pungent, but not unpleasant, perfume. I caught a hint of lavender and assumed that the Italian was attempting to elicit a soporific quality from the use of their odour. He placed the candles at various places in the room, before picking up the small glass bottle. Nodding towards me, he said it contained Holy Water, blessed by Leo XIII himself. The Beasmores whispered *Il Papa* under their breaths and crossed themselves. A strange display of devotion, in my mind."

The doctor paused for a moment, sipping from his brandy and taking a deep breath before continuing. "Whatever was in that bottle, it certainly had an effect. Tinnerello uncorked the bottle and poured a small amount into his palm. Placing the bottle down, he proceeded to flick the Holy Water across Miranda's form, whilst reciting another Latin prayer." Nefferson stared at Holmes for a moment. "What happened, I still can't explain. As the Holy Water touched Miranda's skin, white foam cascaded out of her pores. She screamed as if in pain."

"Did you intervene then?" I asked

"No," he said, his head hanging down in shame. "I know I should have, but I was so intrigued by the spectacle that I found myself rooted to the spot. The bubbling didn't last long, and soon the exorcist wiped the remaining water on a cloth and leaned into Miranda. He whispered into her ear and drew a small cross on her fevered brow. Within moments, she quietened down and fell into a slumber, much to my and her parents' relief. After a moment, Claretha asked whether it was over. To my disappointment, Tinnerello shook his head and said, 'No, the demon inside her is far stronger than thought: One of the major lieutenants of Lucifer's army – Pazuzu, or even Beelzebub. I am unsure. This will take much longer than I had planned. I may even require further assistance from Rome.' Julius stated that he didn't care. Any expense would be met."

I noticed Holmes's expression change at the mention of money. "Expense?" he asked.

"Yes. It seems that these things don't come cheap. The church is all well and good when the coffers are simply filled through the weekly services in their parishes, but these extra duties are costed separately."

"Do you know how much?"

"No. There were no figures thrown around, but I can only assume from Julius's stern look that it was not a small amount."

"Did you examine the girl afterwards?" I asked.

"Yes. She was sleeping deeply. I could almost have assumed she'd been drugged, but I never saw anything administered, so put it down to simple exhaustion."

"Quite so."

"Did you find out when the next session was to occur?"

"Why, yes. Tomorrow night in fact. When Tinnerello suggested tonight, I baulked and said that for the good of the patient she should be allowed to rest after such exertions. The parents actually agreed with me, much to Tinnerello's consternation."

"Good, good. Do you think you would be able to arrange for Watson and me to attend as observers? Perhaps state that you fear for Miranda's mental health after any repeat and would prefer if two of your colleagues could observe. Naturally we will assure them that we will not interfere in any way."

"I will try." He paused for a moment, his anger brewing slightly. "No, of course I will. I'm her physician. If this Italian fellow threatens the safety of my patient, then I will do everything in my power to stop it. You have my word. I will set off directly for the Beasmore residence, first to check in on Miranda, then to ensure that you are allowed access tomorrow night."

"Excellent." Producing a pen and notepad, Holmes asked, "Could you write down the Beasmore address and the time of the ritual, and we will meet you tomorrow night."

Nefferson jotted down the details before sliding the pad and pen across to Holmes, who read it quickly. My doctor friend rose to say his goodbyes but was greeted with one last question. "This Rammier – you mentioned that he had a close relationship with the family. Do you know if he is entertained at their house outside of his clerical duties?"

"Oh yes, the little fellow is there quite often. The Beasmores seem to draw upon his influence as if he can tap into the thoughts of God. As I have stated, I'm no atheist, but this over-reliance on not just the word of God, but also the word of the church, is disturbing to the logical mind."

"Indeed," I replied.

The sun had all but disappeared, bringing with it a late autumn chill, when I found Nefferson standing before the modest three-story Georgian terrace that was the Beasmore residence. The location of their home, in the well-to-do area of Belgravia, spoke loudly about their affluence, which surprised me even more given their reliance on the church for comfort and assurance.

"You didn't mention how well off this family was during your tale," I said to my friend.

Turning to take in the ambience of the house, he replied, "I suppose I hadn't thought of it. I'm fortunate enough that most of my patients reside in premises such as this."

"One wonders how many others take a special interest," I muttered, my mind awash with all sorts of nefarious villains that would be only too willing to take advantage of this family's prosperity. Bringing my thoughts back to the subject at hand, I asked, "Have you had contact with the Beasmores today?"

"Why yes. I performed my regular morning call to check up on Miranda's health and spoke with Claretha. I thought it more prudent to talk with the mother than the father, as he tends to be the more stubborn of the pair. Claretha was at first concerned at bringing in more strangers, but I posed to her that you and Holmes would be as discreet as possible, and would be there as observers, acting only in the direst of circumstances."

"Good. I haven't seen Holmes all day and do hope that he is circumspect in both his manner and garb." As I scanned the area, my concerns evaporated. Holmes strode down the street, resplendent in a morning suit with a matching overcoat, much the same as Nefferson and I wore. I'll admit that my profession isn't one to overdress, but my fellows and I do like to maintain a suitable level of attire.

"What ho, Watson!" Holmes said as he approached, nodding to Nefferson by way of greeting.

"Ah, Holmes, good. Any person on the street would see the three of us as colleagues attending to the same call-out."

"What story have you concocted for our beleaguered family, Nefferson?"

"To ease the concerns of our hostess, I've presented you and Watson as specialists in the study of the mind. Your attendance here tonight will be strictly observational, as part of a favour to me."

"Good," said Holmes. "I merely wish to witness this ritual – mostly to satisfy my curiosity before forming any opinions or producing any solutions."

"Do you wish to discuss what you've been up to for the last day-and-a-half?" I asked.

"At this stage, no. You should know that I'll only announce my findings once I'm fully convinced of the facts." I nodded, expecting exactly that answer. "However, I do have questions." Speaking to Nefferson, he continued. "This Rammier fellow – have you known him long?"

Nefferson nodded. "Only as part of my ministrations to the Beasmore family. He does seem to play a significant role in their lives. He's a regular visitor to this house, and I've found him here quite often now that my cycle of visitations has increased."

"But outside of this immediate circle, you know nothing of him?"

"True. Priest. Catholic. Moderately young. Nothing more really."

Holmes nodded and filed the information away.

"Why?" I asked.

"Nothing for now. Simply building as much of a picture of all the players as I can. The Beasmores? Julius, the patriarch? As far as I can tell, a righteous pillar of society. Lawyer. Well regarded amongst his peers. Money is all his, no inheritance. Puts all his success down to his diligent adherence to the Catholic faith and doctrine."

"Why yes, that would describe him perfectly."

"It's strange though that those who have the most faith are sometimes the same that have the most fears."

"Intriguing thought," added Nefferson.

Once inside, the pleasant atmosphere offered by the house's façade all but evaporated. Luckily, we were first greeted by Mrs. Beasmore who, armed with her prior knowledge, regarded both Holmes and me in an amicable manner. It was upon meeting Mr. Beasmore and the priest, who I immediately found to be extremely sycophantic to the former, that a chill grew in the air to such an extent I was surprised that clouds of vapour didn't appear any time a person spoke.

"Nefferson, I do not see the point of these gentlemen being here," said Julius Beasmore upon our introduction.

"Now, now, dear," said his wife. "I expressed you would have that exact opinion to the Good Doctor when he asked me. I, however, think differently. I would be much more comforted if we have someone here to assist in any medical emergency that may arise. Miranda has slept for two straight days after the last encounter with Father Tinnerello. She hasn't even spoken. I'm very worried about her."

"It's the demon," Beasmore rounded on his wife. "You know that as well as I do. The doctor has failed, it is now for the church to succeed where medicine cannot."

"And I completely understand, Julius, but I will be much more relaxed knowing that we have some of the very best medical minds on hand, in case of anything untoward." The emphasis that Mrs. Beasmore placed on indications of herself in that statement caused Julius Beasmore to wince, and I could immediately tell who held the most sway within the Beasmore family.

Eyeing all three of us with a stare that could have shot bullets, Julius Beasmore retreated up the stairs followed by the rat-like priest. It appeared that the exorcist had already arrived well before all three of us and was already in the girl's room.

"That actually went better than I thought," said Claretha Beasmore quietly, much to my surprise. "Julius does stick solidly to his opinions but will usually accept my advice, albeit begrudgingly." A wry grin came to her face. "He knows how to keep a happy house."

Entering Miranda's room, I was shocked to find the exorcist, resplendent in all black, except for the white dog collar of a priest around his neck, standing next to a sideboard. Nefferson had described him for us, but in person, he was even more of a presence.

"And who are these two fellows?" Tinnerello asked.

"My wife has insisted that these two . . . two doctors, I suppose," Mr. Beasmore struggled to name our fictional profession.

"Psychiatrists," said Holmes, stepping forward and offering his hand to the Italian. "Doctors Holmes and Watson at your service." The exorcist took his hand, shaking it lightly, a confused look on his face.

"Why do we need 'Sickiatrists'?" he asked, his accent slurring the word.

"I have no idea," said Beasmore.

"It was my idea," said Nefferson. "I am still Miranda's physician, and the last rite that you performed left me worried about her mental state. I

264

asked my friends to accompany me here today, to determine if my worries have some foundation."

Waving us away and into the far corner, Tinnerello added, "Fine, but please stay out of the way. There is not much room in here, and I cannot be held responsible for you."

Holmes and I shuffled into the far corner and settled in to watch the proceedings. It was then my sight fell upon the subject of the evening's events. For a girl in her mid-teens, she looked a very poor figure in the bed. Her arms were tied up with soft material to the bedhead, and her feet likewise were bound to the foot. Even in that seemingly uncomfortable posture, she was fast asleep, but her eyes vibrated rapidly behind her closed lids. She was dreaming – a strange state given the description we'd heard from Nefferson. I had expected to see a snarling, violent creature hell-bent on eviscerating all within her reach, not the quietly slumbering form that lay before me.

It was then that a chill ran up the length of my spine. The day had been cool, but the temperature in that room was icy. Breathing out, I half-expected to spy a dense cloud of mist before my face. Glancing at the window, I noticed it was shut, but the external shutters were open. It may be that they had been open prior to our arrival. I rubbed my arms to get the blood flowing.

"The chill is strange, isn't it?" whispered my friend. Looking to my right, I found Holmes standing resolute, observing all the preparations that Tinnerello undertook. The Italian bent to his satchel, sitting on a small table, presumably brought in for that purpose. Out came the crucifix, the leather Bible, and a small glass bottle filled with a clear liquid, supposedly Holy Water. "Intriguing – this fellow must have a store of that Pope-blessed water."

"Why do you say that?"

"The bottle is full. I can only assume that he used copious quantities during the previous ritual."

"You are right," said a surprised Nefferson. "I remember the bottle contained only half that amount at the end of our last meeting."

The exorcist moved around the room, lighting four wax candles and filling the room with the thick but sweet odour of lavender, before picking up his crucifix and Bible and approaching the slumbering girl.

Holding the crucifix only inches above the girl's face, he began a Latin incantation in a low murmuring voice. "*In nómine Pátris, et Fílii, et Spíritus Sancti.* Amen." Finishing with a wave of the crucifix along the four points of the cross, leaving his hand in place at the lower point for a moment. I noticed the girl's eyes flicker before the priest began to incant once more. "*Exsúrgat Deus et dissipéntur inimíci ejus: Et fúgiant qui*

265

odérunt eum a fácie ejus." A low growl emanated from the girl, with her eyes flickering as she began to wake. "*Sicut déficit fumus defíciant. Sicut fluit cera a fácie ígnis, sic péreant peccatóres a fácie Dei.*" The girl's eyes snapped open. A terrified look crossed her face as if waking from a dream into a nightmare. She pulled tentatively at her bonds, a questioning glance at each of her hands. "*Miranda!*" the exorcist snapped. The girl's eyes locked onto his face.

The Italian's voice became deep and commanding, he barked what seemed to be an order. "*Quisquis hanc puellam regit, me aspice! Derelinquamus!*" The effect was immediate. Miranda spat a stream of abuse at the priest. I picked up a few words – most sounded like Latin, but I couldn't be sure. She thrashed at her bonds, straining at each in turn. I stepped forward, afraid she would cut herself. Holmes placed a hand on my chest, restricting my advance. A quick glance at his face was met with a shake of the head.

"Let us observe," he whispered.

Tinnerello repeated the phrase. I listened intently, but my knowledge of conversational Latin was very rusty. I did pick up words for "*eyes*" or "*sight*", and for "*leave*" and "*girl*". I could only assume that it was a command aimed at the supposed-demon to withdraw. Instead, Miranda snarled and snapped, hurling lines of abuse, some in Latin, some in English, at the exorcist. After goading the demon with the same phrase once more, and receiving nothing but a foul stream of swearing, the Italian moved back to the small table, placing the Bible and cross down before retrieving the bottle.

Pouring some of the Holy Water into his left palm, he approached Miranda. "*Virtus Christi urget te!*" he shouted, before flicking the water at the girl, repeating several times and receiving the same responses. Screams came from the girl as if she was driven to agony by the water's touch, and the white bubbling of some effluent flowed from Miranda's pores as the water splashed across her delicate skin.

I cried in anguish, looking from the girl to the parents to my friend. Holmes stood stock still, his hand resting beneath his chin, one finger extended up to his cheek, taking in every detail that could be drawn from the performance before him. When no change appeared in his attitude, I meekly turned my attention back to the outrageous display before me.

The effervescence on Miranda's skin had dissipated, and Tinnerello was back at his table. He wiped the Holy Water off his hand before stepping back towards the girl, who lay with her eyes closed, breathing heavily after her exertions.

The exorcist bent close to the girl, whispering in a voice so low that I could barely hear anything he said, and certainly unable to make out the

266

words. The girl's breathing calmed. With his right thumb, Tinnerello drew a cross upon Miranda's head before touching her top lip and chin. Miranda seemed to slip into a deep sleep, almost immediately.

Rammier stepped up next to his colleague and assisted in clearing away the tools of the trade. Sneaking a glance at Holmes, I hoped to see evidence of his opinion on the matter. He remained resolute, his eyes glancing at the supine figure of the girl before returning to the two priests.

"Well, what did you make of all that?" Nefferson asked.

We stood by the street, outside the Beasmores' front door. Holmes remained quiet, thoughtful. "I'm simply shocked," I said. "I don't know what was more concerning – the strange and awful language coming from that girl. The rage she showed as she struggled against her bonds, or simply the pain that she showed as the ritual went on." I took a breath, still struggling with my own emotions after such an occurrence.

"I agree," said Nefferson. I've never seen someone lose their mind so rapidly, without any form of external stress. Unfortunately, I cannot have her committed unless her parents consent to it. The explanation of possession is all we have at this stage, until I have an actual psychiatrist examine the girl and declare her insane."

My anger welled as I remembered the pain that the girl had suffered during the exorcism. "I'm livid. How can any parent even conceive to allow their child to be subject to such as we saw? Surely after this, they will only be too happy to have her taken somewhere appropriate where she can be treated for her condition. As loathe as I am to admit it, we may have actually witnessed a truly supernatural experience, in which a young girl has been possessed by a demon from the depths of Hell," I said, shaking my head slightly at my own realisation, "but this is not the type of care she should receive."

"Well, I do agree, but as I have explained, Miranda's parents are staunch in their beliefs. I went almost as far as begging them, but my pleas fell on deaf ears. It was all I could do to ensure I was on hand in case anything untoward occurred that threatened the safety of the girl."

"I find it barbaric. Ancient rituals to solve a problem that cannot exist. And to no effect. As you heard, Tinnerello stated that he needs to perform the rite again, as per the doctrine."

"So what happens then? If the third time does not work? Do we simply fob this off as a supernatural problem?"

"What say, you Holmes?" Nefferson asked my colleague.

"I have read of so-called cases of devil possession in some esoteric texts associated with the church, and this had all the hallmarks of such." Smiling a wry grin, Holmes added, "But I will continue to gather all the evidence I need, in order to eliminate every contrary angle. I never dismiss anything, however improbable."

"Foolishness!" huffed my medical friend.

"Do not be hasty to judge," offered Holmes. "I have been presented with many unnatural events, all of which have been found to have their origins in the perfectly normal. There are many elements to this case which may go against that, but there are also numerous probable answers to every uncertainty."

"Then I do hope you discover them quickly."

"Fear not. Even from what I have seen so far, I have severe doubts as to the authenticity of these claims of demons. Let me dig further over the next day or so."

"Should we attend the next ritual?" I asked.

"Oh, yes. I believe that is paramount to the investigation. If there are no mystical causes behind all this, then I would hope to have discovered the causes before this so-called Italian exorcist continues with his unearthly practices."

"Good," said Nefferson. "I'll ensure that you are allowed witness to the supposed 'final' rite. I caught glances of Claretha's horrified face, and I'm sure she is as worried about Miranda's health as she is about her soul. Julius, on the other hand, may be a more delicate matter, but he does defer to his wife on most domestic matters, so that should be fine."

"We shall meet here at the same time in two days, then," said Holmes, and with that, we strode away to find a hansom.

All through the next day, my mind kept replaying the perplexing series of events that we had witnessed. I longed to discuss them in detail with Sherlock Holmes, but was drawn away by a call from a patient and didn't return until later that evening. By then Holmes was nowhere to be seen. I could only assume that he was investigating some matter or another.

In fact, we didn't cross paths again until the next morning where, upon rising from my bed, I came downstairs and found him engaged in several experiments at his chemistry table. As I sauntered across the room, I noticed the bubbling flasks and a small pamphlet on the edge of the table. It was an advertisement for some sideshow in the East End. I gave it no mind and turned my attention to the experiments.

"Good morning. What do you have there? Need I ask?"

Turning, Holmes smiled at me in his enigmatic way and nodded, indicating the bubbling mixtures before him. "You can and you should. These flasks contain several items and chemical compounds drawn from the room – and person of one Miranda Beasmore."

"What?" I said, astounded and fully showing it upon my face, I expect. "How? How did you retrieve those?"

"Ah, well. Let us say that I may have needed to bend the rules of engagement a little. It appears that young Miranda's parents have a habit of visiting their church of an evening. By chance, as I stood outside the house, observing as much as I could from without, I saw them leave. The house itself went rather dark and silent, the servants having retired, so I took the opportunity to enter and make my way to Miranda's room. She was well asleep, probably sedated from one of Dr. Nefferson's tinctures. Having memorised the room during our encounter, I was able to avail myself of samples of the supposed Holy Water, and other possible chemicals used in this play."

"Really? What have you found?"

"I've identified nothing so far. I will require further analysis until I can be completely satisfied."

"As always," I added, "so I shan't rush your examination."

"You may find me missing this afternoon," he explained, "so I will meet you at the Beasmore residence tonight. I have several other avenues to follow up before we attend this final exorcism."

"Very good," I said. "Where else have your investigations taken you?"

Another smile. "Oh, but that would be telling before I have confirmed. I won't suppose on things until I have the evidence and facts before me."

Nodding, I stated, "Yes, I know that, but sometimes I like to be included in the picture."

A slight chuckle emanated from his angular mouth. "Oh, you will be my friend, you will be."

"Have you solved it, Holmes?" asked Nefferson. His face seemed more drawn from worry than on our previous meeting.

"I believe that I'm very close. I would like to see this ritual at least once more to satisfy myself on a few salient points."

"Good. Well, let's hope it is only the one time. I stayed up all last night with worry over the health of that poor girl. She has barely spent an hour awake over the last week. Either I've administered powders to help calm her down, or the stress of these so-called exorcisms have sent her into deep unconsciousness. Sleep is good for the body and mind, but like anything, too much can have dire effects."

"On that point, have either of you brought your medical bags?"

269

I shook my head. I hadn't due to the pretence that we were observers and doctors of the mind, not physicians. To my relief, Nefferson nodded and showed us the satchel that sat behind him, obscured from view.

"Never leave home without it – especially when I visit this place."

"Good, good. I think we may need some of your stimulants once the rite has been performed."

As we entered Miranda's bedroom, the atmosphere became even chillier than the ambient temperature of the room would suggest. Tinnerello, Rammier, and Julius Beasmore all regarded us with piercing stares but begrudgingly bade us enter and move to the same corner as we occupied on the previous evening. Claretha remained in the doorway, her eyes locked with her husband's, in a provocative stare waiting for any resistance to our presence. When he turned away from her look, I knew we would receive no further anguish from Julius.

It was the Italian that voiced his annoyance, but also his reluctant acceptance. "Well, we have an audience once more. Fine. Please, again, do not interfere or make any sound. This third execution of the ancient ritual of exorcism will either rid our beloved Miranda of the foul demon within, or we will lose her forever." Pointing an accusatory finger at us, he added, "It is upon your shoulders how this will progress." I thought long and hard about a response but decided that discretion was the better part of valour and remained silent.

The exorcism routine started as it had the night before. Four candles were placed around the room and lit, filling the area with the almost overpowering and cloying perfume of lavender or some such flower. The girl, Miranda, was silent, still bound by her soft restraints and lost to a deep sleep. It was only when Tinnerello leaned over and whispered in her ear did her eyes flicker open in that same stunned and disoriented way.

It was only as the priest approached with his crucifix and Bible, invoking his Latin chant, and his voice grew louder did Miranda's demeanour change. Within seconds, she went from wild-eyed fright into full-on raving demon-child, sprouting all manner of vile curses and snarling and snapping at the priest as if she was a bound animal, not a young girl.

As the priest droned on, the girl's manner remained. Curses and snarls filled the room, followed by cries of pain as the Holy Water was splashed across her skin, resulting in the same effervescence and bubbling as the previous night. On the final invocation, Tinnerello grasped Miranda's snarling face, holding his hand across her mouth and nose, while repeating a Latin incantation. Finally, the girl's eyes closed, and she fell back into a deep slumber.

270

Silence fell once more upon the room. The only sound came from Tinnerello as he returned his items to the satchel.

It was Claretha that broke the peace. "Is that it? Is the demon gone forever? Will my little girl return to me?"

The Italian shrugged. "I tried to stare into her eyes and see the demon's soul leave, but there was nothing, so I do not know yet. She will rest. I shall return in the morning and perform the last test. If all is well, she will be herself. If not, then I shall consult with the church to determine the next course of action."

"And how much will that cost?"

"What was that?" Tinnerello asked, turning towards Holmes, the source of the question.

"I simply asked how much this next course of action would cost?"

"I don't think that is any of your business," said Rammier.

"That is true, but I understand that the Roman Catholic Church does not charge the members of its congregation for such services as exorcisms." Turning towards Julius Beasmore, whose face showed an expression of surprise, he asked, "How much has Senor Tinnerello requested from you, sir? Five-hundred pounds?"

"A thousand," stammered Beasmore. "But I don't care how much I pay, as long as my Miranda comes back to me, whole and unblemished by this unnatural interloper."

"Ah," said Holmes.

"It is not for me," said Tinnerello. "It is simply to cover my trip to England and the tools of my trade." He looked once at Beasmore, who nodded, then with one last glance at Holmes, Tinnerello turned to consult with Rammier.

I noticed Holmes whisper to Nefferson, who reached for his medical satchel and within moments handed something to my friend. The detective immediately moved across to the bed and sat down next to the reclining figure of Miranda. He unscrewed the lid on the small bottle Nefferson had handed him and held it beneath the sleeping girl's nose. Within a few moments, her eyelids flickered and opened.

"Welcome back, Miranda," Holmes said.

"What are you doing?" shouted Tinnerello, rushing to the bedside. "She needs to rest! The demon has plagued her mind. We need to keep it silent."

Miranda looked around the room, her gaze resting on each person in turn, a confused expression growing on her face.

Her mother stepped forward. "Miranda?"

"It isn't her!" shouted Tinnerello. "It is the demon! Your daughter is in there, but the fiend controls her."

Holmes rose and stepped back. "I apologise for this, my dear girl, but . . . ." He took a deep breath and then repeated one of the Latin phrases Tinnerello had said during the exorcism. "*Quisquis hanc puellam regit, me aspice. Derelinquamus.*" Every person in the room gasped as Miranda, once again, turned from a mildly confused teenage girl into a snarling animal, spouting curses and swear words at all and sundry.

"What are you doing?" shouted Tinnerello. "You have awakened the demon. The girl is in grave danger."

"Is she though?" said Holmes. He bent close to Miranda's snarling face and spoke another Latin phrase. "*Angelus dormies somnum!*" Immediately, Miranda slumped into a deep sleep.

I expected Tinnerello to shout at Holmes once more, but his face was a mask of shock. "How do you know the rites of exorcism? You are not an ordained priest. It is blasphemy for a layman to repeat those phrases!"

"Except that they do not belong to the rites of exorcism, do they?"

"What?" said Julius Beasmore. "What do you mean by that? We've all heard them said here over the last few days. The Father has spoken perfect Latin, and you've seen the effects they have had on the demon within my dear Miranda."

"Ah, yes, that is true, Mr. Beasmore. We have all heard some Latin phrases," said Holmes, pulling a small leather-bound volume from within his jacket pocket. Holding it up, he asked Tinnerello, "Have you seen one of these before, Father?" The priest stood still, unmoving. "You should have. Especially given your station in life." Thumbing through the volume, Holmes added, "This is a copy of the *De Exorcismis et Supplicationibus Quibusdam*. The book which outlines the actual rituals of exorcism, sanctioned by the Roman Catholic Church. I obtained this copy from Cardinal Manning. You would know him as the Archbishop of Westminster. He was very interested in my story about a priest from Rome undertaking exorcisms in the London area."

As I turned to face the priest, I noticed Tinnerello edging towards the doorway. As he reached out for the doorknob, another hand slammed against the door jamb and stopped it from opening. Claretha Beasmore's face was stern, her posture showing an inner strength that belied her slight frame. "I think you should stay, Father. I'd like to hear more from Dr. Holmes. I'd also like to hear an explanation in your words as well."

The supposed Italian's expression dropped. He turned meekly and stood, summoning up as much courage as he could to face his accuser.

"Go on, Doctor," said the Beasmore matriarch.

"It seems there is no record of a Father Tinnerello working here in London – but we shall get to his identity in a moment."

"I knew he was an imposter," said Rammier.

Holmes turned to face the little priest. "I don't think you should be trying to cast an image of innocence, Father. Westminster didn't have any complimentary words for you either. In fact, they were extremely interested to hear that you were also involved in this little escapade as well."

"But – but I . . . I – " stammered Rammier, before closing his mouth lest he put his foot further into it.

"What in the blue blazes is going on here?" cried Julius Beasmore, his face flushed red with anger. "How dare you come into my home and accuse men of the cloth of some egregious act for which you have no proof." He stepped towards the bed and indicated his sleeping daughter. "My daughter is ill – has been for weeks! We have all seen with our own eyes that she is possessed by a demon – a demon that this man – " He pointed to Tinnerello. " – recognised and hopefully has vanquished through the words of the Lord."

"Julius!" snapped Claretha. "Quiet! Let the man speak."

Julius Beasmore's expression changed to abject fear at his wife's voice. I was most impressed at the hold she had over him, though I did feel a little hint of pity for the man. He was mostly bluff and bluster, but was firmly held under his wife's thumb.

"Can you explain what has gone on, Doctor Holmes?" she asked.

"I will also identify myself. It's a good time for it. My name is Sherlock Holmes, as you know, but I am not a physician. I am a consulting detective. Doctor Nefferson requested my involvement, fearing that your daughter might be subject to ill-treatment as part of these rituals." He indicated to me. "This is my colleague, Doctor John Watson – an actual physician, but of the body, not solely of the mind."

He looked from face to face, biding his time and taking in the expressions each before continuing.

"Now, what has gone on here is a charade. Nothing more, nothing less. Your poor daughter has been subject to manipulation of the mind by these two loathsome scoundrels."

"What?" asked Julius. "But Rammier here is a priest. He has been one of our closest confidants for years."

"No doubt – but sometimes even the most pious of men can become tempted by the lure of a better life. Is that not right, Father?" Holmes stared at Rammier, who remained silent, his expression fixed.

"To the ritual played out before us: I'm afraid that this little affair has been ongoing for quite some months. Your daughter's attitude has changed of late, is that right?"

"Yes," said Claretha, "she has grown ever more sullen and withdrawn ever since she turned fifteen."

273

"And you have relied on Father Rammier to console and confide in her, as part of his representation of the church, is that right?"

"Yes. He has been a true comfort to not just Miranda, but all of us as well."

"Is that right, Father?" Holmes directed his question at the quiet priest. "Or have you been preparing Miranda all these many months for this final *denouement* of your plan?"

"What do you mean?" blurted out Julius.

"It was all his bloody idea!" said Tinnerello, pointing at Rammier and suddenly losing his accent and revealing one of a much broader East-End origin.

"Oh, I already know that, don't I, Father Rammier?"

The little priest's head dropped as he realised the game was up.

"What are you going on about?" asked Julius. "This is all very confusing."

"Let me explain, then. Father Tinnerello here is a *mesmerist*. In fact," Holmes stepped towards Tinnerello, "you are better known as 'The Amazing Ernesto'. Isn't that, right? Mr. Ernest Sinister, formerly of the Casartelli Circus from Italy, after spending many years performing in Astley's Amphitheatre, here in London." He slipped the small page I had seen on his chemistry table from his pocket and unfolded it. Nefferson glanced at it, reading quickly.

"I don't believe it," cried Nefferson. "A bloody circus act?"

"Yes. Sinister here was expelled from the Italian circus about five years ago and ended up back in London. He has made a name for himself in the East End as a small-time act in some of the music halls. That is where I believe you may have seen him, Father Rammier? Was it about six months ago? A few weeks before Miranda's emotional state began to surface?"

The priest looked up momentarily before dropping his eyes once more.

"Good Lord!" said Beasmore.

"Ah, yes, I think so," continued Holmes. "After observing Sinister's act on several occasions, Father Rammier conceived his idea. You trained the priest in mesmerism, well enough to seed some vital phrases into poor Miranda's mind. Isn't that, right?"

The mesmerist's face was a mask of grief. "I . . . I didn't know what he was going to do? He promised me money, I . . . I never thought we would hurt anybody?" Sinister dropped his head and stared at his feet.

"This is impossible!" cried Beasmore. "My Miranda? The snarling – the cursing. The rage!"

274

"All implanted in her mind by Father Rammier. It took a second viewing of their act to deduce the phrases and actions, but I feel I have most of them worked out. I brought Miranda out of her sleep with the use of some smelling salts from Doctor Nefferson's bag. Then the phrase I said out loud was one of those that triggered Miranda's delirium and rage. The second was the one used to put her back to sleep. I didn't however use the ether that Sinister has administered as the last part of the ritual, I didn't feel it was required."

"But – but – the bubbling on her skin from the Holy Water!" asked the girl's mother. "Surely, that must be demonic?"

"Ah, now that was clever." Holmes moved around to the bed and pulled a small flask from an inner pocket. "You could not fail to have noticed the lighting of the heavily scented candles that preceded the ritual. That was to mask three significant odours. The smelling salts to rouse her, the ether to subdue her, and this."

Holding up the bottle he uncorked it and dripped several drops of the liquid on Miranda's exposed flesh. Immediately, it began to bubble and sizzle on her skin.

Beasmore groaned.

"A simple chemistry trick. Miranda's skin was prepared with a concentrated solution of sodium bicarbonate. This is vinegar. The acid hitting the alkaline results in the bubbling as we can see. A harmless reaction, except for a minimal amount of heat, but when dressed up as Holy Water splashing onto the skin of a demon-possessed girl, quite a striking effect. The vinegar would have stung our nostrils if it hadn't been for the lavender scent on the air."

"Quite so. This whole affair has been, actually"

"That's quite devilish," said Nefferson.

"And the room's colder temperature?" I asked.

"Frozen carbon dioxide – dry ice – packed into the false priest's bag. It caused enough of a temperature difference that, in that atmosphere, it felt noticeable."

I started to ask another question when the front doorbell rang. A smile grew on Holmes's face. "Ah, Watson, could you? They are right on time."

Within moments I returned with Lestrade and Bradstreet in tow. They were accompanied by a dour-looking man in his fifties, dressed all in a black cassock, with a white priest's collar.

"Ah, good. It's a little crowded, but can you please join us. Bishop Althorp?," Holmes indicated the man in black. "This is Father Rammier. I think you'll be wanting to ask him a lot of questions."

The bishop stared down his nose at the little priest. His anger was palpable. He pivoted towards Julius. "Firstly, I think I will talk with Mr. and Mrs. Beasmore and offer the full apology of the Catholic Church."

"I do hope that the poor girl will regain her senses. Nefferson has had her committed to a sanatorium for the time being, until all this clears from her mind," I said, as we relaxed in the sitting room with late-night brandy and cigarettes.

"Yes. She will need complete rest, and hopefully, Lestrade can pry out of Rammier and Sinister all the phrases they used on the poor girl. Sinister seemed amicable to helping, but Rammier proved himself far more nefarious than his unwitting accomplice."

Nodding, I added, "Well, I'm certainly glad that you unearthed a solution grounded in reality. I am a little sorry that I even entertained the idea that the poor girl was possessed by a demon, but her mental downfall was so sudden and so complete that I couldn't easily fathom any other answer. I can understand why the Beasmores gave it so much credence."

"Some people, no matter their station in life, do sometimes need the comfort of the spiritual realm to make sense of what happens to them in the real world." Holmes took a sip of brandy, a slight grin on his face in response to my own beliefs.

"Bravo. Yes, I am impressed that you approached the matter without any thought of giving credibility to the demon possession angle." I took a drink, before settling back and musing. "I know that over the years, you have been presented with many intriguing cases, supposedly exhibiting some form of supernatural origin, but have always found a rational explanation. Surely there must exist within your mind something that longs for the day when you shall be proven wrong and be presented with something that seems impossible and otherworldly and does indeed exist in the realm of the unknown, and no matter how much you examine it or all the clues you unearth in the quest for knowledge, nothing can drag the solution into a logical and sensible conclusion. Am I right?"

Holmes's face grew stern. I noticed him pause and gaze at me for quite some time before he uttered a single word answer in response.

"No."

The Adventure of the
Haunted Portrait
by Tracy J. Revels

"Mr. Holmes, can a young person be killed by fear?"

The inquiry was spoken by one of the loveliest women ever to grace our Baker Street sitting room. Miss Hannah Sutton was as small and delicate as the first bloom of springtime, crowned with a perfect halo of golden hair. She was clad in the height of fashion, from her hat with its ostrich feature to her mauve walking dress and superbly embroidered gloves. From the moment she entered our chamber, she radiated kindness, curiosity, and, I do confess, a strange vulnerability that made me wish to be her defender. Holmes had, inevitably, noted my attraction. His immunity to female charms perhaps added to his amusement at my admiration. Meanwhile, the lady's mother – stout, ill-clad, and sour-faced – glared at us from her perch upon our divan.

"The Good Doctor would, of course, answer that a sudden bolt of terror, imposed upon a sensitive nervous system, could be fatal," Holmes said. "A man with a weak heart might be done in by such a shock, though the cause of death would be the malfunctioning organ. Fear places an enormous strain upon the body and the mind – no doubt it has led many an invalid to his doom. But for a healthy person to perish from fear alone is impossible."

"See," Mrs. Sutton hissed at her daughter. "I told you there was no such thing. Now we can cease wasting this gentleman's time and return to our shopping."

Holmes held up a hand. "Far be it from me to intrude on your pursuit of items for your trousseau," he chuckled, "but my curiosity has been piqued. Why would a young lady, so recently betrothed to a paragon of British nobility, be worried about dying from fear? It takes no refined deductive skills to understand that you are asking for yourself."

The girl's face turned pink. "Oh . . . I was not aware so many people already knew of my engagement."

I coughed gently. "It was in the society pages this morning."

I retrieved the newspaper from the pile by my chair and, at Holmes's insistence, I read the brief article aloud.

Yet another British noble bachelor has fallen prey to Cupid's bow. The little god of love flutters on Yankee wings these days and must be a livelier chap than his British cousin, whose arrows Lord Waverly has managed to dodge for almost half-a-century. The bride-to-be is Miss Hannah Sutton of Boston, only child of the late American entrepreneur Andrew Jackson Sutton. A summer wedding is planned at the groom's estate, Blackhyll, near Reading.

The lady nodded. "It is all true. And I am happy," she quickly added, with a nervous glance at her mother. "Lord Waverly . . . Augustin . . . is very dear to me. I only wish . . . oh, if he would just not insist on marrying me in *her* presence!"

The mother began to scold and the girl to weep. Holmes rose and masterfully took charge, insisting that there would be no impropriety if Mrs. Sutton visited a few minutes with Mrs. Hudson. The lady clearly loathed to leave the room, but Holmes prevailed, and in a moment returned and closed the door behind him.

"The advantages of having a conspiratorial landlady," he quipped, "but I fear even our good Mrs. Hudson may not be able to keep your mother occupied for long. So, my dear Miss Sutton, please state you case succulently. Who in your future husband's household causes you such terror?"

"Her name is Lady Arabella Waverly. And she has been dead for over two-hundred years!"

Holmes dropped into his seat, pressing his long fingers together. "Ah, that is rather an unexpected development. You have my complete attention."

"You should know that it was Mother's idea to come to London for the season, and to have me presented at court. I would have been content at home, but Mother – Oh, Mr. Holmes, she is obsessed with the idea that I should have a title and a tiara. I tried to avoid any entanglements but – you see how she is. When I met Augustin, well . . . he is kind and gentle, and he says he wants nothing more than to spend the remainder of his life at his estate with a loving spouse. He confessed to me that ours would be a quiet existence, and that we would rarely come to London – but that is what I want. I am a country girl at heart. I would be perfectly happy to remain tucked away somewhere. And if Heaven should bless us with a child, then all would be perfect. Mother could go home and brag about her daughter being Lady Waverly and I could be contented in my new occupation.

"Augustin had us as guests for two weeks before the engagement was announced, though I confess our 'understanding' was common knowledge at Blackhyll, especially to his sister."

"And her name?"

"Mrs. Jane Bartlett – her late husband was an adventurer in South and Central America. She is Augustin's twin sister, and a very interesting lady in her own right. There is a glass case in the house, a little museum filled with artefacts of their journeys. I have marveled over the pictures of her travelling with her husband, meeting with strange tribesmen, and climbing over queer ancient monuments. She has a son, Joffrey, who is away at the University of Berlin. She is quite dedicated to seeing to her brother's happiness, as you might imagine, and she has been most warm and welcoming to me."

"So your fear doesn't spring from her?"

"No sir. I suppose if there is anyone to blame, it is Mrs. Brown, the housekeeper. She is a widowed lady, and something of a historian. I believe she knows the story of every piece of furniture and trinket in the house. It was she who drew my attention to the portrait over the fireplace in the Great Hall.

"It is a fine picture – not a Van Dyck, but perhaps a work by Alexander Crosby. I didn't wish to reveal my uncouthness by asking. It is a portrait of Lady Arabella, of the Stuart Court, with silver hair and a black dress, and a most unpleasant look about her features. Her eyes seem to follow you, wherever you move about the room. It is most unnerving! Mrs. Brown informed me that the lady was a spinster, that her betrothed was executed for being in the Gunpowder Plot. She herself fell under suspicion of treason, leading King James to forbid her from ever marrying. She was so unhappy, it is said, that she will curse any bride who marries in her presence."

The lady shuddered and rubbed her hands tightly against her arms.

"Augustin is most insistent that we wed inside the Great Hall, where all of his ancestors spoke their vows. But according to Mrs. Brown, every Waverly bride who married in that hall has met a horrible fate! Augustin's great-grandmother was drowned mysteriously in the estate's mill pond, his grandmother died from a fall down the staircase, and his mother, poor thing, committed suicide by jumping from the east tower when Augustin and Jane were only babies."

"A tragic set of coincidences," Holmes said.

"Sir, you sound just like Augustin! He has no patience with superstition. He refuses to have the wedding anywhere else, and I dare not press him upon this issue. He is the Lord of the Manor and must have his way."

279

"What about his sister?" I asked. "Surely she would be your ally?"

Miss Sutton shook her head. "Jane also wed in the Great Hall and see what she suffered – widowed when she was only in her thirties! But no, she is insistent that it would be craven to abandon the tradition, and that all the fine people of the neighborhood would question if the wedding – especially one they never thought to see occur, as Augustin was such a confirmed bachelor! – didn't take place in that chamber."

"And your mother's opinion on the matter?" Holmes asked.

"She calls me a silly fool." A single tear rolled down the poor girl's cheek. "What should I do, sir?"

Holmes frowned. "It is difficult to advise you. As you state your case, no crime has occurred, and your fears may well be the nerves of a young American bride who is about to marry into the British nobility. However," my friend quickly and gently added, "a woman's intuition is dismissed at a man's folly. Perhaps your heart is telling you that that if you agree to this wedding, beneath the haunted picture, you will be resigned to always obeying your husband and his family. Is that your will?"

"I feel trapped," the girl whispered. Never have I felt more sympathy for a woman, but I understood Holmes's predicament as well. He could hardly proclaim perfidy where perhaps only insensitivity existed.

"Hannah! Hannah, come at once, or we shall be late for your fitting!" a voice bellowed from the stairwell. Miss Sutton rose and extended her hand.

"Thank you, sir, for at least listening to my case. I will meditate on what you have told me."

Minutes later, Holmes stood at the window, lighting his pipe and watching as the women climbed into a landau embossed with Lord Waverly's Coat-of-arms.

"Poor girl," I whispered.

"Indeed. I saw nothing in the young lady to suggest she deserves to be sold off to a man old enough to be her father, and I question whether the 'quiet life in the country' will truly appeal to her."

"Do you think she is in danger?"

"Of a broken heart and crushed spirit? That goes without saying. Look at the misery so many other American heiresses have endured. Can you imagine how sad the lovely Hatty Doran would have been, if her previous husband hadn't rescued her at the altar?"

"I mean, is there a danger to her life?"

Holmes puffed upon his pipe. "It is a critical error to produce theories in an absence of facts, Watson. I have only the girl's fears and a few quaint myths to go upon. But I am intrigued enough to take it under consideration and conduct some research into the matter."

My professional duties engaged me for almost three days before I could return to Baker Street to hear what Holmes had learned. He had compiled quite a dossier on Lord Augustin Waverly, his immediate family, and his home, Blackhyll. But he began with a photograph of the cursed portrait.

"Miss Sutton was correct – the picture is indeed a work by Alexander Crosby, a fairly undistinguished painter of the early seventeenth century. It appears to have been done in his later period when his talents were said to be waning. Even in his decline, however, he was known for creating portraits that, if failing to flatter the sitter, still created the impression the subject remained alive inside his or her frame, continuing to cast a watchful gaze upon descendants. There are similar pictures in Carlisle Hall and Bickersfield, and even one of James I, reputed to have been done from life, at Windsor."

Holmes slid the photograph across the desk to me. I confess that the painting wouldn't have been one I cared to hang upon a wall. Not only was the subject repulsive and clad in a gruesomely distorted gown, but her expression was one of withering distain.

"Perhaps it is a good thing this lady doesn't reside in the dining chamber. She would certainly quash even the heartiest appetite."

Holmes smiled. "Indeed – she is so disturbing that a myth was devised to explain her."

"So there is no curse?"

"It is true that her intended groom was taken up as a suspect in the Gunpowder Plot, but he died before his trial, and there is no evidence that the lady or the Waverlys ever fell afoul of the Stuarts. It seems more likely that the lady simply chose not to marry, and a legend sprung up around the picture. It is true that the current Lord Waverly's mother died by her own hand, but she was a Morcraft, and insanity runs strong in that line. Two of her siblings and three cousins also died by self-destruction. A family tragedy, quite certainly, but a 'curse' is fanciful. As for the grandmother, she was found dead at the bottom of a staircase, but as the lady was in her nineties at the time, and in poor health, one doesn't immediately suspect a villain beyond Father Time. And the great-grandmother perished, according to all accounts, in her bed of dropsy, at age seventy – no mill pond involved."

I considered the notes Holmes had taken. "Is it possible that someone might be trying to avert the wedding by frightening the bride into breaking her engagement?"

"A much more likely possibility than a bewitchment, is it not? One does immediately suspect the groom's widowed sister. After all, should Lord Waverly succeed in siring an heir with his young wife, Mrs. Bartlett's son would have a much-diminished inheritance. And by all accounts, the lady has enjoyed a long reign as the senior woman at Blackhyll and might not take kindly to being replaced by an American *ingénue*."

"What will you do?" I asked.

"I will send a letter to Miss Sutton, summarizing my findings and advising her to be cautious around her prospective sister-in-law. I can only hope it might give her the courage to return home and find a suitor among the rich American lads."

Holmes composed the letter and posted it that afternoon. The next day, he received a short but courteous reply.

"Has she changed her mind?"

"No – she has examined her heart and is '*determined to do her duty*'. Hardly the words of a lovelorn maiden, Watson. I sense a forceful mother guiding the pen. Well, we have done what we can. Let us move along to more pressing, and resolvable, matters."

And so it rested for that springtime. On occasion, I pointed out notices of parties and receptions the mismatched couple attended. Their wedding date was set for late June, but just a week before the nuptials Holmes was summoned to Paris on a matter of international importance. He insisted that I accompany him, and on some future date I may lay the case before my readers, as it involved a startling combination of ingenuity on the part of the villain and a remarkable escape from death on the part of my friend. We didn't return until the first day of July. While Mrs. Hudson set about preparing a triumphant feast, I began pouring through the back issues of the newspapers, curious as to what had happened in London while we were being pursued by murderous cutthroats through the catacombs of Paris. One startling headline caught my eye.

"Holmes!" I shouted, shoving the newspaper before him. He read the words aloud.

Bride Falls Dead at Wedding

Miss Hannah Sutton, the bride of Lord Augustin Waverly, was fatally stricken just as her vows were being recited in the Great Hall of Blackhyll. The young lady, who was among the fairest of the beautiful American invaders last season, was heard to give a cry before falling senseless at her groom's feet. She was borne to a couch by several of the titled guests, and the illustrious Doctor Joseph Harding, a neighbor to Lord Waverly, hurriedly offered succor. But the lady was beyond his skills, with a look of horror frozen upon her features.

282

The doctor swore that the lady was dead the moment she tumbled to the ground. No wounds were found, and no prior conditions, such as a weak heart, had been noted. Because of the strange nature of her death, the matter was put to the Coroner's Jury, but no evidence was found that the lady was poisoned or met with foul play in any manner. It can only be supposed that the thought of becoming one of England's great ladies was too much for the sensitive young American, and her romantic ambition extracted the ultimate cost.

Holmes's face went white. He threw the paper down as if it had burned him.

That afternoon found us disembarking at Reading Station, where we were met by Inspector Randall Travis, a tall, square-shouldered young man, a fresh face on the Force and a pronounced admirer of my friend. We had found a note from him amid the clutter, and Holmes offered an apology for his tardiness as they shook hands.

"Most understandable, sir," Travis said as we climbed into the very conveyance that we had seen pull away at Baker Street. "And, in truth, there may not be a crime at all. But the girl was so young and beautiful, the picture of health. Just days before the wedding I saw her upon the tennis courts with Mrs. Bartlett, giving her quite a game of it, and Lord Waverly's sister is considered the finest sportswoman in the country."

"A friendly game?" Holmes asked.

"It appeared to be – there was a great deal of laughing involved."

Holmes nodded. "The wedding occurred one week ago yesterday. What can you tell me of that morning and the order of events?"

Travis pulled out a notebook. "The wedding took place at exactly ten in the morning, in the Great Hall of Blackhyll. It was a relatively small affair – only fifty guests were invited – and it was presided over by the Reverend Edgar Forrester of the St. Agnes Parish. A breakfast was to follow in the dining room, and the newlyweds were to depart by rail at four upon their honeymoon.

"Preparations began long before dawn. Lord Waverly's household servants – a housekeeper, three maids, a French cook, and a gardener – were kept in a perfect buzz of work and were all over-excited and exhausted by the time the tragedy occurred. The bride and her mother were lodged in the east wing of the house, and Mrs. Sutton didn't come down the stairs until ten minutes before the bride made her appearance. Lord Waverly met his lady at the foot of the grand staircase and escorted her to the hall."

"Was there anything unusual about Miss Sutton's appearance?" I asked.

"No, Doctor. The witnesses all described her as somewhat pale and nervous, but that is common enough for brides. A few mentioned that halfway down the aisle, Lord Waverly stopped and whispered something in her ear, which seemed to encourage her. They proceeded, the marriage service was read, and the vows exchanged. Lord Waverly slipped the ring upon her finger. The reverend was just about to pronounce them man and wife when the lady collapsed."

"Did she cry out?" Holmes asked.

"Yes, though her mother, who was standing close, described it as more of a startled gasp."

"And the doctor who rushed to her aid could find no cause for her demise?"

"None, sir. Everyone was stunned and mortified – especially as the bride's face had taken on a rather gruesome aspect – a rictus of fear."

"And afterward?"

"I was called within the hour. The lady's body had been carried upstairs and placed in the bedroom. The doctor conducted a more thorough examination but could find no wounds. All of her clothing and toiletries were also examined, very cautiously."

"And none were found poisoned?"

The inspector shook his head. "I know a very clever chemist at Oxford. He was summoned and came that afternoon to collect samples of everything the bride might have consumed, from the dregs of her coffee to the muffin which she had only nibbled upon. Nothing incriminating was discovered. I interviewed all the servants, and soon found that the only people who had seen the bride that morning, before she descended the staircase, were her mother, Mrs. Bartlett, and the housekeeper, all of whom served as tiring-women to help Miss Sutton don her bridal finery. None of them noted any illness or confusion that might have signaled the first hint of poison."

"How did these ladies describe the bride's demeanor that morning?" Holmes asked.

The inspector smiled. "Women are strange in their perceptions – three females will give three different impressions. Mrs. Sutton claimed her daughter was happy and bright, Mrs. Bartlett said that she was poised and patient, the housekeeper claimed the girl was shaking and nervous."

"In other words, each woman saw in her what they wanted to see," Holmes answered. "Hardly a surprise." We had just turned onto a gravel drive, and the fine manor of Blackhyll was visible at the top of a gentle rise. "One final question, Inspector – Was the bride buried here?"

"No. Her mother insisted upon having the body embalmed and returned to America. She departed with her daughter's coffin three days ago."

Holmes scowled. "That was unwise."

"There was nothing we could do to stop her."

"Is Lord Waverly considered her widower?" I asked, wondering why he hadn't objected to this decision.

"The ceremony wasn't complete, nor had they signed the register. Lord Waverly has made it clear he has no expectations of survivorship, considering the bizarre circumstances."

As we drew closer to the mansion, I saw that while it was a beautiful building, in the early Georgian style, with a wealth of glowing yellow marble and numerous windows lining its western façade, it was showing signs of age and badly in need of repair. Like so many old homes, it cried out for attention in its windows, and many of the chimneys were crumbling or fallen. The fountain in the forecourt was dry and cracked, the entryway steps chipped. A butler and a housekeeper, both in somber attire, met us at the door and ushered us into the Great Hall, where Lord Waverly and his sister were seated before the fireplace.

Many of my readers will no doubt recall Lord Augustin Waverly – even in late middle age, he was a handsome and fit man, graced with a mane of dark gray hair and the appearance of a serious scholar. He accepted our condolences and introduced us to his sister.

It was difficult to believe that they were twins. The lady's hair was raven, her skin was without a trace of wrinkles or any sign of age, and even in a mourning dress, she appeared lithe and filled with energy, as if she would have much preferred an afternoon hike to discussing the recent tragedy. The butler withdrew, but the housekeeper lingered, inquiring as to whether we would like tea or coffee. Lord Waverly gently patted her hand and sent her away with a request for tea and scones.

"Agatha has been so distressed since it happened," Lord Waverly said. "At first, I was certain there had been some evil deed done, that it was murder. In the days since, I have accepted that my dear Hannah had a weak heart."

"Nonsense," his sister said. "I have never seen a healthier girl. It is true, Mr. Holmes, that she was a dainty thing, but I put her through her paces over the past month. I wanted to see if she truly meant it when she claimed she would be satisfied with a life in the country. Augustin's happiness is everything to me, and if I had sensed that she was only after him for his title, I would have found a way to send the baggage packing."

Lord Waverly's face colored. "Jane!"

"I see no reason not to speak freely before the only man in England who can get to the bottom of this!" the lady snapped. "Yes, I was suspicious of Hannah, and that cow of a mother. Far too many of these American women have come to our shores looking for titles. And let me be very forward and admit that our family fortunes have declined – Augustin, stop shaking your head, you know it is true. Her American money would have been welcome. But no bank account is worth the misery of a mismatch. Edgar Bartlett lacked money and a title, but we were happy in our life together, travelling the world, exploring the wilds of South America. I have never ceased to mourn him."

"Did your son attend his uncle's wedding?" Holmes asked.

"No, he was in the middle of exams."

I glanced at Lord Waverly. His sister's vehemence seemed to have drained him of all conversation. The housekeeper had returned and was placing the refreshment before him, encouraging him to partake in a most motherly manner.

"Aggy!" Mrs. Bartlett said. "Do stop fussing. Augustin will eat when he wants to."

Holmes was studying the portrait above the fireplace. It was just as Miss Sutton had described it, a very hideous study that would strike fear into the breast of the strongest man. There was a strange sense that the picture's eyes were alive, and as I moved slightly to one side, they appeared to slide with me, keeping me under constant, disapproving surveillance.

"One moment, if you please," Holmes said to the housekeeper, as she started to retire. "Miss Sutton told me you informed her of the family curse?"

The lady nodded guiltily and put the hem of her apron to her eyes. "Oh, sir, if I could only take it back! I was just sharing the family legends, having a bit of fun. I never thought for an instant that she might take them seriously! Oh, sir, if I have killed her – "

"Nonsense," Lord Waverly interrupted, reaching for her plump hand, giving it an affectionate squeeze. "Those stories are so ridiculous, only a credulous child would believe them. No one blames you."

"Yet Miss Sutton *did* believe them," Holmes said, "and she requested that the wedding be staged elsewhere."

The inspector, who had stood back, almost forgotten, now stepped forward.

"Is this true?" he demanded.

"Yes, and why wouldn't it be?" Mrs. Bartlett answered. "All of our family weddings are conducted here. If she wished to be one of us, she had to respect our traditions."

Lord Waverly groaned. "I take responsibility. I insisted. I could tell it was what her mother wanted as well, so there was no reason to indulge her foolish request to go to the church."

I could tell that something had occurred to Holmes. His brows drew tighter, and his features darkened.

"Was the bride placed in the coffin in her wedding dress?"

"No," Mrs. Bartlett said. "Of course, we assumed that would be done, but her mother insisted that she be laid to rest in her court presentation gown instead."

Holmes brightened. "Was the wedding dress retained?"

"It is still in her room," Lord Waverly whispered. "You may see it if you wish."

Holmes thanked him, and the housekeeper led the way to the grand staircase and along the hallway to the east wing. Holmes paused before a glass cabinet that jutted awkwardly along the corridor.

"This must be the 'little museum' that the late Miss Sutton referred to."

The case held a collection of native artefacts, as well as jars, documents, and photographs of the Bartletts in adventurers' attire. I noted what a striking young woman Mrs. Bartlett had been, her chin jutting forward with determination, a rifle resting easily in the crook of her arm.

"This way, sir," the housekeeper called, taking a key from her chatelaine and opening a locked door. "Everything from that day has been kept here, except the items the inspector took away to be tested."

It was a large bedroom with a separate bath, neatly appointed, though showing its age in the faded wallpaper and rather patched draperies. The Oriental carpet was threadbare, but clearly some concern had gone into making the chamber comfortable, including the installation of a new mirror and vanity. It saddened me to see golden hairs in the silver brush and comb that sat on the dressing table, and my heart sank at the appearance of the beautiful white silk dress laid upon the bed. Delicate satin slippers rested on the floor, and a large and heavy veil, still attached to the glittering Waverly tiara, was placed upon the nightstand.

"Were her gloves taken?" Holmes asked.

"No sir – she didn't wear any. There was rather a row with her mother about it, but she said she didn't wish to fumble about with gloves when her Lord put the ring on her finger."

"A sensible girl," Holmes said. He bent down over the frock, subjecting it to a detailed examination with his lens. At last, with a sad sigh, he rose.

"I presume the bouquet was lost."

The housekeeper nodded. "It was fairly crushed in the rush to help her. I found it later, all trampled into bits, and discarded it. Was it important, sir?"

"Only as a tragic souvenir. It was crafted by the local florist, I presume?"

The housekeeper beamed. "Oh no, it is another tradition that a bride's flowers come from the gardens here. I made it up myself, that morning – all red and white roses, with myrtle and baby's breath."

"It was no doubt lovely," Holmes said, his manner suddenly distracted. He signaled to Inspector Travis that there was nothing more he wished to see, and we were being escorted out of the manor by the ancient butler. Holmes noted Lord Waverly walking on the lawn, his head upon his breast, moving like a man with a pressing weight upon his shoulders.

"Allow me a word alone with our host," Holmes said. "I have one final question to put to him, and it might prove embarrassing. Wait for me at the gate."

The inspector and I shared a perplexed look, but we honored the request. Our driver snapped the reins, setting a smart pace away from the manor. I was seated with my back to the driver, and so was able to watch as Holmes approached Lord Waverly. The noble drew himself upright, listened to Holmes for a few moments, then threw his arms over his head. After a moment of violent shaking, he finally dropped his face into his hands, sobbing. Travis ordered the driver to halt the vehicle, for we had reached the manor's gates.

"What did Holmes need to ask?"

"I don't know," I said, "but it appears that he received an answer.".

We had taken lodgings at a local inn, and Holmes insisted upon treating Inspector Travis to dinner. Afterward, Travis accompanied us to our sitting room.

"Is there is no hope of solving the case?" he asked.

"On the contrary," Holmes said. "I have solved it. But short of a confession, which I cannot believe will be forthcoming – for most villains this clever don't willing thrust their heads into nooses – I fear the lovely Miss Hannah Sutton will be forever remembered as a woman killed by her fear of a haunted portrait."

"Please, tell me about your thoughts on this matter," Travis pleaded. "Even if I cannot make an arrest, my mind will never be at ease. I have seen and heard all that you have. What have I missed?"

"Let us review the most essential elements in a murder," Holmes began, with the air of a professor lecturing his students. "They are known to every detective – motive, means, and opportunity."

288

Travis nodded eagerly.

"Now let us consider the principal players in this drama – they would be Lord Waverly, his widowed sister Mrs. Bartlett, the bride's mother Mrs. Sutton, the housekeeper Mrs. Brown, and the bride herself."

"What?" I cried. "Surely you don't think this was a suicide."

"One moment, Watson. We may now consider the cause of death. Clearly the lady was poisoned. No other possibility is admissible. Healthy young lasses may faint, but they don't die of fear, and as this agency doesn't permit supernatural explanations for tragedies, we cannot place the blame upon the painted Lady Arabella, no matter how uncanny her eyes."

"But if it was poison, how was it administered?" Travis asked.

"We shall come to that, because it is tied with opportunity," Holmes said. "Let us return to motive and see if we may remove some suspects. It is possible but not probable that the young lady did away with herself. She was clearly willing to go through with the wedding. Had impulsive self-destruction moments before taking marital vows been her desire, she would have flung herself from the window. As to Mrs. Sutton, it is difficult to envision why she would kill her daughter who was upon the threshold of achieving the much-desired 'title and tiara'. Had Miss Sutton refused to come down for the wedding, we could perhaps envision an unpleasant incident resulting in the bride's demise, but as she was perfectly willing to speak her vows, we must rule out the mother."

Holmes lit his pipe. He rose and moved to the window, trailing blue smoke behind him. "Likewise, the groom had no reason to do away with his bride, except – perhaps – for the financial gain that would come from being her heir. If that was his intention – and nothing in his personality suggests that it was – surely such an intelligent man would have waited until after the marriage was made legal before committing murder. Forgive me for speaking frankly, but it would be much easier to push one's bride overboard on a Mediterranean cruise than to mysteriously poison her on the jaunt down the aisle."

"So it was Mrs. Bartlett," Travis gasped. "I knew it!"

Holmes turned, shaking his head. "Mrs. Bartlett is indeed the most obvious suspect. Her brother's marriage, which might produce heirs, wasn't in her best interest, or her son's. And the means were certainly within her grasp. Indeed, the means originally belonged to her."

"The poison?"

Holmes nodded. "Surely you noted the lady's shrine-like museum to her late husband. There were several jars within it, some even bearing warning insignia. The jungles of South America are notorious for their naturally occurring poisons, which the native tribesmen make clever use of. Some are capable of producing instantaneous death in a sensitive subject."

"So where was Mrs. Bartlett's opportunity?" I asked.

"She had none. According to the inspector, Mrs. Bartlett spent only a few moments with the bride as she was dressing, and she wasn't alone with the bride during that time. Mrs. Bartlett then took in her place downstairs for the half-hour preceding the wedding."

"So the killer was – "

There was a knock at the door. Holmes placed a finger to his lips, then walked over to answer it.

"Ah, Lord Waverly, thanking you for coming. I am grateful that you have honored my request."

Inspector Travis and I exchanged a look of shock. The nobleman seemed to have aged a dozen years in the few hours that had passed since we left Blackhyll. He accepted Holmes's invitation and sagged into the nearest chair. I saw at once that his eyes were bloodshot and his hands trembling.

"I have considered what you said to me, Mr. Holmes. You see clearly into the hidden places of men's hearts. It would be foolish of me to deny what is so clear to you, even if it has been hidden for almost twenty years." He lifted his head slowly, considering us with some trepidation. "Can these gentlemen be trusted? This is a matter that deeply affects my honor."

"You may rest assured that neither of my companions will betray your secret."

"I only ask that you not reveal it until I am in my grave. You will not have to wait long."

Slowly, with painful dignity, Lord Waverly told his story.

"I have always been a scholar, with little time or inclination for social niceties. When I was a youth, at Oxford, an entanglement with a young lady came close to causing a scandal. Fortunately, the affair was discreetly handled by my father, but my confidence was shaken. I vowed to live a monk-like existence, and I soon acquired a reputation as a confirmed bachelor, especially after my parents died and I came into my inheritance. Jane is, as you no doubt inferred, a more hot-blooded individual than I. She married when she was only twenty, and for nearly fifteen years we rarely saw each other, for she was travelling abroad with her husband.

"When I was thirty-five, the elderly lady who had served as both my nurse and housekeeper retired, and I was forced to find a new manager for Blackhyll's domestics. Mrs. Agatha Brown applied for the job. She was recently widowed, and only two years my elder. You might view her as she is now, stout, advanced in years, and the picture of maternal devotion. But when she first came to Blackhyll, she was slender and fair and beautiful, and I had lived a celibate existence for far too long. She was there, and both of us were willing. For years she has been my mistress.

"Of course, we couldn't live openly as lovers, nor could we wed, with her so socially beneath me. We were very discreet, and I made certain that the staff at Blackhyll changed often enough to prevent the spread of rumors. When my sister returned as a widow, we were forced to grow even more cautious. Fortunately, Jane has never suspected, or – if she has – she has never spoken of it to me."

Inspector Travis coughed roughly. "If this arrangement pleased you, then why – "

"Marry? Especially an American girl?" Lord Waverly's face turned ghastly pale. "Without an heir, Blackhyll will pass to my sister's child. For more than a decade I didn't care – but now that Joffrey Bartlett is a young man, I see what he is. Already there have been scandals involving women, and card debts, and drinking. That is why he was sent to Berlin to finish his education, for he had already been expelled from Cambridge. I explained to Agatha that I needed both an heir and the money the American girl could bring in her dowry. If I planned to leave Blackhyll to my future heir, I also needed to restore the estate to its former glory. It wasn't that I loved Agatha less. It was purely a practical arrangement, and Agatha assured me that she understood." He twisted and looked back to Holmes. "You deduced that Agatha was my mistress. Now tell me why you believe she murdered my bride."

"Because she was the only one who *could* have murdered Miss Sutton," Holmes said. "First, she attempted to scare the girl away with the doleful tales of the haunted portrait and the doom that befell all Waverly brides. When that failed, she turned to the resources with which she was familiar as your housekeeper. She constructed the bride's bouquet – the exotic poison was taken from your sister's collection and brushed onto the thorns. A simple pricking of the fingers – inevitable by the bride's lack of protective gloves – would cause her death. It would take a very sharp-eyed coroner to find the tiny pinprick, or to grasp the significance of the single spot of blood that I found upon the bodice of the wedding gown. Mrs. Brown was the only individual with the means and opportunity to do such things. But why murder the bride when the household stood to benefit from the marriage? There was only one logical motive – jealously, of the deepest and most intense type. Jealously sprung from decades of a clandestine love. Mrs. Brown loved the lord of the manor and didn't wish to give him up."

"I should arrest this woman!" Travis said.

Lord Waverly began weeping. "No. No, please, I beg you. She would deny it all, and what proof is there now?"

"None," Holmes said. "With the body gone, the flowers destroyed, and – one imagines – the poison already disposed of, there is no evidence."

I shuddered. It was difficult to picture the placid, sweet-faced housekeeper moving with such stealth, and committing murder in such a cold-blooded fashion.

Lord Waverly rose to his feet. "I will send Agatha away. It isn't justice, but she shall not stay under my roof, or in my heart, a single evening longer."

The door closed behind him. I harrumphed my disgust.

"What a pathetic old sinner! How dare he claim his nephew is too foul to inherit his estate, when he was willing to ruin the life of a young woman he clearly didn't love!"

"A peculiar type of personality," Holmes said. "An alienist would find him a fascinating case study. He has no perception of his faults, but an inflated judgement on the errors of others. And he is matched with a woman who clearly has no morals, a lady capable of killing an innocent girl as easily as she might dispatch a chicken served up for dinner. I am only surprised that this is the first murder than has been done in this household." He turned with a lifted eyebrow. "Murder this cool and calculated generally requires some practice. One wonders, have any pretty housemaids come to untimely ends at Blackhyll? It wouldn't shock me to discover a lass 'accidentally' fallen down the stairs or drowned in a millpond. Perhaps the fictional stories of the Waverly brides had a factual inspiration."

"My God," I whispered.

Our young friend rose to depart, clearly shaken and unnerved by all that he had learned. Holmes had a parting instruction for him.

"Inspector Travis, I would urge you to watch the household carefully."

"Why?"

"Because I fear there might be a further tragedy."

One might assume that my friend was a prophet, as well as a detective. The next morning, as we were stepping out of the inn, bound for the train station, a young boy came dashing up with a message from Travis. Holmes read it, his face turning grim.

"So soon," he whispered.

Lord Waverly had been found dead in his bed at Blackhyll, a bottle of poison and a note on the nightstand beside him. Though the words were barely legible, they spoke of his excessive grief over the loss of his beautiful bride. The note was unsigned. Much to the family's distress, their housekeeper was also dead, lying in repose on the bed beside Lord

292

Waverly. It was theorized that she had found his body early that morning, and, insane with grief, drank down the remaining poison in the bottle.

Holmes bade me not to make a record of the case, out of sensitivity toward the survivors. If you are reading these words now, it is because all the principals in the matter are long since dead, and in writing these lines, I am providing some measure of belated justice to a beautiful and tragic lady, the fair American, Miss Hannah Sutton.

The Crisis of
Count de Vermilion
by Roger Riccard

Chapter I

As the consulting detective Sherlock Holmes's reputation began to gain momentum in the late 1880's, news of his abilities and successful cases spread beyond the shores of the British Isles and onto the Continent. It was in the summer of 1887 and I was dropping in on my friend in Baker Street, having visited a patient nearby. Simultaneous to my arrival, a messenger came with a telegram from France. I accepted delivery just as I was being admitted by my former landlady, Mrs. Hudson. Thus, I was the first to lay eyes upon it. I enquired to Holmes's whereabouts and, assured he was in, I thanked her and trod up the steps to our old flat.

Holmes called out before I could knock with a welcoming, "Come in, Watson!"

I opened the door and saw Holmes was at the deal table near his shelves of indexes, updating one of his many volumes by pasting in newspaper clippings containing the type of information he collected for possible future reference in his work.

"I know better than to ask how you knew it was me," I declared. "Likely you recognized the pace of my tread upon the stairs and knew that I would be one of the few men Mrs. Hudson would admit without announcement. This telegram for you arrived while I was downstairs. It's from Paris."

"Pray, have a seat, Doctor, and read it aloud if you please. My hands are a bit sticky at the moment."

I tore open the form and read as follows:

Sherlock Holmes
221b Baker Street London NW
England

Monsieur,

I wish to consult you on a delicate matter with dire implications. Will arrive Langham Hotel 7 July. Request you leave word when soonest I may call upon you.

Regards,

Jean-Paul Garnier
Count de Vermilon

Holmes wiped his hands clean, selected another volume from his shelf, and walked over to the fireplace mantel where he stuffed his pipe with tobacco from the Persian slipper which hung there. He took the message from me as he passed and read it again for himself while he sat opposite me in his favorite chair.

"Rather short on detail. Let us see what my index of European peerage has to say on this gentleman." He turned the pages at a steady pace until he found the proper entry. He noted the following. "Hmm. I have him listed under the Anglicized version of '*V-e-r-m-i-l-i-o-n*'. Ah, here's why: His mother is an American heiress who married the previous Count de Vermilon. She was widowed when her son was still quite young and fell into the habit of using the American spelling of *Vermilion*. How typical," commented Holmes, shaking his head.

He continued as he ran his pipe stem down the column of text. "Here we are. Jean-Paul Garnier. Unmarried. Born 1863. Inherited the title of Count de Vermilon at the age of eight upon the death of his father, Paul Garnier. Raised by American mother, Ruby Garnier, *nee Redmont* of New York, and Grand-uncle Charles Garnier, architect of the famous opera house, the *Palais Garnier* [1] in Paris. Attended The Université Catholique de Lille, where he studied at the Catholic Institute of Arts and Crafts.

"Under the reign of Napoleon III, entitlements were significantly diminished, though the rank still retains minor holdings. Jean-Paul Garnier is currently employed as an associate curator at the Louvre in Paris."

Holmes closed the book, set it aside, crossed his long legs, and resumed puffing away at his briarwood pipe. I had focused on his reaction from my position on the settee. To my knowledge, he hadn't had a case for some time, and he deplored stagnation. Yet he isn't easily impressed by titles, nor requests lacking specifics.

I was pleasantly surprised when he asked, "Tomorrow is the seventh, and I note your wife isn't currently in residence. Would you be free in the afternoon to meet me at the Langham?"

I tilted my head at him. Even after some time away from Baker Street upon my long journey to San Francisco and subsequent marriage, I thought

I wouldn't be surprised by this habit of his. Yet he had caught me off guard with this proclamation. "You are correct. Constance has gone down to Epsom with her mother for some treatment, so I've decided to accept your invitation to stay for a few days. I've arranged for a *locum*, and I shall be available to join you, except for when I have a few medical obligations. But come, Holmes, how could you possibly know she wasn't at home?"

"There is an odor about you – not an offensive one, I assure you. In fact, just the opposite. It indicates you have spent some bit of time this morning in a restaurant. The variety of smells is too much for a single meal and I know you prefer to take a leisurely breakfast. To not do so with your wife indicates she isn't at home, for you don't fail to spend as much time as possible with her when her health permits. Is she improving?"

His deduction was correct of course, yet it took me a moment to marvel at his talent, even after years of exposure to it. His question was also a surprise, though a pleasant one. His consideration of situations outside the periphery of his investigations was rare. The fact that he enquired after her was warming to my heart.

"The treatments make her feel better for a time. Thank you. As for tomorrow, my last patient is scheduled for one o'clock. I can meet you at the Langham any time after two. Do you intend to surprise this Count by greeting him upon arrival?"

Holmes blew a smoke ring upward, watched it curl toward the dull ceiling, and then replied. "In this particular instance, Watson, with so little detail, I have a rare opportunity to observe our potential client before a formal meeting. It may be most instructive. If he leaves Calais on the first boat of the morning it will be late afternoon before he can arrive in London. However, should he take the last boat this evening and spend the night in Dover before catching the morning train, he could arrive before noon. I shall see to those early hours and will be happy to have your company starting at two o'clock in the lounge."

Having agreed to this plan, we enjoyed a cup of coffee together. The easy camaraderie of our earlier years seemed to continue as if I had never left. Fortunately, his income from his cases and other activities [2] was now sufficient that he could meet the rent without my participation as a roommate. He informed me of some recent assistance he had rendered to Inspector Lestrade of Scotland Yard and the results of a chemical experiment he had conducted for the University of London.

At last, it was time for me to depart for my next appointment and we bid each other *au revoir* until the next afternoon.

Chapter II

My work the following day seemed to drudge by. Morning rounds at Barts, followed by house calls at noon and one o'clock weren't particularly demanding. This was fortunate, as I often found my mind wandering toward the case which lay ahead and may not have been as fully attentive to my patients as I ought.

The fact that this count was an Associate Curator at the Louvre had me speculating toward a myriad of possibilities. Had something been stolen? Did he suspect something on display wasn't authentic? Was something new due to arrive and he sought Holmes's expertise on security measures?

Finally, the two o'clock hour struck just as I walked into the grand reception lounge of the Langham Hotel. The Langham was known as one of the grand hotels of Europe, and its opulence was evident by the crystal chandeliers, the fine furniture, and the marble floors. The brightly lit area was filled with several chairs and settees where guests could take their leisure as they waited for companions, or to be called for dinner reservations at the excellent restaurant. I cast my eyes about, however, I saw no sign of my friend. I took this to mean that possibly the Count had already arrived, and Holmes was with him even now. I checked with a clerk at the desk.

"Pardon me, has a M. Garnier arrived from France today?" I asked the uniformed young man behind the registration desk. Without even looking at the registry, he replied, "I believe you'll wish to speak to the gentleman over there, reading the paper in that chair by the small table near the lift." I turned in the direction the lad had pointed and saw a stout gentleman with mutton chop whiskers curling down into a moustache, and a short, pointed beard. He was wearing a *pince-nez* and reading *The Daily Telegraph*. I thanked the desk clerk and chose to purchase a newspaper before I wandered over to a settee near the fellow. If this was the Count, I obviously didn't wish to introduce myself before Holmes had completed his preliminary observation. If this was someone else following the Count for some nefarious purpose, I thought it best merely to keep an eye upon him.

I had chosen a seat where I could keep the registration desk and the unknown gentleman in my peripheral vision. Unfortunately, I became absorbed in a news story concerning the Zululand annexation and temporarily lost focus on my objective. When I realized a good five minutes had passed since I'd last glanced in that direction, I looked up with some concern. The fellow was no longer where I'd seen him. I anxiously began to observe the rest of the room. Suddenly a voice with a heavy French accent emanated from behind my left shoulder.

"Pardon me, Monsieur. Have you a match?"

I started and turned toward the sound. The very gentleman I sought was addressing me. I cleared my throat and replied, "Why, uh, yes. I believe I do. One moment."

I set the paper down next to me and reached for the pocket where I normally keep my matchbox. By now the fellow had come around in front of me, holding a cigar. I handed him the matchbox and he deftly lit his cheroot. He handed the box back to me, then reached into his pocket and pulled out another cigar. "May I offer you one, Monsieur? I detest smoking alone."

Not knowing how I could refuse his kind offer, I accepted the long roll of tobacco as he sat down on the opposite end of the settee. I lit the cigar and was pleasantly surprised at the taste. He noted my reaction and commented, "The finest in all France, Monsieur – possibly in all Europe. Imported tobacco from distant islands where the tropical climate is ideal for its growth."

He put out his hand. "My name is Guillaume Vernier. May I know to whom I have the pleasure of speaking?"

I shook his hand, attempting not to show the temerity I felt. I hesitated, but then saw no reason for not stating my identity. [3] "Watson. Dr. John Watson. At your service, sir."

Introductions complete, I considered what Holmes might do in this situation. I recalled, from previous observations, he often takes the offensive, if I may use a military term. This allows him to retain control of the conversation and not be put in an awkward position where he is required to answer questions which he would prefer to avoid. Thus, I began.

"Are you in London for business or pleasure, Monsieur?"

"I hope to do a little of the sight-seeing, as you say. But my primary role is to meet with some of your finer restaurants and bistros for the purpose of establishing clients for my family's winery. Perhaps you have heard of Pétri Wines?"

I shook my head, and shrugged my shoulders timidly. "I am afraid not."

"This is no surprise. Don't be embarrassed. We have a modest vineyard in the Loire Valley. However, the competition is so great in France, we have decided to try our hand at exportation. We hope to begin here. If we meet with success, then perhaps expansion to America. We have heard the climate in the state of California is most conducive to vineyards."

298

"Well, I wish you success, Monsieur," I replied. "I visited California last year. I spent most of my time in San Francisco but did manage a tour out to the wine country north of there. It would be an excellent place to establish a vineyard if you can find land for sale. The climate is perfect for grapes to grow. I, for one, always appreciate a fine wine, especially a good merlot."

"Ah, *très bien, Monsieur, le Docteur*. If am successful with the management, perhaps it will not be so long before you may enjoy our wine whenever you stay here."

I wished him well and in that same moment I noticed a gentleman arrive in an obviously French cut suit, accompanied by a porter carrying a large suitcase. My reaction to this sight didn't go unnoticed by my companion. Vernier turned and looked toward the registration desk. Returning his gaze to me he said, "Ah, perhaps this is the person whom you await? I shall not keep you. It was a pleasure speaking with you, Dr. Watson."

He got up and left me as he strolled toward the lift. I noticed the desk clerk give a subtle look and nod in my direction, but he didn't appear to say anything about me to the guest. The gentleman was a small man, perhaps five-foot-six with unruly, curly, light-brown hair. He had a wide moustache and small goatee. His face seemed oddly shaped – almost a stubby, inverted triangle with a wide brow and cheeks suddenly narrowing to a short, rounded chin.

I circled around so as to approach from the rear as he and the porter walked to the lift where the operator was holding the door for them. I went to the desk clerk and verified that the gentleman was Garnier. However, there was no sign of Holmes, so I decided to wait an hour, then return to Baker Street to see if he had left word.

Late that afternoon I was in our old sitting room having tea when Holmes walked in and declared, "Watson, my dear fellow, I owe you a thousand apologies. Please accept this as reparation for leaving you stranded so."

He handed me a box, which I opened with great curiosity. Inside was a bottle of wine. I turned it around to read the label: *Pêtri Vineyards, Merlot, 1882*. I turned to him with what must have been a demanding look upon my face, for he immediately flashed that impish grin of his which comes and goes in an instant. I set the bottle upon the table, folded my arms, crossed my legs, and glared at him with *faux* indignation.

He handed me another of the long cheroot cigars and took a seat opposite. "I must congratulate you for your attempt to steer the conversation in your favour, *le Docteur*. You have come remarkably far in your abilities to participate in these little undercover schemes of mine."

"But why?" I demanded, pointing my now lit cigar at him. "What was the purpose of disguising yourself to me?"

"You have lived away from these rooms for quite some time now. I haven't had the opportunity to test my disguises on anyone who knows me so well. I also wished to see if the opportunity arose to enter into conversation with Count de Vermilon. I came to the realization that to do so incognito would serve my purposes best. Thus, the birth of *M. Vernier*."

"I presume you spoke to the man?" I enquired, stemming the tide of my bruised ego for the moment.

"When the desk clerk nodded in our direction, it was a pre-arranged signal I had with him. While you were circling around, out of Vermilon's line of sight, I stepped into the lift and had the operator hold the door so the Count and I could ride up together – although I should clarify, he isn't using his title on this trip. He is merely Jean-Paul Garnier, Associate Curator, here on business with the British Museum to discuss a temporary exchange of exhibits. At least, this is the story he gave to Monsieur Vernier who struck up a conversation with him in the lift as they rode up and then strolled down the hall toward Garnier's room."

"I know you better than that," I replied. "In addition to this polite conversation, you must have made several observations. What else have you learned?"

The detective smiled at my recognition of his talents, for Holmes doesn't count modesty as a virtue. "I'm sure you noted his complexion is fair, his hands are those of clerk, but with a dash of creativity. They revealed he spends a great deal of time writing, yet there was also a splash of paint on the outer side of his left hand where he must have accidentally touched the canvas of a painting he himself was working on. As it hasn't been washed completely away, it is likely oil-based and its location isn't in plain view unless one is looking for it.

"His manner was polite but tired and there were slight indications of nervousness, as if he might be afraid I was following him. This told me that he is under some sort of threat or fear, whether for himself or someone close to him seemed assured.

"I spoke to him in French, of course, using the same fiction as I did with you. When the lift stopped at his floor, I also got off and saw him to his door, pretending my own room was just down the hall. He tipped the porter in return for his key and indicated he would take his luggage from there. After the young man walked away, he turned and bid me *adieu*. I kept my voice low so we wouldn't be overheard and introduced myself for who I really was.

300

"Garnier looked up and down the hall to ensure we were neither watched nor overheard, then whispered back anxiously, 'Please, Monsieur, come inside.'

"We entered his room and he fairly threw his luggage upon the bed as he bid me take a chair in the sitting area. For a small man he appears to have an inordinate amount of strength. He then sat opposite me, pulled out a large handkerchief, and wiped his wide brow with nervous energy.

"Staring me up and down, he finally asked, "You don't fit the description I was given, Monsieur. Are you really Sherlock Holmes, the detective?"

"In reply, I removed my wig and facial hair. Then I stood and pulled open my shirt so that he might see the padding I was wearing. Before re-taking my seat, I handed him my card. As I lowered myself into my chair, I asked, 'Who was it that gave my description to you, Monsieur?'

"Apparently satisfied at my *bona fides*, he leaned forward and replied, 'You were recommended to me by Lieutenant Andre Allard of the *Sûreté*. He knows nothing of my *difficulté*. I merely communicated with him discreetly to ask who would be best to advise me on security while transporting valuable museum pieces between Paris and London. I have been strictly warned not to go to the police.'

"'Warned by whom?' I asked him.

"'I have no name, Monsieur. What messages I have received are merely signed with a trident. I cannot conceive what it is meant to symbolize. In my mind I associate it with *Diable,* for surely the man is a devil!'"

Chapter III

All this Holmes had relayed to me as we sat, smoking the cheroot cigars he had procured. When he paused after the previous remark, I asked the obvious question: "Did he bring those letters with him for you to examine?"

In reply, he reached into his breast pocket and produced three letters, stating, "He did indeed. In that sense he promises to be a most helpful client. As you know, not all the visitors to these rooms have had the foresight to retain crucial evidence."

He handed the papers across to me and said, "You know my methods, Doctor. What do you make of these?"

I read through them as best I could with my limited knowledge of the French language. I wished now I had paid more attention in school but, as a medical student, I had been more concerned with learning Latin.

After a few minutes, I handed them back to my companion and stated, "From what I can discern, I believe there is a threat against his mother, the Countess, if Garnier doesn't perform as the – shall I say *extortionist* – demands. It appears to be written by an educated man who has access to expensive paper. I would gather that he is left-handed from his handwriting."

"Is that all?" Holmes asked, with a slight shake of his head, as if disappointed with my reply.

I took a sip of my tea, then set the cup in its saucer, took another puff from my cigar, and replied, with some asperity, "I'm sure you will tell me his age, height, and weight – that he walks with a limp, has a pet poodle, and ate waffles for breakfast. But what I've stated is all I can discern."

My remarks, delivered in this minor diatribe, seemed to amuse my friend, for there was a brief smile upon his face as he set the letters on the table next to him. "You're too timid in your deductions," he stated. "And too quick with your examination. You're correct that the writer is an educated man. He not only has access to expensive paper, but he can afford expensive paper and ink, for he is somewhat wealthy in his own right. Here, examine the paper again, but use this."

He handed me the small magnifying lens from his waistcoat pocket along with one of the sheets. I skeptically took them and leaned toward the lamp on the table next to me. As I did so, he remarked, "Be sure to use *all* of your senses."

I gave him a quick, questioning glance, and then brought the paper close to my face to bring the magnifier into focus. As I ticked off the senses in my head, I attempted to ascertain how I could use them in my task. Hearing was certainly out, for neither paper nor ink emitted sound. I wondered if Holmes meant I should imagine what the writer would have sounded like had he been speaking the words he had written. I chose to move on to the other senses before coming back to that. Taste seemed unlikely as well. I was about to concentrate on the obvious ones of touch and sight when I detected an odor. It wasn't strong, for certainly I couldn't smell it when the paper was held at normal reading distance. Having it this close to my face, however, there was something stirring my nostrils. Paper and ink each give off slight odors of their own, of course, but this was different. It had a woodsy smell, liken to pine, yet there was a hint of vanilla – certainly not a natural combination. Thus I concluded it must be some lingering of cologne the writer was wearing.

My expression must have given away my thoughts as Holmes observed, "Ah, you've noticed the trace of cologne. Very good. Keep going."

My magnified examination of the paper indicated it was linen, not rag, which was in line with my original observation it was expensive. I used my sense of touch to rub my fingers upon it, even lightly scraping the fine texture with my fingernail to confirm my deduction. The ink too, was sharp and clear with no fading or inconsistencies, preserving the assumption of wealth.

"Be sure to examine around the edges of the document," chimed in my companion. "They are most instructive."

I gave him a quick glance and manipulated the paper in such a manner to do so. Thanks to the magnification, I was better able to see what was barely visible to the naked eye. In the upper left corner, there were two light finger impressions about an inch or so in from the left. There was also what appeared to be another impression about four inches down the left edge.

I made a mental note of this and continued around the edges. At the bottom I again found an impression. This was much larger, more like the heel of a man's right hand. Out of curiosity, I held that portion to my nose and found the earlier scent I had detected to be stronger in that area.

I sat up again and leaned back, satisfied I had more data, though not sure what to make of it. Before I could voice my thoughts, Holmes handed me the other two letters and advised, "Before you speak, smell these as well."

I retrieved them from his outstretched hand and held each in turn to my face. One had a harsh, peppery odor and the other a musky scent. As I handed them back, he crossed his long legs, pointed his cigar at me, and repeated, "Now, what do make of these?"

I cleared my throat and began again. "The texture of the paper, gleaned by my touch and magnified sight, confirmed it *is* expensive, as is the ink. The odor, and the fact that there are separate odors for each, indicate a member of the gentry who can afford such colognes – especially since he has used different ones over the stretch of time indicated by the dates on these letters, rather than using up one bottle before switching to another. Apparently, he alternates scents on a regular basis. This seems to confirm his wealthy status."

Holmes nodded and waited for me to continue.

I shifted slightly on the soft cushion of the settee and continued, much less sure of myself with the other things I observed. "I've seen the impressions of what appear to be two fingers in the upper left corner and another impression farther down the left side. There also appears to be a mark caused by the heel of a man's right hand under the trident. Could these be the results using a blotter? Perhaps he left the larger impression when he affixed the stamp?"

Holmes, having set his cigar aside, steepled his fingers in front of his lips and tapped his mouth two or three times before replying. He leaned forward with one of the sheets in his hand. "Better, but you have made a singular error. From your initial assumption that the man was left-handed, you denied yourself the opportunity to let other factors receive their true meaning."

To demonstrate he placed the paper on the table between us and took a pencil from his pocket. Holding it above the sheet, he proceeded to pretend to write and said to me, "Note the placement of the first two fingers and thumb of my left hand."

I saw now that his left hand was holding the paper along the same spots I had observed, while his right hand was in a writing posture. "And see how the heel of my right hand would impress upon the paper as I signed it with the trident? Our predator is a right-handed man who either attempted to disguise his handwriting with the unusual slant, or writes that way naturally due to certain personality quirks which are revealed in this result."

I acquiesced to his expertise, but he wasn't finished. "As I mentioned, a detective must use all of his senses when making observations and deductions. While you were diligent in using your fingernail to scrape along the paper, you should have done so near your ear to hear the sound and note the level of roughness. This can determine cheap linen from the more expensive type, which this happens to be. Finally, there is the taste test."

I stopped him there and declared, "Surely you didn't expect me to *eat* the paper?"

He shook his head at me, and replied with a patient sigh. "No, Watson. But anytime you detect an odor such as these, a touch to the tongue may assist you in determining the origin and whether it be citrus, wood, or floral. As a doctor, you know how closely taste and smell are associated."

I heaved my shoulders in resignation, tilted my head in acknowledgement of his superior observations, and replied, "So, where does that leave us? What is the next step?"

Chapter IV

Before replying, Holmes stood and walked over to the sideboard where he poured himself a brandy. Looking back in my direction, I nodded my assent to take one as well, for by now my tea had grown cold. He returned, handing me my snifter, sat back in his chair, and took a sip.

304

Then, looking toward the ceiling, he spoke. "As it is possible M. Garnier may be under observation to ensure he doesn't notify the police, we must take great care in our meeting with him. He certainly cannot be seen coming here, nor would it be advisable for us to meet him at the hotel or any other public place. I have taken certain steps to arrange a clandestine conference in the bowels of the British Museum, where he is expected to go to conduct his business. It will require us to make an early start in the morning. If you care to join me of course?"

I looked at him over the rim of the crystal glass in my hand and replied, "I am at your disposal. My patient load is currently light and can be easily arranged, and Constance isn't due back until next week."

"Excellent!" he replied, raising his glass toward me in salute. "I've set up a meeting in Professor Wooley's offices in the basement. As you are aware, only invited guests and staff may gain entrance to that area. Since both you and I are well-known to the guards, we shall be admitted at eight o'clock, before the museum opens. Should anyone be following our client, they will not know we're there awaiting him. M. Garnier will arrive at nine and ask for the professor. This will be a natural task for him, as Wooley is one of those who must be consulted for any exchange of artworks."

"I was unable to completely translate the language of the letters," I said. "Just what is the nature of this threat against the Count?"

"Ah, forgive me. The letters state that our client must deal in the exchange of certain artworks between the Louvre and the British Museum. During that transfer, he is to substitute a forgery. If he fails to comply, this perpetrator has threatened to abduct his mother, the Countess, and hold her for a ransom equivalent to the value of the artwork he is attempting to steal, which, he assures me, could be several hundred-thousand pounds."

I slowly shook my head at the audacity of it, and then asked, "Just what artwork is he supposed to substitute? Surely not the *Mona Lisa*?"

Holmes smiled. "Nothing quite so bold as that. However, the culprit *is* after a DaVinci. It is one of his later works entitled *Salvator Mundi*. It is apparently a portrait of Christ. Garnier is supposed to arrange for a temporary exchange of it with the British Museum's drawings of *Christ on the Cross* by Michelangelo."

"So someone wishes to obtain this DaVinci. Then what? Will they ransom it back to the museum?"

"A likely scenario," stated Holmes, "although there are those who merely wish to own great masterpieces for their own pleasure, or to satisfy some gap in their collection."

I shook my head. "I've never understood the mind of those who would steal a priceless painting and keep it. They certainly couldn't exhibit it to the admiration of their friends – unless their friends were all lawless men themselves. Are there such men who would deprive the world of such magnificent art, merely for their own ability to view it in secret?"

"The human mind can certainly be unfathomable, as you have witnessed time and again in our little adventures together. I've been meaning to write up a monograph on the subject of thievery and its motives. Let us see if my thoughts on the subject can open your mind to the possibilities in this case."

I took a final sip of my brandy, set the glass aside, and took up pencil and paper to make notes, for this promised to be a significant revelation on my friend's part. He had finished his cigar by this time and he took up his briarwood pipe, stuffed it with tobacco, set it alight, and settled into his chair.

"First there is the mental condition which prompts theft. A Swiss physician, Andre Matthey, I believe was his name, was the first to make note of it some seventy years ago. His term translated in to English as *kleptomania*. It is an abnormal impulsive order which compels a person to steal indiscriminately. Most often it is small or common items which the person could easily pay for, but decides, against all reason, to take in a clandestine fashion. I have rarely been involved in such a case."

He hesitated a moment, then added, "Though there was the affair of Lady Melody's pearls . . . But no matter. In our current case we can eliminate that condition, for kleptomaniacs invariably work alone, rarely steal anything so large, and certainly don't make such demands or threats as we have seen in this instance.

"This brings us to thieves who deliberately plan their actions or seize opportunities which present themselves. Some people will steal out of hardship. They take food because they or a loved one is starving, or they steal money to pay for necessities. Some will steal to finance an addiction, such as alcohol or narcotics. Some will do it to impress others – either peers or perhaps some love interest who has been resistant or unreachable. Such instances can be caused by jealousy or feelings of unworthiness.

"Others will do it out of a false sense of entitlement, such as those who contrive to steal an inheritance which they believe should rightfully be their own. Or, perhaps, someone whom they have no respect for, has something which our thief believes they don't deserve, so he takes it for himself, either to keep, or to give to someone he deems more worthy.

"The most ordinary motive, of course, is to steal something one can use to gain monetary value, either through ransom or by selling it to another party."

Holmes paused to let me catch up on my note-taking and then said, "These are the most common causes and motives. There are several more, which I will denote in my completed monograph. So what do you believe the case here to be?"

I closed my notebook and placed it and my pencil in my pocket. Folding my hands into my lap, I turned my gaze toward the fireplace, contemplating its dancing orange-and-yellow flames for a moment. Then I replied, "Obviously, the final one you mentioned seems apparent. Though why the thief would threaten a kidnapping to achieve his or her goal seems to add an unnecessary complication. If it is money this person is after, why not simply kidnap the countess and obtain a ransom for her? Why the extra step of accepting a painting which in turn will have to be sold? Unless, of course, they intend to keep the painting."

"Ah, Watson, there we delve into the value of a human life. While the Countess may be priceless to her son, she is of a minor rank within the French peerage and isn't a wealthy woman, as seen by the fact her son must work for a living. Our adversary understands this. He knows he can only push so far in demanding money for her, whereas, by using her to demand something of far greater value than our young Count could ever afford, he gains possession of something much more useful to him."

He clamped his jaw down on his pipe and stared at the swirls of smoke. I commented, "So what do we do? You appear to have a 'three-pipe-problem' on your hands."

He removed the briar from his lips and replied, "The pipe-problem cogitation cannot begin until we have more data – Which, I trust, will be forthcoming tomorrow morning."

Suddenly he stood. Setting his pipe aside, he made for the coat rack, donned his hat, and retrieved his cane. I stood and moved toward him, asking, "Where are you off to now? Do you need me to accompany you?"

"Not this trip. I must visit an acquaintance who loathes visitors. But I shall return in time for dinner. Feel free to remain if you wish."

He was out the door before I could reply. I strode over to the window and saw him cross the street, bypass a cab, then take the next in line heading south.

Chapter V

True to his word, Holmes returned just before dinner. I was reading an evening paper when he strode in, poured himself a sherry, and settled into his customary chair before the fire.

I gave him a moment to light his pipe, then enquired, "Were you able to see your unwelcoming friend?"

He gave a quick smirk at my description and replied, "Yes, though it cost me the rest of my *cheroots* to do so. Fortunately, he is a tobacco aficionado and I have never given him cause to distrust my keeping his confidentiality. Thus, he deigned to admit me to his abode. In the world of art collectors he is merely known as the Dutchman, though that doesn't accurately reflect his nationality."

"Very well," said I, setting my paper down. "Was your visit enlightening to your case?"

"One of the Dutchman's useful traits is he has his finger on the pulse of the art world. He himself is an outstanding artist and makes a fair living at providing copies of famous works to various merchants who offer them to the public. To my knowledge – " Here he gave me a wink of an eye. " – he has never been *proven* to have actually forged a painting or passed one of his own works off as an original of any great master.

"When I suggested to him that a famous DaVinci might be the target of some intrigue, he actually stopped in the midst of lighting one of my cigars and stared at me until the vesta burned his fingers.

"He slowly recovered, apparently lost in thought as he almost imperceptibly shook his head and gave a hint of a smile. He successfully lit his cheroot and exhaled a long stream of smoke before he spoke again."

"'*Salvator Mundi* or *Virgin of the Rocks*?' he asked, with the confidence of someone who knows of which he speaks."

I looked at my friend in surprise. "That is incredible! Are you sure he isn't in on this plot?"

Holmes sipped his sherry and shook his head. "He may skirt the edges of the law from time to time, but he would never knowingly be involved in something like this where a life was being threatened. I cannot rule him out completely, as the person who hired him may not have shared these other conditions of the substitution. But for now, he did give me a significant clue as to who may be involved."

"Who?" Then a thought occurred to me. A reminiscence of an earlier case involving the attempted theft of a painting. "Not Professor Moriarty?"

Holmes sighed. "If only that were true. I should very much like to have a case where I could remove that plague from English society. No, our suspect is a well-known art connoisseur who continually makes the rounds between England and the Continent seeking lost works or under-valued treasures to add to his collection. It is one of the finest in the world outside the major museums. There is some suspicion, though no proof, mind you, that not all the works therein were obtained through honest means.

"He is English by birth, though the story goes that his father set off for the gold fields of California in 1849, made his fortune, and brought his wife and baby boy over to live in San Francisco for several years. When the father died, the mother returned to England and their wealth quickly landed the son in the midst of gentrified society. It took some time to smooth out the rough American edges of his nature, but he has adapted well to the land of his birth. The gentleman himself is a welcome figure among society's elite and is a charming fellow. He has been seen in the company of some of the most beautiful women of European society and occasionally royalty, though he has never married."

My ears had perked up at the mention of San Francisco, scene of my recent sojourn and the city where I had found and married Constance Adams before returning to London.

"What is this fellow's name?" I asked with great curiosity.

"Charles Robie. I believe the family roots trace back to a Scottish borderland clan."

"Was his father's name John? There is a John Robie Memorial Library in Eureka Valley."

"I don't know. It wouldn't be surprising, given the family wealth and penchant toward culture. However, I must concentrate on Charles for the moment, to determine if he is indeed behind this plot involving M. Garnier."

I lit my own pipe as I considered Holmes's words. Finally, I exhaled a long trail of smoke and asked, "So how will you go about investigating this gentleman? You cannot just walk up to him and ask if he is blackmailing an Associate Curator of the Louvre."

He seemed to ponder my statement for a moment, then replied, "Perhaps I can do the next best thing. But first things first. Tomorrow, we meet with Wooley and Garnier, and perhaps something will grow out of that."

The next morning, as planned, we were up early and ensconced in the offices of Professor Wooley to await our client. He arrived promptly at nine o'clock.

The professor, his hair and beard now having turned much whiter that when first we met, was still quite stout and his usual effervescent self. One could almost picture him as Father Christmas with his ready smile and eager manner. He greeted M. Garnier warmly and wrapped his thick hands about the gentleman's as he proffered a handshake. Holmes introduced me to the French nobleman as well.

We sat around Wooley's office and the professor began the discussion. "Now, M. Garnier, just what are the details of this temporary exchange you are proposing?"

The Frenchman shuffled his feet and re-crossed his legs in his nervousness, then replied, "I am to arrange a six month exchange of Da

Vinci's *Salvator Mundi* for your drawings of Michelangelo's *Christ on the Cross.*"

"That seems a typical proposal," replied Wooley. "We engage in these sorts of exchanges quite often." He leaned forward and narrowed his eyes at the representative of the Louvre. "Did this thief of yours explain when he planned to substitute the painting?"

Garnier tugged at his collar. "He did not, Monsieur Professor. All I know is, he believes the substitution wouldn't be discovered until the items were returned to their respective museums six months from now. He assures me the crime would be blamed upon your museum and not me."

"Surely he couldn't expect to foist off a forgery upon us from the start."

Garnier answered, "I am supposed to substitute the forgery prior to handing it over to you, Monsieur. He must know that authenticity will be verified prior to the actual exchange, so I can only suppose he believes his forgery to be of such excellence as to pass your inspection, Professor."

Holmes held up a hand to forestall Wooley's response. "Perhaps, but perhaps not. Tell me, gentlemen, how does such an exchange normally take place? Will the DaVinci be brought here, or will the Michelangelo be taken to France for the actual authentication and trade?"

Wooley spoke up first. "It is customary the initiating museum brings their piece to the institution with whom they wish to trade."

Garnier nodded in agreement and Holmes steepled his fingers before his chin as he pondered that scenario. After a few moments he asked another question. "When proposals such as these are made, how long does it usually take the two parties to agree to details? Surely no one would expect an agreement upon a single meeting like this?"

Again, Wooley as the elder and more-experienced expert, answered his former pupil. "You are correct. Such a transaction could require anywhere from two or three days to a fortnight, depending upon the value of the items involved and the security measures which need to be arranged. Insurance companies need to be notified and each museum's Board of Directors must approve."

Holmes turned his look upon the young Frenchman. "The Board at the Louvre had approved this exchange?"

He nodded quickly. "In principle, yes, Monsieur Holmes, or I wouldn't have been allowed to approach the British Museum with the proposal. Of course, the actual details will require final approval."

Holmes was now leaning on his left arm, thumb tucked under his chin and the first two fingers of his left hand extended up his jawbone to the bottom of his ear. His right hand rested upon the other arm of the chair, right index finger slowly tapping the leather upholstery. Suddenly his brought his hands together in his lap, fingers interlaced, and said, "Professor Wooley, I would be much obliged if you would agree, in principle of course, with no actual commitment, to this exchange. I believe we must play along with this perpetrator's game if we are to catch him in the act."

Wooley leaned back in his chair. Garnier anxiously looked on, knowing his mother's life might be dependent upon the professor's answer. Finally, Wooley replied, "If it were anyone other than you, I would have to say 'No!', but I know you will keep our artwork and our reputation safe."

Turning to the Louvre representative, he nodded his assent.

"I agree, Monsieur, as you say 'in principle'. I will put it before our board at tomorrow's meeting and you may come back to see me the day after that to discuss terms and conditions."

Garnier practically leapt from his chair to exchange a handshake with the venerable professor. Having concluded the business at hand, he left us with a lightness to his step. Holmes and I, still wishing to keep our distance from him, stayed with the professor for several more minutes.

After the fellow closed the door upon his departure, Wooley turned to my companion. "Well, what now?"

"Now, Professor, I have some other avenues to explore. I have people keeping an eye on M. Garnier to see if he is notified by anyone whom we may be able to follow. I also intend to meet with Charles Robie."

"Robie!" exclaimed Wooley. "I would have put him high on the list of suspects behind this plot. Won't you're meeting him put him on guard?"

Holmes tilted his head to the side. "Oh, I agree. Robie is a highly questionable character. However, I have never suspected him of anything which was life-threatening. He does have *some* scruples."

I spoke up then. "Well, if you don't suspect him, why go see him?"

He looked at me in a desultory fashion and merely replied, "For the same reason people come to see me, dear Doctor. He is an expert in his field."

Chapter VI

We left the museum a few minutes later and Holmes first stop was a telegraph office, where he dispatched a request to Charles Robie for an appointment. Afterward, we returned to Baker Street, where Holmes perused the morning papers and I organized my notes upon the case thus far. Within the hour, Mrs. Hudson was showing up Wiggins, the leader of the Baker Street Irregulars, that band of youngsters which Holmes used to seek out information and follow persons without attracting attention.

"Ah, Wiggins!" greeted my friend when the boy entered the room. "What have you to report?"

The lad belatedly remembered to take off his hat and nodded to his employer. "We followed the gentleman, Mr. 'Olmes. Just like you told us. He went back to the Langham. Course, we can't be getting' in there through the front door, but I got a friend what works in the kitchen and he snuck us in that way. From there we could see your man take a seat by himself in the dining room and order a big breakfast."

Holmes held up a finger and asked, "Did anyone join him at any time during the meal, even for just a moment?"

Wiggins grinned, satisfied he could give Holmes the answer he was looking for. "Aye, Mr. 'Olmes. About halfway through his meal, a gentleman came by and sat down without waitin' for an invitation. The Count acted surprised to see him and leaned forward to keep his voice low whilst he was talkin'. Seemed like he wanted to man to go away so they wouldn't be seen together."

Holmes tapped his index finger to his lips and asked, "Are you sure that was his attitude? Fear of being seen together, rather than fear of the man himself?"

Wiggins shrugged, the heaving of his shoulders raising the cuffs of his coat sleeves high up his thin, bare wrists. "That's the way it seemed to me. Like he was more angry than afraid. Anyway, this fellow finally got up, but didn't seem in any hurry to go. He wagged his finger at the Count and said something that made your man flinch. Then he walked off. It looked like he was leavin' the hotel 'cause he headed straight through the lobby and didn't turn toward the desk to get a room key."

"Can you describe this man, Wiggins?" asked the detective, motioning to me to take notes.

The lad smiled. "Just like you taught me, sir. He was about two inches taller than the Count, judging by their eye levels when they were seated. Was pretty much a medium build, and about thirty years old with wavy black hair and thick eyebrows. He wore a moustache that curled 'round into a short beard. He wore a dark blue suit and a grey slouch hat. He didn't carry no cane or anything."

Holmes nodded, then asked, "What did Count de Vermilon do then?"

"Well, sir, it looked like whatever his visitor said upset him. He stopped eatin', though he wasn't more 'n halfway through his meal. Motioned for the waiter, signed the check, and walked out. I'd left Oscar out front and when I checked with him, he said the Count never came out, so he likely went up to his room. Oscar is still keepin' an eye out, and I got Jellyfingers Jim to help him while I came to report to you."

312

My companion nodded in approval, fished out some coins from his pocket, and handed them over to the lad. "A good day's work, Wiggins. Share these with your comrades and keep watch until you hear from me. Enlist whomever you need to take turns through the night. And if that other gentleman shows up again, have him followed to see where he's staying. In the meantime, since you have seen this unwelcome visitor in person, I'd like you to go and observe this address – " He jotted it down on a piece of paper and handed it to the lad. " – and see if that same gentleman is either living there, or if he visits the resident."

Wiggins gazed down upon the wages in his hand, smiled broadly, and stuffed them into his pocket. "Aye, Mr. 'Olmes. He won't go nowhere what me and the lads don't know about it."

He gave a knuckle salute and left us. Holmes walked over to the sideboard and poured himself a sherry, as it was approaching lunchtime. He offered the bottle toward me and I nodded my affirmation. Walking back toward the fireplace, he handed me my drink and sat in his familiar chair.

Once seated, he took a sip and spoke. "An interesting turn of events, eh?"

"Indeed. What do you suppose it means? And whose address did you give to Wiggins?"

Holmes shook his head. "Our time could be spent more profitably than to speculate without sufficient data. Garnier will tell us in his own good time. If you wish to spend your time in guesswork, I suggest you use that fertile imagination of yours to put yourself in the criminal's mind and plan how you would steal the painting."

"Surely you have already done so," I replied.

He nodded, but said, "Still, I would value your opinion. As a medical man, you bring a different perspective than I. Also, it will do you good to break out of your cocoon of honesty, which is the result of your upbringing, and get a glimpse of the world of criminal behaviour."

I narrowed my eyes at him. "Just how will that do me 'good'?"

He took on that lecturing tone of his and replied, "You have been exposed to the horrors of war, my friend. Thus, you understand the evil in the world and what men are capable of when encouraged to extremes. But in my world, the criminal mind isn't driven by the forces of nation against nation, but by the depravity of men's darkest thoughts. You expect that all men are inherently good. I know better."

I shook my head. "I've seen enough during your investigations to understand that. It is all I can do to not sink into the depths of depression and suspicion and, frankly, that bent of mind which rules your life and

313

leaves you lonely and morose and without love or family. Is that any way to live? Is that what you're urging on me?"

He tilted his head at me, apparently not expecting such an answer. I felt a twinge of regret at my words, true as they may have been. He finished his drink in one final swallow, looked at the glass as if he might see an answer in its reflection, and then set it down.

Turning to me, he answered, "My dear fellow, I wouldn't wish that upon you for all the world. I am merely appealing to your imagination to expand your horizons. I know you are writing up my cases with the hopes of publishing them someday, but to do so accurately, you must understand the human condition with which I'm forced to deal – the mindset it takes for me to succeed in my work. Trust me when I say that the task I've requested of you will barely scratch the surface and I should hope it certainly will not drag you into the abyss where I dwell."

In more than six years of friendship, we hadn't had such a discussion before and it had become uncomfortable. Thus, I chose to end it by merely agreeing to the task he had assigned me. I took out pencil and paper and began jotting notes.

I was still involved in this task when Mrs. Hudson brought up lunch. I had become so engrossed in my thoughts that I didn't step over to the dining table for several minutes and found the tea lukewarm and the freshly baked bread cool with a hardening crust. Now I understood how Holmes could skip meals so frequently when engaged upon a case.

However, my mind wasn't so disciplined as his, nor my body conditioned to go without food for long periods. Thus, I ate heartily. Holmes merely took up a slice of bread and some cheese and returned to his chair to engage in an extended session of pipe smoking.

The ceiling was shrouded in a heavy blue haze by mid-afternoon when Mrs. Hudson brought up a telegram. She handed it to my companion with a scowl and an exclamation. "Mr. Holmes! Really! It's positively choking in here!" She strode to the window facing the street and threw it open, waving her handkerchief in a futile attempt to carry the poisonous atmosphere outdoors. As she left, she waved the door back and forth a few times, hoping to supplement her previous efforts at creating a cleansing draft

She had barely closed the door when Holmes turned to me and commented, "We have our invitation. Mr. Robie has deigned to see us tonight at eight o'clock."

Chapter VII

That evening, at Holmes's suggestion, we dressed in our finery and set off for Robie's fashionable address in Knightsbridge, arriving at five minutes before the appointed hour. The gentleman's gentleman who admitted us was a large fellow. He appeared to have more of a military look and manner, rather than the usual servitude conduct of a typical butler. He had a maid take our hats, coats, and sticks and escorted us to a great hall where tapestries and paintings adorned the walls and statuary was scattered about on pedestals and tables.

Once there, he declared, "Mr. Robie requests you enjoy the exhibits here as you await his pleasure. He should be along momentarily." He then executed a precision about-face and strode out, closing the door behind him.

I turned to my companion and said quietly, "If that man is a butler, then I am Lord of the Admiralty!"

Holmes gave one of those indulgent smiles of his. "Look around the room, dear fellow. Would you not employ a cadre of soldiers to protect such treasures as these?"

The first thing which struck me was a large bronze statue representing Britannia. The helmeted female form, clad in robes with helmet, shield, and . . . a *trident spear*! I pointed this out to my companion. "Could that be more than just coincidence?"

He gazed upon it and remarked, "For now, it is an interesting fact to be filed away. However, Britannia is such a common representation in art, its significance may be minimal in light of my conclusions regarding Mr. Robie's position."

I took a closer look at our surroundings and noted some of the finest masterpieces I'd ever seen outside of a museum. I walked over to one painting in particular. The plate next to it identified it as *Joanna of Aragon by Raphael 1518*. I looked back at Holmes and said, "Shouldn't this be somewhere in Italy? The Vatican perhaps?"

A voice emanated from behind us, as through another door strode our host. "Indeed, it should, Dr. Watson. Fortunately for collectors like myself, not all artworks were as highly valued by their original owners as they ought to have been. I suppose it is true of every generation that some things which are taken for granted at the time become highly prized with age."

He walked up to us in a friendly manner, first shaking Holmes's hand and then my own. He may have been the handsomest man I have ever met: Roughly six-foot-one, with a trim body with broad chest and shoulders. His dark hair was perfectly combed over dark eyebrows and intelligent eyes. A ready smile framed a broad, clean-shaven face. He wore a burgundy smoking jacket with black lapels and cuffs over his pristine white shirt, *sans* tie, with formal trousers and highly polished patent-leather shoes. His voice was a pleasant baritone and he waved us toward another room.

"Come with me, gentlemen, where we can sit over a good cigar and discuss matters at hand. I had Wirth bring you here just to enjoy the view for a bit. I'm glad you appreciate my pieces, Doctor."

"Some of the finest I have ever seen," I replied as we walked, and I continued to gaze about. At last, we passed through the door from which he had entered and into a parlour with a blazing fire and overstuffed chairs in greens and mauves set in a semi-circle before it. There were a few more pieces in here: Busts and smaller paintings scattered about.

He offered us cigars and I noted they were cheroots, similar to the one Holmes had given me while in disguise. I gave a surreptitious glance at my friend, but he simply accepted the light from our host and commenced to enjoying the fine tobacco. After a puff or two, Holmes commented, "I do enjoy a good French cigar. Do you have these sent over, Mr. Robie?"

Our host was seated now, legs crossed with his left ankle upon his right knee, right wrist resting upon the arm of his chair while he held the cigar next to his cheek as he answered. "Oh, I get over to the Continent several times a year, Mr. Holmes – Greece, Italy, the Netherlands, France." He smiled. "I love the French – especially hearing a Frenchwoman call me *Sharles,* with the soft *Shh* sound."

He smiled wistfully at some memory then returned to the matter at hand. "Now, Mr. Holmes, you said you wished to consult me in a professional capacity. I confess, I am curious. I know you studied with Professor Wooley and may be as talented as me when it comes to detecting forgeries. Just how may I assist you?"

He gave Holmes a hard stare, almost daring the detective to accuse him of some criminal act. I noted that his right hand was within easy reach of a bell upon the table, where he could quickly call for his "butler", Wirth, and perhaps a whole gang of guards.

Holmes remained in a relaxed position and smiled across at the man as he sent a plume of smoke upward. With an off-hand manner he replied, "You are well-aware of the reputation you've garnered in some circles. In my current case, a certain mutual acquaintance has suggested you may be involved, but let me assure you, I'm not here with accusations or innuendo. I am merely aware that to acquire collections such as this, it may be expected that one must skirt the fringes of certain elements of society. I daresay you have likely been contacted by these elements upon occasion, wishing to sell you pieces whose provenance may be suspect."

316

Robie gave a guarded nod with pursed lips in a silent gesture, not truly admitting to anything. He merely stated, "I can guess who that might be. A certain person who has offered his services to me more than once, but whom I have never hired."

Holmes nodded in a tacit understanding and continued. "It is of these elements I wish to speak. I have reason to believe someone is highly interested in obtaining DaVinci's *Salvator Mundi*. So much so, they are willing to resort to extortion and physical threats to achieve their goal."

Robie had taken another puff of his cigar as Holmes spoke and now blew a ring forth prior to commenting. "I find such behaviour abominable, Mr. Holmes. Certainly, no true gentleman would resort to such tactics. It is more along the lines of our 'mutual acquaintance'."

"I was certain you would feel that way, Mr. Robie," Holmes said, "which is why I've come to you. These types are a blemish upon the class of true collectors, such as yourself, and I was hoping you might be able to work with me in keeping your ear to the ground to discover who our perpetrator might be so that we may stop him."

"Or her," Robie replied in what appeared to be an automatic reaction. Noting the reaction upon my face as he said this, he looked at me squarely and continued, "Oh yes, Dr. Watson. There are at least two women I am aware of who have entered the circle of – shall we say – *questionable collectors*, though I've never been aware of any threats of violence in their arsenal. Their methods are more suited to their gender's wiles and ways. Primarily carnal bribes or blackmail."

"Be that as it may, Mr. Holmes," he continued, turning back to my companion, "I shall be happy to assist you if I should hear anything. I presume this person is somehow expecting to remove DaVinci's work from the Louvre? Have you any clue as to how he or she might arrange that?"

Holmes set his cigar in an ashtray and folded his hands into his lap. "That is where the threats come into play. They are expecting an employee to make all the arrangements for them by threatening a close relative."

"That is despicable!" Robie declared. He took a beat, as if making a decision, and then said, "I will reach out to acquaintances I know who, as you say, *skirt the fringes* of that element to see what I may discover. I will send word to you at Baker Street whenever I have something to report."

Holmes nodded his appreciation and replied, "Then my *raison de la rencontre* is complete. I appreciate your time and assistance, Mr. Robie. If you will excuse us, we still have other avenues to follow regarding this case."

Holmes stood to leave and Robie, apparently caught off guard by the whole tone, purpose, and brevity of this meeting, hesitantly rose as well.

317

Almost as if not knowing how to proceed, he stepped over and extended his hand. Holmes took it in a strong grip with a steady gaze upon our host's face, and said, "Thank you, sir. I pray all our future encounters proceed so amicably."

Robie's face broke into a grin. He tilted his head and winked an eye to acknowledge the hidden meaning behind the detective's words. "I trust they will, Mr. Holmes. I should like my reputation to include any assistance I may give to the side of justice."

He shook my hand as well and walked us back to the foyer where Wirth and a maid handed over our accoutrements and we strode out into the night.

Chapter VIII

In the cab back to Baker Street, I asked my friend, "Do you really think he'll help us?"

With no doubt in his voice, he replied, "I am confident he will try. When dealing with a person of that type and personality, it's essential to approach them face-to-face and with a request, rather than a demand or accusation. I have appealed to his gentleman's code of honor. Whether his interpretation of that code differs from others is irrelevant. Unlike hardened criminals, he has boundaries he will not break. To suggest there are others in his particular profession who do, and thus stain that fraternity of honorable thieves, is abhorrent to him, and if he can put them out of the game by helping us, he will."

I nodded and remarked, "It also lessens his competition."

My companion smiled. "And then there is that."

Back in our sitting room, I went to the sideboard and poured us each a brandy. Mrs. Hudson had informed Holmes that a telegram was awaiting him by his chair and he immediately strode to it and tore it open. As he read it, I enquired as to its sender.

"Our client has been warned not to contact the *Sûreté*. I, however, am not so constrained and felt that, so long as I don't mention my client nor the potential crime, I could at last glean some information from my contacts there."

I handed him his snifter and took my customary seat. "And what have you learned?" I asked.

He tossed the telegram on the table, shucked out of his hat and overcoat, and sat down to light his pipe. "Nothing that will lead us to our criminal, I'm afraid. Yet, telling information all the same. Apparently our French friends are unaware of any criminal element who uses a trident as a sign."

"I was wondering about that. I mean, why use a symbol at all? If you aren't identifying yourself, what's the point? If anything, it could provide a damning clue."

He took a sip of his brandy and replied, "It *is* a rather foolish gesture and smacks of amateurs. However, in this case, I believe it was an attempt to instill a higher level of fear into our client. As you have heard, he hasn't identified it as Britannia or Neptune's trident, but rather as the Devil's pitchfork. That in itself may be a clue. It points to the fact our extortionist knows that our client's bend of mind would lead him in that direction, perhaps because of his Catholic University experience."

"So what will you do now?"

"I shall smoke a few pipes upon the matter and pray that more data may be forthcoming on the morrow."

I knew that tone and thus busied myself making more notes and contemplating more theories of my own as Holmes had suggested. About half-past-ten, my mind was trapped in the circle of ideas I'd contemplated and nothing new was coming to me. Thus I took myself off to bed, leaving Holmes wreathed in tobacco smoke and staring at the flames in the fireplace.

The next morning I awoke to the soft knock of Mrs. Hudson upon my bedroom door, enquiring if I desired breakfast. I gazed at the clock, noting it was just after eight, and replied in the affirmative. As I dressed, it came to me that Holmes had likely gone out already, or she wouldn't have made her enquiry herself. I strode into the sitting room and found a fire well-stoked and newspapers scattered about Holmes's chair. I retrieved one he'd left upon the cushion which had a note from him clipped to it. It merely said he had gone out to pursue more data and would be home before lunch.

I had two house calls to make that morning, and would likely be gone until after eleven myself. As Mrs. Hudson arrived with my breakfast tray, she was accompanied by Wiggins who had a message for my companion. I informed him that Holmes wasn't due back until late that morning and so he left it with me.

"If you please, Doctor, you can tell Mr. 'Olmes that the gentleman who met with his client is the same man who lives at that address he told me to keep an eye on."

He gave me a name and I wrote this information down so I could leave it for Holmes, should I not be back before him. I looked upon Wiggins, who seemed pleased to have assisted the detective, and fetched two shillings from my pocket. "You've done good work, Mr. Wiggins. I'm not sure what Holmes would desire, but I imagine keeping an eye on that fellow would be advantageous. Take these and enlist someone to assist you in your task. I suggest one of you report back here at noon to speak to Holmes himself for further instructions. And take this for now." I handed him one of the pieces of toast from my breakfast tray and he held its warm aroma to his nose in appreciation.

Wiggins gave his customary salute and replied, "Aye, Doctor. Thank ye!" Then took off again. I noted the gangly youth politely bow to our landlady as he left. When he was gone, I made a request of her.

"As a doctor, I'm a bit concerned over that young man's health. He should weigh more than he does for his height. Might I offer you some funds to provide him with a substantial lunch when he comes back later?"

"Ach, not necessary, Doctor," she said in her pleasant accent. "Mr. Holmes eats so little when he be on a case there's plenty left to feed an extra mouth. I'll see to it. Don't you worry a bit."

Gratified at her response, I dug into my own hearty meal and was quite satisfied when I left for my first appointment. I did leave a note for my companion regarding Wiggin's discovery and added something which had occurred to me regarding our case and which I desired not to forget to mention. I scribbled *Wooley's Health?,* on the same piece of paper and left it sticking out of the Persian slipper hung on the mantel where Holmes was sure to find it.

At quarter-past-eleven, I returned to Baker Street to find Holmes in his chair just lighting his pipe. The note I had left was on the table beside him. "Ah," he said, "your timing is impeccable. I have just returned myself and found your note. Frankly, Wiggin's discovery wasn't surprising. I merely needed verification. But I am intrigued by the thinking behind your comment regarding Wooley. Pour yourself some libation and pray give me your reasoning."

I chose to take up a glass of sherry as an *apéritif* to lunch and sat across from my friend. "You said I should look at this from my perspective as a medical man. First, I took that to mean as the necessary aspects of an operation. Do I have the proper instruments? Are all the personnel scheduled for the selected time? Am I under a time constraint? Is the patient critical or is this more of an elective surgery which can be done on a more flexible time frame? Then I started to look at it from the standpoint of, *What could go wrong?* That's when the idea of Wooley's health struck me. Is he not the one man who could thwart the whole operation by identifying the forgery too soon? Does that make him vulnerable to some physical threat, such as a poisoning or an accident which gets him out of the way? Perhaps the thief has a bribed appraiser in line who would certify the authenticity of the DaVinci?"

"Bravo, Watson!" said Holmes from his chair. "Now you are thinking like I must do, from the perspective of the criminal. You have made a most excellent point!"

I sat back and took a sip of my sherry, with no little pride at pleasing my friend. "Then you agree, we must be on the lookout for the professor's safety? How will we go about that?"

Holmes tilted his head indulgently. "That isn't the excellent point you made my friend. Of course, you cannot be blamed for your erroneous conclusion about Wooley, for you are unfamiliar with protocols in these transactions. The verification of authenticity is always carried out by a random committee selected by the museum board consisting of no less than three individual experts to ensure there is no collusion with a forger attempting to pass off a fake work of art."

My high spirits suddenly sagged, but Holmes quickly bolstered it again as he leaned forward and reiterated, "The excellent point you made was looking at this escapade as an operation. Think of how many personnel are needed, how many instruments must come into play, the amount of equipment and supplies which may be necessary to pull it off successfully, and the fact everything must take place within specific time frames or it may fail. When you put it like that, your original point from the other day becomes ever more poignant: Why not just kidnap the Countess directly? Less effort, less complications, less chance of anything going wrong."

"So where does that leave us?" I asked.

"With the additional information Wiggins verified as to who met with Garnier in the restaurant. That gentleman is the link which will forge, if you will pardon the pun, the lock on the trap we must set."

Chapter IX

Wiggins arrived sharply at noon and reported that his charge hadn't left his house all that morning and appeared to be working upstairs, as he occasionally walked past a window, apparently stretching his legs. Holmes thanked him for his report and advised him to keep up the surveillance. Before the lad left, I instructed him to see Mrs. Hudson in the kitchen where she would have some food prepared for him.

The lad smiled at that and with a *Thank you*, bounded down the stairs.

Holmes looked upon me after the boy left and said, "If you go about feeding all my spies, you could lose a fortune rather quickly."

I looked at him and replied, "As you had put me in a medical frame of mind, I noted the boy is far underweight for his height, and thus my prescription of a good solid meal."

"*Touché,*" he replied. I went and sat at the dining table to partake of the luncheon Mrs. Hudson had brought up. Holmes wandered over that way, but instead of sitting down to eat, took up a thick slice of bread, wrapped it around a piece of sliced beef, and poured himself some coffee. Then he went back to his chair and folded his long legs into one of his thinking poses.

"Speaking of poor eating habits . . ." I said.

"Shush!" he admonished me. "I must use your operation metaphor and create the best method for a counter-operation. Please leave me be for the next hour-and-a-quarter."

I partook of my lunch as quietly as possible and then retired upstairs to do some reading of a novel – *King Solomon's Mines by* H. Rider Haggard. Allan Quatermain had just led his search party to an oasis when Holmes knocked on my door. Reluctantly, I marked my place and returned to a real-life adventure.

Holmes bade me sit down in my customary spot as he returned to his chair, where a cloud of smoke lingered above. I had grown impatient and spoke. "Well, what has your three-pipe contemplation told you?"

"This one was actually four," he replied. "Every scenario I've contemplated regarding the theft of the DaVinci has ended as an impossibility."

"Surely the thief doesn't think so," I countered. "Unless it was his intention all along to give Garnier an impossible task, so as to have an excuse to kidnap his mother."

"Kidnappers need no excuse," he answered back with some disdain. "They simply take whom they please, when it is convenient to do so. No, there is a different game going on here. Recall what I always say about impossibilities."

I thought a moment, then recalled, "Once they are eliminated, whatever remains, no matter how improbable, must be the truth. But, what remains? If the theft of the DaVinci is impossible, what does the thief hope to gain?"

"That," said my companion, raising an index finger into the air, "is what I hope to discover tonight. With your assistance."

"Anything I can do help."

"Excellent! I knew I could count on my Watson. Tonight, you will have a taste of fatherhood."

"Say again?" I replied, confused as to how this related to the case.

"The gentleman Wiggins was watching today, is, in fact, the Dutchman to whom I referred earlier. It appears our friend Robie was correct when he surmised it might be so. I need to get into his rooms to see

322

how far he's progressed with his forgery and what technique he's using which makes him think he can get away with his plan.

"To do so safely, I shall need to have him watched when he leaves for dinner, for I know he keeps no cook upon his staff and regularly dines out. He may well have seen Wiggins and may become suspicious at a strange boy still hanging about his neighborhood. I've sent him to a clothier who owes me a favour to obtain a set of respectable clothes which he will wear in your company as you go out together as father and son, so as to maintain watch over the Dutchman and give me ample warning before he returns."

"Why not just use one of the other Irregulars?" I asked.

"They wouldn't be able to follow him inside most of the places he prefers to dine – just as Wiggins was unable to enter the Langham without the aid of his friend in the kitchen. With him clean and neatly dressed in your company, he won't be given a second glance. I've engaged a cab driver friend who will take you wherever the Dutchman goes and wait for you. When he's finished his meal, you will be able to hop into your waiting cab and beat him back to his house before he can hail one and follow, thus giving me a few minutes warning.

"It's likely I won't need his entire dinner hour to conduct my investigation into his rooms. However, it's best to be prepared for unforeseen delays."

So it was that Wiggins accompanied me on a father-son expedition to dinner at a nice little restaurant about two miles from the Dutchman's home. We discussed his family circumstances and I learned how he came to join the band of children whom Holmes referred to as his Irregulars.

However, those details are rather personal, so meanwhile I shall stick to the facts of our task that evening, saying only that I gained a good deal of respect for the young man. Holmes in disguise as a plumber (should he be spotted by the Dutchman or questioned by a neighbor) stole his way into the house via the backdoor. The Dutchman had locked the door to his studio on the upper floor, but it quickly gave way to one of Holmes's skeleton keys. Immediately his eyes came to rest upon the answer to the crime involving Count de Vermilon. Still, he made a careful search of the room, leaving no clues as to his presence and was able to leave in mere minutes.

Thus, by the time we were racing back ahead of our quarry, we instead found Holmes hailing us on a corner some three streets from his target. He crowded in beside us, setting his plumbers box upon the four-wheeler's floor. As we made for Baker Street, I asked, "You must have made quick work of your investigation. Did you learn anything significant to put an end to Garnier's troubles?"

A strange look came over the detective's face. Then he replied, "I learned enough to keep the Countess out of danger. I can assure you there will be no kidnapping. We do, however, need to set up another meeting with our client. Do you have rounds at Barts tomorrow?"

"Yes, in the afternoon," I replied. "But I can easily rearrange them if you need me."

He raised his hand. "On the contrary. I should like to use the physician's lounge there as a neutral meeting place. Garnier should feel comfortable that anyone following him would think nothing suspicious of his walking into a hospital. Afternoon shall be perfect, as I have things to arrange in the morning. Would three o'clock be convenient?"

I nodded. "Yes. Generally the afternoon staff take a break around tea time at four, so it should be fairly empty at three."

"Excellent!" cried the detective. "If all goes well, we should have this case wrapped up when he meets with us."

"You've solved it then?"

"I've one or two details to see to, but yes. I now have a full picture and we can lay our hands upon our culprit tomorrow."

He then turned his attention upon our young companion. "Wiggins, you and the lads have done well. Your observation at the Langham dining room was the key to solving the case. You may tell your friends they can stand down. Here is a shilling apiece for each of them."

He pulled a handful of change from his pocket and handed it over to the young man who took it gratefully. "What about these clothes, Mr. 'Olmes? Shall I take them back to your friend tomorrow?"

Holmes shook his head. "No, no, my boy, those are yours to keep. You never know when I may need you to look such a part again."

I thought the lad might shed a tear as he caressed the lapels of his coat. "I don't know what to say Mr. 'Olmes."

Holmes dismissed the emotional tone with a wave of his hand. "A mere 'Thank you' shall suffice, along with the promise that you'll continue your work for me as I need you."

"Absolutely! Thank you, sir!"

"Then there's an end to it. I believe this is your neighborhood. We'll drop you here and I'll let you know when next I need you."

We let the boy out of the cab and continued on to Baker Street. "I'm glad you allowed him to keep the clothes," I said. "I was going to offer to pay for them myself, for he has surely earned them over the years."

"Undoubtedly," was all he acknowledged. Then changed the subject. "Now I am looking forward to a cold supper, a good cigar, and a glass of that *Pétri Merlot* to top off the evening, for tomorrow shall be a busy day."

324

Chapter X

True to his word, Holmes was already out and about when I awoke at eight o'clock the next morning. Dear Mrs. Hudson fixed me a good hot breakfast and I spent the morning with Allan Quatermain and company, until it was time to head off to Barts for my afternoon rounds.

My patients were mostly among London's injured citizens, a combination of broken limbs, cracked ribs, and severe cuts. Fortunately, none were life-threatening, mostly painful and in various stages of healing. Around two-thirty I was called to the front and found myself being greeted by none other than Charles Robie. I cautiously shook the man's hand as I asked for what purpose he had sought me out.

In that pleasant baritone voice he replied, "Our friend, Mr. Holmes, has requested my presence at a meeting at three o'clock. He said I should arrive early, seek you out, and you would provide me with a doctor's coat or apron to wear – something about not wanting to tip his hand too soon. He also said that when we met with him and his companion, you were to refer to me as *Mr. Charles*. Do you know what this is all about?"

I shook my head. "I'm afraid I haven't the slightest idea. It was my impression we were meeting with our client. As Holmes has assured, you aren't involved in this scheme, and I cannot imagine why your presence is required."

Shrugging my shoulders, I continued. "At any rate, I've learned to trust him, no matter how odd his requests, so let us get you fixed up in proper attire."

At five-minutes-to-three, we walked into the physician's lounge and found Holmes. He was quite satisfied with the look I'd given to Robie, but wouldn't answer our questions.

"No time now, gentlemen. Just play along when our guest arrives."

At precisely three o'clock, the door opened slowly and Jean-Paul Garnier's head tentatively poked through the aperture. Once he spotted Holmes, he felt confident enough to enter quickly and shut the door behind him.

"I've come at the hour you suggested, M. Holmes," said the little man, looking nervously about. His eyes came to rest on Robie. "May I enquire as to who this gentleman is? Is he here to help your investigation?"

Holmes nodded. "Mr. Charles is a trusted associate and has connections who are familiar with the types of persons with whom we are dealing. Indeed, the information he's provided has proven crucial to our case."

Holmes waved us all to sit around a table and insisted Garnier sit next to him, while Robie and I took the chairs closest to the door to act as *de facto* guards. The diminutive Count de Vermilon asked, "What information? Is he saying he knows who this *Diable* is?"

Holmes pursed his lips and shook his head. "No, he does not." At which statement Garnier seemed to let out a breath he had been holding. "However," continued the detective, nodding toward Robie, "his information has led me to discover a confederate of your would-be kidnapper. *That* individual is under surveillance by Scotland Yard. He is the forger who was to provide the substitute artwork. It's only a matter of time before he leads us to his employer. Once they meet, we'll have our man. I assure you, your mother is quite safe. But to ensure her continued safety, I've sent a wire to certain colleagues at the *Sûreté* who have been advised of the situation."

A strange look came over the Count's face as Holmes delivered that last remark with a narrow stare into the man's eyes. With a bravado which seemed to me more desperation than indignation, he slammed his fist upon the table and glared at Holmes. "What have you done? You have ruined everything! They are sure to kidnap her now if their plans aren't followed. I will hold you responsible if anything happens to her!"

He stood up and turned to leave, but at a signal from Holmes, I tapped Robie's arm and we both rose and blocked his path to the door. He glared up at us, but I could see the fear in his eyes. Turning back to Holmes he cried, "What is this? You are kidnapping *me* now?"

Holmes merely shook his head and then, with some barely controlled anger in his voice, said, "Do sit down, M. Garnier. Your only chance to escape a ruined reputation and possibly the French judicial system is to tell us the truth. Right here, right now, or I will turn you over to Scotland Yard for extradition back to Paris."

The Frenchman sat down, but still attempted to bully his way out of his predicament. "I've committed no crime. I cannot be arrested."

Holmes leaned over the forearm he rested upon the table, glared at our client, and said in a soft, menacing tone, more powerful than his previous command, "You've committed no crime in England, because I have stopped you. But you can most certainly be detained with the evidence I've gathered. I'm quite sure your accomplice will gladly testify against you in return for a lighter sentence for himself. The Yard will have no choice but to turn you over to the French government for disposition."

His own face turned as red as his name as he cried, "You are bluffing, *Monsieur*!"

Holmes stood and walked over to the window, gazed about for a few seconds as if gathering his thoughts, and then quickly turned upon his prey. "You were seen meeting with the Dutchman after I had already questioned him. This observation revealed you were more angry at his confrontation than fearful of it. This didn't seem natural for man in the situation you claimed to be in. I contacted Mr. Charles, who knows of these matters in the underground art world of Europe, and he suggested the Dutchman might be the perpetrator of your troubles.

"Then there was the scenario you had suggested. These people expected you to foist a forged DaVinci upon the British Museum while they stole away with the real thing. Such an act would be impossible and you, as an associate curator at the Louvre, would know that. Watson will tell you I have a rule about impossibilities. Through my own means, I was able to get a look at what the Dutchman was working on. One glance answered my questions. He wasn't forging the *Salvator Mundi* as you claimed. He was forging the drawings of *Christ on the Cross* by Michelangelo. You knew you couldn't substitute a forgery on the British side of the exchange, but seemed to think you could on your end. Perhaps it was a matter of national pride. You chose to steal from the British instead of from the French."

Holmes walked over to the man's chair, his superior height even more dominating on such a slight figure of a man as Garnier. Crossing his arms and staring down upon him, he made an offer. "Confess your scheme and tell us what has brought you to attempt this desperate solution. It's possible I may be able to help you in a different manner than that for which you originally hired me."

Apparently all the incidents of Garnier's life, where he had been intimidated by men much larger than himself, now boiled up inside him and, possibly for the first time, he refused to give in.

He stood and shook his fist in the detective's face. "Do your worst, M. Holmes! As you say, I've committed no crime. So I am walking out of this room and returning to Paris!"

Holmes heaved a sigh, and resignedly said, "As you wish. Let me open the door for you."

We followed Holmes and Garnier out into the hallway, where upon the detective made a gesture to a man sitting on a bench. When this fellow stood up, I recognized the figure and face of a frequent visitor to Baker Street. He walked up to our little group and said, "Is this the man, Mr. Holmes?"

Holmes gave slight bow and replied, "Jean-Paul Garnier, Count de Vermilon, allow me to introduce Inspector Bradstreet of Scotland Yard. Since you refuse to deal with me, you will be forced to deal with him. He's all yours, Inspector."

Bradstreet grabbed the fellow, spun him around, and slapped a pair of darbies on him quick as a flash. "He'll make a nice cellmate for the Dutchman. Thank you, Mr. Holmes."

A string of what I assumed were French expletives echoed down the hall as our former client was led away. Holmes suggested we return to Baker Street for dinner. Robie spoke up at that. "Gentleman, if I may, I have the most excellent chef on my staff and I would be honored to have you join me for dinner and more of those fine French cigars. Then, Mr. Holmes, I trust you will regale us with the details which will answer all our questions about this case."

Holmes agreed, and by seven o'clock that evening we were again dressed in our best and enjoying the finest of French cuisine at Robie's home. As the first course was being served, our host offered a toast to Holmes with an excellent French champagne. "To your health, sir, and thank you for removing that blight upon the art world."

We drank and, as he set down his glass, he asked, "Now, tell us how you did it. What made you arrive at your conclusions regarding M. Garnier?"

Holmes shook his head modestly and replied, "It was the usual method of how I solve all my cases, Mr. Robie. I take the statements of witnesses or victims and test them for their logicality and accuracy. I observe the circumstances of the crime or threat and make deductions. In many cases, more than one deduction may be possible and I need to test them as hypotheses. I use whatever resources may be necessary, both within and on the edges of the law."

Here he looked pointedly at our host and then continued. "In this case, Watson here made the initial suggestion that the scheme was far too complicated. A threat of kidnapping, or even murder of a loved one, to gain access to a valuable treasure isn't unheard of. I have been involved in a few such cases myself. But this particular treasure was taking things too far. Anyone who appreciates the world of art would know that substituting a forgery during such an exchange with the British Museum is impossible.

"When I went to the Dutchman for his opinion and mentioned the item in question was a DaVinci from the Louvre, he immediately said '*Salvator Mundi* or *Virgin of the Rocks?*' Out of all the DaVinci paintings in the Louvre, he named the one which was the subject of this plot. Watson will tell you how I loathe coincidence. Thus he immediately came under suspicion. When I came to you, you confirmed he would be a likely suspect.

"What took him to the top of the list was his meeting with Garnier at the restaurant in the Langham. When my spies confirmed it was he whom they had observed, I arranged to get a look at his studio to see what he was working on. Instead of *Salvator Mundi,* the Michelangelo sketches were on his easel. I had the last piece of the puzzle and it all became clear: There was no *Diable*. It was Garnier himself all along."

"I made inquiries to French contacts confirmed the state of Count de Vermilon's finances and certain behaviours which had drained his accounts. His mother would allow him no access to the monies she controlled. To actually kidnap her would be insufficient to meet his obligations, for only his uncle had access to her accounts until her death, when Garnier would inherit. He wasn't so cold-blooded as to actually have her killed, so he came up with this threat in order to get his hands on something more valuable than her family fortune."

"But the letters? "I asked. "Are you saying he mailed them to himself?"

"Yes, which is why the handwriting was so unusual. He needed it to look quite different from his own."

Robie pointed his fork at my friend and asked, "But why did he engage your services, Mr. Holmes? Surely that was a foolhardy tactic on his part."

Holmes gazed into his wine glass momentarily, then replied, "In case anything went wrong, Garnier needed proof that he was an unwilling participant. He was afraid the *Sûreté* or Scotland Yard would see into his little scheme. But, if he hired the services of an amateur, he could show he had taken steps to stop the theft and could blame the success of the crime on the fact he couldn't engage professional law enforcement.

"Since the real theft wouldn't take place until he returned to France when, supposedly, his English detective was no longer involved, he felt it was a foolproof plan."

Robie laughed. "I have always believed that the problem with foolproof plans is that not everyone is a fool. Expose your plan to enough people and someone will discover a way to thwart it. "

"Agreed," answered Holmes. Then he turned to me. "I have also recently discovered that there's a need to look at facts from two approaches. One, the logical, analytical aspect, which is my specialty. The other, that of the storyteller, who sees the situation through the artistic mind with emotions and the non-linear thinking of flawed human beings, whose motives can be unfathomable to the logician. You, my dear Doctor, have proven invaluable to me in that method."

Here he raised his glass to me and Robie joined in, proclaiming, "To the partnership of science and art, gentlemen! May your successes continue for years to come."

NOTES

1. At this point in time, the Palais Garnier was renowned for its architecture. It would gain further fame in the Twentieth Century as the setting for the classic 1910 novel by Gaston Leroux, *The Phantom of the Opera*.
2. While still in his athletic prime, Holmes would occasionally supplement his income as an amateur boxer in the underground rings of London. This fact is inferred from *The Sign of the Four*.
3. Among Watson's memorandum on this case was the note that, since he had not yet published any of Holmes cases, he felt his own name would be unknown and not associated with the detective.

The Adventure of
Three-Card Monte
by Anisha Jagdeep

Part I – In Compartment 4D

"That incompetent man! He hasn't the faintest clue what he was talking about! If I were you, Holmes, I wouldn't tolerate this rubbish!"

We had entered Compartment 4D with our luggage. A few days back, Holmes and I had traveled to Bristol to investigate a murder at Rosehill Manor, the details of which I may soon relate to the public. However, at the present moment, in consideration for the important people involved in the affair, my readers must be content with the scarce yet misleading details a two-column print in the newspapers provided.

Of course, I easily acknowledge that I place hard emphasis on the contributions of my friend to the case at hand, the deductive analysis that is present in some variation in every one of my writings and, not to mention, the sensational details that I use to make my writing appeal to both the student and the average reader. Even so, it is particularly difficult for me to ignore the distorted language of the press which gives more attention to the police officials rather than to my friend. This is precisely why I penned my first story, *A Study in Scarlet*.

"It is most inexcusable of Inspector Hartford to snatch your well-earned credit!" I persisted. "Why, the only work he did throughout the entire case was to handcuff that villain, after he bungled the entire case!"

Holmes smiled in his usual gentle manner. "My dear Watson, this cold weather doesn't encourage such outbursts. I do feel that I'm entitled to a little peace and quiet after the end of a successful investigation."

"What is more irritating is your indifference about the whole thing!" I flung the defective newspapers I was reading aside and turned an annoyed look to my friend, who had closed his eyes.

"It was reward enough to be called in for the case. Besides, I believe I owe Inspector Hartford many thanks for allowing me to investigate without any of his slow intellect interfering. Lestrade, on the other hand, isn't nearly as cooperative."

"Lestrade may be a trifle too smart in his words. However, you must agree that he at least holds a meagre appreciation for your intelligence. Once he stops those infernal arguments with Gregson and sees that you do

331

more than spin theories, he is sure to shake your hand someday. And then
– "

I paused as a man entered our compartment. He carried two bags with him which he placed near his legs as he sat down beside me, leaving a small distance in between us. The frosty weather had caused him to dress most warmly. Even so, the fine black overcoat with the velvety fur collar, the gray trousers, the well-cut gloves, and the long brown scarf wrapped thrice around his neck and chin, were of little use, for he was ceaselessly shivering, and his nose blushed as red as a ripe tomato.

"Well sir, it seems as if this weather is especially bitter for you," I remarked, "for I observe that you have a cold."

"Oh, yes sir," he replied with a rough voice, quickly pulling out a handkerchief from his coat pocket. "I have been frightfully taxed of late, and to top it all is this blasted cold! To whom do I have the pleasure of speaking?"

"I am Dr. Watson. The gentleman sitting opposite is my friend, Mr. Sherlock Holmes."

"Mr. Holmes? Why, I have heard a great deal about you, sir. My name is Wallace. James Wallace."

Holmes didn't open his eyes nor acknowledge the outstretched hand of our new companion. It was apparent that he had fallen asleep, quite unconscious of Mr. Wallace's presence. Our companion slowly withdrew his hand and turned to me as if for an explanation which I humbly attempted to give.

"You see, Mr. Wallace. My friend has exerted himself unconditionally these past few days, his mind and body occupied in solving a rather extraordinary case. I think it only fair that we excuse Mr. Holmes and allow him some rest."

"Of course, of course," he said in a visibly good humor. "Anyway, I'm certain that neither I nor my problems are interesting enough to be the subject of Mr. Holmes's attention. However, it is fortunate that *you* are awake, Dr. Watson, for you may be able to suggest some medication for me."

"It is an ordinary cold, Mr. Wallace. I don't perceive any congestion or any hoarseness in your voice, so laryngitis can be dismissed. When you reach home tonight, prepare a mustard plaster and some hot water with lemon or pepper. The most important thing is to get plenty of rest, so if you're feeling tired, you can sleep now. I don't think Holmes here would mind."

"I'm not very tired now, but I'm certain by the end of this train ride, I will be. As to the other treatments you mention, unfortunately, it will be quite difficult for me to arrange for them, as I'm not returning home."

332

"My dear sir," I said, quite taken aback at his remark, "one doesn't need to be a doctor to tell you that you shouldn't be traveling in your condition."

"Yes, you're right, Doctor," he said with much emotion. "But I have no alternative. I'm unfortunate, as most elderly folk are. You see . . . but it isn't right for me to spoil your journey with my personal troubles."

"No, no, please go on, Mr. Wallace. I assure you I am interested."

"It is kind of you to listen. You see, my beloved wife died a year ago. Some years earlier, my son, Jacob, had traveled to Philadelphia to set up some industrial firm. I, being a simple watercolor artist, had no sort of education in the field of business, but the interests of young people conflict with those of their parents in many instances, and Jacob was impatient to find his own place in the world – one far away from the musty life of paintbrushes and inkpots. He returned about two months ago. He had become very wealthy in the States from making successful investments in . . . some companies that I learned were very prosperous. I should have been a very proud and happy father if not for, what I still consider, a rash indiscretion on the part of my son. He had married a theater actress while living in Philadelphia, so I had the opportunity to see both him and his wife, Nora, at my doorstep that day. I was, as you can imagine Dr. Watson, startled upon seeing her, as it was agreed, before he left, that Jacob would be married to the eligible daughter of my friend, Mr. Hawthorne, when he returned. I didn't say a word about it until after dinner, when I chanced to be alone with my son in his room. I may haven't chosen my words correctly, but his coolness made me furious.

"'What is of great concern is that I'm now placed in a most awkward position,' I told him. 'How can I tell Mr. Hawthorne of this fresh incident? When I received your letter in which you wrote that you were coming back, I immediately wrote to his family, and they have been busy ever since, preparing for the wedding!'

"'Well then, it seems we *both* have been very hasty!' said he with a chuckle that irritated me so. 'In any case, Dad, I was never eager to marry Miss Hawthorne. As far as I'm concerned, you can tell them the truth or a fabrication. What Mr. Hawthorne thinks of me is of no consequence to me. Now if you'll excuse me, Dad, I'm rather tired from the journey. Good night!'

"The conversation ended there, but I wasn't at all satisfied with my son's relaxed manner about it. For me, it was a matter of losing my friend's trust and respect. To think that I could have no control over my own son!"

"But what did you tell Mr. Hawthorne?" I asked him.

"I decided it was only fair to visit him instead of simply writing. I went to his house and told him that there was a sudden change of plans, and Jacob had to remain in the States due to unforeseen business developments. When he asked if I had any inkling of when he would be able to return, I said I had none and remarked that now that Ella, Mr. Hawthorne's daughter, is of marriageable age, he should try to find someone else instead of waiting for Jacob."

"What effect did the news have on poor Miss Hawthorne?" I remarked, trying to extract as much information as I could from my companion in order to converse with Holmes later about this interesting narrative.

"She had gone to market, so I couldn't speak to her, but Mr. Hawthorne assured me that she would be informed. I didn't learn of their plans, for a week later, we moved. My son sold our old house and purchased a small house in the country. I was, at first, not willing to leave my home in which I have lived for over thirty-five years, but my son insisted on my staying with him and Nora, for he hoped I would be able to know Nora better. He was right! I discovered that she was extremely extravagant and spoiled and especially hostile towards me. Jacob wasn't willing to accept my protests. I could see that his attraction towards Nora overshadowed his concern for my complete comfort. I know that I'm old, and I didn't want to be a burden to a young couple, so I spoke very little and decided to allow Jacob to take full charge of expenses and all of that, and Nora to take charge of the household.

"This morning after breakfast, I thought I would visit Mr. and Mrs. Burton. They are the couple that bought our old house. My pesky cold had started last night, but I was unusually restless. Oh, if only I hadn't gone! I would have been spared all this . . . this . . . this mess!

"I found out that Mr. Hawthorne had sent me a couple of letters. I was surprised to see that he had mistaken the address, for I had written a letter to him about my shifting to a new house and Jacob had posted it. I read the letters in the cab. They gave me, Dr. Watson, a most terrible shock, one that I wasn't prepared for."

Mr. Wallace gave a brief summary of the letters on our train journey. A duration of seven months has passed since the ending of this case, and as to the privacy of the people concerned in what had been a singular affair, as my readers will soon understand, I need not go through great pains to conceal any delicate or even compromising information, since the entire matter has been made public. Therefore, I can now take the liberty of presenting my readers with reproductions of the actual letters written by Mr. Hawthorne to Mr. Wallace.

The two letters are as follows:

38 Aldbourne Street
Bristol
January 4th

Dear Jim,

I hope that young Jacob's business in the States is doing well, acknowledging that I have trained him well and knowing his dedication and spirit, I am confident that he has addressed the financial difficulties, which you spoke of, most excellently. Please give my warmest regards to him.

My next point concerns our dear Ella. Immediately after you left our house that day, she returned from the market. Apparently, she had met one of her old admirers and entered into an argument with him. For thirty minutes, she talked my ears off about how "that rascal had the nerve to say that Jacob had forgotten her and wouldn't come back for her had she been the Princess of Wales" and how "she passionately fought back such offences by educating him on the truth that Jacob was coming home, and they would soon be married". It was a foolish little squabble, but you know how young girls are. She concluded her mighty chronicle by declaring her "utmost trust for Jacob" and that "he would never betray her affections". I think you will agree with me, James, that, at that moment, it wouldn't have been very tactful to let her know about the unfortunate delay in Jacob's return.

A couple of days passed before I told her. She took the news much better than I expected, but I did notice disappointment in her face even though she endeavored admirably to conceal it. The announcement of "Jacob's return" to the States had reached the ears of every one of her friends as well as the florist, the baker, and even the clergyman, so the next few days Ella spent in retracting those words she had made in some haste.

I felt she needed a bit of cheering up, so I suggested that she travel to the States and visit Jacob who, if I remember correctly, is in Philadelphia at the moment. As you would expect, she was thrilled with the suggestion. She is to leave for the States in a few days, so I'm writing to ask you if you would kindly give us the information of Jacob's whereabouts in Philadelphia. I am certain it would be a wonderful surprise to

335

him when he meets Ella, whom he hasn't seen for two-and-a-half years.

Faithfully yours,
Grover Hawthorne

* * * * *

38 Aldbourne Street
Bristol
January 12th
Re: Jacob's Address

Dear Jim,

I did not receive a reply from you the last time I wrote. I hope that you are in fine health and all is well. My Ella has safely crossed the Atlantic – although the ship was hindered by a rather heavy storm for two nights and therefore delayed – and has taken up lodgings in a hotel in Haddonfield, New Jersey. Her plans, as she related to me in her letter, are to visit a few relatives around the area and then call on Jacob. Please reply to this letter with Jacob's address or the savings that I invested into this intercontinental journey would have been a waste. Unhappily, my wife has taken ill, and I cannot afford to leave her side for the present. If not for this spell of misfortune, I would have gladly visited you.

Faithfully yours,
Grover Hawthorne

"This was a fine pickle, Dr. Watson! A very fine one! I boiled with rage at the actions of my son. One unwarranted misstep of his had sparked difficulties for me and for the Hawthornes! A young girl was stuck in America, earnestly searching for a wretch of a boy who is now an ocean apart from her! This was too much for an old man to stand!"

"Mr. Wallace, on learning of these happenings – if I'm not prying – what was your next step?"

"I ordered the cab to reroute and travel to Aldbourne Street. I believe it started to snow just then. Once I reached my friend's house, I related to Mr. Hawthorne the blatant truth with no added embellishment. I'm partly to blame, for it was I who made such a fine yarn of the whole thing, and I

336

now had to face an even greater humiliation from him, whose face, rightly so, showed every feature of offense and disenchantment upon hearing of my son's marriage. Had Mrs. Hawthorne been present at this meeting, she would have broken into quite a pretty tantrum! Mr. Hawthorne who, on the contrary, was softer by nature, said more in his eyes than in his words, and yet, he reproached me about how freely Ella's feelings have been played with by that unruly boy. I pleaded for forgiveness and offered to pay compensation for Ella's journey to the States and the financial inconvenience caused by the wedding arrangements. Mr. Hawthorne, who didn't want to make a scene of it in front of Mrs. Hawthorne who had called her husband from her room upstairs to see who had come, patted me on the shoulder and suggested in a most stiff and cold voice that I leave. I then sadly left the house and set off for home, all the while blazing with anger and disgrace.

"I was prepared to lecture Jacob about his misconduct till his ears dropped off! However, fortunately for him but not so for me, only Nora was at home. She told me that Jacob had gone into town. I wasn't very pleased to wait, for I feared that my temper would cool down at the elapse of time and I wouldn't be so harsh with the boy, but only twenty minutes had passed when the door opened and in came Jacob."

Mr. Wallace coughed slightly in his handkerchief and continued, "Now there isn't much to tell. I confronted Jacob, we had a bitter argument, and it ended with my leaving the house for good."

"You have my sympathy, Mr. Wallace," I said. "I trust you will recover your somewhat fragmented friendship with Mr. Hawthorne."

"Thank you, Dr. Watson. I think the best I can yearn for is compassion, which you have amply supplied, and my watercolors. I think I'll step out to the passage and have a cigarette. I'll just be back in a moment."

"Of course, Mr. Wallace." I laid back, gazing at the bleak darkness of the night outside. The snowflakes had ceased their merciless cascade, yet the atmosphere remained severely cold and demanding. How hard-hearted a son had to be to send his own father out of the house on a night like that, an aged man who wasn't keeping good health! My thoughts were still occupied in Mr. Wallace's little anecdote when a voice across from me interrupted my reflections.

"What do you make of it all?"

I looked up, astonished to see my friend smiling, his eyes mischievously iridescent. I said to him, "Why, Holmes, were you listening this entire time? I thought you were asleep!"

"On many an occasion have I closed my eyes for long hours, not in a sound sleep, but in a tranquil yet insightful meditation. I would have

337

smoked had I not desired that our companion should believe that I was asleep."

"Holmes! Why on Earth? He seems a perfectly genuine gentleman!"

Disregarding my exclamations, Holmes sat silently for a moment and stared reflectively at Mr. Wallace's bags kept on the floor of the train. Then, he looked at me and repeated his last query. "What do you make of his story?"

"I don't think there is anything to make of it. The poor man has been much harassed of late. He simply communicated the circumstances – "

"With admirable detail! And he wasn't even a client!"

"I should think that when he sees another who is ready to offer much desired consolation, a distraught man will pour out all his woes, giving as much description as possible in his passion."

"Even so, Watson, even so! To a stranger, even a very amiable one such as yourself, one is typically wary of divulging private information, let alone erupting into intense outbursts." He paused and laid back, his face showing mixed signs of confusion and interest. "I believe he would have gone further if he didn't check himself from time to time. After all, he concluded his monologue rather suddenly. An interesting specimen of a Bristolian, what?"

"Nevertheless, it is quite commonplace in comparison to the Rosehill Manor case you have just solved. A domestic affair involving a rash son, an anguished father, and two women who are each at the opposite ends of the spectrum. One is beautiful and ill-disposed and the other innocent and devoted, and predictably, the young man was attracted to the former. In the end, the broken father has to pay a dear price. The whole tangled predicament is pitiable, yet unexceptional."

"It is often the case that the most commonplace state of affairs, while it may elude the publicity of the newspapers due to its unoriginal nature, suppresses the inexplicable and grotesque within. The responsibility of the logician is to, whenever duly appropriate, extract the mysterious from the commonplace, like a nut from its shell. The more stubborn the shell, the greater pains we have to take to crack it open."

"But I see no reason for any suspicion of Mr. Wallace's story or the man himself."

"Did you not observe his behavior when he placed his bags on the floor and settled down? He hastily fished out his handkerchief from his pocket and held it to his nose."

"What of it? He has a serious chill."

"Ah, but his manner changed slightly when he thought I was asleep. He relaxed his hold on the handkerchief for a slight second. This I could faintly discern as I let my eyes open a bit when you began to explain to him of my trying exertions. When he turned to you to resume the conversation, he once again pressed it tightly to his nose. It was subtle yet perceptible to a trained eye. For the entire duration of the narration, he covered his nose or parts of his face with that handkerchief. That small square of blue cloth is very suggestive and has served a tender and careful purpose."

"You would be doing Mr. Wallace a disservice if he is an innocent man. Surely, these conjectures may be products of your inclination to see everything in the perspective of your line of work."

"No, not conjectures. Observations! One other remarkable point is that – "

Holmes, in an instant, paused and gently laid back his head on the wall of the compartment as Mr. Wallace reentered and resumed his seat. He still had his handkerchief at his nose, but he seemed refreshed and was more genial rather than remorseful. He noticed that Holmes was awake and said to him, "Ah, Mr. Holmes! I hope you have had a pleasant rest! I too have been somewhat reinvigorated, but I think a good night's sleep, as you suggested before, Dr. Watson, will help me get over those recent occurrences in my life."

Holmes smiled but said nothing. In another hour, we reached London and, at the station, I helped Mr. Wallace with his luggage, and we alighted from the train. "It was a fine journey!" said Mr. Wallace. "I wish you gentlemen a very good night!"

"The same to you, Mr. Wallace," I responded. "Take care of your health."

In the hansom on our way to Baker Street, I turned to Holmes and, with whatever little authority I may have had to rebuke him, I made it quite clear to him that I didn't approve his coldness towards Mr. Wallace, to which he replied, "I don't see why I should bestow any kind attention on a man who is trying his best to deceive me."

The matter was closed for the night, but my mind was yet to be satisfied, for it was plain to see that Holmes had noticed more about our train companion than what was discernable to me. I, in the first place, couldn't imagine any motive for deception or any profit Mr. Wallace would achieve if we had blindly swallowed his story, for we were strangers to each other, and the story, as I have already discussed with Holmes, was fairly commonplace. However, I didn't allow myself to lose a good night's sleep over such a matter and managed to rest a few hours with as much comfort as can be felt during the icy winters of London.

It was nearing eight when I joined Holmes for breakfast. The sky had cleared to regain its light cerulean tinge of the morning, but not without garlanding each and every rooftop and sidewalk with snow. It was a most perfect day for staying indoors and enjoying the solace of a warm fire, and Holmes, who hadn't said a word during our meal, had just picked up his violin when Mrs. Hudson entered, bearing a tray on which was placed a note. Holmes, upon reading it, glanced with a serious face in my direction and said, "Apparently, it was unwise for us to have returned to Baker Street. My suspicions yesterday, which you felt were unfounded, have suddenly gained some ground to go upon."

"Why, what is the matter?"

"The body of Jacob Wallace has been discovered near his house in Winterbourne, Bristol."

Part II – The Case

It wasn't unusual for two cases to materialize in quick succession, one after the other between an interval of at most a day. Yet I was, I must confess, quite irked at the idea of journeying back to a place where we had found ourselves just hours before, but such a startling discovery demanded our presence which couldn't be delayed. We found ourselves on a snow-covered path, lined with trees, that led to the main road into town. There were several constables, led by Inspector Hartford of the Bristol Constabulary, all collected around at the edge of a creek near a small, abandoned cottage. As we came closer, we saw the body of a man, the right side of his forehead red with blood and his legs and upper part of his body lying on the frozen bridge that was built over the creek. His head, facing down, lay immediately where the bridge ended onto the path. Thick carpet had been placed on the bridge to allow the constables to cross the bridge without any trouble.

"Ah, Mr. Holmes, Dr. Watson!" said Hartford when he saw us advance to the position where the body of the unfortunate man lay. "We haven't moved him, so you can see exactly how his end came. It was a most unnecessary death. It seems that Mr. Jacob Wallace slipped while on this bridge and hit his head on this beauty here." He pointed to a stone statue of a woman, a Greek goddess to be precise, that was placed to the right of the edge of the bridge. It was invariably a garden ornament and would have been beautiful to behold, if not for the fact that the elbow of the stone damsel was stained with a small, red patch that was evidently caused by the fall of the now-dead man on that rough point.

"The butler discovered the body at about four this morning," continued the inspector. "He had had the evening off yesterday and had gone to the tavern and fallen asleep from the drink until he woke up and saw the time. Then he went back to the house to find a disturbing sight."

"It is now more difficult than usual to give a proper estimation of the time of death," I intervened. "Due to the extremely low temperature, his body heat must have declined rapidly."

"But he must have been dead for at least eight hours," added Holmes, examining the wound. "His body is completely covered with a layer of snow and, if I'm not mistaken, the snowfall ended at about the time when we reached Baker Street – that is, 11:15."

The inspector chuckled pleasantly and said, "As simple as your deduction is, Mr. Holmes, I'm justified in not figuring it out myself, for I was snoring my head off at 11:15. After the work of the Rosehill Manor case, I needed all the rest I could get!"

I gazed disdainfully at the inspector while Holmes simply smiled. He lifted the body a little and turned it over a bit. The face was covered in snow, but I could make out its pleasant if somewhat mature features. Holmes brushed off some snow from the forehead and examined a small, dull spot of discoloration. After his study of the forehead, he stood up, saying, "You were certainly indispensable in our previous case, as you say, but I don't see how you thought that I would be of any use here. You yourself say it was an accident."

"Ah, well . . . Mr. Holmes, it definitely appears to be so."

"Then why has the body not been taken away long before?"

"The fact is that one member of this household is absent. This man's father had been at the Bristol Temple Meads Station last evening, and he had bought a ticket to London. There must be some background to this affair, and it is that which makes us uneasy. The point is to clear up everything where death is concerned, as you've no doubt taught me, Mr. Holmes." On perceiving no effect of flattery in Holmes's rather icy eyes, the inspector continued, "In fact, the conductor of the train Mr. Wallace was in says that he was in the same compartment that you and Dr. Watson were in. I thought perhaps that if you had talked with the elder Wallace, you would be able to give some information about why Mr. Jacob Wallace was out here in the snow and why his father was heading for London. I also must add that Mrs. Wallace, the deceased's wife . . . uh . . . has strong suspicions as well about this affair. Still, I must apologize for bringing you back here, Mr. Holmes and you, Dr. Watson, on a day like this."

"On the contrary, Inspector," said Holmes, now eagerly studying the statue. "I must confess you have done us a great favor, one that I'm sure Dr. Watson here will be thankful for. Am I not right, Watson? I would be glad to share my knowledge with you, but I think we must first interview Mrs. Wallace."

We continued down the path to a lonely yet respectable cottage, the residence of Master Wallace. We found Mrs. Wallace sitting on the settee, wiping the tears that fell from her delicate brown eyes. Domestic obligations and the simple pastoral atmosphere hadn't done much to mask any show of the stage glamor from her appearance. She still had the sophisticated beauty of an actress. "No doubt I have heard of you, Mr. Holmes," she said, directing a tearful glance at my friend. "Even though I have lived in England for only a short while, I have heard of you, and I want you to tell me that I am correct – that my husband's death wasn't an accident."

"My dear lady, I am bound to go by evidence, and if your judgement doesn't crumble in the face of solid facts, I'm willing to try my best to aid you. You must, however, relate to me everything you know that led up to the tragic event."

"My husband came home late in the afternoon. His father had already returned from his outing about thirty minutes before. As soon as I came out to meet Jacob . . . ."

"I beg your pardon, Mrs. Wallace. Where were you when your husband returned?"

"I was in the . . . kitchen."

"Pray continue."

"When I came out to meet Jacob, his father began making wild statements that conveyed nothing to my mind. I stayed in the room for a couple of minutes, and I then left them alone. I still heard yelling from both my husband and his father. After about a half-an-hour, I came out into this room on hearing a loud slam of a door. The room was empty, and I went up to Jacob's bedroom and saw him at his own table, his head in his hands. He was evidently disturbed and upset."

"Was there anything to signify that he was intoxicated? A bottle perhaps?"

"No, of course not!" said Mrs. Wallace in an indignant tone. "What makes you ask such a question?"

"I beg your pardon, Mrs. Wallace, but I'm sure you understand that a man, upset and under the influence of drink, will, in most cases, not walk properly. His muddled movements could have accounted for his sudden slip on the bridge. Never mind. Please continue."

"As I was saying, he looked terribly distressed. When he saw me, he laid aside some letters he'd been examining and told me that his father had just left the house. I insisted upon knowing what the argument was about, but he kept on shaking his head as if he was ashamed of telling me. After about a quarter-of-an-hour, he told me had to leave and bring his father back, and no protest of mine could prevent him from doing so. He left, and quite troubled myself, I immediately went to bed, not knowing that at probably the time I had changed into my nightgown, poor Jacob was already lying dead on that bridge. Oh, how horrible it is!"

"I don't suppose you would know where your husband had intended to go," added the inspector.

"It may have been to Mr. Hawthorne's place."

"How do you know this?" said Hartford, quite startled.

"I . . . I . . . ." stammered Mrs. Wallace, "By accident, I glanced at the signature of the two letters on his table."

The inspector and I looked at each other, while Holmes stared with a grave expression at Mrs. Wallace, who had bent her head. He then asked, "I'm still quite puzzled as to why you believe your husband was murdered. What do you believe happened to him?"

"I . . . uh . . . Jacob's father may have concealed himself somewhere nearby and made Jacob stumble or trip over some string or shovel. Or he might have come from behind and pushed Jacob's head on that stone statue multiple times and left him there dead. Oh, he always despised me! I knew he was terribly furious from what little I heard of the beginning of that argument! And he looks a frightfully strong man!"

"But Madam," interrupted Hartford, "you did tell us before that Jacob was alive, and his father had left the house quite some time before the accident happened."

"He might have come back somehow, in time to meet Jacob outside. There might have been another scuffle, and this time he killed him!"

"I'm afraid it is impossible, Mrs. Wallace," said Holmes. "Dr. Watson and I met the elder Wallace on the train. He had decided to travel to London."

Mrs. Wallace, upon hearing these words, glanced at me as if to see if I corroborated my friend's statements, and perceiving my small nod of assent, she bent her head, sighed, and continued to wipe the soft tears that bathed her cheeks. "We will no longer trouble you, Mrs. Wallace," said Holmes. "I think it will now be best to speak with the butler."

Luther, the butler, was a small, decent-looking man who at first glance, appeared to be naturally inclined to speak the truth. He immediately answered all the questions Holmes posed to him.

"Yes, sir, I had the evening off yesterday. It was the first evening I've had free since I started working for Mr. Wallace. After a little dinner, it started to snow, and I thought I would warm myself up with a couple of drinks. I don't know what came over me, sir. After waking up, I discovered it was four in the morning. I rushed back to the house, and to my horror, I saw Mr. Jacob Wallace lying on the bridge, covered with snow and with a deep cut in his head."

"What did you do immediately after you discovered your master?"

"I was quite shaken, Mr. Holmes, but thankfully I was composed enough to carefully tread the bridge and enter the house. I then knocked on the door of the elder Mr. Wallace, my master's father, and as I received no answer, I opened the door to find the room empty. Astonished as I was, I knocked on Mrs. Wallace's door. I told her of the unhappy accident, and she at once told me to fetch the police."

"You know nothing of the events leading up to the accident?"

"Yes sir, now I do. Mrs. Wallace has told me something of them."

"Mrs. Wallace also tells us that she believes her husband's father is involved in this matter. Do you also think so?"

"I cannot see how Mr. Wallace could have been involved, sir, from what I've heard. It appears very much to be an accident. Hitting one's head suddenly on the elbow of that statue might cause instantaneous death, or if he lost consciousness on hitting the statue, he must have died of hypothermia. After all," added Luther, looking ashamed, "he was there all night."

"Thank you, Luther. Now, if you please, I think it wise to examine the rooms of young Jacob Wallace and his father."

The ill-fated man's chamber was quite plain and homely. A mahogany desk and chair were placed in a small corner of the room, adjacent to the bed, and a cabinet and bookcase stood on the left side of the window. Holmes focused his attention on the desk which supported a bundle of papers, a pen, and an ink pot. He thoroughly examined the related documents – business papers they seemed to be – and stacked them, then looked with keen interest at two of them. "Look Watson – these must be the letters of which Mrs. Wallace spoke. They're from Mr. Hawthorne."

"That's right," said the inspector. "They probably have some connection to the argument last night. I don't suppose Mr. Wallace would want them back, Mr. Holmes?"

"I don't believe so," said Holmes. "If he wanted them, he would have remembered to take them with him. I suppose that I can retain these for a while, Inspector?"

Without waiting for a reply, Holmes put the letters in his pocket and then proceeded to the room of the elder Wallace. It was quite empty of course, for Mr. Wallace had remarked yesterday that he would never return to the house again. The wooden table in the room was discolored with small blots of red, blue, and black, indicating that a watercolor artist had indeed resided in the room. Holmes glanced around and said, "It seems there isn't much data here, Inspector."

"Yes, Mr. Holmes," said Hartford. "He must have taken his personal items with him. I suppose this hinders your investigation."

"On the contrary," said Holmes with a soft smile. "In this case, nothing can be more helpful than lack of data, that too in the right place."

He glanced around once more with a small gleam of satisfaction in his eye and quitted the room. Then, he progressed downstairs to the kitchen which was at the very back of the house. Holmes examined the fireplace in the far end of the kitchen. The logs in the fire were consumed. Holmes opened a covered iron pot which was suspended over the fire. It contained a roast and vegetables. On seeing a good dinner gone to waste, Hartford said, "It's a shame. Mrs. Wallace must have forgotten about the roast when her husband left. It's quite natural."

Holmes said nothing. He examined the contents of the pot quite thoroughly and then replaced the lid. He then led us out of the kitchen and back to the main room. Once there, he turned to Mrs. Wallace and asked, "You mentioned earlier, Madam, that once your husband left the house, you immediately went to your own room and to bed. You are sure on that point? You didn't, perhaps, return to the kitchen?"

"No, Mr. Holmes. I forgot all about dinner. I had a sudden headache after everything that happened, so I went to sleep immediately."

"Then when was the fire in your wood stove put out?"

"Oh yes, I put it out in the middle of the night. I went to the kitchen for a glass of water and saw that the fire was burning. Well . . . I was too tired to worry about the roast, so I simply adjusted the logs and let the fire die down. It was already quite low."

"I see. Thank you, Mrs. Wallace."

We then proceeded outside where Holmes turned to the inspector and asked, "Your final verdict, Inspector?"

"I'm sure that the house so far hasn't offered a shred of evidence in favor of foul play. I believe I've been quite thorough, Mr. Holmes. All the evidence outside the house clearly points to an accident.

"I respect your authority too much, Inspector, to repeat any investigation you've done. I would, however, in order to justify my superfluous presence here, give you a small suggestion: Don't inform the elder Wallace of the death of his son just yet. And let this affair not be put in the papers until I say it cannot hurt to do so. I suppose the news of this hasn't reached the ears of any of the journalists."

"No, Mr. Holmes, it hasn't. I suppose the least I can do is to act upon your words, in view of the fact that you and Dr. Watson were knocked up so early to come all the way back here! It was, as you said, 'superfluous'!"

Upon leaving the house, we immediately went to the newspaper office and Holmes made some inquiries which I didn't hear. A secretary brought him some old newspapers which he perused for a short while. Then, as we entered a cab, Holmes said, "I feel it is rather redundant to return to Baker Street immediately. It's quite good that we have brought our luggage from our last trip. What do you say we stay here in Bristol for a short while?"

"If it's all the same to you," I answered, quite unexcited about the idea. "I'd really rather go back to London."

"Could it be that this cold weather has weakened your appetite for adventure? That is disappointing!"

"I don't see any adventure, let alone a case to solve. The young Mr. Wallace did repent for his impetuousness before his death. Poor man! On hearing about Miss Hawthorne's travel to America and on ordering his father out of the house, he was troubled and regretful enough to go out in the snow and bring his father back. No doubt in his hurry and grief, he slipped on that icy bridge."

"But it is odd, is it not, that a much older man, our old acquaintance from the train, had crossed that very same bridge to hail the carriage to town? He was also very upset, not to mention furious, when he left the house. Moreover, he was carrying luggage. It would make much more sense had the elder Wallace slipped on the bridge instead of his son."

"That is logical, but a slip is a slip. Perhaps the elder Wallace was more careful. Or perhaps he did slip but was fortunate enough not to hit his head on the statue. Anyway, why do you suggest that we not return to Baker Street?"

"I wish to dig a little deeper into this matter, purely as an analytical study of truth and fabrication, and I think I would achieve the most satisfying results here in Winterbourne. If you would be obliging enough to accompany me, I promise you the first thing we do now is find a good restaurant."

I could see that Holmes was excited, but not a word would he tell me until we had taken our seats at a small café. "Now," he began. "Let us start from the very beginning: The elder Mr. Wallace from the train has left the house and, in spite of his emotions, has somehow crossed that bridge unscathed. A while later, the younger Wallace, in his repentance, decides to leave as well. An unfortunate tragedy occurs, and he is left in the snow until morning. And while all of this happens, the elder Wallace is chatting pleasantly with you.

"Let us take things one by one, in the order in which we were introduced to them. First, the behavior of Mr. Wallace on the train. When one takes his verbal behavior and his physical behavior together, one wonders at both his openness and his secrecy."

"I'm not sure I follow you."

"The man is confusing. He first somehow finds the impulse to relate his whole life story to you, a most descriptive account too, and yet he never

346

allows anyone to see his entire face at any moment. It seems that he overdid his alibi, if he thought he was going to need one."

"You don't mean he knew that his son would be killed and – "

"I mean nothing until I'm certain. I only suggest explanations for what I observed and what I found unnatural, such as the small, ugly mauve-colored patch on the forehead of the deceased. You recall that this bruise is on the left side of the forehead while the deadly gash caused by the statue is on the right side. The two wounds are almost collinear."

"That patch would have a simple explanation. It doesn't look as if it would kill a person, Holmes."

"Perhaps. But let us return to the fascinating Mr. Wallace. He not only gives a clear account of his troubles, but he names many people he knows. What for? Why all those names? Why the whole story in fact?"

"I did answer on that point in the train."

"I'm not satisfied. I think we have to go down the list. We've met Mrs. Wallace and Luther. Let us, after lunch, meet the Burtons."

Mr. Wallace's old residence differed from the house we had just visited, but it evoked a genial and tranquil atmosphere more so due to its two inhabitants, the Burtons, who were as eager to answer Holmes's questions as he was to ask them.

"It's such an unfortunate thing to have happen," said Mr. Burton upon hearing the news from Holmes. "He seemed a fine man when I met him."

"Yes, Mr. Holmes," said his wife, "Most cordial in fact. He said he and his father would take care of the entire moving business, in fact. All we had to do was pay the price and move in."

Holmes, who predicted a digression from his central focus, changed the subject to one with which we were both familiar. "I beg your pardon, Mrs. Burton, but my concerns are entirely about the young man's father. Did he come here yesterday?"

"Oh yes he did, Mr. Holmes. He came for a friendly visit."

"What time did he come?"

"About two."

"You had, I understand, some letters to give to him?"

"Yes," interjected Mr. Burton. "I would have forwarded the letters to him sooner if I had known the new address. I should say he was slightly perturbed. I informed him of some advertisements we put in the agony column which I suppose neither his son nor he saw."

At this, Holmes frowned. For one who knew Holmes's verdict on the legitimacy of Mr. Wallace, I could see that his crumpled brows betrayed his confusion on Mr. Burton's statements, which seemed to validate the story we heard on our train journey.

"Mr. Burton, do you remember the postmarks of those letters to Mr. Wallace?"

"Oh, I'm sorry. You see, it so happened that we were out visiting our relatives for two weeks. Our maid, Bertha, took in our mail and she, being a rather foolish girl, didn't notice the postmark or the name of the receiver. She just kept all the mail in a stack, and we sorted it out when we returned. But we failed to notice the postmark. I'm sure it was early in January though. We weren't at home the first weeks of January."

Holmes made every effort to suppress his annoyance and rose hastily. We left the Burtons and hailed a cab for 38 Aldbourne Street, the residence of Mr. Hawthorne. We were told he was engaged and wouldn't be able to see us, so we made our way to a hotel.

I was glad that I hadn't unpacked my luggage after returning home after the Rosehill Manor affair. After we obtained our rooms, I decided to first unpack my case, but when I opened it, to my astonishment, my night-clothes, shaving kit, and other necessaries were missing. I found instead a Reeves watercolor box, a number of paintbrushes and other painting implements, and a few large boards of canvas (which were painted on). There were also a shaving kit and an unfamiliar dressing gown and slippers. I immediately called Holmes and showed him the case. He smiled, looked at me merrily, and said, "I say, I should have believed you of all my acquaintances were quite incapable of being so careless."

"But Holmes! I distinctly remember picking up my case on leaving that train!"

"And I remember also that your case was almost identical to that of Mr. Wallace."

"What am I to do? And what is Mr. Wallace to do without his painting supplies?"

"There is nothing you nor Mr. Wallace can do now. I suggest we eat some dinner and have a night cap."

"I suppose that when we leave tomorrow, we can sort matters out at the station. Or we can quickly go to the station now and at least drop this case off . . . ."

"No, Watson, no, no! That lunch we had wasn't very nourishing. I would, if you don't mind, have some dinner now."

I saw a slight twinkle in his eye as he said this, and yet despite his saying he was impatient to dine, he ate very little and even set off on a little stroll in the moonlight. I didn't question him and set to the task of sleeping as comfortably as I could without my usual night-clothes.

It was a little after lunchtime when we found ourselves in the main room of Mr. Hawthorne's house. On hearing of Jacob Wallace's death, he said, "How dreadful! He was an extremely intelligent man. Very gifted indeed! It's a pity!"

"He wasn't a very faithful young man," said Holmes, "as you no doubt know, from what you were told by Mr. Wallace."

"I may not have forgiven him when he was alive, but now that he is dead . . . You see, I don't speak ill of the dead."

"Of course, Mr. Hawthorne. Is Mrs. Hawthorne at home? I would be honored to meet her."

Mr. Hawthorne looked at Holmes with wide eyes, but he replied quickly, "No, I'm sorry. She isn't well and in bed."

"Oh, I'm sorry to hear that. If I may ask you a question, Mr. Hawthorne: Did you send two letters to Mr. Wallace's old address early this month?"

"Yes, I did."

"You did not know of the fact that Mr. Wallace had moved to the country?"

"No, I did not. No one informed me of the fact."

"But Mr. Wallace told me that he had written a letter to you about his moving."

"Yes, he told me so as well. It seems that his son had neglected to post it. I suppose he didn't want to be bothered by me, and I certainly would have bothered them if I had come to know sooner. That must be the reason why they moved. If I had paid them a visit, it would have been a terrible shock to see Jacob here with his wife. I'm assuming, you know the details about the . . . the situation."

"Yes, Mr. Wallace gave a most instructive sermon on the train that night. Do you know where he is at the moment?"

"No, I don't. If you'll excuse me, gentlemen, I must go and attend to my wife. Please give my condolences to Mrs. Wallace."

We left the house and began to walk along the street. Holmes, his voice almost reaching the quality of a growl, said, "All the ways I can think of to discover inconsistencies have been demolished! I have talked to everyone mentioned by Mr. Wallace and so far, they all verify his story and those letters – even the fact that Mrs. Hawthorne is ill! Everything is annoyingly accurate!"

"Why shouldn't they be? You sound as if you're desperate to find some irregularity."

"I am. Irregularities are the flies in the soup bowl. They shouldn't be there, of course, and when you find one fly, you immediately pick it out. Ah! But you don't stop there! No! You are eager to make sure that there isn't another fly or anything else unpleasant in the soup before you're satisfied. Now I have found one irregularity. I'm simply searching for more until I'm satisfied that everything is right."

"You are becoming too metaphorical of late. I should be alert myself, lest I start to agree with you about Mr. Wallace."

Holmes smiled. "Perhaps we shall find an irregularity right back where we've started from: The residence of the late Jacob Wallace."

Luther opened the door to us when we arrived. Nora Wallace was sitting in the same place we had seen her when we first came. She looked up at us with a very tired expression. "Mr. Holmes, I do hope you'll understand that I'm not in a state for conversation."

"Forgive us, Mrs. Wallace. My profession requires me to do all I can to clear any doubts where a death of a man is concerned."

"I have already told you of my doubts regarding my father-in-law. I have no more to tell."

"You said that you were in the room for some time at the beginning of the argument between your husband and his father. You must remember something of what was said between them."

"No, Mr. Holmes, nothing definite. I only remember hearing Mr. Wallace telling Jacob what a wretched man he was and repeating the name 'Ella'. He was incoherent in his anger. My husband kept asking what the matter was, and he glanced at me and gave me a small sign which indicated I should leave them alone."

"You didn't think anything of a woman's name involved in the argument?"

Mrs. Wallace gave a proud look at Holmes and said, "I'm not one to jump to distasteful conclusions when I am not aware of any context."

"Yes, but you did glance at those letters on your late husband's table."

"I was simply curious to see who had sent them. That is all."

"Your curiosity didn't get the better of you, I suppose?"

"Certainly not! I had thought of asking my husband about it when he returned, but he did not, so I know nothing about the matter."

"Quite so. Please forgive my impertinence, Madam. I only ask these questions as a matter of verification, nothing more."

She stared at him, showing every sign of annoyance. Holmes rose and said, "Thank you, Mrs. Wallace. I offer you my apologies for trying you like this. And I am sorry you came to our country to witness a tragedy. May I ask if you're planning to return to the United States?"

Again, I saw that grand look, a look expressive of her marvelous theatrical background. "I thank you, Mr. Holmes, for your sympathies. I can assure you that I can look after myself here in England just as well as I can there."

We came out of the house and I said to my friend, "She is a remarkable woman, but she didn't like us coming here again, that is certain."

"And yet when we first saw her, she was quite impatient to hear what I had to say about the death of her husband. She was eager for me to acknowledge her own theories about the affair. You see, now we have two instances of confusing behavior: That of the elder Wallace and that of Mrs. Wallace. A fine irregularity we have come across, don't you think so?"

"It isn't exactly a worthy specimen of an irregularity."

"Perhaps not." Holmes walked a few paces and peered into the window of the house. His face showed deep interest, and I followed him and looked in as well. Luther had come into the room, and Mrs. Wallace had stood up. I don't usually mince words, but let me say that she was conversing with him in a way that made it look intimate rather than formal. Luther then took her hand, and they both went into a different room.

"I'm sure this would interest our good friend, Inspector Hartford."

That afternoon, the inspector visited us at our hotel. "Mr. Holmes, I think I have a fairly decent theory about the entire thing," said he, taking the teacup I handed him. "Accepting that there was no accident, I believe it must be the butler, Luther, who has murdered his employer."

"Why do you say that, Inspector?"

"What you clearly saw was a critical development in this case. There is definitely intimacy between Luther and Mrs. Wallace. Luther may have become infatuated with her when he first entered the household, and it was inevitable that she also developed affections for him. He is a handsome man, much more handsome than his master, who looked quite older than him. They decided that for their happiness, they must get rid of young Jacob Wallace.

"Luther is in the house when the elder Wallace and his son are arguing over matters which you have been fortunate to hear of in the train. He hears scraps of conversation, realizing that his master and the elder Wallace are now estranged. He sees the elder Wallace leave the house. Now, we are made to believe that Master Jacob retired to his own room immediately after this. However, I suggest that he walked out after his father and stood on the bridge, shouting or pleading for him to come back. Luther follows him to the bridge, taking care that he isn't seen. At that moment, when the elder Wallace is now out of sight, Luther seizes his opportunity. He pounces on his master from behind and takes his head and hits it on the elbow of the statue. Luther looks a strong man, so Jacob Wallace wouldn't be able to shake him off, if he was lucky to even have a chance to look at him. Luther then makes it appear to be an accident."

351

"You've forgotten that Luther has an alibi," I said after hearing the inspector's theory. "He was at the local tavern until four in the morning."

"Ah, Doctor, I went to the tavern to verify his alibi. The bartender says he had seen him that day. He didn't pay much attention to him, naturally, as there are always many people in a tavern, and one cannot keep track of everybody. But he doesn't believe there was any man of Luther's description in the tavern after nine in the evening. I know that the murder must have been committed before seven. That's the time when you met Mr. Wallace on the train, but even then, Luther's alibi is by no means irrefutable."

"But if the plan all along was to disguise the murder as an accident, and if Mrs. Wallace is complicit in the foul affair, why should she insist that the elder Wallace is the murderer? She simply complicated what at first would seem a fairly simple matter." I was conscious of a fleeting approbation in the eyes of Holmes as he glanced at me and then back at the inspector. I must have imagined at the time that my friend had instinctively styled himself the judge of this debate, silently evaluating the intelligence of my questions to Hartford and Hartford's responses to them.

"Ah yes, that is a fair question, Dr. Watson. I suppose that she wanted to direct Mr. Holmes's attention to the letters. Then, if for some reason, an investigation was made, the investigation would be centered around the elder Wallace instead of her and her lover. I believe it is a small, spontaneous impulse on her part, considering that Luther didn't attempt to implicate James Wallace. It gives credit to her excellent skills in acting."

Holmes usually doesn't entertain a view from the police for so long, and I normally don't conduct such conversations with the officials. However, this time I found the inspector's reasoning to be quite complete, and I fancied Holmes did as well. Otherwise, his impatience would have shown by now. It was only after Hartford finished his statements regarding Nora Wallace and took up his now-lukewarm cup of tea that Holmes spoke.

"Inspector," he said, "your suggestions seem to very well cover the facts, with the exception of one: I haven't received a telegram from Charing Cross Station saying that Mr. Wallace has come to enquire about his case."

"What case?"

"This one here," said Holmes, pointing to it, still open on the table. "The station master at Charing Cross Station has promised to notify me when Mr. Wallace comes to enquire about it. I've not yet heard from him . . . even after two days."

"But Mr. Wallace may not have noticed."

352

"I gave him two days, Inspector. Being an ardent watercolor artist, he wouldn't ignore his profession for any significant period of time. What is an even more definite point is that he doesn't plan on returning to his son's house nor is he acquainted with the sad fact that his son is dead. Why should he not have unpacked his luggage by now?"

With a sudden positive feeling, I exclaimed, "Holmes, you exchanged the cases deliberately, didn't you?"

Holmes merely glanced at me, smiled briefly, and restored his attention to the inspector, who was shaking his head.

"The official police cannot afford to take such liberties as you do, Mr. Holmes. If even the smallest unorthodox act of ours is publicized by the papers, we would be drowned in a quicksand of humiliation."

"I have no reason to worry, for the press is obliging enough to refrain from reporting any acts of mine."

Hartford caught none of the tartness that laced Holmes's remark and continued, "Even so, Mr. Holmes, I, in my own paltry judgement, say that you shouldn't have done what you did. It was quite crude and unoriginal. Something children might do, if I may speak straight."

"You are focusing too much on the action rather than its consequence. I do not ask, 'What do you make of it?' to too many people, Inspector. You would be deciding on a point on which the entire case hinges if you were to answer my query."

"I haven't the remotest idea what to make of this affair."

Holmes turned to me and seeing that I too had no opinion to give, began, "On the basis of the fact that Mr. Wallace hasn't enquired about his case, we can conclude that he hasn't opened it. A keen artist doesn't let his paintbrushes gather dust, and I could confirm, by an inspection of his color-soaked table and of the remarkable detail of his paintings, that he was a keen artist. Of course – "

"As if the brushes could gather dust in two days!" Hartford said laughingly. "It is natural that he didn't paint immediately after an episode that upset him – being thrown out of his own house."

"Yes, that is the most obvious explanation. But Watson saw a dressing gown and a shaving kit when he opened the case. Don't tell me that in his despair, he has ceased to shave or sleep."

"He wasn't very close to his son or his wife in the weeks spent in the new house," I noted. "Mr. Wallace himself told me that he didn't feel much grief, only frustration."

"I don't think we can rely entirely on his word," added Holmes, "but fortunately, we can rely on his actions – or in this case, his inactions. His failure to reclaim his case is suspicious. More so is the untidiness of his luggage. The dressing gown was jammed into the case, along with painting tools that weren't even arranged neatly. They weren't even arranged, as a matter of fact. The shaving tools looked as if they were individually thrown in. You can see the razor has made a tear in one of the canvasses. It seems that the case was packed by a man who hadn't the slightest care of the condition of the articles."

"How does any of this refute my original theory about the butler?" Hartford questioned.

"I wasn't attempting to refute your theory, Inspector. What gave you that idea?"

Hartford had no answer, and Holmes maintained, "I only meant to bring up the gravity of a disregarded issue. It may, however, if analyzed carefully and correctly, throw your theory off its ground. I myself feel that the idea of a romance is too unrefined and weak to be compatible with the extraordinary precautions that have been taken in this case."

There was a moment of silence which allowed Hartford and myself to wonder about what precautions Holmes was alluding to. Then Holmes said, "I think, Inspector, that we have spent much time in this discussion. I suggest you resume your investigation of Luther in any way you deem fit." Hartford merely got up, thanked us for the tea, and left the room.

"Watson, come sit here," said Holmes, indicating the chair in which Inspector Hartford had occupied. "I only hope I'm right in my deduction."

"And you gather your deductions, of which I am ignorant, solely from this case?"

"It provides the most important clue. If I'm correct, it changes the case entirely. There are some points of which I'm still puzzled, so I think it would be premature to tell you of my theory."

"Very well, but if you don't mind, I would like to ask you one question: You give so much importance to the contents of this case. What if you had taken Mr. Wallace's *second* case instead of this one? Would you have been equally satisfied?"

"There is a chance I would have been. The other case may have been even more helpful, but I took the one that looked similar to yours."

The soft amusement that had sparkled in his eyes as he had exchanged arguments with Hartford had faded by now and expired into a serious meditation. He stretched his long, thin arm for his pipe and lit it, the unmistakable preamble to an evening of silent analysis. He then crossed his legs on his chair and closed his eyes, remaining so for three-quarters-of-an-hour. Sleep had slowly begun to take hold of me, so I finally stood up, not wishing now to be vanquished by it. The moment when I took my hat and cane in preparation for an evening walk, my companion said, his eyes still closed, "You aren't leaving now?"

"I certainly won't, now that you're free to talk."

354

"If you would be good enough to resume your seat, my friend, we shall analyze the confounding situation in its entirety."

I sat down once more as Holmes uncrossed his legs. "Now," he began, "even you will not be able to fathom the myriad directions to which my mind has turned during this past hour, trying to find one solid thread that covers all facts and clearly illuminates when and why people have chosen to lie. Yes, more than one person has lied. There has been careful planning to ensure that I don't discover any fresh discrepancy regarding this matter. That is why I don't agree with the inspector's idea about Mrs. Wallace and the butler. The thing seems too intricate and convoluted to boil down to a cheap love affair."

"But you were the one to point out the understanding between the two people. Surely a butler who knows his place doesn't – "

"Yes, yes, but there is more to it than that. It was pure chance that I saw them talking to each other. To form a conclusion solely on that event, as Inspector Hartford has confidently done, is a mistake. But I must say his theory is rather justified if one ignores the abundant physical evidence. I mean of course this insightful trunk of Mr. Wallace's, and also what was discovered at his son's house as well."

"Ah yes, you were quite occupied with the examination of the house – rather more so than even the examination of the body. You didn't disclose any thoughts at the time."

"It is an intellectual delight for a logician to analyze the combat between observation and testimony. When all persons of relevance provide statements that haven't conflicted and instead have matched in every degree, the application of any circumstantial data weakens. One must devote one's time and one's pipe to making sense of a mess of a situation and untangle the obstinate knots in the chain. It would have seemed rather silly at the time had I pitted a metal cooking pot against the convincing stories of two persons of the case."

"That pot on the wood stove in the kitchen?"

"Precisely. The kitchen. Mrs. Wallace says she was in the kitchen when her husband returned. You noticed the hesitation when she mentioned she was in the kitchen. Anyway, she came out into the main room and, after a lapse of a few minutes, she left them. After she heard Mr. Wallace leave, she went to her husband's room and then to her own. You no doubt remember that she also claimed she went to the kitchen and put out the fire. The iron vessel and its contents show, however, that her claims aren't true. Did you by any chance observe the roast and the vegetables?"

"I'm afraid I only noticed that they were inedible."

355

"That they were. But that is the general picture. Details, Watson, details! The top half of the roast was more than fully cooked. If you looked carefully, you would have seen that the bottom half wasn't cooked at all. But if the fire was burning – and it was, proven by the fact that the logs were consumed entirely – then the bottom half must have been especially cooked – blackened to the crisp for that matter. Why, when I examine the pot, do I see the top half cooked and the bottom half undercooked? It leads me to infer that the roast was replaced upside-down in the pot at some time. But the quantity of potatoes and carrots in the pot were also cooked very unevenly, not at all fit for eating. One situation that would explain these facts would be that the pot was upset and the contents spilled out of it. The roast was flipped and placed back, and the vegetables were carelessly tossed back in."

"But what is the relevance of this? Why did the pot grab your attention in the first place?"

"That discoloration on the forehead of the body."

"I didn't inspect the body carefully, but it was my impression that it was a mark left by a small thump or burn."

"Yes, you've hit it! A burn! Quite fresh too! When I saw that the logs in the wood stove were consumed, it struck me that the pot, when fiery hot, can cause a burn like that in an instant. If the pot touched the man's forehead even for a second, a dull purple, grey mark would appear. Now, the only reasonable way that it can happen is that the pot was swung at the man, and it hit him. I remarked before that the fatal wound is in the same line as the burn. What I gather from this is that the pot was swung at him, and it hit him on the left area of the forehead. The man, upon such a violent hit, turned backwards and as he fell, he hit himself on a sharp edge, perhaps the point of a table. That was the fatal blow.

"It caused him to collapse dead. If a man falls in the way I just described and the burn is on the left part of the forehead, then the wound caused by the edge would be in the middle of the forehead or towards the right part of it, which it was on this body. The curious state of the dinner corroborates this inference. The scalding pot was snatched from its place, and when it was swung, the roast and the vegetables fell out. And this fits in with the supposition that the things were then placed back rather negligently or sloppily thrown back in the vessel similar to the way the shaving implements were thrown in the case. We now have a more serious case. Either the act was done in a moment of desperation or the intention was to murder. This is what I have gathered from the physical evidence presented to us.

"Now come the people involved. The gruesome scenario set in the kitchen dispute the statements given by two people, our acquaintance of the train and Mrs. Wallace. We cannot exclude the butler either. The statements of everyone we've seen – the Wallace of the train, Mrs. Wallace, Mr. Hawthorne, and the Burtons – all agree on the point of the letters. Let us come to that. We can accept that two letters were sent by Mr. Hawthorne . . . ."

Holmes stopped. He sighed and crumpled his brows, giving every impression of perplexity. I was still thinking over the kitchen episode and ventured a remark. "You say the man was killed by hitting his forehead on a sharp edge in the kitchen, not that statue by the bridge. Then, the argument must have taken place in the kitchen, and the only explanation is that the elder Wallace killed his son."

"Does Mrs. Wallace seem like a woman that would be persuaded by any means to protect her father-in-law when he has killed her husband? Yes, she gave the impression that she believed her father-in-law to be the murderer, but overall, her statement agrees with that of Mr. Wallace. Why should she not tell the truth if what you say is true? She has no attachment to the elder Wallace."

"What if she was threatened?"

"The man was in London when we questioned her. She would have run minimal risk on telling us the truth. Moreover, she doesn't appear to be a woman who would be frightened by threats."

I nodded slowly in agreement and put my chin in my hand in deep thought. Holmes smiled and said, "You don't seem to have realized the important meaning of the case, even after all my rambling."

I looked up at his clear, bright face. "This case is too complicated. Every single object throws a fresh twist."

"Our old acquaintance must be located. I haven't heard any news from Scotland Yard as yet – I informed them yesterday to track him down. It is more than likely that he is still in London." He suddenly stood up and took his coat and hat. "I expect Inspector Hartford to be at the police station. I'll be back shortly."

Two hours had passed when Holmes came into our room. "I must say my continual presence in the house of the Wallaces is now irritating the butler. It is absolutely amusing to see how I am a nuisance to so many in the pursuit of justice."

"What did you go back to the house for?"

"I was told that Hartford was there. He had made some investigation of his own and gone back to the house to question Luther. I was just in time to hear what the man had to say for himself. His performance was as laudable as Mrs. Wallace's, if not more."

"I beg you to elaborate."

"The inspector began with the safe, less-provoking questions first. He asked the man, 'When did you first start working for the late Mr. Wallace, Luther?'

"'I was hired a little over a week before Mr. Wallace purchased this house, sir.'

"'You and your master were on amiable terms?'

"'Of course, sir. I had much respect for him.'

"Here, I interrupted, 'Was this same respect felt towards your master's father?'

"'No, if I may so, sir. He wasn't much trouble. He would mostly sit in his room all day painting, but whenever he sat in the living room or at the dinner table, he would be grumbling and muttering to himself, always with a bitter frown on his face. I simply couldn't possess a good opinion of him, but I had respect for his age and experience, sir.'

"I had apparently ruined Hartford's organized attack with my interruption. He turned an annoyed glance at me and artfully redirected the interview. 'And your master's wife?' he said. 'Did you have any . . . for the sake of variety, let me use a word other than 'respect'. Let me see . . . any 'admiration' for her?'

"Luther remained silent. His face betrayed confusion, and his bold brown eyes looked up at Hartford as if requesting him to explain himself, which he promptly did. 'I mean, has the death of your master made it more convenient for you?'

"Luther glanced proudly at the two of us with his dignity in no way unruffled and answered, 'I must say, sir, that the implication of your question is offensive. I may be a subordinate, but you have no right to ask me such a question.'

"'You were seen talking with Mrs. Wallace and taking her hand. What have you to say about this?'

"The man looked up with slight alarm and then fixed his eyes at me. I could see that he knew that it was I who had witnessed the unbecoming scene, and a wave of resentment passed his face. He again looked at Hartford and replied, 'Mrs. Wallace is a stranger in this country. She has no friends, and she has set foot in Bristol only to be a victim of sorrow. You mistake my sympathy to be affection.' He then suddenly, on seeing that the inspector was unconvinced, filled up with anger and exclaimed, 'I will not have it, sir! I will not have Mrs. Wallace's nor my own honor to be scarred in this way!'

"'Then sir, answer this. We have checked your alibi. You were in Sommers' Tavern as you had said, but the bartender, Mr. Sommers, says he didn't see you after nine. And yet you claim that you came home and found the body at four in the morning.'

358

"'Mr. Sommers! He is a man who drains clean two bottles for his breakfast! If he didn't see me, then he didn't see anybody! Many times, his nephew takes his place for a while. I have only once before set foot in that tavern, but I've heard the ways of the place. I was there, sir, and nowhere else. I admit, I don't remember much of that night – had one drink too many – but I was there! And . . . and . . . besides, you know that the elder Wallace had left at about seven, and my master died shortly after. You say that Mr. Sommers didn't see me after nine.'

"'The tavern was busy that evening, and no one was paying any attention to you. You may have left before seven, come home to find the perfect opportunity for murdering your master, done the deed, made it appear to be an accident with the help of Mrs. Wallace, and snuck back to the tavern. Then, perhaps an hour later, you returned home. The tavern isn't far from this house.'

"'You are wrong, sir! Wrong in every detail!'

"At that moment, Mrs. Wallace entered. It was evident that she had just come from the burial ceremony. On seeing the three of us, she said, 'What is this? Inspector, is my house not to know any peace?'

"'We are only making our enquiries, Mrs. Wallace.'

"The episode ended with Luther and Mrs. Wallace being taken into custody as suspicious persons. There is no definite proof as yet, but I'm glad that I have at least convinced the inspector that it wasn't an accident. We may have to release them if we don't get any further. The case cannot escape the newspapers now, and I rather think the exposure will do us good. What is of great importance is that Mr. Wallace should be found."

"I should say it's very difficult to find him."

"Yes, more so, because he is an intelligent man, and if he is guilty, he will be elusive. But I should denounce him a wretch if he isn't in London."

"But why has he not found out yet that he has the wrong case?"

"He may have found out, but it may now dangerous for him to do anything about it. He cannot advertise for it. If he does so, we can easily get him, but he isn't so feather-brained. If he had reported it that same evening before we left for Bristol, or at most that morning, he would have foiled my trick. It is more probable that he still hasn't found out. But he didn't open his case immediately. That was his mistake. He didn't open it because the contents within didn't belong to him."

"This is fantastic, Holmes! It is hardly believable."

"Yes, but this piece of luggage is all that is needed to arrive at the fact that the Wallace we met isn't James Wallace, the watercolor artist. He is Master Jacob. The dead man is the real James Wallace. It is amazing indeed that the murderer resorted to switching identities. They must have thought it was a risk that simply had to be taken. Even so, there was no reason for anyone to doubt their word that the body was Master Jacob's. No reason at all to confirm identification when the statements of two people agreed, and 'Mr. Wallace' was actually seen at the train station and in the train."

"I did notice when you turned the body over, that he looked older than I had expected. A bit too old to be the husband of a young girl."

"It isn't uncommon for men to marry women much younger than them. And our friend from the train did well to appear elderly so that the body could pass off has his son. One further point: Mr. Jacob has just come back from the United States. Only the Burtons could have pointed out that he was a young man. No one in the country would know. But even so, even if they didn't think they were taking a risk, I cannot help but marvel how the three of them have held on this long.

"This is what I have reasoned, and I must admit that even now, it has a few holes, but in time, we can fill them up. Mr. James Wallace visits the Burtons. He is given the two letters written by Mr. Hawthorne. He discovers that Mr. Hawthorne's daughter is in America. He then goes to his friend to apologize and returns home. Mrs. Wallace is in the kitchen, and Mr. Wallace probably goes to the kitchen to vent his anger on her. Jacob Wallace now enters, hears his father shouting, and joins the two of them. He sends his wife out and quarrels with his father. His father tells him of everything that happened and probably shows a little too much of his temper. Jacob, in his desperation, reaches for the iron pot – note that he just came from outside and is still wearing gloves, so the pot doesn't burn him – and swings it at his father. The man dies in the method I have stated before. Now comes the problem. If Mr. James Wallace is found dead, suspicion is sure to be thrown on Jacob. Mr. Hawthorne, who now resents Jacob, will definitely not conceal any information. They decide that Jacob must leave the place, but not as himself. He wears his father's clothes and wraps that scarf to conceal his face. He also pretends he has a cold, so he can use that handkerchief as extra protection. They then concoct the entire story of Mr. James Wallace leaving the house after the quarrel and Jacob going out after his father. This story gives "James Wallace" an alibi.

"They then pack two suitcases with the real Mr. James Wallace's things. I infer that they burned some of the clothes in the wood stove. This explains the fact that the logs are consumed, and yet the bottom of the roast being undercooked. The pot was put back on the stove after the logs were consumed. They then plant the letters in Jacob's room and finally execute their plan of making it appear to be an accident by placing the body on the bridge and smearing some blood on the statue. Jacob then leaves to catch the train to London. I suspect Luther must have returned a little after nine or even before, and Mrs. Wallace tells him everything. She probably knows that he loves her, and she takes advantage of this. He cannot refuse her. The stage is set, the performers are prepared, and cue the three-ring circus! I as an audience member sincerely applaud the three of them. It was a story most ingenious, and they have all kept it afloat."

"Ingenious as you say, but I think the precise word is 'imaginative'. How could they dream up all this in so short a period of time? And why to such lengths to make it so elaborate? If you look at it in this way, it hardly seems intelligent."

"I'm afraid I can only adjust my analysis to accommodate a person's intelligence, not their foolishness. You can appreciate that. There may be some history to this of which I have no way of knowing. But I at least am sure of the guilt of three people."

"What will you do now?"

"It will not be efficient to disinter the body of Mr. Wallace, and besides, it is highly improbable that we will be granted permission for it, as we haven't yet been able to prove that there was foul play. Our reasoning will simply be thrown back in our faces."

"That's unfortunate, for that would have been the most helpful course of action."

"I must put the blame on myself for being so slow. Only yesterday, we would have had access to the body. I could have asked the Burtons to identify him. But what's done is done. Now I'm anxious for Scotland Yard to find that impostor, Jacob Wallace."

"Why don't you return to London then and aid the police?"

"My friend, two out of three culprits are here in Winterbourne. We cannot leave now."

"Why don't *you* return to London?" I asked. "I'll stay behind."

Holmes suddenly turned his head and smiled slowly and softly. He nodded, pondering over the matter, and said, "Yes. I must tell you that I didn't think of that."

The next morning, after giving his instructions, Holmes started off for the capital, while I went to the police station to find Inspector Hartford. "Ah, Dr. Watson," said he as he saw me, "Isn't Mr. Holmes with you?"

"No, no, he has gone back to London. I find the country quite pleasant and quiet, so I decided to stay back for a while."

"I see. Well, between us, I find you quite easier to talk to. Mr. Holmes is rather like a rabbit. Can't tell what he thinks or what he plans to do, possibly because he keeps all the clues to himself."

"He did tell you of the case."

"On that subject, I dare say Mr. Wallace may have advertised for it in our town's newspapers, but since it has fallen into Mr. Holmes's hands, he will never get it back, will he? He may as well consider it fallen into the sea. Moreover, he must be wondering at this moment why you haven't asked for *your* case."

"Holmes has his reasons for doing what he does."

"Yes, and I have mine, Doctor. You know we arrested Mrs. Wallace and the butler yesterday. No positive proof yet, but they will remain in our custody. We may have to let them go soon and rule this one a death by accident."

It is just as well to keep Holmes's actions secret – as was his faithful custom – to ensure each case receives its share of drama. The reader may also appreciate that whatever steps Holmes takes, they earn their due admiration from the police only at the end, when everything comes to light.

I went back to the hotel and hadn't yet reached my room when Mr. Hawthorne stepped toward me. "Oh, I'm extremely sorry, Dr. Watson!" said he hastily. "Terribly sorry. I need to speak to Mr. Holmes immediately, sir."

"I'm afraid he isn't here."

"When . . . when will he be back? Please, I must see him urgently."

"I'm sorry, Mr. Hawthorne, but Mr. Holmes is in London."

"What is he doing there?"

"He's a very busy man. I'm staying here for a while. Can I be of any service to you?"

"Uh, well yes, I . . . ."

"The man was obviously in some state of torment, [I would write later to Holmes] *but he seemed hesitant to say anything. Either he, on an impulse, rushed to our rooms and when he reached here, began to realize doubts of seeking aid, or he found it would be more of use to speak to you rather than me. But there was something on his mind, and I tried my best to figure out what it was . . . ."*

"Mr. Hawthorne, please sit down," I said, pouring a glass of brandy. "I'm sure I may be able to do something for you. What is the matter?"

"I'm afraid that even if I tell you, you won't be able to do anything about it. I mean no offense, Dr. Watson. I am now in fact relieved that I found you alone. I suppose that the death of Jacob has only now hit me, and I'm in a state of nerves." He paused and then continued. "I'm sorry for my intrusion. I'll go now."

"If there's anything I can do, Mr. Hawthorne – "

"No, no. It's all right. I must get home to my wife."

"Before you go, sir, may I ask if you have received any letter from Mr. Wallace?"

"No . . . no I haven't. I don't know where he is."

"Now that the tragedy is covered in local papers, I think it would be only fair to personally write to Mr. Wallace of the death of his only son. Are you sure you don't know where he is?"

"No, Dr. Watson. But you're right. It is my duty to find out."

With that, he murmured his farewells and departed, leaving me pondering about his manner. I decided to follow him, taking care to keep some distance between us. He hailed a hansom and told the driver to go to Sommers' Tavern, so I did the same.

When we reached there, Hawthorne sat at a table and called a young man whom I took to be the bartender. He spoke a few words to him. The bartender left and returned with a mug of ale. By this time, I had taken a seat at a table behind Hawthorne. The bartender was bent over, conversing with him in a very quiet, suspicious way. It was as if Hawthorne was giving directions, and the bartender was keenly listening to them, nodding his head to show that he understood. Because I sat behind the man, I couldn't clearly make out what was going on, but after a few minutes, I thought I saw Hawthorne handing something over to the young man, who then went away. Hawthorne then finished the ale and walked out of the place as I was doing my best to remain unnoticed.

All this I wrote in my letter to Mr. Holmes that evening. The episode was certainly of some importance in the whole matter which I didn't grasp until the next day when the papers revealed with clear clarity its effect:

> *Inspector Hartford of the Bristol Constabulary had only yesterday, as announced in the local papers, arrested two persons, Francis Oak Luther and Mrs. Nora Wallace, in connection with the death of Mr. Jacob Wallace, which has recently produced suspicions among the police force that the death wasn't accidental. The persons aforementioned were detained in custody on the strength of such evidence as described in yesterday's papers, and the investigation was to continue until conclusive incriminating evidence could be produced. Ironically, the proof that was obtained served as evidence of innocence, resulting in the two suspects to be released from custody. Mr. Bradley Sommers, the nephew of Mr. Jack Sommers, the owner of Sommers' Tavern, offered his statements which are printed as follows:*
>
> *I was serving on the evening of January 19 (evening of death of Mr. Wallace). My uncle was in his cups and half*

asleep, so I took over. Many people there that night. Didn't notice 'em much, except one man whom now I know is Mr. Luther. Looked more like a gentleman than the others, so I noticed him. Drank one glass after another as if he was compensating for a dull, sober Christmas. But he was there all night for sure, Guv'nor. There was a scene after that, but I'm darned if he'll remember. But Bess – she's our barmaid – I think took a fancy to him. Tried to serenade him, so to speak, and some – including my uncle – were put off. Heck of a time cleaning the mess, I'll say. Mr. Luther just sat quietly, keeping to himself. Soon, everyone shut up like a clam and there was peace, and I don't know when he left, but he was there at nine-thirty when the scene ended. I didn't know anything about it until the papers told me he was arrested for an accident that happened that night, so I came forward. Don't know what Uncle Jack told you, but I wasn't there then, or I would have told you then what really happened."

Due to the conclusiveness of this evidence, the case, which has so far been pursued as a possible instance of murder, causing the recruit of not only Inspector Hartford but also Sherlock Holmes, the well-known detective, has now officially closed.

I, for my part, stayed put, knowing it best to wait until Holmes returned – for he notified me that he was returning in his letter – rather than to act alone. It wasn't until next evening, when Holmes, Inspector Hartford, and I were taking tea at our hotel, that my singular observations passed into official hands.

"A clear-cut incident of the simplest yet brightest example of cause-and-effect!" Holmes remarked. "Watson, I again must congratulate you for your foresight. If you hadn't followed Mr. Hawthorne, we wouldn't have been furnished with such salacious information."

"I don't know what prompted me to start following him," I answered, quite glad in my heart, "and I'm blessed if I know what made me hail a hansom when I heard he was going to a tavern."

"There are other taverns nearer to the hotel than Sommers' Tavern. Why should he select that one?"

"So we are faced with the possibility that Mr. Hawthorne bribed that young Sommers chap to lie about Luther," said the inspector.

"There is no doubt of it," said Holmes, "No doubt that what Mr. Hawthorne pressed into the fellow's hand was a packet of money."

"But why? What could be the reason for Mr. Hawthorne to mix himself up in this? There is no reason why he should do it for Luther, and even less reason why he should do it for Mrs. Wallace."

"I share your confusion, Inspector. When I analyzed this case, I never found a way to add Mr. Hawthorne into the equation."

"I suppose it would look absurd if I detained them a second time."

"The papers will not spare you, Inspector, if you are bold enough to do that."

"Yes, you should see what's already circulating among some of the locals. 'The coppers picking on innocent people! Busybodies turning the peaceful countryside into a dog park for their precious sleuthhounds!' Pah! Because of this and our evergreen, immortal folly in the Rosehill Manor case! No respect for the police, I say!"

Holmes chuckled at Hartford's wit and consoled him, "You will be able to arrest the pair once we have actual proof of their guilt. Unfortunately, that proof is as slippery as an eel. He is a cunning devil!"

"Who do you mean?"

"Mr. Wallace."

"But he can't be connected in this."

"That's what I thought about Mr. Hawthorne."

"How is Scotland Yard faring?" I interjected. "Do they have any clue as to his whereabouts?"

"He isn't in London. They're following his tracks. He's hidden himself very carefully. I've sent a cable to the Philadelphia Police Department to see if they can give me some information about Jacob Wallace, and I've yet to hear from them. But I will gain some knowledge in the meantime."

"Jacob Wallace? He is the dead man!" exclaimed the inspector.

"Watson can tell you about that later. The only thing to do now is to see Mrs. Wallace, Luther, and Mr. Hawthorne together."

Part III – The Assembly

A complicated case such as this one in which my friend Sherlock Holmes showed his astounding intellectual reasoning and skill for deep analysis was bound to end his way, with him raising the curtain to reveal the cast of characters that made this affair a splendid sensation among those who regard what he has now made a science – armchair investigation. That was virtually what this case came down to: Quiet, careful study and probing in an armchair amidst an atmosphere of pipe smoke.

Holmes went to the desk to write a note and, as he did so, he told Hartford, "Inspector, can you arrange for Mrs. Wallace and Luther to be present here in fifty minutes? But first send someone to give this note to Mr. Hawthorne. I want him here alone first."

When the inspector left, my friend turned to me and said, "We're nearing the end of the investigation in which you have played a most significant role. It has been one of the most fascinating we've had the opportunity to undertake, a fine study of the scheming mind."

"All this was motivated by what? What is the history that lies behind this?"

"We will know in a quarter-of-an-hour or so."

At the end of that time, Mr. Hawthorne was at the door, and Holmes offered him a chair. "Mr. Hawthorne," he said, "I'm sorry that I wasn't able to see you yesterday. I was in London, but Dr. Watson informed me that you wished my assistance."

"Yes, Mr. Holmes," replied Mr. Hawthorne, "I did come here, wanting to see you, but when Dr. Watson here gave me some brandy, my nerves were calmed. I think I only then faced the fact that poor Jacob is dead. I'm sorry to have troubled you, Dr. Watson, and you Mr. Holmes. It's nothing at all. I'm deeply sorry for causing you to return from London just to see me."

"No need for the apology. The journey back here wasn't at all fruitless. But are you sure it was the brandy that restored you to your senses?"

"What do you mean? Of . . . of course it was." There was, I sensed, a layer of confusion and fright in those words.

"Not for example, anything else in this room?"

Mr. Hawthorne looked around the room, his eyebrows crossed in puzzled apprehension, and said to Holmes, "I think I shall go now if I may. Thank you for inviting me here, but now that we've explained everything, I have no longer need to bother you gentlemen."

"You come here to ask for my service for something related to this whole affair. But when you come in, you suddenly change your mind. My absence didn't discourage you, of that I'm sure. You became suspicious that I had discovered something that I wasn't meant to discover. It was the case that brought forth those suspicions, wasn't it? Your friend, Mr. James Wallace's case?"

Mr. Hawthorne's face turned pale, but he didn't lose his full composure as yet. His gray eyes showed defiance, and he pulled himself together. "I only noticed the painting articles. It wasn't my business to question why they were in your possession."

"It was your business to question – that is if you had thought that Mr. James Wallace was in London. But you know he wasn't."

What happened next, I can only describe as a spectacle. As Holmes ended his statement, Mr. Hawthorne's ashy complexion whitened, his hands sprang to his forehead, clutching his hair and, giving vent to innumerable groans, he staggered to the chair and fell. His hands impetuously clawed at his face, and if he hadn't been wearing thick gloves, I believe he would have almost scratched his eyes out. When he did will himself to speak, it was in an exhausted, despaired tone. "I am an unhappy man! If you knew everything, you would have spared me this. Or do you know everything and yet torment me?"

"I'm afraid, Mr. Hawthorne, what you're suffering now cannot be worse than what James Wallace, your dear friend, had to suffer."

On hearing his friend's name, Mr. Hawthorne's head sank down lower and tears began to fill his eyes. "I've missed him, Mr. Holmes, but I couldn't do anything, I couldn't say anything."

"It isn't hard to understand why an evil man does evil. I reasoned out the guilt of three people, and because I knew they were guilty, I knew why they did what they did. But as I believed you innocent, Mr. Hawthorne, I couldn't connect you in all this. I pity James Wallace. On all sides, he was surrounded by people he couldn't trust, even after death."

"Believe me, Mr. Holmes. I – "

It was just then that Inspector Hartford arrived with Mrs. Nora Wallace and Luther. When Mrs. Wallace saw Mr. Hawthorne, her face suddenly changed. She bit her lips and hastily looked away. Holmes caught it, and I'm sure he immediately guessed the answer to what confused him, but he didn't reveal anything at that moment.

"Thank you, Inspector. Now, Mrs. Wallace – "

"If I may sir," interrupted Luther, "this thing is now becoming quite intolerable. This is clear abuse on your part."

"Let us not resort to fancy terms, Mr. Luther. Please don't interrupt me. I think I should first say that your husband, Mrs. Wallace, isn't in London."

She stared, her mouth open, and turned to Mr. Hawthorne, who still had his face in his hands. Her big, lovely eyes were blazing with anger. "You . . . you told him! I know you did! You told him and betrayed us!"

"He did nothing of the kind, Madam. I already knew."

"What do you mean he isn't in London?" said Luther, his eyes wrinkled with shock, "He must be."

"He is not. He has disappeared."

"The rat!" shouted Luther. "The double-crossing old devil!" He was about ready to break everything in the room, and if we hadn't restrained him, he would have done so.

Mrs. Wallace's expression showed that she was equally shocked, but her nature hadn't instigated her to lose her temper. She instead sank into a chair and let the tears slowly stain her red cheeks. She stammered, her voice grievous, "But . . . but he said he would come back for me. He said he would . . . for me."

"It isn't easy, I assure you, Madam, to tell you that you have done so much effort, used so much energy, to protect a man who isn't worth protecting. Risked your neck for a wretch – a wretch who doesn't care who is in the dock as long as it isn't him."

Turning to Mr. Hawthorne, my friend continued, "You, Mr. Hawthorne, did what you did, not for the sake of Jacob Wallace, but for your daughter, Ella, who by now I have realized is Mrs. Nora Wallace."

Mr. Hawthorne, still in despair, didn't reply, so Holmes turned to Luther, the last member of the gang, and said, "You, sir, also played a hand in this, again not for your master's sake, but for that of his wife. I have high regard for your performance as a butler, for I'm sure that isn't what you really are."

In response, the man lifted his head and said, "I was one of Ella's suitors. And you speak wrongly to use the term, 'performance'. A butler is basically what I was to that traitor. All those years, the tyrant treated me as his servant!" The man growled with distinct fury.

"It is amazing to see how so much was done for the sake of another!" marveled Holmes, "Everyone involved in this mess gambled their own good names so that another could keep his. And that one has fled, leaving you all here."

"He said once he found a safe place in London, he would arrange to fetch us," said Luther. "Then we would probably leave the country. If I knew he would double-cross us like this, I wouldn't have done this! None of us would have!"

"Do you know exactly what you've done?" said Holmes, turning a stern, cold look at Luther. "You've helped a murderer escape, and once he did just that, you continued to protect him! And he now has taken advantage of your loyalty! What was the use of your efforts? Tell me, Mrs. Wallace!"

There was complete silence. Holmes was now the sole master of the scene, and the inspector and I couldn't help but show our admiration for him and how he subdued three persons who until now, hadn't been easy to intimidate. Holmes looked at the three of them, one by one, and said, "I think it would be wise to explain the history of this. Mrs. Wallace, you should go first.

Mrs. Wallace passed her handkerchief over her eyes, heaved a sigh, and spoke. "My father and Mr. Wallace had been very good friends, so Jacob and I had known each other since childhood. When Jacob grew older, he became an apprentice to my father, who is in the steel business. He was a very ambitious man, and he had a dream of traveling to the United States – Philadelphia, in fact – to earn his fortune. It was decided that upon his return to England, we would be married.

"It so happened that Jacob wrote to his father that he would return to England because he wasn't having much luck, and that is what caused Mr. Wallace to inform my father that he would be coming back. But he suddenly changed his mind, a sudden brainwave perhaps, and he continued to stay in America. My father, hearing from Mr. Wallace of this change of plans, then wrote the first letter that you found on Jacob's table.

"Mr. Holmes, I was a young girl. I loved him, and I missed him terribly. I was harassed by my many admirers who said that Jacob had probably fallen in love with an American girl and gotten married to her, and that he had forgotten me. Or what if his ambition got the better of him, and he would never come back to England? I was very anxious to go to him and marry him immediately. I didn't tell my father everything, so he assumed I was simply going to pay a visit, and he found my desire reasonable. After all, it had been two-and-a-half years since Jacob had left us. I departed for America and went to New Jersey, where some relatives of mine were living. My father said he would wire me Jacob's address in Philadelphia once he received the information from Mr. Wallace. In the meantime, a friend of one of my relatives was visiting us, and he was a manager of an acting troupe. I . . . I suppose he was quite taken with me and suggested I should be on the stage.

"I was reluctant to at first, and it took a lot of persuasion, but in the end, I suppose Jacob's ambition rubbed off on me, and I agreed to give it a try. It so happened that I was a natural actress on stage, and I joined the troupe. We then went to Philadelphia to perform there, and one night, luck favored me, for I saw Jacob sitting in the audience, and he too recognized me. He was also young and foolish, so we got married the following week. I thought I would stay in America for a couple of months and then return, but my father wrote to me that my mother was terribly ill, and I had to leave Jacob and the stage to go back to England. I didn't see my husband for another two years." She paused and said, "I think Fred, you'd better continue."

She turned to the man – who I'll continue to call Luther – who said, "I must say that I too was an apprentice of Mr. Hawthorne. I wasn't as bright as Jacob, but when it came to ambition, I was on the same level with him. When I heard that he had gone to America, I thought I would too. I worked in the same company he worked, and even though there had been competition between us, I let that fade, and we became friends. I was there when Ella married him. He is an extremely intelligent fellow, and after Ella returned to England, he started working to put his 'brainwave' into action. He, along with myself and another two chaps, started a partnership. Together we created a small coke production company in which we used the beehive ovens to produce coke. Then we would supply the coke to the steel mills nearby.

"Again, being a very enterprising man, Jacob made some smart investments, and he became the manager of the company. He employed me as assistant manager. It was then that his success went to his head. He became arrogant, insufferably arrogant. He would quarrel with our two partners when they accused him of cheating them out of their rightful share of the profits. The workers complained of harsh treatment, strict schedules, and low pay, and when I would confront him, he would lash out, so deaf was he to everything but the sweet sound of money. Most of the workers didn't even have time to eat. In one incident, one worker sat down to eat a sandwich, and when Jacob caught him, he threw the sandwich into one of the ovens and made sure the man received no pay that week. I nearly went mad, worrying that the workers would begin a strike.

"He was more paranoid than I was about the idea. If he heard news about his workers simply having a discussion, he would arrange for the band to be broken up immediately. I must say that the workers were very resentful against a man they thought was too young to treat them as if they were his wretched servants.

"One day, a few men suffered an accident on the job – I won't go into weary details – and Jacob was piled with several lawsuits. I was very close to him, so I saw him work day and night to keep his reputation from being marred. One of the men, who was more seriously injured and belonged to the union, tried to blackmail him, saying that the matter would be hushed up if he was reasonably compensated. Otherwise, he would recommend to his partners that they should go on strike. Jacob asked for my aid, and I gave it to him. I don't know what I should have done otherwise. I arranged for the payments week after week until I found out that the man had disappeared, vanished. This was to be nothing short of a scandal. The union made numerous threats. The police were suspicious – the whole thing was a mess!"

Luther stopped, his face haggard with reminiscing about the past, and Mrs. Wallace said, "By now, I was in Philadelphia again after telling my father that I wanted to visit him again. But I was busy on the stage."

Luther continued, "Eventually, there was a strike in which many men were killed. Jacob himself was behind most of the deaths, and I suppose I was too because I protected him for the sake of Ella. I thought it best that with the money we had, we should flee to England, which is just what we did. We secretly boarded a ship back here. Jacob had written to his father that we were returning, and Mr. Wallace wished for us to stay with him for a while, now that his wife had passed. None of us thought there would be a harm in it, since Mr. Wallace was a simple man who kept very much to himself and was only devoted to his painting. We moved to the country where we felt safer and to get away from Mr. Hawthorne. We didn't inform him that Ella had come back. The scandal was too fresh for such admissions and details. It was safe for all concerned that Mr. Hawthorne believed that we were still in America."

Here, Mr. Hawthorne took his turn in the unraveling of the history. "Being also an affiliate of the steel trade, it was only a matter of time that I learned that Jacob was entangled in massive scandals relating to the strike at his company and then the disappearance. Of course, I had my doubts about it, but they didn't stop me from writing two letters to my friend, explaining my concerns. These didn't reach Mr. Wallace promptly as you know already."

"Mr. Wallace then came home and confronted me," said Mrs. Wallace. "He kept on screaming and yelling. I . . . I never knew him to have such a temper. Jacob came home, and they continued the argument in the kitchen. And . . . ."

"And then your husband killed him by taking the pot that was on the fire and swinging it at him," said Holmes.

"It could have been sheer impulse on his part, Mr. Holmes! Mr. Wallace said he would expose him to the police – his own son!"

Holmes didn't reply to this argument and went on, "So then you and your husband thought of this ingenious plan to make it appear to be an accident, and if the police did have any suspicions, it would be rooted in romance rather than the steel business scandal which, since it was fresh and recent, had to be concealed. Jacob Wallace couldn't afford such exposure, so he staged this rather elaborate charade, planting those two letters which were written years ago (but early in January of an earlier year), when you, Madam, first traveled to America. Ah yes, one point needs to be clarified: How were such old letters kept? Did Mr. Wallace preserve his mail, Mr. Hawthorne?"

"He did have the habit of preserving and cataloguing letters, Mr. Holmes," said Mr. Hawthorne who then lowered his eyes and added, "Especially those written by me."

"I see. Anyway, the trick worked brilliantly, because Mr. Hawthorne indeed had sent two letters recently, letters with more dangerous contents about the steel business scandal. Your husband then collected some of his father's belongings, packed them in the cases, and burned the rest of them in the fire in the kitchen. That is why the logs were fully consumed, and the roast wasn't cooked properly. He then disguised himself as an old man, probably with your help, Mrs. Wallace, since you are an actress. I gather that is all he had time to do, for he had to catch the train. Subsequently, when you, Mr. Fred, came from the tavern, you helped to move the body where you claimed you found it in the morning. You were now Francis Oak Luther and Nora Wallace. You changed your names for this farce. Sometime that evening, you, Madam, must have gone to your father's house to explain everything and recruit him in your plan. And finally, you Mr. Hawthorne, didn't take the example of your friend, who had more integrity than you did. He had no hesitation in giving up his only son, but you aided in covering up his murder to save your daughter."

"I wouldn't have sent those two blasted letters if I knew that Ella was already married to Jacob! But she was innocent, Mr. Holmes! She did all this to help the man she loved. Unfortunately, he wasn't worthy of her."

"I'm afraid I cannot argue with people who thought it justified to protect a murderer, not to mention a cheat and a rogue," replied Holmes. He then turned to Luther, "You, especially, put yourself at great risk, for you were Jacob Wallace's partner in Philadelphia, and your name too surely must have been involved in those deaths. You will now have to stand trial for that scandal."

"I don't mind standing trial for murder!" snarled Luther. "After I wring the traitor's neck, I don't care what happens to me – leaving Ella behind and running away like a coward!"

"He may not have had a choice," remarked Hartford. "After all, the bit about the switched case . . . he may have been suspicious."

"But he could have written, Inspector," said Holmes. "And anyway, the other case – the one on the train that he still has – must have contained money and his own things. It is most likely that it was already in his head to leave his wife and confidante to face the music. The case that is in Watson's possession contained his father's things, and he was going to get rid of it anyway. Why should he open it if it was going to be destroyed?"

I saw Mrs. Wallace and Luther turn pale at realizing how Holmes played that simple trick. My friend again looked around and rested his eyes on Mr. Hawthorne. He said, "I pity you, Mr. Hawthorne, for getting mixed up in something which shouldn't have concerned you. If you had stayed true to your poor, courageous friend and played it straight, you all, at least, would have been spared this humiliation. But your weakness overpowered you. You resorted to bribery to get your daughter released, and you acted very convincingly all along. I must say I admire the way you remembered the contents of your old letter, to the very small detail too. Is your wife really ill at this moment?"

"No, Mr. Holmes," he said with his eyes again filling with tears. "She is as fit as a fiddle!"

Part IV – Three-Card Monte

"Ah, I'm sure you're immensely happy to be in Baker Street once more."

"That is a great understatement. I feel I shall never want to go to Bristol again – although I don't mean to take anything away from your success. A most tangled affair indeed!"

"It was extremely gratifying! We were dealing with a snake! If you have time, read the answer to my cable to the Philadelphia Police Department. Horrendous accusations! But it was very much a gratifying case. Do you remember when I remarked that this was a three-ring circus? On reflection, that is a very theatrical and artificial term for such master work. It was, I should say, Three-Card Monte."

"How do you mean?"

"A great con game played between two locations, London and Bristol! In Three-Card Monte, the three cards are mixed up on the table, and the victim tries to find the money card. Of course, he will never guess correctly. The three cards in our affair were Luther, Mrs. Wallace, and Mr. Hawthorne."

"What about Jacob Wallace?"

"He was the conman who invited us, taking us for a couple of suckers, to play his version of Three-Card Monte. He showed the cards to us, shuffled them, and put them on the table. That was what he was doing when he was entertaining you with that fairy tale on the train. You realize he made sure we knew everyone including the Burtons because he knew that whatever they said would support his story. The main premise of the story, such as Jacob marrying another woman and the argument between father and son over the marriage, he must have discussed with his wife beforehand. His wife then informed Mr. Hawthorne, so everyone knew their parts perfectly. That night, Jacob Wallace was making his escape, and finding us already in the compartment, he began his little performance. He thought we would fall for it, and we did."

"*You* didn't, Holmes."

"My dear friend, my suspicions were reasonable but not at all established. I must admit that it was an impulse that made me trade your cases, nothing else. But you see, that didn't hinder his escape. Ha! When he stepped out to smoke, he must have been laughing his head off! It would have regaled him to see us running around in Winterbourne. Whatever card we chose, we were wrong. We could have chosen Mrs. Wallace or Luther, and we did. We might even have chosen Hawthorne. It was of no consequence, because the real money card was Jacob Wallace. And because all three of his puppets were so admirably loyal to him or to each other, we were all tricked. Ah well, another failure for your collection."

"I don't regard it at all as a failure, Holmes. The police are still searching for him. And we have the others. They were also difficult to catch."

"Yes, and they helped to create a wonderful study of human behavior. For example, you remember my remark about Mrs. Wallace's change when we visited her for a second time in her house. In the beginning, she tried her best to play a doting wife, weeping her heart out, and giving her own theories to become more convincing. That was the touch of the actress in her. But the second time, she wasn't as passionate. She was irritated with us for not letting the thing go as an accident. She was very much trying to discourage us then, and that encouraged me even more to find out the truth.

"But their trials will come soon. I don't know what the results will be, and I won't try to guess either. I'll do my part, though. But it generates a most annoying feeling to know that when you cast your net into the water and pull it up, you see the big fish wriggle out, and you're left with tadpoles!"

I laughed heartily and said to him, "I tell you what: You cast your net again into the river and hope that you catch my case, for that's probably where it is now. In the river."

"I promise you I will never try that trick again as long as I live."

I continued to tease him, "You know my expenses from purchasing new night-clothes, a shaving kit, and other things."

"Yes, and don't you worry," he replied with a sly, mischievous smile. "I've given the bill to Inspector Hartford. He'll be ready with your money the next time we visit the lovely, peaceful Bristol countryside!"

The Adventure of the Armchair Detective
by John McNabb

In the many years that I have been reporting the remarkable career of my friend Mr. Sherlock Holmes, I have laid before the reading public cases which have ranged from the horrific to the truly bizarre. Under the first head I well recall the appalling case of Japhet Gillray the Finsbury Park poisoner, whom Holmes apprehended by catching out the myna bird in a lie. Under the second head there was the case of Professor Wyndblown-Smythe, the celebrated archaeologist from Camford University. As he entered a newly discovered chamber in the ancient British barrow at Addleton there was a rush of air, and all the lamps were extinguished. When they were relit, the professor lay stone cold dead upon the flagging, transformed into a wizened old man.

But one question is continuously asked of me: Why did Sherlock Holmes not take up the case of Jack the Ripper, that fiend who terrorised the East End of London in the autumn of 1888? Did Scotland Yard not seek out his advice? Why had his brother Mycroft not engaged him on behalf of the British Government? Was there no telegram from the Home Secretary, Sir Henry Mathews, requesting Holmes to apprehend the fiend and restore public order? Like many others, I had been surprised at the official silence, and I quizzed Holmes on the matter, more than once.

"I have told you, Watson," was always the reply, "Jack the Ripper will be caught not by deduction, but by good old fashioned police work – detection, leavened with a large measure of luck."

"Luck?"

"Indeed – either this blackguard is the cleverest man to haunt the streets of London, or he has the Devil's own luck. How is it that he evades discovery in a district teeming with nocturnal life? No! Slapping the bracelets on this fellow will be no easy task."

How the Ripper evaded capture was indeed a mystery. The newspapers were only too keen to lay the blame at the door of the police and the Criminal Investigation Department. Yet, I for one couldn't see what more they could have done. Every lead was followed. Every suspect investigated, and there was no shortage of those. Extra constables had been drafted in to add to the many already on the Whitechapel beat. Moreover, vigilantes roamed the streets organised by a local resident, a Mr. George

Lusk. It was even rumoured that police constables were dressing up as women to ensnare the killer. Then again, Whitechapel itself was a district that never slept. At all hours of the day and night, street cleaners and market porters were constantly going to and from their work. Carmen and delivery drivers were everywhere abouts. To add to the mix, there were those who haunted the streets at night unable to find a place in the many communal lodging houses. They wandered like somnambulists, aimlessly seeking a dry corner out of the wind in which to sleep. Yet the Ripper continued to evade detection and capture. It beggared belief.

The autumn of that year was a busy time for Holmes – I have already chronicled a number of cases from that period, "The Greek Interpreter" and *The Sign of the Four*, and that other encounter with evil-incarnate: The deranged owner of the Baskerville hound. Although his talents were occupied elsewhere, Holmes wasn't unaware of the events as they unfolded in Whitechapel, nor was he insensitive to them. I would often find him sitting on the rug in our Baker Street rooms, wrapped in his shabby mouse-coloured dressing gown, surrounded by open newspapers as he absorbed all that he could from the daily reporting of the case.

So it was one morning later in November that I came down to breakfast to find Holmes sitting in the middle of the floor corralled by neatly stacked piles of newspapers, six of them to be exact. His breakfast lay ignored on the table. It was a bright and sunny autumn morning, but Holmes had the windows shut fast. A positive fug of stale tobacco smoke filled the room. Holmes was oblivious to the poisonous atmosphere. Coughing, I threw open the windows and settled down to a hasty slice of toast and a rasher or two, now thoroughly smoked.

"In answer to your question, each pile is the collected newspaper accounts for one of Jack the Ripper's victims," he said matter-of-factly. "That was your next question, was it not?"

I shrugged in response, not wishing to admit that he was right, as usual. But to find him engaged with the case was good news.

"Have your services been retained?" I asked hopefully, but he shook his head.

"No. The police are diligent in their duties as best they may be. There is little for me to do." He waved at the newspaper stacks. "Yet there is a pattern here, if I could but see it. You are familiar with the last murder? That of Mary Jane Kelly. A ghastly and wicked killing."

I nodded. Like all of London, I had been horrified by the callous brutality that the Ripper had shown to the bodies of his victims, but this latest was particularly horrific. The poor woman had been almost completely eviscerated. Unlike the earlier crimes, this one had taken place indoors, 13 Miller's Court, off Dorset Street, Whitechapel – a thoroughfare which already had a dark reputation. Free of prying eyes or the threat of disturbance, the killer had taken his time to conduct his grizzly business across the early hours of Friday, the ninth of November. Internal organs had been arranged around the body and beneath it, and her face had been extensively mutilated. Her heart was missing.

"There are full, if slightly contradictory, reports of the inquest in *The Times* and *The Daily Telegraph*," said Holmes as he scooped two newspapers off the top of the nearest pile and passed them across to me. "Also," he began, throwing another copy of *The Times* across, "take note of the statement of one George Hutchinson, delivered to the police on Monday the twelfth."

I quickly read through the reporting of the inquest. A resident of Miller's Court, unable to sleep, had allegedly heard a woman crying "Murder!" at about four o'clock in the morning. Another resident agreed with her. Neither took the cry seriously, as this was a common-enough occurrence in Whitechapel and rarely true. Yet it seemed others in Miller's Court who had been awake at that time had heard nothing.

Mr. Hutchinson's evidence was at first sight impressive. He had met the murder victim Mary Kelly near the corner of Thrawl Street and Commercial Street at two o'clock in the morning. They were old friends. He had seen a man stop her. The two spoke for a few moments and then walked back towards Hutchinson. He had gotten a good look at the fellow as they passed. He described a man in his middle thirties of dark complexion and with a small dark moustache, otherwise clean-shaven. What had attracted Hutchinson's curiosity was that he was well dressed. A long coat trimmed with astrakhan fur and neat shoes with gaiters. He had a gold watch chain with a big seal attached to it from which a red stone hung. He was carrying a small parcel fastened by a strap or band.

Hutchinson had followed Mary Kelly and the man to Dorset Street, whereupon they had gone into the passageway that led into Miller's Court. He'd waited outside until two-forty-five or three o'clock, but astrakhan-man hadn't reappeared and Hutchinson had lost interest. He even thought he had seen the man again on Sunday morning in Petticoat Lane, and so believed he must be a resident of the area.

I looked up at Holmes. "But then they must surely have him, for there cannot be many men who fit such a description in the district."

"You would think so, wouldn't you?" replied Holmes. "I cabled Lestrade for some insight this very morning. He has sent a veritable dossier back by messenger boy." He indicated a thick buff-coloured folder lying on the breakfast table. On the front cover was a hastily scribbled note: "*For S.H. Eyes Only. Any help you can offer greatly appreciated. Regards,*

Abberline". And below that, in another hand: "*Any help at all – Please.*"
It was signed *L* – so that was Lestrade.

"Inspector Frederick Abberline of Scotland Yard is in charge of the case," said Holmes. "He has interviewed this Hutchinson and seems to think he's a credible witness. I am less certain. I suspect that the rather flowery descriptions of the suspect's dress may have been added later for the press." Here Holmes smiled ruefully. "His testimony is unusually detailed. Suspiciously so."

Reading the document, I had to agree with Holmes's observation, but there was still much that appeared valuable in Hutchinson's statement. "Surely the time of death is neatly established between the woman who heard the cry of 'Murder!' at four o'clock and the fact that this Hutchinson chap watched them enter Miller's Court and then stood outside the entrance for at least three-quarters of an hour."

Holmes nodded absently. "True, but does it not strike you as odd that Hutchinson should stand there for all that time just waiting for the man to emerge? To what end?"

I had to admit it was true, but then the fellow had missed his place in the doss house. There was little alternative but to tramp the streets until dawn.

"Do you suspect him of some other motive?" I asked.

"I think Lestrade does. He is less convinced of the fellow than is Abberline. Reading between the lines, I think Lestrade believes Hutchinson planned on robbing the man when he came out." Holmes shrugged his shoulders. "If you cannot relieve a man of his valuables, then denouncing him to the newspapers as Jack the Ripper will still turn a pretty penny. Yes, friend Hutchinson's testimony is rather suspect, I feel."

There was a logic to Holmes's sentiments. "There is a hefty reward on offer, and the newspapers will pay well for any new story about the Ripper," I replied.

"You'll note more than a hint of anti-Semitism in his deposition too," said Holmes.

"Anti-Semitism?" I queried. "What has that to do with the Whitechapel outrages?"

"Mark my words, you will find race somewhere at the heart of this ghastly business."

It was common knowledge that racial tension, fuelled by poverty and depravation simmered fitfully just below the surface of Whitechapel. In the last twenty years, there had been a huge influx of Eastern Europeans into the area, many of them Jewish, all fleeing from oppression at home. Jack the Ripper had opened up the divisions between neighbours. The newspapers did little to ease the situation. Some like *The Star* were

378

actively stoking the fires of resentment and hatred. There were too many people more than willing to put a match to this powder keg. Perhaps George Hutchinson was such a one?

Holmes cast around looking for his pipe. "Did you note the red handkerchief that astrakhan-man gave Mary Kelly?"

I nodded. Just before disappearing down the passageway into Miller's Court, Mary had complained she had lost her handkerchief and the man had given her his. Holmes uttered a cryptic, "That may be significant later."

He tossed the paper he was reading back on its pile. "Having read the details of Mary Kelly's death, there is one thing of which I am now certain: We have seen the last of Saucy Jack!"

I looked up from my reading, astounded. "Holmes?"

"You may count on it," was the response. "Each horror he perpetrated was more savage than the last. The devil was evolving his technique, culminating in the unprecedented disembowelment visited on poor Mary Kelly. But now he has sated himself, attained his apotheosis. Whatever he once was has been left behind, and in his mind, he occupies some new plane of existence."

I shuddered. "The very thought sends shivers down my spine. It was as if the monster was searching for something in the body of his victims? Why take her heart?"

Holmes fixed me a curious stare. "That is very astute, Doctor. You may well have something there.

"But let us look at the facts," he continued. "Martha Tabram is attacked in George Yard, off Whitechapel Road, on the seventh of August. The time of death was estimated at the *post mortem* as just after two-thirty in the morning. She was stabbed from the front with a small-bladed knife, although a heavier and thicker-bladed weapon may also have been used. There is no evidence of a sexual assault. Multiple stab wounds, in the abdomen and elsewhere, but none of the slashing that characterised the Ripper's later killings. She was last seen in the company of a soldier at eleven-forty-five the previous night, but there are many hours unaccounted for between then and the time of her death. The killer has made his first move, but he isn't happy with his *modus operandi* – too messy, too much chance of being covered in his victim's blood.

"So when he strikes again on the thirty-first of August, Mary Anne Nichols, also known as Polly, is attacked from behind, likely strangled, and her body laid on the ground. He then cuts her throat and proceeds to mutilate her," Holmes paused, having discovered his pipe under a pile of newsprint. He reached for the Persian slipper containing his rough-cut shag mixture. Once the pipe was lit, he continued. "As a medical man, you will see the significance of that."

I thought for a moment and then nodded, seeing exactly what Holmes was driving at. "If she was already dead by strangulation, then there would be no spray of arterial blood when he leaned over her to cut the poor woman's throat."

Holmes nodded blowing out his wax vesta. "Capital. Yes, his technique is definitely evolving.

"Mary's body was first discovered by a cart driver on his way to work as he proceeded along Bucks Row. He saw what he thought was a tarpaulin on the pavement in front of the gated entrance to a yard. As he did so, another driver, who was unknown to him, passed by. He called to him. Together they investigated and realised it was a woman's body. The first man touched her hand to see if she was still alive, believing she might be drunk or the victim of some mundane attack. She was still warm. The other man touched her chest to see if she was still breathing and thought she was, faintly. They went in search of a constable. They found Constable Mizen in Bakers Row, who proceeded straight to Bucks Row. The men had no way of knowing the time. In the meantime, a Constable Neil had also discovered the body, as Bucks Row was on his beat. He put the time at quarter-to-four in the morning. He had last visited the spot at quarter-past-three and the body hadn't been there then. If we assume no more than five minutes elapsed between the two cabmen finding the body and their meeting Constable Mizen, then they must have discovered the body at about twenty-minutes-to-four o'clock. Given the warmth of the body, the attack must have occurred only a few minutes before that. The two cart drivers were adamant that there was no one else in the street with them, and neither of the two constables had seen anyone acting suspiciously or running away."

"But the blackguard couldn't just vanish into thin air," I said.

Holmes grunted. "Yet, seemingly, he did, and left no witnesses. Her throat had been cut, and no one in the area heard or saw anything suspicious. Her abdomen had been slashed and repeatedly stabbed all with the same long-bladed knife." Holmes replied looking up. "He has his method now, and he is buoyed by his first grizzly success."

He blew out a long plume of smoke and reached for a paper from the top of another pile. "Now with the murder of Annie Chapman, we see something new in the devil's approach. This takes place in the back yard of a house, Number 29 Hanbury Street, on Saturday the eighth of September. This time he cuts his way into the poor woman's abdomen, and for the first time he lays her organs out on her body. He also takes a part of her away – a portion of her uterus and bladder were missing from the body."

I must confess I shuddered at this point. Even as a medical man and an army doctor used to the horrors of combat surgery, there was something devilishly alien about the murderer's actions. Many had opined that such horrific slaughter couldn't be the work of an Englishman. No true son of Albion could conceive of such horrors, let alone carry them out. They said it had to be a foreigner – an immigrant, possibly a Jew.

Holmes continued oblivious to my discomfort. "Positioning internal organs on the body and removing body parts will become a part of the killer's method from this point forward – a new stage in his evolution."

Suddenly, Holmes stood and walked over to the breakfast table. He scowled at the cold breakfast but took a mouthful from his coffee cup and shuddered. "Cold" he announced. "I feel the creative juices flowing. More stimulus is needed." With that he was at the door of our rooms and on the landing. "Mrs. Hudson!" he roared. "More coffee if you please!" He resumed his place on the floor and puffed furiously on his pipe, deep in thought.

"Annie Chapman was last seen alive by Mrs. Elizabeth Long at half-past-five in the morning. The Police Surgeon, Dr. Phillips, estimated the time of death at about four-thirty in the morning, but was concerned that the coldness of the morning air might have affected the body, and so his estimate. A Mr. John Richardson was in the back yard of No. 29 at twenty-to-five and saw nothing untoward in the yard at that time. The body was discovered by a Mr. John Davis who lives in the property not long after a quarter-to-six."

Holmes blew out a long plume of tobacco smoke before continuing. "Now a Mr. Cadosch, who lived next door at No. 27 Hanbury Street, went into the back yard of his house to use the outside toilet at twenty-past-five. He heard someone on the other side of the fence say, '*No!*'. He has a medical condition and had to come out again a few minutes later when he heard something fall against the fence between the two yards."

"But then he must have heard the murder actually being committed?" I cried.

"So it would seem," was Holmes's response, "but he thought nothing more of it. You note the discrepancy in the timings?"

I nodded. The estimated time of death was four-thirty, but Mrs. Long had seen Annie alive at five-thirty. She had been certain of her time as a local clock had struck the half-hour. Cadosch's evidence suggested the murder was slightly earlier.

"Nevertheless, it would seem that Annie Chapman was murdered sometime between twenty-past-five and a few minutes after half-past."

"I agree, but with this outrage, we also have our first real glimpse of the killer. Mrs. Long saw Annie talking to a man as she passed by the street door of No. 29. His back was turned to her so she couldn't see his face, but she described him as being a little taller than Annie, who was five-foot in height. He had a dark complexion, was over forty years in age, and wore a deerstalker hat. She also described the man as 'shabby-genteel' and possibly 'foreign' looking."

I was surprised by this. "For a passing glance from behind, that is a rather detailed description," I said. "Particularly since there was no reason at that time for her to remember the incident."

Holmes nodded in agreement. "The suggestion that the man was foreign looking is interesting. I wonder whether gossip and the gutter press had already influenced Mrs. Long's powers of observation.

"Here, this might be of interest" Holmes tossed a copy of *The Star* across at me for the tenth of September. He summarised aloud as I perused the article he indicated. "Despite protestations by the residents, the backyard of No. 29 was indeed a favoured spot for prostitutes. A Miss Emily Walter told the *Star's* reporter that she was treated rather roughly by a 'foreign man' in the same yard not long before the attack on Annie."

"Do you suspect the Ripper?" I asked.

"No, I think not. But what I do suspect is that the backyard was one of Annie's 'spots'. The Ripper may well have been an old customer of hers, and the locality known to him. The familiarity would have made it seem safer."

At this point Mrs. Hudson, our long-suffering landlady, entered with fresh coffee and cups on a tray. She tutted at Holmes's untouched breakfast and, on trying to clear up, she was promptly shooed out of the room by Holmes.

"Now where were we?" he continued. "Ah, yes. This brings us to the double murder – the morning of Sunday the thirtieth of September. Elizabeth Stride's body was discovered in Berner Street at about one o'clock in the morning, and three-quarters-of-an-hour later, Catherine Eddowes in Mitre Square.

He skimmed several newspapers off two of the piles in front of him. "Again, there is good coverage of the inquests in *The Times* and *The Daily Telegraph*."

I read through the reports while Holmes dug out more copy from the stacks of the morning afternoon and evening editions of London's many newspapers.

At about one o'clock in the morning, on the thirtieth of September, a Mr. Lewis Diemschutz, the steward of a socialist meeting group (I confess I tutted disapprovingly here), the *International Working Men's Education*

Society, steered his horse and cart into the narrow entrance of Dutfield's Yard, in Berner Street. The yard was dark despite the lights of the surrounding houses, as well as those from the socialist club itself. This was a three-storey building to the right of the yard as one went in. Suddenly, Diemschutz' horse shied away. There was something lying on the ground up against the wall of the club. Diemschutz lit a match and saw it was a woman's body. He rushed into the club for help. Now, with the light of a candle, they could see blood everywhere. Diemschutz ran into Berner Street, calling for a policeman. He met a man who accompanied him back to the yard. This man lifted the head of the body slightly and they saw a cut across the throat.

I read the remainder of the inquest report in both newspapers. It seemed that only her throat had been cut, probably after she had been forced to the ground. Police were acting on the assumption that the arrival of the horse and cart had disturbed the killer before he could get to his grizzly work. He may even have been lurking in the shadows while Diemschutz examined the body and then fled when Diemschutz went into the club for help.

I looked up, confused. "There seems to be an inconsistency here."

He eased himself into the armchair before the fireplace and steepled his fingers, elbows resting on the chair's arms. "What concerns you?"

"It's the time of death again. The two medical men attending, Dr. Blackwell and Dr. Phillips, both fix the time of death as between twelve-forty-five and twelve-fifty-five am. Diemschutz finds the body at one o'clock. That leaves a window of between five and perhaps more than ten minutes for the Ripper to mutilate his victim. Yet he does not. Why?"

"Why indeed? You have it in a nutshell."

"Perhaps he was disturbed by others?"

Holmes nodded thoughtfully. "There is plenty of witness testimony to prove it was a busy thoroughfare, even at that time of the morning. The killer may well have feared interruption from the street, or perhaps from the social club itself via the door that opened into the yard.

"Unlike the previous cases, the problem here is too much evidence. We must be selective. It's clear that Elizabeth Stride spent her last few hours in the vicinity of Berner Street, and indeed her final hour may have been confined to that street alone. There are multiple sightings of her in the company of a man or men. Their descriptions don't tally, so we cannot be certain whether it is the same one or many. Some of the testimony bares particular notice. I refer you to the inquest report of Constable William Smith."

I quickly re-read that section. Constable Smith was in Berner Street between twelve-thirty and twelve-thirty-five. He saw someone with

383

Elizabeth Stride, but since they weren't behaving suspiciously, he didn't take much notice. He described a youngish man in his late twenties, respectably dressed in dark clothes, about five-foot-seven inches tall. What is more, he was wearing a deerstalker. Smith went onto say the man carried a small parcel in one hand. Suddenly I felt a small jolt of electricity down my spine.

"Holmes, astrakhan-man carried a parcel, and the man seen with Annie Chapman was wearing a deerstalker."

"Well done! I was hoping you wouldn't miss those."

"What is the significance of the parcel?" I asked. "Do you think it's the killer carrying the tools of his trade?"

"It is possible, but you know my feelings on speculating before the facts are all in. If nothing else, these inquest reports are a likely source for some of George Hutchinson's embellishments."

Holmes tapped his nose thoughtfully with one finger. "Once more the concern here is the timing. Several members of the socialist club came and went through Dutfield's yard between five and ten minutes of Constable Smith seeing Elizabeth Stride and deerstalker-man together. There was certainly no body in the yard then."

I looked back over the Annie Chapman reports, and those for Liz Stride. "Although the descriptions of deerstalker man aren't exact matches, they aren't wildly dissimilar. They could be the same person: Dark complexion, middle height, and early middle aged."

Holmes nodded absently. "Indeed, they could well be the same person, but here is why speculation is premature: It seems that this fellow may not be our man. There is another piece of the puzzle: Here we have witness testimony that wasn't introduced into the inquest."

Holmes walked over to the table and began to leaf through the Scotland Yard documents until he found what he was looking for. He passed it across to me along with a copy of *The Star* newspaper for the first of October. "Read Lestrade's missive first. He got it straight from Abberline."

It seemed that a man named Israel Schwartz had presented himself at Leman Street Police Station. He was a Hungarian Jew who spoke no English, but he had brought an interpreter with him. On the night of the murder, he had been walking down Berner Street at a quarter-to-one in the morning. As he passed the gate to Dutfield's Yard, he saw a man who had been walking ahead of him stop and try to pull Elizabeth Stride into the street. He positively identified her body in the mortuary. She had been standing in the gateway. He spun her around and threw her to the pavement. She screamed three times but not loudly. Schwartz thought it was a husband and wife quarrelling, so he crossed to the other side of the street. He noticed a second man now on the same side of the road as him lighting a pipe. The assailant apparently called out to the pipe-man, "Lipski!" Schwartz walked on, but, on turning 'round, noticed that pipe-man was following him. Frightened, he ran off down the street, but pipe-man didn't follow him.

"Great Scott!" I said. "This Schwartz chap actually got a look at Jack the Ripper!"

"The timing – think of the timing."

"Ah, yes, I see what you mean. It still doesn't bring us close to the time of death, if it was nearer to one o'clock when the body was found. But look here: A doctor's estimate of the time of death is just that – an estimate. It depends on a number of things including the rate of cooling of the body. Many factors can affect that,: The local air temperature for example, even a slight breeze at pavement level can affect the estimate. You recall this was a concern of the attending physician in Annie Chapman's case."

Holmes looked up at me over the tops of his fingertips "Yes, I am aware of that. I admit it's unclear when precisely poor Lizzie was killed. Read the descriptions of the men."

Scanning the document, I read out loud. "*The assailant was about thirty years old, and short in stature, about five-feet-five-inches tall. He was well built with a fair complexion, dark hair, and a small moustache. He wore dark clothing and jacket, and had a cap with a peak*'," I scanned the next paragraph. "'*Pipe-man was taller, about five-foot-eleven-inches, also dressed in dark clothes, had on a dark overcoat and a black hat with a wide brim*'."

On Holmes's urging, I then perused the copy of *The Star*. Although the incident was clearly the same one, it was embellished with details not in the report that Israel Schwartz gave to the police. In the newspaper version, pipe man was coming out of a public house, he shouted out the warning to the assailant, and moreover he had a knife in his hand.

"I think we can discount the newspaper story," said Holmes, and I concurred.

"Now the salient points are these." He ticked them off on his long fingers. "First, there are two men, one shorter and one taller. Both have dark or brown hair, both have moustaches. One is of lighter complexion than the other. Second, both men are wearing dark clothes. The assailant has a jacket on, which I take to mean a shorter garment, while pipe-man has an overcoat on – a longer garment. Third, pipe-man may be named 'Lipski', and so could be east European – it is a common enough Hungarian name, but one also found in Russia."

Glancing over Abberline's report, as paraphrased for us by Lestrade, I pointed out that the shouted word may not have been a name.

Holmes nodded in agreement. "Abberline is of the opinion that it may have been uttered as a warning to Schwartz to mind his own business. Apparently, it is a common enough racial slur in the East End, and aimed at Jews."

"But why?" I asked

"You recall the Israel Lipski case? The man was hanged last year. He was a poisoner. There was a great deal of unrest after that – rioting in the streets, and extra police had to be drafted in to break it up. The next road along is Batty Street, where Israel Lipski perpetrated his foul crime. Once more the spectre of race and anti-Semitism raises its ugly head.

"Now my fourth point is that Stride cried out three times, but not very loudly. What does that suggest?"

"She perhaps knew her assailant?"

"Agreed. Had she been in mortal terror of her life, would she not have screamed out loudly for aid? But if it was a man she knew, perhaps an old client, she may well have known him to be violent, but not murderous, so at that point she didn't believe she was in mortal danger. I fear women like Lizzie Stride are habituated to violence directed against them by men."

"Then what are you suggesting? That this *wasn't* Jack the Ripper? Or worse, there are *two* of them?"

"Both are possible," he steepled his fingers once more and stared into the grate. "Currently there are three hypotheses I would entertain: The first is that one or both men are indeed Jack the Ripper, perhaps one acting as watchman for the other. The second is that neither of them are the murderer. That would be deerstalker-man. The third is that Lizzie Stride wasn't killed by the Ripper at all. It was perpetrated by someone who wanted to stir up racial hatred by pretending to be the Ripper."

"In which case what of pipe-man and his compatriot then?" I asked, a little bewildered.

It was a moment before Holmes answered. "Perhaps members of one of the local gangs who routinely extort money from prostitutes as protection. Since Lizzie was south of Whitechapel High Street, she may have entered new territory and been recognised as a new face by some gang members who happened past."

"That would explain why she wasn't in fear of her life, believing that the worse that could happen to her was a beating."

"Yes, a good point there," said Holmes, and I must admit I blushed. Praise from him was rare and always welcome.

He continued, "There is a precedent for this. Emma Elizabeth Smith was murdered on the third of April this year, attacked by three men in a

386

particularly vicious and brutal way. The police consider it a protection-type slaying. But we also have an instance of such in this very case."

He threw another copy of *The Star* across at me. Early in September, the paper had run a series of articles following on from the police investigation of a suspect known as Leather Apron. He was a particularly violent character, especially toward women and often carried a knife. He may well have been part of a protection racket aimed at street prostitutes. *The Star* described him as a Jew and painted an unflattering picture of his appearance and character. The articles caused much alarm and further fuelled anti-Semitic unrest in the East End.

"Surely it is inconceivable that someone would copy such a ghastly crime just for the purposes of fermenting disturbance?"

He looked at me for a moment. "Sadly, it is only too possible, I fear. Need I remind you of the lengths that Dr. Grimesby Roylott or the loathsome Enoch Drebber were willing to go to.

"Nevertheless, it is odd that this crime is to the south of Whitechapel High Street when all the others are to the north? It is located in an area already noted for anti-Hebrew rioting. The outrage is perpetrated on premises where a Jewish socialist newspaper is printed, associated with a socialist club whose political membership was largely Jewish. Other Jews in the area use it as a social club. There is often singing and dancing after a political lecture.

"The choice of murder site couldn't be more clear. And it was premeditated too. The killer – or killers – took with them a knife of the sort they thought was described in the published newspaper accounts and carefully placed it where it would be found."

I pounced on one of the open newspapers in front of me. "Ah, yes, the knife found by Thomas Coram and Constable Drage in Whitechapel Road." I quickly leafed through the inquest report in *The Daily Telegraph* ". . . At – let me see, yes here it is – twelve-thirty, Constable Drage reported seeing a man, Coram, pick up a long-bladed knife from the steps in front of a laundry. Its handle was wrapped in a blood-stained handkerchief, but one of the doctors who later performed the autopsy on Lizzie Stride opined that the knife couldn't be the murder weapon because it had a rounded tip and the blade that took Lizzie's life would more likely have a sharp point."

Holmes pointed to the relevant passages in the two newspapers. "*The Daily Telegraph's* account implies that Stride's neck was cut with a shorter knife. *The Times* is less clear on the point."

I looked up at this. "Martha Tabram was killed with a short-bladed knife."

Holmes nodded. "Quite so. Lizzie Stride's murderer probably used a shorter knife with a point. Newspaper reports had already described the kind of long-bladed knife the Ripper favoured. The killer – or killers – found one they thought suited their purposes. They smeared it in blood for effect and then left it on the laundry steps, clearly visible to any passer-by. Mark my words, it was placed there to be found.

It took me a moment to follow Holmes's line of reasoning. "In which case," I added, "the cry of 'Lipski' was indeed a racial slur against Mr. Schwartz."

Holmes nodded but said nothing further. For a full minute he was quiet, an expression of intense concentration on his face, but then let out a heartfelt cry of exasperation.

"No, no, this will not do! I am caught by the very snare I have made it my life's business to avoid: Speculation. With so many contradictions and so much missing information, we cannot connect the different lines of evidence together." And with that he propelled himself out of his chair, an explosion of frustrated nervous energy. He paced restlessly up and down like a caged animal.

He drove one fist into an open palm. "There is nothing for it. We must apply Occam's celebrated Law of Parsimony. We must decide which is the solution with the least number of contradictions."

He sat down heavily in his chair again and, with a quick smile and wave of the hand, said, "Watson, I cede the floor to you. Proceed."

I was momentarily surprised by my friend's instruction. He wasn't one to welcome my theorising in the normal course of events, but I was beginning to appreciate his earlier comment that hunting for the Ripper was more old-fashioned detection than deduction. Holmes looked across at me expectantly and I felt a moment of fluttering unease. Concentrating, I arranged the facts as seemed right to me.

"Well, two killers would make sense of the contradictions between the different knives used," I said, and Holmes nodded encouragingly. "It also resolves some of the differences between the witness's descriptions. I'm also persuaded by your argument about the anti-Semitic aspect of Lizzie Stride's murder. Perhaps this too is part of the Ripper's evolution – or at least one of them." Here I had a moment of inspiration. "Or our *two* murderers have slightly different aims."

Holmes nodded again. "Good Watson, good!"

I continued. "Deerstalker-man in Berner Street is a coincidence. It is an unusual but not uncommon headwear. His carrying a parcel is also a coincidence, although George Hutchinson drew from it for his own embellished yarn to the newspapers.

"Our murderers are pipe-man and his friend," I said with a confidence I did not quite feel.

Here I paused a moment, for two problems had simultaneously occurred to me: The first was why had Elizabeth Stride been in Berner's Street, and the second was if there was enough time to mutilate the body, then why didn't they?

I took a leaf out of Holmes's book and paced up and down the room, applying myself to the problem.

"How did they know they would meet Elizabeth Stride at the yard's gates? Did they leave it to chance? Was she simply unlucky and in the wrong place at an inconvenient time?" I clicked my fingers as an alternative came to me. "No, they had pre-arranged it, perhaps at an earlier chance meeting in the day. That was why Lizzie hung around the general area, and why she kept to Berner Street after twelve-thirty in the morning. Like Annie Chapman, Lizzie knew her murderer and had made a prior arrangement."

Holmes gave a cry of pleasure. "Capital, my dear fellow, capital! So our killers set up Lizzie to be where they wanted her to be. Pray continue."

"I admit the timings are uncertain, but if Israel Schwartz walked behind the assailant at twelve-forty-five and then fled the scene, that could have taken up two minutes. So it is possible that poor Lizzie was pushed into the yard just before ten minutes to one o'clock."

On an impulse I quickly perused *The Star* for the first of October. To my delight there was a report on an interview with Israel Schwartz. I scanned it quickly to ascertain why he was confident of the time he saw the assailant attack Lizzie. All that was stated was that the incident occurred "about" a quarter-to-one. There was in fact no exact or corroborated time.

"Holmes," I began, somewhat hesitantly, "if there is some uncertainty about the time of death and about just when Lizzie was attacked in the street, it is possible that the murder actually took place closer to one o'clock. But that still leaves enough time to kill her and mutilate the body. Yet they do not."

"Yes. If your scenario is correct, she is killed about ten-minutes-to-one or just after, but something prevents them from beginning the mutilation of the body."

"But what?"

He shrugged. "That we will never know."

I thought for a moment. "That would mean that the theory the killer was interrupted could still hold good. If one stood as sentry for the other, they may have been warned that someone was coming. Quite possibly Lewis Diemschutz in his pony and cart had entered the street. It may have taken him a few minutes to reach the yard."

389

I watched Holmes's face carefully for some sign of displeasure, but he remained impassive. His fingers were steepled before him once more. His eyes were closed and from long familiarity I knew this meant he was concentrating intensely. Encouraged, I continued. However, now I encountered another problem with my theorising: If the real time of death was closer to one o'clock, how would these assassins avoid detection and affect their escape unnoticed? Diemschutz would have seen them flee the yard.

Holmes looked up. "You are stumbling on how to get the villains out without being seen, eh? I can be of some service there." He moved over to the table and slid several large-scale Ordinance Survey Maps across. They were of Dutfield's Yard, Berner Street, and several other adjacent streets.

"Look to the left-hand side of the yard," he said.

For a moment I couldn't fathom his meaning. "Ah," I said at last. "The outside toilets in the yard."

Holmes nodded. "It would take Diemschutz perhaps two minutes to reach the yard from the end of the street. A warning from the look-out would give plenty of time to hide themselves away. That would further reduce the time available for the fiends to begin to mutilate Lizzie's body. When Diemschutz went for help on discovering the body, they could have slipped out of the yard altogether."

I agreed enthusiastically. I had also noticed from the maps that about four or five doors up from the yard was a footpath that led to Batty Gardens, a cut-through in the middle of the block of dwellings which contained Dutfield's Yard. It gave access to the next street to the west and was certainly a safer escape route than Berner Street with its high chance of bumping into Constable Smith on his patrol.

"A logical escape route," Holmes agreed. "Batty Gardens would bring our killers onto Backchurch Lane, then northwards to Commercial Road East, and thence back to Whitechapel High Street.

"But here is a puzzle: Why did the killers not cross the High Street and disappear north into Whitechapel? Why continue north-west to Aldgate and Mitre Square?"

Here I had a possible answer to Holmes's question. "One or both of the murderers may well have still been consumed by unsated blood-lust. According to the papers, Aldgate High Street and the area around St. Botolph's Church are notorious for prostitutes."

Holmes nodded and fixed me with a penetrating look. I was awaiting a sarcastic remark, and for him to tell me that I had missed almost every salient point in the case. Instead, he smiled and clapped me lightly on the back.

"Watson, we may make a detective out of you yet. Now I see the morning has escaped us. I propose Mrs. Hudson furnish us with a spot of light lunch, and then it is a hansom to the East End."

The cab dropped us at the meeting point of Commercial Road, Commercial Street, and Whitechapel High Street. The day was still bright, and standing on the busy pavement in the sunlight, it was hard to believe that within a few hours the confidence of the day would give way to the uncertainty of what the night might conceal.

"We will walk westwards toward Aldgate and Mitre Square, but first I wish to conduct a small experiment. Do you see the two women selling flowers a few yards ahead of us. And there further on, on the opposite side of the street there is a woman selling matches. Now wait here for five minutes and approach each of them and ask whether a friend of yours has passed this way heading for the station. Give them a description of me."

"Holmes," I said, somewhat taken aback, "what is this all about?"

But rather than answer me, he said, "Remember now – five minutes." And with that he was off up the street. I watched him stop and engage the flower sellers in conversation. They pointed in the direction we were headed, and he departed. A minute later I saw him on the other side of the road talking with the match seller. She too pointed toward Aldgate.

I waited five minutes by my watch then enquired of my friend from the two flower sellers. I had by now divined the purpose of Holmes's little experiment.

"Excuse me, ladies," I said. "I was wondering if a friend of mine had passed this way. We were heading for Aldgate Station and got separated. He is a tall man, clean-shaven, and wearing a long dark coat and a hat."

"Oh yes, dear," said one of the two. "A gent did stop and ask the way to the station, but 'e 'ad a short coat on and a funny old-fashioned sort of 'at. One of them old 'unting 'ats."

At which point her friend interrupted. "But he wasn't tall, he was more your height. I do remember his hat though. It was dark and had a peak. But he had a moustache." Then she thought better of it. "Maybe he didn't have a moustache. I can't remember."

"Anyway, 'e went off in that direction," said the first woman. "You'll catch him if you are quick."

I thanked them and bought some flowers, and then crossed the road. As luck would have it the match seller already had a customer, a non-descript man in a short jacket and a round flat cap with a peak. I waited until he left and then enquired of Holmes. Yes, she had seen him, and proceeded to give me an exact description of the previous customer except that he was wearing a funny old hat. I thanked her and gave her the flowers. "Oh dearie!" was all I heard as I hastened away.

"Well?" asked Holmes, whom I found perched on the wall of St. Botolph's Church.

"If your purpose was to show the imprecision of human memory and the discrepancies between witness testimony, you have succeeded."

He looked pleased. "But sometimes the memory can be deliberately tricked. Very often a simple device like a noticeable hat can focus the memory on that alone to the detriment of other significant features. Take our two miscreants. By the simple device of a tall man and a shorter man exchanging a hat or coat, they can be recalled as a completely different people."

I would have found Mitre Square a dreary place even if I hadn't known of the murder of Catherine Eddowes. We entered via the main approach from Mitre Street, flanked on both sides by tall three-story buildings, shop fronts and private dwellings which fronted onto Mitre Street. Directly facing us and taking up the whole of the opposite side of the Square was a warehouse belonging to Kearley and Tonge Tea Importers. The furthest half of the Square's left side was another of Kearley and Tonge's warehouses, while to our immediate left, the Square held two private houses. The right side also had a warehouse, while that half to our immediate right was a low wall, topped by a high wooden fence with a gate in the corner, behind which were the back yards of more houses. It was up against this wall beside the gate that Catherine Eddowes' body had been found. In the top right-hand corner of the Square was an alley-way, Church Passage, giving on to Duke's Street beyond. In the top left-hand corner was another alley, St. James' Passage, which led to another Square of the same name.

Holmes looked around, his expression unreadable. "Abberline calculated it would take someone walking at a steady pace some twelve to fifteen minutes to get from Berner Street to here. The murderers would wish to be quit of the place quickly, yet not draw attention to themselves. Since the police are focused on looking for one man, two walking in an unhurried way would attract less attention. So they would have arrived in this area around one-fifteen in the morning.

"At one-thirty, Constable Watkins of the City of London Police came into the Square through the entrance from Mitre Street. This is part of his beat. He walked around the Square, looking in the corners but found nothing. He may have chatted a moment with the night watchman in Kearley and Tonge before continuing on his beat. Lestrade thinks he occasionally stopped for a brew of tea with the watchman, a man called Morris and an ex-police constable himself.

392

"This next item is somewhat unclear," Holmes continued. "Duke Street, which lies behind Kearley and Tonge's warehouse, is part of the beat of a constable called Harvey. He didn't possess a watch. His timings are reconstructed from his seeing the Post Office clock in Aldgate High Street as he proceeded along his beat. This part of his route brought him in from Duke Street, down Church Passage to the Square, but not into it. He seems to have been here about the same time as Watkins, or perhaps a little later since the two didn't see each other. How much later is a matter of some concern to the constabulary.

"Constable Watkins returns at sixteen minutes to two o'clock and finds the body in this corner. The Ripper has killed her following his usual method, then mutilated her, laying some of her internal organs on her body. He removed one of her kidneys and most of her uterus and took them away. Now we see a new feature: This time, he mutilates her face and cuts her eye lids. Once more his technique is evolving.

"If Constable Watkins is to be believed, and there is no reason why he shouldn't be, the murder and mutilation all took place within the space of about ten minutes. At the inquest, one of the attending physicians suggested it would be possible to carry out these atrocities in the space of five minutes or so."

I nodded. "With even a basic knowledge of human anatomy, that would be possible. But it astonishes me that the killer could see to carry out his work. Its gloomy enough in here mid-afternoon, let alone at night."

"There is a lamp yonder at the entrance to Church Passage," said Holmes, "but it is faulty, and another there on the left side of the Square in front of Kearley and Tonge. Neither throws a particularly wide light. However, the corner wasn't totally in the dark, it would seem. There was enough light for the murderer to work by."

"Then why did Constable Harvey not see Catherine and her killer?" I asked.

"Why not indeed?" came the terse reply. "It may well be that looking into the Square from the end of Church Passage, and standing under the light of even a poor gas lamp, it was just not possible to see into the gloomy corner. On the other hand, and reading between the lines, I think Lestrade is of the opinion that Harvey may have skimmed a little off his beat and only looked down Church Passage from the Duke Street end. In which case, he would be very unlikely to have seen anything in the corner."

"If he was here not long after Watkins left," I said, "that means he was here as the murder was actually being committed."

"In all likelihood," Holmes nodded. "Our finest chance to have put the cuffs on the beggar. Bah!" he exclaimed with feeling. "Now, we can refine the time a little more. As in Berner Street, there was a witness."

393

With that, Holmes strode across the Square toward Church Passage. I took one last glance back. It was indeed a chill place. Even in the mid-afternoon sun, the towering three-storey buildings on all sides cast it in permanent shadow. As I learned later, there had been another murder here when a monastery had occupied the site. A mad monk had murdered a woman, and her ghost was said to still haunt the Square.

At the end of church passage, we came out on Duke Street.

"Now, I want you to stand just here." Holmes positioned me just to one side of the entrance to the alley-way. He pointed with his stick. "At one-thirty in the morning, a man called Joseph Lawende and two of his friends were in the Imperial Club, just across the road there. They finished their drinks, checked their watches by the club clock, and donned their coats. Within a few minutes they were in the street and walking past this point, so no later than thirty-five minutes past the hour. They saw Catherine Eddowes standing where you are, with her back to them, talking to a man."

"How did they know it was Eddowes?" I asked.

"They identified her clothing in the mortuary. This is the description of the man she was talking to," said Holmes. "About five-foot-seven tall, thirtyish in age, a fair complexion, a small moustache, a greyish cap with a peak, and a short greyish jacket. He was wearing a red handkerchief knotted round his neck."

Several points intruded on my thoughts at the same time. "That is a very similar description to the man described by Israel Schwartz in Berner Street. The red handkerchief – that is what astrakhan-man was seen giving to Mary Jane Kelly."

Holmes nodded grimly. "The handkerchief may be another motif that George Hutchinson took from the newspapers. However, the physical descriptions do tally, or at least are close enough. Both Lestrade and Abberline are satisfied with Mr. Lawende being a credible witness. If Catherine is seen alive at one-thirty-five, here in Duke Street, and constable Watkins finds her body at one-forty-four, then that leaves nine or ten minutes for her murderer to take her into the Square, attack and kill her, and then mutilate her. Applying Occam's Razor again, the man Lawende saw has to be the murderer. There isn't enough time for her to find another customer.

"I am convinced we have our man."

Though the two descriptions weren't exact matches, there was a strong similarity between Joseph Lawende's description and that of Israel Schwartz. Given the vagaries of human memory, as Holmes had just proved, I was satisfied that the two descriptions were of the same man. But then where was pipe-man, I asked?

He nodded. "Somewhere close by, I'll warrant, secreted in one of these doorways and unnoticed by Mr. Lawende and his friends. He may well have been on lookout duty, warning the killer of Constable Harvey's approach as soon as he turned into Duke Street on his beat.

I snapped my fingers. Holmes had hit upon it. As at Berner Street with ample warning, there was enough time for the murderers to hide themselves out of sight, or to make good their escape.

"Now are you game for the last piece of the puzzle?

I'd read the reports and I knew immediately to what he was referring.

"Goulston Street?" I asked, and he nodded.

We headed eastwards, taking the very same streets that the Ripper may have taken in making his escape from Mitre Square. We talked as we walked.

"Something is puzzling me. Mitre Square seems a foolish choice for a murder site. There are two constables who regularly patrol this area. Twice the chance of being caught."

"I too have wondered about that," was his reply. "I did wonder if the wooden gate next to her body was normally unfastened, but for some reason was locked that night. It would provide a quiet place away from the prying eyes," he shrugged his shoulders. "I suppose we will never know.

"I have only recently learned that on the night of the murder, there were two firemen stationed in St. James Square, on the other side of St. James' Passage. They heard nothing, and would have certainly raised the alarm if they'd seen any suspicious characters fleeing the Square." He paused a moment. "So the killers must have exited through Church Passage as we did."

I was beginning to appreciate Holmes's earlier comments about the Ripper having the Devil's own luck, but then I had a thought. "I wonder if we are looking at this from the wrong perspective? We have assumed the Ripper had unnatural good fortune in not encountering a constable, or that he had done his homework well. But what if he was relying on the knowledge of the unfortunate women he prayed upon. Catherine Eddowes would surely be familiar with the police routines on her own territory, as it were."

"Upon my word, Watson, you are quite the detective today!" my friend replied. "Yes, that had occurred to me also. Many of these women have their own beat too. When Joseph Lawende saw Eddowes and the man talking, she had her hand laid gently on his breast. Lawende heard no raised voices or quarrelling when he passed them. I wonder whether she was urging him to be patient. She would have known that Constable Watkins would have just quit the Square, while Constable Harvey wasn't yet due. They could have wandered down Church Passage and hidden out of sight, knowing that Harvey was unlikely to walk all the way down Church Passage and look into the Square."

"My word, you are quite the speculator today!"

"*Touché*, Doctor!" came the riposte.

Mitre Square lay within the jurisdiction of the City of London Police Force, whereas Whitechapel and the remainder of London fell under the Metropolitan Police Force. The border was Middlesex Street. We crossed this line and were once again in the territory of the Met. New Goulston Street brought us into the upper end of Goulston Street itself. We pulled up in front of a dingy entrance-way, a small sign announced apartments 108 through 119. This was Wentworth Model Dwellings: New housing built to replace slum clearances. The building was a series of tenement apartments which opened onto landings. I was told later that it was mainly Jewish families who lived in the tenements. The right half of the entrance was taken up by a stairway, slightly recessed, and on the left a doorway. The vertical jambs of the entrance were painted black, but just behind them the lower half of the brickwork was darker in colour, and lighter above.

"At about twenty-past-two in the morning," Holmes began, "a Constable Long was walking past this entrance-way. He looked down casually as he passed and saw nothing. At this time, he wasn't aware of the murder in Mitre Square. A detective constable named Halse, who passed this way at around the same time, and who was definitely searching for Catharine Eddowes' killer, also saw nothing of note.

"When Long's beat brought him round again at five-minutes-to-three, he saw what turned out to be a blood-stained piece of cloth. It lay on the floor up against the dark brickwork. The blood on it was still wet. He searched the landings of the building but found nothing more. While looking around he noticed some chalk writing on the black coloured brickwork, directly above the cloth:

The Jews are the men that will not be blamed for nothing.

"Long wrote it down in his notebook at the time. He was joined by another police constable who must have told him about the Mitre Square murder. He then took the cloth to the Commercial Street Police Station." Here he paused a moment and looked thoughtful. "There is disagreement as to how the word '*Jews*' was spelt, and indeed disagreement about the exact order of the words. But that is immaterial. The implication is as clear as daylight: The author of those words believed the Jews to be guilty of something. What it is we do not know."

I looked up at him surprised. "Do you mean to imply that this was a further attempt to implicate the Jews in the Ripper slayings?"

396

"I do. Both of the killings on the thirtieth of September attempted that," Holmes pointed with his stick to the north. Just ahead of us was Wentworth Street, which on the morning of the murder would have been preparing for its famous street market – Petticoat Lane.

"This is the very heart of the Jewish East End. There are, by repute, some one-hundred-thousand Jews crammed into the streets around us. With racial tensions strained to breaking point, a message like this in such a visible spot and tied to a bloody memento of the slaying of a Gentile woman could have been the final spark. Little wonder then that Sir Charles Warren, the Metropolitan Police Commissioner, ordered the message to be removed before anyone saw it. He was convinced there would be a riot. He may well have been right."

"How can you be sure the Ripper wrote the words?" I asked.

"That is an apposite question, and of course I cannot. The message was written in chalk on the lower black coloured bricks. Who carries a piece of chalk with them? If not a teacher, then someone who intends leaving a message. In truth, there is other such graffiti in the area. But as with the wording, it doesn't really matter who wrote it. The placement of the bloodstained rag next to it was enough to get the message across."

I was about to ask another question, but then I recalled the significance of the discovery. The rag was in fact a part of the apron that Catherine Eddowes had been wearing and had been cut away by her murderer. The two cut portions were matched together some hours after the body was brought to the morgue, and the match was exact.

"Current opinion on the blood-stained apron cloth is that the killer used it to wipe his hands or clean his knife. But why do that an hour after he had killed poor Catherine, and here of all places. Why carry that around on your person for such a time? No, it will not do. The apron was taken for another reason than to clean his blade.

"There is nothing more we can do here," said Holmes with a sigh. "What do you say to a refreshing glass of ale and a brandy to restore our spirits. Come, Watson, I'll stand a round at The Ten Bells.

I nodded acceptance, eager to be quit of the place. We made our way north-westwards through dingy narrow streets with small over-crowded houses and endless tenement buildings. Neither of us were much in the mood for conversing. I watched the gangs of dirty ill-fed children playing in the gutters while their mothers and elder sisters wearing the only clothes they owned gathered at street corners. Here and there a body would lie in the entrance to an alley-way, a drunk sleeping it off. No one took any notice. Lone women or sometimes in pairs smiled at us as we passed, hoping to entice us into a clandestine tryst in an alley-way or back-yard. It made me shudder. Did they not fear for their very lives with this maniac still on the loose?

"There are still bellies to be filled and a bed in a communal lodging house to be paid for," said Holmes quietly at my side, his clairvoyance no longer surprising me. "Fourpence or sixpence to be earned."

We passed many public houses, hearing the hubbub of conversation from within. Prostitutes would move from pub to pub, seeking a new client or taking temporary solace in beer and gin. Men stood outside, as begrimed as their women folk, staring at us with resentful eyes. Had it been darker, I feel we would have been in greater peril, but Holmes seemed unconcerned. Outside the doss houses, the queues for a night's bed were already long even though it was only late afternoon. Everywhere there were faces devoid of hope – men and women for whom life held little joy and the promise of tomorrow was just the same as yesterday's empty belly. Unrelenting hopelessness.

Although Mary Jane Kelly and Elizabeth Stride may have earned their living by soliciting, the other women only sold themselves when they had to, and that for the price of a bed in one of the communal lodging houses. Was it any wonder that women, with no other recourse, would turn to casual prostitution just to eat and find somewhere to sleep? Was it any wonder that Jack the Ripper could rise like a phantom from the midst of this misery? Yet not three miles to the west, polite society was sitting down to tea and scones in chintz drawing rooms. How could two such contrasting worlds live cheek-by-jowl in the same country, let alone the same city? London was the heart of a great civilising empire. Yet to the gentle folk of Mayfair, the people of Whitechapel were as strange as the natives from the furthest reaches of British rule. The border that separated the two parts of the city was invisible, but more impermeable than if it had been made of steel and stone – class and birth.

At last, Holmes broke the silence as we walked. "The Ripper was made in these streets. His home is somewhere here. His knowledge of the area, and the way he avoids detection, makes it certain. Where did he go for just over an hour between murdering Catherine Eddowes and placing the blood-stained cloth in Goulston Street? He went home and probably changed his clothes and cleaned himself up."

I had been wondering about the missing hour myself. I also recalled that George Hutchinson had claimed to have seen astrakhan-man on the Sunday after Mary's murder in the Petticoat Lane market.

"But then somebody must know something," I replied. "Surely a neighbour or a friend has suspicions?"

"If they do, they have said nothing," was the terse reply.

This brought my thoughts back to Holmes's earlier querying of the Ripper's luck. Even with two of them to ward each other's backs, it was still a mystery as to how the fiends had eluded everyone.

As if anticipating my train of thought, Holmes spoke as we turned into Commercial Street. "I do not but wonder if we are missing something in our reasoning?"

"How so?"

"What if one or both of our fellows are policemen?"

I stopped dead in my tracks. "You cannot be serious!" I said, shocked.

"But I am old chap, deadly serious. A constable or a CID man could come and go as he pleased and could well have blood on his clothes, but who would challenge him?"

"But surely a strange face would be noticed by his fellows on the beat?" I said.

"Don't forget that extra constables have been drafted in for this emergency. This would work distinctly to his advantage. Then again, a prostitute would be more inclined to accept the favours of a policeman than a stranger – particularly if he was an old customer."

I had to admit that as Holmes explained it, the idea seemed less preposterous than I had first thought. But it also depressed me greatly that someone could so abuse a sacred oath and murder those he was sworn to protect. Yet the more I considered it, the more the suggestion took on solid form. A police officer could come and go with impunity. If seen with compromising materials, or blood on his tunic, he would merely say he was about his official business.

Then I recalled something from the inquest of Lizzie Stride. One of the witnesses who identified her body was a Mrs. Mary Malcolm, but she had confused Lizzy with her own estranged sister, a Mrs. Elizabeth Watts. Mrs. Malcolm had described her sister's life, confusing much of it with details from Lizzie Stride's own sad story. The coroner, I recalled, had been sceptical about the veracity of Mrs. Malcolm's evidence, and he had been right to be so. In a later sitting of the inquest, the real Elizabeth Watts had appeared in high dudgeon over the way her sister had characterised her. I said as much to Holmes as we made for Spitalfields and The Ten Bells.

"What I do recall from Mary Malcolm's testimony," I continued, "was a tale that Elizabeth Stride had appeared on her doorstep one day with a babe in arms. She claimed the child's father was a policeman she had known when she had been in service in the West End of London. Perhaps there we have a motive – if Mary Malcolm is to be believed."

Holmes nodded. "Lestrade's notes on Mrs. Malcolm were most enlightening. He believes that Stride deliberately played on Mary

399

Malcolm's confusion and poor memory. She falsely presented herself as Malcolm's long estranged sister, mixing up enough of her own life with what she could glean of that of Malcolm's real sister."

"But why?" I asked.

"Lizzie Stride was in the habit of visiting Mary Malcolm once a week for a handout. When you have nothing, even a little is something. A few shillings can buy gin and beer and a bed for the night."

"And the story of the policeman's child?"

Holmes shrugged his shoulders. "Sadly, we will probably never know. It may have been true. Or it may have been a ruse on Lizzie Stride's part. Perhaps it was a figment of Mrs. Malcolm's imagination."

A thought struck me. Rather than actual policemen, perhaps the two men were posing as plain clothed constables, or even CID. With all the men drafted in from other divisions, they wouldn't arouse suspicion. Perhaps a warrant card was not difficult to fake.

"Ah, here we are," Holmes suddenly announced, breaking my train of thought.

We had arrived at the pub and pushed the door open. The conversation died for a moment as we entered. We were clearly not locals. The hostelry had a circular bar in the middle of the floor, and tables and chairs arranged around the walls. We ordered our drinks and found a table in a quiet corner. Suspicious eyes regarded us warily. In and amongst the ordinary working men enjoying a glass of beer after work, were pickpockets pimps and prostitutes, thieves, illegal bookmakers, and probably worse. The public house was a favourite of unfortunate women as the newspapers described them. Mary Jane Kelly was known to have solicited custom on the pavement outside, and had been in here the night before she died. It was reputed that Annie Chapman had also drunk here the day before she was killed.

"All of the Ripper's victims are of the same class of person," Holmes began in a low voice. "Women whose husbands are dead or who have thrown them out for one reason or another. They are mothers who have left their children. They have had a succession of lovers and are all addicted to alcohol. They work when they can, charring, or selling trinkets on the street, but all too often it isn't enough, and they must make a few pennies some other way."

"Then the Ripper is picking his victims carefully," I said. "Surely that must help us to narrow down his identity. The victims must have been known to him?"

But he shook his head. "Sadly, such tales of woe are ten-a-penny here. Just look around. More than half the women in here will share the same story."

His words depressed me greatly. "How can this be? I was brought up to believe the English race had a civilizing mission, given to us by God, to bring peace and prosperity to the world. I fought at Maiwand for Queen and Empire, sure in my belief of our moral superiority. We decry other nations and other peoples for living as uneducated savages, yet here on our very doorstep we ignore the lives of people whose existence is as brutal as those of our primitive ancestors. We shut our eyes to them."

"My dear fellow, don't taken on so," said Holmes. "Don't forget that there are innumerable folk in the East End who are good and decent people. Their circumstances may be harsh, but they retain their dignity and human self-respect – ordinary decent men and women of many faiths and many communities who live God-fearing lives."

It was a very valid point, and I was grateful to Holmes for making it. Another thought struck me. "I fail to understand what it is the Ripper wants, and why in the name of God is this other man helping him?"

"He may well be more than a lookout," said Holmes. "A disciple perhaps? Two murderers would explain differences in the knife work between the victims," he finished looking pointedly at me. "And why Lizzie Stride wasn't strangled from behind first. As to what he or they are seeking, I do not pretend to understand. It will be a long time before medical science can map the mind of the criminally insane. The removal of body parts is significant, I feel sure. You yourself opined that the killer might have been searching for something. With Mary Jane Kelly, he found it. Perhaps they both did."

I shuddered with horror. It was beyond the understanding of any sane man or woman. Holmes was about to say more when a shadow loomed over our table. I looked up into the gnarled face of a short and powerful-looking man wearing grey trousers and a waistcoat, with a flat cap. My attention was drawn to his broad weather-beaten face and his nose which had clearly been broken many times.

"I know who you are, Mr. Sherlock Holmes," he said a low gravelly voice. My heart sank. "Do you remember me then?"

Holmes, unfazed, looked at him for a moment. "Yes, I do. You are James Bolton, the Houndsditch Hammer. I recall we once went five rounds in a ring at the back of The Horn of Plenty. I had you in front of the magistrate in '84 for the Camberwell art heist."

"I did three years hard labour for that," was the slow reply. I tensed, ready for the inevitable fisticuffs.

"Anyways," Bolton continued. "me and the lads were wondering what you was doing here. Then Hiram there, he said you'd be after Saucy Jack, so we wanted to say good luck, and if you want our help, then just give us a shout. He don't belong here, and he ain't wanted here neither."

401

At which point two brandies appeared on our table from Mr. Bolton and his companions. With a touch at the peak of his cap, he returned to his table.

"You see, there are good people everywhere," Holmes said with some irony. "Nevertheless, prudence suggests we drink up and take our leave."

On the pavement in front of The Ten Bells we buttoned ourselves into our coats. "The one thing we haven't discussed," I said, "is the actual identity of the Ripper – or should I say *Rippers*."

"I am afraid that will be a secret that the Whitechapel's streets will keep for a long time yet. And now an adversary far more dangerous that the Houndsditch Hammer has espied us. I think it time we beat a hasty retreat to Baker Street."

I looked in the direction he indicated. With a loud "Halloa!" I perceived the match-seller still clutching her bouquet of flowers waving and making a bee-line for us.

It was time to leave Whitechapel.

NOTES

Afterword

In researching my story, I have only used newspaper articles, inquest reports, and police documentation that had been written up to the end of November 1888, but not after. In other words, Holmes and Watson know only what the police and the public knew at the time of the Ripper murders. With a few exceptions, I have deliberately avoided subsequent Ripper scholarship. One of the exceptions was Megan Coles' web site suggesting that the Ripper might have been a police officer. The suggestion is not new. Bernard Brown suggested the killer was a railway transport police officer. The notion that a police officer could be involved was one I had thought up myself but quickly came across Coles' interesting ideas when I began to look into the subject in more detail.

In writing a story like this, I am conscious that I have drawn from a wide variety of ideas that are in the sources I consulted below. I do not claim that any of what I have written is original, and if I have pinched your idea and not acknowledged that as such, then please accept my sincerest apologies. The notion that Elizabeth Stride was playing Mary Malcolm is drawn directly from Rubenhold's book, *The Five*.

This is not intended as a serious contribution to Ripperology. It is just a story.

My one real concern is whether my fictionalising the deaths of the six women discussed here is disrespectful to their memory and to the awful fate they met. Rubenhold's book *The Five* goes a long way to re-humanising these women, so that they no longer appear as unflattering sketches from the *Police Gazette*, or dehumanised images from mortuary slabs. They now have stories. They experienced lives that were ultimately tragic and full of despair. They were certainly victims of poverty and the callousness of their times. Jack London's chilling *People of the Abyss* (1903), written nearly fifteen years later, makes one clear point if no other: True poverty is having no choices at all. These women knew such poverty. They survived as best they could in the same way as thousands of other women did then (and still do). It is ironic that we know their names only because they were murdered. They are the silenced ambassadors of a faceless and voiceless multitude whose names and stories have been forever lost. Whoever they were, they all deserve our respect.

Acknowledgements

I am grateful to a number of people who read various drafts of the story and made comments. I did not always follow your advice, but I listened and I thought about it. My thanks go to Rob Hosfield, Jonathan McCafferty, Elaine McCafferty, and my own Sherlock, Helena Silver.

References

Begg, P., Fido, M. and Skinner, K. 2015 E-book edition. *The Complete Jack the Ripper A to Z*. John Blake Publishing Limited. London.

Coles, M. 2016. *Ripper Killings: Could A Cop Have Done It? - Megan Coles, Streatham and Clapham High School.*
https://www.thisislocallondon.co.uk/youngreporter/14820369.ripper-killings-could-a-cop-have-done-it-megan-coles-streatham-and-clapham-high-school/ Last accessed 03/06/22.

Evans, S.P and Skinner, K. 2001 (paperback). *The Ultimate Jack the Ripper Source Book. An Illustrated Encyclopaedia*. Robinson. London.

London, J. 1903. *The People of the Abyss*. Macmillan & Co. Ltd. London.

Morley, C.J. 2005. *Jack the Ripper a Suspect Guide.* The full 2005 text is available from the web-site *Casebook: Jack the Ripper*. Here I include the link to the "Railway Policeman Theory" by Bernard Brown, which is cited by Coles and briefly reviewed by Morley.
https://www.casebook.org/ripper_media/book_reviews/non-fiction/cjmorley/150.html Last accessed 03/06/22
(NOTE: This link only seems to work if cut and pasted into a browser).

Rubenhold, H. 2019. *The Five. The Untold Lives of the Women Killed by Jack the Ripper*. Penguin. London.

Ryder, S.P. and Johnno 1996-2022. *Casebook: Jack the Ripper*.
https://www.casebook.org/index.html Last accessed 03/06/22

J.M.

About the Contributors

The following contributors appear in this volume:
The MX Book of New Sherlock Holmes Stories
Part XXXIV – "However Improbable . . . ." (1878-1888)

Tim Newton Anderson is a former senior daily newspaper journalist and PR manager who has recently started writing fiction. In the past six months, he has placed fourteen stories in publications including *Parsec Magazine*, *Tales of the Shadowmen*, *SF Writers Guild*, *Zoetic Press*, *Dark Lane Books*, *Dark Horses Magazine*, *Emanations*, and *Planet Bizarro*.

Brian Belanger, PSI, is a publisher, illustrator, graphic designer, editor, and author. In 2015, he co-founded Belanger Books publishing company along with his brother, author Derrick Belanger. His illustrations have appeared in *The Essential Sherlock Holmes* and *Sherlock Holmes: A Three-Pipe Christmas*, and in children's books such as *The MacDougall Twins with Sherlock Holmes* series, *Dragonella*, and *Scones and Bones on Baker Street*. Brian has published a number of Sherlock Holmes anthologies and novels through Belanger Books, as well as new editions of August Derleth's classic Solar Pons mysteries. Brian continues to design all of the covers for Belanger Books, and since 2016 he has designed the majority of book covers for MX Publishing. In 2019, Brian received his investiture in the PSI as "Sir Ronald Duveen." More recently, he illustrated a comic book featuring the band The Moonlight Initiative, created the logo for the Arthur Conan Doyle Society and designed *The Great Game of Sherlock Holmes* card game. Find him online at:
www.belangerbooks.com and
www.redbubble.com/people/zhahadun and
zhahadun.wixsite.com/221b

Thomas A. Burns Jr. writes *The Natalie McMasters Mysteries* from the small town of Wendell, North Carolina, where he lives with his wife and son, four cats, and a Cardigan Welsh Corgi. He was born and grew up in New Jersey, attended Xavier High School in Manhattan, earned B.S degrees in Zoology and Microbiology at Michigan State University, and a M.S. in Microbiology at North Carolina State University. As a kid, Tom started reading mysteries with The Hardy Boys, Ken Holt, and Rick Brant, then graduated to the classic stories by authors such as A. Conan Doyle, Dorothy Sayers, John Dickson Carr, Erle Stanley Gardner, and Rex Stout, to name a few. Tom has written fiction as a hobby all of his life, starting with *The Man from U.N.C.L.E.* stories in marble-backed copybooks in grade school. He built a career as technical, science, and medical writer and editor for nearly thirty years in industry and government. Now that he's a full-time novelist, he's excited to publish his own mystery series, as well as to write stories about his second most favorite detective, Sherlock Holmes. His Holmes story, "The Camberwell Poisoner", appeared in the March-June 2021 issue of *The Strand Magazine*. Tom has also written a Lovecraftian horror novel, *The Legacy of the Unborn*, under the pen name of Silas K. Henderson – a sequel to H.P. Lovecraft's masterpiece *At the Mountains of Madness*. His Natalie McMasters novel *Killers!* won the Killer Nashville Silver Falchion Award for Best Book of 2021.

Leslie Charteris was born in Singapore on May 12th, 1907. With his mother and brother, he moved to England in 1919 and attended Rossall School in Lancashire before moving on to Cambridge University to study law. His studies there came to a halt when a publisher accepted his first novel. His third one, entitled *Meet the Tiger*, was written when he was twenty years old and published in September 1928. It introduced the world to Simon Templar, *aka* The Saint. He continued to write about The Saint until 1983 when the last book, *Salvage for The Saint*, was published. The books, which have been translated into over thirty languages, number nearly a hundred and have sold over forty-million copies around the world. They've inspired, to date, fifteen feature films, three television series, ten radio series, and a comic strip that was written by Charteris and syndicated around the world for over a decade. He enjoyed travelling, but settled for long periods in Hollywood, Florida, and finally in Surrey, England. He was awarded the Cartier Diamond Dagger by the *Crime Writers' Association* in 1992, in recognition of a lifetime of achievement. He died the following year.

Ian Dickerson was just nine years old when he discovered The Saint. Shortly after that, he discovered Sherlock Holmes. The Saint won, for a while anyway. He struck up a friendship with The Saint's creator, Leslie Charteris, and his family. With their permission, he spent six weeks studying the Leslie Charteris collection at Boston University and went on to write, direct, and produce documentaries on the making of *The Saint* and *Return of The Saint,* which have been released on DVD. He oversaw the recent reprints of almost fifty of the original Saint books in both the US and UK, and was a co-producer on the 2017 TV movie of *The Saint*. When he discovered that Charteris had written Sherlock Holmes stories as well – well, there was the excuse he needed to revisit The Canon. He's consequently written and edited three books on Holmes' radio adventures. For the sake of what little sanity he has, Ian has also written about a wide range of subjects, none of which come with a halo, including talking mashed potatoes, Lord Grade, and satellite links. Ian lives in Hampshire with his wife and two children. And an awful lot of books by Leslie Charteris. Not quite so many by Conan Doyle, though.

Sir Arthur Conan Doyle (1859-1930) *Holmes Chronicler Emeritus*. If not for him, this anthology would not exist. Author, physician, patriot, sportsman, spiritualist, husband and father, and advocate for the oppressed. He is remembered and honored for the purposes of this collection by being the man who introduced Sherlock Holmes to the world. Through fifty-six Holmes short stories, four novels, and additional Apocryphal entries, Doyle revolutionized mystery stories and also greatly influenced and improved police forensic methods and techniques for the betterment of all. *Steel True Blade Straight.*

Steve Emecz's main field is technology, in which he has been working for about twenty-five years. Steve is a regular speaker at trade shows and his tech career has taken him to more than fifty countries – so he's no stranger to planes and airports. In 2008, MX published its first Sherlock Holmes book, and MX has gone on to become the largest specialist Holmes publisher in the world with over 500 books. MX is a social enterprise and supports three main causes. The first is Happy Life, a children's rescue project in Nairobi, Kenya, where he and his wife, Sharon, spend every Christmas at the rescue centre in Kasarani. They have written two editions of a short book about the project, *The Happy Life Story*. The second is Undershaw, Sir Arthur Conan Doyle's former home, which is a school for children with learning disabilities for which Steve is a patron. Steve has been a mentor for the World Food Programme for several years, and was part of the Nobel Peace Prize winning team in 2020.

Mark A. Gagen BSI is co-founder of Wessex Press, sponsor of the popular *From Gillette to Brett* conferences, and publisher of *The Sherlock Holmes Reference Library* and many other fine Sherlockian titles. A life-long Holmes enthusiast, he is a member of *The Baker Street Irregulars* and *The Illustrious Clients of Indianapolis*. A graphic artist by profession, his work is often seen on the covers of *The Baker Street Journal* and various BSI books.

James Gelter is a director and playwright living in Brattleboro, VT. His produced written works for the stage include adaptations of *Frankenstein* and *A Christmas Carol*, several children's plays for the New England Youth Theatre, as well as seven outdoor plays co-written with his wife, Jessica, in their *Forest of Mystery* series. In 2018, he founded The Baker Street Readers, a group of performers that present dramatic readings of Arthur Conan Doyle's original Canon of Sherlock Holmes stories, featuring Gelter as Holmes, his longtime collaborator Tony Grobe as Dr. Watson, and a rotating list of guests. When the COVID-19 pandemic stopped their live performances, Gelter transformed the show into The Baker Street Readers Podcast. Some episodes are available for free on Apple Podcasts and Stitcher, with many more available to patrons at *patreon.com/bakerstreetreaders*.

Denis Green was born in London, England in April 1905. He grew up mostly in London's Savoy Theatre where his father, Richard Green, was a principal in many Gilbert and Sullivan productions, A Flying Officer with RAF until 1924, he then spent four years managing a tea estate in North India before making his stage debut in *Hamlet* with Leslie Howard in 1928. He made his first visit to America in 1931 and established a respectable stage career before appearing in films – including minor roles in the first two Rathbone and Bruce Holmes films – and developing a career in front of and behind the microphone during the golden age of radio. Green and Leslie Charteris met in 1938 and struck up a lifelong friendship. Always busy, be it on stage, radio, film or television, Green passed away at the age of fifty in New York.

John Atkinson Grimshaw (1836-1893) was born in Leeds, England. His amazing paintings, usually featuring twilight or night scenes illuminated by gas-lamps or moonlight, are easily recognizable, and are often used on the covers of books about The Great Detective to set the mood, as shadowy figures move in the distance through misty mysterious settings and over rain-slicked streets.

Arthur Hall was born in Aston, Birmingham, UK, in 1944. He discovered his interest in writing during his schooldays, along with a love of fictional adventure and suspense. His first novel, *Sole Contact*, was an espionage story about an ultra-secret government department known as "Sector Three", and was followed, to date, by three sequels. Other works include seven Sherlock Holmes novels, *The Demon of the Dusk*, *The One Hundred Percent Society*, *The Secret Assassin*, *The Phantom Killer*, *In Pursuit of the Dead*, *The Justice Master*, and *The Experience Club* as well as three collections of Holmes *Further Little-Known Cases of Sherlock* Holmes, *Tales from the Annals of Sherlock* Holmes, and *The Additional Investigations of Sherlock Holmes*. He has also written other short stories and a modern detective novel. He lives in the West Midlands, United Kingdom.

Stephen Herczeg is an IT Geek, writer, actor, and film-maker based in Canberra Australia. He has been writing for over twenty years and has completed a couple of dodgy novels, sixteen feature-length screenplays, and numerous short stories and scripts. Stephen was very successful in 2017's International Horror Hotel screenplay competition, with his scripts *TITAN* winning the Sci-Fi category and *Dark are the Woods* placing second in the horror category. His two-volume short story collection, *The Curious Cases of Sherlock Holmes*, was published in 2021. His work has featured in *Sproutlings – A Compendium of Little Fictions* from Hunter Anthologies, the *Hells Bells* Christmas horror anthology published by the Australasian Horror Writers Association, and the *Below the Stairs*, *Trickster's Treats, Shades of Santa, Behind the Mask*, and *Beyond the Infinite* anthologies from *OzHorror.Con, The Body Horror Book, Anemone Enemy*, and *Petrified Punks* from Oscillate Wildly Press, and *Sherlock Holmes In the Realms of H.G. Wells* and *Sherlock Holmes: Adventures Beyond the Canon* from Belanger Books.

Paul Hiscock is an author of crime, fantasy, horror, and science fiction tales. His short stories have appeared in a variety of anthologies, and include a seventeenth-century whodunnit, a science fiction western, a clockpunk fairytale, and numerous Sherlock Holmes pastiches. He lives with his family in Kent (England) and spends his days taking care of his two children. He mainly does his writing in coffee shops with members of the local NaNoWriMo group, or in the middle of the night when his family has gone to sleep. Consequently, his stories tend to be fuelled by large amounts of black coffee. You can find out more about Paul's writing at *www.detectivesanddragons.uk*.

Anisha Jagdeep is a 21-year-old senior at Rutgers University, currently pursuing a degree in Computer Engineering. With her twin sister, Ankita, a fellow Sherlock Holmes enthusiast, she enjoys watching classic films and writing short stories inspired by notable short story writers such as Dame Agatha Christie, John Kendrick Bangs, O. Henry, and Saki. They are also students of Indian classical music and dance. Anisha expresses her gratitude to Sir Arthur Conan Doyle for his unparalleled contributions to mystery literature with his exceptional characters, Sherlock Holmes and Dr. Watson.

Roger Johnson, BSI, ASH, PSI, etc, is a member of more Holmesian societies than he can remember, thanks to his (so far) 16 years as editor of *The Sherlock Holmes Journal*, and thirty-two years as editor of *The District Messenger*. The latter, the newsletter of *The Sherlock Holmes Society of London*, is now in the safe hands of Jean Upton, with whom he collaborated on the well-received book, *The Sherlock Holmes Miscellany*. Roger is resigned to the fact that he will never match the Duke of Holdernesse, whose name was followed by *"half the alphabet"*.

Gordon Linzner is founder and former editor of *Space and Time Magazine*, and author of three published novels and dozens of short stories in *F&SF, Twilight Zone, Sherlock Holmes Mystery Magazine*, and numerous other magazines and anthologies, including *Baker Street Irregulars II, Across the Universe*, and *Strange Lands*. He is a member of *HWA* and a lifetime member of *SFWA*.

David Marcum plays *The Game* with deadly seriousness. He first discovered Sherlock Holmes in 1975 at the age of ten, and since that time, he has collected, read, and chronologicized literally thousands of traditional Holmes pastiches in the form of novels, short stories, radio and television episodes, movies and scripts, comics, fan-fiction, and unpublished manuscripts. He is the author of over one-hundred Sherlockian pastiches, some published in anthologies and magazines such as *The Strand*, and others collected in his own books, *The Papers of Sherlock Holmes, Sherlock Holmes and A Quantity of Debt, Sherlock Holmes – Tangled Skeins, Sherlock Holmes and The Eye of Heka*, and *The Collected Papers of Sherlock Holmes*. He has edited over sixty books, including several dozen traditional Sherlockian anthologies, such as the ongoing series *The MX Book of New Sherlock Holmes Stories*, which he created in 2015. This collection is now at thirty-six volumes, with more in preparation. He was responsible for bringing back August Derleth's Solar Pons for a new generation with his collection of authorized Pons stories, *The Papers of Solar Pons*. His new collection, *The Further Papers of Solar Pons*, will be published in

2022. Pons's return was further assisted by his editing of the reissued authorized versions of the original Pons books, and then several volumes of new Pons adventures. He has done the same for the adventures of Dr. Thorndyke, and has plans for similar projects in the future. He has contributed numerous essays to various publications, and is a member of a number of Sherlockian groups and Scions, as well as The Mystery Writers of America. His irregular Sherlockian blog, *A Seventeen Step Program*, addresses various topics related to his favorite book friends (as his son used to call them when he was small), and can be found at *http://17stepprogram.blogspot.com/* He is a licensed Civil Engineer, living in Tennessee with his wife and son. Since the age of nineteen, he has worn a deerstalker as his regular-and-only hat. In 2013, he and his deerstalker were finally able make his first trip-of-a-lifetime Holmes Pilgrimage to England, with return Pilgrimages in 2015 and 2016, where you may have spotted him. If you ever run into him and his deerstalker out and about, feel free to say hello!

John McNabb is a Welshman and an archaeologist, and a proud member of *The Sherlock Holmes Society of London*. He has published academic analysis of aspects of Conan Doyle's work, as well as its broader context. Mac also has a long-standing interest in Victorian and Edwardian scientific romances and the portrayal of human origins in early science fiction.

Will Murray has built a career on writing classic pulp characters, ranging from Tarzan of the Apes to Doc Savage. He has penned several milestone crossover novels in his acclaimed Wild Adventures series. *Skull Island* pitted Doc Savage against King Kong, which was followed by *King Kong Vs. Tarzan. Tarzan, Conqueror of Mars* costarred John Carter of Mars. His 2015 Doc Savage novel, *The Sinister Shadow*, revived the famous radio and pulp mystery man. Murray reunited them for *Empire of Doom*. His first Spider novel, *The Doom Legion*, revived that infamous crime buster, as well as James Christopher, AKA Operator 5, and the renowned G-8. His second *Spider, Fury in Steel*, guest-stars the FBI's Suicide Squad. Ten of his Sherlock Holmes short stories have been collected as *The Wild Adventures of Sherlock Holmes*. He is the author of the non-fiction book, *Master of Mystery: The Rise of The Shadow*. For Marvel Comics, Murray created the Unbeatable Squirrel Girl. Website: *www.adventuresinbronze.com*

Sidney Paget (1860-1908), a few of whose illustrations are used within this anthology, was born in London, and like his two older brothers, became a famed illustrator and painter. He completed over three-hundred-and-fifty drawings for the Sherlock Holmes stories that were first published in *The Strand* magazine, defining Holmes's image forever after in the public mind.

Tracy J. Revels, a Sherlockian from the age of eleven, is a professor of history at Wofford College in Spartanburg, South Carolina. She is a member of *The Survivors of the Gloria Scott* and *The Studious Scarlets Society*, and is a past recipient of the Beacon Society Award. Almost every semester, she teaches a class that covers The Canon, either to college students or to senior citizens. She is also the author of three supernatural Sherlockian pastiches with MX (*Shadowfall*, *Shadowblood*, and *Shadowwraith*), and a regular contributor to her scion's newsletter. She also has some notoriety as an author of very silly skits: For proof, see "The Adventure of the Adversarial Adventuress" and "Occupy Baker Street" on YouTube. When not studying Sherlock, she can be found researching the history of her native state, and has written books on Florida in the Civil War and on the development of Florida's tourism industry.

411

Roger Riccard's family history has Scottish roots, which trace his lineage back to Highland Scotland. This British Isles ancestry encouraged his interest in the writings of Sir Arthur Conan Doyle at an early age. He has authored the novels, *Sherlock Holmes & The Case of the Poisoned Lilly*, and *Sherlock Holmes & The Case of the Twain Papers.* In addition he has produced several short stories in *Sherlock Holmes Adventures for the Twelve Days of Christmas* and the series *A Sherlock Holmes Alphabet of Cases.* A new series will begin publishing in the Autumn of 2022, and his has another novel in the works. All of his books have been published by Baker Street Studios. His Bachelor of Arts Degrees in both Journalism and History from California State University, Northridge, have proven valuable to his writing historical fiction, as well as the encouragement of his wife/editor/inspiration and Sherlock Holmes fan, Rosilyn. She passed in 2021, and it is in her memory that he continues to contribute to the legacy of the *"man who never lived and will never die"*.

Nicholas Rowe was born in Edinburgh Scotland and attended Eton before receiving a Bachelor of Arts degree from the University of Bristol. He has performed in a many films, television shows, and theatrical productions. In 1985, he was Sherlock Holmes in *Young Sherlock Holmes*, and he also appeared as the "Matinee Holmes" in 2015's *Mr. Holmes*.

Dan Rowley practiced law for over forty years in private practice and with a large international corporation. He is retired and lives in Erie, Pennsylvania, with his wife Judy, who puts her artistic eye to his transcription of Watson's manuscripts. He inherited his writing ability and creativity from his children, Jim and Katy, and his love of mysteries from his parents, Jim and Ruth.

Award winning poet and author **Joseph W. Svec III** enjoys writing, poetry, and stories, and creating new adventures for Holmes and Watson that take them into the worlds of famous literary authors and scientists. His *Missing Authors* trilogy introduced Holmes to Lewis Carroll, Jules Verne, H.G. Wells, and Alfred Lord Tennyson, as well as many of their characters. His transitional story *Sherlock Holmes and the Mystery of the First Unicorn* involved several historical figures, besides a Unicorn or two. He has also written the rhymed and metered Sherlock Holmes Christmas adventure, *The Night Before Christmas in 221b*, sure to be a delight for Sherlock Holmes enthusiasts of all ages. Joseph won the Amador Arts Council 2021 Original Poetry Contest, with his Rhymed and metered story poem, "The Homecoming". Joseph has presented a literary paper on Sherlock Holmes/Alice in Wonderland crossover literature to the Lewis Carroll Society of North America, as well as given several presentations to the Amador County Holmes Hounds, Sherlockian Society. He is currently working on his first book in the *Missing Scientist Trilogy, Sherlock Holmes and the Adventure of the Demonstrative Dinosaur*, in which Sherlock meets Professor George Edward Challenger. Joseph has Masters Degrees in Systems Engineering and Human Organization Management, and has written numerous technical papers on Aerospace Testing. In addition to writing, Joseph enjoys creating miniature dioramas based on music, literature, and history from many different eras. His dioramas have been featured in magazine articles and many different blogs, including the North American Jules Verne society newsletter. He currently has 57 dioramas set up in his display area, and has written a reference book on toy castles and knights from around the world. An avid tea enthusiast, his tea cabinet contains over 500 different varieties, and he delights in sharing afternoon tea with his childhood sweetheart and wonderful wife, who has inspired and coauthored several books with him.

DJ Tyrer dwells on the northern shore of the Thames estuary, close to the world's longest pleasure pier in the decaying seaside resort of Southend-on-Sea, and is the person behind Atlantean Publishing. They studied history at the University of Wales at Aberystwyth and have worked in the fields of education and public relations. Their fiction featuring Sherlock Holmes has appeared in volumes from MX Publishing and Belanger Books, and in an issue of *Awesome Tales*, and they have a forthcoming story in *Sherlock Holmes Mystery Magazine*. DJ's non-Sherlockian mysteries have appeared in anthologies such as *Mardi Gras Mysteries* (Mystery and Horror LLC) and *The Trench Coat Chronicles* (Celestial Echo Press).

DJ Tyrer's website is at *https://djtyrer.blogspot.co.uk/*
DJ's Facebook page is at *https://www.facebook.com/DJTyrerwriter/*
The Atlantean Publishing website is at *https://atlanteanpublishing.wordpress.com/*

Emma West joined Undershaw in April 2021 as the Director of Education with a brief to ensure that qualifications formed the bedrock of our provision, whilst facilitating a positive balance between academia, pastoral care, and well-being. She quickly took on the role of Acting Headteacher from early summer 2021. Under her leadership, Undershaw has embraced its new name, new vision, and consequently we have seen an exponential increase in demand for places. There is a buzz in the air as we invite prospective students and families through the doors. Emma has overseen a strategic review, re-cemented relationships with Local Authorities, and positioned Undershaw at the helm of SEND education in Surrey and beyond. Undershaw has a wide appeal: Our students present to us with mild to moderate learning needs and therefore may have some very recent memories of poor experiences in their previous schools. Emma's background as a senior leader within the independent school sector has meant she is well-versed in brokering relationships between the key stakeholders, our many interdependences, local businesses, families, and staff, and all this whilst ensuring Undershaw remains relentlessly child-centric in its approach. Emma's energetic smile and boundless enthusiasm for Undershaw is inspiring.

Marcia Wilson is a freelance researcher and illustrator who likes to work in a style compatible for the color blind and visually impaired. She is Canon-centric, and her first MX offering, *You Buy Bones*, uses the point-of-view of Scotland Yard to show the unique talents of Dr. Watson. This continued with the publication of *Test of the Professionals: The Adventure of the Flying Blue Pidgeon* and *The Peaceful Night Poisonings*. She can be contacted at: *gravelgirty.deviantart.com*

*The following contributors appear
in the companion volumes:*
The MX Book of New Sherlock Holmes Stories
Part XXXV – "However Improbable . . . ." (1889-1896)
Part XXXVI – "However Improbable . . . ." (1897-1919)

Donald Baxter has practiced medicine for over forty years. He resides in Erie, Pennsylvania with his wife and their dog. His family and his friends are for the most part lawyers who have given him the ability to make stuff up, just as they do.

Josh Cerefice has followed the exploits of a certain pipe-smoking sleuth ever since his grandmother bought him *The Complete Sherlock Holmes* collection for his twenty-first birthday, and he has devotedly accompanied the Great Detective on his adventures ever since. When he's not reading about spectral hellhounds haunting the Devonshire moors, or the Machiavellian machinations of Professor Moriarty, you can find him putting pen to paper and challenging Holmes with new mysteries to solve in his own stories.

Chris Chan is a writer, educator, and historian. He works as a researcher and "International Goodwill Ambassador" for Agatha Christie Ltd. His true crime articles, reviews, and short fiction have appeared (or will soon appear) in *The Strand*, *The Wisconsin Magazine of History*, *Mystery Weekly*, *Gilbert!*, *Nerd HQ*, Akashic Books' *Mondays are Murder* web series, *The Baker Street Journal*, *The MX Book of New Sherlock Holmes Stories*, *Masthead: The Best New England Crime Stories*, *Sherlock Holmes Mystery Magazine*, and multiple Belanger Books anthologies. He is the creator of the Funderburke mysteries, a series featuring a private investigator who works for a school and helps students during times of crisis. The Funderburke short story "The Six-Year-Old Serial Killer" was nominated for a Derringer Award. His first book, *Sherlock & Irene: The Secret Truth Behind "A Scandal in Bohemia"*, was published in 2020 by MX Publishing. His second book, *Murder Most Grotesque: The Comedic Crime Fiction of Joyce Porter* will be released by Level Best Books in 2021, and his first novel, *Sherlock's Secretary*, was published by MX Publishing in 2021. *Murder Most Grotesque* was nominated for the Agatha and Silver Falchion Awards for Nonfiction Writing, and *Sherlock's Secretary* was nominated for the Silver Falchion for Best Comedy. He is also the author of the anthology of Sherlock Holmes stories *Of Course He Pushed Him*.

Leslie Charteris also has a story in Part XXXIV.

Martin Daley was born in Carlisle, Cumbria in 1964. He cites Doyle's Holmes and Watson as his favourite literary characters, who continue to inspire his own detective writing. His fiction and non-fiction books include a Holmes pastiche set predominantly in his home city in 1903. In the adventure, he introduced his own detective, Inspector Cornelius Armstrong, who has subsequently had some of his own cases published by MX Publishing. For more information visit *www.martindaley.co.uk*

The Davies Brothers are Brett and Nicholas Davies, twin brothers who share a love of books, films, history, and the Wales football team. Brett lived in four different countries before settling in Japan, where he teaches English and Film Studies at a university in Tokyo. He also writes for screen and stage, as well as articles for a variety of publications on cinema, sports, and travel. Nicholas is a freelance writer and PhD researcher based in Cardiff. He previously worked for the Arts Council of Wales, focusing on theatre and drama. He now writes for stage and screen, as well as articles for arts and football magazines. They are the authors of the novels *Hudson James and the Baker Street Legacy* (based upon an ancient puzzle set by Sherlock Holmes himself!) and *The Phoenix Code*. They also serve as the "literary agents" for Dr Watson's newly uncovered adventures, *Sherlock Holmes: The Centurion Papers*.

Ian Dickerson also has a foreword in Part XXXIV.

Alan Dimes was born in North-West London and graduated from Sussex University with a BA in English Literature. He has spent most of his working life teaching English. Living in the Czech Republic since 2003, he is now semi-retired and divides his time between Prague and his country cottage. He has also written some fifty stories of horror and fantasy and thirty stories about his husband-and-wife detectives, Peter and Deirdre Creighton, set in the 1930's.

414

Anna Elliott is an author of historical fiction and fantasy. Her first series, *The Twilight of Avalon* trilogy, is a retelling of the Trystan and Isolde legend. She wrote her second series, *The Pride and Prejudice Chronicles*, chiefly to satisfy her own curiosity about what might have happened to Elizabeth Bennet, Mr. Darcy, and all the other wonderful cast of characters after the official end of Jane Austen's classic work. She enjoys stories about strong women, and loves exploring the multitude of ways women can find their unique strengths. She was delighted to lend a hand with the "Sherlock and Lucy" series, and this story, firstly because she loves Sherlock Holmes as much as her father, co-author Charles Veley, does, and second because it almost never happens that someone with a dilemma shouts, "Quick, we need an author of historical fiction!" Anna lives in the Washington, D.C .area with her husband and three children.

Matthew J. Elliott is the author of *Big Trouble in Mother Russia* (2016), the official sequel to the cult movie *Big Trouble in Little China*, *Lost in Time and Space: An Unofficial Guide to the Uncharted Journeys of Doctor Who* (2014), *Sherlock Holmes on the Air* (2012), *Sherlock Holmes in Pursuit* (2013), *The Immortals: An Unauthorized Guide to* Sherlock *and* Elementary (2013), and *The Throne Eternal* (2014). His articles, fiction, and reviews have appeared in the magazines *Scarlet Street*, *Total DVD*, *SHERLOCK*, and *Sherlock Holmes Mystery Magazine*, and the collections *The Game's Afoot*, *Curious Incidents 2*, *Gaslight Grimoire*, *The Mammoth Book of Best British Crime 8*, and *The MX Book of New Sherlock Holmes Stories – Part III: 1896-1929*. He has scripted over 260 radio plays, including episodes of *Doctor Who*, *The Further Adventures of Sherlock Holmes*, *The Twilight Zone*, *The New Adventures of Mickey Spillane's Mike Hammer*, *Fangoria's Dreadtime Stories*, and award-winning adaptations of *The Hound of the Baskervilles* and *The War of the Worlds*. He is the only radio dramatist to adapt all sixty original stories from The Canon for the series *The Classic Adventures of Sherlock Holmes*. Matthew is a writer and performer on *RiffTrax.com*, the online comedy experience from the creators of cult sci-fi TV series *Mystery Science Theater 3000* (*MST3K* to the initiated). He's also written a few comic books.

John Farrell Jr. was born and raised in San Pedro, California. He became interested in Sherlock Holmes in the late 1960's. He joined *The Non-Canonical Calabashes* (A Sherlock Holmes scion Society) where he met and became friends with another Sherlockian, Sean Wright. He collaborated with Mr. Wright on *The Sherlock Holmes Cookbook*. Later he was a member of *The Goose Club of the Alpha Inn*. He submitted articles to *The Baker Street Journal*. *The Baker Street Irregulars* awarded him the title The Tiger of San Pedro in 1981. He was proud to include "*BSI*" after his name. John made his living as a classical music and play reviewer for multiple newspapers in the Los Angeles area. He passed away in 2015 while he was writing a review. He left behind his family and many friends. He has been accurately described by those that knew him as larger than life.

Paul D. Gilbert was born in 1954 and has lived in and around London all of his life. His wife Jackie is a Holmes expert who keeps him on the straight and narrow! He has two sons, one of whom now lives in Spain. His interests include literature, ancient history, all religions, most sports, and movies. He is currently employed full-time as a funeral director. His books so far include *The Lost Files of Sherlock Holmes* (2007), *The Chronicles of Sherlock Holmes* (2008), *Sherlock Holmes and the Giant Rat of Sumatra* (2010), *The Annals of Sherlock Holmes* (2012), *Sherlock Holmes and the Unholy Trinity* (2015), *Sherlock Holmes: The Four Handed Game* (2017), *The Illumination of Sherlock Holmes* (2019), and *The Treasure of the Poison King* (2021).

415

Hal Glatzer is the author of the Katy Green mystery series set in musical milieux just before World War II. He has written and produced audio/radio mystery plays, including the all-alliterative adventures of Mark Markheim, the Hollywood hawkshaw. He scripted and produced the Charlie Chan mystery *The House Without a Key* on stage, and he adapted "The Adventure of the Devil's Foot" into a stage and video play called *Sherlock Holmes and the Volcano Horror*. In 2022, after many years on the Big Island of Hawaii, he returned to live on his native island – Manhattan. See more at: *www.halglatzer.com*

Denis Green also has a story in Part XXXIV.

Arthur Hall *also has stories in Parts XXXV and XXXVI.*

In the year 1998 **Craig Janacek** took his degree of Doctor of Medicine at Vanderbilt University, and proceeded to Stanford to go through the training prescribed for pediatricians in practice. Having completed his studies there, he was duly attached to the University of California, San Francisco as Associate Professor. The author of over seventy medical monographs upon a variety of obscure lesions, his travel-worn and battered tin dispatch-box is crammed with papers, nearly all of which are records of his fictional works. To date, these have been published solely in electronic format, including two non-Holmes novels (*The Oxford Deception* and *The Anger of Achilles Peterson*), the trio of holiday adventures collected as *The Midwinter Mysteries of Sherlock Holmes*, the Holmes story collections *The First of Criminals*, *The Assassination of Sherlock Holmes*, *The Treasury of Sherlock Holmes*, *Light in the Darkness*, *The Gathering Gloom*, *The Travels of Sherlock Holmes*, and the Watsonian novels *The Isle of Devils* and *The Gate of Gold*. Craig Janacek is a *nom de plume*.

Christopher James was born in 1975 in Paisley, Scotland. Educated at Newcastle and UEA, he was a winner of the UK's National Poetry Competition in 2008. He has written three full length Sherlock Holmes novels, *The Adventure of the Ruby Elephant*, *The Jeweller of Florence*, and *The Adventure of the Beer Barons*, all published by MX.

Naching T. Kassa is a wife, mother, and writer. She's created short stories, novellas, poems, and co-created three children. She resides in Eastern Washington State with her husband, Dan Kassa. Naching is a member of *The Horror Writers Association*, *Mystery Writers of America*, *The Sound of the Baskervilles*, *The ACD Society*, *The Crew of the Barque Lone Star*, and *The Sherlock Holmes Society of London*. She's also an assistant and staff writer for Still Water Bay at Crystal Lake Publishing. You can find her work on Amazon. *https://www.amazon.com/Naching-T-Kassa/e/B005ZGHTI0*

Amanda Knight was born and grew up in Sydney Australia. At the age of nineteen, she decided to travel and spent a wonderful time in the UK in the 1980's. Travelling through Scotland and Wales, as well as living and working in England for an extended period, and working in pubs, which is almost obligatory if you are an Australian in the UK. As a long-time fan of Sherlock Holmes, she spent many a pleasant hour investigating many of the places mentioned by Conan Doyle in the Sherlock Holmes stories. Amanda still lives in Australia and is enjoying the invigorating mountain air where she now resides. Amanda is the author of *The Unexpected Adventures of Sherlock Holmes* (2004)

Susan Knight's newest novel, *Mrs. Hudson goes to Paris*, from MX publishing, is the latest in a series which began with her collection of stories, *Mrs. Hudson Investigates* (2019) and the novel *Mrs. Hudson goes to Ireland* (2020). She has contributed to several of the MX anthologies of new Sherlock Holmes short stories and enjoys writing as Dr. Watson as much as she does Mrs. Hudson. Susan is the author of two other non-Sherlockian story collections, as well as three novels, a book of non-fiction, and several plays, and has won several prizes for her writing. Mrs. Hudson's next adventure, still evolving, will take her to Kent, the Garden of England, where she is hoping for some peace and quiet. In vain, alas. Susan lives in Dublin.

David L. Leal PhD is Professor of Government and Mexican American Studies at the University of Texas at Austin. He is also an Associate Member of Nuffield College at the University of Oxford and a Senior Fellow of the Hoover Institution at Stanford University. His research interests include the political implications of demographic change in the United States, and he has published dozens of academic journal articles and edited nine books on these and other topics. He has taught classes on Immigration Politics, Latino Politics, Politics and Religion, Mexican American Public Policy Studies, and Introduction to American Government. In the spring of 2019, he taught British Politics and Government, which had the good fortune (if that is the right word) of taking place parallel with so many Brexit developments. He is also the author of three articles in *The Baker Street Journal* as well as letters to the editor of the *TLS: The Times Literary Supplement*, *Sherlock Holmes Journal*, and *The Baker Street Journal*. As a member of the British Studies Program at UT-Austin, he has given several talks on Sherlockian and Wodehousian topics. He most recently wrote a chapter, "Arthur Conan Doyle and Spiritualism," for the program's latest book in its *Adventures with Britannia* series (Harry Ransom Center/IB Tauris/Bloomsbury). He is the founder and Warden of "MA, PhD, Etc," the BSI professional scion society for higher education, and he is a member of *The Fourth Garrideb*, *The Sherlock Holmes Society of London*, *The Clients of Adrian Mulliner*, and *His Last Bow (Tie)*.

David Marcum *also has stories in Parts XXXV and XXXVI*

Mark Mower is a long-standing member of the *Crime Writers' Association, The Sherlock Holmes Society of London,* and *The Solar Pons Society of London.* To date, he has written 33 Sherlock Holmes stories, and his pastiche collections include *Sherlock Holmes: The Baker Street Case-Files, Sherlock Holmes: The Baker Street Legacy,* and *Sherlock Holmes: The Baker Street Archive* (all with MX Publishing). His non-fiction works include the best-selling book *Zeppelin Over Suffolk: The Final Raid of the L48* (Pen & Sword Books). Alongside his writing, Mark maintains a sizeable collection of pastiches, and never tires of discovering new stories about Sherlock Holmes and Dr. Watson.

Tracy J. Revels *also has stories in Parts XXXV and XXXVI*

Dan Rowley *also has stories in Parts XXXV and XXXVI*

Jane Rubino is the author of *A Jersey Shore* mystery series, featuring a Jane Austen-loving amateur sleuth and a Sherlock Holmes-quoting detective, *Knight Errant, Lady Vernon and Her Daughter,* (a novel-length adaptation of Jane Austen's novella *Lady Susan,* co-authored with her daughter Caitlen Rubino-Bradway, *What Would Austen Do?,* also co-authored with her daughter, a short story in the anthology *Jane Austen Made Me Do It, The Rucastles' Pawn, The Copper Beeches from Violet Turner's POV,* and, of course, there's the Sherlockian novel in the drawer – who doesn't have one? Jane lives on a barrier island at the New Jersey shore.

Alisha Shea has resided near Saint Louis, Missouri for over thirty years. The eldest of six children, she found reading to be a genuine escape from the chaotic drudgery of life. She grew to love not only Sherlock Holmes, but the time period from which he emerged. In her spare time, she indulges in creating music via piano, violin, and Native American flute. Sometimes she thinks she might even be getting good at it. She also produces a wide variety of fiber arts which are typically given away or auctioned off for various fundraisers.

Geri Schear is a novelist and short story writer. Her work has been published in literary journals in the U.S. and Ireland. Her first novel, *A Biased Judgement: The Diaries of Sherlock Holmes 1897* was released to critical acclaim in 2014. The sequel, *Sherlock Holmes and the Other Woman* was published in 2015, and *Return to Reichenbach* in 2016. She lives in Kells, Ireland.

Robert V. Stapleton was born in Leeds, England, and served as a full-time Anglican clergyman for forty years, specialising in Rural Ministry. He is now retired, and lives with his wife in North Yorkshire. This is the area of the country made famous by the writings of James Herriot, and television's *The Yorkshire Vet*, to name just a few. Amongst other things, he is a member of the local creative writing group, Thirsk Write Now (TWN), and regularly produces material for them. He has had more than fifty stories published, of various lengths and in a number of different places. He has also written a number of stories for *The MX Book of New Sherlock Holmes Stories*, and several published by Belanger Books. Several of these Sherlock Holmes pastiches have now been brought together and published in a single volume by MX Publishing, under the title of *Sherlock Holmes: A Yorkshireman in Baker Street*. Many of these stories have been set during the Edwardian period, or more broadly between the years 1880 and 1920. His interest in this period of history began at school in the 1960's when he met people who had lived during those years and heard their stories. He also found echoes of those times in literature, architecture, music, and even the coins in his pocket. The Edwardian period was a time of exploration, invention, and high adventure – rich material for thriller writers.

Liese Sherwood-Fabre knew she was destined to write when she got an A+ in the second grade for her story about Dick, Jane, and Sally's ruined picnic. After obtaining her PhD, she joined the federal government and worked and lived internationally for more than fifteen years. Returning to the states, she seriously pursued her writing career, garnering such awards as a finalist in the Romance Writers of America's Golden Heart contest and a Pushcart Prize nomination. A recognized Sherlockian scholar, her essays have appeared in newsletters, *The Baker Street Journal*, and *Canadian Holmes*. She has recently turned to a childhood passion: Sherlock Holmes. *The Adventure of the Murdered Midwife*, the first book in *The Early Case Files of Sherlock Holmes* series, was the CIBA Mystery and Mayhem 2020 first-place winner. *Publishers Weekly* has described her fourth book in the series, *The Adventure of the Purloined Portrait*, as "*a truly unique, atmospheric tale that is Sherlockian through and through.*" More about her writing can be found at *www.liesesherwoodfabre.com*.

Tim Symonds was born in London. He grew up in the rural English counties of Somerset and Dorset, and the British Crown Dependency of Guernsey. After several years travelling widely, including farming on the slopes of Mt. Kenya in East Africa and working on the Zambezi River in Central Africa, he emigrated to Canada and the United States. He studied at the Georg-August University (Göttingen) in Germany, and the University of California, Los Angeles, graduating *cum laude* and Phi Beta Kappa. He is a Fellow of the Royal Geographical Society and a Member of The Society of Authors. His detective novels include *Sherlock Holmes And The Dead Boer At Scotney Castle*, *Sherlock Holmes And The Mystery Of Einstein's Daughter*, *Sherlock Holmes And The Case Of The Bulgarian Codex*, *Sherlock Holmes And The Sword Of Osman*, *Sherlock Holmes And The Nine-Dragon Sigil*, six Holmes and Watson short stories under the title *A Most Diabolical Plot*, and his novella *Sherlock Holmes and the Strange Death of Brigadier-General Delves*.

Kevin P. Thornton was shortlisted six times for the Crime Writers of Canada best unpublished novel. He never won – they are all still unpublished, and now he writes short stories. He lives in Canada, north enough that ringing Santa Claus is a local call and winter is a way of life. This is his twelfth short story in *The MX Book of New Sherlock Holmes Stories*. By the time you next hear from him, he hopes to have written his thirteenth.

William Todd has been a Holmes fan his entire life, and credits *The Hound of the Baskervilles* as the impetus for his love of both reading and writing. He began to delve into fan fiction a few years ago when he decided to take a break from writing his usual Victorian/Gothic horror stories. He was surprised how well-received they were, and has tried to put out a couple of Holmes stories a year since then. When not writing, Mr. Todd is a pathology supervisor at a local hospital in Northwestern Pennsylvania. He is the husband of a terrific lady and father to two great kids, one with special needs, so the benefactor of these anthologies is close to his heart.

Charles Veley has loved Sherlock Holmes since boyhood. As a father, he read the entire Canon to his then-ten-year-old daughter at evening story time. Now, this very same daughter, grown up to become acclaimed historical novelist Anna Elliott, has worked with him to develop new adventures in the *Sherlock Holmes and Lucy James Mystery Series*. Charles is also a fan of Gilbert & Sullivan, and wrote *The Pirates of Finance*, a new musical in the G&S tradition that won an award at the New York Musical Theatre Festival in 2013. Other than the Sherlock and Lucy series, all of the books on his Amazon Author Page were written when he was a full-time author during the late Seventies and early Eighties. He currently works for United Technologies Corporation, where his main focus is on creating sustainability and value for the company's large real estate development projects.

Margaret Walsh was born Auckland, New Zealand and now lives in Melbourne, Australia. She is the author of *Sherlock Holmes and the Molly-Boy Murders*, *Sherlock Holmes and the Case of the Perplexed Politician*, and *Sherlock Holmes and the Case of the London Dock Deaths*, all published by MX Publishing. Margaret has been a devotee of Sherlock Holmes since childhood and has had several Holmesian related essays printed in anthologies, and is a member of the online society *Doyle's Rotary Coffin*. She has an ongoing love affair with the city of London. When she's not working or planning trips to London. Margaret can be found frequenting the many and varied bookshops of Melbourne.

I.A. Watson, great-grand-nephew of Dr. John H. Watson, has been intrigued by the notorious "black sheep" of the family since childhood, and was fascinated to inherit from his grandmother a number of unedited manuscripts removed circa 1956 from a rather larger collection reposing at Lloyds Bank Ltd (which acquired Cox & Co Bank in 1923). Upon discovering the published corpus of accounts regarding the detective Sherlock Holmes from which a censorious upbringing had shielded him, he felt obliged to allow an interested public access to these additional memoranda, and is gradually undertaking the task of transcribing them for admirers of Mr. Holmes and Dr. Watson's works. In the meantime, I.A. Watson continues to pen other books, the latest of which is *The Incunabulum of Sherlock Holmes*. A full list of his seventy or so published works are available at:

DeForeest Wright III has a day job as a baker for Ralphs grocery stores. It helps support his love for books. A long-time lover of literature, especially of the Sherlock Holmes tales, he spends his time away from the oven hunched over novels, poetry, anthologies, or any tome on philosophy, mathematics, science, or martial arts he can find, sipping an espresso if one is to hand. He writes prose and poetry in his off hours and currently hosts "The Sunless Sea Open-Mic: Spoken Word and Poetry Show" at the Unurban Coffee House in Santa Monica. He was glad to team up writing with his father.

Sean Wright makes his home in Santa Clarita, a charming city at the entrance of the high desert in Southern California. For sixteen years, features and articles under his byline appeared in *The Tidings* – now *The Angelus News*, publications of the Roman Catholic Archdiocese of Los Angeles. Continuing his education in 2007, Mr. Wright graduated from Grand Canyon University, attaining a Bachelor of Arts degree in Christian Studies with a *summa cum laude*. He then attained a Master of Arts degree, also in Christian Studies. Once active in the entertainment industry, and in an abortive attempt to revive dramatic radio in 1976 with his beloved mentor, the late Daws Butler, directing, Mr. Wright co-produced and wrote the syndicated *New Radio Adventures of Sherlock Holmes*, starring the late Edward Mulhare as the Great Detective. Mr. Wright has written for several television quiz shows and remains proud of his work for *The Quiz Kid's Challenge* and the popular TV quiz show *Jeopardy!* for which the Academy of Television Arts and Sciences honored him in 1985 with an Emmy nomination in the field of writing. Honored with membership in The Baker Street Irregulars as "The Manor House Case" after founding The Non-Canonical Calabashes, the Sherlock Holmes Society of Los Angeles in 1970, Mr. Wright has written for *The Baker Street Journal* and *Mystery Magazine*. Since 1971, he has conducted lectures on Sherlock Holmes's influence on literature and cinema for libraries, colleges, and private organizations, including MENSA. Mr. Wright's whimsical *Sherlock Holmes Cookbook* (Drake), created with John Farrell, BSI, was published in 1976, and a mystery novel, *Enter the Lion: a Posthumous Memoir of Mycroft Holmes* (Hawthorne), "edited" with Michael Hodel, BSI, followed in 1979. As director general of The Plot Thickens Mystery Company, Mr .Wright originated hosting "mystery parties" in homes, restaurants, and offices, as well as producing and directing the very first "Mystery Train" tours on Amtrak, beginning in 1982.

The MX Book of New Sherlock Holmes Stories
Edited by David Marcum
(MX Publishing, 2015-   )

"This is the finest volume of Sherlockian fiction I have ever read, and I have read, literally, thousands." – Philip K. Jones

"Beyond Impressive . . . This is a splendid venture for a great cause!
– Roger Johnson, Editor, *The Sherlock Holmes Journal,*
The Sherlock Holmes Society of London

Part I: 1881-1889
Part II: 1890-1895
Part III: 1896-1929
Part IV: 2016 Annual
Part V: Christmas Adventures
Part VI: 2017 Annual
Part VII: Eliminate the Impossible (1880-1891)
Part VIII – Eliminate the Impossible (1892-1905)
Part IX – 2018 Annual (1879-1895)
Part X – 2018 Annual (1896-1916)
Part XI – Some Untold Cases (1880-1891)
Part XII – Some Untold Cases (1894-1902)
Part XIII – 2019 Annual (1881-1890)
Part XIV – 2019 Annual (1891-1897)
Part XV – 2019 Annual (1898-1917)
Part XVI – Whatever Remains . . . Must be the Truth (1881-1890)
Part XVII – Whatever Remains . . . Must be the Truth (1891-1898)
Part XVIII – Whatever Remains . . . Must be the Truth (1898-1925)
Part XIX – 2020 Annual (1882-1890)
Part XX – 2020 Annual (1891-1897)
Part XXI – 2020 Annual (1898-1923)
Part XXII – Some More Untold Cases (1877-1887)
Part XXIII – Some More Untold Cases (1888-1894)
Part XXIV – Some More Untold Cases (1895-1903)
Part XXV – 2021 Annual (1881-1888)
Part XXVI – 2021 Annual (1889-1897)
Part XXVII – 2021 Annual (1898-1928)
Part XXVIII – More Christmas Adventures (1869-1888)
Part XXIX – More Christmas Adventures (1889-1896)
Part XXX – More Christmas Adventures (1897-1928)
Part XXXI – 2022 Annual Part (1875-1887)
XXXII – 2022 Annual (1888-1895)
Part XXXIII – 2022 Annual (1896-1919)
Part XXXIV "However Improbable . . . ." (1878-1888)
Part XXXV "However Improbable . . . ." (1889-1896)
Part XXXVI "However Improbable . . . ." (1897-1919)

In Preparation

Part XXXVI (and XXXVIII and XXXIX???) – 2023 Annual

. . . and more to come!

The MX Book of New Sherlock Holmes Stories
Edited by David Marcum

(MX Publishing, 2015-   )

<u>*Publishers Weekly*</u> says:

Part VI: *The traditional pastiche is alive and well . . . .*

Part VII: *Sherlockians eager for faithful-to-the-canon plots and characters will be delighted.*

Part VIII: *The imagination of the contributors in coming up with variations on the volume's theme is matched by their ingenious resolutions.*

Part IX: *The 18 stories . . . will satisfy fans of Conan Doyle's originals. Sherlockians will rejoice that more volumes are on the way.*

Part X: *. . . new Sherlock Holmes adventures of consistently high quality.*

Part XI: *. . . an essential volume for Sherlock Holmes fans.*

Part XII: *. . . continues to amaze with the number of high-quality pastiches.*

Part XIII: *. . . Amazingly, Marcum has found 22 superb pastiches . . . This is more catnip for fans of stories faithful to Conan Doyle's original*

Part XIV: *. . . this standout anthology of 21 short stories written in the spirit of Conan Doyle's originals.*

Part XV: *Stories pitting Sherlock Holmes against seemingly supernatural phenomena highlight Marcum's 15th anthology of superior short pastiches.*

Part XVI: *Marcum has once again done fans of Conan Doyle's originals a service.*

Part XVII: *This is yet another impressive array of new but traditional Holmes stories.*

Part XVIII: *Sherlockians will again be grateful to Marcum and MX for high-quality new Holmes tales.*

Part XIX: *Inventive plots and intriguing explorations of aspects of Dr. Watson's life and beliefs lift the 24 pastiches in Marcum's impressive 19th Sherlock Holmes anthology*

Part XX: *Marcum's reserve of high-quality new Holmes exploits seems endless.*

Part XXI: *This is another must-have for Sherlockians.*

Part XXII: *Marcum's superlative 22nd Sherlock Holmes pastiche anthology features 21 short stories that successfully emulate the spirit of Conan Doyle's originals while expanding on the canon's tantalizing references to mysteries Dr. Watson never got around to chronicling.*

Part XXIII: *Marcum's well of talented authors able to mimic the feel of The Canon seems bottomless.*

Part XXIV: *Marcum's expertise at selecting high-quality pastiches remains impressive.*

Part XXVIII: *All entries adhere to the spirit, language, and characterizations of Conan Doyle's originals, evincing the deep pool of talent Marcum has access to. Against the odds, this series remains strong, hundreds of stories in.*

Part XXXI: *. . . yet another stellar anthology of 21 short pastiches that effectively mimic the originals . . . Marcum's diligent searches for high-quality stories has again paid off for Sherlockians.*

The MX Book of New Sherlock Holmes Stories
Edited by David Marcum
(MX Publishing, 2015-   )

MX Publishing

MX Publishing is the world's largest specialist Sherlock Holmes publisher, with over five-hundred titles and over two-hundred authors creating the latest in Sherlock Holmes fiction and non-fiction

The catalogue includes several award winning books, and over two-hundred-and-fifty have been converted into audio.

MX Publishing also has one of the largest communities of Holmes fans on Facebook, with regular contributions from dozens of authors.

www.mxpublishing.com

@mxpublishing on Facebook, Twitter, and Instagram

CPSIA information can be obtained
at www.ICGtesting.com
Printed in the USA
LVHW010439201122
733440LV00001B/2